Charles Reade

A Simpleton, and the Wandering Heir

A novel

Charles Reade

A Simpleton, and the Wandering Heir
A novel

ISBN/EAN: 9783337048716

Printed in Europe, USA, Canada, Australia, Japan

Cover: Foto ©Andreas Hilbeck / pixelio.de

More available books at **www.hansebooks.com**

A SIMPLETON,

AND

THE WANDERING HEIR.

BY

CHARLES READE.

HOUSEHOLD EDITION.

BOSTON:
JAMES R. OSGOOD AND COMPANY,
(LATE TICKNOR & FIELDS, AND FIELDS, OSGOOD, & CO.)
1873.

CONTENTS.

A SIMPLETON.

CHAPTER I.

A YOUNG lady sat pricking a framed canvas in the drawing-room of Kent Villa, a mile from Gravesend. She was making, at a cost of time and tinted wool, a chair-cover, admirably unfit to be sat upon — except by some peevish artist bent on obliterating discordant colors. To do her justice, her mind was not in her work; for she rustled softly with restlessness as she sat, and she rose three times in twenty minutes, and went to the window. Thence she looked down over a trim flowery lawn, and long sloping meadows, on to the silver Thames, alive with steamboats ploughing, white sails bellying, and great ships carrying to and fro the treasures of the globe. From this fair landscape and epitome of commerce she retired each time with listless disdain. She was waiting for somebody.

Yet she was one of those whom few men care to keep waiting. Rosa Lusignan was a dark but dazzling beauty, with coal-black hair and glorious dark eyes that seemed to beam with soul all day long; her eyebrows, black, straightish, and rather thick, would have been majestic, and too severe, had the other features followed suit; but her black brows were succeeded by long silky lashes, a sweet oval face, two pouting lips studded with ivory, and an exquisite chin, as feeble as any man could desire in the partner of his bosom. Person straight, elastic, and rather tall. Mind, nineteen. Accomplishments, numerous: a poor French scholar, a worse German, a worst English; an admirable dancer, an inaccurate musician, a good rider, a bad draughtswoman; a bad hairdresser, at the mercy of her maid; a hot theologian, knowing nothing; a sorry accountant, no housekeeper, no seamstress, a fair embroideress, a capital geographer, and no cook.

Collectively, namely, mind and body, the girl we kneel to.

This ornamental member of society now glanced at the clock once more, and then glided to the window for the fourth time. She peeped at the side a good while with superfluous slyness, or shyness; and presently she drew back, blushing crimson: then she peeped again, still more furtively, then retired softly to her frame, and, for the first time, set to work in earnest. As she plied her harpoon, smiling now, the large and vivid blush that had suffused her face and throat turned from carnation to rose, and melted away slowly but perceptibly, and ever so sweetly; and somebody knocked at the street-door.

The blow seemed to drive her deeper into her work. She leaned over it, graceful as a willow, and so absorbed she could not even see the door of the room open, and Dr. Staines come in.

All the better; her not perceiving that slight addition to her furniture gives me a moment to describe him.

A young man, five feet eleven inches high, very square-shouldered and deep-chested, but so symmetrical and light in his movements that his size hardly struck one at first. He was smooth shaved, all but a short, thick auburn whisker; his hair was brown. His features no more than comely; the brow full; the eyes wide apart and deep-seated; the lips rather thin, but expressive; the chin solid and square. It was a face of power, and capable of harshness, but leavened by an eye of an unusual color, between hazel and gray, and wonderfully tender. In complexion he could not compare with Rosa: his cheek was clear but pale; for few young men had studied night and day so constantly. Though but twenty-eight years of age, he was literally a learned physician, deep in hospital practice, deep in books, especially deep in German science, — too often neglected or skimmed by English physicians. He had delivered a course of lectures at a learned university with general applause.

As my reader has divined, Rosa was preparing the comedy of a cool reception; but, looking up, she saw his pale cheek tinted with a lover's beautiful joy at the bare sight of her, and his soft eye so divine with love that she had not the heart to chill him. She gave him her hand kindly, and smiled brightly on him instead of remonstrating. She lost nothing by it; for the very first thing he did was to excuse himself eagerly. "I am behind time: the fact is, just as I was mounting my horse, a poor man came to the gate to consult me. He had a terrible disorder I have sometimes succeeded in arresting. I attack the cause instead of the symptoms, which is the old practice

and so that detained me. You forgive me?"

"Of course. Poor man! Only you said you wanted to see papa, and he always goes out at two."

When she had been betrayed into saying this, she drew in suddenly, and blushed with a pretty consciousness.

"Then don't let me lose another minute," said the lover. "Have you prepared him for — for what I am going to have the audacity to say?"

Rosa answered, with some hesitation, "I *must* have, a little. When I refused Col. Bright — you need not devour my hand quite; he is forty."

Her sentence ended; and away went the original topic, and grammatical sequence along with it. Christopher Staines recaptured them both. "Yes, dear, when you refused Col. Bright —

"Well, papa was astonished; for everybody says the colonel is a most eligible match. Don't you hate that expression? I do. Eligible!"

Christopher made due haste, and recaptured her. "Yes, love, your papa said" —

"I don't think I will tell you. He asked me was there anybody else; and of course I said, 'No.'"

"Oh!"

"Oh, that is nothing! I had not time to make up my mind to tell the truth. I was taken by surprise; and you know one's first impulse is to fib — about *that*."

"But did you really deceive him?"

"No. I blushed; and he caught me: so he said, 'Come now, there was.'"

"And you said, 'Yes, there is,' like a brave girl as you are."

"What! plump like that? No: I was frightened out of my wits, like a brave girl as I am not, and said I should never marry any one he could disapprove; and then — oh! then I believe I began to cry.

Christopher, I'll tell you something. I find people leave off teasing you when you cry — gentlemen, I mean. Ladies go on all the more. So then dear papa kissed me, and told me I must not be imprudent and throw myself away, that was all; and I promised him I never would. I said he would be sure to approve my choice, and he said he hoped so. And so he will."

Dr. Staines looked thoughtful, and said he hoped so too. "But now it comes to the point of asking him for such a treasure, I feel my deficiencies."

"Why, what deficiencies? You are young and handsome and good, and ever so much cleverer than other people. You have only to ask for me, and insist on having me. Come, dear, go and get it over." She added, mighty coolly, "There is nothing so *dreadful* as suspense."

"I'll go this minute," said he, and took a step toward the door; but he turned, and in a moment was at her knees. He took both her hands in his, and pressed them to his beating bosom, while his beautiful eyes poured love into hers point blank. "May I tell him you love me? Oh! I know you cannot love me as I love you; but I may say you love me a little, may I not? That will go farther with him than any thing else. May I, Rosa, may I? — a little?"

His passion mastered her. She drooped her head sweetly on his shoulder, and murmured, "You know you may, my own. Who would not love you?"

He parted lingeringly from her, then marched away, bold with love and hope, to demand her hand in marriage.

Rosa leaned back in her chair, and quivered a little with new emotions. Christopher was right: she was not capable of loving like him; but still the actual contact of so strong a passion made her woman's nature vibrate. A dewy tear hung on the fringes of her long lashes; and she leaned back in her chair, and fluttered a while.

That emotion, almost new to her, soon yielded, in her girlish mind, to a complacent languor, and that, in its turn, to a soft reverie. So she was going to be married! To be mistress of a house, settle in London (*that* she had quite determined long ago); be able to go out into the streets all alone, to shop or visit; have a gentleman all her own, whom she could put her finger on any moment, and make him take her about, even to the opera and the theatre; to give dinner-parties her own self, and even a little ball once in a way; to buy whatever dresses she thought proper, instead of being crippled by an allowance; have the legal right of speaking first in society, even to gentlemen rich in ideas but bad starters, instead of sitting mum-chance and mock-modest; to be mistress instead of miss — contemptible title; to be a woman instead of a girl; and all this rational liberty, domestic power, and social dignity were to be obtained by merely wedding a dear fellow who loved her, and was so nice: and the bright career to be ushered in with several delights, each of them dear to a girl's very soul, — presents from all her friends; as many beautiful new dresses as if she was changing her body or her hemisphere instead of her name; *éclat;* going to church, which is a good English girl's theatre of display and temple of vanity, and there tasting delightful publicity and whispered admiration, in a heavenly long veil, which she could not wear even once if she remained single.

This bright variegated picture of holy wedlock and its essential features, as revealed to young ladies by feminine tradition, though not enumerated in the Book of Common Prayer composed by males, so entranced her that time flew by unheeded, and Christopher Staines came back from her father. His step was heavy: he looked pale and deeply distressed; then stood like a statue, and did not come close to her, but cast a piteous look, and gasped out one word, that seemed almost to choke him,—"REFUSED!"

Miss Lusignan rose from her chair, and looked almost wildly at him with her great eyes. "Refused?" said she faintly.

"Yes," said he sadly. "Your father is a man of business; and he took a mere business view of our love: he asked me directly what provision I could make for his daughter and her children. Well, I told him I had three thousand pounds in the Funds, and a good profession; and then I said I had youth, health, and love, boundless love, the love that can do or suffer, the love that can conquer the world."

"Dear Christopher! And what *could* be say to all that?"

"He ignored it entirely. There, I'll give you his very words. He said, 'In that case, Dr. Staines, the simple question is, what does your profession bring you in per annum?'"

"Oh! There, I always hated arithmetic; and now I abominate it."

"Then I was obliged to confess I had scarcely received a hundred pounds in fees this year; but I told him the reason: this is such a small district, and all the ground occupied. London, I said, was my sphere."

"And so it is," said Rosa eagerly; for this jumped with her own little designs. "Genius is wasted in the country. Besides, whenever anybody worth curing is ill down here, they always send to London for a doctor."

"I told him so, dearest," said the lover. "But he answered me directly, then I must set up in London; and, as soon as my books showed an income to keep a wife and servants and children, and

insure my life for five thousand pounds"—

"Oh, that is so like papa! He is director of an insurance company; so all the world must insure their lives."

"No, dear, he was quite right there: professional incomes are most precarious. Death spares neither young nor old, neither warm hearts nor cold. I should be no true physician if I could not see my own mortality." He hung his head, and pondered a moment; then went on sadly, "It all comes to this: until I have a professional income of eight hundred a year at least, he will not hear of our marrying: and the cruel thing is, he will not even consent to an engagement. But," said the rejected, with a look of sad anxiety, "you will wait for me without that, dear Rosa?"

She could give him that comfort; and. she gave it him with loving earnestness. "Of course I will; and it shall not be very long. While you are making your fortune to please papa, I will keep fretting and pouting and crying till be sends for you."

"Bless you, dearest. Stop! not to make yourself ill! not for all the world." There spoke the lover and the physician.

He came, all gratitude, to her side; and they sat, hand in hand, comforting each other; indeed, parting was such sweet sorrow that they sat, and very close to one another, till Mr. Lusignan, who thought five minutes quite enough for rational beings to take leave in, walked into the room and surprised them. At sight of his gray head and iron-gray eyebrows, Christopher Staines started up and looked confused: he thought some apology necessary, so he faltered out, "Forgive me, sir; it is a bitter parting to me, you may be sure."

Rosa's bosom heaved at these simple words. She flew to her father, and cried, "O papa! papa! you were never cruel before," and hid her burning face on his shoulder; and then burst out crying, partly for Christopher, partly because she was now ashamed of herself for having taken a young man's part so openly.

Mr. Lusignan looked sadly discomposed at this outburst: she had taken him by his weak point; he told her so. "Now, Rosa," said he, rather peevishly, "you know I hate a noise."

Rosa had actually forgotten that trait for a single moment; but, being reminded of it, she reduced her sobs in the prettiest way, not to offend a tender parent who could not bear noise. Under this homely term, you must know he included all scenes, disturbances, rumpuses, passions, and expected all men, women, and things in Kent Villa to go smoothly, or go elsewhere.

"Come, young people," said he, "don't make a disturbance. Where's the grievance? Have I said he should never marry you? Have I forbidden him to correspond, or even to call, say twice a year? All I say is, no marriage, nor contract of marriage, until there is an income." Then he turned to Christopher. "Now, if you can't make an income without her, how could you make one with her, weighed down by the load of expenses a wife entails? I know her better than you do. She is a good girl, but rather luxurious and self-indulent. She is not cut out for a poor man's wife; and pray don't go and fancy that nobody loves my child but you. Mine is not so hot as yours, of course; but believe me, sir, it is less selfish. You would expose her to poverty and misery; but I say no. It is my duty to protect her from all chance of them; and, in doing it, I am as much your friend as hers, if you could but see it. Come, Dr. Staines, be a man, and see the world as it is. I have told you how to earn my daughter's hand and my esteem: you must gain both or neither.

1*

Dr. Staines was never quite deaf to reason: he now put his hand to his brow, and said, with a sort of wonder and pitiful dismay, "My love for Rosa selfish! Sir, your words are bitter and hard." Then, after a struggle, and with rare and touching candor, "Ay, but so are bark and steel; yet they are good medicines." Then, with a great glow in his heart, and tears in his eyes, "My darling shall not be a poor man's wife, — she who would adorn a coronet, ay, or a crown. Good-by, Rosa, for the present." He darted to her, and kissed her hand with all his soul. "Oh, the sacrifice of leaving you!" he faltered: "the very world is dark to me without you. Ah, well, I must earn the right to come again!" He summoned all his manhood, and marched to the door. There he seemed to turn calmer all of a sudden, and said, firmly yet humbly, "I'll try and show you, sir, what love can do."

"And I'll show you what love can suffer," said Rosa, folding her beautiful arms superbly.

It was not in her to have shot such a bolt except in imitation; yet how promptly the mimic thunder came, and how grand the beauty looked, with her dark brows and flashing eyes and folded arms! much grander and more inspired than poor Staines, who had only furnished the idea.

But between these two figures, swelling with emotion, the representative of common sense, Lusignan *père*, stood cool and impassive: he shrugged his shoulders, and looked on both lovers as a couple of ranting novices he was saving from each other and almshouses.

For all that, when the lover had torn himself away, papa's composure was suddenly disturbed by a misgiving. He stepped hastily to the stair-head, and gave it vent. "Dr. Staines," said he, in a loud whisper (Staines was half-way down the stairs: he stopped), "I trust to you, as a gentleman, not to mention this; it will never transpire here. Whatever we do, no noise!"

CHAPTER II.

ROSA LUSIGNAN set herself pining as she had promised, and she did it discreetly for so young a person; she was never peevish, but always sad and listless. By this means she did not anger her parent, but only made him feel she was unhappy, and the house she had hitherto brightened exceeding dismal.

By degrees this noiseless melancholy undermined the old gentleman; and he well nigh tottered.

But one day, calling suddenly on a neighbor with six daughters, he heard peals of laughter, and found Rosa taking her full share of the senseless mirth. She pulled up short at sight of him, and colored high; but it was too late, for he launched a knowing look at her on the spot, and muttered something about seven foolish virgins.

He took the first opportunity when they were alone, and told her he was glad to find she was only dismal at home.

But Rosa had prepared for him. "One can be loud without being gay at heart," said she, with a lofty, languid air. "I have not forgotten your last words to *him.* We were to hide our broken hearts from the world. I try to obey you, dear papa; but, if I had my way, I would never go into the world at all. I have but one desire now, — to end my days in a convent."

"Please begin them first. A convent! Why, you'd turn it out of window. You are no more fit to be a nun than — a pauper."

Not having foreseen this facer, Rosa had nothing ready: so she received it with a sad, submissive, helpless sigh, as one who should say, "Hit me, papa: I have no friend now." So then he was sorry he had been so clever; and, indeed, there is one provoking thing about "a woman's weakness," it is invincible.

The next minute what should come but a long letter from Dr. Staines, detailing his endeavors to purchase a practice in London, and his ill-success. The letter spoke the language of love and hope, but the facts were discouraging; and indeed a touching sadness pierced through the veil of the brave words.

Rosa read it again and again, and cried over it before her father, to discourage him in his heartless behavior.

About ten days after this, something occurred that altered her mood.

She became grave and thoughtful, but no longer lugubrious. She seemed desirous to atone to her father for having disturbed his cheerfulness. She smiled affectionately on him, and often sat on a stool at his knee, and glided her hand into his.

He was not a little pleased, and said to himself, "She is coming round to common sense."

Now, on the contrary, she was farther from it than ever.

At last he got the clew. One afternoon he met Mr. Wyman coming out of the villa. Mr. Wyman was the consulting surgeon of that part.

"What! anybody ill?" said Mr. Lusignau: "one of the servants?"

"No: it is Miss Lusignan."

"Why, what is the matter with her?"

Wyman hesitated. "Oh, nothing very alarming! Would you mind asking her?"

"Why?"

"The fact is, she requested me not to tell you, — made me promise."

"And I insist upon your telling me."

"I think you are quite right, sir, as her father. Well, she is troubled with a little spitting of blood."

Mr. Lusignan turned pale. "My child! spitting of blood! God forbid!"

"Oh, do not alarm yourself! It is nothing serious."

"Don't tell me," said the father. "It is always serious. And she kept this from me!"

Masking his agitation for the time, he inquired how often it had occurred, — this grave symptom.

"Three or four times this last month. But I may as well tell you at once, I have examined her carefully, and I do not think it is from the lungs."

"From the throat, then?"

"No, from the liver. Every thing points to that organ as the seat of derangement: not that there is any lesion; only a tendency to congestion. I am treating her accordingly, and have no doubt of the result."

"Who is the ablest physician hereabouts?" asked Lusignan abruptly.

"Dr. Snell, I think."

"Give me his address."

"I'll write to him if you like, and appoint a consultation." He added, with vast but rather sudden alacrity, "It will be a great satisfaction to my own mind."

"Then send to him, if you please, and let him be here to-morrow morning; if not, I shall take her to London for advice at once."

On this understanding they parted; and Lusignan went at once to his daughter. "O my child!" said he, deeply distressed, "how could you hide this from me?"

"Hide what, papa?" said the girl, looking the picture of unconsciousness.

"That you have been spitting blood."

"Who told you that?" said she sharply.

"Wyman; he is attending you."

Rosa colored with anger. "Chatterbox! He promised me faithfully not to."

"But why, in Heaven's name? What! would you trust this terrible thing to a stranger, and hide it from your poor father?"

"Yes," replied Rosa quietly.

The old man would not scold her now: he only said sadly, "I see how it is: because I will not let you marry poverty, you think I do not love you." And he sighed.

"O papa! the idea!" said Rosa. "Of course I know you love me. It was not that, you dear, darling, foolish papa. There, if you must know, it was because I did not want you to be distressed. I thought I might get better with a little physic; and if not, why then I thought, 'Papa is an old man; la! I dare say I shall last his time;' and so, why should I poison your latter days with worrying about *me?*"

Mr. Lusignan stared at her, and his lip quivered; but he thought the trait hardly consistent with her superficial character. He could not help saying, half-sadly, half-bitterly, "Well, but of course you have told Dr. Staines."

Rosa opened her beautiful eyes like two suns. "Of course I have done nothing of the sort. He has enough to trouble him without that. Poor fellow! there he is, worrying and striving to make his fortune and gain your esteem: 'they go together,' you know you told him so." (Young cats will scratch when least expected.) "And for me to go and tell him I am in danger! Why, he would go wild; he would think of nothing but me and my health; he would never make his fortune; and so then, even when I am gone, he will never get a wife, because he has only got genius and goodness and three thousand pounds. No, papa, I have not told poor Christopher. I may tease those I love; I have been teasing *you* this ever so long: but frighten them and make them miserable? No."

And here, thinking of the anguish that was perhaps in store for those she loved, she wanted to cry; it almost choked her not to. But she fought it bravely down: she reserved her tears for lighter occasions and less noble sentiments.

Her father held out his arms to her; she ran her footstool to him, and sat nestling to his heart.

"Please forgive me my misconduct. I have not been a dutiful daughter ever since you — But now I will. Kiss me, my own papa. There! Now we are as we always were."

Then she purred to him on every possible topic but the one that now filled his parental heart, and bade him good-night at last with a cheerful smile.

Wyman was exact; and ten minutes afterward Dr. Snell drove up in a carriage and pair. He was intercepted in the hall by Wyman, and, after a few minutes' conversation, presented to Mr. Lusignan.

The father gave vent to his paternal anxiety in a few simple but touching words, and was proceeding to state the symptoms as he had gathered them from his daughter; but Dr. Snell interrupted him politely, and said he had heard the principal symptoms from Mr. Wyman. Then, turning to the latter, he said, "We had better proceed to examine the patient."

"Certainly," said Mr. Lusignan. "She is in the drawing-room;" and he led the way, and was about to enter the room, when Wyman informed him that it was against etiquette for him to be present at the examination.

"Oh, very well!" said he. "Yes, I see the propriety of that. But oblige me by asking her if she has any thing on her mind."

Dr. Snell bowed a lofty assent; for to receive a hint from a layman was to confer a favor on him.

The men of science were closeted full half an hour with the patient. She was too beautiful to be slurred over, even by a busy doctor: he felt her pulse, looked at her tongue, and listened attentively to her lungs, to her heart, and to the organ suspected by Wyman. He left her at last with a kindly assurance that the case was perfectly curable.

At the door they were met by the anxious father, who came, with throbbing heart, and asked the doctor's verdict.

He was coolly informed that could not be given until the consultation had taken place; the result of that consultation would be conveyed to him.

"And pray why can't I be present at the consultation? The grounds on which two able men agree or disagree must be well worth listening to."

"No doubt," said Dr. Snell; "but," with a superior smile, "my dear sir, it is not the etiquette."

"Oh, very well!" said Lusignan. But he muttered, "So, then, a father is nobody."

And this unreasonable person retired to his study, miserable, and gave up the dining-room to the consultation.

They soon rejoined him.

Dr. Snell's opinion was communicated by Wyman. "I am happy to tell you, that Dr. Snell agrees with me entirely; the lungs are not affected, and the liver is congested, but not diseased."

"Is that so, Dr. Snell?" asked Lusignan anxiously.

"It is so, sir." He added, "The treatment has been submitted to me, and I quite approve it."

He then asked for a pen and paper, and wrote a prescription. He assured Mr. Lusignan that the case had no extraordinary feature whatever; he was not to alarm himself. Dr. Snell then drove away, leaving the parent rather puzzled, but, on the whole, much comforted.

And here I must reveal an extraordinary circumstance, —

Wyman's treatment was by drugs.

Dr. Snell's was by drugs.

Dr. Snell, as you have seen, entirely approved Wyman's treatment.

His own had nothing in common with it. The arctic and antarctic poles are not farther apart than was his prescription from the prescription he thoroughly approved.

Amiable science! In which complete diversity of practice did not interfere with perfect uniformity of opinion.

All this was kept from Dr. Staines; and he was entirely occupied in trying to get a position that might lead to fortune and satisfy Mr. Lusignan. He called on every friend he had, to inquire where there was an opening. He walked miles and miles in the best quarters of London, looking for an opening; he let it be known in many quarters that he would give a good premium to any physician who was about to retire, and would introduce him to his patients.

No; he could hear of nothing.

Then, after a great struggle with himself, he called upon his uncle, Philip Staines, a retired M.D., to see if he would do any thing for him. He left this to the last, for a very good reason; Dr. Philip was an irritable old bachelor, who had assisted most of his married relatives; but, finding no bottom to the well, had turned rusty and crusty, and now was apt to administer kicks instead of checks to all who were near and dear to him. However, Christopher was the old gentleman's favorite, and was now desperate; so he mustered courage and went. He was graciously received, — warmly indeed. This gave him great hopes, and he told his tale.

The old bachelor sided with Mr. Lusignan. "What!" said he, "do you want to marry, and propagate pauperism? I thought you had more sense. Confound it all! I had just one nephew whose knock at my street-door did not make me tremble: he was a bachelor and a thinker, and came for a friendly chat; the rest are married men, highwaymen, who come to say, 'Stand and deliver;' and now even you want to join the giddy throng. Well, don't ask me to have any hand in it. You are a man of promise; and you might as well hang a millstone around your neck as a wife. Marriage is a greater mistake than ever now; the women dress more, and manage worse. I met your cousin Jack the other day and his wife, with seventy pounds on her back, and next door to paupers. No; while you are a bachelor, like me, you are my favorite, and down in my will for a lump. Once marry, and you join the noble army of footpads, leeches, vultures, paupers, gone coons, and babblers about brats, and I disown you."

There was no hope from old Crusty. Christopher left him, snubbed and heart-sick. At last he met a sensible man, who made him see there was no short-cut in that profession. He must be content to play the up-hill game; must settle in some good neighborhood, marry if possible, since husbands and fathers of families prefer married physicians; and so be poor at thirty, comfortable at forty, and rich at fifty — perhaps.

Then Christopher came down to his lodgings at Gravesend, and was very unhappy; and, after some days of misery, he wrote a letter to Rosa in a moment of impatience, despondency, and passion.

Rosa Lusignan got worse and worse. The slight but frequent hemorrhage was a drain upon her system, and weakened her visibly. She began to lose her rich complexion, and sometimes looked almost sallow; and a slight circle showed itself under her eyes. These symptoms were unfavorable; nevertheless Dr. Snell and Mr. Wyman accepted them cheerfully, as fresh indications that nothing was affected but the liver. They multiplied and varied their prescriptions; the malady ignored those prescriptions, and went steadily on. Mr. Lusignan was terrified, but helpless; Rosa resigned and reticent.

But it was not in human nature that a girl of this age could always, and at all hours, be mistress of herself. One evening in particular she stood before the glass in the drawing-room, and looked at herself a long time with horror. "Is that Rosa Lusignan?" said she aloud. "It is her ghost."

A deep groan startled her. She turned; it was her father. She thought he was fast asleep; and so indeed he had been : but he was just awaking, and heard his daughter utter her real mind. It was a thunder-clap. "O my child! what shall I do?" he cried.

Then Rosa was taken by surprise in her turn. She spoke out. "Send for a great physician, papa. Don't let us deceive ourselves · it is our only chance."

"I will ask Mr. Wyman to get a physician down from London."

"No, no; that is no use: they will put their heads together; and he will say whatever Mr. Wyman tells him. La, papa! a clever man like you not to see what a cheat that consultation was! Why, from what you told me, one can see it was managed so that Dr. Snell could not possibly have an opinion of his own. No; no more echoes of Mr. Chatterbox. If you really want to cure me, send for Christopher Staines."

"Dr. Staines! He is very young."

"But he is very clever, and he is not an echo. He won't care how many doctors he contradicts when I am in danger. Papa, it is your child's one chance."

"I'll try it," said the old man eagerly. "How confident you look! your color has come back. It is an inspiration. Where is he?"

"I think by this time he must be at his lodgings in Gravesend. Send to him to-morrow morning."

"Not I. I'll go to him to-night. It is only a mile, and a fine clear night."

"My own, good, kind papa! Ah, well, come what may, I have lived long enough to be loved. Yes, dear papa, save me. I am very young to die ; and he loves me so dearly."

The old man bustled away, to put on something warmer for his night walk ; and Rosa leaned back, and the tears welled out of her eyes, now he was gone.

Before she had recovered her composure, a letter was brought her; and this was the letter from Christopher Staines alluded to already.

She took it from the servant with averted head, not wishing it to be seen she had been crying; and she started at the handwriting. It seemed such a coincidence that it should come just as she was sending for him.

"MY OWN BELOVED ROSA,—I now write to tell you, with a heavy heart, that all is vain. I cannot make or purchase a connection, except as others do, by time and patience. Being a bachelor is quite against a young physician. If I had a wife, and such a wife as you, I should be sure to get on. You would increase my connection very soon. What, then, lies before us? I see but two things : to wait till we are old, and our pockets are filled, but our hearts chilled or soured ; or else to marry at once, and climb the hill together. If you love me as I love you, you will be saving till the battle is over ; and I feel I could find energy and fortitude for both. Your father, who thinks so much of wealth, can surely settle something on *you*; and I am not too poor to furnish a house and start fair. I am not quite obscure,—my lectures have given me a name; and to you, my own love, I hope I may say that I know more than many of my elders, thanks to good schools, good method, a genuine love of my noble profession, and a tendency to study from my childhood. Will you not risk something on my ability? If not, God help me! for I shall lose you; and what is life, or fame, or wealth, or any mortal thing to me, without you. I cannot accept your father's decision: *you* must decide my fate.

"You see, I havekept away from you until I can do so no more. All this time the world to me has seemed to want the sun; and my heart pines and sickens for one sight of you. Darling Rosa, pray let me look at your face once more.

"When this reaches you, I shall be at your gate. Let me see you, though but for a moment, and let me hear my fate from no lips but yours.

"My own love,
"Your heart-broken lover,
"CHRISTOPHER STAINES."

This letter stunned her at first. Her mind of late had been turned away from love to such stern realities. Now she began to be sorry she had not told him. "Poor thing!" she said to herself; "he little thinks that now all is changed. Papa, I sometimes think, would deny me nothing now. It is I who would not marry him, to be buried by him in a month or two. Poor Christopher!"

The next moment she started up in dismay. Why, her father would miss him. No, perhaps catch him waiting for her. What would he think? What would Christopher think? That she had shown her papa his letter.

She rang the bell hard. The footman came.

"Send Harriet to me this instant. Oh! and ask papa to come to me!"

Then she sat down, and dashed off a line to Christopher. This was for Harriet to take out to him. Any

thing better than for Christopher to be caught doing what was wrong.

The footman came back first. "If you please, miss, master has gone out."

"Run after him, the road to Gravesend."

"Yes, miss."

"No. It is no use. Never mind."

"Yes, miss."

Then Harriet came in. "Did you want me, miss?"

"Yes. No, never mind now."

She was afraid to do any thing, for fear of making matters worse. She went to the window and stood looking anxiously out, with her hands working. Presently she uttered a little scream, and shrank away to the sofa. She sank down on it, half-sitting, half-lying, hid her face in her hands, and waited.

Staines, with a lover's impatience, had been more than an hour at the gate, or walking up and down close by it, his heart now burning with hope, now freezing with fear that she would decline a meeting on these terms.

At last the postman came, and then he saw his mistake; but now in a few minutes Rosa would have his letter, and then he should soon know whether she would come or not. He looked up at the drawing-room windows. They were full of light. She was there, in all probability. Yet she did not come to them. But why should she, if she was coming out?

He walked up and down the road. She did not come. His heart drooped; and perhaps it was owing to this that he almost ran against a gentleman who was coming the other way. The moon shone bright on both faces.

"Dr. Staines!" said Mr. Lusignan, surprised. Christopher uttered an ejaculation more eloquent than words.

They stared at each other.

"You were coming to see us?"

"N — no," stammered Christopher.

Lusignan thought that odd; however, he said, politely, "No matter; it is fortunate. Would you mind coming in ?"

"No," faltered Christopher, and stared at him ruefully, puzzled more and more; but beginning to think, after all, it might be a casual meeting.

They entered the gate; and in one moment he saw Rosa at the window, and she saw him.

Then he altered his opinion again. Rosa had sent her father out to him. But how was this ? The old man did not seem angry. Christopher's heart gave a leap inside him, and he began to glow with the wildest hopes. For what could this mean but relenting ?

Mr. Lusignan took him first into the study, and lighted two candles himself. He did not want the servants prying.

The lights showed Christopher a change in Mr. Lusignan. He looked ten years older.

"You are not well, sir," said Christopher gently.

"My health is well enough, but I am a broken-hearted man. Dr. Staines, forget all that passed here at your last visit. All that is over. Thank you for loving my poor girl as you do. Give me your hand. God bless you ! Sir, I am sorry to say it is as a physician I invite you now. She is ill, sir, — very, very ill ! "

"Ill, and not tell me ? "

"She kept it from you, my poor friend, not to distress you ; and she tried to keep it from me, but how could she ? For two months she has had some terrible complaint : it is destroying her. She is the ghost of herself. Oh, my poor child ! my child ! "

The old man sobbed aloud. The young man stood trembling and ashy pale. Still, the habits of his profession and the experience of dangers overcome, together with a certain sense of power, kept him up; but, above all, love and duty said, "Be firm." He asked for an outline of the symptoms.

They alarmed him greatly.

"Let us lose no more time," said he: "I will see her at once."

"Do you object to my being present ? "

"Of course not."

"Shall I tell you what Dr. Snell says it is, and Mr. Wyman ? "

"By all means, after I have seen her."

This comforted Mr. Lusignan. He was to get an independent judgment, at all events.

When they reached the top of the stairs, Dr. Staines paused, and leaned against the baluster. "Give me a moment," said he. "The patient must not know how my heart is beating ; and she must see nothing in my face but what I choose her to see. Give me your hand once more, sir; let us both control ourselves. Now announce me."

Mr. Lusignan opened the door, and said, with forced cheerfulness, "Dr. Staines, my dear ! come to give you the benefit of his skill."

She lay on the sofa, just as we left her, only her bosom began to heave.

Then Christopher Staines drew himself up; and the majesty of knowledge and love together seemed to dilate his noble frame. He fixed his eye on that reclining, panting figure, and stepped lightly but firmly across the room, to know the worst, — like a lion walking up to levelled lances.

CHAPTER III.

The young physician walked steadily up to his patient, without taking his eye off her, and drew a chair to her side.

Then she took down one hand, — the left, — and gave it to him, averting her face tenderly, and still covering it with the right, "For," said she to herself, "I am such a fright now." This opportune reflection, and her heaving bosom, proved that she at least felt herself something more than his patient. Her pretty consciousness made his task more difficult: nevertheless, he only allowed himself to press her hand tenderly with both his palms one moment, and then he entered on his functions bravely. "I am here as your physician."

"Very well," said she softly.

He gently detained the hand, and put his finger lightly to her pulse; it was palpitating, and a fallacious test. Oh, how that beating pulse, by love's electric current, set his own heart throbbing in a moment!

He put her hand gently, reluctantly down, and said, "Oblige me by turning this way." She turned: and he winced internally at the change in her; but his face betrayed nothing. He looked at her full; and, after a pause, put her some questions; one was as to the color of the hemorrhage. She said it was bright red.

"Not a tinge of purple?"

"No," said she hopefully, mistaking him.

He suppressed a sigh.

Then he listened at her shoulder-blade and at her chest, and made her draw her breath while he was listening. The acts were simple and usual in medicine; but there was a deep, patient, silent intensity about his way of doing them.

Mr. Lusignan crept nearer, and stood with both hands on a table, and his old head bowed, awaiting, yet dreading the verdict.

Up to this time Dr. Staines, instead of tapping and squeezing and pulling the patient about, had never touched her with his hand, and only grazed her with his ear: but now he said, "Allow me," and put both hands to her waist, more lightly and reverently than I can describe: "now draw a deep breath, if you please."

"There!"

"If you could draw a deeper still," said he insinuatingly.

"There, then," said she a little pettishly.

Dr. Staines's eye kindled.

"Hum!" said he. Then, after a considerable pause, "Are you better or worse after each hemorrhage?"

"La!" said Rosa; "they never asked me that. Why, better."

"No faintness?"

"Not a bit."

"Rather a sense of relief, perhaps?"

"Yes. I feel lighter and better."

The examination was concluded.

Dr. Staines looked at Rosa, and then at her father. The agony in that aged face, and the love that agony implied, won him; and it was to the parent he turned to give his verdict.

"The hemorrhage is from the lungs" —

Lusignan interrupted him: "From the lungs?" cried he in dismay.

"Yes: a slight congestion of the lungs."

"But not incurable! Oh! not incurable, doctor!"

"Heaven forbid! It is curable —easily — by removing the cause."

"And what is the cause?"

"The cause?" He hesitated, and looked rather uneasy. "Well, the cause, sir, is — tight stays."

The tranquillity of the meeting was instantly disturbed. "Tight stays! Me!" cried Rosa. "Why, I am the loosest girl in England! Look, papa!" and, without any apparent effort, she drew herself in, and poked her little fist between her sash and her gown. "There!"

Dr. Staines smiled sadly and a little sarcastically: he was evidently shy of encountering the lady in this argument; but he was more at his ease with her father; so he turned toward him, and lectured him freely.

"That is wonderful, sir; and

the first four or five female patients that favored me with it made me disbelieve my other senses; but Miss Lusignan is now about the thirtieth who has shown me that marvellous feat, with a calm countenance that belies the Herculean effort. Nature has her every-day miracles: a boa-constrictor, diameter seventeen inches, can swallow a buffalo; a woman, with her stays bisecting her almost, and lacerating her skin, can yet for one moment make herself seem slack, to deceive a juvenile physician. The snake is the miracle of expansion; the woman is the prodigy of contraction."

"Highly grateful for the comparison," said Rosa. "Women and snakes!"

Dr. Staines blushed, and looked uncomfortable. "I did not mean to be offensive: it certainly was a very clumsy comparison."

"What does that matter?" said Mr. Lusignan impatiently. "Be quiet, Rosa, and let Dr. Staines and me talk sense."

"Oh! then I am nobody in the business!" said this wise young lady.

"You are everybody," said Staines soothingly. "But," suggested he obsequiously, "if you don't mind, I would rather explain my views to your father — on this one subject."

"And a pretty subject it is."

Dr. Staines then invited Mr. Lusignan to his lodgings, and promised to explain the matter anatomically. "Meantime," said he, "would you be good enough to put your hands to my waist, as I did to the patient's."

Mr. Lusignan complied; and the patient began to titter directly, to put them out of countenance.

"Please observe what takes place when I draw a full breath."

"Now apply the same test to the patient. Breathe your best, please, Miss Lusignan."

The patient put on a face full of saucy mutiny.

"To oblige us both."

"Oh, how tiresome!"

"I am aware it is rather laborious," said Staines a little dryly; "but to oblige your father!"

"Oh, any thing to oblige papa!" said she spitefully. "There! And I do hope it will be the last. La! no; I don't hope that, neither."

Dr. Staines politely ignored her little attempts to interrupt the argument. "You found, sir, that the muscles of my waist, and my lower ribs themselves, rose and fell with each inhalation and exhalation of air by the lungs."

"I did; but my daughter's waist was like dead wood, and so were her lower ribs."

At this volunteer statement, Rosa colored to her temples. "Thanks, papa! Pack me off to London, and sell me for a big doll!"

"In other words," said the lecturer, mild and pertinacious, "with us the lungs have room to blow, and the whole bony frame expands elastic with them, like the wood-work of a blacksmith's bellows; but with this patient, and many of her sex, that noble and divinely-framed bellows is crippled and confined by a powerful machine of human construction; so it works lamely and feebly: consequently too little air, and of course too little oxygen, passes through that spongy organ whose very life is air. Now mark the special result in this case: being otherwise healthy and vigorous, our patient's system sends into the lungs more blood than that one crippled organ can deal with. A small quantity becomes extravasated at odd times. It accumulates, and would become dangerous; then Nature, strengthened by sleep and by some hours' relief from the diabolical engine, makes an effort, and flings it off; that is why the hemorrhage comes in the morning, and why she is the better for it, feeling neither faint nor sick, but relieved of a weight. This, sir, is the *rationale* of the complaint; and it is to you

I must look for the cure. To judge from my other female patients, and from the few words Miss Lusignan has let fall, I fear we must not count on any very hearty co-operation from her; but you are her father, and have great authority. I conjure you to use it to the full, as you once used it, to my sorrow, in this very room.. I am forgetting my character. I was asked here only as her physician. Good-evening."

He gave a little gulp, and hurried away, with an abruptness that touched the father, and offended the sapient daughter.

However, Mr. Lusignan followed him, and stopped him before he left the house, and thanked him warmly, and, to his surprise, begged him to call again in a day or two.

"Well, Rosa, what do you say?"

"I say that I am very unfortunate in my doctors. Mr. Wyman is a chatter-box, and knows nothing. Dr. Snell is Mr. Wyman's echo. Christopher is a genius, and they are always full of crotchets. A pretty doctor! Gone away and not prescribed for me!"

Mr. Lusignan admitted it was odd. "But, after all," said he, "if medicine does you no good?"

"Ah! but any medicine *he* had prescribed would have done me good; and that makes it all the unkinder."

"If you think so highly of his skill, why not take his advice? if can do no harm."

"No harm? Why, if I was to leave them off, I should catch a dreadful cold; and that would be sure to settle on my chest, and carry me off in my present delicate state. Besides, it is so unfeminine not to wear them."

This staggered Mr. Lusignan, and he was afraid to press the point; but what Staines had said fermented in his mind.

Dr. Snell and Mr. Wyman continued their visits and their prescriptions.

The patient got a little worse.

Mr. Lusignan hoped Christopher would call again; but he did not.

When Dr. Staines had satisfied himself that the disorder was easily curable, then wounded pride found an entrance even into his loving heart. That two strangers should have been consulted before him! He was only sent for because they could not cure her.

As he seemed in no hurry to repeat his visit, Mr. Lusignan called on him, and said, politely, he had hoped to receive another call ere this. "Personally," said he, "I was much struck with your observations: but my daughter is afraid she will catch cold if she leaves off her corset; and that, you know, might be very serious."

Dr. Staines groaned. And, when he had groaned, he lectured. "Female patients are wonderfully monotonous in this matter: they have a programme of evasions; and, whether the patient is a lady or a house-maid, she seldom varies from that programme. You find her breathing life's air with half a bellows, and you tell her so. 'Oh, no!' says she, and does the gigantic feat of contraction we witnessed that evening at your house. But, on inquiry, you learn there is a raw red line plowed in her flesh by the cruel stays. 'What is that?' you ask, and flatter yourself you have pinned her. Not a bit. 'That was the last pair. I changed them because they hurt me.' Driven out of that by proofs of recent laceration, they say, 'If I leave them off, I should catch my death of cold;' which is equivalent to saying there is no flannel in the shops, no common-sense nor needles at home."

He then laid before him some large French plates, showing the organs of the human trunk, and bade him observe in how small a space and with what skill the Creator has packed so many large yet delicate organs, so that they shall be free and secure from friction, though so close to each other. He showed him the liver, an organ weighing four pounds and of a large circumference; the lungs, a very large organ suspended in the chest, and impatient of pressure; the heart, the stomach, the spleen, all of them too closely and artfully packed to bear any further compression.

Having thus taken him by the eye, he took him by the mind.

" Is it a small thing for the creature to say to her Creator, ' I can pack all this egg-china better than you can,' and thereupon to jam all those vital organs close by a powerful, a very powerful and ingenious machine? Is it a small thing for that sex, which, for good reasons, the Omniscient has made larger in the waist than the male, to say to her Creator, ' You don't know your business; women ought to be smaller in the waist than men, and shall be throughout the civilized world ? ' " .

In short, he delivered so many true and pointed things on this trite subject that the old gentleman was convinced, and begged him to come over that very evening and convince Rosa.

Dr. Staines shook his head dolefully; and all his fire died out of him at having to face the fair. " Reason will be wasted. Authority is the only weapon. My profession and my reading have both taught me that the whole character of her sex undergoes a change the moment a man interferes with their dress. From Chaucer's day to our own, neither public satire nor private remonstrance has ever shaken any of their monstrous fashions. Easy, obliging, pliable, and weaker of will than men in other things, do but touch their dress, however objectionable, and rock is not harder, iron is not more stubborn, than these soft and yielding creatures. It is no earthly use my coming. I'll come."

He came that very evening, and saw directly she was worse. " Of course," said he sadly, " you have not taken my advice."

Rosa replied with a toss and an evasion, " I was not worth a prescription ? "

" A physician can prescribe without sending his patient to the druggist; and, when he does, then it is his words are gold."

Rosa shook her head with an air of lofty incredulity.

He looked ruefully at Mr. Lusignan, and was silent. Rosa smiled sarcastically; she thought he was at his wit's end.

Not quite: he was cudgelling his brains in search of some horribly unscientific argument that might prevail; for he felt science would fall dead upon so fair an antagonist. At last his eye kindled: he had hit on an argument unscientific enough for anybody, he thought. Said he, ingratiatingly, " You believe the Old Testament ? "

" Of course I do. Every syllable."

" And the lessons it teaches ? "

" Certainly."

" Then let me tell you a story from that book. A Syrian general had a terrible disease. He consulted Elijah by deputy. Elijah said, ' Bathe seven times in a certain river, Jordan, and you will get well.' The general did not like this at all : he wanted a prescription; wanted to go to the druggist; 'didn't believe in hydropathy to begin, and, in any case, turned up his nose at Jordan. What, bathe in an Israelitish brook, when his own country boasted noble rivers, with a reputation for sanctity into the bargain? In short, he preferred his leprosy to such irregular medicine. But it happened, by some immense fortuity, that one of his servants, though an Oriental, was a friend instead of a flatterer; and this sensible fellow said, ' If the prophet told you to do some great and difficult thing to get rid of this fearful malady, would not you do it, however distasteful? and can you hesitate when he merely says, "Wash in Jordan, and be healed?"' The general listened to good sense, and cured himself. Your case is parallel. You would take quantities of foul medicine, you would submit to some painful operation, if life and health depended on it; then why not do a small thing for a great result? You have only to take off an unnatural machine, which cripples your growing frame, and was unknown to every one of the women whose forms in parian marble the world admires. Off with that monstrosity, and your cure is as certain as the Syrian general's; though science, and not inspiration, dictates the easy remedy."

Rosa had listened impatiently, and now replied with some warmth, "This is shockingly profane. The idea of comparing yourself to Elijah, and me to a horrid leper! Much obliged. Not that I know what a leper is."

"Come, come, that is not fair," said Mr. Lusignan. "He only compared the situation, not the people."

"But, papa, the Bible is not to be dragged into the common affairs of life."

"Then what on earth is the use of it?"

"O papa! Well, it is not Sunday; but I have had a sermon. This is the clergyman, and you are the commentator. He! he! And so now let us go back from divinity to medicine. I repeat" (this was the first time she had said it) "that my other doctors give me real prescriptions, written in hieroglyphics. You can't look at them without feeling there *must* be something in them."

An angry spot rose on Christopher's cheek; but he only said, "And are your other doctors satisfied with the progress your disorder is making under their superintendence?"

"Perfectly. Papa, tell him what they say; and I'll find him their prescriptions." She went to a drawer and rummaged, affecting not to listen.

Lusignan complied. "First of all, sir, I must tell you they are confident it is not the lungs, but the liver."

"The what?" shouted Christopher.

"Ah?" screamed Rosa. "Oh, don't!—bawling!"

"And don't you screech," said her father, with a look of misery and apprehension impartially distributed on the resounding pair.

"You must have misunderstood them," murmured Staines, in a voice that was now barely audible a yard off. "The hemorrhage of a bright red color, and expelled without effort or nausea?"

"From the liver, they have assured me again and again," said Lusignan.

Christopher's face still wore a look of blank amazement, till Rosa herself confirmed it positively.

Then he cast a look of agony upon her, and started up in a passion, forgetting, once more, that his host abhorred the sonorous. "Oh, shame! shame!" he cried, "that the noble profession of medicine should be disgraced by ignorance such as this!" Then he said sternly: "Sir, do not mistake my motives; but I decline to have any thing further to do with this case until those two gentlemen have been relieved of it; and as this is very harsh, and on my part unprecedented, I will give you one reason out of many I *could* give you. Sir, there is no road from the liver to the throat by which blood can travel in this way, defying the laws of gravity; and they knew from the patient that no strong expellant force has ever been in operation. Their diagnosis, therefore, implies agnosis, or ignorance too great to be forgiven. I will not share my patient with two gentlemen who know so little of medicine, and know nothing of anatomy, which is the A B C of medicine. Can I see their prescriptions ? "

These were handed to him. "Good heavens ! " said he, " have you taken all these ? "

" Most of them."

" Why, then, you have drunk about two gallons of unwholesome liquids, and eaten a pound or two of unwholesome solids. These medicines have co-operated with the malady. The disorder lies not in the hemorrhage, but in the precedent extravasation ; that is, a drain on the system. And how is the loss to be supplied ? Why, by taking a little more nourishment than before. There is no other way ; and probably Nature, left to herself, might have increased your appetite to meet the occasion. But those two worthies have struck that weapon out of Nature's hand ; they have peppered away at the poor ill-used stomach with drugs and draughts, not very deleterious, I grant you, but all more or less indigestible, and all tending not to whet the appetite, but to clog the stomach, or turn the stomach, or pester the stomach, and so impair the appetite, and so co-operate, indirectly, with the malady."

" This is good sense," said Lusignan. " I declare I — I wish I knew how to get rid of them."

" Oh, I'll do that papa ! "

" No, no : it is not worth a rumpus."

" I'll do it too politely for that. Christopher, you are very clever, terribly clever. Whenever I threw their medicines away, I was always a little better that day. I will sacrifice them to you. It *is* a sacrifice. They are both so kind and chatty, and don't grudge me hieroglyphics : now you do.'

She sat down and wrote two sweet letters to Dr. Snell and Mr. Wyman, thanking them for the great

attention they had paid her : but finding herself getting steadily worse, in spite of all they had done for her, she proposed to discontinue her medicines for a time, and try change of air.

" And suppose they call to see whether you are changing the air ? "

" In that case, papa. 'Not at home.' "

The notes were addressed and despatched.

Then Dr. Staines brightened up, and said to Lusignan," I am now happy to tell you that I have overrated the malady. The sad change I see in Miss Lusignan is partly due to the great bulk of unwholesome esculents she has been eating and drinking under the head of medicines. These discontinued, she might linger on for years, existing, though not living : the tight-laced cannot be said to live. But, if she would be healthy and happy, let her throw that diabolical machine into the fire. It is no use asking her to loosen it ; she can't. Once there, the temptation is too strong. Off with it : and, take my word, you will be one of the healthiest and most vigorous young ladies in Europe."

Rosa looked rueful, and almost sullen.

She said she had parted with her doctors for him, but she really could not go about without stays. " They are as loose as they can be. See ! "

" That part of the programme is disposed of," said Christopher. " Please go on to No. 2. How about the raw red line where the loose machine has sawed your skin ? '

" What red line ? Oh ! oh ! oh ! Somebody or other has been peeping in at my window. I'll have the ivy cut down to-morrow."

" Simpleton ! " said Mr. Lusignan, angrily. " You have let the cat out of the bag. There is such a mark, then ; and this extraordinary young man has discerned it with the eye of science."

"He never discerned it at all," said Rosa, red as fire; "and, what is more, he never will."

"I don't want to. I should be very sorry to. I hope it will be gone in a week."

"I wish *you* were gone now, exposing me in this cruel way," said Rosa, angry with herself for having said an idiotic thing, and furious with him for having made her say it.

"O Rosa!" said Christopher, in a voice of tenderest reproach.

But Mr. Lusignan interfered promptly. "Rosa, no noise. I will not have you snapping at your best friend and mine. If you are excited, you had better retire to your own room and compose yourself. I hate a clamor."

Rosa made a wry face at this rebuke, and then began to cry quietly.

Every tear was like a drop of blood from Christopher's heart. "Pray don't scold her, sir," said he, ready to snivel himself. "She meant nothing unkind: it is only her pretty, sprightly way; and she did not really imagine a love so reverent as mine"—

"Don't *you* interfere between my father and me," said this reasonable young lady, now in an ungovernable state of feminine irritability.

"No, Rosa," said Christopher humbly. "Mr. Lusignan," said he, "I hope you will tell her that from the very first I was unwilling to enter on this subject with *her*. Neither she nor I can forget my double character. I have not said half as much to her as I ought, being her physician; and yet you see I have said more than she can bear from me, who, she knows, loves her and reveres her. Then, once for all, do pray let me put this delicate matter into your hands: it is a case for parental authority."

"Unfatherly tyranny, that means," said Rosa. "What business have gentlemen interfering in such things? It is unheard of. I will not submit to it even from papa."

"Well, you need not scream at me," said Mr. Lusignan; and he shrugged his shoulders to Staines. "She is impracticable, you see. If I do my duty, there will be a disturbance."

Now this roused the bile of Dr. Staines. "What, sir," said he, "you could separate her and me by your authority, here in this very room; and yet, when her life is at stake, you abdicate. You could part her from a man who loved her with every drop of his heart, and she said she loved him, or at all events preferred him to others, and you cannot part her from a miserable corset, although you see in her poor wasted face that it is carrying her to the churchyard. In that case, sir, there is but one thing for you to do: withdraw your opposition, and let me marry her. As her lover, I am powerless; but invest me with a husband's authority, and good-by corset! You will soon see the roses return to her cheek, and her elastic figure expanding, and her eye beaming with health and physical happiness."

Mr. Lusignan made an answer neither of his hearers expected. He said, "I have a great mind to take you at your word. I am too old and fond of quiet to drive a simpleton in single harness."

This contemptuous speech, and above all the word "simpleton," which had been applied to her pretty freely by young ladies at school, and always galled her terribly, inflicted so intolerable a wound on Rosa's vanity that she was ready to burst: on that, of course, her stays contributed their might of physical uneasiness. Thus irritated, mind and body, she burned to strike in return; and, as she could not slap her father in the presence of another, she gave it to Christopher backhanded.

"You can turn me out of doors," said she, "if you are tired of your daughter; but I am not such a *simpleton* as to marry a tyrant. No: he has shown the cloven foot in time. A husband's *authority*, indeed!" Then she turned her hand, and gave it him direct. "You told me a different story when you were paying your court to me; then you were to be my servant,—all hypocritical sweetness. You had better go and marry a Circassian slave. They don't wear stays, and they do wear trowsers; so she will be unfeminine enough even for you. No English lady would let her husband dictate to her about such a thing. I can have as many husbands as I like, without falling into the clutches of a tyrant. You are a rude, indelicate — And so please understand it is all over between you and me."

Both her auditors stood aghast; for she uttered this conclusion with a dignity of which the opening gave no promise. and the occasion, weighed in masculine balances, was not worthy.

"You do not mean that. You cannot mean it," said Dr. Staines aghast.

"I do mean it," said she firmly; "and, if you are a gentleman, you will not compel me to say it twice,—three times, I mean."

At this dagger-stroke, Christopher turned very pale; but he maintained his dignity. "I am a gentleman," said he quietly, "and a very unfortunate one. Good-by, sir; thank you kindly. Good-by, Rosa; God bless you! Oh, pray take a thought! Remember, your life and death are in your own hand now. I am powerless."

And he left the house in sorrow, and just, but not pettish, indignation.

When he was gone, father and daughter looked at each other; and there was the silence that succeeds a storm.

Rosa, feeling the most uneasy, was the first to express her satisfaction. "There, *he* is gone; and I am glad of it. Now you and I shall never quarrel again. I was quite right. Such impertinence! Such indelicacy! A fine prospect for me if I had married such a man! However, he is gone; and so there's an end of it. The idea! telling a young lady, before her father, she is tight-laced. If you had not been there, I could have forgiven him. But I am not; it is a story. Now," suddenly exalting her voice, "I know you believe him!"

"I say nothing," whispered papa, hoping to still her by example. This *ruse* did not succeed.

"But you look volumes," cried she; "and I can't bear it; I won't bear it. If you don't believe *me*, ask my *maid*." And, with this felicitous speech, she rang the bell.

"You'll break the wire, if you don't mind," suggested her father piteously.

"All the better! Why should not wires be broken as well as my heart? Oh, here she is! Now, Harriet, come here."

"Yes, miss."

"And tell the truth. *Am* I tight-laced?"

Harriet looked in her face a moment, to see what was required of her, and then said, "That you are not, miss. I never dressed a young lady as wore 'em easier than you do."

"There, papa. That will do, Harriet."

Harriet retired as far as the key-hole: she saw something was up.

"Now," said Rosa, "you see I was right; and, after all, it was a match you did not approve. Well, it is all over; and now you may write to your favorite, Colonel Bright. If he comes here, I'll box his old ears. I hate him. I hate them all. Forgive your wayward girl. I'll stay with you all my days. I dare say that will not be long, now I have quarrelled with my guardian angel: and all for what? Papa! papa! how *can* you sit there and not speak me one word of comfort?

'*Simpleton!*' Ah! that I am, to throw away a love a queen is scarcely worthy of: and all for what? Really, if it wasn't for the ingratitude and wickedness of the thing, it is too laughable. Ha! ha!—oh! oh! oh!—ha! ha! ha!"

And off she went into hysterics, and began to gulp and choke frightfully.

Her father cried for help, in dismay. In ran Harriet, saw, and screamed, but did not lose her head. This veracious person whipped a pair of scissors off the table, and cut the young lady's stay-laces directly. Then there was a burst of imprisoned beauty; a deep, deep sigh of relief came from a bosom that would have done honor to Diana; and the scene soon concluded with fits of harmless weeping, renewed at intervals.

When it had settled down to this, her father, to soothe her, said he would write to Dr. Staines, and bring about a reconciliation if she liked.

"No," said she, "you shall kill me sooner. I should die of shame."

She added, "Oh, pray, from this hour never mention his name to me!"

And then she had another cry.

Mr. Lusignan was a sensible man: he dropped the subject for the present; but he made up his mind to one thing,—that he would never part with Dr. Staines as a physician.

Next day Rosa kept her own room until dinner-time, and was as unhappy as she deserved to be. She spent her time in sewing on stiff flannel linings, and crying. She half-hoped Christopher would write to her, so that she might write back that she forgave him. But not a line.

At half-past six, her volatile mind took a turn, real or affected. She would cry no more for an ungrateful fellow,—ungrateful for not seeing through the stone walls how she had been employed all the morning, and making it up; so she bathed her red eyes, made a great alteration in her dress, and came dancing into the room, humming an Italian ditty.

As they were sitting together in the dining-room after dinner, two letters came by the same post to Mr. Lusignan,—from Mr. Wyman and Dr. Snell.

Mr. Wyman's letter.

"DEAR SIR,—I am sorry to hear from Miss Lusignan that she intends to discontinue medical advice. The disorder was progressing favorably, and nothing to be feared, under proper treatment.

"Yours, etc."

Dr. Snell's letter.

"DEAR SIR,—Miss Lusignan has written to me somewhat impatiently, and seems disposed to dispense with my visits. I do not, however, think it right to withdraw without telling you candidly that this is an unwise step. Your daughter's health is in a very precarious condition.

"Yours, etc."

Rosa burst out laughing. "I have nothing to fear; and I'm on the brink of the grave. That comes of writing without a consultation. If they had written at one table, I should have been neither well nor ill. Poor Christopher!" and her sweet face began to work piteously.

"There, there: drink a glass of wine."

She did, and a tear with it, that ran into the glass like lightning.

Warned by this that grief sat very near the bright hilarious surface, Mr. Lusignan avoided all emotional subjects for the present. Next day, however, he told her she might dismiss her lover; but no power should make him dismiss his pet physician, unless her health improved.

. "I will not give you that excuse

for inflicting him on me again," said the young hypocrite.

She kept her word. She got better and better, stronger, brighter, gayer.

She took to walking every day, and increasing the distance, till she could walk ten miles without fatigue.

Her favorite walk was to a certain cliff that commanded a noble view of the sea : to get to it, she must pass through the town of Gravesend ; and we may be sure she did not pass so often through that city without some idea of meeting the lover she had used so ill, and eliciting an *apology* from him. Sly puss !

When she had walked twenty times or thereabouts through the town and never seen him, she began to fear she had offended him past hope. Then she used to cry at the end of every walk.

But by-and-by bodily health, vanity, and temper combined to rouse the defiant spirit. . Said she, " If he really loved me, he would not take me at my word in such a hurry. And, besides, why does he not watch me, and find out what I am doing and where I walk ? "

At last she really began to persuade herself that she was an ill-used and slighted girl. She was very angry at times, and disconsolate at others, — a mixed state, in which hasty and impulsive young ladies commit life-long follies.

Mr. Lusignan observed the surface only. He saw his invalid daughter getting better every day, till at last she became a picture of health and bodily vigor. Relieved of his fears, he troubled his head but little about Christopher Staines. Yet he esteemed him, and had got to like him ; but Rosa was a beauty, and could do better than marry a struggling physician, however able. He launched out into a little gayety, resumed his quiet dinner parties, and, after some persuasion, took his now blooming daughter to a

ball given by the officers at Chatham.

She was the belle of the ball beyond dispute, and danced with ethereal grace and athletic endurance. She was madly fond of waltzing ; and here she encountered what she was pleased to call a divine dancer. It was a Mr. Reginald Falcon, a gentleman who had retired to the sea-side to recruit his health and finances, sore tried by London and Paris. Falcon had run through his fortune, but had acquired, in the process, certain talents, which, as they cost the acquirer dear, so they sometimes repay him, especially if he is not overburdened with principle, and adopts the notion, that, the world having plucked him, he has a right to pluck the world. He could play billiards well, but never so well as when backing himself for a heavy stake. He could shoot pigeons well ; and his shooting improved under that which makes some marksmen miss, — a heavy bet against the gun. He danced to perfection ; and being a well-bred, experienced, brazen, adroit fellow, who knew a little of every thing that was going, he had always plenty to say ; above all, he had made a particular study of the fair sex ; had met with many successes, many rebuffs, and at last, by keen study of their minds, and a habit he had acquired of watching their faces, and shifting his helm accordingly, had learned the great art of pleasing them. They admired his face : to me the short space between his eyes and his hair, his aquiline nose, and thin straight lips, suggested the bird of prey a little too much ; but to fair doves, born to be clutched, this similitude perhaps was not very alarming, even if they observed it.

Rosa danced several times with him, and told him he danced like an angel. He informed her that was because, for once, he was dancing with an angel. She laughed and blushed. He flattered deliciously, and it cost him little; for he fell in love with her that night deeper than he had ever been in his whole life of intrigue. He asked leave to call on her: she looked a little shy at that, and did not respond. He instantly withdrew his proposal, with an apology and a sigh that raised her pity. However, she was not a forward girl, even when excited by dancing and charmed with her partner; so she left him to find his own way out of that difficulty.

He was not long about it. At the end of the next waltz, he asked her if he might venture to solicit an introduction to her father.

"Oh, certainly!" said she. "What a selfish girl I am! this is terribly dull for him."

The introduction being made, and Rosa being engaged for the next three dances, Mr. Falcon sat by Mr. Lusignan and entertained him. For this little piece of apparent self-denial, he was paid in various coin: Lusignan found out he was the son of an old acquaintance, and so the door of Kent Villa opened to him. Meantime, Rosa Lusignan never passed him, even in the arms of a cavalry officer, without bestowing a glance of approval and gratitude on him. "What a good-hearted young man!" thought she. "How kind of him to amuse papa! and now I can stay so much longer."

Falcon followed up the dance by a call, and was infinitely agreeable; followed up the call by another, and admired Rosa with so little disguise that Mr. Lusignan said to her, "I think you have made a conquest. His father had considerable estates in Essex. I presume he inherits them."

"Oh, never mind his estates!" said Rosa. "He dances like an angel, and gossips charmingly, and *is so nice*."

Christopher Staines pined for this girl in silence; his fine frame got thinner, his pale cheek paler, as she got rosier and rosier; and how? Why, by following the very advice she had snubbed him for giving her. At last he heard she had been the belle of a ball, and that she had been seen walking miles from home, and blooming as a Hebe. Then his deep anxiety ceased, his pride stung him furiously; he began to think of his own value, and to struggle with all his might against his deep love. Sometimes he would even inveigh against her, and call her a fickle, ungrateful girl, capable of no strong passion but vanity. Many a hard term he applied to her in his sorrowful solitude, but not a word when he had a hearer. He found it hard to rest: he kept dashing up to London and back. He plunged furiously into study. He groaned and sighed, and fought the hard and bitter fight that is too often the lot of the deep that love the shallow. Strong, but single-hearted, no other lady could comfort him. He turned from their female company, and shunned all for the fault of one.

The inward contest wore him. He began to look very thin and wan, and all for a simpleton.

Mr. Falcon prolonged his stay in the neighborhood, and drove a handsome dog-cart over twice a week to visit Mr. Lusignan.

He used to call on that gentleman at four o'clock; for at that hour Mr. Lusignan was always out, and his daughter always at home.

She was at home at that hour, because she took her long walks in the morning. While her new admirer was in bed, or dressing, or breakfasting, she was springing along the road with all the elasticity of youth and health and native vigor, braced by daily exercise.

Twenty-one of these walks did she take with no other result than health and appetite: but the twenty-second was more fertile, extremely fertile. Starting later than usual, she passed through Gravesend while Reginald Falcon was smoking at his front window. He saw her, and instantly doffed his dressing-gown and donned his coat to follow her. He was madly in love with her; and, being a man who had learned to shoot pigeons and opportunities flying, he instantly resolved to join her in her walk, get her clear of the town, by the sea-beach, where beauty melts, and propose to her. Yes, marriage had not been hitherto his habit; but this girl was peerless. He was pledged by honor and gratitude to Phœbe Dale; but hang all that now. "No man should marry one woman when he loves another; it is dishonorable." He got into the street, and followed her as fast as he could without running.

It was not so easy to catch her. Ladies are ·not built for running; but a fine, tall, symmetrical girl, who has practised walking fast, can cover the ground wonderfully in walking —if she chooses. It was a sight to see how Rosa Lusignan squared her shoulders and stepped out from the loins, like a Canadian girl skating, while her elastic foot slapped the pavement as she spanked along.

She had nearly cleared the town before Falcon came up with her.

He was hardly ten yards from her when an unexpected incident occurred. She whisked round the corner of Bird Street, and ran plump against Christopher Staines; in fact, she darted into his arms, and her face almost touched the breast she had wounded so deeply.

----◆----

CHAPTER IV.

Rosa cried, "Oh!" and put up her hands to her face in lovely confusion, coloring like a peony.

"I beg your pardon," said Christopher stiffly, but in a voice that trembled.

"No," said Rosa: "it was I ran against you. I walk so fast now. Hope I did not hurt you."

"Hurt me?"

"Well, then, frighten you?"

No answer.

"Oh, please don't quarrel with me in the *street!*" said Rosa, cunningly implying that he was the quarrelsome one. "I am going on the beach. Good-by." This adieu she uttered softly, and in a hesitating tone, that belied it. She started off, however, but much more slowly than she was going before; and, as she went, she turned her head with infinite grace, and kept looking askant down at the pavement two yards behind her: moreover, she went close to the wall, and left room at her side for another to walk.

Christopher hesitated a moment; but the mute invitation, so arch yet timid, so pretty, tender, sly, and womanly, was too much for him, as it has generally proved for males; and the philosopher's foot was soon in the very place to which the simpleton with the mere tail of her eye directed it.

They walked along side by side in silence, Staines agitated, gloomy, confused; Rosa radiant and glowing; yet not knowing what to say for herself, and wanting Christopher to begin. So they walked along without a word.

Falcon followed them at some distance, to see whether it was an admirer or only an acquaintance; a lover, he never dreamed of, she had shown such evident pleasure in his company, and had received his visits alone so constantly.

However, when the pair had got to the beach, and were walking slower and slower, he felt a pang of rage and jealousy, turned on his heel with an audible curse, and found Phœbe Dale a few yards behind him with a white face and a peculiar look. He knew what the look meant. He had brought it to that faithful face before to-day.

"You are better, Miss Lusignan."

"Better, Dr. Staines? I am health itself, thanks to— Hem!"

"Our estrangement has agreed with you?" This very bitterly.

"You know very well it is not that. Oh, please don't make me cry in the streets!"

This humble petition, or rather meek threat, led to another long silence. It was continued till they had nearly reached the shore. But meantime, Rosa's furtive eyes scanned Christopher's face; and her conscience smote her at the signs of suffering. She felt a desire to beg his pardon with deep humility; but she suppressed that weakness. She hung her head with a pretty, sheepish air, and asked him if he could not think of something agreeable to say to one after deserting one so long.

"I am afraid not." said Christopher bluntly. "I have an awkward habit of speaking the truth; and some people can't bear that, not even when it is spoken for their good."

"That depends on temper and nerves and things," said Rosa deprecatingly; then softly, "I could bear any thing from you now."

"Indeed!" said Christopher, grimly. "Well, then, I hear you had no sooner got rid of your old lover, for loving you too well, and telling you the truth, than you took up another, — some flimsy man of fashion, who will tell you any lie you like."

"It is a story, a wicked story," cried Rosa, thoroughly alarmed. "Me, a lover? He dances like an angel. I can't help that."

"Are his visits at your house like angels', few and far between?" And the true lover's brow lowered black upon her for the first time.

Rosa changed color; and her eyes fell a moment. "Ask papa," said she. "His father was an old friend of papa's."

"Rosa, you are prevaricating. Young men do not call on old gentlemen when there is an attractive young lady in the house."

The argument was getting too close, so Rosa operated a diversion. "So," said she, with a sudden air of lofty disdain, swiftly and adroitly assumed, "you have had me watched."

"Not I : I only hear what people say."

"Listen to gossip, and not have me watched! That shows how little you really cared for me. Well, if you had, you would have made a little discovery; that is all."

"Should I?" said Christopher puzzled. "What?"

"I shall not tell you. Think what you please. Yes, sir, you would have found out that I take long walks every day, all alone; and what is more, that I walk through Gravesend hoping, like a goose, that somebody really loved me, and would meet me, and beg my pardon; and, if he had, I should have told him it was only my tongue and my nerves and things. My heart was his, and my gratitude; and, after all, what do words signify when I am a good, obedient girl at bottom? So that is what you have lost by not condescending to look after me. Fine love! Christopher, beg my pardon."

"May I ask for what?"

"Why, for not understanding me; for not knowing that I should be sorry the moment you were gone. I took them off the very next day, to please you."

"Took off whom? Oh, I understand! You did? Then you *are* a good girl."

"Didn't I tell you I was? A good obedient girl, and any thing but a flirt."

"I don't say that."

"But I do. Don't interrupt. It is to your good advice I owe my health; and to love anybody but you, when I owe you my love and my life, I must be a heartless ungrateful, worthless— O Christopher forgive me!　No, no; I mean, beg my pardon."

"I'll do both," said Christopher, taking her in his arms.　"I beg your pardon, and I forgive you."

Rosa leaned her head tenderly on his shoulder, and began to sigh. "Oh, dear, dear, I am a wicked, foolish girl, not fit to walk alone!"

On this admission, Christopher spoke out, and urged her to put an end to all these unhappy misunderstandings, and to his new torment, jealousy, by marrying him.

"And so I would this very minute, if papa would consent.　But," said she shyly, "you never can be so foolish to wish it.　What! a wise man like you marry a simpleton!"

"Did I ever call you that?" asked Christopher, reproachfully.

"No, dear; but you are the only one who has not; and perhaps I should lose even the one, if you were to marry me.　Oh, husbands are not so polite as lovers!　I have observed that, simpleton or not."

Christopher assured her that he took quite a different view of her character: he believed her to be too profound for shallow people to read all in a moment; he even intimated that he himself had experienced no little difficulty in understanding her at odd times. "And so," said he, "they turn round upon you, and instead of saying, 'We are too shallow to fathom you,' they pretend you are a simpleton."

This solution of the mystery had never occurred to Rosa, nor, indeed, was it likely to occur to any creature less ingenious than a lover.　It pleased her hugely : her fine eyes sparkled ; and she nestled closer still to the strong arm that was to parry every ill, from mortal disease to galling epithets.

She listened with a willing ear to all his reasons, his hopes, his fears ; and, when they reached her father's door, it was settled that he should dine there that day, and urge his suit to her father after dinner.　She would implore the old gentleman to listen to it favorably.

The lovers parted ; and Christopher went home like one who has awakened from a hideous dream to daylight and happiness.

He had not gone far before he met a dashing dog-cart driven by an exquisite.　He turned to look after it, and saw it drive up to Kent Villa.

In a moment, he divined his rival ; and a sickness of heart came over him.　But he recovered himself directly, and said, "If that is the fellow, she will not receive him now."

She did receive him, though : at all events, the dog-cart stood at the door, and its master remained inside.

Christopher stood and counted the minutes : five — ten — fifteen — twenty minutes ; and still the dog-cart stood there.

It was more than he could bear. He turned savagely, and strode back to Gravesend, resolving that all this torture should end that night, one way or other.

Phœbe Dale was the daughter of a farmer in Essex, and one of the happiest young women in England till she knew Reginald Falcon, Esq.

She was reared on wholesome food, in wholesome air, and used to churn butter, make bread, cook a bit now and then, cut out and sew all her own dresses, get up her own linen, make hay, ride any thing on four legs, and, for all that, was a great reader, and taught in the Sunday school to oblige the vicar ; wrote a neat hand, and was a good arithmetician ; kept all the house accounts and farm accounts.　She was a musician too — not profound, but very correct; she would take her turn at the harmonium in church, and when she was there you never heard a wrong note in the bass, nor an inappropriate flourish, nor bad time. She could sing too, but never would, except her part in a psalm. Her voice was a deep contralto; and she chose to be ashamed of this heavenly organ because a pack of envious girls had giggled, and said it was like a man's.

In short, her natural ability, and the range and variety of her useful accomplishments, were considerable; not that she was a prodigy, but she belonged to a small class of women in this island who are not too high to use their arms, nor too low to cultivate their minds; and, having a faculty and a habit deplorably rare among her sex, viz., attention, she had profited by her miscellaneous advantages.

Her figure and face both told her breed at once: here was an old English pastoral beauty; not the round-backed, narrow-chested cottager, but the well-fed, erect rustic, with broad, full bust and massive shoulder, and arm as hard as a rock with health and constant use; a hand finely cut, though neither small nor very white, and just a little hard inside compared with Luxury's soft palm; a face honest, fair, and rather large than small; not beautiful, but exceedingly comely; a complexion not pink and white, but that delicately blended, brick-dusty color which tints the whole cheek in fine gradation, outlasts other complexions twenty years, and beautifies the true Northern even in old age. Gray, limpid, honest, point-blank, searching eyes; hair true nut brown, without a shade of red or black, and a high smooth forehead, full of sense. Across it ran one deep wrinkle that did not belong to her youth; that wrinkle was the brand of trouble, the line of agony. It had come of loving above her, yet below her, and of loving an egotist.

Three years before our tale commenced a gentleman's horse ran away with him, and threw him on a heap of stones by the roadside, not very far from Farmer Dale's gate. The farmer had him taken in: the doctor said he must not be moved. He was insensible; his cheek like delicate wax; his fair hair like silk stained with blood. He became Phœbe's patient, and, in due course, her convalescent: his pale, handsome face and fascinating manners gained one charm more from weakness; his vices were in abeyance.

The womanly nurse's heart yearned over her child, for he was feeble as a child; and when he got well enough to amuse his weary hours by making love to her, and telling her a pack of arrant lies, she was a ready dupe. He was to marry her as soon as ever his old uncle died and left him the means, etc., etc. At last he got well enough to leave her, and went away, her open admirer and secret lover. He borrowed twenty pounds of her the day he left.

He used to write her charming letters, and feed the flame: but one day her father sent her up to London, on his own business, all of a sudden; and she called on Mr. Falcon at his feigned address. She found he did not live there—only received letters. However, half a crown soon bought his real address, and thither Phœbe proceeded, with a troubled heart; for she suspected that her true lover was in debt or trouble, and obliged to hide. Well, he must be got out of it, and hide at the farm meantime.

So the loving girl knocked at the door, asked for Mr. Falcon, and was shown in to a lady rather showily dressed, who asked her business, and introduced herself as Mrs. Falcon.

Phœbe Dale stared at her, and then turned pale as ashes. She was paralyzed, and could not find her tongue.

"Why, what is the matter now?" said the other sharply.

"Are you married to Reginald Falcon?"

"Of course I am. Look at my wedding-ring."

"Then I am not wanted here," faltered Phœbe, ready to sink on the floor.

"Certainly not, if you are one of the by-gones," said the woman coarsely; and Phœbe Dale waited to hear no more, but found her way, Heaven knows how! into the street, and there leaned, half fainting, on a rail, till a policeman came and told her she had been drinking, and suggested a cool cell as the best cure.

"Not drink; only a breaking heart," said she, in her low mellow voice that few could resist.

He got her a glass of water, drove away the boys that congregated directly, and she left the street. But she soon came back again, and waited about for Reginald Falcon.

It was night when he appeared. She seized him by the breast, and taxed him with his villany.

What with her iron grasp, pale face, and flashing eyes, he lost his cool impudence, and blurted out excuses. It was an old and unfortunate connection; he would give the world to dissolve it, if he could do it like a gentleman.

Phœbe told him to please himself; he must part with one or the other.

"Don't talk nonsense," said this man of brass. "I'll un-Falcon her on the spot."

"Very well," said Phœbe. "I am going home, and if you are not there by to-morrow at noon"— She said no more, but looked a great deal. Then she departed, and refused him her hand at parting. "We will see about that by and by," said she.

By noon my lord came down to the farm, and, unfortunately for Phœbe, played the penitent so skilfully for about a month that she forgave him, and loved him all the more for having so nearly parted with him.

Her peace was not to endure long. He was detected in an intrigue in the very village.

The insult struck so home that Phœbe herself, to her parents' satisfaction, ordered him out of the house at once.

But when he was gone she had fits of weeping, and could settle to nothing for a long time.

Months had elapsed, and she was getting a sort of dull tranquillity, when one evening, taking a walk she had often taken with him, and mourning her solitude and wasted affection, he waylaid her, and clung to her knees, and shed crocodile tears on her hands, and after a long resistance, violent at first, but fainter and fainter, got her in his power again, and that so completely that she met him several times by night, being ashamed to be seen with him in those parts by day.

This ended in fresh promises of marriage, and in a constant correspondence by letter. This pest knew exactly how to talk to a woman, and how to write to one. His letters fed the unhappy flame: and, mind you, he sometimes deceived himself and thought he loved her; but it was only himself he loved. She was an invaluable lover, a faithful, disinterested friend : hers was a vile bargain; his an excellent one, and he clung to it.

And so they went on. She detected him in another infidelity, and reproached him bitterly; but she had no longer the strength to break with him. Nevertheless, this time she had the sense to make a struggle. She implored him on her very knees to show her a little mercy in return for all her love. "For pity's sake, leave me!" she cried. "You are strong, and I am weak. You can end it forever; and pray do. You don't want me; you don't value me: then leave me once and for all, and end this hell you keep me in."

No; he could not or he would not leave her alone. Look at a bird's wings!—how like an angel's! Yet so vile a thing as a bit of bird-lime subdues them utterly : and such was the fascinating power of this mean man over this worthy woman. She was a reader, a thinker, a model of respectability, industry, and sense; a business woman, keen and practical; could encounter sharp hands in sharp trades; could buy or sell hogs, calves, or beasts with any farmer or butcher in the country; yet no match for a cunning fool. She had enshrined an idol in her heart; and that heart adored it and clung to it, though the superior head saw through it, dreaded it, despised it.

No wonder three years of this had drawn a tell-tale wrinkle across the polished brow.

Phœbe Dale had not received a letter for some days: that roused her suspicion and stung her jealousy; she came up to London by fast train, and down to Gravesend directly.

She had a thick veil that concealed her features; and, with a little inquiring and bribing, she soon found out that Mr. Falcon was there with a showy dog-cart. "Ah!" thought Phœbe, "he has won a little money at play or pigeon-shooting; so now he has no need of me."

She took lodgings opposite him, but observed nothing till this very morning, when she saw him throw off his dressing-gown all in a hurry, and fling on his coat. - She tied on her bonnet as rapidly, and followed him until she discovered the object of his pursuit. It was a surprise to her, and a puzzle, to see another man step in, as if to take her part. But, as Reginald still followed the loitering pair, she followed Reginald, till he turned and found her at his heels, white and lowering.

She confronted him in threatening silence for some time, during which he prepared his defence.

"So it is a *lady* this time." said she, in her low, rich voice, sternly.

"Is it?"

"Yes, and I should say she is bespoke. That tall, fine-built gentleman. But I suppose you care no

more for his feelings than you do for mine."

"Phœbe," said the egotist, "I will not try to deceive you. You have often said you are my true friend."

"And I think I have proved it."

"That you have. Well, then, be my true friend now. I am in love —really in love — this time. You and I only torment each other; let us part friends. There are plenty of farmers in Essex that would jump at you. As for me, I'll tell you the truth; I have run through every farthing; my estate mortgaged beyond its value — two or three writs out against me — that is why I slipped down here. My only chance is to marry Money. Her father knows I have land, and he knows nothing about the mortgages; she is his only daughter. Don't stand in my way, that is a good girl; be my friend as you always were. Hang it all, Phœbe, can't you say a word to a fellow that is driven into a corner, instead of glaring at me like that: there, I know it is ungrateful — but what can a fellow do? I must live like a gentleman, or else take a dose of prussic acid; you don't want to drive me to that. Why, you proposed to part, last time, yourself."

She gave him one majestic, indescribable look, that made even his callous heart quiver, and turned away.

Then the scamp admired her for despising him, and could not bear to lose her. He followed her, and put forth all those powers of persuading and soothing which had so often proved irresistible. But this time it was in vain. The insult was too savage and his egotism too brutal for honeyed phrases to blind her.

After enduring it a long time with a silent shudder, she turned and shook him fiercely off her, like some poisonous reptile.

"Do you want me to kill you? I'd liever kill myself for loving such a thing as *thou*. Go thy ways, man, and let me go mine." In her passion, she dropped her cultivation for once, and went back to the thou and thee of her grandam.

He colored up, and looked spiteful enough; but he soon recovered his cynical egotism, and went off whistling an operatic passage.

She crept to her lodgings, and buried her face in her pillow, and rocked herself to and fro for hours in the bitterest agony the heart can feel, groaning over her great affection wasted, flung into the dirt.

While she was thus, she heard a little commotion. She came to the window and saw Falcon, exquisitely dressed, drive off in his dog-cart, attended by the acclamations of eight boys. She saw at a glance he was going courting. Her knees gave way under her; and, such is the power of the mind, this stalwart girl lay weak as water on the sofa, and had not the power to go home, though just then she had but one wish, one hope, to see her idol's face no more, nor hear his wheedling tongue, that had ruined her peace.

The exquisite Mr. Falcon was received by Rosa Lusignan with a certain tremor that flattered his hopes. He told her, in charming language, how he had admired her at first sight, then esteemed her, then loved her.

She blushed and panted, and showed more than once a desire to interrupt him, but was too polite. She heard him out, with rising dismay, and he offered her his hand and heart.

But, by this time, she had made up her mind what to say. "O Mr. Falcon!" she cried, "how can you speak to me in this way? Why, I'm engaged! Didn't you know?"

"No; and I am sure you are not, or you would never have given me the encouragement you have."

"Oh, all engaged young ladies flirt, — a little! and everybody here knows I am engaged to Dr. Staines."

"Why, I never saw him here!"

Rosa's tact was a quality that came and went; so she blushed and faltered out, "We had a little tiff, as lovers will."

"And you did me the honor to select me as cat's-paw, to bring him on again. Was not that rather heartless?"

Rosa's fitful tact returned to her.

"Oh, sir, do not think so ill of me! I am not heartless, I am only unwise. And you are so superior to the people about you I could not help appreciating you: and I thought you knew I was engaged; and so I was less on my guard. I hope I shall not lose your esteem, though I have no right to any thing more. Ah! I see by your face I have behaved very ill: pray forgive me."

And with this she turned on the waters of the Nile, better known to you perhaps as "crocodile tears."

Falcon was a gentleman on the surface, and knew he should only make matters worse by quarrelling with her. So he ground his teeth, and said, "May your own heart never feel the pangs you have inflicted! I shall love you and remember you till my dying day."

He bowed ceremoniously, and left her. "Ay," said he to himself, "I *will* remember you, you heartless jilt, and the man you have jilted me for. Staines is his d——d name, is it?"

He drove back crest-fallen, bitter, and, for once in his life, heart-sick, and drew up at his lodgings. Here he found attendants waiting to receive him.

A sheriff's officer took his dog-cart and horse under a judgment; the disturbance this caused collected a tidy crowd, gaping and grinning, and brought Phoebe's white face and eyes swollen with weeping to the window.

Falcon saw her, and brazened it out. "Take them," said he, with an oath. "I'll have a better turn-out by to-morrow, breakfast-time."

The crowd cheered him for his spirit.

He got down, lit a cigar, chaffed the officer and the crowd, and was, on the whole, admired.

Then another officer, who had been hunting him in couples with the other, stepped forward and took *him* for the balance of a judgment debt.

Then the swell's cigar fell out of his mouth, and he was seriously alarmed. "Why, Cartwright," said he, "this is too bad! You promised not to see me this month. You passed me full in the Strand."

"You are mistaken, sir," said Cartwright, with sullen irony, "I've got a twin brother, a many takes him for me, till they finds the difference." Then, lowering his voice, "What call had you to boast in your club you had made it right with Bill Cartwright, and he'd never see you? That got about, and so I was bound to see you or lose my bread. There's one or two I don't see; but then they are real gentle-men, and thinks of me as well as theirselves, and doesn't blab."

"I must have been drunk," said Falcon apologetically.

"More likely blowing a cloud. When you young gents gets a-smok-ing together, you'd tell on your own mothers. Come along, colonel; off we go to Merrimashee."

"Why, it is only twenty-six pounds. I have paid the rest."

"More than that; there's the costs."

"Come in, and I'll settle it."

"All right, sir; Jem, watch the back."

"Oh, I shall not try that game with a sharp hand like you, Cart-wright!"

"You had better not, sir," said Cartwright; but he was softened a little by the compliment.

When they were alone, Falcon be-gan by saying it was a bad job for him.

"Why, I thought you was a-go-ing to pay it all in a moment!"

"I can't: but I have got a friend over the way that could, if she chose. She has always got money somehow."

"Oh! if it is a she, it is all right"

"I don't know. She has quar-reled with me; but give me a little time. Here, have a glass of sherry and a biscuit, while I try it on."

Having thus muffled Cartwright, this man of the world opened his window and looked out. The crowd had followed the captured dog-cart, so he had the street to himself. He beckoned to Phœbe; and, after con-siderable hesitation, she opened her window.

"Phœbe," said he, in tones of tender regret, admirably natural and sweet, "I shall never offend you again; so forgive me this once. I have given that girl up."

"Not you," said Phœbe sullenly.

"Indeed I have. After our quar-rel I started to propose to her, but I had not the heart: I came back and left her."

"Time will show. If it is not her, it will be some other, you false, heartless villain."

"Come, I say, don't be so hard on me in trouble. I am going to prison."

"So I suppose."

"Ah, but it is worse than you think! I am only taken for a pal-try thirty pounds or so."

"Thirty-three, fifteen, five," sug-gested Cartwright, in a muffled whisper, his mouth being full of biscuit.

"But once they get me to a sponging-house, detainers will pour in, and my cruel creditors will con-fine me for life."

"It is the best place for you. It will put a stop to your wickedness, and I shall be at peace. That's what I have never known, night or day, this three years."

"But you will not be happy if you see me go to prison before your eyes. Were you ever inside a prison? Just think what it must be to be cooped up in those cold grim cells all alone; for they use a debtor like a criminal now."

Phœbe shuddered; but she said bravely, "Well, tell *them* you have been a-courting. There was a time I'd have died sooner than see a hair of your head hurt; but it is all over now: you have worn me out."

Then she began to cry.

Falcon heaved a deep sigh. "It is no more than I deserve," said he. "I'll pack up my things and go with the officer. Give me one kind word at parting; and I'll think of it in my prison night and day."

He withdrew from the window with another deep sigh, told Cartwright, cheerfully, it was all right, and proceeded to pack up his traps.

Meantime Phœbe sat at her window and cried bitterly. Her words had been braver than her heart.

Falcon managed to pay the trifle he owed for the lodgings; and presently he came out with Cartwright, and the attendant called a cab. His things were thrown in, and Cartwright invited him to follow. Then he looked up and cast a genuine look of terror and misery at Phœbe. He thought she would have relented before this.

Her heart gave way: I am afraid it would, even without that piteous and mute appeal. She opened the window, and asked Mr. Cartwright if he would be good enough to come and speak to her.

Cartwright committed his prisoner to the subordinate, and knocked at the door of Phœbe's lodgings. She came down herself and let him in. She led the way upstairs, motioned him to a seat, sat down by him, and began to cry again. She was thoroughly unstrung.

Cartwright was human, and muttered some words of regret that a poor fellow must do his duty.

"Oh, it is not that!" sobbed Phœbe; "I can find the money. I have found more for him than that many's the time." Then, drying her eyes, "But you must know the world; and I dare say you can see how 'tis with me."

"I can," said Cartwright gravely. "I overheard you and him; and, my girl, if you take my advice, why, let him go. He is a gentleman skin deep, and dresses well, and can palaver a girl, no doubt; but, bless your heart! I can see at a glance he is not worth your little finger,—an honest, decent young woman like you. Why, it is like butter fighting with stone! Let him go; or I will tell you what it is, you will hang for him some day, or else make away with yourself."

"Ay, sir," said Phœbe, "that's likelier; and, if I was to let him go to prison, I should sit me down and think of his parting look: and I should fling myself into the water for him before I was a day older."

"Ye mustn't do that, any way. While there's life there's hope."

Upon this, Phœbe put him a question, and found him ready to do any thing for her, in reason,—provided he was paid for it. And the end of it all was, the prisoner was conveyed to London. Phœbe got the requisite sum; Falcon was deposited in a third-class carriage bound for Essex. Phœbe paid his debt, and gave Cartwright a present; and away rattled the train conveying the handsome egotist into temporary retirement, to wit, at a village five miles from the Dales' farm. She was too ashamed of her young gentleman and herself to be seen with him in her native village. On the road down, he was full of little practical attentions; she received them coldly. His mellifluous mouth was often at her ear, pouring thanks and praises into it; she never vouchsafed a word of reply. All she did was to shudder now and then, and cry at intervals. Yet, whenever he left her side, her whole body became restless; and, when he came back to her, a furtive thrill announced the insane complacency his bare contact gave her. Surely of all the forms in which love torments the heart, this was the most terrible and pitiable.

Mr. Lusignan found his daughter in tears.

"Why, what is the matter now?" said he, a little peevishly. "We have had nothing of this sort of thing lately."

"Papa, it is because I have misconducted myself. I am a foolish, imprudent girl. I have been flirting with Mr. Falcon; and he has taken a *cruel* advantage of it, — proposed to me, this very afternoon, actually!"

"Has he? Well, he is a fine fellow, and has a landed estate in Norfolk. There's nothing like land. They may well call it real property: there is something to show. You can walk on, it, and ride on it, and look out of window at it: that *is* property."

"O papa! What are you saying? Would you have me marry one man, when I belong to another?"

"But you don't belong to any one, except to me."

"Oh, yes, I do! I belong to my dear Christopher."

"Why, you dismissed him before my very eyes; and very ill you behaved, begging your pardon! The man was your able physician and your best friend, and said nothing that was not for your good; and you treated him like a dog."

"Yes, but he has apologized."

"What for? for being treated like a dog?"

"Oh, don't say so, papa! At all events, he has apologized, as a gentleman should whenever — whenever" —

"Whenever a lady is in the wrong."

"Don't, papa; and I have asked him to dinner."

"With all my heart. I shall be downright glad to see him again. You used him abominably."

"But you need not keep saying so," whined Rosa. "And that is not all, dear papa; the worst of it is, Mr. Falcon proposing to me has opened my eyes. I am not fit to be trusted alone. I am too fond of dancing; and flirting will follow somehow. Oh, think how ill I was a few months ago, and how unhappy you were about me! They were killing me. He came and saved me. Yes, papa, I owe all this health and strength to Christopher. I did take them off the very next day, and see the effect of it, and my long walks. I owe him my life, and, what I value far more, my good looks. La! I wish I had not told you that; and, after all this, don't I belong to my Christopher? How could I be happy, or respect myself, if I married any one else? And O papa! he looks wan and worn. He has been fretting for his simpleton. Oh, dear! I mustn't think of that; it makes me cry; and you don't like scenes, do you?"

"Hate 'em!"

"Well, then," said Rosa coaxingly, "I'll tell you how to end them. Marry your simpleton to the only man who is fit to take care of her. O papa! think of his deep, deep affection for me, and pray don't snub him if — by any chance — after dinner — he should *happen* to ask you — something."

"Oh! then it is possible that, by the merest chance, the gentleman you have accidentally asked to dinner may, by some strange fortuity, be surprised into asking me a second time for something very much resembling my daughter's hand, eh?"

Rosa colored high. "He might, you know. How can I tell what gentlemen will say when the ladies have retired, and they are left alone with — with" —

"With the bottle. Ay, that's

true! when the wine is in, the wit is out."

Said Rosa, "Well, if he should happen to be so foolish, pray think of *me*; of all we owe him, and how much I love him, and ought to love him." She then bestowed a propitiatory kiss, and ran off to dress for dinner : it was a much longer operation to-day than usual.

Dr. Staines was punctual. Mr. Lusignan commented favorably on that.

"He always is," said Rosa eagerly.

They dined together. Mr. Lusignan chatted freely; but Staines and Rosa were under a feeling of restraint, Staines in particular: he could not help feeling that before long his fate must be settled. He would either obtain Rosa's hand, or have to resign her to some man of fortune who would step in; for beauty such as hers could not long lack brilliant offers. Longing, though dreading, to know his fate, he was glad when dinner ended.

Rosa sat with them a little while after dinner, then rose, bestowed another propitiatory kiss on her father's head, and retired with a modest blush, and a look at Christopher that was almost divine.

It inspired him with the courage of lions; and he commenced the attack at once.

CHAPTER V.

"Mr. Lusignan," said he, "the last time I was here, you gave me some hopes that you might be prevailed on to trust that angel's health and happiness to my care."

"Well, Dr. Staines, I will not beat about the bush with you. My judgment is still against this marriage : you need not look so alarmed; it does not follow I shall forbid it. I feel I have hardly a right to; for my Rosa might be in her grave now but for you. And another thing, when I interfered between you two, I had no proof you were a man of ability : I had only your sweetheart's word for that; and I never knew a case before where a young lady's swan did not turn out a goose. Your rare ability gives you another chance in the professional battle that is before you; indeed, it puts a different face on the whole matter. I still think it premature. Come, now, would it not be much wiser to wait, and secure a good practice before you marry a mere child ? There — there — I only advise; I don't dictate: you shall settle it together, you two wiseacres. Only I must make one positive condition : I have nothing to give my child during my lifetime; but one thing I have done for her; years ago I insured my life for six thousand pounds; and you must do the same. I will not have her thrown on the world a widow, with a child or two perhaps, to support, and not a farthing; you know the insecurity of mortal life."

"I do, I do. Why, of course I will insure my life, and pay the annual premium out of my little capital until income flows in !"

"Will you hand me over a sum sufficient to pay that premium for five years ? "

"With pleasure."

"Then I fear," said the old gentleman with a sigh, "my opposition to the match must cease here. I still recommend you to wait: but, there I might just as well advise fire and tow to live neighbors, and keep cool."

To show the injustice of this simile, Christopher Staines started up, with his eyes all aglow, and cried out, rapturously, "O sir ! may I tell her ? "

"Yes, you may tell her," said Lusignan with a smile. "Stop ! what are you going to tell her ? "

"That you consent, sir. God bless you ! God bless you ! Oh !"

"Yes, but that I advise you to wait."

"I'll tell her all," said Staines, and rushed out even as he spoke, and upset a heavy chair with a loud thud.

"Ah! ah!" cried the old gentleman in dismay, and put his fingers in his ears. "Too late. I see," said he, "there will be no peace and quiet now till they are out of the house." He lighted a soothing cigar, to counteract the fracas.

"Poor little Rosa!—a child but yesterday, and now to encounter the cares of a wife, and perhaps a mother. Ah! she is but young, but young."

The old gentleman prophesied truly; from that moment he had no peace till he withdrew all semblance of dissent, and even of procrastination.

Christopher insured his life for six thousand pounds, and assigned the policy to his wife. Four hundred pounds was handed to Mr. Lusignan to pay the premiums until the genius of Dr. Staines should have secured him that large professional income, which does not come all at once even to the rare physician, who is *Capax Efficax Sugar.*

The wedding-day was named. The bridemaids were selected, the guests invited. None refused but Uncle Philip. He declined, in his fine bold hand, to countenance in person an act of folly he disapproved. Christopher put his letter away with a momentary sigh, and would not show it Rosa. All other letters they read together, — charming pastime of that happy period. Presents poured in. Silver tea-pots, coffee-pots, sugar-basins, cream-jugs, fruit-dishes, silver-gilt inkstands, albums, photograph-books, little candlesticks, choice little services of china, shell salt-cellars in a case lined with maroon-velvet; a Bible, superb in binding and clasps and every thing, but the text,—that was illegible; a silk scarf from Benares; a gold chain from Delhi, six feet long or nearly; a maltese necklace; a ditto in exquisite filigree, from Genoa; English brooches, a trifle too big and brainless: apostle-spoons; a treble-lined parasol, with ivory stick and handle; an ivory card-case, richly carved; work-box of sandal-wood and ivory, &c. Mr. Lusignan's city friends, as usual with these gentlemen, sent the most valuable things. Every day one or two packages were delivered; and, on opening them, Rosa invariably uttered a peculiar scream of delight, and her father put his fingers in his ears; yet there was music in this very scream — if he would only have listened to it candidly, instead of fixing his mind on his vague theory of screams — so formed was she to please the ear as well as eye.

At last came a parcel she opened and stared at, smiling: and coloring like a rose, but did not scream, being too dumb-foundered and perplexed; for lo! a tea-pot of some base material, but simple and elegant in form, being an exact reproduction of a melon; and inside this tea-pot a canvas bag containing ten guineas in silver, and a wash-leather bag containing twenty guineas in gold, and a slip of paper, which Rosa, being now half recovered from her stupefaction, read out to her father and Dr. Staines.

"People that buy presents blindfold give duplicates and triplicates; and men seldom choose to a woman's taste: so be pleased to accept the enclosed tea-leaves, and buy for yourself. The tea-pot you can put on the hob; for it is nickel."

Rosa looked sore puzzled again. "Papa," said she timidly, "have we any friend that is — a little — deranged?"

"A lot."

"Oh, then, that accounts!"

"Why no, love," said Christopher. "I have heard of much learning making a man mad, but never of much good sense."

"What! Do you call this sensible?"

"Don't you?"

"I'll read it again," said Rosa. "Well—yes—I declare—it is not so mad as I thought; but it is very eccentric."

Lusignan suggested there was nothing so eccentric as common-sense, especially in time of wedding. "This," said he, "comes from the city. It is a friend of mine, some old fox: he is throwing dust in your eyes with his reasons. His real reason was that his time is money; it would have cost the old rogue a hundred pounds' worth of time—you know the city, Christopher—to go out and choose the girl a present; so he has sent his clerk out with a cheek to buy a pewter teapot, and fill it with specie."

"Pewter!" cried Rosa. "No such thing! It's nickel. What is nickel, I wonder?"

The handwriting afforded no clew, so there the discussion ended: but it was a nice little mystery, and very convenient, made conversation. Rosa had many an animated discussion about it with her female friends.

The wedding-day came at last. The sun shone—*actually*, as Rosa observed. The carriages drove up. The bridemaids, principally old school-fellows and impassioned correspondents of Rosa, were pretty, and dressed alike, and delightfully: but the bride was peerless; her southern beauty literally shone in that white satin dress and veil, and her head was regal with the crown of orange blossoms. Another crown she had, true virgin modesty. A low murmur burst from the men the moment they saw her; the old women forgave her beauty on the spot, and the young women almost pardoned it; she was so sweet and womanly, and so sisterly to her own sex.

When they started for the church, she began to tremble, she scarce knew why; and when the solemn words were said, and the ring was put on her finger, she cried a little, and looked half-imploringly at her bridemaids once, as if scared at leaving them for an untried and mysterious life with no woman near.

They were married. Then came the breakfast, that hour of uneasiness and blushing to such a bride as this; but at last she was released. She sped up stairs, thanking goodness it was over. Down came her last box. The bride followed in a plain travelling dress, which her glorious eyes and brows and her rich glowing cheeks seemed to illumine. She was handed into the carriage; the bridegroom followed. All the young guests clustered about the door, armed with white shoes,—slippers are gone by.

They started: the ladies flung their white shoes right and left with religious impartiality, except that not one of their missiles went at the object. The men, more skilful, sent a shower on to the roof of the carriage, which is the lucky spot. The bride kissed her hand, and managed to put off crying, though it cost her a struggle. The party hurrahed. Enthusiastic youths gathered fallen shoes, and ran and hurled them again with cheerful yells; and away went the happy pair, the bride leaning sweetly and confidingly with both her white hands on the bridegroom's shoulder, while he dried the tears that would run now at leaving home and parent forever, and kissed her often, and encircled her with his strong arm, and murmured comfort and love and pride and joy and sweet vows of life-long tenderness into her ears, that soon stole nearer his lips to hear, and the fair cheek grew softly to his shoulder.

CHAPTER VI.

Dr. Staines and Mrs. Staines visited France, Switzerland, and the Rhine, and passed a month of Elysium, before they came to London to face their real destiny and fight the battle of life.

And here, methinks a reader of novels may, perhaps, cry out and say, "What manner of man is 'this, who marries his hero and heroine, and then, instead of leaving them happy for life, and at rest from his uneasy pen, and all their other troubles, flows coolly on with their adventures?"

To this I can only reply that the old English novel is no rule to me, and life is; and I respectfully propose an experiment: catch eight old married people, four of each sex, and say unto them, "Sir," or "Madame, did the more remarkable events of your life come to you before marriage or after?" Most of them will say "after," and let that be my excuse for treating the marriage of Christopher Staines and Rosa Lusignan as merely one incident in their lives, — an incident which, so far from ending their story, led by degrees to more striking events than any that occurred to them before they were man and wife.

They returned then from their honey-tour; and Staines, who was methodical, and kept a diary, made the following entry therein: —

"We have now a life of endurance and self-denial and economy before us: we have to rent a house, and furnish it, and live in it, until professional income shall flow in and make all things easy; and we have two thousand five hundred pounds left to do it with."

They came to a family hotel; and Doctor Staines went out, directly after breakfast, to look for a house. Acting on a friend's advice, he visited the streets and places north of Oxford Street, looking for a good commodious house adapted to his business. He found three or four at fair rents, neither cheap nor dear, the district being respectable and rather wealthy, but no longer fashionable. He came home with his notes, and found Rosa, beaming in a crisp *peignoir*, and her lovely head its natural size and shape, high-bred and elegant. He sat down, and with her hand in his, proceeded to describe the houses to her, when a waiter threw open the door—"Mrs. John Cole."

"Florence!" cried Rosa, starting up.

In flowed Florence: they both uttered a little squawk of delight, and went at each other like two little tigresses, and kissed in swift alternation with a singular ardor, drawing their crests back like snakes, and then darting them forward and inflicting what, to the male philosopher looking on, seemed hard kisses, violent kisses, rather than the tender ones to be expected from two tender creatures embracing each other.

"Darling," said Rosa, "I knew you would be the first. Didn't I tell you so, Christopher? My husband, my darling Florry! Sit down, love, and tell me every thing: he has just been looking out for a house. Ah! you have got all that over long ago: she has been married six months. Florry, you are handsomer than ever; and what a beautiful dress! Ah, London is the place. Real Brussels, I declare;" and she took hold of her friend's lace, and gloated on it.

Christopher smiled good-naturedly, and said, "I dare say you ladies have a good deal to say to each other."

"Oceans!" said Rosa.

"I will go and hunt houses again."

"There's a good husband," said Mrs. Cole, as soon as the door closed on him; "and such a fine man. Why, he must be six feet! Mine is rather short. But he is very good; refuses me nothing. My will is law."

"That is all right, you are so sensible; but I want governing a little:

and I like it—actually. Did the dressmaker find it, dear?"

"Oh, no! I had it by me. I bought it at Brussels, on our wedding-tour: it is dearer there than in London."

She said this, as if "dearer" and "better" were synonymous.

"But about your house, Rosie dear?"

"Yes, darling, I'll tell you all about it. I never saw a moire this shade before; I don't care for them in general; but this is so *distingue*."

Florence rewarded her with a kiss.

"The house," said Rosa. "Oh! he has seen one in Portman Street, and one in Gloucester Place."

"Oh, that will never do!" cried Mrs. Cole. "It is no use being a physician in those out-of-the-way places. He must be in Mayfair."

"Must he?"

"Of course. Besides, then my Johnnie can call him in, when they are just going to die. Johnnie is a general prac., and makes two thousand a year; and he shall call your one in: but he must live in Mayfair. Why, Rosa, you would not be such a goose as to live in those places! they are quite gone by."

"I shall do whatever you advise me, dear. Oh, what a comfort to have a dear friend! and six months married, and knows things. How richly it is trimmed! Why, it is nearly all trimmings!"

"That is the fashion."

"Oh!"

And, after that big word, there was no more to be said.

These two ladies in their conversation gravitated toward dress, and fell flat on it every half minute. That great and elevating topic held them by a silken cord: but it allowed them to flutter upward into other topics; and in those intervals, numerous though brief, the lady who had been married six months found time to instruct the matrimonial novice with great authority, and even a shade of pomposity. "My dear, the way ladies and gentlemen get a house — in the first place, you don't go about yourself like that, and you never go to the people themselves, or you are sure to be taken in, but to a respectable house-agent."

"Yes, dear, that must be the best way, one would think."

"Of course it is; and you ask for a house in Mayfair; and he shows you several, and recommends you the best, and sees you are not cheated."

"Thank you, love," said Rosa: "now I know what to do; I'll not forget a word. And the train is so beautifully shaped! Ah, it is only in London or Paris they can make a dress flow behind like that," &c., &c.

Dr. Staines came back to dinner in good spirits: he had found a house in Harewood Square; good entrance hall, where his gratuitous patients might sit on benches; good dining-room, where his superior patients might wait, and good library, to be used as a consulting-room. Rent only £85 per annum.

But Rosa told him that would never do; a physician must be in the fashionable part of the town.

"Eventually," said Christopher; "but surely at first starting; and you know they say little boats should not go too far from shore."

Then Rosa repeated all her friend's arguments, and seemed so unhappy at the idea of not living near her, that Staines, who had not yet said the hard word "No" to her, gave in, consoling his prudence with the reflection that, after all, Mr. Cole could put many a guinea in his way; for Mr. Cole was middle-aged — though his wife was young — and had really a very large practice.

So next day the newly-wedded pair called on a house-agent in Mayfair, and his son and partner went with them to several places. The rents of houses equal to that in Harewood Square were £300 a year at least, and a premium to boot.

. Christopher told him these were quite beyond the mark. "Very well," said the agent. "Then I'll show you a Bijou."

Rosa clapped her hands. "That is the thing for us. We don't want a large house, only a beautiful one, and in Mayfair."

"Then the Bijou will be sure to suit you."

He took them to the Bijou.

The Bijou had a small dining-room with one very large window in two sheets of plate-glass, and a projecting balcony full of flowers; a still smaller library, which opened on a square yard enclosed. Here were a great many pots, with flowers dead or dying from neglect. On the first floor a fair-sized drawing-room, and a tiny one at the back; on the second floor one good bedroom, and a dressing-room, or little bedroom; three garrets above.

Rosa was in ecstasies. "It is a nest," said she.

. "It is a bank-note," said the agent, simulating equal enthusiasm, after his fashion, "You can always sell the lease again for more money."

Christopher kept cool. "I don't want a house to sell, but to live in, and do my business; I am a physician. Now, the drawing-room is built over the entrance to a mew. The back-rooms all look into a mew: we shall have the eternal noise and smell of a mew. My wife's rest will be broken by the carriages rolling in and out. The hall is fearfully small and stuffy. The rent is abominably high; and what is the premium for, I wonder?"

"Always a premium in Mayfair, sir. A lease is property here: the gentleman is not acquainted with this part, madam."

"Oh, yes, he is!" said Rosa, as boldly as a six years' wife; "he knows every thing."

"Then he knows that a house of this kind at £130 a year, in Mayfair, is a bank-note."

Staines turned to Rosa. "The poor patients, where am I to receive them?"

"In the stable," suggested the house-agent.

"Oh!" said Rosa, shocked.

"Well, then, the coach-house. Why, there's plenty of room for a brougham and one horse, and fifty poor patients at a time. Beggars mustn't be choosers. If you give them physic gratis, that is enough: you ain't bound to find 'em a palace to sit down in, and hot coffee and rump-steaks all around, doctor."

This tickled Rosa so that she burst out laughing, and thenceforward giggled at intervals, wit of this refined nature having all the charm of novelty for her.

They inspected the stables, which were indeed the one redeeming feature in the horrid little Bijou : and then the agent would show them the kitchen and the new stove. He expatiated on this to Mrs. Staines. "Cook a dinner for thirty people, madam."

"And there's room for them to eat it, — in the road," said Staines.

The agent reminded him there were larger places to be had by a very simple process; namely, paying for them.

Staines thought of the large comfortable house in Harewood Square. "£130 a year for this pokey little hole?" he groaned.

"Why, it is nothing at all for a Bijou."

"But it is too much for a band-box."

Rosa laid her hand on his arm, with an imploring glance.

"Well," said he, "I'll submit to the rent, but I really cannot give the premium; it is too ridiculous. He ought to bribe me to rent it, not I him."

"Can't be done without, sir."

"Well, I'll give £100, and no more."

"Impossible, sir."

"Then good-morning. Now, dearest, just come and see the house at Harewood Squa e; £85 and no premium."

"Will you oblige me with your address, doctor?" said the agent.

"Dr. Staines, Morley's Hotel."

And so they left Mayfair.

Rosa sighed, and said, "Oh, the nice little place! and we have lost it for £200."

"Two hundred pounds is a great deal for us to throw away."

"Being near the Coles would soon have made that up to you: and such a cosey little nest."

"Well, the house will not run away."

"But somebody is sure to snap it up. It is a Bijou." She was disappointed, and half-inclined to pout. But she vented her fee ings in a letter to her beloved Florry, and appeared at dinner as sweet as usual.

During dinner, a note came from the agent, accepting Dr. Staines's offer. He glozed the matter thus: he had persuaded the owner it was better to take a good tenant at a moderate loss than to let the Bijou be uninhabited during the present rainy season. An assignment of the lease, which contained the usual covenants, would be prepared immediately; and Doctor Staines could have possession in forty-eight hours, by paying the premium.

Rosa was delighted; and as soon as dinner was over, and the waiters gone, she came and kissed Christopher. He smiled, and said, "Well, you are pleased; that is the principal thing. I have saved £200, and that is something. It will go toward furnishing."

"La, yes!" said Rosa; "I forgot. We shall have to get furniture now. How nice!" It was a pleasure the man of forecast could have willingly dispensed with; but he smiled at her, and they discussed furniture. And Christopher, whose retentive memory had picked up a little of every thing, said there were wholesale upholsterers in the city, who sold cheaper than the West End houses; and he thought the best way was to measure the rooms in the Bijou, and go to the city with a clear idea of what they wanted, ask the prices of various necessary articles, and then make a list, and demand a discount of fifteen per cent on the whole order, being so considerable, and paid for in cash.

Rosa acquiesced, and told Christopher he was the cleverest man in England.

About nine o'clock Mrs. Cole came in to condole with her friend, and heard the good news. When Rosa told her how they thought of furnishing, she said, "Oh, no! you must not do that; you will pay double for every thing! That is the mistake Johnnie and I made; and, after that, a friend of mine took me to the auction-rooms, and I saw every thing sold. Oh, such bargains! — half, and less than half, their value. She has furnished her house almost entirely from sales; and she has the loveliest things in the world, — such ducks of tables, and *jardinières* and things, and beautiful rare china: her house swarms with it, for an old song. A sale is the place, and then so amusing."

"Yes, but," said Christopher, "I should not like my wife to encounter a public room."

"Not alone, of course; but with me. La! Dr. Staines, they are too full of buying and selling to trouble their heads about us."

"O Christopher! do let me go with her. Am I always to be a child?"

Thus appealed to before a stranger, Staines replied warmly, "No, dearest, no; you cannot please me better than by beginning life in earnest. If you two ladies together can face an auction-room, go by all means; only I must ask you not to buy china, or ormolu, or any thing that will break or spoil, but only solid, good furniture."

"Won't you come with us?"

"No, or you might feel yourself in leading-strings. Remember the Bijou is a small house: choose your furniture to fit it ; and then we shall save something by its being so small."

This was Wednesday. There was a weekly sale in Oxford Street on Friday ; and the ladies made the appointment accordingly.

Next day, after breakfast, Christopher was silent and thoughtful a while, and at last said to Rosa, "I'll show you I don't look on you as a child : I'll consult you on a delicate matter."

Rosa's eyes sparkled.

"It is about my Uncle Philip. He has been very cruel : he has wounded me deeply ; he has wounded me through my wife. I never thought he would refuse to come to our marriage."

"And did he? You never showed me his letter."

"You were not my wife then. I kept an affront from you ; but now, you see, I keep nothing."

"Dear Christie ! "

"I am so happy, I have got over that sting — almost ; and the memory of many kind acts come back to me ; and — I don't know what to do. It seems ungrateful not to visit him : it seems almost mean to call."

"I'll tell you ; take me to see him directly. He won't hate us forever, if he sees us often. We may as well begin at once. Nobody hates me long."

Christopher was proud of his wife's courage and wisdom. He kissed her, begged her to put on the plainest dress she could ; and they went together to call on Uncle Philip.

When they got to his house in Gloucester Place, Portman Square, Rosa's heart began to quake ; and she was right glad when the servant said, "Not at home."

They left their cards and address ; and she persuaded Christopher to take her to the salesroom to see the things.

A lot of brokers were there, like vultures ; and one after another stepped forward and pestered them to employ him in the morning. Dr. Staines declined their services civilly but firmly ; and he and Rosa looked over a quantity of furniture, and settled what sort of things to buy.

Another broker came up, and, whenever the couple stopped before an article, proceeded to praise it as something most extraordinary. Staines listened in cold, satirical silence, and told his wife, in French, to do the same. Notwithstanding their marked disgust, the impudent, intrusive fellow stuck to them, and forced his venal criticism on them, and made them uncomfortable, and shortened their tour of observation.

"I think I shall come with you to-morrow," said Christopher, " or I shall have these blackguards pestering you."

"Oh, Florry will send them to the right about ! She is as brave as a lion."

Next day Dr. Staines was sent for into the city at twelve, to pay the money, and receive the lease of the Bijou ; and this and the taking possession occupied him till four o'clock, when he came to his hotel.

Meantime, his wife and Mrs. Cole had gone to the auction-room.

It was a large room, with a good sprinkling of people, but not crowded, except about the table. At the head of this table, full twenty feet long, was the auctioneer's pulpit ; and the lots were brought in turn to the other end of the pulpit for sight and sale.

"We must try and get a seat," said the enterprising Mrs. Cole, and pushed boldly in. The timid Rosa followed strictly in her wake, and so evaded the human waves her leader clove. They were importuned at every step by brokers thrusting catalogues on them, with offers of their services, yet they soon got to the table. A gentleman resigned one chair, a broker another, and they were seated.

Mrs. Staines let down half her veil; but Mrs. Cole surveyed the company point-blank.

The broker who had given up his seat, and now stood behind Rosa, offered her his catalogue. "No, thank you," said Rosa, "I have one;" and she produced it, and studied it, yet managed to look furtively at the company.

There were not above a dozen private persons visible from where Rosa sat; perhaps as many more in the whole room. They were easily distinguishable by their cleanly appearance. The dealers, male and female, were more or less rusty, greasy, dirty, aquiline. Not even the amateurs were brightly dressed: that fundamental error was confined to Mesdames Cole and Staines. The experienced, however wealthy, do not hunt bargains in silk and satin.

The auctioneer called "Lot 7. Four sauce-pans, two trays, a kettle, a boot-jack, and a towel-horse."

These were put up at two shillings, and speedily knocked down for five, to a fat old woman in a greasy velvet jacket; blind industry had sewed bugles on it, not artfully, but agriculturally.

"The lady on the left!" said the auctioneer to his clerk. That meant, "Get the money."

The old lady plunged a huge paw into a huge pocket, and pulled out a huge handful of coin, — copper, silver, and gold, and paid for the lot; and Rosa surveyed her dirty hands and nails with innocent dismay. "Oh, what a dreadful creature!" she whispered; "and what can she want with those old rubbishy things? I saw a hole in one from here." The broker overheard, and said, "She is a dealer, ma'am; and the things were given away. She'll sell them for a guinea, easy."

"Didn't I tell you?" said Mrs. Co'e.

Soon after this, the superior lots came on; and six very neat bedroom chairs were sold to all appearance for fifteen shillings.

The next lot was identical; and Rosa hazarded a bid, "Sixteen shillings."

Instantly some dealer, one of the hooked-nosed that gathered round each lot as it came to the foot of the table, cried, "Eighteen shillings."

"Nineteen," said Rosa.

"A guinea," said the dealer.

"Don't let it go," said the broker behind her. "Don't let it go, ma'am."

She colored at the intrusion, and left off bidding directly, and addressed herself to Mrs. Cole. "Why should I give so much, when the last were sold for fifteen shillings?"

The real reason was, that the first lot was not bid for at all except by the proprietor. However, the broker gave her a very different solution; he said, "The trade always runs up a lady or a gentleman. Let me bid for you: they won't run me up; they know better."

Rosa did not reply, but looked at Mrs. Co'e.

"Yes, dear," said that lady, "you had much better let him bid for you."

"Very well," said Rosa. "You can bid for this chest of drawers, — Lot 25."

When Lot 25 came on, the broker bid in the silliest possible way, if his object had been to get a bargain: he began to bid early and ostentatiously; the article was protected by somebody or other there present, who now, of course, saw his way clear. He ran it up audaciously; and it was purchased for Rosa at about the price it could have been bought for at a shop.

The next thing she wanted was a set of oak chairs.

They went up to twenty-eight pounds; then she said, "I shall give no more, sir."

"Better not lose them," said the agent; "they are a great bargain," and bid another pound for her on his own responsibility. They were still run up; and Rosa peremptorily refused to give any more. She lost them accordingly, by good luck. Her faithful broker looked blank; so did the proprietor.

But, as the sale proceeded, she being young, the competition, though most of it sham, being artful and exciting, and the traitor she employed constantly puffing every article, she was drawn into wishing for things, and bidding by her feelings.

Then her traitor played a game that has been played a hundred times, and the perpetrators never once lynched, as they ought to be, on the spot: he signalled a confederate with a hooked nose. The Jew rascal bid against the Christian scoundrel; and so they ran up the more enticing things to twice their value under the hammer.

Rosa got flushed; and her eye gleamed like a gambler's, and she bought away like wild-fire. In which sport she caught sight of an old gentleman with little black eyes, that kept twinkling at her.

She complained of these eyes to Mrs. Cole.

"Why does he twinkle so? I can see it is at me, I am doing something foolish — I know I am."

Mrs. Cole turned and fixed a haughty stare on the old gentleman. Would you believe it? Instead of sinking through the floor, he sat his ground, and retorted with a cool, clear grin.

But now, whenever Rosa's agent bid for her, and the other man of straw against him, the black eyes twinkled; and Rosa's courage began to ooze away. At last she said, —

"That is enough for one day. I shall go. Who could bear those eyes?"

The broker took her address; so did the auctioneer's clerk. The auctioneer asked her for no deposit;

her beautiful, innocent, and high-bred face was enough for a man who was always reading faces and interpreting them.

And so they retired.

But this charming sex is like that same auctioneer's hammer, it cannot go abruptly. It is always going — going — going — a long time before it is gone. I think it would perhaps loiter at the door of a jail, with the order of release in its hand, after six years' confinement. Getting up to go quenches in it the desire to go. So these ladies, having got up to go, turned and lingered, and hung fire so long that at last another set of oak chairs came up. "Oh! I must see what those go for," said Rosa, at the door.

The bidding was mighty languid now Rosa's broker was not stimulating it; and the auctioneer was just knocking down twelve chairs — oak and leather — and two arm-chairs, for twenty pounds, when, casting his eyes around, he caught sight of Rosa looking at him rather excited. He looked inquiringly at her. She nodded slightly; he knocked them down to her at twenty guineas, and they were really a great bargain.

"Twenty-two," cried a dealer.

"Too late," said the auctioneer.

"I spoke with the hammer, sir."

"After the hammer, Isaacs."

"S'help me God, we was together."

One or two more of his tribe confirmed this pious falsehood, and clamored to have them put up again.

"Call the next lot," said the auctioneer peremptorily. "Make up your mind a little quicker next time, Mr. Isaacs; you have been long enough at it to know the value of oak and morocco."

Mrs. Staines and her friend now started for Morley's Hotel, but went round by Regent Street, whereby they got glued at Peter Robinson's window and nine other windows; and it was nearly five o'clock when they reached Morley's. As they came near the door of their sitting-room, Mrs. Staines heard somebody laughing and talking to her husband. The laugh, to her subtle ears, did not sound musical and genial, but keen, satirical, unpleasant: so it was with some timidity she opened the door; and there sat the old chap with the twinkling eyes. Both parties stared at each other a moment.

"Why, it is them!" cried the old gentleman; "ha! ha! ha! ha! ha!"

Rosa colored all over, and felt guilty somehow, and looked miserable.

"Rosa dear," said Doctor Staines, "this is our Uncle Philip."

"Oh!" said Rosa, and turned red and pale by turns: for she had a great desire to propitiate Uncle Philip.

"You were in the auction-room, sir," said Mrs. Cole severely.

"I was, madam. He! he!"

"Furnishing a house?"

"No, ma'am. I go to a dozen sales a week; but it is not to buy: I enjoy the humors. Did you ever hear of Robert Burton, ma'am?"

"No. Yes, a great traveller, isn't he? Discovered the Nile — or the Niger — or *something*."

This majestic vagueness staggered old Crusty at first; but he recovered his equilibrium, and said, "Why, yes, now I think of it, you are right; he has travelled farther than most of us; for about two centuries ago he visited that bourn whence no traveller returns. Well, when he was alive — he was a student of Christ Church — he used to go down to a certain bridge over the Isis and enjoy the chaff of the bargemen. Now there are no bargemen left to speak of: the mantle of Bobby Burton's bargees has fallen on the Jews and demi-semi-Chris-

tians, that buy and sell furniture at the weekly auctions: thither I repair, to hear what little coarse wit is left us: used to go to the House of Commons, but they are getting too civil by half for my money. Besides, characters come out in an auction. For instance, only this very day I saw two ladies enter, in gorgeous attire, like heifers decked for sacrifice, and reduce their spoliation to a certainty by employing a broker to bid. Now, what is a broker? A fellow who is to be paid a shilling in the pound for all articles purchased. What is his interest then? To buy cheap? Clearly not. He is paid in proportion to the dearness of the article."

Rosa's face began to work piteously.

"Accordingly, what did the broker in question do? He winked to another broker, and these two bid against one another, over their victim's head, and ran every thing she wanted up at least a hundred per cent above the value. So open and transparent a swindle I have seldom seen, even in an auction-room. Ha! ha! ha! ha! ha!"

His mirth was interrupted by Rosa going to her husband, hiding her head on his shoulder, and meekly crying.

Christopher comforted her like a man. "Don't you cry, darling," said he; "How should a pure creature like you know the badness of the world all in a moment? If it is my wife you are laughing at, Uncle Philip, let me tell you this is the wrong place. I'd rather, a thousand times, have her as she is, than armed with the cunning and suspicions of a hardened old worldling like you."

"With all my heart," said Uncle Philip, who, to do him justice, could take blows as well as give them; "but why employ a broker? why pay a scoundrel five per cent to make you pay a hundred per cent? why pay a noisy fool a farthing to open his mouth for you when you have taken the trouble to be there yourself, and have got a mouth of your own to bid discreetly with? Was ever such an absurdity?" He began to get angry.

"Do you want to quarrel with me, Uncle Philip?" said Christopher firing up; "because sneering at my Rosa is the way, and the only way, and the sure way."

"Oh, no!" said Rosa interposing. "Uncle Philip was right. I am very foolish and inexperienced; but I am not so vain as to turn from good advice. I will never employ a broker again, sir."

Uncle Philip smiled, and looked pleased.

Mrs. Cole caused a diversion by taking leave, and Rosa followed her down stairs. On her return she found Christopher telling his uncle all about the bijou, and how he had taken it for £130 a year and £100 premium, and Uncle Philip staring fearfully.

At last he found his tongue. "The bijou!" said he. "Why, that is a name they gave to a little den in Dear Street, Mayfair. You haven't been and taken that! Built over a mews."

Christopher groaned. "That is the place, I fear."

"Why, the owner is a friend of mine; an old patient. Stables stunk him out. Let it to a man; I forget his name. Stables stunk *him* out. He said, 'I shall go.' 'You can't,' said my friend; 'you have taken a lease.' 'Lease be d——d,' said the other; 'I never took *your* house; here's quite a large stench not specified in your description of the property: *it can't be the same place:*' flung the lease at his head, and cut like the wind to foreign parts less odoriferous. I'd have got you the hole for ninety; but you are like your wife, you must go to an agent. What! don't you know that an agent is a man acting for you with an interest opposed to yours? Employing an agent. It is like a

Trojan seeking the aid of a Greek. You needn't cry, Mrs. Staines; your husband has been let in deeper than you have. Now you are young people beginning life: I'll give you a piece of advice. Employ others to do what you can't do, and it must be done; but never to do any thing you can do better for yourselves. Agent! the word is derived from a Latin word, 'agere,' to do: and agents act up to their etymology; for they invariably *do* the nincompoop that employs them, or deals with them in any mortal way. I'd have got you that beastly little bijou for £90 a year."

Uncle Philip went away crusty, leaving the young couple finely mortified and discouraged.

This did not last very long. Christopher noted the experience and Uncle Phil's wisdom in his diary, and then took his wife on his knee, and comforted her, and said, "Never mind; experience is worth money, and it always has to be bought. Those who cheat us will die poorer than we shall, if we are honest and economical. I have observed that people are seldom ruined by the vices of others; these may hurt them, of course; but it is only their own faults and follies that can destroy them."

"Ah, Christie!" said Rosa, "you are a man. Oh, the comfort of being married to *a man!* A man sees the best side. I adore men. Dearest, I will waste no more of your money. I will go to no more sales."

Christopher saw 'she was deeply mortified; and he said quietly, "On the contrary, you will go to the very next. Only take Uncle Philip's advice; employ no broker, and watch the prices things fetch when you are not bidding, and keep cool."

She caressed his ears with both her white hands, and thanked him for giving her another trial. So that trouble melted in the sunshine of conjugal love.

Notwithstanding the agent's solemn assurance, the bijou was out of repair. Doctor Staines detected internal odors, as well as those that flowed in from the mews. He was not the man to let his wife perish by miasma; so he had the drains all up and actually found brick drains and a cesspool; he stopped that up, and laid down new pipe-drains, with a good fall, and properly trapped. The old drains were hidden, after the manner of builders. He had the whole course of his new drains marked upon all the floors they passed under and had several stones and boards hinged, to faciliate examination at any period.

But all this, with the necessary cleaning, whitewashing, painting, and papering, ran away with money. Then came Rosa's purchases, which, to her amazement, amounted to £190, and not a carpet, curtain, or bed, among the lot. Then there was the carriage home from the auction-room, an expense one avoids by buying at a shop, and the broker claimed his shilling in the pound. This, however, Staines refused. The man came and blustered. Rosa, who was there, trembled. Then, for the first time, she saw her husband's brow lower; he seemed transfigured, and looked terrible. "You scoundrel," said he, "you set another villain like yourself to bid against you, and you betrayed the innocent lady that employed you. I could indict you and your confederate for a conspiracy: I take the goods out of respect of my wife's credit, but you shall gain nothing by swindling her. Be off, you heartless miscreant, or I'll " —

" I'll take the law if you do."

" Take it, then : I'll give you something to howl for;" and he seized him with a grasp so tremendous that the fellow cried out in dismay, " Oh! don't hit me sir; pray don't."

On this abject appeal, Staines tore the door open with his left hand, and spun the broker out into the passage with his right. Two movements of the angry Hercules, and the man was literally whirled out of sight with a rapidity and swiftness almost ludicrous; it was like a trick in a pantomime : a clatter on the stairs betrayed that he had gone down the first steps in a wholesale and irregular manner, though he had just managed to keep his feet.

As for Staines, he stood there still lowering like thunder, and his eyes like hot coals; but his wife threw her arms around him, and begged him consolingly not to mind.

She was trembling like an aspen.

" Dear me," said Christopher, with a ludicrous change to marked politeness and respect; " I forgot *you* in my righteous indignation." Next he becomes uxurious. " Did they frighten her, a duck? Sit on my knee, darling, and pull my hair for not being more considerate — there — there."

This was followed by the whole absurd soothing process as practised by manly husbands upon quivering and somewhat hysterical wives; and ended with a formal apology. " You must not think that I am passionate; on the contrary, I am always practising self-government. My maxim is, *Animum rege qui nisi paret imperat;* and that means, Make your temper your servant, or else it will be your master. But to ill-use my dear little wife, it is unnatural, it is monstrous, it makes my blood boil."

" Oh, dear! don't go into another. It is all over. I can't bear to see you in a passion; you are so terrible, so beautiful. Ah! they are fine things, courage and strength. There is nothing I admire so much."

" Why, they are as common as dirt. What I admire is modesty, timidity, sweetness; the sensitive cheek that pales or blushes at a word, the bosom that quivers, and clings to a fellow whenever any thing goes wrong."

"Oh, that is what you admire, is it?" said Rosa dryly.

"Admire it? said Christopher, not seeing the trap; "I adore it."

"Then, Christie dear, you are a simpleton: that is all. And we are made for one another."

The house was to be furnished and occupied as soon as possible; so Mrs. Staines and Mrs. Cole went to another sale-room. Mrs. Staines remembered all Uncle Philip had said, and went plainly dressed; but her friend declined to sacrifice her showy dress to her friend's interests. Rosa thought that a little unkind, but said nothing.

In this auction-room they easily got a place at the table: but they did not find it heaven; for a number of second-hand carpets were in the sale, and these, brimful of dust, were all shown on the table, and the dirt choked and poisoned our fair friends. Brokers pestered them, until, at last, Rosa, smarting under her late exposure, addressed the auctioneer quietly, in her silvery tones: "Sir, these gentlemen are annoying me by forcing their services on me. I do not intend to buy at all unless I can be allowed to bid for myself."

When Rosa, blushing and amazed at her own boldness, uttered these words, she little foresaw their effect. She had touched a popular sore.

"You are right, madam," said a respectable tradesman opposite her. "What right have these dirty fellows, without a shilling in their pocket, to go and force themselves on a lady against her will?"

"It has been complained of in the papers again and again," said another.

"What, mayn't we live as well as you?" retorted a broker.

"Yes, but not to force yourself on a lady. Why, she'd give you in charge of the police if you tried it on outside."

Then there was a downright clamor of discussion and chaff.

Presently uprises very slowly a countryman so colossal that it seemed as if he never would have done getting up, and gives his experiences. He informed the company, in a broad Yorkshire dialect, that he did a bit in furniture, and at first starting these brokers buzzed about him like flies, and pestered him. "Ah damned 'em pretty hard," said he, "but they didn't heed any. So then ah spoke 'em civil, and ah said, ' Well, lads, ah dinna come fra Yorkshire to sit like a dummy and let you buy wi' my brass: the first that pesters me again ah'll just fell him on t' plaace, like a caulf, and ah'm not very sure he'll get up again in a hurry.' So they dropped me like a hot potato; never pestered me again. But if they won't give over pestering you, mistress, ah'll come round, and just stand behind your chair, and bring neive with me," showing a fist like a leg of mutton.

"No, no," said the auctioneer, "that will not do. I will have no disturbance here. Call the policeman."

While the clerk went to the door for the bobby, a gentleman reminded the auctioneer that the journals had repeatedly drawn attention to the nuisance.

"Fault of the public, not mine, sir. Policeman, stand behind that lady's chair, and, if anybody annoys her, put him quietly into the street."

"This auction-room will be to let soon," said a voice at the end of the table.

"This auction-room," said the auctioneer, master of the gay or grave at a moment's notice, "is supported by the public and the trade; it is not supported by paupers."

A Jew upholsterer put in his word. "I do my own business; but I like to let a poor man live."

"Jonathan," said the auctioneer to one of his servants, "after this sale you may put up the shutters; we have gone and offended Mr. Jacobs. He keeps a shop in Blind Alley, Whitechapel. Now then, Lot 69."

Rosa bid timidly for one or two lots, and bought them cheap.

The auctioneer kept looking her way, and she had only to nod.

The obnoxious broker got opposite her, and ran her up a little out of spite; but as he had only got half a crown about him, and no means of doubling it, he dared not go far.

On the other side of the table was a figure to which Rosa's eyes often turned with interest: a fair young boy about twelve years old; he had golden hair, and was in deep mourning. His appearance interested Rosa, and she wondered how he came there, and why: he looked like a lamb wedged in among wolves, a flower among weeds. As the lots proceeded, the boy seemed to get uneasy; and at last, when Lot 73 was put up, anybody could see in his poor little face that he was there to bid for it.

"Lot 73, an arm-chair covered in morocco. An excellent and most useful article. Should not be at all surprised if it was made by Gillow."

"Gillow would, though," said Jacobs, who owed him a turn.

Chorus of dealers. — " Haw ! haw !"

The auctioneer. — " I like to hear some people run a lot down; shows they are going to bid for it in earnest. Well, name your own price. Five pounds to begin ?"

Now, if nobody had spoken, the auctioneer would have gone on, " Well, four pounds then, three, two, whatever you like," and at last obtained a *bona fide* offer of thirty shillings; but the moment he said, " Five pounds to begin," the boy in black lifted up his childish treble, and bid thus, " Five pound ten," — " six pounds," — " six pound ten," — " seven pounds,"

— " seven pound ten," — " eight pounds," — " eight pound ten," — " nine pounds," — " nine pound ten," — " ten pounds ! " without interruption, and indeed, almost in a breath.

There was a momentary pause of amazement, and then an outburst of chaff.

" Nice little boy ! "

" Didn't he say his lesson well ? "

" Favor us with your card, sir. You are a gent as knows how to buy."

" What did he stop for ? If it's worth ten, it is worth a hundred."

" Bless the child ! " said a female dealer kindly, " what made you go on like that ? Why, there was no bid against you ! you'd have got it for two pounds, — a rickety old thing."

Young master began to whimper. " Why, the gentleman said, ' Five pounds to *begin.*' It was the chair poor grandpapa always sat in, and all the things are sold, and mamma said it would break her heart to lose it. She was too ill to come, so she sent me. She told me I was not to let it be sold away from us for less than ten pounds, or she sh — should be m — mi — miserable," and the poor little fellow began to cry. Rosa followed suit promptly but unobtrusively.

" Sentiment always costs money," said Mr. Jacobs gravely.

" How do you know ? " asked Mr. Cohen. " Have *you* got any on hand ? I never seen none at your shop."

Some tempting things now came up, and Mrs. Staines bid freely ; but all of a sudden she looked down the table, and there was Uncle Philip twinkling as before. " Oh, dear ! what am I doing now ? " thought she. " I have got no broker."

She bid on, but in fear and trembling because of those twinkling eyes. At last she mustered courage, wrote on a leaf of her pocketbook, and passed it down to him.

"It would be only kind to warn me. What am I doing wrong?"

He sent her back a line directly: "Auctioneer running you up himself. Follow his eye when he bids; you will see there is no *bona fide* bidder at your prices."

Rosa did so, and found that it was true.

She nodded to Uncle Philip; and, with her expressive face, asked him what she should do.

The old boy must have his joke. So he wrote back, "Tell him, as you see he has a fancy for certain articles, you would not be so discourteous as to bid against him."

The next article but one was a drawing-room suit Rosa wanted; but the auctioneer bid against her; so, at eighteen pounds, she stopped.

"It is against you, madam," said the auctioneer.

"Yes, sir," said Rosa; "but as you are the only bidder, and you have been so kind to me, I would not think of opposing you."

The words were scarcely out of her mouth when they were greeted with a roar of Homeric laughter that literally shook the room, and this time not at the expense of the innocent speaker.

"That's into your mutton, governor."

"Sharp's the word this time."

"I say, governor, don't you want a broker to bid for ye?"

"Wink at me next time, sir; I'll do the office for you."

"No greenhorns left now."

"That lady won't give a ten-pound note for her grandfather's armchair."

"Oh, yes, she will, if it's stuffed with bank-notes!"

"Put the next lot up with the owner's name and the reserve price. Open business."

"And sing a psalm at starting."

"A little less noise in Judæa, if you please," said the auctioneer, who had now recovered from the blow. "Lot 97."

This was a very pretty marqueterie cabinet; it stood against the wall, and Rosa had set her heart upon it. Nobody would bid. She had muzzled the auctioneer effectually.

"Your own price."

"Two pounds," said Rosa.

A dealer offered guineas, and it advanced slowly to four pounds and half a crown, at which it was about to be knocked down to Rosa, when suddenly a new bidder arose in the broker Rosa had rejected. They bid slowly and sturdily against each other, until a line was given to Rosa from Uncle Philip.

"This time it is your own friend, the snipe-nosed woman. She telegraphed a broker."

Rosa read, and crushed the note. "Six guineas," said she.

"Six-ten."

"Seven."

"Seven-ten."

"Eight."

"Eight-ten."

"Ten guineas," said Rosa; and then, with feminine cunning, stealing a sudden glance, caught her friend leaning back and signalling the broker not to give in.

"Eleven pounds."

"Twelve."

"Thirteen."

"Fourteen."

"Sixteen."

"Eighteen."

"Twenty."

"Twenty guineas."

"It is yours, my faithful friend," said Rosa, turning suddenly round on Mrs. Cole with a magnificent glance no one would have thought her capable of.

Then she rose, and stalked away.

Dumfoundered for the moment, Mrs. Cole followed her, and stopped her at the door.

"Why, Rosie dear, it is the only thing I have bid for. There I've sat by your side like a mouse."

Rosa turned gravely toward her. "You know it is not that. You had only to tell me you wanted it. I would never have been so mean as to bid against you."

"Mean, indeed!" said Florence, tossing her head.

"Yes, mean; to draw back and hide behind the friend you were with, and employ the very rogue she had turned off. But it is my own fault. Cecilia warned me against you. She always said you were a treacherous girl."

"And I say you are an impudent little minx. Only just married, and going about like two vagabonds, and talk to me like that!"

"We are not going about like two vagabonds. We have taken a house in Mayfair."

"Say a stable."

"It was by your advice, you false-hearted creature."

"You are a fool."

"You are worse: you are a traitress."

"Then don't you have any thing to do with me."

"Heaven forbid I should. You treacherous thing."

"You insolent — insolent — I hate you."

"And I despise you."

"I always hated you at bottom."

"That's why you pretended to love me, you wretch."

"Well, I pretend no more. I am your enemy for life.

"Thank you. You have told the truth for once in your life."

"I have. And he shall never call in your husband; so you may leave Mayfair as soon as you like."

"Not to please you, madam. We can get on without traitors."

And so they parted, with eyes that gleamed like tigers.

Rosa drove home in great agitation, and tried to tell Christopher, but choked, and became hysterical. The husband physician coaxed and and scolded her out of that; and presently in came Uncle Philip, full of the humors of the auction-room. He told about the little boy with a

delight that disgusted Mrs. Staines; and then was particularly merry on female friendships. "Fancy a man going to a sale with his friend, and bidding against him on the sly."

"She is no friend of mine. We are enemies for life."

"And you were to be friends till death," said Staines with a sigh.

Philip inquired who she was.

"Mrs. John Cole."

"Not of Curzon Street?"

"Yes."

"And you have quarrelled with her?"

"Yes."

"Well, but her husband is a general practitioner."

"She is a traitress."

"But her husband could put a good deal of money in Christopher's way."

"I can't help it. She is a traitress."

"And you have quarrelled with her about an old wardrobe."

"No, for her disloyalty, and her base good-for-nothingness. Oh! oh! oh!"

Uncle Philip got up, looking sour. "Good-afternoon, Mrs. Christopher," said he very dryly.

Christopher accompanied him to the foot of the stairs.

Well, Christopher," said he, "matrimony is a blunder at the best; and you have not done the thing by halves. You have married a simpleton. She will be your ruin."

"Uncle Philip, since you only come here to insult us, I hope in future-you will stay at home."

"Oh! with pleasure, sir. Good-by."

CHAPTER VII.

Christopher Staines came back looking pained and disturbed. "There," said he, "I feared it would come to this. I have quarrelled with Uncle Philip."

"Oh! how could you?"

"He affronted me."

"What about?"

"Never you mind. Don't let us say any thing more about it, darling. It is a pity, a sad pity—he was a good friend of mine once."

He paused, entered what had passed in his diary, and then sat down with a gentle expression of sadness on his manly features. Rosa hung about him, soft and pitying, till it cleared away, at all events for the time.

Next day they went together to clear the goods Rosa had purchased. While the list was being made out in the office, in came the fair-haired boy with a ten-pound note in his very hand. Rosa caught sight of it, and turned to the auctioneer with a sweet, pitying face: "Oh! sir, surely you will not take all that money from him, poor child, for a rickety old chair."

The auctioneer stared with amazement at her simplicity, and said, "What would the vendors say to me?"

She looked distressed, and said, "Well, then, really we ought to raise a subscription, poor thing!"

"Why, ma'am," said the auctioneer, "he isn't hurt: the article belonged to his mother and her sister; the brother-in-law isn't on good terms; so he demanded a public sale. She will get back four pun ten out of it." Here the clerk put in his word. "And there's five pounds paid, I forgot to tell you."

"Oh! left a deposit, did he?"

"No, sir. But the Laughing Hyena gave you five pounds at the end of the sale."

"The Laughing Hyena, Mr. Jones?"

"Oh! beg pardon: that is what we call him in the room. He has got such a curious laugh."

"Oh! I know the gent. He is a retired doctor. I wish he'd laugh less and buy more; and *he* gave you five pounds toward the young gentleman's arm-chair! Well, I should

as soon have expected blood from a flint. You have got five pounds to pay, sir: so now the chair will cost your mamma ten shillings. Give him the order and the change, Mr. Jones."

Christopher and Rosa talked this over in the room while the men were looking out their purchases. "Come," said Rosa; "now I forgive him sneering at me; his heart is not really hard, you see." Staines, on the contrary, was very angry. "What!" he cried, "pity a boy who made one bad bargain, that, after all, was not a very bad bargain; and he had no kindness, nor even common humanity, for my beautiful Rosa, inexperienced as a child, and buying for her husband, like a good, affectionate, honest creature, among a lot of sharpers and hard-hearted cynics —like himself."

"It *was* cruel of him," said Rosa, altering her mind in a moment, and half inclined to cry.

This made Christopher furious. "The ill-natured, crotchety, old— The fact is, he is a misogynist."

"Oh, the wretch!" said Rosa warmly. "And what is that?"

"A woman-hater."

"Oh! is that all? Why, so do I —after that Florence Cole. Women are mean, heartless things. Give me men! they are loyal and true."

"All of them?" inquired Christopher a little satirically. "Read the papers."

"Every soul of them," said Mrs. Staines, passing loftily over the proposed test. "That is, all the ones *I* care about; and that is my own, own one."

Disagreeable creatures to have about one—these simpletons!

Mrs. Staines took Christopher to shops to buy the remaining requisites: and in three days more the house was furnished, two female servants engaged, and the couple took their luggage over to the Bijou.

Rosa was excited and happy at

the novelty of possession and authority, and that close sense of house proprietorship which belongs to woman. By dinner-time she could have told you how many shelves there were in every cupboard, and knew the Bijou by heart in a way that Christopher never knew it. All this ended, as running about and excitement generally does, with my lady being exhausted, and lax with fatigue. So then he made her lie down on a little couch, while he went through his accounts.

When he had examined all the bills carefully he looked very grave, and said, "Who would believe this? We began with £3000. It was to last us several years—till I got a good practice. Rosa, there is only £1440 left." Oh, impossible!" said Rosa. "Oh dear! why did I ever enter a sale-room?"

"No, no, my darling; you were bitten once or twice, but you made some good bargains too. Remember there was £400 set apart for my life policy."

"What a waste of money!"

"Your father did not think so. Then the lease; the premium; repairs of the drains that would have poisoned my Rosa; turning the coach-house into a dispensary; painting, papering and furnishing; china and linen and every thing to buy. We must look at this seriously. Only £1440 left. A slow profession. No friends. I have quarrelled with Uncle Philip: you with Mrs. Cole; and her husband would have launched me."

"And it was to please her we settled here. Oh, I could kill her: nasty cat!"

"Never mind; it is not a case for despondency, but it is for prudence. All we have to do is to look the thing in the face, and be very economical in every thing. I had better give you an allowance for housekeeping; and I earnestly beg you to buy things yourself while you are a poor man's wife, and pay ready money for every

thing. My mother was a great manager, and she always said, 'There is but one way; be your own market-woman, and pay on the spot; never let the tradesmen get you on their books, or what with false weight, double charges, and the things your servants order that never enter the house, you lose more than a hundred a year by cheating.'"

Rosa yielded a languid assent to this part of his discourse, and it hardly seemed to enter her mind; but she raised no objection, and in due course he made her a special allowance for housekeeping.

It soon transpired that medical advice was to be had gratis at the Bijou from eight till ten, and there was generally a good attendance. But a week passed, and not one patient came of the class this couple must live by. Christopher set this down to what people call the "Transition period:" his Kent patients had lost him; his London patients not found him. He wrote to all his patients in the country, and many of his pupils at the university, to let them know where he was settled · and then he waited.

Not a creature came.

Rosa bore this very well for a time, so long as the house was a novelty; but, when that excitement was worn out, she began to be very dull, and used to come and entice him out to walk with her: he would look wistfully at her, but object that if he left the house he should be sure to lose a patient.

"Oh, they won't come any more for our staying in — tiresome things!" said Rosa.

But Christopher would kiss her, and remain firm, "My love," said he, "you do not realize how hard a fight there is before us. How should you? You are very young. No, for your sake, I must not throw a chance away. Write to your female friends: that will while away an hour or two."

"What, after that Florence Cole?"

"Write to those who have not made such violent professions."

"So I will, dear. Especially to those that are married and come to London. Oh, and I'll write to that cold-blooded thing, Lady Cicely Treherne! Why do you shake your head?"

"Did I? I was not aware. Well, dear, if ladies of rank were to come here, I fear they might make you discontented with your lot."

"All the women on earth could not do that. However, the chances are she will not come near me; she left the school quite a big girl, an immense girl, when I was only twelve. She used to smile at my capriccios, and once she kissed me—actually. She was an awful Sawney, though, and so affected. I think I will write to her."

These letters brought just one lady, a Mrs. Turner, who talked to Rosa very glibly about herself, and amused Rosa twice: at the third visit Rosa tried to change the conversation. Mrs. Turner instantly got up and went away. She could not bear the sound of the human voice, unless it was talking about her and her affairs.

And now Staines began to feel downright uneasy. Income was steadily going out: not a shilling coming in. The lame, the blind, and the sick frequented his dispensary, and got his skill out of him gratis, and sometimes a little physic, a little wine, and other things that cost him money: but of the patients that pay, not one came to his front-door.

He walked round and round his little yard, like a hyena in its cage, waiting, waiting, waiting: and oh! how he envied the lot of those who can hunt for work, instead of having to stay at home and wait for others to come, whose will they can not influence. His heart began to sicken with hope deferred and dim

5*

forebodings of the future; and he saw, with grief, that his wife was getting duller and duller, and that her days dragged more heavily far than his own; for he could study.

At last his knocker began to show signs of life: his visitors were physicians. His lectures on "Diagnosis" were well known to them; and one after another found him out. They were polite, kind, even friendly; but here it ended: these gentlemen, of course, did not resign their patients to him; and the inferior class of practitioners avoided his door like a pestilence.

Mrs. Staines, who had always lived for amusement, could strike out no fixed occupation; her time hung like lead; the house was small; and in small houses the faults of servants ran against the mistress, and she can't help seeing them, and all the worse for her. It is easier to keep things clean in the country, and Rosa had a high standard, which her two servants could never quite attain. This annoyed her, and she began to scold a little. They answered civilly, but, in other respects, remained imperfect beings: they laid out every shilling they earned in finery; and this, I am ashamed to say, irritated Mrs. Staines, who was wearing out her wedding garments, and had no excuse for buying, and Staines had begged her to be economical. The more they dressed, the more she scolded; they began to answer. She gave the cook warning; the other, though not on good terms with the cook, had a gush of *esprit du corps* directly, and gave Mrs. Staines warning.

Mrs. Staines told her husband all this: he took her part, though without openly interfering; and they had two new servants, not as good as the last.

This worried Rosa sadly; but it was a flea-bite to the deeper nature and more forecasting mind of her husband, still doomed to pace that miserable yard, like a hyena, chafing, seeking, longing for the patient that never came.

Rosa used to look out of his dressing-room window, and see him pace the yard. At first tears of pity stood in her eyes. By and by she got angry with the world; and at last, strange to say, a little irritated with him. It is hard for a weak woman to keep up all her respect for the man that fails.

One day, after watching him a long time unseen, she got excited, put on her shawl and bonnet, and ran down to him. She took him by the arm: "If you love me, come out of this prison, and walk with me; we are too miserable. I shall be your first patient if this goes on much longer." He looked at her, saw she was very excited, and had better be humored; so he kissed her, and just said, with a melancholy smile, "How poor are they that have not patience!" Then he put on his hat, and walked in the Park and Kensington Gardens with her. The season was just beginning. There were carriages enough, and gay Amazons enough, to make poor Rosa sigh more than once.

Christopher heard the sigh, and pressed her arm, and said, "Courage, love: I hope to see you among them yet."

"The sooner the better," said she a little hardly.

"And, meantime, which of them all is as beautiful as you?"

"All I know is, they are more attractive. Who looks at me? walking tamely by."

Christopher said nothing: but these words seemed to imply a thirst for admiration, and made him a little uneasy.

By and by the walk put the swift-changing Rosa in spirits, and she began to chat gayly, and hung prattling and beaming on her husband's arm, when they entered Curzon Street. Here, however, occurred an incident, trifling in itself, but un-

pleasant. Dr. Staines saw one of his best Kentish patients get feebly out of his carriage, and call on Dr. Bar. He started, and stopped. Rosa asked what was the matter. He told her. She said, "*We are unfortunate.*"

Staines said nothing; he only quickened his pace, but he was greatly disturbed. She expected him to complain that she had dragged him out, and lost him that first chance. But he said nothing. When they got home he asked the servant had anybody called.

"No, Sir."

"Surely you are mistaken, Jane. A gentleman in a carriage!"

"Not a creature have been since you went out, sir."

"Well, then, dearest," said he sweetly, "we have nothing to reproach ourselves with." Then he knit his brow gloomily. "It is worse than I thought. It seems even one's country patients go to another doctor when they visit London. It is hard. It is hard."

Rosa leaned her head on his shoulder, and curled round him, as one she would shield against the world's injustice; but she said nothing; she was a little frightened at his eye that lowered, and his noble frame that trembled a little, with ire suppressed.

Two days after this a brougham drove up to the door, and a tallish, fattish, pasty-faced man got out, and inquired for Dr. Staines.

He was shown into the dining-room, and told Jane he had come to consult the doctor.

Rosa had peeped over the stairs, all curiosity; she glided noiselessly down, and with love's swift foot got into the yard before Jane. "He is come! he is come! Kiss me."

Dr. Staines kissed her first, and then asked who was come.

"Oh, nobody of any consequence! *Only* the first patient. Kiss me again."

Dr. Staines kissed her again, and

then was for going to the first patient.

"No," said she; "not yet. I met a doctor's wife at Dr. Mayne's, and she told me things. You must always keep them waiting, or else they think nothing of you. Such a funny woman! 'Treat 'em like dogs, my dear,' she said. But I told her they wouldn't come to be treated like dogs or any other animal."

"You had better have kept that to yourself, I think."

"Oh! if you are going to be disagreeable, good-by. You can go to your patient, sir. Christie dear, if he is very, very ill — and I'm sure I hope he is — oh, how wicked I am! — may I have a new bonnet?"

"If you really want one."

On the patient's card was "Mr. Pettigrew, 47 Manchester Square."

As soon as Staines entered the room the first patient told him who and what he was, a retired civilian from India; but he had got a son there still, a very rising man; wanted to be a parson, but he would not stand that; bad profession; don't rise by merit; very hard to rise at all — no, India was the place. "As for me, I made my fortune there in ten years. Obliged to leave it now — invalid this many years; no *tone*. Tried two or three doctors in this neighborhood; heard there was a new one, had written a book on something. Thought I would try *him*."

To stop him, Staines requested to feel his pulse, and examine his tongue and eye.

"You are suffering from indigestion," said he. "I will write you a prescription; but, if you want to get well, you must simplify your diet very much."

While he was writing the prescription, off went this patient's tongue, and ran through the topics of the day, and into his family history again.

Staines listened politely. He could afford it, having only this one.

At last the first patient, having delivered an octavo volume of nothing, rose to go; but it seems that speaking an infinite deal of nothing exhausts the body, though it does not affect the mind; for the first patient sank down in his chair again. "I have excited myself too much — feel rather faint."

Staines saw no signs of coming syncope; he rang the bell quietly, and ordered a decanter of sherry to be brought; the first patient filled himself a glass; then another; and went off, revived, to chatter elsewhere. But at the door he said, "I had always a running account with Dr. Mivar. I suppose you don't object to that system. Double fee the first visit, single afterward."

Dr. Staines bowed a little stiffly; he would have preferred the money. However, he looked at the Blue-Book, and found his visitor lived at 47 Manchester Square; so that removed his anxiety.

The first patient called every other day, chattered nineteen to the dozen, was exhausted, drank two glasses of sherry, and drove away.

Soon after this a second patient called. This one was a deputy patient — Collett, a retired butler — kept a lodging-house, and waited at parties; he lived close by, but had a married daughter in Chelsea. Would the doctor visit her, and he would be responsible?

Staines paid the woman a visit or two, and treated her so effectually that soon her visits were paid to him. She was cured, and Staines, who by this time wanted to see money, sent to Collett.

Collett did not answer.

Staines wrote warmly.

Collett dead silent.

Staines employed a solicitor.

Collett said he had recommended the patient, that was all; he had never said he would pay her debts. That was her husband's business.

Now, her husband was the mate

of a ship; would not be in England for eighteen months.

The woman, visited by lawyer's clerk, cried bitterly, and said she and her children had scarcely enough to eat.

Lawyer advised Staines to abandon the case, and pay him two pounds fifteen shillings, expenses. He did so.

"This is damnable," said he. "I must get it out of Pettigrew: by the by, he has not been here this two days."

He waited another day for Pettigrew, and then wrote to him. No answer. Called. Pettigrew gone abroad. House in Manchester Square to let.

Staines went to the house-agent with his tale. Agent was impenetrable at first, but at last, won by the doctor's manner and his unhappiness, referred him to Pettigrew's solicitor; the solicitor was a respectable man, and said he would forward the claim to Pettigrew in Paris.

But by this time Pettigrew was chatting and guzzling in Berlin; and thence he got to St. Petersburg. In that stronghold of gluttony he gormandized more than ever, and, being unable to chatter it off the stomach, as in other cities, had apoplexy, and died.

But, long before this, Staines saw his money was as irrecoverable as his sherry; and he said to Rosa. "I wonder whether I shall ever live to curse the human race?

"Heaven forbid!" said Rosa. "Oh! they use you cruelly, my poor, poor Christie?"

Thus for months the young doctor's patients bled him, and that was all.

And Rosa got more and more moped at being in the house so much, and pestered Christopher to take her out, and he declined; and, being a man hard to beat, took to writing on medical subjects, in hopes of getting some money from the various medical and scientific publications; but he found it as hard to get the wedge in there as to get patients.

At last Rosa's remonstrance began to rise into something that sounded like reproaches. One Sunday she came to him in her bonnet, and interrupted his studies to say he might as well lay down the pen and talk. Nobody would publish any thing he wrote.

Christopher frowned, but contained himself; and laid down the pen.

"I might as well not be married at all as to be a doctor's wife. You are never seen out with me, not even to church. Do behave like a Christian, and come to church with me now."

Dr. Staines shook his head.

"Why, I wouldn't miss church for all the world. Any excitement is better than always moping. Come over the water with me. The time Jane and I went, the clergyman read a paper that Mr. Brown had fallen down in a fit. There was such a rush directly, and I'm sure fifty ladies went out — fancy, all Mrs. Browns! Wasn't that fun?"

"Fun? I don't see it. Well, Rosa, your mind is evidently better adapted to diversion than mine is. Go you to church, love; and I'll continue my studies."

"Then all I can say is, I wish I was back in my father's house. Husband! friend! companion!— I have none."

Then she burst out crying violently; and being shocked at what she had said, and at the agony it had brought into her husband's face, she went off into hysterics; and as his heart would not let him bellow at her, or empty a bucket on her as he could on another patient, she had a good long bout of them, and got her way; for she broke up his studies for that day, at all events.

Even after the hysterics were got

under, she continued to moan and sigh very prettily, with her lovely, languid head pillowed on her husband's arm; in a word, though the hysterics were real, yet this innocent young person had the presence of mind to postpone entire convalescence, and lay herself out to be petted all day. But fate willed it otherwise. While she was sighing and moaning, came to the door a scurrying of feet, and then a sharp, persistent ringing that meant something. The moaner cocked eye and ear, and said, in her every-day voice, which, coming so suddenly, sounded very droll, " What is that, I wonder ? "

Jane hurried to the street-door, and Rosa recovered by magic; and, preferring gossip to hysterics, in an almost gleeful whisper ordered Christopher to open the door of the study The Bijou was so small that the following dialogue rang in their ears : —

A boy in buttons gasped out, " Oh ! if you please, will you ast the doctor to come round directly ? there's a haccident."

" La, bless me ? " said Jane ; and never budged.

" Yes, miss. It's our missus's little girl fallen right off an i chair, and cut her head dreadful, and smothered in blood."

" La, to be sure ? " And she waited steadily for more.

" Ay, and missus she fainted right off; and I've been to the regler doctor, which he's out; and Sarah, the house-maid, said I had better come here : you was only just set up, she said ; you wouldn't have so much to do, says she."

" That is all *she* knows," said Jane. " Why, our master they pulls him in pieces which is to have him fust."

" What an awful liar ! " " Oh, you good girl ! " whispered Dr. Staines and Rosa in one breath.

" Ah, well ! " said Buttons, "anyway, Sarah says she knows you are clever, cos her little girl as lives with her mother, and calls Sarah aunt, has bin to your · 'spensary with ringworm, and you cured her right off."

" Ay, and a good many more," said Jane loftily. She was a housemaid of imagination ; and while Staines was putting some lint and an instrument into his pocket, she proceeded to relate a number of miraculous cures. Doctor Staines interrupted them by suddenly emerging, and inviting Buttons to take him to the house.

Mrs. Staines was so pleased with Jane for cracking up the doctor, that she gave her five shillings ; and after that used to talk to her a great deal more than to the cook, which in due course set all three by the ears.

Buttons took the doctor to a fine house in the same street, and told him his mistress's name on the way, — Mrs. Lucas. He was taken up to the nursery, and found Mrs. Lucas seated, crying and lamenting, and a woman holding a little girl of about seven, whose brow had been cut open by the fender, on which she had fallen from a chair; it looked very ugly, and was even now bleeding.

Dr. Staines lost no time; he examined the wound keenly, and then said kindly to Mrs. Lucas, " I am happy to tell you it is not serious." He then asked for a large basin and some tepid water, and bathed it so softly and soothingly that the child soon became composed ; and the mother discovered the artist at once. He compressed the wound, and explained to Mrs. Lucas that the principal thing really was to avoid an ugly scar. " There is no danger," said he. He then bound the wound neatly up, and had the girl put to bed. " You will not wake her at any particular hour, nurse. Let her sleep. Have a little strong beef tea ready, and give it her at any hour, night or day, she asks for it. But do not force it on her, or you will do her more harm than good. She had better sleep before she eats."

Mrs. Lucas begged him to come every morning; and, as he was going, she shook hands with him, and the soft palm deposited a hard substance wrapped in paper. He took it with professional gravity and seeming unconsciousness; but, once outside the house, went home on wings. He ran up to the drawing-room, and found his wife seated, and playing at reading. He threw himself on his knees, and the fee into her lap ; and, while she unfolded the paper with an ejaculation of pleasure, he said, "Darling, the first real patient — the first real fee. It is yours to buy the new bonnet."

"Oh, I'm so glad!" said she, with her eyes glistening. "But I'm afraid one can't get a bonnet fit to wear — for a guinea."

Dr. Staines visited his little patient every day, and received his guinea. Mrs. Lucas also called him in for her own little ailments, and they were the best possible kind of ailments : being almost imaginary, there was no limit to them.

Then did Mrs. Staines turn jealous of her husband. "They never ask me," said she; "and I am moped to death."

"It is hard," said Christopher sadly. "But have a little patience. Society will come to you long before practice comes to me."

About two o'clock one afternoon a carriage and pair drove up, and a gorgeous footman delivered a card, " Lady Cicely Treherne."

Of course Mrs. Staines was at home, and only withheld by propriety from bounding into the passage to meet her school-fellow. However, she composed herself in the drawing-room ; and presently the door was opened, and a very tall young woman, richly but not gayly dressed, drifted into the room, and stood there a statue of composure.

Rosa had risen to fly to her ; but the reverence a girl of eighteen strikes into a child of twelve hung about her still ; and she came timidly forward, blushing and sparkling, a curious contrast in color and mind to her visitor ; for Lady Cicely was Languor in person — her hair white-brown, her face a fine oval, but almost colorless ; her eyes a pale gray, her neck and hands incomparably white and beautiful — a lymphatic young lady, a live antidote to emotion. However, Rosa's beauty, timidity, and undisguised affectionateness were something so different from what she was used to in the world of fashion that she actually smiled, and held out both her hands a little way. Rosa seized them and pressed them ; they let her, and remained passive and limp.

"O Lady Cicely!" said Rosa, "how kind of you to come ! "

"How kind of you to send to me," was the polite but perfectly cool reply. "But how you are gwown, and—may I say impwoved? —you la petite Lusignan! It is incwedible," lisped her ladyship very calmly.

"I was only a child," said Rosa. "You were always so beautiful and tall, and kind to a little monkey like me. Oh, pray sit down, Lady Cicely, and talk of old times."

She drew her gently to the sofa, and they sat down hand in hand; but Lady Cicely's high-bred reserve made her a very poor gossip about any thing that touched herself and her family; so Rosa, though no egotist, was drawn into talking about herself more than she would have done had she deliberately planned the conversation. But here was an old school-fellow, and a singularly polite listener ; and so out came her love, her genuine happiness, her particular griefs, and especially the crowning grievance, no society, moped to death, &c.

Lady Cicely could hardly understand the sentiment in a woman who so evidently loved her husband. "Society!" said she, after due reflection, "why, it is a boa." (And here I may as well explain that Lady Cicely spoke certain words falsely, and others affectedly; and as for the letter *r*, she could say it if she made a hearty effort, but was generally too lazy to throw her leg over it.) "Society! I'm dwenched to death with it. If I could only catch fiah like other women, and love somebody, I would rather have a *tête-à-tête* with him, than to go teawing about all day and all night, from one unintwisting cwowd to another. To be sure," said she, puzzling the matter out, "you are a beauty, and would be more looked at."

"The idea! and,—oh, no! no! it is not that. But even in the country we had always some society."

"Well, dyah believe me, with your appeawance, you can have as much society as you please; but it will boa you to death, as it does me, and then you will long to be left quiet with a sensible man who loves you."

Said Rosa, "When shall I have another *tête-à-tête* with *you*, I wonder? Oh, it has been such a comfort to me! Bless you for coming. There — I wrote to Cecilia, and Emily, and Mrs. Bosanquest that is now, and all my sworn friends, and to think of you being the one to come,—you that never kissed me but once, and an earl's daughter into the bargain."

"Ha! ha! ha!" Lady Cicely actually laughed for once in a way, and she did not feel the effort. "As for kissing," said she, "if I fall shawt, fawgive me. I was nevaa vewy demonstwative."

"No; and I have had a lesson. That Florence Cole — Florence Whiting that was, you know — was always kissing me, and she has turned out a traitor. I'll tell you all about her." And she did.

Lady Cicely thought Mrs. Staines a little too unreserved in her conversation, but was so charmed with her sweetness and freshness that she kept up the acquaintance, and called on her twice a week during the season. At first she wondered that her visits were not returned; but Rosa let out that she was ashamed to call on foot in Grosvenor Square.

Lady Cicely shrugged her beautiful shoulders a little at that; but she continued to do the visiting, and to enjoy the simple, innocent rapture with which she was received.

This lady's pronunciation of many words was false or affected. She said "good-murning" for "good-morning," and turned other vowels into diphthongs, and played two or three pranks with her "r's." But we cannot be all imperfection: with her pronunciation her folly came to a full stop. I really believe she lisped less nonsense and bad taste in a year, than some of us articulate in a day. To be sure, folly is generally uttered in a hurry, and she was too deplorably lazy to speak fast on any occasion whatever.

One day Mrs. Staines took her up stairs, and showed her from the back window her husband pacing the yard waiting for patients. Lady Cicely folded her arms, and contemplated him at first with a sort of zoölogical curiosity. Gentleman pacing back yard like hyena she had never seen before.

At last she opened her mouth in a whisper, "What is he doing?"

"Waiting for patients."

"Oh! Waiting—for—patients?"

"For patients that never come, and never will come."

"Cuwious! — How little I know of life!"

"It is that all day, dear, or else writing"

Lady Cicely, with her eyes fixed on Staines, made a motion with her hand that she was attending.

"And they won't publish a word he writes."

"Poor man !"

"Nice for me, is it not ? "

"I begin to understand," said Lady Cicely quietly, and soon after retired with her invariable composure.

Meantime Dr. Staines, like a good husband, had thrown out occasional hints to Mrs. Lucas that he had a wife, beautiful, accomplished, moped. More than that, he went so far as to regret to her that Mrs. Staines, being in a neighborhood new to him, saw so little society; the more so as she was formed to shine, and had not been used to seclusion.

All these hints fell dead on Mrs. Lucas. A handsome and skilful doctor was welcome to her : his wife — that was quite another matter.

But one day Mrs. Lucas saw Lady Cicely Treherne's carriage standing at the door. The style of the whole turn-out impressed her. She wondered whose it was.

On another occasion she saw it drive up, and the lady get out. She recognized her; and the very next day this *parvenue* said adroitly, "Now, Dr. Staines, really you can't be allowed to hide your wife in this way." (Staines stared.) "Why not introduce her to me next Wednesday ? It is my night. I would give a dinner expressly for her, but I don't like to do that while my husband is in Naples."

When Staines carried the invitation to his wife she was delighted, and kissed him with childish frankness.

But the very next moment she became thoughtful, uneasy, depressed. "Oh, dear ! I've nothing to wear."

"Oh, nonsense, Rosa ! Your wedding outfit."

"The idea ! I can't go as a bride. It's not a masquerade."

"But you have other dresses."

"All gone by, more or less ; or not fit for such parties as *she* gives. A hundred carriages ! "

"Bring them down, and let me see them."

"Oh, yes!" And the lady who had nothing to wear paraded a very fair show of dresses.

Staines saw something to admire in all of them Mrs. Staines found more to object to in each.

At last he fell upon a silver-gray silk, of superlative quality.

"That ! It is as old as the hills," shrieked Rosa.

"It looks just out of the shop. Come, tell the truth : how often have you worn it ? "

"I wore it before I was married."

"Ay, but how often ? "

"Twice. Three times, I believe."

"I thought so. It is as good as new."

"But I have had it so long by me. I had it two years before I made it up."

"What does that matter ? Do you think the people can tell how long a dress has been lurking in your wardrobe ? This is childish, Rosa. There, with that dress as good as new, and your beauty, you will be as much admired, and perhaps hated, as your heart can desire."

"I am afraid not," said Rosa naïvely. "Oh, how I wish I had known a week ago ! "

"I am very thankful you did not," said Staines dryly.

At ten o'clock Mrs. Staines was nearly dressed ; at quarter past ten she demanded ten minutes ; at half past ten she sought a reprieve ; at a quarter to eleven, being assured that the street was full of carriages which had put down at Mrs. Lucas's she consented to emerge ; and in a minute they were at the house.

They were shown first into a cloak-room, and then into a tea-room, and then mounted the stairs. One scr-vant took their names, and bawled them out to another four yards off, he to another about as near, and so on; and they edged themselves into the room, not yet too crowded to move in.

They had not taken many steps, on the chance of finding their hostess, when a slight buzz arose, and seemed to follow them.

Rosa wondered what that was, but only for a moment; she observed a tall, stout, aquiline woman fix an eye of bitter, diabolical, malignant hatred on her; and, as she advanced ugly noses were cocked disdainfully, and scraggy shoulders elevated at the risk of sending the bones through the leather, and a titter or two shot after her. A woman's instinct gave her the key at once; the sexes had complimented her at sight, each in its way — the men with respectful admiration, and the women with their inflammable jealousy, and ready hatred in another of the quality they value most in themselves. But the country girl was too many for them: for she would neither see nor hear, but moved sedately on, and calmly crushed them with her southern beauty. Their dry powdered faces would not live by the side of her glowing skin, with Nature's delicate gloss upon it, and the rich blood mantling below it. The got-up beauties — i. e., the majority — seemed literally to fade and wither as she passed.

Mrs. Lucas got to her, suppressed a slight maternal pang, having daughters to marry, and took her line in a moment: here was a decoy-duck. Mrs. Lucas was all graciousness, made acquaintance, and took a little turn with her, introducing her to one or two persons; among the rest, to the malignant woman, Mrs. Barr. Mrs. Barr, on this, ceased to look daggers, and substituted icicles; but, on the hateful beauty moving away, dropped the icicles, and resumed the poniards.

The rooms filled; the heat be-

came oppressive, and the mixed odors of flowers, scents, and perspiring humanity, sickening. Some, unable to bear it, trickled out of the room, and sat all down the stairs.

Rosa began to feel faint. Up came a tall, sprightly girl, whose pertness was redeemed by a certain *bonhomie*, and said, "Mrs. Staines, I believe? I am to make myself agreeable to you. That is the order from head-quarters."

"Miss Lucas," said Staines.

She jerked a little off-hand bow to him, and said, "Will you trust her to me for five minutes?"

"Certainly." But he did not much like it.

Miss Lucas carried her off, and told Dr. Staines, over her shoulder, now he could flirt to his heart's content.

"Thank you," said he dryly. "I'll await your return."

"Oh! there are some much greater flirts here than I am," said the ready Miss Lucas; and, whispering something in Mrs. Staines's ear, suddenly glided with her behind a curtain, pressed a sort of button fixed to a looking-glass door. The door opened, and behold they were in delicious place, for which I can hardly find a word, since it was a boudoir and a conservatory in one: a large octagon, the walls lined from floor to ceiling with looking-glasses of moderate width at intervals, and with creepers that covered the intervening spaces of the wall, and were trained so as to break the outline of the glasses without greatly clouding the reflection. Ferns, in great variety, were grouped in a deep crescent, and in the bight of this green bay were a small table and chairs. As there were no hot-house plants, the temperature was very cool, compared with the reeking oven they had escaped; and a little fountain bubbled and fed a little meandering gutter that trickled away among the ferns; it ran crystal clear over little bright pebbles and shells. It did not always run, you understand; but Miss Lucas turned a secret tap, and started it.

"Oh, how heavenly!" said Rosa, with a sigh of relief, "and how good of you to bring me here!"

"Yes: by rights I ought to have waited till you fainted; but there is no making acquaintance among all those people. Mamma will ask such crowds; one is like a fly in a glue-pot."

Miss Lucas had good nature, smartness, and animal spirits; hence arose a vivacity and fluency that were often amusing, and passed for very clever. Reserve she had none; would talk about strangers or friends, herself, her mother, her God, and the last buffoon singer, in a breath. At a hint from Rosa she told her who the lady in the pink dress was, and the lady in the violet velvet, and so on; for each lady was defined by her dress, and, more or less, quizzed by the show-woman, not exactly out of malice, but because it is smarter and more natural to decry than to praise, and a little *médisance* is the spice to gossip, belongs to it, as mint-sauce to lamb. So they chattered away, and were pleased with each other, and made friends, and there, in cool grot, quite forgot the sufferings of their fellow-creatures in the adjacent Turkish bath, yclept Society. It was Rosa who first recollected herself. "Will not Mrs. Lucas be angry with me if I keep you all to myself?"

"Oh, no! but I am afraid we must go into the hothouse again. I like the greenhouse best, with such a nice companion."

They slipped noiselessly into the throng again, and wriggled about, Miss Lucas presenting her new friends to several ladies and gentlemen.

Presently Staines found them, and then Miss Lucas wriggled away; and, in due course, the room was thinned by many guests driving off home, or to balls and other receptions, and Dr. Staines and Mrs. Staines went home to the Bijou. Here the physician prescribed bed; but the lady would not hear of such a thing until she had talked it over. So they compared notes, and Rosa told him how well she had got on with Miss Lucas and made a friendship. "But for that," said she, "I should be sorry I went among those people, such a dowdy."

"Dowdy!" said Staines. "Why, you stormed the town; you were the great success of the night, and, for all I know, of the season." The wretch delivered this with unbecoming indifference.

"It is too bad to mock me, Christie. Where were your eyes?"

"To the best of my recollection they were one on each side of my nose."

"Yes, but some people are eyes, and no eyes."

"I scorn the imputation; try me."

"Very well. Then, did you see that lady in sky-blue silk, embroidered with flowers and flounced with white velvet, and the corsage point lace; and oh! such emeralds?"

"I did; a tall, skinny woman, with eyes resembling her jewels in color, though not in brightness."

"Never mind her eyes; it is her dress I am speaking of. Exquisite; and what a coiffure! Well, did you see *her* in the black velvet, trimmed so deep with Chantilly lace, wave on wave, and her headdress of crimson flowers, and such a *rivière* of diamonds; oh, dear! oh, dear!"

"I did, love. The room was an oven, but her rubicund face and suffocating costume made it seem a furnace."

"Stuff! Well, did you see the lady in the corn-colored silk, and poppies in her hair?"

"Of course I did. Ceres in person. She made me feel very hot too; but I cooled myself at her pale, sickly face."

"Never mind their faces; that is not the point."

"Oh, excuse me! it is always a point with us benighted males, all eyes and no eyes."

"Well, then, the lady in white, with cherry velvet bands, and a white tunic looped with crimson, and head-dress of white illusion *à la vierge*, I think they call it."

"It was very refreshing, and adapted to that awful atmosphere. It was the nearest approach to nudity I ever saw, even among fashionable people."

"It was lovely; and then, that superb figure in white illusion and gold, with all those narrow flounces over her slip of white silk *glacé* and a wreath of white flowers, with gold wheat-ears among them, in her hair; and oh! oh! oh! her pearls, Oriental, and as big as almonds!"

"And oh! oh! oh! her nose! reddish, and as long as a woodcock's."

"Noses! noses! stupid! That is not what strikes you first in a woman dressed like an angel."

"Well, if you were to run up against that one, as I nearly did, her nose *would* be the thing that would strike you first. Nose! it was a rostrum! the spear-head of Goliath."

"Now don't, Christopher. This is no laughing matter. Do you mean you were not ashamed of your wife? I was."

"No, I was not: you had but one rival — a very young lady, wise before her age, a blonde, with violet eyes. She was dressed in light mauve-colored silk, without a single flounce, or any other tomfoolery to fritter away the sheen and color of an exquisite material; her sunny hair was another wave of color, wreathed with a thin line of white jasmine flowers closely woven, that scented the air. This girl was the moon of that assembly, and you were the sun."

"I never even saw her."

"Eyes, and no eyes. She saw you, and said, 'Oh, what a beautiful creature!' for I heard her. As for the old stagers, whom you admire so, their faces were all clogged with powder, the pores stopped up, the true texture of the skin abolished. They looked downright nasty whenever you or that young girl passed by them. Then it was you saw to what a frightful extent women are got up in our day, even young women, and respectable women. No, Rosa, dress can do little for you; you have beauty — real beauty."

"Beauty! That passes unnoticed unless one is well dressed."

"Then what an obscure pair the Apollo Belvidere and the Venus de Medicis must be!"

. "Oh! they are dressed — in marble."

Christopher Staines then smiled.

"Well done," said he admiringly. "That is a knock-down blow. So now you have silenced your husband, go you to bed directly. I can't afford you diamonds; so I will take care of that little insignificant trifle, your beauty."

Mrs. Staines and Mrs. Lucas exchanged calls, and soon Mrs. Staines could no longer complain she was out of the world. Mrs. Lucas invited her to every party, because her beauty was an instrument of attraction she knew how to use; and Miss Lucas took a downright fancy to her; drove her in the Park, and on Sundays to the Zoölogical Gardens, just beginning to be fashionable.

The Lucases rented a box at the opera; and if it was not let at the library by six o'clock, and if other engagements permitted, word was sent round to Mrs. Staines, as a matter of course, and she was taken to the opera. She began almost to live at the Lucases', and to be oftener fatigued than moped.

The usual order of things was inverted; the maiden lady educated the matron; for Miss Lucas knew all about everybody in the Park, honorable or dishonorable; all the scandals, and all the flirtations; and whatever she knew, she related point-blank. Being as inquisitive as voluble, she soon learned how Mrs. Staines and her husband were situated. She took upon her to advise her in many things, and especially impressed upon her that Dr. Staines must keep a carriage if he wanted to get on in medicine. This piece of advice accorded so well with Rosa's wishes that she urged it on her husband again and again.

He objected that no money was coming in, and therefore it would be insane to add to their expenses. Rosa persisted, and at last worried Staines with her importunity. He began to give rather short answers. Then she quoted Miss Lucas against him. He treated the authority with marked contempt; and then Rosa fired up a little. Then Staines held his peace; but did not buy a carriage to visit his no patients.

So at last Rosa complained to Lady Cicely Treherne, and made her the judge between her husband and herself.

Lady Cicely drawled out a prompt but polite refusal to play that part. All that could be elicited from her, and that with difficulty, was, "Why quall with your husband about a cawwige? He is your best friend."

"Ah, that he is!" said Rosa; "but Miss Lucas is a good friend, and she knows the world. We don't; neither Christopher nor I."

So she continued to nag at her husband about it, and to say that he was throwing his only chance away.

Galled as he was by neglect, this was irritating, and, at last, he could not help telling her she was unreasonable. "You live a gay life, and I a sad one. I consent to this, and let you go about with these Lucases, because you were so dull; but you should not consult them in our private affairs. Their interference is indelicate and improper. I will not set up a carriage till I have patients to visit. I am sick of seeing our capital dwindle, and no income created. I will never set up a carriage till I have taken a hundred-guinea fee."

"Oh! Then we shall go splashing through the mud all our days."

"Or ride in a cab," said Christopher, with a quiet doggedness that left no hope of his yielding.

One afternoon Miss Lucas called for Mrs. Staines to drive in the Park, but did not come up stairs; it was an engagement, and she knew Mrs. Staines would be ready, or nearly. Mrs. Staines, not to keep her waiting, came down rather hastily, and, in the very passage, whipped out of her pocket a little glass, and a little powder-puff, and puffed her face all over in a trice. She was then going out; but her husband called her into the study. "Rosa, my dear," said he, "you were going out with a dirty face."

"Oh," cried she, "give me a glass!"

"There is no need of that. All you want is a basin and some nice rain-water. I keep a little reservoir of it."

He then handed her the same with great politeness. She looked in his eye, and saw he was not to be trifled with. She complied like a lamb, and the heavenly color and velvet gloss that resulted were admirable.

He kissed her, and said, "Ah! now you are my Rosa again. Oblige me by handing over that powder-puff to me." She looked vexed, but complied. "When you come back I will tell you why."

"You are a pest," said Mrs. Staines, and so joined her friend, rosy with rain water and a rub.

"Dear me, how handsome you

look to day!" was Miss Lucas's first remark.

Rosa never dreamed that rain-water and a rub could be the cause of her looking so well.

"It is my tiresome husband," said she. "He objects to powder, and he has taken away my puff."

"And you stood that?"

"Obliged to."

"Why, you poor-spirited little creature. I should like to see a husband presume to interfere with me in those things. Here, take mine."

Rosa hesitated a little. "Well — no — I think not."

Miss Lucas laughed at her, and quizzed her so on her allowing a man to interfere in such sacred things as dress and cosmetics that she came back irritated with her husband, and gave him a short answer or two. Then he asked what was the matter.

"You treat me like a child — taking away my very puff."

"I treat you like a beautiful flower that no bad gardener shall wither while I am here."

"What nonsense! How could that wither me? It is only violet powder — what they put on babies."

"And who are the Herods that put it on babies?"

"Their own mothers, that love them ten times more than the fathers do."

"And kill a hundred of them for one a man ever kills. Mothers! — the most wholesale homicides in the nation. We will examine your violet powder. Bring it down here."

While she was gone, he sent for a breakfast-cupful of flour; and when she came back he had his scales out, and begged her to put a teaspoonful of flour into one scale, and of violet powder into another. The flour kicked the beam, as Homer expresses himself.

"Put another spoonful of flour."

The one spoonful of violet powder outweighed the two of flour.

"Now," said Staines, "does not

6*

that show you the presence of a mineral in your vegetable powder? I suppose they tell you it is made of white violets dried, and triturated in a diamond mill. Let us find out what metal it is. We need not go very deep into chemistry for that." He then applied a simple test, and detected the presence of lead in large quantities. Then he lectured her: "Invisible perspiration is a process of nature necessary to health and to life. The skin is made porous for that purpose. You can kill anybody in an hour or two by closing the pores. A certain infallible ass, called Pope Leo XII., killed a little boy in two hours by gilding him to adorn the pageant of his first procession as pope. But what is death to the whole body must be injurious to a part. What madness, then, to clog the pores of so large and important a surface as the face, and check the invisible perspiration: how much more to insert lead into your system every day of your life: accumulative poison, and one so deadly and so subtle that the Sheffield file-cutters die in their prime from merely hammering on a leaden anvil. And what do you gain by this suicidal habit? No plum has a sweeter bloom or more delicious texture than the skin of your young face; but this mineral filth hides that delicate texture, and substitutes a dry, uniform appearance, more like a certain kind of leprosy than health. Nature made your face the rival of peaches, roses, lilies; and you say, 'No; I know better than my Creator and my God; my face shall be like a dusty miller's. Go into any flour-mill, and there you shall see men with faces exactly like your friend Miss Lucas's. But before a miller goes to his sweetheart, he always washes his face. You ladies would never get a miller down to your level in brains. It is a miller's *dirty* face our monomaniacs of women imitate, not the face a miller goes-a-courting with."

"La! what a fuss about nothing!"

"About nothing! Is your health nothing? Is your beauty nothing? Well, then, it will cost you nothing to promise me never to put powder on your face again."

"Very well, I promise. Now, what will you do for me?"

"Work for you — write for you — suffer for you — be self-denying for you — and even give myself the pain of disappointing you now and then — looking forward to the time when I shall be able to say 'Yes' to every thing you ask me. Ah, child! you little know what it costs me to say 'No' to *you*."

Rosa put her arms around him, and acquiesced. She was one of those who go with the last speaker; but, for that very reason, the eternal companionship of so flighty and flirty a girl as Miss Lucas was injurious to her.

One day Lady Cicely Treherne was sitting with Mrs. Staines, smiling languidly at her talk, and occasionally drawling out a little plain good sense, when in came Miss Lucas, with her tongue well hung, as usual, and dashed into twenty topics at once.

This young lady, in her discourse, was like those oily little beetles you see in small ponds, whose whole life is spent in tacking — confound them! — generally at right angles. What they are in navigation was Miss Lucas in conversation: tacked so eternally from topic to topic that no man on earth, and not every woman, could follow her.

At the sight and sound of her, Lady Cicely congealed and stiffened. Easy and unpretending with Mrs. Staines, she was all dignity, and even majesty, in the presence of this chatterbox; and the smoothness with which the transfiguration was accomplished marked that accomplished actress the high-bred woman of the world.

Rosa, better able to estimate the change of manner than Miss Lucas was, who did not know how little this Sawney was afflicted with misplaced dignity, looked wistfully and distressed at her. Lady Cicely smiled kindly in reply, rose, without seeming to hurry — catch her condescending to be rude to Charlotte Lucas — and took her departure, with a profound and most gracious courtesy to the lady who had driven her away.

Mrs. Staines saw her down stairs, and said ruefully, "I am afraid you do not like my friend Miss Lucas. She is a great rattle, but so good-natured and clever."

Lady Cicely shook her head. "Clevaa people don't talk so much nonsense before stangaas."

"Oh, dear!" said Rosa. "I was in hopes you would like her."

"Do *you* like her."

"Indeed I do; but I shall not, if she drives an older friend away."

"My dyah, I'm not easily dwiven from those I esteem. But you undarstand that is not a woman for me to mispwonownce my 'ah's' befaw — NOR FOR YOU TO MAKE A BOSOM FRIEND OF — ROSA STAINES."

She said this with a sudden maternal solemnity and kindness that contrasted nobly and strangely with her yea-nay style, and Mrs. Staines remembered the words years after they were spoken.

It so happened that, after this, Mrs. Staines received no more visits from Lady Cicely for some time, and that vexed her. She knew her sex enough to be aware that they are very jealous, and she permitted herself to think that this high-minded Sawney was jealous of Miss Lucas.

This idea, founded on a general estimate of her sex, was dispelled by a few lines from Lady Cicely, to say her family and herself were in deep distress: her brother, Lord Aycough, lay dying from an accident.

Then Rosa was all remorse, and ran down to Staines to tell him. She found him with an open letter in his hand. It was from Dr. Barr, and on the same subject. The doctor, who had always been friendly to him, invited him to come down at once to Hallowtree Hall, in Huntingdonshire, to a consultation. There was a friendly intimation to start at once, as the patient might die any moment.

Husband and wife embraced each other in a tumult of surprised thankfulness. A few necessaries were thrown into a carpet-bag, and Dr. Staines was soon whirled into Huntingdonshire. Having telegraphed beforehand, he was met at the station by the earl's carriage and people, and driven to the Hall. He was received by an old silver-haired butler, looking very sad, who conducted him to a boudoir, and then went and tapped gently at the door of the patient's room. It was opened and shut very softly, and Lady Cicely, dressed in black, and looking paler than ever, came into the room.

"Dr. Staines, I think?"

He bowed.

"Thank you for coming so promptly. Dr. Barr is gone. I fear he thinks — he thinks — O Dr. Staines, no sign of life but in his poor hands, that keep moving day and night."

Staines looked very grave at that.

Lady Cicely observed it, and, faint at heart, could say no more, but led the way to the sick-room.

There, in a spacious chamber, lighted by a grand oriel-window and two side windows, lay rank, title, wealth, and youth, stricken down in a moment by a common accident. The sufferer's face was bloodless, his eyes fixed, and no signs of life but in his thumbs, and they kept working with strange regularity.

In the room were a nurse and the surgeon; the neighboring physician, who had called in Dr. Barr, had just paid his visit and gone away.

Lady Cicely introduced Dr. Staines and Mr. White, and then Dr Staines stood and fixed his eyes on the patient in profound silence.

Lady Cicely scanned his countenance searchingly, and was struck with the extraordinary power and intensity it assumed in examining the patient; but the result was not encouraging. Dr. Staines looked grave and gloomy.

At last, without removing his eye from the recumbent figure, he said quietly to Mr. White, "Thrown from his horse, sir?"

"Horse fell on him, Dr. Staines."

"Any visible injuries?"

"Yes. Severe contusions, and a rib broken and pressed upon the lungs. I replaced and set it. Will you see?"

"If you please."

He examined and felt the patient, and said it had been ably done.

Then he was silent and searching.

At last he spoke again. "The motion of the thumbs corresponds exactly with his pulse."

"Is that so, sir?"

"It is. The case is without a parallel. How long has he been so?"

"Nearly a week."

"Impossible!"

"It is so, sir."

Lady Cicely confirmed this.

"All the better," said Staines, upon reflection. "Well, sir," said he, "the visible injuries having been ably relieved, I shall look another way for the cause." Then, after another pause, "I must have his head shaved."

Lady Cicely demurred a little to this; but Dr. Staines stood firm, and his lordship's valet undertook the job.

Staines directed him where to begin; and when he had made a circular tonsure on the top of the head, had it sponged with tepid water.

"I thought so," said he. "Here is the mischief;" and he pointed to a very slight indentation on the left side of the pia mater. "Observe," said he, "there is no corresponding indentation on the other side. Underneath this trifling depression a minute piece of bone is doubtless pressing on the most sensitive part of the brain. He must be trephined."

Mr. White's eyes sparkled.

"You are a hospital surgeon, sir?"

"Yes, Dr. Staines. I have no fear of the operation."

"Then I hand the patient over to you. The case at present is entirely surgical."

White was driven home, and soon returned with the requisite instruments. The operation was neatly performed, and then Lady Cicely was called in. She came trembling; her brother's fingers were still working, but not so regularly.

"That is only *habit*," said Staines; "it will soon leave off, now the cause is gone."

And truly enough, in about five minutes the fingers became quiet. The eyes became human next, and within half an hour after the operation the earl gave a little sigh.

Lady Cicely clasped her hands, and uttered a little cry of delight.

"This will not do," said Staines. "I shall have you screaming when he speaks."

"O Dr. Staines! will he ever speak?"

"I think so; and very soon. So be on your guard."

This strange scene reached its climax soon after by the earl saying quietly, —

"Are her knees broke, Tom?"

Lady Cicely uttered a little scream, but instantly suppressed it.

"No, my lord," said Staines smartly; "only rubbed a bit. You can go to sleep, my lord. I'll take care of the mare."

"All right," said his lordship, and composed himself to slumber.

Dr. Staines, at the earnest request of Lady Cicely, staid all night; and in course of the day advised her how to nurse the patient, since both physician and surgeon had done with him.

He said the patient's brain might be irritable for some days, and no women in silk dresses, or crinoline, or creaking shoes, must enter the room. He told her the nurse was evidently a clumsy woman, and would be letting things fall. She had better get some old soldier used to nursing. "And don't whisper in the room," said he; "nothing irritates them worse; and don't let anybody play a piano within hearing; but in a day or two you may try him with slow and continuous music on the flute or violin, if you like. Don't touch his bed suddenly; don't sit on it or lean on it. Dole sunlight into his room by degrees; and ,when he can bear it, drench him with it. Never mind what the old school tell you. About these things they know a good deal less than nothing."

Lady Cicely received all this like an oracle.

The cure was telegraphed to Dr. Barr, and he was requested to settle the fee. He was not the man to undersell the profession, and was jealous of nobody, having a large practice and a very wealthy wife. So he telegraphed back — "Fifty guineas, and a guinea a mile from London."

So, as Christopher Staines sat at an early breakfast, with the carriage waiting to take him to the train, two notes were brought him on a salver.

They were both directed by Lady Cicely Treherne. One of them contained a few kind and feeling words of gratitude and esteem; the other a check, drawn by the earl's steward, for one hundred and thirty guineas.

He bowled up to London, and told it all to Rosa. She sparkled with pride, affection, and joy.

"Now, who says you are not a

genius?" she cried. "A hundred and thirty guineas for one fee! Now, if you love your wife as she loves you, you will set up a brougham."

———◆———

CHAPTER VIII.

Dr. Staines begged leave to distinguish : he had not said he would set up a carriage at the first one hundred guinea fee, but only that he would not set up one before. There are misguided people who would call this logic; but Rosa said it was equivocating, and urged him so warmly that at last he burst out, "Who can go on forever saying 'No' to the only creature he loves?"—and caved. In forty-eight hours more a brougham waited at Mrs. Staines's door. The servant engaged to drive it was Andrew Pearman, a bachelor, and hitherto an undergroom. He readily consented to be coachman, and do certain domestic work as well. So Mrs. Staines had a man-servant as well as a carriage.

Ere long three or four patients called or wrote, one after the other. These Rosa set down to brougham, and crowed. She even crowed to Lady Cicely Treherne, to whose influence, and not to brougham's, every one of these patients was owing. Lady Cicely kissed her, and demurely enjoyed the poor soul's self-satisfaction.

Staines himself, while he drove to or from these patients, felt more sanguine, and, buoyed as he was by the consciousness of ability, began to hope that he had turned the corner.

He sent an account of Lord Aycough's case to a medical magazine; and so full is the world of flunkyism that this article, though he withheld the name, retaining only the title, got the literary wedge in for him at once; and in due course he became a paid contributor to two medical organs, and used to study and write more, and indent the little stone yard less, than heretofore.

It was about this time, circumstances made him acquainted with Phœbe Dale. Her intermediate history I will dispose in fewer words than it deserves. Her Ruin, Mr. Reginald Falcon, was dismissed from his club for marking high cards on the back with his nail. This stopped his remaining resource—borrowing; so he got more and more out at elbows till at last he came down to hanging about billiard-rooms, and making a little money by concealing his game; from that, however, he rose to be a marker.

Having culminated to that, he wrote and proposed marriage to Miss Dale, in a charming letter. She showed it to her father with pride.

Now if his vanity, his disloyalty, his falsehood, his ingratitude, and his other virtues, had not stood in the way, he would have done this three years ago, and been jumped at.

But the offer came too late; not for Phœbe—she would have taken him in a moment—but for her friends. A bated hook is one thing, a bare hook is another. Farmer Dale had long discovered where Phœbe's money went : he said not a word to her, but went up to town like a shot; found Falcon out, and told him he mustn't think to eat his daughter's bread. She should marry a man who could make a decent livelihood; and if she was to run away with *him*, why they'd starve together. The farmer was resolute, and spoke very loud, like one that expects opposition, and comes prepared to quarrel. Instead of that, this artful rogue addressed him with deep respect and an affected veneration that quite puzzled the old man; acquiesced in every word, expressed contrition for his past misdeeds, and told the farmer he had quite determined to labor with his hands. "You know, farmer," said he, "I am not the only gentleman who has come to that in the present day. Now, all my friends who have seen my sketches assure me I am a born painter; and a painter I'll be — for love of Phœbe."

The farmer made a wry face. "Painter! that is a sorry sort of a trade."

"You are mistaken. It's the best trade going. There are gentlemen making their thousands a year by it"

"Not in our parts, there bain't. Stop a bit. What be ye going to paint, sir? Housen, or folk?"

"Oh, hang it! not houses. Figures, landscapes."

"Well, ye might just make a shift at it, I suppose, with here and there a signboard. They are the best paid, our way; but, Lord bless ye, *they* wants head-piece! Well, sir, let me see your work. Then we'll talk further."

"I'll go to work this afternoon," said Falcon eagerly; then, with affected surprise, "Bless me! I forgot. I have no palette, no canvas, no colors. You couldn't lend me a couple of sovereigns to buy them, could you?"

"Ay, sir, I could, but I won't. I'll lend ye the things, though, if you have a mind to go with me and buy 'em."

· Falcon agreed, with a lofty smile, and the purchases were made.

Mr. Falcon painted a landscape or two out of his imagination. The dealer to whom he took them declined them; one advised the gentleman painter to color tea-boards; "That's your line," said he.

"The world has no taste," said the gentleman painter; "but it has got lots of vanity: I'll paint portraits."

He did — and formidable ones. His portraits were, amazingly like the people, and yet unlike men and women, especially about the face. One thing, he didn't trouble with lights and shades, but went slap at the features.

His brush would never have kept him: but he carried an instrument in the use of which he was really an artist, viz., his tongue. By wheedling and underselling — for he only charged a pound for the painted canvas — he contrived to live; then he aspired to dress as well as live. With this second object in view, he hit upon a characteristic expedient.

He used to prowl about; and when he saw a young woman sweeping the afternoon streets with a long silk train, and, in short, dressed to ride in the park, yet parading the streets, he would take his hat off to her with an air of profound respect, and ask permission to take her portrait. Generally he met a prompt rebuff; but if the fair was so unlucky as to hesitate a single moment, he told her a melting tale: he had once driven his four-in-hand, but by indorsing his friend's bills was reduced to painting likenesses — admirable likenesses in oils, only a guinea each.

His piteous tale provoked more jibes than pity; but as he had no shame, the rebuffs went for nothing. He actually did get a few sitters by his audacity, and some of the sitters actually took the pictures and paid for them; others declined them with fury as soon as they were finished. These he took back with a piteous sigh that sometimes extracted half a crown. Then he painted over the rejected one, and let it dry; so that sometimes a paid portrait would present a beauty enthroned on the *débris* of two or three rivals, and that is where few beauties would object to sit.

All this time he wrote nice letters to Phœbe, and adopted the tone of the struggling artist, and the true lover, who wins his bride by patience, perseverance, and indomitable industry; a babbled of "Self-help."

Meantime Phœbe was not idle; an excellent business woman, she took immediate advantage of a new station that was built near the farm to send up milk, butter, and eggs to London. Being genuine, they sold like wild-fire. Observing that, she extended her operations by buying of other farmers and forwarding to London; and then, having, of course, an eye to her struggling artist, she told her father she must have a shop in London, and somebody in it she could depend upon.

"With all my heart, wench," said he; "but it must not be thou. I can't spare thee."

"May I have Dick, father?"

"Dick! He is rather young."

"But he is very quick, father, and minds every word I tell him."

"Ay, he is as fond of thee as ever a cow was of a calf. Well, you can try him."

So the love-sick woman of business set up a little shop, and put her brother Dick in it, and all to see more of her struggling artist. She staid several days, to open the little shop and start the business. She advertised pure milk, and challenged scientific analysis of every thing she sold. This came of her being a reader. She knew, by the journals, that we live in a sinful and adulterating generation; and any thing pure must be a Godsend to the poor poisoned public.

Now Dr. Staines, though known to the profession as a diagnost, was also an analyst, and this challenge brought him down on Phœbe Dale. He told her he was a physician, and in search of pure food for his own family — would she really submit the milk to analysis?

Phœbe smiled an honest country smile, and said, "Surely, sir." She gave him every facility, and he applied those simple tests which are commonly used in France, though hardly known in England.

He found it perfectly pure, and told her so; and gazed at Phœbe for a moment, as a phenomenon.

She smiled again at that, her broad country smile. "That is a wonder in London, I dare say. It's my belief half the children that die here are perished with watered milk. Well, sir we sha'n't have that on our souls, father and I: he is a farmer in Essex. This comes a many miles, this milk."

Staines looked in her face with kindly approval marked on his own eloquent features. She blushed a little at so fixed a regard. Then he asked her if she would supply him with milk, butter, and eggs.

"Why, if you mean sell you them, yes, sir, with pleasure. But for sending them home to you in this big town, as some do, I can't, for there's only brother Dick and me: it is an experiment like."

"Very well," said Staines: "I will send for them."

"Thank you kindly, sir. I hope you won't be offended, sir; but we only sell for ready money."

"All the better: my order at home is, no bills."

When he was gone, Phœbe, assuming vast experience, though this was only her third day, told Dick that was one of the right sort. "And O Dick!" said she, "did you notice his eye?"

"Not particklar, sister."

"There, now! the boy is blind. Why, 'twas like a jewel. Such an eye I never saw in a man's head, nor a woman's neither."

Staines told his wife about Phœbe and her brother, and spoke of her with a certain admiration that raised Rosa's curiosity, and even that sort of vague jealousy that fires at bare praise. "I should like to see this phenomenon," said she. "You shall," said he· "I have to call on Mrs. Manly. She lives near. I will drop you at the little shop, and come back for you."

He did so, and that gave Rosa a quarter of an hour to make her purchases. When he came back he found her conversing with Phœbe as if they were old friends, and Dick glaring at his wife with awe and admiration. He could hardly get her away.

She was far more extravagant in her praises than Dr. Staines had been. "What a good creature!" said she. "And how clever! To think of her setting up a shop like that all by herself; for her Dick is only seventeen."

Dr. Staines recommended the little shop wherever he went, and even extended its operations. He asked Phœbe to get her own wheat ground at home, and send the flour up in bushel bags. "These assassins, the bakers," said he, " are putting copper into the flour now as well as alum. Pure flour is worth a fancy price to any family. With that we can make the bread of life. What you buy in the shops is the bread of death."

Dick was a good, sharp boy, devoted to his sister. He stuck to the shop in London, and handed the money to Phœbe when she came for it. She worked for it in Essex, and extended her country connection for supply as the retail business increased.

Staines wrote an article on pure food, and incidentally mentioned the shop as a place where flour, milk, and butter were to be had pure. This article was published in the *Lancet*, and caused quite a run upon the little shop. By and by Phœbe enlarged it, for which there were great capabilities, and made herself a pretty little parlor, and there she and Dick sat to Falcon for their portraits; here, too, she hung his rejected landscapes. They were fair in her eyes; what matter whether they were like nature? his hand had painted them. She knew from him that everybody else had rejected them. With all the more pride and love did she have them framed in gold, and hung up with the portraits in her little sanctum.

For a few months Phœbe Dale was as happy as she deserved to be. Her lover was working, and faithful to her — at least she saw no reason to doubt it. He came to see her every evening, and seemed devoted to her; would sit quietly with her, or walk with her, or take her to a play, or a music-hall — at her expense.

She now lived in a quiet elysium, with a bright and rapturous dream of the future; for she saw she had hit on a good vein of business, and should soon be independent, and able to indulge herself with a husband, and ask no man's leave.

She sent to Essex for a dairymaid, and set her to churn milk into butter, *coram populo*, at a certain hour every morning. This made a new sensation. At other times the woman was employed to deliver milk and cream to a few favored customers.

Mrs. Staines dropped in now and then, and chatted with her. Her sweet face and her naïveté won Phœbe's heart; and one day, as happiness is apt to be communicative, she let out to her, in reply to a feeler or two as to whether she was quite alone, that she was engaged to be married to a gentleman; "but he is not rich, ma'am," said Phœbe plaintively; "he has had trouble — obliged to work for his living, like me; he painted these pictures, *every one of them*. If it was not making too free, and you could spare a guinea — he charges no more for the picture, only you must go to the expense of the frame."

"Of course I will," said Rosa warmly, "I'll sit for it here any day you like."

Now, Rosa said this out of her ever-ready kindness, not to wound Phœbe; but, having made the promise, she kept clear of the place for some days, hoping Phœbe would forget all about it. Meantime she sent her husband to buy.

In about a fortnight she called again, primed with evasions if she should be asked to sit; but nothing of the kind was proposed. Phœbe was dealing when she went in. The customers disposed of, she said to Mrs. Staines, "O ma'am! I am glad you are come. I have something I should like to show you." She took her into the parlor, and made her sit down; then she opened a drawer, and took out a very small substance that looked like a tear of ground glass, and put it on the table before her. "There, ma'am," said she, "that is all he has had for painting a friend's picture."

"Oh! what a shame!"

"His friend was going abroad — to Natal; to his uncle that farms out there, and does very well. It is a first-rate part, if you take out a little stock with you, and some money; so my one gave him credit, and when the letter came with that postmark he counted on a five-pound note; but the letter only said he had got no money yet, but sent him something as a keepsake; and there was this little stone. Poor fellow! he flung it down in a passion; he was so disappointed."

Phœbe's great gray eyes filled; and Rosa gave a little coo of sympathy that was very womanly and lovable.

Phœbe leaned her cheek on her hand and said thoughtfully, "I picked it up, and brought it away; for, after all, don't you think, ma'am, it is very strange that a friend should send it all that way if it was worth nothing at all?"

"It is impossible. He could not be so heartless."

"And do you know, ma'am, when I take it up in my fingers it doesn't feel like a thing that is worth nothing."

"No more it does; it makes my fingers tremble. May I take it home and show it to my husband? he is a great physician and knows every thing."

7

"I am sure I should be much obliged to you, ma'am."

Rosa drove home on purpose to show it to Christopher. She ran into his study. "O Christopher! please look at that. You know that good creature we have our flour and milk and things of. She is engaged, and he is a painter. Oh, such daubs! He painted a friend, and the friend sent that home all the way from Natal; and he dashed it down, and *she* picked it up, and what is it? ground glass, or a pebble, or what?"

"Humph! by its shape, and the great — brilliancy, — and refraction of light upon this angle, where the stone has got polished by rubbing other stones in the course of ages, I'm inclined to think it is — a diamond."

"A diamond!" shrieked Rosa. "No wonder my fingers trembled. Oh! can it be? Oh, you good, cold-blooded Christie! Poor thing! Come along, Diamond! Oh, you beauty! Oh, you duck!"

"Don't be in such a hurry. I only said I thought it was a diamond. Let me weigh it against water, and then I shall *know*."

He took it to his little laboratory, and returned in a few minutes, and said, "Yes. It is just three times and a half heavier than water. It is a diamond."

"Are you positive?"

"I'll stake my existence."

"What is it worth?"

"My dear, I'm not a jeweller; but it is very large and pear-shaped, and I see no flaw: I don't think you could buy it for less than three hundred pounds."

"Three hundred pounds! It is worth £300."

"Or sell it for more than £150."

"A hundred and fifty! It is worth £150."

"Why, my dear, one would think you had invented 'the diamond.' Show me how to crystallize carbon, and I will share your enthusiasm."

"Oh! I leave you to carbonize crystal. I prefer to gladden hearts; and I will do it this minute, with my diamond."

"Do, dear; and I will take that opportunity to finish my second article on Adulteration."

Rosa drove off to Phœbe Dale.

Now, Phœbe was drinking tea with Reginald Falcon, in her little parlor. "Who is that, I wonder?" she said, when the carriage drew up.

Reginald drew back a corner of the gauze curtain which had been drawn across the little glass door leading from the shop.

"It is a lady, and a beautiful — Oh! let me get out." And he rushed out at the door leading to the kitchen, not to be recognized.

This set Phœbe all in a flutter; and the next moment Mrs. Staines tapped at the little door, then opened it, and peeped. "Good news! may I come in?"

"Surely," said Phœbe, still troubled and confused by Reginald's strange agitation.

"There! It is a diamond!" screamed Rosa. "My husband knew it directly. He knows every thing. If ever you are ill, go to him and nobody else — by the refraction, and the angle, and its being three times and a half as heavy as water. It is worth £300 to buy, and £150 to sell."

"Oh!"

"So don't you go throwing it away, as he did." (In a whisper) "Two tea-cups! Was that him? I have driven him away. I am so sorry. I'll go; and then you can tell him. Poor fellow!"

"O ma'am, don't go yet!" said Phœbe, trembling. "I haven't half thanked you."

"Oh, bother thanks! Kiss me; that is the way."

"May I?"

"You may, and must. There — and there — and there. Oh, dear, what nice things good luck and happiness are, and how sweet to bring them for once!"

Upon this Phœbe and she had a nice little cry together, and Mrs. Staines went off refreshed thereby, and as gay as a lark, pointing slyly at the door, and making faces to Phœbe that she knew he was there, and she only retired, out of her admirable discretion, that they might enjoy the diamond together.

When she was gone, Reginald, whose eye and ear had been at the key-hole, alternately gloating on the face and drinking the accents of the only woman he had ever really loved, came out, looking pale and strangely disturbed, and sat down at the table without a word.

Phœbe came back to him full of the diamond, "Did you hear what she said, my dear? It is a diamond; it is worth £150 at least. Why, what ails you? Ah! to be sure! you know the lady."

"I have cause to know her. Cursed jilt!"

"You seem a good deal put out at the sight of her."

"It took me by surprise, that is all."

"It takes me by surprise too. I thought you were cured. I thought *my* turn had come at last."

Reginald met this in sullen silence. Then Phœbe was sorry she had said it; for, after all, it wasn't the man's fault if an old sweetheart had run into the room, and given him a start. So she made him some fresh tea, and pressed him kindly to try her home-made bread and butter.

My lord relaxed his frown and consented; and, of course, they talked diamond.

He told her loftily, he must take a studio; and his sitters must come to him, and must no longer expect to be immortalized for £1. It must be £2 for a bust, and £3 for a kit-cat.

"Nay, but, my dear," said Phœbe, "they will pay no more because you have a diamond."

"Then they will have to go un-painted," said Mr. Falcon.

This was intended for a threat. Phœbe instinctively felt that it might not be so received ; she coun-selled moderation. "It is a great thing to have earned a diamond," said she : "but 'tis only once in a life. Now, be ruled by me : go on just as you are. Sell the diamond, and give me the money to keep for you. Why, you might add a little to it, and so would I, till we made it up £200. And if you could only show £200 you had made and laid by father would let us marry, and I would keep this shop — it pays well, I can tell you — and keep my gen-tleman in a sly corner : you need never be seen in it."

"Ay, ay," said he, "that is the small game. But I am a man that have always preferred the big game. I shall set up my studio, and make enough to keep us both. So give me the stone, if you please. I shall take it round to them all, and the rogues won't get it out of *me* for a hundred and fifty ; why, it is as big as a nut."

"No, no, Reginald. . Money has always made mischief between you and me. You never had fifty pounds yet, you didn't fall into temptation. Do pray let me keep it for you ; or else sell it — I know how to sell ; nobody better — and keep the money for a good occasion."

"Is it yours, or mine ?" said he sulkily.

"Why, yours, dear ; you earned it."

"Then give it me, please." And he almost forced it out of her hand.

So now she sat down and cried over this piece of good luck, for her heart filled with forebod-ings.

He laughed at her. But, at last, had the grace to console her, and assure her she was tormenting her-self for nothing.

"Time will show," said she sadly.

Time did show.

Three or four days he came, as usu-al, to laugh at her for her forebodings. But presently his visits ceased. She knew what that meant : he was liv-ing like a gentleman, melting his diamond, and playing her false with the first pretty face he met.

This blow, coming after she had been so happy, struck Phœbe Dale stupid with grief. The line on her high forehead deepened ; and at night she sat with her hands be-fore her, sighing, and sighing, and listening for the footsteps that never came.

"O Dick !" she said, "never you love any one. I am aweary of my life. And to think that, but for that diamond — oh, dear ! oh, dear ! oh, dear ! "

Then Dick used to try and com-fort her in his way, and often put his arm round her neck, and gave her his rough but honest sympathy. Dick's rare affection was her one drop of comfort : it was something to relieve her swelling heart.

"O Dick !" she said to him one night, "I wish I had married him."

"What, to be ill-used ?"

"He couldn't use me worse. I have been wife and mother and sweatheart and all to him, and to be left like this. He treats me like the dirt beneath his feet."

"'Tis your own fault, Phœbe, partly. You say the word, and I'll break every bone in his carcass."

"What, do him a mischief ! Why, I'd rather die than harm a hair of his head. You must never lift a hand to him, or I shall hate you."

"Hate *me*, Phœbe ? "

"Ay, boy, I should. God for-give me, 'tis no use deceiving our-selves ; when a woman loves a man she despises, never you come between them : there's no reason in her love, so it is incurable. One comfort ; it can't go on forever ; it must kill me before my time, and so best. If I was only a mother, and had a little Reginald to dandle on my knee and gloat upon till he spent his money and came back to me. That is why I said I wished I was his wife. Oh! why does God fill a poor woman's bosom with love, and nothing to spend it on but a stone? for sure his heart must be one. If I had only something that would let me always love it — a little toddling thing at my knee, that would always let me look at it, and love it — something too young to be false to me, too weak to run away from my long—ing arms — and — yearn—ing heart!" Then came a burst of agony, and moans of desolation, till poor Dick blubbered loudly at her grief, and then her tears flowed in streams.

Trouble on trouble. Dick himself got strangely out of sorts, and complained of shivers. Phœbe sent him to bed early, and made him some white wine whey very hot. In the morning he got up, and said he was better; but after breakfast he was violently sick, and suffered several returns of nausea before noon. "One would think I was poisoned," said he.

At one o'clock he was seized with a kind of spasm in the throat that lasted so long it nearly choked him.

Then Phœbe got frightened, and sent to the nearest surgeon. He did not hurry, and poor Dick had another frightful spasm just as he came in.

"It is hysterical," said the surgeon. "No disease of the heart is there. Give him a little sal volatile every half hour."

In spite of the sal volatile these terrible spasms seized him every half hour; and now he used to spring off the bed with a cry of terror when they came; and each one left him weaker and weaker; he had to be carried back by the women.

A sad, sickening fear seized on Phœbe. She left Dick with the maid, and, tying on her bonnet in a moment, rushed wildly down the street, asking the neighbors for a great doctor, the best that could be had for money. One sent her east a mile, another west, and she was almost distracted, when, who should drive up but Doctor and Mrs. Staines, to make purchases. She did not know his name, but she knew he was a doctor. She ran to the window, and cried, "O doctor, my brother! Oh, pray, come to him! Oh! oh!"

Doctor Staines got quickly but calmly out, told his wife to wait, and followed Phœbe up stairs. She told him, in a few agitated words, how Dick had been taken, and all the symptoms; especially what had alarmed her so, his springing off the bed when the spasm came.

Doctor Staines told her to hold the patient up. He lost not a moment, but opened his mouth resolutely, and looked down.

"The glottis is swollen," said he: then he felt his hands, and said, with the grave, terrible calm of experience, "He is dying."

"Oh, no! no! O doctor, save him! save him!"

"Nothing can save him, unless we had a surgeon on the spot. Yes, I might save him, if you have the courage: opening his windpipe before the next spasm is his one chance."

"Open his windpipe! O doctor, it will kill him! Let me look at you."

She looked hard in his face. It gave her confidence.

"Is it the only chance?"

"The only one: and it is flying while we chatter."

"Do it."

He whipped out his lancet.

"But I can't look on it. I trust to you and my Saviour's mercy."

She fell on her knees, and bowed her head in prayer.

Staines seized a basin, put it by

the bedside, made an incision in the windpipe, and got Dick down on his stomach, with his face over the bedside. Some blood ran, but not much. "Now!" he cried cheerfully, "a small bellows! There's one in your parlor. Run."

Phœbe ran for it, and, at Dr. Staines direction, lifted Dick a little, while the bellows, duly cleansed, were gently applied to the aperture in the windpipe, and the action of the lungs delicately aided by this primitive but effectual means.

He showed Phœbe how to do it, tore a leaf out of his pocket-book, wrote a hasty direction to an able surgeon near, and sent his wife off with it in the carriage.

Phœbe and he never left the patient till the surgeon came with all the instruments required; among the rest, with a big, tortuous pair of nippers, with which he could reach the glottis and snip it. But they consulted, and thought it wiser to continue the surer method; and so a little tube was neatly inserted into Dick's windpipe, and his throat bandaged; and by this aperture he did his breathing for some little time.

Phœbe nursed him like a mother; and the terror and the joy did her good; and made her less desolate.

Dick was only just well when both of them were summoned to the farm, and arrived only just in time to receive their father's blessing and his last sigh.

Their elder brother, a married man, inherited the farm, and was executor. Phœbe and Dick were left £1500 apiece, on condition of their leaving England and going to Natal.

They knew directly what that meant. Phœbe was to be parted from a bad man; and Dick was to comfort her for the loss.

When this part of the will was read to Phœbe, she turned faint, and only her health and bodily vigor kept her from swooning right away.

But she yielded. "It is the will of the dead," said she; "and I will obey it; for, oh, if I had but listened to him more when he was alive to advise me, I should not sit here now, sick at heart and dry-eyed, when I ought to be thinking only of the good friend that is gone."

When she had come to this, she became feverishly anxious to be gone.

She busied herself in purchasing agricultural machines, and stores, and even stock; and, to see her pinching the beasts' ribs to find their condition, and parrying all attempts to cheat her, you would never have believed she could be a love-sick woman.

Dick kept her up to the mark. He only left her to bargain with the master of a good vessel; for it was no trifle to take out horses, and cows, and machines, and bales of cloth, cotton, and linen.

When that was settled they came into town together, and Phœbe bought shrewdly, at wholesale houses in the city, for cash, and would have bargains: and the little shop in ———Street was turned into a warehouse.

They were all ardor, as colonists should be: and, what pleased Dick most, she never mentioned Falcon; yet he learned from the maid that worthy had been there twice, looking very seedy.

The day drew near. Dick was in high spirits.

"We shall soon make our fortune out there," he said: "and I'll get you a good husband."

She shuddered, but said nothing.

The evening before they went to sail, Phœbe sat alone, in her black dress, tired with work, and asking herself, sick at heart, could she ever really leave England, when the door opened softly, and Reginald Falcon, shabbily dressed, came in, and threw himself into a chair.

She started up with a scream, then sank down again, trembling, and turned her face to the wall.

“So you are going to run away from me?” said he savagely.

“Ay, Reginald,” said she meekly.

“This is your fine love; is it?”

“You have worn it out, dear,” she said softly, without turning her head.

“I wish I could say as much: but, curse it, every time I leave you, I learn to love you more. I am never really happy but when I am with you.”

“Bless you for saying that, dear. I often thought you *must* find that out one day; but you took too long.”

“Oh, better late than never, Phœbe! Can you have the heart to go to the Cape, and leave me all alone in the world with nobody that really cares for me? Surely you are not obliged to go?”

“Yes; my father left Dick and me £1,500 apiece to go: that was the condition. Poor Dick loves his unhappy sister. He won’t go without me—I should be his ruin—poor Dick that really loves me; and he lay a-dying here, and the good doctor and me—God bless him!—we brought him back from the grave. Ah! you little know what I have gone through. You were not here. Catch you being near me when I am in trouble. There, I must go. I must go. I will go; if I fling myself into the sea half-way.”

“And if you do, I’ll take a dose of poison; for I have thrown away the truest heart, the sweetest, most unselfish, kindest, generous—oh! oh! oh!”

And he began to howl.

This set Phœbe sobbing. “Don’t cry, dear,” she murmured through her tears: “if you have really any love for me, come with me.”

“What, leave England, and go to a desert?”

“Love can make a desert a garden.”

“Phœbe, I’ll do any thing else. I’ll swear not to leave your side, I’ll never look at any other face but yours. But I can’t live in Africa.”

“I know you can’t. It takes a little real love to go there with a poor girl like me. Ah, well, I’d have made you so happy. We are not poor emigrants. I have a horse for you to ride, and guns to shoot; and me and Dick would do all the work for you. But there are others here you can’t leave for me. Well, then, good-by, dear. In Africa or here I shall always love you; and many a salt tear I shall shed for you yet; many a one I have, as well you know. God bless you! Pray for poor Phœbe, that goes against her will to Africa, and leaves her heart with thee.”

This was too much even for the selfish Reginald. He kneeled at her knees, and took her hand and kissed it, and actually shed a tear or two over it.

She could not speak. He had no hope of changing her resolution: and presently he heard Dick’s voice outside; so he got up to avoid him. “I’ll come again in the morning before you go.”

“Oh, no, no!” she gasped; “unless you want me to die at your feet. I am almost dead now.”

Reginald slipped out by the kitchen.

Dick came in, and found his sister leaning with her head back against the wall. “Why, Phœbe,” said he, “whatever is the matter?” and he took her by the shoulder.

She moaned, and he felt her all limp and powerless.

“What is it, lass? Whatever is the matter? Is it about going away?”

She would not speak for a long time.

When she did speak, it was to say something for which my male reader perhaps may hardly be prepared.

“O Dick, forgive me!”

“Why, what for?”

“Forgive me, or else kill me: I don’t care which.”

"I do, though. There, I forgive you. Now what's the crime?"

"I can't go. Forgive me."

"Can't go?"

"I can't. Forgive me."

"I'm blest if I don't believe that vagabond has been here tormenting of you again."

"Oh! don't miscall him. He is penitent. Yes, Dick, he has been here crying to me—and I can't leave him. I can't—I can't. Dear Dick, you are young and stout-hearted; take all the things over, and make your fortune out there; and leave your poor foolish sister behind. I should only fling myself into the salt sea if I left him now, and that would be peace to me, but a grief to thee."

"Lord sake! Phœbe, don't talk so. I can't go without you. And do but think. Why the horses are on board now, and all the gear. It's my belief a good hiding is all you want to bring you to your senses; but I hain't the heart to give you one, worse luck! Blessed if I know what to say or do."

"I won't go!" cried Phœbe, turning violent all of a sudden. "No, not if I am dragged to the ship by the hair of my head. Forgive me." And with that word she was a mouse again.

"Eh, but women are kittle cattle to drive," said poor Dick ruefully. And down he sat at a nonplus, and very unhappy.

Phœbe sat opposite, sullen, heart-sick, wretched to the core, but determined not to leave Reginald.

Then came an event that might have been foreseen, yet it took them both by surprise.

A light step was heard, and a graceful, though seedy, figure entered the room, with a set speech in his mouth: "Phœbe, you are right. I owe it to your long and faith-ful affection to make a sacrifice for you. I will go to Africa with you. I will go to the end of the world sooner than you shall say I care for any woman on earth but you."

Both brother and sister were so unprepared for this that they could hardly realize it at first.

Phœbe turned her great, inquiring eyes on the speaker; and it was a sight to see amazement, doubt, and happiness animating her features, one after another.

"Is this real?" said she.

"I'll sail with you to-morrow, Phœbe; and I will make you a good husband, if you will have me."

"That is spoke like a man," said Dick. "You take him at his word, Phœbe; and if he ill-uses you out there, I'll break every bone in his skin."

"How dare you threaten him?" said Phœbe. "You had best leave the room."

Out went poor Dick, with the tear in his eye at being snubbed so. While he was putting up the shutters, Phœbe was making love to her pseudo-penitent. "My dear," said she, "trust yourself to me. You don't know all my love yet; for I have never been your wife, and I would not be your jade; that is the only thing I ever refused you. Trust yourself to me. Why, you never found happiness with others; try it with me. It shall be the best day's work you ever did, going out in the ship with me. You don't know how happy a loving wife can make her husband. I'll pet you out there as man was never petted. And besides, it isn't for life; Dick and me will soon make a fortune out there, and then I'll bring you home, and see you spend it any way you like but one. Oh, how I love you! do you love me a little? I worship the ground you walk on. I adore every hair of your head!" Her noble arm went round his neck in a moment, and the grandeur of her passion elec-trified him so far that he kissed her affectionately, if not quite so warmly as she did him: and so it was all settled. The maid was discharged that night, instead of the morning, and Reginald was to occupy her bed. Phœbe went up stairs with her heart literally on fire, to prepare his sleeping-room, and so Dick and Reginald had a word.

"I say, Dick, how long will this voyage be?"

"Two months, sir, I'm told."

"Please to cast your eyes on this suit of mine. Don't you think it is rather seedy — to go to Africa with? Why, I shall disgrace you on board the ship. I say, Dick, lend me three sovs., just to buy a new suit at the slop-shop."

"Well, brother-in-law," said Dick, "I don't see any harm in that. I'll go and fetch them for you."

What does this sensible Dick do but go up stairs to Phœbe, and say, "He wants three pounds to buy a suit; am I to lend it him?"

Phœbe was shaking and patting her penitent's pillow. She dropped it on the bed in dismay. "O Dick, not for all the world! Why, if he had three sovereigns he'd desert me at the water's edge. O God help me, how I love him! God forgive me, how I mistrust him! Good Dick! kind Dick! say we have suits of clothes, and we'll fit him like a prince, as he ought to be, on board ship: but not a shilling of money; and, my dear, don't put the weight on me. You understand?"

"Ay, mistress. I understand."

"Good Dick!"

"Oh, all right! and then, don't you snap this here good, kind Dick's nose off at a word again."

"Never. I get wild if anybody threatens him. Then I'm not myself. Forgive my hasty tongue. You know I love you, dear!"

"Oh, ay! you love well enough. But seems to me your love is precious like cold veal; and your love for that chap is hot roast beef."

"Ha! ha! ha! ha!"

"Oh! ye can laugh now, can ye?"

"Ha! ha! ha!"

"Well, the more of that music the better for me."

"Yes, dear; but go and tell him."

Dick went down, and said, "I've got no money to spare, till I get to the Cape; but Phœbe has got a box full of suits, and I made her promise to keep it out. She will dress you like a prince, you may be sure."

"Oh! that is it, is it?" said Reginald dryly.

Dick made no reply.

At nine o'clock they were on board the vessel; at ten she weighed anchor, and a steam-vessel drew her down the river about thirty miles, then cast off, and left her to the southeasterly breeze. Up went sail after sail; she nodded her lofty head, and glided away for Africa.

Phœbe shed a few natural tears at leaving the shores of Old England; but they soon dried. She was demurely happy, watching her prize, and asking herself had she really secured it, and all in a few hours?

They had a prosperous voyage: were married at Cape Town, and went up the country, bag and baggage, looking out for a good bargain in land. Reginald was mounted on an English horse, and allowed to zigzag about, and shoot, and play, while his wife and brother-in-law marched slowly with their cavalcade.

What with air, exercise, wholesome food, and smiles of welcome, and delicious petting, this egotist enjoyed himself finely. He admitted as much. Says he one evening, to his wife, who sat by him for the pleasure of seeing him feed, "It sounds absurd; but I never was so happy in all my life."

At that, the celestial expression of her pastoral face, and the maternal gesture with which she drew her pet's head to her queenly bosom, was a picture for celibacy to gnash the teeth at.

CHAPTER IX.

DURING this period, the most remarkable things that happened to Dr. and Mrs. Staines were really those which I have related as connecting them with Phœbe Dale and her brother; to which I will now add that Dr. Staines detailed Dick's case in a remarkable paper, entitled *Œdema of the Glottis*, and showed how the patient had been brought back from the grave by tracheotomy and artificial respiration. He received a high price for this article.

To tell the truth, he was careful not to admit that it was he who had opened the windpipe; so the credit of the whole operation was given to Mr. Jenkyn; and this gentleman was naturally pleased, and threw a good many consultation fees in Staines's way.

The Lucases, to his great comfort — for he had an instinctive aversion to Miss Lucas — left London for Paris in August, and did not return all the year.

In February he reviewed his year's work and twelve months' residence in the Bijou. The pecuniary result was — outgoings, £950; income, from fees, £280; writing, £90.

He showed these figures to Mrs. Staines, and asked her if she could suggest any diminution of expenditure. Could she do with less housekeeping money?

"Oh, impossible! You cannot think how the servants eat; and they won't touch our home-made bread."

"The fools! Why?"

"Oh! because they think it costs us less. Servants seem to me always to hate the people whose bread they eat."

"More likely it is their vanity. Nothing that is not paid before their eyes seems good enough for them. Well, dear, the bakers will revenge us. But is there any other item we could reduce? Dress?"

"Dress! Why, I spend nothing."

"Forty-five pounds this year."

"Well, I shall want none next year."

"Well, then, Rosa, as there is nothing we can reduce, I must write more, and take more fees, or we shall be in the wrong box. Only £860 left of our little capital; and, mind, we have not another shilling in the world. One comfort, there is no debt. We pay ready money for every thing."

Rosa colored a little, but said nothing.

Staines did his part nobly. He read; he wrote; he paced the yard; he wore his old clothes in the house. He took off his new ones when he came in. He was all genius, drudgery, patience.

How Phœbe Dale would have valued him, co-operated with him, and petted him, if she had had the good luck to be his wife!

The season came back, and with it Miss Lucas, towing a brilliant bride, Mrs. Vivian, young, rich, pretty, and gay, with a waist you could span, and a thirst for pleasure.

This lady was the first that ever made Rosa downright jealous. She seemed to have every thing the female heart could desire; and she was No. 1 with Miss Lucas this year. Now, Rosa was No. 1 last season, and had weakly imagined that was to last forever. But Miss Lucas had always a sort of female flame, and it never lasted two seasons.

Rosa did not care so very much for Miss Lucas before, except as a convenient friend; but now she was mortified to tears at finding Miss Lucas made more fuss with another than with her.

This foolish feeling spurred her to attempt a rivalry with Mrs. Vivian in the very things where rivalry was hopeless.

Miss Lucas gave both ladies tickets for a flower-show, where all the great folk were to be, princes and princesses, &c.

"But I have nothing to wear," sighed Rosa.

"Then you must get something, and mind it is not pink, please; for we must not clash in color. You know I'm dark, and pink becomes me." (The selfish young brute was not half as dark as Rosa.) "Mine is coming from Worth's, in Paris, on purpose. And this new Madam Cie, of Regent Street, has such a duck of a bonnet, just come from Paris. She wanted to make me one from it; but I told her I would have none but the pattern bonnet — and she knows very well she can't pass a copy off on me. Let me drive you up there, and you can see mine, and order one if you like it."

"Oh, thank you! let me just run and speak to my husband first."

Staines was writing for the bare life, and a number of German books about him, slaving to make a few pounds, when in comes the buoyant figure and beaming face his soul delighted in.

He laid down his work, to enjoy the sunbeam of love.

"O darling! I've only come in for a minute. We are going to a flower-show on the 13th; everybody will be so beautifully dressed — especially that Mrs. Vivian. I have got ten yards of beautiful blue silk in my wardrobe, but that is not enough to make a whole dress. Every thing takes so much stuff now. Madame Cie does not care to make up dresses unless she finds the silk, but Miss Lucas says she thinks, to oblige a friend of hers, she would do it for once in a way. You know, dear, it would only take a few yards more, and it would last as a dinner-dress for ever so long."

Then she clasped him round the neck, and leaned her head upon his shoulder, and looked lovingly up into his face. "I know you would like your Rosa to look as well as Mrs. Vivian."

"No one ever looks as well — in my eyes — as my Rosa. There, the dress will add nothing to your beauty; but go and get it, to please yourself: it is very considerate of you to have chosen something of which you have ten yards already. See, dear, I'm to receive twenty pounds for this article; if research was paid, it ought to be a hundred. I shall add it all to your allowance for dresses this year. So no debt, mind; but come to me for every thing."

The two ladies drove off to Madame Cie's, a pretty shop, lined with dark velvet and lace draperies.

In the back room they were packing a lovely bridal dress, going off, the following Saturday, to New York.

"What! send from America to London!"

"Oh, dear, yes!" exclaimed Madame Cie. "The American ladies are excellent customers. They buy every thing of the best and the most expensive."

"I have brought you a new customer," said Miss Lucas; "and I want you to do a great favor, and that is to match a blue silk, and make her a pretty dress for the flower-show on the 13th."

Madame Cie produced a white muslin polonaise, which she was just going to send home to the Princess ——, to be worn over mauve.

"Oh, how pretty and simple!" exclaimed Miss Lucas.

"I have some lace exactly like that," said Mrs. Staines.

"Then, why don't you have a polonaise? The lace is the only expensive part, the muslin is a mere nothing; and it is such a useful dress, it can be worn over any silk."

It was agreed Madame Cie was to send for the blue silk and the lace, and the dresses were to be tried on on Thursday.

On Thursday, as Rosa went gayly into Madame Cie's back room to have the dresses tried on, Madame Cie said, "You have a beautiful lace shawl, but it wants arranging: in five minutes I could astonish you with what I could do to that shawl."

"Oh, pray do!" said Mrs. Staines.

The dress-maker kept her word. By the time the blue dress was tried on, Madame Cie had, with the aid of a few pins, plaits, and a bow of blue ribbon, transformed the half-lace shawl into one of the smartest and most *distingué* things imaginable; but when the bill came in at Christmas, for that five minutes' labor and *distingué* touch, she charged one pound eight.

Before they left, Mrs. Staines ordered a bonnet like the pattern bonnet from Paris; and Madame Cie, with oily tongue, persuaded her to let her send home the pink bonnet, which was so becoming to her; it was only slightly soiled, and there were certainly two good wears out of it, and they would not quarrel about the price, which the Simpleton understood to mean the price was to be small; whereas it meant this, "I, in my brutal egotism, cannot conceive that you object to any price I charge, however high."

Madame Cie then told the ladies, in an artfully confidential tone, she had a quantity of black silk coming home, which she had purchased considerably below cost price; and that she should like to make them each a dress — not for her own sake, but theirs — as she knew they would never meet such a bargain again.

"You know, Miss Lucas," she continued, "we don't want our money when we know our customer. Christmas is soon enough for us."

"Christmas is a long time off," thought the young wife, "nearly ten months. I think I'll have a black dress, Madame Cie; but I must not say any thing to the doctor about it just yet, or he might think me extravagant."

"No one can ever think a lady extravagant for buying a black silk; it's such a useful dress; lasts forever — almost."

Days, weeks, and months rolled on, and with them an ever-rolling tide of flower-shows, dinners, at-homes, balls, operas, lawn-parties, concerts, and theatres.

Strange that in one house there should be two people who loved each other, yet their lives ran so far apart, except while they were asleep: the man all industry, self-denial, patience; the woman all frivolity, self-indulgence, and amusement; both chained to an oar, only one in a working-boat, the other in a painted galley.

The woman got tired first, and her charming color waned sadly. She came to him for medicine to set her up. "I feel so languid!"

"No, no," said he; "no medicine can do the work of wholesome food and rational repose. You lack the season of all natures, sleep. Dine at home three days running, and go to bed at ten."

On this the doctor's wife went to a chemist for advice. He gave her a pink stimulant; and, as stimulants have two effects, viz., first, tn stimulate, and then to weaken, this did her no lasting good. Doctor Staines cursed the London season, and threatened to migrate to Liverpool.

But there was worse behind.

Returning one day to his dressing-room, just after Rosa had come down stairs, he caught sight of a red stain in a washhand-basin. He examined it; it was arterial blood.

He went to her directly, and expressed his anxiety.

"Oh, it is nothing!" said she.

"Nothing! Pray how often has it occurred?"

"Once or twice. I must take your advice, and be quiet, that is all."

Staines examined the housemaid; she lied instinctively at first, seeing he was alarmed; but, being urged to tell the truth, said she had seen it repeatedly, and had told the cook.

He went down stairs, and sat down, looking wretched.

"Oh, dear!" said Rosa. "What is the matter now?"

"Rosa," said he very gravely, "there are two people a woman is mad to deceive, — her husband and her physician. You have deceived both."

I suspect Dr. Staines merely meant to say that she had concealed from him an alarming symptom for several weeks; but she answered in a hurry, to excuse herself, and let the cat out of the bag — excuse my vulgarity.

"It was all that Mrs. Vivian's fault. She laughed at me so for not wearing them; and she has a waist you can span — the wretch!"

"Oh! then, you have been wearing stays clandestinely?"

"Why, you know I have. Oh, what a stupid! I have let it all out."

"How could you do it, when you know, by experience, it is your death?"

"But it looks so beautiful — a tiny waist."

"It looks as hideous as a Chinese foot, and, to the eye of science, far more disgusting; it is the cause of so many nasty diseases."

"Just tell me one thing. Have you looked at Mrs. Vivian?"

"Minutely. I look at all your friends — with great anxiety, knowing no animal more dangerous than a fool. Vivian — a skinny woman, with a pretty face, lovely hair, good teeth, dying eyes — yes, lovely. A sure proof of a disordered stomach — and a waist pinched in so unnaturally, that I said to myself, ' Where on earth does this idiot put her liver?' Did you ever read of the frog who burst trying to swell to an ox? Well, here is the rivalry reversed. Mrs. Vivian is a bag of bones in a balloon; she can machine herself into a wasp; but a fine young woman like you, with flesh and muscle, must kill yourself three or four times before you can make your body as meagre, hideous, angular, and unnatural as Vivian's. But all you ladies are monomaniacs. One might as well offer the truth to a gorilla. It brought you to the edge of the grave. I saved you. Yet you could go and — God grant me patience! So I suppose these unprincipled women lent you their stays, to deceive your husband?"

"No. But they laugh at me so that — O Christie! I'm a wretch; I kept a pair at the Lucases', and a pair at Madame Cie's, and I put them on now and then."

"But you never appeared here in them"

"What, before my tyrant? Oh, no, I dared not!"

"So you took them off before you came home?"

Rosa hung her head, and said, "Yes," in a reluctant whisper.

"You spent your daylight dressing. You dressed to go out; dressed again in stays; dressed again without them; and all to deceive your husband, and kill yourself, at the bidding of two shallow, heartless women, who would dance over your grave without a pang of remorse, or sentiment of any kind, since they live, like midges, *only to dance in the sun, and suck some worker's blood!*"

"O Christie! I'm so easily led, I am too great a fool to live. Kill me!"

And she kneeled down, and renewed the request, looking up in his face with an expression that might have disarmed Cain *ipsum*.

He smiled superior. "The question is, Are you sorry you have been so naughty?"

"Yes, dear. Oh! oh!"

"Will you be very good, to make up?"

"Oh, yes! Only tell me how, for it does not come natural to poor me."

"Keep out of those women's way for the rest of the season."

"I will."

"Bring your stays home, and allow me to do what I like with them."

"Of course. Cut them in a million pieces."

"Till you are recovered you must be my patient, and go nowhere without me."

"That is no punishment, I am sure."

"Punishment! Am I the man to punish you? I only want to save you."

"Well, darling, it won't be the first time."

"No; but I do hope it will be the last."

CHAPTER X.

Sublata causa tollitur effectus. The stays being gone, and dissipation moderated, Mrs. Staines bloomed again, and they gave one or two unpretending little dinners at the Bijou. Dr. Staines admitted no false friends to these. They never went beyond eight; five gentlemen, three ladies. By this arrangement the terrible discursiveness of the fair, and man's cruel disposition to work a subject threadbare, were controlled and modified, and a happy balance of conversation established. Lady Cicely Treherne was always invited, and always managed to come; for she said, "They were the most agweeable little paaties in London, and the host and hostess both so intewesting." In the autumn Staines worked double tides with the pen, and found a vehicle for medical narratives in a weekly magazine that did not profess medicine.

This new vein put him in heart. His fees, toward the end of the year, were less than last year, because there was no hundred guinea fee; but there was a marked increase in the small fees, and the unflagging pen had actually earned him £200, or nearly. So he was in good spirits.

Not so Mrs. Staines; for some time she had been uneasy, fretful, and like a person with a weight on her mind.

One Sunday she said to him, "Oh, dear, I do feel so dull! Nobody to go to church with me, nor yet to the Zoo."

"I'll go with you," said Staines.

"You will? To which?"

"To both: in for a penny, in for a pound."

So to church they went; and Staines, whose motto was "*Hoc age,*" minded his book. Rosa had some intervals of attention to the words, but found plenty of time to study the costumes.

During the Litany in bustled Clara, the housemaid, with a white jacket on so like her mistress's that Rosa clutched her own convulsively to see whether she had not been skinned of it by some devilish sleight of hand.

No, it was on her back; but Clara's was identical.

In her excitement Rosa pinched Staines, and with her nose, that went like a water-wagtail, pointed out the malefactor. Then she whispered, "Look! How dare she? My very jacket! Ear-rings too, and brooches, and dresses her hair like mine."

"Well, never mind," whispered Staines. "Sunday is her day. We have got all the week to shine. There, don't look at her. 'From all evil speaking, lying, and slandering'" —

"I can't keep my eyes off her."

"Attend to the Litany. Do you know, this is really a beautiful composition?"

"I'd rather do the work fifty times over myself."

"Hush! people will hear you."

When they walked home, after church, Staines tried to divert her from the consideration of her wrongs; but no — all other topics were too flat by comparison.

She mourned the hard fate of

mistresses — unfortunate creatures that could not do without servants.

"Is not that a confession that servants are good, useful creatures, with all their faults? Then, as to the mania for dress, why, that is not confined to them. It is the mania of the sex. Are you free from it?"

"No, of course not. But I am a lady."

"Then she is your intellectual inferior, and more excusable. Any way, it is wise to connive at a thing we can't help."

"What, keep her, after this? — no, never"

"My dear, pray do not send her away, for she is tidy in the house, and quick, and better than any one we have had this last six months; and you know you have tried a great number."

"To hear you speak, one would think it was my fault that we have so many bad servants."

"I never said it was your fault; but I *think*, dearest, a little more forbearance in trifles" —

"Trifles! trifles — for a mistress and maid to be seen dressed alike in the same church? You take the servant's part against me, that you do."

"You should not say that, even in jest. Come now, do you really think a jacket like yours can make the servant look like you, or detract from your grace and beauty? There is a very simple way: put your jacket by for a future occasion, and wear something else in its stead at church."

"A nice thing, indeed, to give in to these creatures! I won't do it."

"Why won't you, this once?"

"Because I won't — there!"

"That is unanswerable," said he.

Mrs. Staines said that, but, when it came to acting, she deferred to her husband's wish; she resigned her intention of sending for Clara and giving her warning; on the contrary, when Clara let her in, and the white jackets rubbed together in the narrow passage, she actually said nothing, but stalked to her own room, and tore her jacket off, and flung it on the floor.

Unfortunately, she was so long dressing for the Zoo, that Clara came in to arrange the room. She picks up the white jacket, takes it in both hands, gives it a flap, and proceeds to hang it up in the wardrobe.

Then the great feminine heart burst its bounds.

"You can leave that alone. I shall not wear that again."

Thereupon ensued an uneven encounter, Clara being one of those of whom Scripture says, "The poison of asps is under their tongues."

"La, ma'am," said she, "why, t'ain't so very dirty."

"No; but it is too common."

"Oh! because I've got one like it. Ay, missises can't abide a good-looking servant, nor to see 'em dressed becoming."

"Mistresses do not like servants to forget their place, nor wear what does not become their situation."

"My situation! Why, I can pay my way, go where I will. I don't tremble at the tradesman's knock, as some do."

"Leave the room! Leave it this moment."

"Leave the room, yes — and I'll leave the house too, and tell all the neighbors what I know about it."

She flounced out, and slammed the door, and Rosa sat down, trembling.

Clara rushed to the kitchen, and there told the cook and Andrew Pearman how she had given it to the mistress, and every word she had said to her, with a good many more she had not.

The cook laughed, and encouraged her.

But Andrew Pearman was wroth, and said, "You to affront our mistress like that! Why, if I had heard you, I'd have twisted your neck for ye."

"It would take a better man than

you to do that. You mind your own business. Stick to your one-horse shay."

"Well, I'm not above my place, for that matter. But you gals must always be aping your betters."

"I have got proper pride, that is all, and you haven't. You ought to be ashamed of yourself to do two men's work,—drive a brougham and wait on a horse, and then come in and wait at table. You are a tea-kettle groom, that is what you are. Why, my brother was coachman to Lord Fitz-James, and gave his lordship notice the first time he had to drive the children. Says he, 'I don't object to the children, my lord, but with her ladyship in the carriage.' It's such servants as you as spoil places. No servant as knows what's due to a servant ought to know you. They'd scorn your 'quaintance, as I do, Mr. Pearman."

"You are a stuck-up hussy and a soldier's jade," roared Andrew.

"And you are a low tea-kettle groom."

This expression wounded the great equestrian heart to the quick; the rest of Sunday he pondered on it. The next morning he drove the doctor as usual, but with a very heavy soul.

Meantime the cook made haste and told the baker, Pearman had "got it hot" from the housemaid, and she had called him a tea-kettle groom; and in less than half an hour after that it was in every stable in the mews Why, as Pearman was taking the horse out of the brougham, didn't two little red-headed urchins call out, "Here, come and see the tea-kettle groom!" and at night some mischievous boy chalked on the black door of the stable a large white tea-kettle, and next morning a drunken, idle fellow, with a clay pipe in his mouth, and a dirty pair of corduroy trowsers, no coat, but a shirt very open at the chest, showing inflamed skin, the effect of drink, inspected that work of art with blinking eyes and vacillating toes, and said, "This comes of a chap doing too much. A few more like you and work would be scarce. A fine thing for gentlefolks to make one man fill two places! but it ain't the gentlefolks' fault, it's the man as humors 'em."

Pearman was a peaceable man, and made no reply, but went on with his work, only during the day he told his master that he should be obliged to him if he would fill his situation as soon as convenient. The master inquired the cause; and the man told him, and said the mews was too hot for him.

The doctor offered him five pounds a year more, knowing he had a treasure; but Pearman said, with sadness and firmness, that he had made up his mind to go, and go he would.

The doctor's heart fairly sank at the prospect of losing the one creature he could depend upon.

Next Sunday evening Clara was out, and fell in with friends, to whom she exaggerated her grievance.

Then they worked her up to fury, after the manner of servants' *friends*. She came home, packed her box, brought it down, and then flounced into the room to Doctor and Mrs. Staines, and said, "I sha'n't sleep another night in this house."

Rosa was about to speak, but Dr. Staines forbade her: he said, "You had better think twice of that. You are a good servant, though for once you have been betrayed into speaking disrespectfully. Why forfeit your character and three weeks' wages?"

"I don't care for my wages. I won't stay in such a house as this."

"Come, you must not be impertinent."

"I don't mean to, sir," said she, lowering her voice suddenly; then, raising it as suddenly, "There are my keys, ma'am, and you can search my box."

"Mrs. Staines will not search your box; and you will retire at once to your own part of the house."

"I'll go farther than that," said she, and soon after the street-door was slammed; the Bijou shook.

At six o'clock next morning she came for her box. It had been put away for safety. Pearman told her she must wait till the doctor came down. She did not wait, but went at eleven, A.M., to a police magistrate, and took out a summons against Dr. Staines, for detaining a box containing certain articles specified — value under fifteen pounds.

When Dr. Staines heard she had been for her box, but left no address, he sent Pearman to hunt for her. He could not find her. She avoided the house, but sent a woman for her diurnal love-letters. Dr. Staines sent the woman back to fetch her. She came, received her box, her letters, and the balance of her wages, which was small, for Staines deducted the three weeks' wages.

Two days afterward, to his surprise, the summons was served.

Out of respect for a court of justice, however humble, Dr. Staines attended next Monday, to meet the summons.

The magistrate was an elderly man, with a face shaped like a hog's, but much richer in color, being purple and pimply: so foul a visage Staines had rarely seen, even in the lowest class of the community.

Clara swore that her box had been opened, and certain things stolen out of it; and that she had been refused the box next morning.

Staines swore that he had never opened the box, and that if any one else had, it was with her consent, for she had left the keys for that purpose. He bade the magistrate observe, that if a servant went away like this, and left no address, she put it out of the master's *power* to send her box after her; and he proved he had some trouble to force the box on her.

The pig-faced beak showed a manifest leaning toward the servant; but there wasn't a leg to stand on; and he did not believe, nor was it credible, that any thing had been stolen out of her box.

At this moment Pearman, sent by Rosa, entered the court with an old gown of Clara's that had been discovered in the scullery, and a scribbling-book of the doctor's, which Clara had appropriated and written amorous verses in, very superior — in number — to those that have come down to us from Anacreon.

"Hand me those," said the pig-faced beak. "What are they, Dr. Staines?"

"I really don't know. I must ask my servant."

"Why, more things of mine that have been detained," said Clara.

"Some things that have been found since she left," said Staines.

"Oh! those that hide know where to find."

"Young woman," said Staines, do not insult those whose bread you have eaten, and who have given you many presents besides your wages. Since you are so ready to accuse people of stealing, permit me to say, that this book is mine, and not yours; and yet, you see, it is sent after you because you have written your trash in it."

The purple, pig-faced beak went instantly out of the record, and wasted a great deal of time reading Clara's poetry, and trying to be witty. He raised the question whose book this was. The girl swore it was given her by a lady who was now in Rome. Staines swore he bought it of a certain stationer, and, happening to have his pass-book in his pocket, produced an entry corresponding with the date of the book.

The pig-faced beak said that the doctor's was an improbable story, and that the gown and the book were quite enough to justify the summons. Verdict, one guinea costs.

"What, because two things she never demanded have been found and sent after her? This is monstrous. I shall appeal to your superiors."

"If you are impertinent, I'll fine you five pounds."

"Very well, sir. Now hear me: if this is an honest judgment, I pray God I may be dead before the year's out; and if it isn't, I pray God you may be."

Then the pig-faced beak fired up, and threatened to fine him for blaspheming.

He deigned no reply, but paid the guinea, and Clara swept out of the court with a train a yard long, and leaning on the arm of a scarlet soldier, who avenged Dr. Staines with military promptitude.

Christopher went home raging internally, for hitherto he had never seen so gross a case of injustice.

One of his humble patients followed him, and said, "I wish I had known, sir; you shouldn't have come here to be insulted. Why, no gentleman can ever get justice against a servant-girl when *he* is sitting. It is notorious, and that makes these hussies so bold. I've seen that jade here with the same story twice afore."

Staines reached home more discomposed than he could have himself believed. The reason was that barefaced injustice in a court of justice shook his whole faith in man. He opened the street-door with his latch-key, and found two men standing in the passage. He inquired what they wanted.

"Well, sir," said one of them civilly enough, "we only want our due."

"For what?"

"For goods delivered at this house, sir. Balance of account." And he handed him a butcher's bill, £88 11s. 5½d.

"You must be mistaken; we run

no bills here. We pay ready money for every thing."

"Well, sir," said the butcher, "there have been payments; but the balance has always been gaining; and we have been put off so often, we determined to see the master. Show you the books, sir, and welcome."

"This instant, if you please." He took the butcher's address, who then retired, and the other tradesman, a grocer, told him a similar tale; balance, sixty pounds odd.

He went to the butcher's, sick at heart, inspected the books, and saw that, right or wrong, they were incontrovertible; that debt had been gaining slowly but surely almost from the time he confided the accounts to his wife. She kept faith with him about five weeks, no more.

The grocer's books told a similar tale.

The debtor put his hand to his heart, and stood a moment. The very grocer pitied him, and said, "There's no hurry, doctor; a trifle on account, if settlement in full is not convenient just now. I see you have been kept in the dark."

"No, no," said Christopher; "I'll pay every shilling." He gave one gulp, and hurried away.

At the fishmonger's the same story, only for a smaller amount.

A bill of nineteen pounds at the very pastry-cook's; a p'ace she had promised him, as her physician, never to enter.

At the draper's, thirty-seven pounds odd.

In short, wherever she had dealt, the same system, — partial payments, and ever-growing debt.

Remembering Madame Cie, he drove in a cab to Regent Street, and asked for Mrs. Staines's account.

"Shall I send it, sir?"

"No: I will take it with me."

"Miss Edwards, make out Mrs. Staines's account, if you please."

Miss Edwards was a good while making it out; but it was ready at last. He thrust it into his pocket, without daring to look at it then; but he went into Verrey's, asked for a cup of coffee, and then pursued the document.

Mrs. Dr. Staines,
To Madame Cie, Dr.

	£	s.	d.
To 1 black silk costume..........	23	8	0
To 1 costume of reseda failie, with cashmere polonaise........	20	10	0
To 1 bonnet of pink velvet, with plume..............	5	5	6
To making trained dress of blue gros grain................	5	0	0
To 12 yards of gros grain for do., with trimmings.................	19	0	0
To draping lace shawl.............		8	0
To 1 Sicilenne Dolman.............	8	3	6
To 1 round hat of failie and crape	4	0	0
To 1 cashmere morning dress.....	8	5	0
To 2 camisoles	3	2	6
To 1 crinoline bustle.............	1	6	0
Total......................	99	8	6

He went home, and into his studio, and sat down on his hard beech chair; he looked round on his books and his work, and then, for the first time, remembered how long and how patiently he had toiled for every hundred pounds he had made; and he laid the evidences of his wife's profusion and deceit by the side of those signs of painful industry and self-denial, and his soul filled with bitterness. "Deceit! Deceit!"

Mrs. Staines heard he was in the house, and came to know about the trial. She came hurriedly in, and caught him with his head on the table, in an attitude of prostration, quite new to him; he raised his head directly he heard her, and revealed a face pale, stern, and wretched.

"Oh! what is the matter now?" said she

"The matter is what it has always been, if I could only have seen it. You have deceived me, and disgraced yourself. Look at those bills."

"What bills?—oh!"

"You have had an allowance for housekeeping."

"It wasn't enough."

"It was plenty, if you had kept faith with me, and paid ready money. It was enough for the first five weeks. I am housekeeper now, and I shall allow myself two pounds a week less, and not owe a shilling, either."

"Well, all I know is, I couldn't do it; no woman could."

"Then you should have come to me and said so; and I should have shown you how. Was I in Egypt, or at the North Pole, that you could not find me, and treat me like a friend? You have ruined us; these debts will sweep away the last shilling of our little capital; but it isn't that, oh, no! it is the miserable deceit."

Rosa's eye caught the sum total of Madame Cie's bill, and she turned pale. "Oh, what a cheat that woman is!"

But she turned paler when Christopher said, "That is the one honest bill, for I gave you leave. It is these that part us; these; these. Look at them, false heart! There, go and pack up your things. We can live here no longer: we are ruined. I must send you back to your father."

"I thought you would, sooner or later," said Mrs. Staines, panting, trembling, but showing a little fight. "He told you I wasn't fit to be a poor man's wife."

"An honest man's wife, you mean: that is what you are not fit for. You shall go home to your father, and I shall go into some humble lodging to work for you. I'll contrive to keep you and find you a hundred a year to spend in dress,—the only thing your heart can really love. But I won't have an enemy here in disguise of a friend; and I won't have a wife about me I must treat like a servant and watch like a traitor."

The words were harsh, but the agony with which they were spoken distinguished them from vulgar vituperation.

They overpowered poor Rosa: she had been ailing a little for some time; and from remorse and terror, conpled with other causes, nature gave way. Her lips turned white, she gasped inarticulately, and with a little piteous moan, tottered, and swooned dead away.

He was walking wildly about, ready to tear his hair, when she tottered; he saw her just in time to save her, and laid her gently on the floor and kneeled over her.

Away went anger and every other feeling but love and pity for the poor weak creature, that, with all her faults, was so lovable and so loved. He applied no remedies at first; he knew they were useless and unnecessary; he laid her head quite low, and opened door and window, and loosened all her dress, sighing deeply all the time at her condition.

While he was thus employed, suddenly a strange cry broke from him; a cry of horror, remorse, joy, tenderness, all combined; a cry compared with which language is inarticulate. His swift and practical cye had made a discovery.

He kneeled over her, with his eyes dilating and his hands clasped, —a picture of love and tender remorse.

She stirred.

Then he made haste and applied his remedies, and brought her slowly back to life: he lifted her up and carried her in his arms quite away from the bills and things, that when she came too she might see nothing to revive her distress. He carried her to the drawing-room, and kneeled down, and rocked her in his arms, and pressed her again and again gently to his heart, and cried over her. "Oh, my dove, my dove! the tender creature God gave me to love and cherish, and I have used it harshly? If I had only known! if I had only known!"

While he was thus bemoaning her, and blaming himself, and cry-ing over her like the rain,—he, whom she had never seen shed a tear before in all his troubles,—she was coming to entirely, and her quick ears caught his words, and she opened her lovely eyes upon him

"I forgive you, dear," she said feebly. "BUT I HOPE YOU WILL BE A KINDER FATHER THAN A HUSBAND."

These quiet words, spoken with rare gravity and softness, went through the great heart like a knife.

He gave a sort of shiver, but said not a word.

But that night he made a solemn vow to God that no harsh word from his lips should ever again strike a being so weak, so loving, and so beyond his comprehension. Why look for courage and candor in a creature so timid and shy she could not even tell her husband *that* until, with her subtle sense, she saw he had discovered it?

———◆———

CHAPTER XI.

To be a father; to have an image of his darling Rosa and a fruit of their love to live and work for: this gave the sore heart a heavenly glow, and elasticity to bear. Should this dear object be born to an inheritance of debt, of poverty? Never.

He began to act as if he was even now a father. He entreated Rosa not to trouble or vex herself; he would look into their finances, and set all straight.

He paid all the bills, and put by a quarter's rent and taxes. Then there remained of his little capital just £10.

He went to his printers, and had a thousand order-checks printed. These forms ran thus:

"Dr. Staines, of 13 Dear Street, Mayfair (blank for date), orders of (blank here for tradesman and goods ordered), for cash. Received same time (blank for tradesman's receipt). Notice. —Dr. Staines disowns all orders not printed on this form, and paid for at date of order."

He exhibited these forms, and warned all the tradespeople before a witness whom he took round for that purpose.

He paid off Pearman on the spot. Pearman had met Clara, dressed like a pauper, her soldier having emptied her box to the very dregs; and he now offered to stay, but it was too late.

Staines told the cook Mrs. Staines was in delicate health, and must not be troubled with any thing. She must come to him for all orders.

"Yes, sir," said she. But she no sooner comprehended the check system fully than she gave warning. It put a stop to her wholesale pilfering. Her cooks had made full £100 out of Rosa among them since she began to keep accounts.

Under the male housekeeper every article was weighed on delivery; and this soon revealed that the butcher and the fishmonger had habitually delivered short weight from the first, besides putting down the same thing twice. The things were sent back that moment, with a printed form, stating the nature and extent of the fraud.

The washer-woman, who had been pilfering wholesale so long as Mrs. Staines and her sloppy-headed maids had counted the linen, and then forgot it, was brought up with a run, by trip icate forms, and by Staines counting the things before two witnesses, and compelling the washer-woman to count them as well, and verify or dispute on the spot. The laundress gave warning, — a plain confession that stealing had been a part of her trade.

He kept the house well for £3 a week, exclusive of coals, candles, and wine. His wife had had £5, and whatever she asked for dinnerparties, yet found it not half enough upon her method.

He kept no coachman. If he visited a patient, a man in the yard drove him at a shilling per hour.

By these means, and by working like a galley-slave, he dragged his expenditure down almost to a level with his income.

Rosa was quite content at first, and thought herself lucky to escape reproaches on such easy terms.

But by and by so rigorous a system began to gall her. One day she fancied a Bath bun; sent the new maid to the pastry-cook's. Pastrycook asked to see the doctor's order. Maid could not show it, and came back bunless.

Rosa came into the study to complain to her husband.

"A Bath bun," said Staines. "Why, they are colored with annatto, to save an egg, and annatto is adulterated with chromates that are poison. Adulteration upon adulteration. I'll make you a real Bath bun." Off coat, and into the kitchen, and made her three, pure, but rather heavy. He brought them her in due course. She declined them languidly. She was off the notion, as they say in Scotland.

"If I can't have a thing when I want it, I don't care for it at all." Such was the principle she laid down for his future guidance.

He sighed, and went back to his work; she cleared the plate.

One day, when she asked for the carriage, he told her the time was now come for her to leave the carriage exercise. She must walk with him every day instead.

"But I don't like walking."

"I am sorry for that. But it is necessary to you, and by and by your life may depend on it."

Quietly, but inexorably, he dragged her out walking every day.

In one of those walks she stopped at a shop window, and fell in love with some baby's things. "Oh! I

must have that," said she. "I must.
I shall die if I don't; you'll see now."

"You shall," said he, "when I
can pay for it," and drew her away.

The tears of disappointment stood
in her eyes, and his heart yearned
over her. But he kept his head.

He changed the dinner-hour to six,
and used to go out directly afterward.

She began to complain of his leaving her alone like that.

"Well, but wait a bit," said he;
"suppose I am making a little
money by it, to buy you something
you have set your heart on, poor
darling!"

In a very few days after this, he
brought her a little box with a slit
in it. He shook it, and money rattled; then he unlocked it, and poured
out a little pile of silver. "There,"
said he, "put on your bonnet, and
come and buy those things."

She put on her bonnet, and on the
way she asked how it came to be all
in silver.

"That is a puzzler," said he,
"isn't it?"

"And how did you make it, dear;
by writing?"

"No."

"By fees from poor people?"

"What, undersell my brethren!
Hang it, no! My dear, I made it
honestly, and some day I will tell
you how I made it; at present, all I
will tell you is this: I saw my darling longing for something she had
a right to long for; I saw the tears
in her sweet eyes, and — oh, come
along, do! I am wretched till I see
you with the things in your hand."

They went to the shop; and
Staines sat and watched Rosa buying baby clothes. Oh! it was a
pretty sight to see this modest young
creature, little more than a child herself, anticipating maternity, but
blushing every now and then, and
looking askant at her lord and master. How his very bowels yearned
over her!

And when they got home, she
spread the things on the table, and
they sat hand in hand, and looked
at them, and she leaned her head on
his shoulder, and went quietly to
sleep there.

And yet, as time rolled on, she became irritable at times and impatient, and wanted all manner of
things she could not have, and made
him unhappy.

Then he was out from six o'clock
till one, and she took it into her head
to be jealous. So many hours to
spend away from her! Now that
she wanted all his comfort.

Presently Ellen, the new maid,
got gossiping in the yard, and a
groom told her her master had a
sweetheart on the sly, he thought;
for he drove the brougham out every
evening himself; "and," said the
man, "he wears a mustache at
night."

Ellen ran in, brimful of this, and
told the cook; the cook told the
washer-woman; the washer-woman
told a dozen families, till about two
hundred people knew it.

At last it came to Mrs. Staines in
a round-about way, at the very
moment when she was complaining
to Lady Cicely Treherne of her hard
lot. She had been telling her she
was nothing more than a lay figure
in the house.

"My husband is housekeeper
now, and cook and all, and makes
me delicious dishes, I can tell you;
such curries! I couldn't keep the
house with five pounds a week, so
now he does it with three: and I
never get the carriage, because walking is best for me; and he takes it
out every night to make money. I
don't understand it."

Lady Cicely suggested that perhaps Dr. Staines thought it best for
her to be relieved of all worry, and
so undertook the house-keeping.

"No, no, no," said Rosa; "I used
to pay them all a part of their bills,
and then a little more, and so I kept
getting deeper; and I was ashamed
to tell Christie, so that he calls de-

ccit; and oh, he spoke to me so cruelly once! But he was very sorry afterward, poor dear! Why are girls brought up so silly? a. piano, and no sense; and why are men sillier to go and marry such silly things? A wife! I am not so much as a servant. Oh! I am finely humiliated, and," with a sudden hearty naïveté all her own, "it serves me just right."

While Lady Cicely was puzzling this out, in came a letter. Rosa opened it, read it, and gave a cry like a wounded deer.

"Oh!" she cried, "I am a miserable woman. What will become of me?"

The letter informed her bluntly that her husband drove his brougham out every night to pursue. a criminal amour.

While Rosa was wringing her hands in real anguish of heart, Lady Cicely read the letter carefully.

"I don't believe this," said she quietly.

"Not true! Why, who would be so wicked as to stab a poor, inoffensive wretch like me if it wasn't true?"

"The first ugly woman would, in a minute. Don't you see the writer can't tell you where he goes? Dwives his bougham out! That is all your infaumant knows."

"Oh, my dear friend, bless you! What have I been complaining to you about? All is light except to lose his love. What shall I do? I will never tell him. I will never affront him by saying I suspected him."

"Wosa, if you do that, you will always have a serpent gnawing you. No; you must put the letter quietly into his hand, and say, 'Is there any twuth in that?'"

"Oh, I could not! I haven't the courage. If I do that, I shall know by his face is there any truth in it."

"Well, and you must know the twuth. You shall know it. I want to know it too; for, if he does not love you twuly, I will nevaa twust myself to any thing so deceitful as a man."

Rosa, at last, consented to follow this advice.

After dinner she put the letter into Christopher's hand, and asked him quietly was there any truth in that: then her hands trembled, and her eyes drank him.

Christopher read it, and frowned; then he looked up, and said, "No, not a word. What scoundrels there are in the world! To go and tell you that, now! Why, you little goose, have you been silly enough to believe it?"

"No," said she irresolutely. "But *do* you drive the brougham out every night?"

"Except on Sunday."

"Where?"

"My dear wife, I never loved you as I love you now, and if it was not for you I should not drive the brougham out of nights. That is all I shall tell you at present; but some day I'll tell you all about it."

He took such a calm high hand with her about it, that she submitted to leave it there; but from this moment the serpent doubt nibbled her.

It had one curious effect, though. She left off complaining of trifles.

Now, it happened one night that Lady Cicely Treherne and a friend were at a concert in Hanover Square. The other lady felt rather faint, and Lady Cicely offered to take her home. The carriage had not yet arrived, and Miss Macnamara said to walk a few steps would do her good. A smart cabman saw them from a distance, and drove up, and, touching his hat, said, "Cab, ladies?"

It seemed a very superior cab, and Miss Macnamara said, "Yes" directly.

The cabman bustled down and opened the door; Miss Macnamara got in first, then Lady Cicely; her eye fell on the cabman's face, which was lighted full by a street lamp, and it was Christopher Staines !

He started and winced, but the woman of the world never moved a muscle.

"Where to ?" said Staines, averting his head.

She told him where, and, when they got out, said, "I'll send it you by the servant."

A flunky soon after appeared with half a crown, and the amateur coachman drove away. He said to himself, "Come, my mustache is a better disguise than I thought."

Next day, and the day after, he asked Rosa, with affected carelessness, had she heard any thing of Lady Cicely.

"No, dear: but I dare say she will call this afternoon; it is her day."

She did call at last, and, after a few words with Rosa, became a little restless, and asked if she might consult Dr. Staines.

"Certainly, dear; come to his studio."

"No; might I see him here ?"

"Certainly." She rang the bell, and told the servant to ask Dr. Staines if he would be kind enough to step into the drawing-room.

Dr. Staines came in, and bowed to Lady Cicely, and eyed her a little uncomfortably.

She began, however, in a way that put him quite at his ease. "You remember the advice you gave us about my little cousin Tadcastah."

"Perfectly; his life is very precarious ; he is bilious, consumptive, and, if not watched, will be epileptical ; and he has a fond, weak mother, who will let him kill himself."

"Exactly: and you wecommended a sea-voyage, with a medical attendant to watch his diet, and contwol his habits. Well, she took other advice, and the youth is worse; so now she is fwightened, and a month ago she asked me to pwopose to you to sail about with Tadcastah; and she offered me a thousand pounds a year. I put on my stiff look, and said, 'Countess, with every desiah to oblige you, I must decline to cawwy that offah to a man of genius, learning, and weputation, who has the ball at his feet in London.'"

"Lord forgive you ! Lady Cicely."

"Lord bless her ! for standing up for my Christie."

Lady Cicely continued : " Now, this good lady, you must know, is not exactly one of us; the late earl mawwied into cotton, or wool, or something. So she said, 'Name your price for him. I shwugged my shoulders, smiled affably, and as affectedly as you like, and changed the subject. But since then things have happened. I am afwaid it is my duty to make you the judge whether you choose to sail about with that little cub— Rosa, I can beat about the bush no longer. Is it a fit thing that a man of genius, at whose feet we ought all to be sitting with reverence, should drive a cab in the public streets? Yes, Rosa Staines, your husband drives his brougham out at night, not to visit any other lady, as that anonymous wretch told you, but to make a few miserable shillings for you."

"O Christie ! "

"It is no use, Dr. Staines ; I must and will tell her. My dear, he drove me three nights ago. He had a cabman's badge on his poor arm. If you knew what I suffered in those five minutes ! Indeed, it seems cruel to speak of it — but I could not keep it from Rosa, and the reason I muster courage to say it before you, sir, is because I know she has other friends who keep you out of their consultations ; and after all it is the world that ought to blush, and not you."

Her ladyship's kindly bosom heaved, and she wanted to cry; so she took her handkerchief out of her pocket without the least hurry, and pressed it delicately to her eyes, and did cry quietly, but without any disguise, like a brave lady, who neither cried nor did any thing else she was ashamed to be seen at.

As for Rosa, she sat sobbing round Christopher's neck, and kissed him with all her soul.

"Dear me!" said Christopher. "You are both very kind. But, begging your pardon, it is 'much ado about nothing.'"

Lady Cicely took no notice of that observation. "So, Rosa dear," said she, "I think you are the person to decide whether he had not better sail about with that little cub, than — Oh!"

"I will settle that," said Staines. "I have one beloved creature to provide for. I may have another, I *must* make money. Turning a brougham into a cab, whatever you may think, is an honest way of making it, and I am not the first doctor who has coined his brougham at night. But, if there is a good deal of money to be made by sailing with Lord Tadcaster, of course I should prefer that to cab-driving, for I have never made above twelve shillings a night."

"Oh! as to that, she shall give you fifteen hundred a year."

"Then I jump at it."

"What! and leave *me!*"

"Yes, love : leave you — for your good ; and only for a time. Lady Cicely, it is a noble offer. My darling Rosa will have every comfort — ay, every luxury, till I come home, and then we will start afresh, with a good balance, and with more experience than we did at first."

Lady Cicely gazed on him with wonder. She said, "Oh, what stout hearts men have! No, no; don't let him go. See, he is acting. His great heart is torn with agony. I will have no hand in parting man and wife — no not for a day." And she hurried away in rare agitation.

Rosa fell on her knees, and asked Christopher's pardon for having been jealous; and that day she was a flood of divine tenderness. She repaid him richly for driving the cab. But she was unnaturally cool about Lady Cicely; and the exquisite reason soon come out. "Oh, yes! She is very good, very kind; but it is not for me now! .No, you shall not sail about with her cub of a cousin, and leave me at such a time."

Christopher groaned.

"Christie, you shall not see that lady again. She came here to part us. *She is in love with you.* I was blind not to see it before."

Next day, as Lady Cicely sat alone in the morning-room thinking over this very scene, a footman brought in a card and a note. "Dr. Staines begs particularly to see Lady Cicely Treherne."

The lady's pale cheek colored; she stood irresolute a single moment. "I will see Dr. Staines," said she.

Dr. Staines came in, looking pale and worn; he had not slept a wink since she saw him last.

She looked at him full, and divined this at a glance. She motioned him to a seat and sat down herself, with her white hand pressing her forehead, and her head turned a little away from him.

CHAPTER XII.

He told her he had come to thank her for her great kindness, and to accept the offer.

She sighed. "I hoped it was to decline it. Think of the misery of separation, both to you and her."

"It will be misery. But we are not happy as it is; and she cannot bear poverty. Nor is it fair she should, when I can give her every comfort by just playing the man for a year or two." He then told Lady Cicely there were more reasons than he chose to mention : go he must and would; and he implored her not to let the affair drop. In short, he was sad but resolved, and she found she must go on with it, or break faith with him. She took her desk, and wrote a letter concluding the bargain for him. She stipulated for half the year's fee in advance. She read Dr. Staines the letter.

"You *are* a friend," said he. "I should never have ventured on that: it will be a godsend to my poor Rosa. You will be kind to her when I am gone?"

"I will."

"So will Uncle Philip, I think. I will see him before I go, and shake hands. He has been a good friend to me; but he was too hard on *her*, and I could not stand that."

Then he thanked and blessed her again, with the tears in his eyes, and left her more disturbed and tearful than she had ever been since she grew to woman. "Oh, cruel Poverty!" she thought; "that such a man should be torn from his home, and thank me for doing it — all for a little money — and here are we poor commonplace creatures rolling in it."

Staines hurried home and told his wife. She clung to him convulsively, and wept bitterly; she made no direct attempt to shake his resolution: she saw by his iron look that she could only afflict, not turn him.

Next day came Lady Cicely to see her. Lady Cicely was very uneasy in her mind, and wanted to know whether Rosa was reconciled to the separation.

Rosa received her with a forced politeness and an icy coldness that petrified her. She could not stay long in face of such a reception. At parting, she said sadly. "You look on me as an enemy."

"What else can you expect, when you part my husband and me?" said Rosa with quiet sternness.

"I meant well," said Lady Cicely sorrowfully; "but I wish I had never interfered."

"So do I;" and she began to cry. Lady Cicely made no answer. She went quietly away, hanging her head sadly.

Rosa was unjust, but she was not rude nor vulgar; and Lady Cicely's temper was so well governed that it never blinded her heart. She withdrew, but without the least idea of quarrelling with her afflicted friend, or abandoning her. She went quietly home, and wrote to Lady ——, to say that she should be glad to receive Dr. Staines's advance as soon as convenient, since Mrs. Staines would have to make fresh arrangements and the money might be useful.

The money was forth-coming directly. Lady Cicely brought it to Dear Street, and handed it to Dr. Staines. His eyes sparkled at the sight of it.

"Give my love to Rosa," said she softly, and cut her visit very short.

Staines took the money to Rosa, and said, "See what our best friend has brought us. You shall have four hundred, and I hope after the bitter lessons you have had you will be able to do with it for some months. The two hundred I shall keep as a reserve fund for you to draw on."

"No, no!" said Rosa. "I shall go and live with my father, and never spend a penny. O Christie, if you knew how I hate myself for the folly that is parting us! Oh, why don't they teach girls sense and money, instead of music and the globes?"

But Christopher opened a banking account for her, and gave her a check-book, and entreated her to pay every thing by check, and run no bills whatever; and she promised. He also advertised the Bijou, and put a bill in the window: "The lease of this house and furniture to be sold."

Rosa cried bitterly at the sight of it, thinking how high in hope they were when they had their first dinner there, and also when she went to the first sale to buy the furniture cheap.

And now every thing moved with terrible rapidity. The *Amphitrite* was to sail from Plymouth in five days; and meantime there was so much to be done that the days seemed to gallop away.

Dr. Staines forgot nothing. He made his will in duplicate, leaving all to his wife; he left one copy at Doctors' Commons, and another to his lawyer: inventoried all his furniture and effects in duplicate too; wrote to Uncle Philip, and then called on him to seek reconciliation. Unfortunately Dr. Philip was in Scotland. At last this sad pair went down to Plymouth together, there to meet Lord Tadcaster, and go on board H. M. S. *Amphitrite*, lying at anchor at Hamoaze, under orders for the Australian station.

They met at the inn, as appointed, and sent word of their arrival on board the frigate, asking to remain on shore till the last minute.

Dr. Staines presented his patient to Rosa; and after a little while drew him apart and questioned him professionally. He then asked for a private room. Here he and Rosa really took leave; for what could the poor things say to each other on a crowed quay? He begged her forgiveness on his knees for having once spoken harshly to her; and she told him, with passionate sobs, he had never spoken harshly to her; her folly had parted them.

Poor wretches! they clung to each other with a thousand vows of love and constancy. They were to pray for each other at the same hours; to think of some kind words or loving act at other stated hours; and so they tried to fight with their suffering minds against the cruel separation: and if either should die, the other was to live wedded to memory, and never listen to love from other lips; but no! God was pitiful; he would let them meet again ere long, to part no more. They rocked in each other's arms; they cried over each other — it was pitiful.

At last the cruel summons came; they shuddered, as if it was their death-blow. Christopher, with a face of agony, was yet himself, and would have parted then: and so best. But Rosa could not. She would see the last of him, and became almost wild and violent when he opposed.

Then he let her come with him to Milbay Steps, but into the boat he would not let her step.

. The ship's boat lay at the steps, manned by six sailors, all seated, with their oars tossed in two vertical rows. A smart middy in charge conducted them, and Doctor Staines and Lord Tadcaster got in, leaving Rosa, in charge of her maid, on the quay.

"Shove off" —" Down "—" Give way."

Each order was executed so swiftly and surely, that, in as many seconds, the boat was clear, the oars struck the water with a loud splash, and the husband was shot away like an arrow, and the wife's despairing cry rang on the stony quay, as many a poor woman's cry had rung before.

In half a minute the boat shot under the stern of the frigate.

They were received on the quarterdeck by Capt. Hamilton: he introduced them to the officers — a torture to poor Staines, to have his mind taken for a single instant from his wife — the first lieutenant came aft, and reported, "Ready for making sail, sir."

"Staines seized the excuse, rushed to the other side of the vessel, leaned over the taffrail, as if he would fly ashore, and stretched out his hands to his beloved Rosa; and she stretched out her hands to him. They were so near he could read the expression of her face. It was wild and troubled, as one who did not yet realize the terrible situation, but would not be long first.

"HANDS MAKE SAIL — WAY ALOFT — UP ANCHOR," rang in Christopher's ears as if in a dream. All his soul and senses were bent on that desolate young creature. How young and amazed her lovely face! Yet this bewildered child was about to become a mother. Even a stranger's heart might have yearned with pity for her: how much more her miserable husband's!

The capstan was manned, and worked to a merry tune that struck chill to the bereaved; yards were braced for casting, anchor hove, catted, and fished, sail was spread with amazing swiftness, the ship's head dipped, and slowly and gracefully paid off toward the Breakwater, and she stood out to sea under swiftly swelling canvas and a light north-westerly breeze.

Staines only felt the motion: his body was in the ship, his soul with his Rosa. He gazed, he strained his eyes to see her eyes, as the ship glided from England and her. While he was thus gazing and trembling all over, up came to him a smart second lieutenant, with a brilliant voice that struck him like a sword: "Captain's orders to show you berths. Please choose for Lord Tadcaster and yourself."

The man's wild answer made the young officer stare. "Oh, sir! not now — try and do my duty when I have quite lost her — my poor wife — a child — a mother — there — sir — on the steps — there! — there!"

Now, this officer always went to sea singing "Oh, be joyful!" But a strong man's agony, who can make light of it? It was a revelation to him, but he took it quickly. The first thing he did, being a man of action, was to dash into his cabin, and come back with a short, power-ful, double glass. "There!" said he, roughly but kindly, and shoved it into Staines's hand. He took it, stared at it stupidly, then used it, without a word of thanks, so wrapped was he in his anguish.

This glass prolonged the misery of that bitter hour. When Rosa could no longer tell her husband from another, she felt he was really gone, and she threw her hands aloft and clasped them above her head, with the wild abandon of a woman who could never again be a child; and Staines saw it, and a sharp sigh burst from him, and he saw her maid and others gather round her. He saw the poor young thing led away, with her head all down, as he had never seen her before, and supported to the inn; and then he saw her no more.

His heart seemed to go out of his bosom in search of her, and leave nothing but a stone behind: he hung over the taffrail like a dead thing. A steady footfall slapped his ear. He raised his white face and filmy eyes, and saw Lieut. Fitzroy marching to and fro like a sentinel, keeping everybody away from the mourner, with the steady, resolute, business-like face of a man in whom sentiment is confined to action; its phrases and its flourishes being literally *terra incognita* to the honest fellow.

Staines staggered toward him, holding out both hands, and gasped out, "God bless you! Hide me somewhere — must not be seen so — got duty to do — Patient — can't do it yet — one hour to draw my breath — oh, my God, my God! — one hour, sir. Then do my duty if I die — as you would."

Fitzroy tore him down into his own cabin, shut him in, and ran to the first lieutenant, with a tear in his eye. "Can I have a sentry, sir?"

"Sentry? What for?"

"The doctor — awfully cut up at leaving his wife; got him in my cabin. Wants to have his cry to himself."

"Fancy a fellow crying at going to sea!"

"It is not that, sir; it is leaving his wife."

"Well, is he the only man on board has got a wife?"

"Why, no, sir. It *is* odd, now I think of it. Perhaps he has only got that *one*."

"Curious creatures, landsmen," said the first lieutenant. "However, you can stick a marine there."

"Yes, sir."

"And I say, show the *youngster* the berths, and let him choose, as the doctor's aground."

"Yes, sir."

So Fitzroy planted his marine, and then went after Lord Tadcaster: he had drawn up alongside his cousin, Capt. Hamilton. The captain, being an admirer of Lady Cicely, was mighty civil to his little lordship, and talked to him more than was his wont on the quarterdeck; for though he had a good flow of conversation, and dispensed with ceremony in his cabin, he was apt to be rather short on deck. However, he told little Tadcaster he was fortunate; they had a good start, and, if the wind held, might hope to be clear of the Channel in twenty-four hours. "You will see Eddystone Lighthouse about four bells," said he.

"Shall we go out of sight altogether?" inquired his lordship.

"Of course we shall, and the sooner the better." He then explained to the novice that the only danger to a good ship was from the land.

While Tadcaster was digesting this paradox, Capt. Hamilton proceeded to descant on the beauties of blue water, and its fine medicinal qualities, which, he said, were particularly suited to young gentlemen with bilious stomachs; but presently, catching sight of Lieut. Fitzroy standing apart, but with the manner of a lieutenant not there by accident, he stopped, and said, civilly but sharply, "Well, sir."

Fitzroy came forward directly, saluted, and said he had orders from the first lieutenant to show Lord Tadcaster the berths. His lordship must be good enough to chose, because the doctor — couldn't."

"Why not?"

"Brought to, sir — for the present — by — well, by grief."

"Brought to by Grief! Who the deuce is Grief? No riddles on the quarter-deck, if you please, sir."

"Oh, no, sir! I assure you he is awfully cut up, and he is having his cry out in my cabin."

"Having his cry out! why, what for?"

"Leaving his wife, sir."

"Oh! is that all?"

"Well, I don't wonder," cried little Tadcaster warmly. "She is, oh, so beautiful!" and a sudden blush overspread his pasty cheeks. "Why on earth didn't we bring her along with us here?" said he, suddenly opening his eyes with astonishment at the childish omission.

"Why, indeed?" said the captain comically, and dived below, attended by the well-disciplined laughter of Lieut. Fitzroy, who was too good an officer not to be amused at his captain's jokes. Having acquitted himself of that duty — and it is a very difficult one sometimes — he took Lord Tadcaster to the maindeck, and showed him two comfortable sleeping-berths that had been screened off for him and Dr. Staines. One of these was fitted with a standing bedplace, the other had a cot swung in it. Fitzroy offered him the choice, but hinted that he himself preferred a cot.

"No, thank you," says my lord mighty dryly.

"All right," said Fitzroy cheerfully. "Take the other, then, my lord."

His little lordship cocked his eye like a jackdaw, and looked almost as cunning. "You see," said he, "I have been reading up for this voyage."

"Oh, indeed! Logarithms?"

"Of course not."

"What then?"

"Why, *Peter Simple*, to be sure."

"Ah, ha!" said Fitzroy, with a chuckle that showed plainly he had some delicious reminiscences of youthful study in the same quarter.

The little lord chuckled too, and put one finger on Fitzroy's shoulder, and pointed at the cot with another. "Tumble out the other side, you know — slippery hitches — cords cut — down you come flop in the middle of the night."

Fitzroy's eye flashed merriment, but only for a moment. His countenance fell the next. "Lord bless you!" said he sorrowfully, "all that game is over now. Her majesty's ship!—it is a church afloat. The service is going to the devil, as the old fogies say."

"Ain't you sorry?" says the little lord, cocking his eye again just like the bird hereinbefore mentioned.

"Of course I am."

"Then I'll take the standing hed."

"All right. I say, you don't mind the doctor coming down with a run, eh?"

"He is not ill—I am. He is paid to take care of me—I am not paid to take care of him," said the young lord sententiously.

"I understand," replied Fitzroy dryly. "Well, every one for himself, and Providence for us all, as the elephant said when he danced among the chickens."

Here my lord was summoned to dinner with the captain. Staines was not there, but he had not forgotten his duty. In the midst of his grief he had written a note to the captain, hoping that a bereaved husband might not seem to desert his post if he hid for a few hours the sorrow he felt himself unable to control. Meantime he would be grateful if Capt. Hamilton would give or-

ders that Lord Tadcaster should eat no pastry, and drink only six ounces of claret, otherwise he should feel that he was indeed betraying his trust.

The captain was pleased and touched with this letter. It recalled to him how his mother sobbed when she launched her little middy, swelling with his first cocked hat and dirk.

There was champagne at dinner, and little Tadcaster began to pour out a tumbler. "Hold on!" said Capt. Hamilton. "You are not to drink that;" and he quietly removed the tumbler. "Bring him six ounces of claret."

While they were weighing the claret with scientific precision, Tadcaster remonstrated; and being told it was the doctor's order, he squeaked out, "Confound him! why did he not stay with his wife? She is beautiful." Nor did he give it up without a struggle, "Here's hospitality!" said he. "Six ounces."

Receiving no reply, he inquired of the third lieutenant, which was generally considered the greatest authority in a ship — the captain or the doctor?

The third lieutenant answered not, but turned his head away, and, by violent exertion, succeeded in not splitting.

"I'll answer that," said Hamilton politely. "The captain is the highest in his department, and the doctor in his. Now, Dr. Staines is strictly within his department, and will be supported by me and my officers. You are bilious and epileptical, and all the rest of it; and you are to be cured by diet and blue water."

Tadcaster was inclined to snivel. However, he subdued that weakness with a visible effort, and in due course returned to the charge. "How would you look," quavered he "if there was to be a mutiny in this ship of yours, and I was to head it?"

"Well, I should look *sharp—*

hang all the ringleaders at the yard-arm, clap the rest under hatches, and steer for the nearest prison."

"Oh!" said Tadcaster, and digested this scheme a bit. At last he perked up again, and made his final hit. "Well, I shouldn't care, for one, if you didn't flog us."

"In that case," said Capt. Hamilton, "I'd flog you—and stop your six ounces."

"Then curse the sea; that is all I say."

"Why, you have not seen it; you have only seen the British Channel." It was Mr. Fitzroy who contributed this last observation.

After dinner all but the captain went on deck, and saw the Eddystone light-house ahead and to leeward. They passed it. Fitzroy told his lordship its story, and that of its unfortunate predecessors. Soon after this Lord Tadcaster turned in.

Presently the captain observed a change in the thermometer, which brought him on deck. He scanned the water and the sky; and as these experienced commanders have a subtle insight into the weather, especially in familiar latitudes, he remarked to the first lieutenant that it looked rather unsettled; and, as a matter of prudence, ordered a reef in the topsails, and the royal yards to be sent down. Ship to be steered W. by S. This done, he turned in, but told them to call him if there was any change in the weather.

During the night the wind gradually headed; and at four bells in the middle watch, a heavy squall came up from the southwest.

This brought the captain on deck again; he found the officer of the watch at his post, and at work. Sail was shortened, and the ship made snug for heavy weather.

At 4, A.M.; it was blowing hard, and, being too near the French coast, they wore the ship.

Now, this operation was bad for little Tadcaster. While the vessel was on the starboard tack, the side kept him snug; but when they wore her, of course he had no lee board to keep him in. The ship gave a lee lurch, and shot him clean out of his bunk into the middle of the cabin.

He shrieked and shrieked, with terror and pain, till the captain and Staines, who were his nearest neighbors, came to him, and they gave him a little brandy, and got him to bed again. Here he suffered nothing but violent sea-sickness for some hours.

As for Staines, he had been swinging heavily in his cot; but such was his mental distress that he would have welcomed sea-sickness, or any reasonable bodily suffering. He was in that state when the sting of a wasp is a touch of comfort.

Worn out with sickness, Tadcaster would not move. Invited to breakfast, he swore faintly, and insisted on dying in peace. At last exhaustion gave him a sort of sleep, in spite of the motion, which was violent, for it was now blowing great guns, a heavy sea on, and the great waves dirty in color and crested with raging foam.

They had to wear ship again, always a ticklish manœuvre in weather like this.

A tremendous sea stuck her quarter, stove in the very port abreast of which the little lord was lying, and washed him clean out of bed into the lee scuppers, and set all swimming round him.

Didn't he yell, and wash about the cabin, and grab at all the chairs and tables and things that drifted about, nimble as eels, avoiding his grasp!

In rushed the captain, and in staggered Staines. They stopped his "voyage au tour de sa chambre," and dragged him into the after-saloon.

He clung to them by turns, and begged, with many tears, to be put on the nearest land; a rock would do.

"Much obliged," said the captain; "now is the very time to give rocks a wide berth."

"A dead whale, then — a lighthouse — any thing but a beast of a ship."

They pacified him with a little brandy, and for the next twenty-four hours he scarcely opened his mouth, except for a purpose it is needless to dwell on. We can trust to our terrestrial readers' personal reminiscences of lee lurches, weather rolls, and their faithful concomitant.

At last they wriggled out of the channel, and soon after the wind abated, and next day veered round to the northward, and the ship sailed almost on an even keel. The motion became as heavenly as it had been diabolical, and the passengers came on deck.

Staines had suffered one whole day from sea-sickness, but never complained. I believe it did his mind more good than harm.

As for Tadcaster, he continued to suffer, at intervals, for two days more; but, on the fifth day out, he appeared with a little pink tinge on his cheek, and a wolfish appetite. Dr. Staines controlled his diet severely as to quality and, when they had been at sea just eleven days, the physician's heavy heart was not a little lightened by the marvellous change in him. The unthinking, who believe in the drug system, should have seen what a physician can do with air and food, when circumstances enable him to *enforce* the diet he enjoins. Money will sometimes buy even health, if you *avoid drugs entirely*, and go another road.

Little Tadcaster went on board pasty, dim-eyed, and very subject to fits, because his stomach was constantly overloaded with indigestible trash, and the blood in his brain-vessels was always either galloping or creeping, under the first or second effect of stimulants administered at first by thoughtless physi-cians. Behold him now — bronzed, pinky, bright-eyed, elastic; and only one fit in twelve days.

The quarter-deck was hailed from the "lookout" with a cry that is sometimes terrible, but, in this latitude and weather, welcome and exciting. "Land, ho!"

"Where away?" cried the officer of the watch.

"A point on the lee bow, sir."

It was the Island of Madeira: they dropped anchor in Funchal Roads, furled sails, squared yards, and fired a salute of twenty-one guns for the Portuguese flag.

They went ashore, and found a good hotel, and were no longer dosed, as in former days, with oil, onions, garlic, eggs. But the wine queer, and no *Madeira* to be got.

Staines wrote home to his wife: he told her how deeply he had felt the bereavement, but did not dwelt on that, his object being to cheer her. He told her it promised to be a rapid and wonderful cure, and one that might very well give him a fresh start in London. They need not be parted a whole year, he thought. He sent her a very long letter, and also such extracts from his sea journal as he thought might please her. After dinner they inspected the town; and what struck them most was to find the streets paved with flag-stones, and most of the carts drawn by bullocks on sledges. A man every now and then would run forward and drop a greasy cloth in front of the sledge to lubricate the way.

Next day, after breakfast, they ordered horses — these, on inspection, proved to be of excellent breed, either from Australia or America — very rough shod, for the stony road. Started for the Grand Canal — peeped down that mighty chasm, which has the appearance of an immense mass having been blown out of the centre of the mountain.

They lunched under the Great Dragon-Tree near its brink, then rode back, admiring the bold mountain scenery. Next morning, at dawn, rode on horses up the hill to the convent. Admired the beautiful gardens on the way. Remained a short time; then came down in the hand-sled — little baskets slung on sledges, guided by two natives; these sledges run down hill with surprising rapidity, and the men guide them round corners by sticking out a foot to port or starboard.

Embarked at 11.30, A.M.

At 1.30, the men having dined, the ship was got under way for the Cape of Good Hope, and all sail made for a southerly course, to get into the N.E. trades.

The weather was now balmy and delightful, and so genial that everybody lived on deck, and could hardly be got to turn in to their cabins, even for sleep.

Dr. Staines became a favorite with the officers. There is a great deal of science on board a modern ship of war; and of course, on some points, Staines, a Cambridge wrangler, and man of many sciences and books, was an oracle. On others he was quite behind, but a ready and quick pupil. He made up to the navigating officer, and learned, with his help, to take observations. In return, he was always at any youngster's service in a trigonometrical problem; and he amused the midshipmen and young lieutenants with analytical tests; some of these were applicable to certain liquids dispensed by the paymaster. Under one of them the port-wine assumed some very droll colors, and appearances not proper to grape juice.

One lovely night that the ship clove the dark sea into a blaze of phosphorescence, and her wake streamed like a comet's tail, a waggish middy got a bucketful hoisted on deck, and asked the doctor to analyze that. He did not much like it, but yielded to the general request; and by dividing it into smaller vessels, and dropping in various chemicals, made rainbows and silvery flames and what not. But he declined to repeat the experiment: "No, no; once is philosophy; twice is cruelty. I've slain more than Samson already."

As for Tadcaster, science had no charms for him; but fiction had; and he got it galore; for he cruised about the forecastle, and there the quartermasters and old seamen spun him yarns that held him breathless.

But one day my lord had a fit on the quarter-deck, and a bad one; and Staines found him smelling strong of rum. He represented this to Capt. Hamilton. The captain caused strict inquiries to be made; and it came out that my lord had gone among the men with money in both pockets, and bought a little of one man's grog and a little of another, and had been sipping the furtive but transient joys of solitary intoxication.

Capt. Hamilton talked to him seriously; told him it was suicide.

"Never mind, old boy," said the young monkey; "a short life and a merry one."

Then Hamilton represented that it was very ungentlemanlike to go and tempt poor Jack with his money to offend discipline and get flogged. "How will you feel, Tadcaster, when you see their backs bleeding under the cat?"

"Oh! d—n it all, George, don't do that," says the young gentleman, all in a hurry.

Then the commander saw he had touched the right chord. So he played on till he got Lord Tadcaster to pledge his honor not to do it again.

The little fellow gave the pledge, but relieved his mind as follows: "But it is a cursed tyrannical hole, this tiresome old ship. You can't do any thing you like in it."

"Well, but no more you can in the grave; and that is the agreeable residence you were hurrying to but for this tiresome old ship."

"Lord! no more you can," said, Tadcaster, with sudden candor. "*I forgot that.*"

The airs were very light; ship hardly moved. It was beginning to get dull, when one day a sail was sighted on the weather bow, standing to the eastward. On nearing her, she was seen by the cut of her sails to be a man-of-war, evidently homeward bound; so Capt. Hamilton ordered the main-royal to be lowered (to render signal more visible) and the "Demand" hoisted. No notice being taken of this, a gun was fired to draw her attention to the signal. This had the desired effect; down went her main-royal and up went her "Number." On referring to the signal-book she proved to be the *Vindictive*, from the Pacific station.

This being ascertained, Capt. Hamilton, being that captain's senior, signalled, "Close, and prepare to receive letters:" in obedience to this she bore up, ran down, and rounded to; the sail in *Amphitrite* was also shortened, the main top-sail laid to the mast, and a boat lowered. The captain having finished his, dispatches, they, with the letter-bags, were handed into the boat, which shoved off, pulled to the lee side of the *Vindictive*, and left the despatches, with Capt. Hamilton's compliments. On its return, both ships made sail on their respective course, exchanging "Bon voyage" by signal; and soon the upper sails of the homeward-bounder were seen dipping below the horizon: longing eyes followed her, on board the *Amphitrite*.

How many hurried missives had been written and despatched in that hour! But as for Staines, he was a man of forethought, and had a volume ready for his dear wife.

Lord Tadcaster wrote to Lady Cicely Treherne. His epistle, though brief, contained a plum or two.

He wrote: "What with sailing, and fishing, and eating nothing but roast meat, I'm quite another man."

This amused her ladyship a little, but not so much as the postscript, which was indeed the neatest thing in its way she had met with, and she had some experience too.

"P.S. — I say, Cicely, I think I should like to marry you. Would you mind?"

Let us defy time and space to give you Lady Cicely's reply: "I should enjoy it of all things, Taddy. But, alas! I am too young."

N.B. — She was twenty-seven, and Tad sixteen. To be sure, Tad was four feet eleven, and she was only five feet six and a half.

To return to my narrative (with apologies), this meeting of the vessels caused a very agreeable excitement that day; but a greater was in store. In the afternoon Tadcaster, Staines, and the principal officers of the ship, being at dinner in the captain's cabin, in came the officer of the watch, and reported a large spar on the weather bow.

"Well, close it if you can; and let me know if it looks worth picking up."

He then explained to Lord Tadcaster, that, on a cruise, he never liked to pass a spar, or any thing that might possibly reveal the fate of some vessel or other.

In the middle of his discourse the officer came in again, but not in the same cool, business way: he ran in excitedly, and said, "Captain, the signal-man reports it *alive!*"

"Alive? — a spar! What do you mean? Something alive *on* it, eh?"

"No, sir; alive itself."

"How can that be? Hail him again. Ask him what it is."

The officer went out, and hailed the signal-man at the mast-head. "What is it?"

"Sea-sarpint, I think."

This hail reached the captain's ears faintly. However, he waited quietly till the officer came in and reported it ; then he burst out, "Absurd ! — there is no such creature in the universe. What do you say, Dr. Staines ? It is in your department."

" The universe in my department, captain ? "

" Haw ! haw ! haw !" went Fitzroy and two more.

" No, you rogue, the serpent."

Dr. Staines, thus appealed to, asked the captain if he had ever seen small snakes out at sea.

" Why, of course. Sailed through a mile of them once in the Archipelago."

" Sure they were snakes ? "

" Quite sure : and the biggest was not eight feet long "

" Very well, captain ; then sea-serpents exist, and it becomes a mere question of size. Now, which produces the larger animals in every kind, land or sea ? The grown elephant weighs, I believe, about two tons. The very smallest of the whale tribe weighs ten ; and they go as high as forty tons. There are smaller fish than the whale that are four times as heavy as the elephant. " Why doubt, then, that the sea can breed a snake to eclipse the boa-constrictor ? Even if the creature had never been seen, I should, by mere reasoning from analogy, expect the sea to produce a serpent excelling the boa-constrictor, as the lobster excells the cray-fish of our rivers. See how large things grow at sea ! The salmon born in our rivers weighs in six months a quarter of a pound, or less ; it goes out to sea, and comes back in one year weighing seven pounds. So far from doubting the large sea-serpents, I believe they exist by the million. The only thing that puzzles me is, why they should ever show a nose above water ; they must be very numerous, I think."

Capt. Hamilton laughed, and said, " Well, this *is* new. Doctor, in compliment to your opinion, we will go on deck and inspect the reptile you think so common." He stopped at the door, and said, " Doctor, the salt-cellar is by you. Would you mind bringing it on deck ? We shall want a little to secure the animal."

So they all went on deck right merrily.

The captain went up a few ratlines in the mizzen rigging, and looked to windward, laughing all the time ; but all of a sudden there was a great change in his manner.

" Good Heavens, it is alive — LUFF ! "

The helmsman obeyed ; the news spread like wild-fire. Mess kids, grog kids, pipes, were all let fall, and soon three hundred sailors clustered on the rigging like bees, to view the long-talked-of monster.

It was soon discovered to be moving lazily along, the propelling part being under water, and about twenty-five feet visible. It had a small head for so large a body ; and, as they got nearer, rough scales were seen, ending in smaller ones farther down the body. It had a mane, but not like a lion's, as some have pretended. If you have ever seen a pony with a hog-mane, that was more the character of this creature's mane — if mane it was.

They got within a hundred yards of it, and all saw it plainly, scarce believing their senses.

When they could get no nearer for the wind, the captain yielded to that instinct which urges man always to kill a curiosity, " to encourage the rest," as saith witty Voltaire. " Get ready a gun. Best shot in the ship lay and fire it."

This was soon done. Bang went the gun ; the shot struck the water close to the brute, and may have struck him under water, for aught I know. Anyway, it sorely disturbed him ; for he reared into the air a column of serpent's flesh that looked as thick as the main-topmast of a seventy-four, opened a mouth that looked capacious enough to swallow the largest bacoy anchor in the ship, and, with a strange grating noise between a bark and a hiss, dived, and was seen no more.

When he was gone they all looked at one another, like men awakening from a dream.

Staines alone took it quite coolly. It did not surprise him in the least. He had always thought it incredible that the boa-constrictor should be larger than any sea-snake. That idea struck him as monstrous and absurd. He noted the sea-serpent in his journal, but with this doubt, "Semble — more like a very large eel."

Next day they crossed the line. Just before noon a young gentleman burst into Staines's cabin, apologizing for want of ceremony; but if Dr. Staines would like to see the line, it was now in sight from the mizzen-top.

"Glad of it, sir," said Staines; "collect it for me in the ship's buckets, if you please. I want to send a *line* to friends at home."

Young gentleman buried his hands in his pockets, walked out in solemn silence, and resumed his position on the lee side of the quarter-deck.

Nevertheless, the opening, coupled with what he had heard and read, made Staines a little uneasy, and he went to his friend Fitzroy, and said, —

"Now look here: I am at the service of you experienced and humorous mariners. I plead guilty at once to the crime of never having passed the line; so make ready your swabs, and lather me; your ship's scraper, and shave me; and let us get it over. But Lord Tadcaster is nervous, sensitive, prouder than he seems, and I'm not going to have him driven into a fit for all the Neptunes and Amphitrites in creation."

Fitzroy heard him out, then burst out laughing. "Why, there is none of that game in the Royal Navy," said he. "Hasn't been this twenty years."

"I'm so sorry!" said Dr. Staines.

"If there is a form of wit I revere, it is practical joking."

"Doctor, you are a satirical beggar."

Staines told Tadcaster, and he went forward and chaffed his friend the quartermaster, who was one of the forecastle wits. "I say, quartermaster, why doesn't Neptune come on board?"

Dead silence.

"I wonder what has become of poor old Nep?"

"Gone ashore!" growled the seaman. "Last seen in the Ratcliff Highway. Got a shop there — lends a shilling in the pound on seamen's advance tickets."

"Oh! and Amphitrite?"

"Married the sexton at Wapping."

"And the Nereids?"

"Neruds!" (scratching his head) "I harn't kept my eye on them small craft. But I *believe* they are selling oysters in the port of Leith."

A light breeze carried them across the equator; but soon after they got becalmed, and it was dreary work, and the ship rolled, gently but continuously, and upset Lord Tadcaster's stomach again, and quenched his manly spirit.

At last they were fortunate enough to catch the S.E. trade, but it was so languid at first that the ship barely moved through the water, though they set every stitch, and studding-sails alow and aloft, till really she was acres of canvas.

While she was so creeping along, a man in the mizzen-top noticed an enormous shark gliding steadily in her wake. This may seem a small incident, yet it ran through the ship like wildfire, and caused more or less uneasiness in three hundred stout hearts: so near is every seaman to death, and so strong the persuasion in their superstitious minds, that a shark does not follow a ship pertinaciously without a prophetic instinct of calamity.

Unfortunately, the quarter-master conveyed this idea to Lord Tadcaster, and confirmed it by numerous examples, to prove that there was death at hand when a shark followed the ship.

Thereupon Tadcaster took it into his head that he was under a relapse, and the shark was waiting for his dead body. He got quite low-spirited. Staines told Fitzroy. Fitzroy said, "Shark be hanged! I'll have him on deck in half an hour." He got leave from the captain. A hook was baited with a large piece of pork, and towed astern by a stout line, experienced old hands attending to it by turns.

The shark came up leisurely, surveyed the bait, and, I apprehend, ascertained the position of the hook: at all events, he turned quietly on his back, sucked the bait off, and retired to enjoy it.

Every officer in the ship tried him in turn, but without success; for if they got ready for him, and the moment he took the bait jerked the rope hard, in that case he opened his enormous mouth so wide that the bait and hook came out clear. But sooner or later, he always got the bait, and left his captors the hook.

This went on for days, and his huge dorsal fin always in the ship's wake.

Then Tadcaster, who had watched these experiments with hope, lost his spirit and his appetite.

Staines reasoned with him, but in vain. Somebody was to die; and although there were three hundred and more in the ship, he must be the one. At last he actually made his will, and threw himself into Staines's arms, and gave him messages to his mother and Lady Cicely, and ended by frightening himself into a fit.

This roused Staines's pity, and also put him on his mettle. What, science be beaten by a shark!

He pondered the matter with all his might, and at last an idea came to him.

He asked the captain's permission to try his hand. This was accorded immediately, and the ship's stores placed at his disposal very politely, and with a sly, comical grin.

Dr. Staines got from the carpenter some sheets of zinc and spare copper and some flannel. These he cut into three-inch squares, and soaked the flannel in acidulated water. He then procured a quantity of bell-wire, the greater part of which he insulated by wrapping it round with hot gutta-percha. So eager was he that he did not turn in all night.

In the morning he prepared what he called an electric fuse. He filled a soda-water bottle with gunpowder, attaching some cork to make it buoyant, put in the fuse and hung, made it water-tight, connected and insulated his main wires, enveloped the bottle in pork, tied a line to it and let the bottle overboard.

The captain and officers shook their heads mysteriously. The tars peeped and grinned from every rope to see a doctor try and catch a shark with a soda-water bottle and no hook; but somehow the doctor seemed to know what he was about, so they hovered around, and waited the result, mystified but curious, and showing their teeth from ear to ear.

"The only thing I fear," said Staines, "is that the moment he takes the bait, he will cut the wire before I can complete the circuit and fire the fuse."

Nevertheless, there was another objection to the success of the experiment. The shark had disappeared.

"Well," said the captain, "at all events you have frightened him away."

"No," said little Tadcaster, white as a ghost: "he is only under water, I know; waiting — waiting."

"There he is!" cried one in the ratlines.

There was a rush to the taffrail —great excitement.

"Keep clear of me," said Staines, quietly but firmly. "It can only be done at the moment before he cuts the wire."

The old shark swam slowly round the bait.

He saw it was something new.

He swam round and round it.

"He won't take it," said one.

"He suspects something."

"Oh, yes! he will take the meat somehow, and leave the pepper. Sly old fox."

"He has eaten many a poor Jack, that one."

The shark turned slowly on his back, and, instead of grabbing the bait, seemed to draw it by gentle suction into that capacious throat, ready to blow it out in a moment if it was not all right.

The moment the bait was drawn out of sight, Staines completed the circuit: the bottle exploded with a fury that surprised him and everybody who saw it; a ton of water flew into the air, and came down in spray, and a gory carcass floated belly uppermost, visibly staining the blue water.

There was a roar of amazement and applause.

The carcass was towed alongside, at Tadcaster's urgent request, and then the power of the explosion was seen. Confined, first by the bottle, then by the meat, then by the fish, and lastly by the water, it had exploded with tenfold power, had blown the brute's head into a million atoms, and had even torn a great furrow in its carcass, exposing three feet of the backbone.

Taddy gloated on his enemy, and began to pick up again from that hour.

The wind improved, and, as usual in that latitude, scarcely varied a point. They had a pleasant time. Private theatricals, and other amusements, till they got to latitude 26° S., and longitude 27°. Then the trade-wind deserted them. Light and variable winds succeeded.

The master complained of the chronometers, and the captain thought it his duty to verify or correct them: and so shaped his course for the island of Tristan d'Acunha, then lying a little way out of his course. I ought, perhaps, to explain to the general reader that the exact position of this island, being long. ago recorded, it was an infallible guide to go by in verifying a ship's chronometers.

Next day the glass fell all day, and the captain said he should double reef-topsails at night-fall, for something was brewing.

The weather, however, was fine, and the ship was sailing very fast, when, about half an hour before sunset, the mast-head man hailed that there was a balk of timber in sight, broad on the weather-bow.

The signal-man was sent up, and said it looked like a raft.

The captain, who was on deck, levelled his glass at it, and made it out a raft, with a sort of rail to it, and the stump of a mast.

He ordered the officer of the watch to keep the ship as close to the wind as possible. He should like to examine it if he could.

The master represented respectfully that it would be unadvisable to beat to windward for that. "I have no faith in our chronometers, sir, and it is important to make the island before dark: fogs rise here so suddenly."

"Very well, Mr. Bolt: then I suppose we must let the raft go."

"MAN ON THE RAFT TO WINDWARD!" hailed the signal-man.

This electrified the ship. The captain ran up the mizzen rigging and scanned the raft, now nearly abeam.

"It *is* a man !" he cried, and was about to alter the ship's course when, at that moment the signal man hailed again :

"It is a corpse."

"How d'ye know ? "

"By the gulls."

Then succeeded an exciting dialogue between the captain and the master, who, being in his department, was very firm ; and went so far as to say he would not answer for the safety of the ship if they did not sight the land before dark.

The captain said, " Very well," and took a turn or two. But at last he said, " No. Her Majesty's ship must not pass a raft with a man on it, dead or alive."

He then began to give the necessary orders, but before they were out of his mouth, a fatal interruption occured.

Tadcaster ran into Dr. Staines's cabin, crying, " A raft with a corpse close by ! "

Staines sprang to the quarter-port to see ; and, craning eagerly out, the lower port chain, which had not been well secured, slipped, the port gave way, and, as his whole weight rested on it, canted him headlong into the sea.

A smart seaman in the fore-chains saw the accident, and instantly roared out, " Man overboard ! " a cry that sends a thrill through a ship's very ribs.

Another smart fellow cut the life-buoy adrift so quickly that it struck the water within ten yards of Staines.

The officer of the watch, without the interval of half a minute, gave the right orders in the voice of a Stentor :—

" Let go life-buoy.

" Life-boat's crew away.

" Hands shorten sail.

" Mainsail up.

" Main-topsail to mast."

These orders were executed with admirable swiftness. Meantime there was a mighty rush of feet throughout the frigate, every hatch-way was crammed with men eager to force their way on deck.

In five seconds the middy of the watch and half her crew were in the lee cutter fitted with Clifford's apparatus.

" Lower away ! " cried the excit ed officer ; " the others will come down by the pendants."

The man stationed, sitting on the bottom boards, eased away roundly, when suddenly there was a hitch — the boat would go no farther.

" Lower away there in the cutter ! Why don't you lower ? screamed the captain, who had come over to leeward expecting to see the boat in the water.

" The rope has swollen, sir, and pendants won't unreeve," cried the middy in agony.

" Volunteers for the weather-boat ! " shouted the first lieutenant ; but the order was unnecessary, for more than the proper number were in her already.

" Plug in — lower away."

But mishaps never come singly. Scarcely had this boat gone a foot from the davit than the volunteer who was acting as cockswain, in reaching out for something, inadvertently let go the line which, in Kynaston's apparatus, keeps the tackles hooked ; consequently, down went the boat and crew twenty feet, with a terrific crash ; the men were struggling for their lives, and the boat was stove.

But meantime, more men having been sent into the lee cutter, their weight caused the pendants to render, and the boat got afloat, and was soon employed picking up the struggling crew.

Seeing this, Lieut. Fitzroy collected some hands, and lowered the life-boat gig, which was fitted with common tackles, got down into her himself by the falls, and, pulling round to windward, shouted to the signal-man for directions.

The signal-man was at his post, and had fixed his eye on the man overboard, as his duty was : but his messmate was in the stove boat, and he had cast one anxious look down to see if he was saved, and, sad to relate, in that one moment he had lost sight of Staines : the sudden darkness — there was no twilight — confused him more, and the ship had increased her drift.

Fitzroy, however, made a rapid calculation, and pulled to windward with all his might. He was followed in about a minute by the other sound boat powerfully manned ; and both boats melted away into the night.

There was a long and anxious suspense, during which it became pitch-dark, and the ship burned blue-lights to mark her position more plainly to the crews that were groping the sea for that beloved passenger.

Capt. Hamilton had no doubt that the fate of Staines was decided, one way or other, long before this ; but he kept quiet until he saw the plain signs of a squall at hand. Then, as he was responsible for the safety of boats and ship, he sent up rockets to recall them.

The cutter came alongside first. Lights were poured on her ; and quavering voices asked, " Have you got him ? "

The answer was dead silence, and sorrowful, drooping heads.

Sadly and reluctantly was the order given to hoist the boat in.

Then the gig came alongside. Fitzroy seated in her, with his hands before his face ; the men gloomy and sad.

" Gone ! Gone ! "

Soon the ship was battling a heavy squall.

At midnight all quiet again, and hove to. Then, at the request of many, the bell was tolled, and the ship's company mustered bare-headed, and many a stout seaman in tears, as the last service was read for Christopher Staines.

CHAPTER XIII.

Rosa fell ill with grief at the hotel, and could not move for some days ; but, the moment she was strong enough, she insisted on leaving Plymouth : like all wounded things, she must drag herself home.

But what a home ! How empty it struck, and she heart-sick and desolate ! Now all the familiar places wore a new aspect: the little yard, where he had so walked and waited, became a temple to her ; and she came out and sat in it, and now first felt to the full how much he had suffered there — with what fortitude ! She crept about the house, and kissed the chair he had sat in, and every much-used place and thing of the departed.

Her shallow nature deepened and deepened under this bereavement, of which, she said to herself with a shudder, she was the cause. And this is the course of nature : there is nothing like suffering to enlighten the giddy brain, widen the narrow mind, improve the trivial heart.

As her regrets were tender and deep, so her vows of repentance were sincere. Oh, what a wife she would make when he came back ! how thoughtful ! how prudent ! how loyal ! and never have a secret. She who had once said, " What is the use of your writing ? nobody will publish it," now collected and perused every written scrap. With simple affection she even looked up his very waste-paper basket, full of fragments he had torn, or useless papers he had thrown there before he went to Plymouth.

In the drawer of his writing-table she found his diary. It was a thick quarto : it began with their marriage, and ended with his leaving home — for then he took another volume. This diary became her Bible : she studied it daily, till her tears hid his lines. The entries were very miscellaneous, very exact.

It was a map of their married life. But what she studied most was his observations on her own character, so scientific, yet so kindly; and his scholar-like and wise reflections. The book was an unconscious picture of a great mind she had hitherto but glanced at: now she saw it all plain before her; saw it, understood it, adored it, mourned it. Such women are shallow, not for want of a head upon their shoulders, but of *attention*. They do not really study any thing; they have been taught at their schools the bad art of skimming; but let their hearts compel their brains to think and think, the result is considerable. The deepest philosopher never fathomed a character more thoroughly than this poor child fathomed her husband when she had read his journal ten or eleven times, and bedewed it with a thousand tears.

One passage almost cut her more intelligent heart in twain:—

"This dark day I have done a thing incredible. I have spoken with brutal harshness to the innocent creature I have sworn to protect. She had run into debt, through inexperience, and that unhappy timidity which makes women conceal an error until it ramifies, by concealment, into a fault; and I must storm and rave at her till she actually fainted away. Brute! Ruffian! Monster? And she, how did she punish me, poor Lamb? By soft and tender words — like a lady, as she is. Oh, my sweet Rosa, I wish you could know how you are avenged! Talk of the scourge — the cat! I would be thankful for two dozen lashes. Ah! there is no need, I think, to punish a man who has been cruel to a woman. Let him alone. He will punish himself more than you can, if he really is a man."

From the date of that entry this self-reproach and self-torture kept cropping up every now and then in the diary; and it appeared to have been not entirely without its influence in sending Staines to sea, though the main reason he gave was that his Rosa might have the comforts and luxuries she had enjoyed before she married him.

One day, while she was crying over this diary, Uncle Philip called, but not to comfort her, I promise you. He burst on her, irate, to take her to task. He had returned, learned Christopher's departure, and settled the reason in his own mind. That uxorious fool was gone to sea, by a natural re-action; his eyes were open to his wife at last, and he was sick of her folly; so he had fled to distant climes, as who would not that could?

"*So*, ma'am," said he, "my nephew is gone to sea, I find — all in a hurry. Pray, may I ask what he has done that for?"

It was a very simple question, yet it did not elicit a very plain answer. She only stared at this abrupt inquisitor, and then cried piteously, "O Uncle Philip!" and burst out sobbing.

"Why, what is the matter?"

"You *will* hate me now. He is gone to make money for *me;* and I would rather have lived on a crust. Uncle, don't hate me. I'm a poor, bereaved, heart-broken creature, that repents."

"Repents! heigho! why, what have you been up to now, ma'am? No great harm, I'll be bound. Flirting a little — with some *fool* —eh?"

"Flirting! Me! a married woman!"

"Oh, to be sure! I forgot. Why, surely he has not deserted you."

"My Christopher desert me! He loves me too well; far more than I deserve, but not more than I will. Uncle Philip, I am too confused and wretched to tell you all that has happened; but I know you love him though you had a tiff. Uncle, he called on you, to shake hands and ask your forgiveness, poor fellow! He was so sorry you were away. Please read his diary: it will tell you all, better than his poor foolish wife can. I know it by heart. I'll show you where you and he quarrelled about me. There, see." And she showed him the passage with her finger. "He never told me it was that, or I would have come and begged your pardon on my knees. But see how sorry he was. There, see.

"And now I'll show you another place, where my Christopher speaks of your many, many acts of kindness. There, see. And now please let me show you how he longed for reconciliation. There, see. And it is the same through the book. And now I'll show you how grieved he was to go without your blessing. I told him I was sure you would give him that, and him going away. Ah, me! will he ever return? Uncle dear, don't hate me. You are his only relative; and what shall I do, now he is gone, if you disown me? Why, you are the only Staines left me to love."

"Disown you, ma'am! that I'll never do. You are a good-hearted young woman, I find. There, run and dry your eyes, and let me read Christopher's diary all through. Then I shall see how the land lies."

Rosa complied with this proposal; and left him alone while she bathed her eyes, and tried to compose herself, for she was all trembling at this sudden irruption.

When she returned to the drawing-room he was walking about looking grave and thoughtful.

"It is the old story," said he rather gently: "a *misunderstanding.* How. wise our ancestors were that first used that word to mean a quarrel! for look into twenty quarrels, and you shall detect a score of mis-under-standings. Yet our American cousins must go and substitute the unideaed word, 'difficulty;' that is wonderful. I had

no quarrel with him; delighted to see either of you. But I had called twice on him; so I thought he ought to get over his temper, and call on a tried friend like me. A misunderstanding! Now, my dear, let us have no more of these misunderstandings. You will always be welcome at my house; and I shall often come here; and look after you and your interests. What do you mean to do, I wonder?"

"Sir, I'm to go home to my father, if he will be troubled with me. I have written to him."

"And what is to become of the Bijou?"

"My Christie thought I should like to part with it and the furniture; but his own writing-desk and his chair, no, I never will; and his little clock. Oh! oh! oh! But I remember what you said about agents, and I don't know what to do; for I shall be away."

"Then leave it to me. I'll come and live here with one servant: and I'll soon sell it for you."

"You, Uncle Philip!"

"Well, why not?" said he roughly.

"That will be a great trouble and discomfort to you, I'm afraid."

"If I find it so, I'll soon drop it. I'm not the fool to put myself out for anybody. When you are ready to go out, send me word, and I'll come in."

Soon after this he bustled off. He gave her a hurried kiss at parting, as if he was ashamed of it, and wanted it over as quickly as possible.

Next day her father came, condoled with her politely, assured her there was nothing to cry about; husbands were a sort of functionaries that always went to sea at some part of their career, and no harm ever came of it. On the contrary, "Absence makes the heart grow fonder," said this judicious parent.

10*

This sentiment happened to be just a little too true, and set the daughter crying bitterly; but she fought against it. "Oh, no!" said she. "*I mustn't.* I will not be always crying in Kent Villa."

"Lord forbid!"

"I shall get over it in time—a little."

"Why, of course you will. But as to your coming to Kent Villa, I am afraid you would not be very comfortable there. You know, I am superannuated. Only get my pension now."

"I know that, papa; and—why, that is one of the reasons. I have a good income now; and I thought if we put our means together."

"Oh! that is a very different thing. You will want a carriage, I suppose. I have put mine down."

"No carriage, no horse, no footman, no luxury of any kind, till my Christie comes back. I abhor dress, I abhor expense; I detest every thing I once liked too well! I hate every folly that has parted us; and I hate myself worst of all. Oh! oh! oh! Forgive me for crying so."

"Well, I think you had better come at once. I dare say there are associations about this place that upset you. I shall go and make ready for you, dear; and then you can come as soon as you like."

He bestowed a paternal kiss on her brow, and glided doucely away before she could possibly cry again.

The very next week Rosa was at Kent Villa, with the relics of her husband about her: his chair, his writing-table, his clock, his waste-paper basket, a very deep and large one. She had them all in her bed-room at Kent Villa.

Here the days glided quietly but heavily. She derived some comfort from Uncle Philip. His rough friendly way was a tonic, and braced her. He called several times about the Bijou; told her he had put up enormous boards all over the house, and puffed it finely. "I have had a hundred agents at me," said he; "and the next thing, I hope, will be one customer; that is about the proportion." At last he wrote her he had hooked a victim, and sold the lease and furniture for nine hundred guineas. Staines had assigned the lease to Rosa, so she had full powers; and Philip invested the money, and two hundred more she gave him, in a little mortgage at six per cent.

Now came the letter from Madeira. It gave her new life. Christopher was well, contented, hopeful. His example should animate her. She would bravely bear the present, and share his hopes of the future. With these brighter views, nature co-operated. The instincts of approaching maternity brightened the future. She fell into gentle reveries, and saw her husband return, and saw herself place their infant in his arms with all a wife's, a mother's, pride.

In due course came another long letter from the equator, with a full journal, and more words of hope. Home in less than a year, with reputation increased by this last cure: home, to part no more.

Ah! what a changed wife he should find! how frugal, how candid, how full of appreciation, admiration, and love of the noblest, dearest husband that ever breathed!

Lady Cicely Treherne waited some weeks, to let kinder sentiments return. She then called in Dear Street, but found Mrs. Staines was gone to Gravesend. She wrote to her.

In a few days she received a reply, studiously polite and cold.

This persistent injustice mortified her at last. She said to herself, "Does she think his departure was no loss to *me?* It was to her interests, as well as his, I sacrificed my own selfish wishes. I will write to her no more."

This resolution she steadily maintained. It was shaken for a moment, when she heard, by a side wind, that Mrs. Staines was fast approaching the great pain and peril of women. Then she wavered. But no: she prayed for her by name in the liturgy, but she troubled her no more.

This state of things had lasted some six weeks, when she received a letter from her Cousin Tadcaster, close on the heels of his last, to which she had replied as I have indicated. She knew his handwriting, and opened it with a smile.

That smile soon died off her horror-stricken face. The letter ran thus : —

"TRISTAN D'ACUNHA, Jan. 5.

"DEAR CICELY, — A terrible thing has just happened. We signalled a raft, with a body on it ; and poor Dr. Staines leaned out of the port-hole, and fell overboard. Three boats were let down after him ; but it all went wrong somehow, or it was too late. They could never find him ; he was drowned ; and the funeral service was read for the poor fellow.

" We are all sadly cut up. Everybody loved him. It was dreadful, next day at dinner, when his chair was empty. The very sailors cried at not finding him.

"First of all, I thought I ought to write to his wife. I know where she lives ; it is called Kent Villa, Gravesend. But I was afraid : it might kill her ; and you are so good and sensible, I thought I had better write to you, and perhaps you could break it to her by degrees, before it gets in all the papers.

" I send this from the island, by a small vessel, and paid him ten pounds to take it.

"Your affectionate cousin,
"TADCASTER."

Words are powerless to describe a blow like this : the amazement, the stupor, the reluetance to believe, — the rising, swelling, surging horror. She sat like a woman of stone, crumpling the letter. " Dead ! dead ! "

For a long time this was all her mind could realize, — that Christopher Staines was dead. He who had been so full of life and thought and genius, and worthier to live than all the world, was dead ; and a million nobodies were still alive, and he was dead.

It revealed to her, in one withering flash, that she loved him. She loved him, and he was dead.

She lay back on the sofa, and all the power left her limbs. She could not move a hand.

But suddenly she started up ; for a noble instinct told her this blow must not fall on the wife as it had on her, and in her time of peril.

She had her bonnet on in a moment, and, for the first time in her life, darted out of the house without her maid. She flew along the streets, scarcely feeling the ground. She got to Dear Street, and obtained Philip Staines's address. She flew to it, and there learned he was down to Kent Villa. Instantly she telegraphed to her maid to come down to her at Gravesend, with things for a short visit, and wait for her at the station ; and she went down by train to Gravesend.

Hitherto she had walked on air, driven by one overpowering impulse. Now, as she sat in the train, she thought a little of herself. What was before her ? To break to Mrs. Staines that her husband was dead. To tell her all her misgivings were more than justified. To encounter her cold civility, and let her know, inch by inch, it must be exchanged for curses and tearing of hair : her husband was dead. To tell her this, and in the telling of it, perhaps reveal that it was *her* great bereavement, as well as the wife's; for she had a deeper affection for him than she ought.

Well, she trembled like an aspen-leaf — trembled like one in an ague, even as she sat; but she persevered.

A noble woman has her courage; not exactly the same as that which leads forlorn hopes against bastions bristling with rifles, and tongued with flames and thunderbolts, yet not inferior to it.

Tadcaster, small and dull, but noble by birth and instinct, had seen the right thing for her to do; and she of the same breed, and nobler far, had seen it too; and the great soul steadily drew the recoiling heart and quivering body to this fiery trial, this act of humanity, to do which was terrible and hard, to shirk it cowardly and cruel.

She reached Gravesend, and drove in a fly to Kent Villa.

The door was opened by a maid.

"Is Mrs. Staines at home?"

"Yes ma'am, she is *at home;* but"—

"Can I see her?"

"Why, no, ma'am: not at present."

"But I must see her. I am an old friend. Please take her my card. Lady Cicely Treherne."

The maid hesitated, and looked confused. "Perhaps you don't know, ma'am. Mrs. Staines, she is — the doctor have been in the house all day."

"Ah, the doctor! I believe Dr. Philip Staines is here."

"Why, that *is* the doctor, ma'am. Yes, he is here."

"Then pray let me see him — or no; I had better see Mr. Lusignan."

"Master have gone out for the day, ma'am; but, if you'll step in the drawing-room, I'll tell the doctor."

Lady Cicely waited in the drawing-room some time, heart-sick and trembling.

At last Doctor Philip came in, with her card in his hand, looking evidently a little cross at the interruption. "Now, madam, please tell me, as briefly as you can, what I can do for you."

"Are you Dr. Philip Staines?"

"I am, madam, at your service — for five minutes. Can't quit my patient long, just now."

"O sir, thank God I have found you! Be prepared for ill news — sad news — a terrible calamity — I can't speak. Read that, sir." And she handed him Tadcaster's note.

He took it and read it.

He buried his face in his hands.

"Christopher! my poor, poor boy!" he groaned. But suddenly a terrible anxiety seized him. "Who knows of this!" he asked.

"Only myself, sir. I came here to break it to her."

"You are a good, kind lady, for being so thoughtful. Madam, if this gets to my niece's ears it will kill her, as sure as we stand here."

"Then let us keep it from her. Command me, sir. I will do any thing. I will live here — take the letters in — the journals — any thing."

"No, no; you have done your part, and God bless you for it. I must stay here. Your ladyship's very presence, and your agitation, would set the servants talking, and some idiot-fiend among them babbling; there is nothing so terrible as a fool."

"May I stay at the inn, sir, just one night?"

"Oh, yes, I wish you would! and I will run over, if all is well with her — well with her? poor unfortunate girl!"

Lady Cicely saw he wished her gone, and she went directly.

At nine o'clock that same evening, as she lay on a sofa in the best room of the inn, attended by her maid, Dr. Philip Staines came to her. She dismissed her maid.

Dr. Philip was too old — in other words, had lost too many friends — to he really broken down by a bereavement; but he was strangely subdued. The loud tones were out of him, and the loud laugh, and even the keen sneer. Yet he was the same man, but with a gentler surface; and this was not without its pathos.

"Well, madam," said he gravely and quietly, "it is as it always has been. 'As is the race of leaves, so that of man.' When one falls, another comes. Here's a little Christopher come, in place of him that is gone — a brave, beautiful boy, ma'am; the finest but one I ever brought into the world. He is come to take his father's place in our hearts, — I see you valued his poor father, ma'am, — but he comes too late for me. At your age, ma'am, friendships come naturally; they spring like loves in the soft heart of youth : at seventy, the gate is not so open; the soil is more sterile. I shall never care for another Christopher; never see another grow to man's estate."

"The mother, sir," sobbed Lady Cicely : "the poor mother ? "

"Like them all, poor creature! in heaven, madam; in heaven. New life! new existence! a new character. All the pride, glory, rapture, and amazement of maternity — thanks to her ignorance, which we must prolong, or I would not give one straw for her life, or her son's. I shall never leave the house till she does know it, and, come when it may, I dread the hour. She is not framed by nature to bear so deadly a shock."

"Her father, sir, — would he not be the best person to break it to her ? He was out to-day "

"Her father, ma'am ? I shall get no help from him. He is one of those soft, gentle creatures that come into the world with what your canting fools call a mission; and his mission is to take care of number one. Not dishonestly, mind you, nor violently, nor rudely, but doucely and calmly. The care a brute like me takes of his vitals, that care Lusignan takes of his outer cuticle. His number one is a sensitive plant. No scenes, no noise : nothing painful — by the by, the little creature that writes in the papers, and calls calamities *painful*, is of Lusignan's breed. Out to-day! of course he was out, ma'am : he knew from me his daughter would be in peril all day, so he visited a friend. He knew his own tenderness, and evaded paternal sensibilities : a self-defender. I count on no help from that charming man."

"A man! I call such men weptiles!" said Lady Cicely, her ghastly cheek coloring for a moment.

"Then you give them false importance."

In the course of this interview, Lady Cicely accused herself sadly of having interfered between man and wife, and, with the best intentions, brought about this cruel calamity. "Judge, then, sir," said she, "how grateful I am to you for undertaking this cruel task. I was her school-fellow, sir, and I love her dearly; but she has turned against me, and now, oh, with what horror she will regard me!"

"Madam," said the doctor, "there is nothing more mean and unjust than to judge others by events that none could foresee. Your conscience is clear. You did your best for my poor niece : she has many virtues, but justice is one you must not look for in that quarter. Justice requires brains. It's a virtue the heart does not deal in. You must be content with your own good conscience, and an old man's esteem. You did all for the best; and this very day you have done a good kind action. God bless you for it!

Then he left her; and next day she went sadly home, and for many a long day the hollow world saw nothing of Cicely Treherne.

When Mr. Lusignan came home that night, Dr. Philip told him the miserable story, and his fears. He received it not as Philip had expected. The bachelor had counted without his dormant paternity. He was terror-stricken — abject — fell into a chair, and wrung his hands, and wept piteously. To keep it from his daughter till she should be stronger seemed to him chimerical, impossible. However, Philip insisted it must be done; and he must make some excuse for keeping out of her way, or his manner would rouse her suspicions. He consented readily to that, and, indeed, left all to Dr. Philip.

Dr. Philip trusted nobody, not even his own confidential servant. He allowed no journal to come into the house without passing through his hands; and he read them all before he would let any other soul in the house see them. He asked Rosa to let him be her secretary, and open her letters, giving as a pretext that it would be as well she should have no small worries or trouble just now.

"Why," said she, "I was never so well able to bear them. It must be a great thing to put me out now. I am so happy, and live in the future. Well, dear uncle, you can if you like — what does it matter? — only there must be one exception: my own Christie's letters, you know."

"Of course," said he wincing inwardly.

The very next day came a letter of condolence from Miss Lucas. Dr. Philip intercepted it, and locked it up, to be shown her at a more fitting time.

But how could he hope to keep so public a thing as this from entering the house in one of a hundred newspapers?

He went into Gravesend, and searched all the newspapers, to see what he had to contend with. To his horror, he found it in several dailies and weeklies, and in two illustrated papers. He sat aghast at the difficulty and the danger.

The best thing he could think of was to buy them all, and cut out the account. He did so, and brought all the papers, thus mutilated, into the house, and sent them into the kitchen. He said to his old servant, "These may amuse Mr. Lusignan's people, and I have extracted all that interests me."

By these means he hoped that none of the servants would go and buy any more of these same papers elsewhere.

Notwithstanding these precautions, he took the nurse apart, and said, " Now, you are an experienced woman, and to be trusted about an excitable patient. Mind, I object to any female servant entering Mrs. Staines's room with gossip. Keep them outside the door for the present, please. Oh! and nurse, if any thing should happen likely to grieve or worry her, it must be kept from her entirely: can I trust you?"

"You may, sir."

"I shall add ten guineas to your fee if she gets through the month without a shock or disturbance of any kind."

She stared at him inquiringly. Then she said, —

"You may rely on me, doctor."

"I feel I may. Still, she alarms me. She looks quiet now, but she is very excitable."

Not all these precautions gave Dr. Philip any real sense of security; still less did they to Mr. Lusignan. He was not a tender father, in small things; but the idea of actual danger to his only child was terrible to him; and he now passed his life in a continual tremble.

This is the less to be wondered at when I tell you that even the stout Philip began to lose his nerve, his appetite, his sleep, under this hourly terror and this hourly torture.

Well did the great imagination

of antiquity feign a torment too great for the mind long to endure, in the sword of Damocles suspended by a single hair over his head. Here the sword hung over an innocent creature, who smiled beneath it fearless; but these two old men must sit and watch the sword, and ask themselves how long before that subtle salvation shall snap.

"Ill news travel fast," says the proverb. "The birds of the air shall carry the matter," says Holy Writ; and it is so. No bolts nor bars, no promises nor precautions, can long shut out a great calamity from the ears it is to blast, the heart it is to wither. The very air seems full of it, until it falls.

Rosa's child was more than a fortnight old, and she was looking more beautiful than ever, as is often the case with a very young mother, and Dr. Philip complimented her on her looks. "Now," said he, "you reap the advantage of being good and obedient, and keeping quiet. In another ten days or so, I may take you to the sea-side for a week. I have the honor to inform you that from about the fourth to the tenth of March there is always a week of fine weather, which takes everybody by surprise except me. It does not astonish me, because I observe it is invariable. Now, what would you say if I gave you a week at Herne Bay, to set you up altogether?"

"As you please, dear uncle," said Mrs. Staines, with a sweet smile. "I shall be very happy to go or to stay. I shall be happy everywhere with my darling boy and the thought of my husband. Why, I count the days till he shall come back to me. No, to us — to us, my pet. How dare a naughty mammy say 'to me,' as if 'me' was half the "portance of oo, a precious pets."

Dr. Philip was surprised into a sigh.

"What is the matter, dear?" said Rosa very quickly.

"The matter?"

"Yes, dear, the matter. You sighed — you, the laughing philosopher."

"Did I?" said he, to gain time. "Perhaps I remembered the uncertainty of human life, and of all mortal hopes. The old will have their thoughts, my dear. They have seen so much trouble."

"But, uncle dear, he is a very healthy child."

"Very."

"And you told me yourself carelessness was the cause so many children die."

"That is true."

She gave him a curious and rather searching look; then, leaning over her boy, said, "Mammy's not afraid. Beautiful Pet was not born to die directly. He will never leave his mamma. No, uncle, he never can. For my life is bound in his and his dear father's. It is a triple cord: one go, go all."

She said this with a quiet resolution that chilled Uncle Philip.

At this moment the nurse, who had been bending so pertinaciously over some work that her eyes were invisible, looked quickly up, cast a furtive glance at Mrs. Staines, and, finding she was employed for the moment, made an agitated signal to Dr. Philip. All she did was to clinch her two hands and lift them half-way to her face, and then cast a frightened look toward the door; but Philip's senses were so sharpened by constant alarm and watching that he saw at once something serious was the matter. But, as he asked himself what he should do in case of some sudden alarm, he merely gave a nod of intelligence to the nurse, scarcely perceptible, then rose quietly from his seat, and went to the window. "Snow coming, I think," said he. "For all that, we shall have the March summer in ten days. You mark my words." He then went leisurely out of the room. At the door he turned, and, with, all the cunning he was master of, said, "Oh! by the by, come to my room, nurse, when you are at leisure."

"Yes, doctor," said the nurse, but never moved. She was too bent on hiding the agitation she really felt.

"Had you not better go to him, nurse?"

"Perhaps I had, madam."

She rose with feigned indifference, and left the room. She walked leisurely down the passage, then casting a hasty glance behind her, for fear Mrs. Staines should be watching her, burst into the doctor's room. They met at once in the middle of the room; and Mrs. Briscoe burst out, "Sir, it is known all over the house!"

"Heaven forbid! What is known?"

"What you would give the whole world to keep from her. Why, sir, the moment you cautioned me, of course I saw there was trouble; but little I thought—sir, not a servant in the kitchen or the stable but knows that her husband — poor thing! poor thing! Ah! there goes the house-maid — to have a look at her."

"Stop her!"

Mrs. Briscoe had not waited for this; she rushed after the woman, and told her Mrs. Staines was sleeping, and the room must not be entered on any account.

"Oh, very well!" said the maid rather sullenly.

Mrs. Briscoe saw her return to the kitchen, and came back to Dr. Staines: he was pacing the room in torments of anxiety.　　.

"Doctor," said she, "it is the old story: 'Servants' friends, the master's enemies.' An old servant came here to gossip with her friend the cook (she never could abide her while they were together, by all accounts), and told her the whole story of his being drowned at sea."

Dr. Philip groaned. "Cursed chatterbox!" said he. "What is to be done? Must we break it to her now? Oh, if I could only buy a few days more! The heart to be crushed while the body is weak! It is too cruel. Advise me, Mrs. Briscoe. You are an experienced woman, and I think you are a kind-hearted woman."

"Well, sir," said Mrs. Briscoe, "I had the name of it when I was younger, before Briscoe failed, and I took to nursing; which nursing hardens, sir, by use, and along of the patients themselves; for sick folk are lumps of selfishness: we see more of them than you do, sir. But this I *will* say, 'tisn't selfishness that lies now in that room, waiting for the blow that will bring her to death's door, I'm afraid, but a sweet, gentle, thoughtful creature, as ever supped sorrow: for I don't know how 'tis doctor, nor why 'tis, but an angel like that has always to sup sorrow."

"But you do not advise me," said the doctor, in agitation, "and something must be done."

"Advise you, sir! it is not for me to do that. I am sure I'm at my wits' end, poor thing! Well, sir, I don't see what you can do but try and break it to her. Better so than let it come to her like a clap of thunder. But I think, sir, I'd have a wet-nurse ready before I said much; for she is very quick, and ten too one but the first word of such a thing turns her blood to gall. Sir, I once knew a poor woman — she was a carpenter's wife — a-nursing her child, in the afternoon; and in runs a foolish woman, and tells her he was killed dead, off a scaffold. 'Twas the man's sister told her. Well, sir, she was knocked stupid like; and she sat staring, and nursing of her child, before she could take it in rightly. The child was dead before supper-time, and the woman was not long after. The whole family was swept away;

sir, in a few hours, and I mind the table was not cleared he had dined on when they came to lay them out. Well-a-day, nurses see sorrow!"

"We all see sorrow that live long, Mrs. Briscoe. I am heart-broken myself; I am desperate. You are a good soul, and I'll tell you. When my nephew married this poor girl I was very angry with him, and I soon found she was not fit to be a struggling man's wife, and then I was very angry with her. She had spoiled a first-rate physician, I thought. But since I knew her better it is all changed, she is so lovable. How I shall ever tell her this terrible thing, God knows. All I know is, that I will not throw a chance away. Her body *shall* be stronger before I break her heart. Cursed idiots, that could not save a single man with their boats in a calm sea! Lord forgive me for blaming people when I was not there to see! I say I will give her every chance. She shall not know it till she is stronger — no, not if I live at her door, and sleep there, and all. Good God! inspire me with something. There is always something to be done, if one could but see it."

Mrs. Briscoe sighed and said, "Sir, I think any thing is better than for her to hear it from a servant; and they are sure to blurt it out. Young women are such fools."

"No, no: I see what it is," said Dr. Philip. "I have gone all wrong from the first. I have been acting like a woman, when I should have acted like a man. Why, I only trusted *you* by halves. There was a fool for you. Never trust people by halves."

"That is true, sir."

"Well, then, now I shall go at it like a man. I have a vile opinion of servants, but no matter. I'll try them: they are human, I suppose. I'll hit them between the eyes like a man. Go to the kitchen,

Mrs. Briscoe, and tell them I wish to speak to all the servants, in-doors or out."

"Yes, sir."

She stopped at the door, and said, "I had better get back to her as soon as I have told them."

"Certainly."

"And what shall I tell her, sir? Her first word will be to ask me what you wanted me for. I saw that in her eye. She was curious: that is why she sent me after you so quick."

Doctor Philip groaned. He felt he was walking among pitfalls. He rapidly flavored some distilled water with orange-flower, then tinted it a beautiful pink, and bottled it. "There," said he: "I was mixing a new medicine. Table-spoon four times a day: had to filter it. Any lie you like."

Mrs. Briscoe went to the kitchen and gave her message, then went to Mrs. Staines with the mixture. Dr. Philip went down to the kitchen, and spoke to the servants very solemnly. He said, "My good friends, I am come to ask your help in a matter of life and death. There is a poor young woman up stairs: she is a widow, and does not know it, and must not know it yet. If the blow fell now, I think it would kill her: indeed, if she hears it all of a sudden at any time, that might destroy her. We are in so sore a strait that a feather may turn the scale. So we must try all we can to gain a little time, and then trust to God's mercy after all. Well, now what do you say? Will you help me keep it from her till the tenth of March, say? and then I will break it to her by degrees. Forget she is your mistress. Master and servant, that is all very well at a proper time; but this is the time to remember nothing but that we are all one flesh and blood. We lie down together in the church-yard, and we hope to rise together where there will be no master and servant. Think of the poor unfortunate creature as your own flesh and blood, and tell me, will you help me try and save her under this terrible blow ? "

" Ay, doctor, that we will," said the footman. " Only you give us our orders, and you will see."

" I have no right to give you orders; but I entreat you not to show her, by word or look, that calamity is upon her. Alas! it is only a reprieve you can give to her and to me. The bitter hour *must* come when I must tell her she is a widow, and her boy an orphan. When that day comes, I will ask you all to pray for me that I may find words. But now I ask you to give me that ten days' reprieve. Let the poor creature recover a little strength before the thunder-bolt of affliction falls on her head. Will you promise me ? "

They promised heartily; and more than one of the women began to cry.

" A general assent will not satisfy me," said Dr. Philip. " I want every man and every woman to give me a hand upon it; then I shall feel sure of you."

The men gave him their hands at once. The women wiped their hands with their aprons, to make sure they were clean, and gave him their hands too. The cook said, " If any one of us goes from it, this kitchen will be too hot to hold her."

" Nobody will go from it, cook," said the doctor. " I'm not afraid of that; and now, since you have promised me, out of your own good hearts, I'll try and be even with you. If she knows nothing of it by the tenth of March, five guineas to every man and woman in this kitchen. You shall see, that, if you can be kind, we can be grateful."

He then hurried away. He found Mr. Lusignan in the drawing-room, and told him all this.

Lusignan was fluttered, but grateful. " Ah, my good friend," said he, " this is a hard trial to two old men like you and me."

" It is," said Philip. " It has shown me my age. I declare I am trembling, — I, whose nerves were iron. But I have a particular contempt for servants. Mercenary wretches! I think Heaven inspired me to talk to them. After all, who knows ? perhaps we might find a way to their hearts, if we did not eternally shock their vanity, and forget that it is, and must be, far greater than our own. The women gave me their tears, and the men were earnest. Not one hand lay cold in mine. As for your kitchen-maid, I'd trust my life to that girl What a grip she gave me ! What strength ! What fidelity was in it ! My hand was never *grasped* before. I think we are safe for a few days more."

Lusignan sighed. " What does it all come to ? We are pulling the trigger gently, that is all."

" No, no ; that is not it. Don't let us confound the matter with similes, please. Keep them for children."

Mrs. Staines left her bed, and would have left her room, but Dr. Philip forbade her strictly.

One day, seated in her arm-chair, she said to the nurse, before Dr. Philip, " Nurse, why do the servants look so curiously at me ? "

Mrs. Briscoe cast a hasty glance at Dr. Philip, and then said, " I don't know, madam. I never noticed that."

" Uncle, why did nurse look at you before she answered such a simple question ? "

" I don't know. What question ? "

" About the servants."

" Oh, about the servants ! " said he contemptuously.

" You should not turn up your nose at them, for they are all most kind and attentive. Only I catch them looking at me so strangely; really — as if they" —

"Rosa, you are taking me quite out of my depth. The looks of servant-girls! Why, of course a lady in your condition is an object of especial interest to them. I dare say they are saying to one another, 'I wonder when my turn will come?' A fellow-feeling makes us wondrous kind; that is a proverb, is it not?"

"To be sure. I forgot that."

She said no more, but seemed thoughtful, and not quite satisfied.

On this, Dr. Philip begged the maids to go near her as little as possible. "You are not aware of it," said he; "but your looks and your manner of speaking rouse her attention; and she is quicker than I thought she was, and observes very subtlely."

This was done; and then she complained that nobody came near her. She insisted on coming down stairs: it was so dull.

Dr. Philip consented, if she would be content to receive no visits for a week."

She assented to that; and now passed some hours every day in the drawing-room. In her morning wrappers, so fresh and crisp, she looked lovely, and increased in health and strength every day.

Dr. Philip used to look at her, and his very flesh to creep at the thought, that, ere long, he must hurl this fair creature into the dust of affliction; must, with a word, take the ruby from her lips, the rose from her cheeks, the sparkle from her glorious eyes, — eyes that beamed on him with sweet affection, and a mouth that never opened but to show some simplicity of the mind or some pretty burst of the sensitive heart.

He put off, and put off; and at last cowardice began to whisper, "Why tell her the whole truth at all? Why not take her through stages of doubt, alarm, and, after all, leave a grain of hope till her child gets so rooted in her heart that" — But conscience and good sense interrupted this temporary thought, and made him see to what a horrible life of suspense he should condemn a human creature, and live a perpetual lie, and be always at the edge of some pitfall or other.

One day, while he sat looking at her, with all these thoughts, and many more, coursing through his mind, she looked up at him, and surprised him. "Ah!" said she gravely.

"What is the matter, my dear?"

"Oh, nothing!" said she cunningly.

"Uncle dear," said she presently, "when do we go to Herne Bay?"

Now, Dr. Philip had given that up. He had got the servants at Kent Villa on his side, and he felt safer here than in any strange place; so he said, "I don't know: that all depends. There is plenty of time."

"No, uncle," said Rosa gravely. "I wish to leave this house. I can hardly breath in it."

"What! your native air?"

"Mystery is not my native air, and this house is full of mystery. Voices whisper at my door, and the people don't come in. The maids cast strange glances at me, and hurry away. I scolded that pert girl, Jane, and she answered me as mad as Moses. I catch you looking at me, with love, and something else. What is that something? It is pity: that is what it is. Do you think, because I am called a simpleton, that I have no eyes, nor ears, nor sense? What is this secret which you are all hiding from one person, and that is me? Ah! Christopher has not written this five weeks. Tell me the truth, for I will know it," and she started up in wild excitement.

Then Dr. Philip saw the hour was come.

He said, "My poor girl, you have read us aright. I am anxious about Christopher, and all the servants know it."

"Anxious, and not tell *me* — his wife — the woman whose life is bound up in his!"

"Was it for us to retard your convalescence, and set you fretting, and perhaps destroy your child? Rosa, my darling, think what a treasure Heaven has sent you, to love and care for."

"Yes," said she, trembling, "Heaven has been good to me; I hope Heaven will always be as good to me. I don't deserve it; but I tell God so. I am very grateful, and very penitent. I never forget that if I had been a good wife, my husband — five weeks is a long time. Why do you tremble so? Why are you so pale — a strong man like you? Calamity! calamity!"

Dr. Philip hung his head.

She looked at him, started wildly up, then sank back into her chair. So the stricken deer leaps, then falls. Yet even now she put on a deceitful calm, and said, "Tell me the truth. I have a right to know."

He stammered out, "There is a report of an accident at sea."

She kept silence.

"Of a passenger drowned — out of that ship. This, coupled with his silence, fills our hearts with fear."

"It is worse — you are breaking it to me — you have gone too far to stop. One word, is he alive? Oh, say he is alive!"

Philip rang the bell hard, and said, in a troubled voice, "Rosa, think of your child."

"Not when my husband — is he alive, or dead?"

"It is hard to say, with such a terrible report about, and no letters," faltered the old man, his courage failing him.

"What are you afraid of? Do you think I can't die, and go to him? Alive, or dead?" and she stood before him, raging and quivering in every limb.

The nurse came in.

"Fetch her child," he cried. "God have mercy on her!"

"Ah, then, he is dead," said she, with stony calmness. "I drove him to sea, and he is dead."

The nurse rushed in, and held the child to her.

She would not look at it.

"Dead!"

"Yes, our poor Christie is gone; but his child is here, the image of him. Do not forget the mother. Have pity on his child and yours."

"Take it out of my sight!" she screamed. "Away with it, or I shall murder it, as I have murdered its father. My dear Christie, before all that live! I have killed him. I shall die for him. I shall go to him." She raved and tore her hair. Servants rushed in. Rosa was carried to her bed, screaming and raving, and her black hair all down on both sides, a piteous sight.

Swoon followed swoon; and that very night, brain-fever set in with all its sad accompaniments. A poor bereaved creature, tossing and moaning; pale, anxious, but resolute faces of the nurse and the kitchen-maid watching; on one table a pail of ice, and on another, alas! the long, thick, raven hair of our poor simpleton, lying on clean silver paper. Dr. Philip had cut it all off with his own hand; and he was now folding it up, and crying over it; for he thought to himself, "Perhaps in a few days more, only this will be left of her on earth."

CHAPTER XIV.

STAINES fell head-foremost into the sea with a heavy plunge. Being an excellent swimmer, he struck out the moment he touched the water; and that arrested his dive, and brought him up with a slant, shocked and panting, drenched and confused. The next moment he saw, as through a fog — his eyes being full of water — something fall from the ship. He breasted the big waves, and swam toward it: it rose on the top of a wave, and he saw it was a life-buoy. Encumbered with wet clothes, he seemed impotent in the big waves; they threw him up so high, and down so low.

Almost exhausted, he got to the life-buoy, and clutched it with a fierce grasp and a wild cry of delight. He got it over his head, and, placing his arms round the buoyant circle, stood with his breast and head out of water, gasping.

He now drew a long breath, and got his wet hair out of his eyes, already smarting with salt-water, and, raising himself on the buoy, looked out for help.

He saw, to his great concern, the ship already at a distance. She seemed to have flown; and she was still drifting fast away from him.

He saw no signs of help. His heart began to turn as cold as his drenched body. A horrible fear crossed him.

But presently he saw the weather-boat filled, and fall into the water; and then a wave rolled between him and the ship, and he only saw her topmast.

The next time he rose on a mighty wave, he saw the boats together astern of the vessel, but not coming his way; and the gloom was thickening, the ship becoming indistinct, and all was doubt and horror.

A life of agony passed in a few minutes.

He rose and fell like a cork on the buoyant waves, — rose and fell, and saw nothing but the ship's lights, now terribly distant.

But at last, as he rose and fell, he caught a few fitful glimpses of a smaller light rising and falling like himself. "A boat!" he cried, and, raising himself as high as he could, shouted, cried, implored, for help. He stretched his hands across the water. "This way, this way!"

The light kept moving; but it came no nearer. They had greatly underrated the drift. The other boat had no light.

Minutes passed of suspense, hope, doubt, dismay, terror. Those minutes seemed hours.

In the agony of suspense the quaking heart sent beads of sweat to the brow, though the body was immersed

And the gloom deepened, and the cold waves flung him up to heaven with their giant arms, and then down again to hell; and still that light, his only hope, was several hundred yards from him.

Only for a moment at a time could his eyeballs, straining with agony, catch this will-o'-the-wisp, — the boat's light. It groped the sea up and down, but came no nearer.

When what seemed days of agony had passed, suddenly a rocket rose in the horizon: so it seemed to him.

The lost man gave a shriek of joy; so prone are we to interpret things hopefully.

Misery! The next time he saw that little light, that solitary spark of hope, it was not quite so near as before. A mortal sickness fell on his heart. The ship had recalled the boats by rocket.

He shrieked, he cried, he screamed, he raved, "O Rosa, Rosa! for her sake, men, men, do not leave me. I am here, here!"

In vain. The miserable man saw the boat's little light retire, recede, and melt into the ship's larger light; and that light glided away.

Then a cold, deadly stupor fell on him. Then Death's icy claw seized his heart, and seemed to run from it to every part of him. He was a dead man. Only a question of time. Nothing to gain by floating.

But the despairing mind could not quit the world in peace; and even here in the cold, cruel sea the quivering body clung to this fragment of life, and winced at Death's touch, though more merciful.

He despised this weakness; he raged at it; he could not overcome it.

Unable to live or to die, condemned to float slowly, hour by hour, down into Death's jaws.

To a long, death-like stupor succeeded frenzy. Fury seized this great and long-suffering mind. It rose against the cruelty and injustice of his fate. He cursed the world, whose stupidity had driven him to sea; he cursed remorseless nature; and at last he railed on the God who made him, and made the cruel water that was waiting for his body. "God's justice! God's mercy! God's power! they are all lies," he shouted, "dreams, chimeras, like him, the all-powerful and good, men babble of by the fire. If there was a God more powerful than the sea, and only half as good as men are, he would pity my poor Rosa and me, and send a hurricane to drive those caitiffs back to the wretch they have abandoned. Nature alone is mighty. Oh! if I could have her on my side, and only God against me! But she is as deaf to prayer as he is, as mechanical and remorseless. I am a bubble melting into the sea. Soul I have none: my body will soon be nothing, nothing. So ends an honest, loving life. I always tried to love my fellow-creatures. Curse them! curse them! Curse the earth! Curse the sea! Curse all nature! there is no other God for me to curse."

The moon came out.

He raised his head and staring eyeballs, and cursed her.

The wind began to whistle, and flung spray in his face.

He raised his fallen head and staring eyeballs, and cursed the wind.

While he was thus raving, he became sensible of a black object to windward.

It looked like a rail, and a man leaning on it.

He stared; he cleared the wet hair from his eyes, and stared again.

The thing being larger than himself, and partly out of water, was drifting to leeward faster than himself.

He stared and trembled; and at last it came nearly abreast, black, black.

He gave a loud cry, and tried to swim toward it; but, encumbered with his life-buoy, he made little progress. The thing drifted abreast of him but ten yards distant.

As they each rose high upon the waves, he saw it plainly.

It was the very raft that had been the innocent cause of his sad fate.

He shouted with hope, he swam, he struggled; he got near it, but not to it; it drifted past, and he lost his chance of intercepting it. He struggled after it. The life-buoy would not let him catch it.

Then he gave a cry of agony, rage, despair, and flung off the life-buoy, and risked all on this one chance.

He gains a little on the raft.

He loses.

He gains. He cries, "Rosa, Rosa!" and struggles with all his soul, as well as his body: he gains.

But, when almost within reach, a wave half drowns him, and he loses.

He cries, "Rosa, Rosa!" and swims high and strong. "Rosa, Rosa, Rosa!"

He is near it. He cries, "Rosa, Rosa!" and, with all the energy of love and life, flings himself almost out of the water, and catches hold of the nearest thing on the raft.

It was the dead man's leg.

It seemed as if it would come away in his grasp. He dared not try to pull himself up by that. But he held on by it, panting, exhausting, faint.

This faintness terrified him. "Oh," thought he, "if I faint now, all is over."

Holding by that terrible and strange support, he made a grasp, and caught hold of the wood-work at the bottom of the rail. He tried to draw himself up. Impossible.

He was no better off than with his life-buoy.

But in situations so dreadful men think fast. He worked gradually round the bottom of the raft by his hands, till he got to leeward, still holding on. There he found a solid block of wood at the edge of the raft. He pried himself carefully up: the raft in that part then sank a little. He got his knee upon the timber of the raft, and, with a wild cry, seized the nearest upright, and threw both arms round it, and clung tight. Then first he found breath to speak. "THANK GOD!" he cried, kneeling on the timber, and grasping the upright post, — "OH, THANK GOD, THANK GOD!"

----•----

CHAPTER XV.

"THANK God?" why, according to his theory, it should have been "Thank Nature." But I observe, that, in such cases, even philosophers are ungrateful to the mistress they worship.

Our philosopher not only thanked God, but, being on his knees, prayed forgiveness for his late ravings, — prayed hard, with one arm curled round the upright, lest the sea, which ever and anon rushed over the bottom of the raft, should swallow him up in a moment.

Then he rose carefully, and wedged himself into the corner of the raft opposite to that other figure, ominous relic of the wild voyage the new-comer had entered upon. He put both arms over the rail, and stood erect.

The moon was now up; but so was the breeze. Fleecy clouds flew with vast rapidity across her bright face, and it was by fitful though vivid glances Staines examined the raft and his companion.

The raft was large, and well made of timbers tied and nailed together; and a strong rail ran round it resting on several uprights. There were also some blocks of a very light wood screwed to the horizontal timbers; and these made it float high.

But what arrested and fascinated the man's gaze was his dead companion, — sole survivor, doubtless, of a horrible voyage; since the raft was not made for one, nor by one.

It was a skeleton, or nearly, whose clothes the sea-birds had torn, and pecked every limb in all the fleshy parts: the rest of the body had dried to dark leather on the bones. The head was little more than an eyeless skull; but, in the fitful moonlight, those huge hollow caverns seemed gigantic lamp-like eyes, and glared at him fiendishly, appallingly.

He sickened at the sight. He tried not to look at it; but it would be looked at, and threaten him in the moonlight with great lack-lustre eyes.

The wind whistled, and lashed his face with spray torn off the big waves; and the water was nearly always up to his knees; and the raft tossed so wildly, it was all he could do to hold on in his corner. In which struggle still those monstrous lack-lustre eyes, like lamps of death, glared at him in the moon, and all else dark, except the fiery crests of the black mountain billows, tumbling and raging all around.

What a night!

But before morning the breeze sank, the moon set, and a sombre quiet succeeded, with only that grim figure in outline dimly visible. Owing to the motion still retained by the waves, it seemed to nod and rear, and be ever preparing to rush upon him.

The sun rose glorious on a lovely scene; the sky was a very mosaic of colors sweet and vivid, and the tranquil, rippling sea, peach-colored to the horizon, with lines of diamonds where the myriad ripples broke into smiles.

Staines was asleep, exhausted. Soon the light awoke him, and he looked up. What an incongruous picture met his eye!—that Heaven of color all above and around, and right before him, like a devil stuck in mid-heaven, that grinning corpse, whose fate foreshadowed his own.

But daylight is a great strengthener of the nerves. The figure no longer appalled him, a man who had long learned to look with Science's calm eye upon the dead. When the sea became like glass, and from peach-color deepened to rose, he walked along the raft, and inspected the dead man. He found it was a man of color, but not a black. The body was not kept, in its place, as he had supposed, merely by being jammed into the angle caused by the rail: it was also lashed to the corner upright by a long, stout belt. Staines concluded this had kept the body there, and its companions had been swept away.

This was not lost on him. He removed the belt for his own use: he then found it was not only a belt, but a receptacle. It was nearly full of small hard substances that felt like stones.

When he had taken it off the body, he felt a compunction. "Ought he to rob the dead, and expose it to be swept into the sea at the first wave, like a dead dog?"

He was about to replace the belt, when a middle course occurred to him. He was a man who always carried certain useful little things about him; viz., needles, thread, scissors, and string. He took a piece of string, and easily secured this poor light skeleton to the raft. The belt he strapped to the rail, and kept for his own need.

And now hunger gnawed him. No food was near. There was nothing but the lovely sea and sky, mosaic with color, and that grim, ominous skeleton.

Hunger comes and goes many times before it becomes insupportable. All that day and night, and the next day, he suffered its pangs; and then it became torture, but the thirst maddening.

Toward night fell a gentle rain. He spread a handkerchief and caught it. He sucked the handkerchief.

This revived him, and even allayed in some degree the pangs of hunger.

Next day was cloudless. A hot sun glared on his unprotected head, and battered down his enfeebled frame.

He resisted as well as he could. He often dipped his head, and as often the persistent sun, with cruel glare, made it smoke again.

Next day the same; but the strength to meet it was waning. He lay down and thought of Rosa, and wept bitterly. He took the dead man's belt, and lashed himself to the upright. That act, and his tears for his beloved, were almost his last acts of perfect reason; for next day came the delusions and the dreams that succeed when hunger ceases to torture, and the vital powers begin to ebb. He lay and saw pleasant meadows, with meandering streams, and clusters of rich fruit that courted the hand, and melted in the mouth.

Ever and anon they vanished, and he saw grim Death looking down on him with those big cavernous eyes.

By and by—whether his body's eye saw the grim skeleton, or his mind's eye the juicy fruits, green meadows, and pearly brooks — all was shadowy.

So in a placid calm, beneath a blue sky, the raft drifted dead, with its dead freight, upon the glassy purple; and he drifted, too, toward the world unknown.

There came across the waters to that dismal raft a thing none too common by sea or land, — a good man.

He was tall, stalwart, bronzed, and had hair like snow, before his time; for he had known trouble. He commanded a merchant steamer bound for Calcutta, on the old route.

The man at the mast-head descried a floating wreck, and hailed the deck accordingly. The captain altered his course without one moment's hesitation, and brought up alongside, lowered a boat, and brought the dead and the breathing man on board.

A young middy lifted Staines in his arms from the wreck to the boat. He whose person I described in Chapter I. weighed now no more than that.

Men are not always rougher than women. Their strength and nerve enable them now and then to be gentler than butter-fingered angels, who drop frail things through sensitive agitation, and break them. These rough men saw Staines was hovering between life and death, and they handled him like a thing the ebbing life might be shaken out of in a moment. It was pretty to see how gingerly the sailors carried the sinking man up the ladder; and one fetched swabs, and the others laid him down softly on them at their captain's feet.

"Well done, men!" said he. "Poor fellow! Pray Heaven we may not have come too late. Now stand aloof a bit. Send the surgeon aft."

The surgeon came, and looked, and felt the heart. He shook his head, and called for brandy. He had Staines's head raised, and got half a spoonful of diluted brandy down his throat. But there was an ominous gurgling.

After several such attempts at intervals, he said plainly the man's life could not be saved by ordinary means.

"Then try extraordinary," said the captain. "My orders are that he is to be saved. There is life in him. You have only got to keep it there. He *must* be saved; he *shall* be saved."

"I should like to try Dr. Staines's remedy," said the surgeon.

"Try it, then: what is it?"

"A bath of beef-tea. Dr. Staines says he applied it to a starved child — in the *Lancet.*"

"Take a hundred-weight of beef, and boil it in the coppers."

Thus encouraged, the surgeon went to the cook, and very soon beef was steaming on a scale and at a rate unparalleled.

Meantime Capt. Dodd had the patient taken to his own cabin; and he and his servant administered weak brandy and water with great caution and skill.

There was no perceptible result. But, at all events, there was life and vital instinct left, or he could not have swallowed.

Thus they hovered about him for some hours, and then the bath was ready.

The captain took charge of the patient's clothes; the surgeon and a sailor bathed him in lukewarm beef-tea, and then covered him very warm with blankets next the skin. Guess how near a thing it seemed to them when I tell you they dared not rub him.

Just before sunset his pulse became perceptible. The surgeon administered half a spoonful of egg-flip. The patient swallowed it.

By and by he sighed.

"He must not be left day or night," said the captain. "I don't know who or what he is; but he is a man; and I could not bear him to die now."

That night Capt. Dodd overhauled the patient's clothes, and looked for marks on his linen. There were none.

"Poor devil!" said Capt. Dodd. "He is a bachelor."

Capt. Dodd found his pocketbook, with bank-notes £200. He took the numbers, made a memorandum of them, and locked the notes up.

He lighted his lamp, examined the belt, unripped it, and poured out the contents on his table.

They were dazzling. A great many large pieces of amethyst, and some of white topaz and rock-crystal, a large number of smaller stones, carbuncles, chrysolites, and not a few emeralds. Dodd looked at them with pleasure, sparkling in the lamplight.

"What a lot!" said he. "I wonder what they are worth." He sent for the first mate, who, he knew, did a little private business in precious stones. "Masterton," said he, "oblige me by counting these stones with me, and valuing them."

Mr. Masterton stared, and his mouth watered. However, he named the various stones, and valued them. He said there was only one stone, a large emerald without a flaw, that was worth a heavy sum by itself; but the pearls, very fine; and, looking at the great number, they must be worth a thousand pounds.

Capt. Dodd then entered the whole business carefully in the ship's log. The living man he described thus, "About five feet six in height, and about fifty years of age." Then he described the notes and the stones very exactly, and made Masterton, the valuer, sign the log.

Staines took a good deal of egg-flip that night, and next day ate solid food; but they questioned him in vain. His reason was entirely in abeyance: he had become an eater, and nothing else. Whenever they gave him food, he showed a sort of fawning animal gratitude. Other sentiment he had none; nor did words enter his mind any more than a bird's. And, since it is not pleasant to dwell on the wreck of a fine understanding, I will only say that they landed him at Cape Town, out of bodily danger, but weak, and his mind, to all appearance, a hopeless blank.

They buried the skeleton, read the service of the English Church over a Malabar heathen.

Dodd took Staines to the hospital, and left twenty pounds with the governor of it to cure him. But he deposited Staines's money and jewels with a friendly banker, and begged that the principal cashier might see the man, and be able to recognize him should he apply for his own.

The cashier came and examined him, and also the ruby ring on his finger,—a parting gift from Rosa,—and remarked this was a new way of doing business.

"Why, it is the only one, sir," said Dodd. "How can we give you his signature? He is not in his right mind."

"Nor never will be."

"Don't say that, sir. Let us hope for the best, poor fellow."

Having made these provisions, the worthy captain weighed anchor with a warm heart and a good conscience. Yet the image of the man he had saved pursued him; and he resolved to look after him next time he should coal at Cape Town, homeward bound.

Staines recovered his strength in about two months; but his mind returned in fragments, and very slowly. For a long, long time he remembered nothing that had preceded his great calamity. His mind started afresh, aided only by certain fixed habits; for instance, he could read and write. But, strange as it may appear, he had no idea who he was; and, when his memory cleared a little on that head, he thought his surname was Christie; but he was not sure.

Nevertheless, the presiding physician discovered in him a certain progress of intelligence, which gave him great hopes. In the fifth month, having shown a marked interest in the other sick patients, coupled with a disposition to be careful and attentive, they made him a nurse, or rather a sub-nurse under the special orders of a responsible nurse I really believe it was done at first to avoid the alternative of sending him adrift, or transferring him to the insane ward of the hospital. In this congenial pursuit he showed such watchfulness and skill that by and by they found they had got a treasure. Two months after that, he began to talk about medicine, and astonished them still more. He became the puzzle of the establishment. The doctor and surgeon would converse with him, and try and lead him to his past life; but, when it came to that, he used to put his hands to his head, with a face of great distress; and it was clear some impassable barrier lay between his growing intelligence and the past events of his life. Indeed, on one occasion, he said to his kind friend the doctor, " The past! —a black wall, a black wall ! "

Ten months after his admission he was promoted to be an attendant, with a salary.

He put by every shilling of it; for he said, "A voice from the dark past tells me money is every thing in this world."

A discussion was held by the authorities as to whether he should be informed he had money and jewels at the bank or not.

Upon the whole, it was thought advisable to postpone this information, lest he should throw it away. But they told him he had been picked up at sea, and both money and jewels found on him · they were in safe hands; only the person was away for the time. Still he was not to look upon himself as either friendless or moneyless.

At this communication he showed an almost childish delight, that confirmed the doctor in his opinion he was acting prudently, and for the real benefit of an amiable and afflicted person not yet to be trusted with money and jewels.

———◇———

CHAPTER XVI.

In his quality of attendant on the sick, Staines sometimes conducted a weak but convalescent patient into the open air; and he was always pleased to do this, for the air of the Cape carries health and vigor on its wings. He had seen its fine recreative properties; and he divined, somehow, that the minds of convalescents ought to be amused; and so he often begged the doctor to let him take a convalescent abroad. Sooner than not, he would draw the patient several miles in a Bath chair. He rather liked this; for he was a Hercules, and had no egotism or false pride where the sick were concerned.

Now, these open-air walks exerted a beneficial influence on his own darkened mind. It is one thing to struggle from idea to idea; it is another when material objects mingle with the retrospect. they seem to supply stepping-stones in the gradual resuscitation of memory and reason.

The ships going out of port were such a stepping-stone to him; and a vague consciousness came back to him of having been in a ship.

Unfortunately, along with this reminiscence came a desire to go in one again; and this sowed discontent in his mind; and, the more that mind enlarged, the more he began to dislike the hospital and its confinement. The feeling grew, and bade fair to disqualify him for his humble office. The authorities could not fail to hear of this; and they had a little discussion about parting with him; but they hesitated to turn him adrift, and they still doubted the propriety of trusting him with money and jewels.

While matters were in this state, a remarkable event occurred. He drew a sick patient down to the quay one morning, and watched the business of the port with the keenest interest. A ship at anchor was unloading, and a great heavy boat was sticking to her side like a black leech. Presently this boat came away, and moved sluggishly toward the shore, rather by help of the tide than of the two men, who went through the form of propelling her with two monstrous sweeps, while a third steered her. She contained English goods: agricultural implements, some cases, four horses, and a buxom young woman with a thorough English face. The woman seemed a little excited; and, as she neared the landing-place, she called out in jocund tones to a young man on the shore, "It is all right, Dick: they are beauties." And she patted the beasts as people do who are fond of them.

She stepped lightly ashore; and then came the slower work of landing her imports. She bustled about like a hen over her brood, and wasn't always talking, but put in her word every now and then, never crossly, and always to the point.

Staines listened to her, and examined her with a sort of puzzled look; but she took no notice of him, her whole soul was in the cattle.

They got the things on board well enough; but the horses were frightened at the gangway, and jibbed. Then a man was for driving them, and poked one of them in the quarter: he snorted and reared directly.

"Man alive!" cried the young woman, "that is not the way. They are docile enough, but frightened. Encourage 'em, and let 'em look at it. Give 'em time. More haste, less speed, with timorsome cattle."

"That is a very pleasant voice," said poor Staines, rather more dictatorially than became the present state of his intellect. He added softly, "A true woman's voice;" then, gloomily, "a voice of the past, — the dark, dark past."

At this speech intruding itself upon the short sentences of business, there was a roar of laughter; and Phœbe Falcon turned sharply round to look at the speaker. She stared at him; she cried "Oh!" and clasped her hands, and colored all over. "Why, sure," said she, "I can't be mistook. Those eyes — 'tis you, doctor, isn't it?"

"Doctor!" said Staines with a puzzled look. "Yes: I think they called me doctor once. I'm an attendant in the hospital now."

"Dick!" cried Phœbe in no little agitation. "Come here this minute!"

"What, afore I get the horses ashore?"

"Ay, before you do another thing, or say another word. Come here now!" So he came; and she told him to take a good look at the man. "Now," said she, "who is that?"

"Blest if I know," said he.

"What, not know the man that saved your own life! O Dick! what are your eyes worth?"

This discourse brought the few persons within hearing into one band of excited starers.

Dick took a good look, and said, "I'm blest if I don't, though. It is the doctor that cut my throat."

This strange statement drew forth quite a shout of ejaculations.

"Oh! better breathe through a slit than not at all," said Dick. "Saved my life with that cut, he did — didn't he, Pheeb?"

"That he did, Dick! Dear heart, I hardly know whether I am in my senses or not, seeing him a-looking so blank. You try him."

Dick came forward. "Sure you remember me, sir. Dick Dale. You cut my throat, and saved my life."

"Cut your throat! Why, that would kill you."

"Not the way you done it. Well, sir, you ain't the man you was, that is clear: but you was a good friend to me; and there's my hand."

"Thank you, Dick," said Staines, and took his hand. "I don't remember *you*. Perhaps you are one of the past. The past is a dead-wall to me, — a dark dead-wall." And he put his hands to his head with a look of distress.

Everybody there now suspected the truth; and some pointed mysteriously to their own heads.

Phœbe whispered an inquiry to the sick person.

He said a little pettishly, "All I know is, he is the kindest attendant in the ward, and very attentive."

"Oh! then he is in the public hospital."

"Of course he is."

The invalid, with the selfishness of his class, then begged Staines to take him out of all this bustle down to the beach. Staines complied at once with the utmost meekness, and said, "Good-by, old friends; forgive me for not remembering you. It is my great affliction that the past is gone from me, — gone, gone." And he went sadly away, drawing his sick charge like a patient mule.

Phœbe Falcon looked after him, and began to cry.

"Nay, nay, Phœbe," said Dick: "don't ye take on about it."

"I wonder at you," sobbed Phœbe. "Good people, I'm fonder of my brother than he is of himself, it seems; for I can't take it so easy. Well, the world is full of trouble. Let us do what we are here for. But I shall pray for the poor soul every night, that his mind may be given back to him."

So then she bustled, and gave herself to getting the cattle on shore, and the things put on board her wagon.

But, when this was done, she said to her brother, "Dick, I did not think any thing on earth could take my heart off the cattle and the

things we have got from home; but I can't leave this without going to the hospital about our poor dear doctor; and it is late for making a start, any way. And you mustn't forget the newspapers for Reginald, he is so fond of them; and you must contrive to have one sent out regular after this; and I'll go to the hospital."

She went, and saw the head doctor, and told him he had got an attendant there she had known in England in a very different condition. And she had come to see if there was any thing she could do for him; for she felt very grateful to him, and grieved to see him so.

The doctor was pleased and surprised, and put several questions.

Then she gave him a clear statement of what he had done for Dick in England.

"Well," said the doctor, "I believe it is the same man; for, now you tell me this — yes, one of the nurses told me he knew more medicine than she did. His name, if you please."

"His name, sir?"

"Yes, his name. Of course you know his name. Is it Christie?"

"Doctor," said Phœbe, blushing, "I don't know what you will think of me; but I don't know his name. Laws forgive me, I never had the sense to ask it."

A shade of suspicion crossed the doctor's face.

Phœbe saw it, and colored to the temples. "O sir!" she cried piteously, "don't go for to think I have told you a lie! Why should I? And indeed I am not of that sort, nor Dick neither. Sir, I'll bring him to you, and he will say the same. Well, we were all in terror and confusion, and I met him accidentally in the street. He was only a customer till then, and paid ready money: so that is how I never knew his name; but, if I hadn't been the greatest fool in England, I should have asked his wife."

“What! he has a wife?”

“Ay, sir, the loveliest lady you ever clapped eyes on, and he is almost as handsome: has eyes in his head like jewels; 'twas by them I knew him on the quay; and I think he knew my voice again, — said as good as he had heard it in past times.”

“Did he? Then we have got him,” cried the doctor energetically.

“La, sir.”

“Yes: if he knows your voice, you will be able, in time, to lead his memory back: at least, I think so. Do you live in Cape Town?”

“Dear heart, no! I live at my own farm, a hundred and eighty miles from this.”

“What a pity!”

“Why, sir?”

“Well — hum!”

“Oh! if you think I could do the poor doctor good by having him with me, you have only to say the word, and out he goes with Dick and me to-morrow morning. We should have started for home to-night but for this.”

“Are you in earnest, madam?” said the doctor, opening his eyes. “Would you really encumber yourself with a person whose reason is in suspense, and may never return?”

“But that is not his fault, sir. Why, if a dog had saved my brother's life, I'd take it home, and keep it all its days; and this is a man, and a worthy man. O sir! when I saw him brought down so, and his beautiful eyes clouded like, my very bosom yearned over the poor soul. A kind act done in dear old England — who could see the man in trouble here, and not repay it, ay, if it cost one's blood? But, indeed, he is strong and healthy, and hands always scarce our way; and the odds are he will earn his meat one way or t'other; and, if he doesn't, why, all the better for me: I shall have the pleasure of serving him for nought that once served me for neither money nor reward.”

“You are a good woman,” said the doctor warmly.

“There's better, and there's worse,” said Phœbe quietly, and even a little coldly.

“More of the latter,” said the doctor dryly. “Well, Mrs.”—

“Falcon, sir.”

“We shall hand him over to your care; but first, — just for form, — if you are a married woman, we should like to see Dick here: he is your husband, I presume.”

Phœbe laughed merrily. “Dick is my brother; and he can't be spared to come here   Dick! he'd say black was white if I told him to.”

“Then let us see your husband about it, — just for form.”

“My husband is at the farm. I could not venture so far away, and not leave him in charge.” If she had said, “I will not bring him into temptation,” that would have been nearer the truth. “Let that fly stick on the wall, sir. What I do my husband will approve.”

“I see how it is. You rule the roost.”

Phœbe did not reply point-blank to that: she merely said, “All my chickens are happy, great and small;” and an expression of lofty, womanly, innocent pride illuminated her face, and made it superb for a moment.

In short, it was settled that Staines should accompany her next morning to Dale's Kloof Farm, if he chose. On inquiry, it appeared that he had just returned to the hospital with his patient. He was sent for, and Phœbe asked him sweetly if he would go with her to her house, one hundred and eighty miles away, and she would be kind to him.

“On the water?”

“Nay, by land; but 'tis a fine country, and you will see beautiful deer, and things running across the plains, and”—

“Shall I find the past again, the past again?”

“Ay, poor soul, that we shall,

God willing. You and I, we will hunt it together."

He looked at her, and gave her his hand. "I will go with you. Your face belongs to the past, so does your voice."

He then inquired, rather abruptly, had she any children. She smiled.

"Ay, that I have, the loveliest little boy you ever saw. When you are as you used to be, you will be his doctor, won't you?"

"Yes, I will nurse him, and you will help me find the past."

Phœbe then begged Staines to be ready to start at six in the morning. She and Dick would take him up on their way.

While she was talking to him, the doctor slipped out; and, to tell the truth, he went to consult with another authority whether he should take this opportunity of telling Staines that he had money and jewels at the bank. He himself was half inclined to do so; but the other, who had not seen Phœbe's face, advised him to do nothing of the kind. "They are always short of money, these colonial farmers," said he: "she would get every shilling out of him."

"Most would; but this is such an honest face!"

"Well; but she is a mother, you say."

"Yes."

"Well, what mother could be just to a lunatic with her own sweet angel babes to provide for?"

"That is true," said Dr. ——. "Maternal love is apt to modify the conscience."

"What I would do, I would take her address, and make her promise to write if he gets well; and, if he does get well, then write to *him* and tell him all about it."

Dr. —— acted on this shrewd advice, and ordered a bundle to be made up for the traveller out of the hospital stores: it contained a nice light summer suit, and two changes of linen.

CHAPTER XVII

NEXT morning Staines and Dick Dale walked through the streets of Cape Town side by side. Dick felt the uneasiness of a sane man, not familiar with the mentally afflicted, who suddenly finds himself alone with one. Insanity turns men oftenest into sheep and hares; but it does now and then make them wolves and tigers; and that has saddled the insane in general with a character for ferocity. Young Dale, then, cast many a suspicious glance at his comrade as he took him along. These glances were re-assuring.. Christopher's face had no longer the mobility, the expressive changes, that mark the superior mind. His countenance was monotonous; but the one expression was engaging. There was a sweet, patient, lamblike look, the glorious eye a little troubled and perplexed, but wonderfully mild. Dick Dale looked and looked; and his uneasiness vanished. And the more he looked the more did a certain wonder creep over him, and make him scarce believe the thing he knew; viz., that a learned doctor had saved him from the jaws of death by rare knowledge, sagacity, courage, and skill combined, and that mighty man of wisdom was brought down to this lamb, and would go north, south, east, or west, with sweet and perfect submission, even as he, Dick Dale, should appoint. With these reflections honest Dick felt his eyes get a little misty; and to use those words of Scripture, which nothing can surpass or equal, his bowels yearned over the man.

As for Christopher, he looked straight forward, and said not a word till they cleared the town; but when he saw the vast flowery vale, and the far-off violet hills, like Scotland glorified, he turned to Dick with an ineffable expression of sweetness and good-fellowship, and said,

"Oh, beautiful! We'll hunt the past together."

"We — will — so," said Dick with a sturdy, and indeed almost a stern resolution.

Now, this he said, not that he cared for the past, nor intended to waste the present by going upon its predecessor's trail; but he had come to a resolution — full three minutes ago — to humor his companion to the top of his bent, and say "Yes" with hypocritical vigor to every thing not directly and immediately destructive to him and his.

The next moment they turned a corner, and came upon the rest of their party, hitherto hidden by the apricot hedge and a turning in the road. A blue-black Caffre with two yellow Hottentot drivers, man and boy, was harnessing, in the most primitive mode, four horses on to the six oxen attached to the wagon; and the horses were flattening their ears, and otherwise resenting the incongruity. Meantime a fourth figure, a colossal young Caffre woman, looked on superior with folded arms like a sable Juno, looking down with that absolute composure upon the struggles of man and other animals, which Lucretius and his master Epicurus assigned to the divine nature. Without jesting, the grandeur, majesty, and repose of this figure, were unsurpassable in nature, and such as have vanished from sculpture two thousand years and more.

Dick Dale joined the group immediately, and soon arranged the matter. Meantime Phœbe descended from the wagon, and welcomed Christopher very kindly, and asked him if he would like to sit beside her, or to walk.

He glanced into the wagon: it was covered and curtained, and dark as a cupboard. "I think," said he timidly, "I shall see more of the past out here."

"So you will, poor soul," said Phœbe kindly, "and better for your health. But you must not go far from the wagon, for I'm a fidget; and I have got the care of you now, you know, for want of a better. Come, Ucatella, you must ride with me, and help me sort the things: they are all higgledy-piggledy." So those two got into the wagon through the back curtains. Then the Caffre driver flourished his kambok, or long whip, in the air, and made it crack like a pistol, and the horses reared, and the oxen started, and slowly bored in between them, for they whinnied and kicked, and spread out like a fan all over the road: but a flick or two from the terrible kambok soon sent them bleeding and trembling, and rubbing shoulders, and the oxen mildly but persistently gorging their recalcitrating haunches, the intelligent animals went ahead, and revenged themselves by breaking the harness; but that goes for little in Cape travel.

The body of the wagon was long and low and very stout. The tilt strong and tight made. The roof inside, and most of the sides, lined with green baize. Curtains of the same to the little window and the back. There was a sort of hold literally built full of purchases, a small fire-proof safe, huge blocks of salt, saws, axes, pickaxes, adzes, flails, tools innumerable, bales of wool and linen stuff, hams, and two hundred empty sacks strewn over all. In large pigeon-holes fixed to the sides were light goods, groceries, collars, glaring cotton handkerchiefs for Phœbe's aboriginal domestics, since not every year did she go to Cape Town, — a twenty-days' journey by wagon: things dangled from the very roof; but no hard goods there, if you please, to batter one's head in a spill. Outside were latticed grooves with tent, tent-poles, and rifles. Great pieces of cork and bags of hay and corn hung dangling from mighty hooks; the latter to feed the cattle, should they be compelled to camp out on some sterile spot in the Veldt, and, methinks, to act as buffers, should the whole concern roll down a nullah, or little precipice, —no very uncommon incident in the blessed region they must pass to reach Dale's Kloof.

Harness mended; fresh start. The Hottentots and Caffre vociferated and yelled, and made the unearthly row of a dozen wild beasts wrangling. The horses drew the bullocks, they the wagon: it crawled and creaked, and its appendages wabbled finely.

Slowly they creaked and wabbled past apricot-hedges and detached houses and huts, and got into an open country without a tree, but here and there a stunted camel-thorn. The soil was arid, and grew little food for man or beast, yet, by a singular freak of nature, it put forth abundantly things that here at home we find it harder to raise than homely grass and oats. The ground was thickly clad with flowers of delightful hues; pyramids of snow or rose-color bordered the track; yellow and crimson stars bejewelled the ground; and a thousand bulbous plants burst into all imaginable colors, and spread a rainbow carpet to the foot of the violet hills : and all this glowed and gleamed and glittered in a sun shining with incredible brightness and purity of light, but, somehow, without giving a headache, or making the air sultry.

Christopher fell to gathering flowers, and interrogating the past by means of them; for he had studied botany. The past gave him back some pitiably vague ideas. He sighed. "Never mind," said he to Dick, and tapped his forehead : it is here : it is only locked up."

"All right," said Dick : "nothing is lost when you know where 'tis."

"This is a beautiful country," suggested Christopher. "It is all flowers. It is like the garden of — the garden of — Locked up."

"It is de—light—ful," replied

the self-compelled optimist sturdily. But here nature gave way. He was obliged to relieve his agricultural bile by getting into the cart, and complaining to his sister. " 'Twill take us all our time to cure him. He have been bepraising this here soil, which it is only fit to clean the women's kettles. 'Twouldn't feed three larks to an acre, I know; no, *nor half so many*."

"Poor soul ! Mayhap the flowers have took his eye. Sit here a bit, Dick. I want to talk to you about a many things."

While these two were conversing, Ucatella, who was very fond of Phœbe, but abhorred wagons, stepped out, and stalked by the side like an ostrich, a camelopard, or a Taglioni ; nor did the effort with which she subdued her stride to the pace of the procession appear : it was the poetry of walking. Christopher admired it a moment ; but the noble expanse tempted him, and he strode forth like a giant, his lungs inflating in the glorious air, and soon left the wagon far behind.

The consequence was, that when they came to a halt, and Dick and Phœbe got out to release and water the cattle, there was Christopher's figure retiring into space.

"Hanc rem ægrè tulit Phœbe," as my old friend Livy would say. "Oh, dear! oh, dear! If he strays so far from us, he will be eaten up at nightfall by jackals or lions or something. One of you must go after him."

"Me go, missy," said Ucatella zealously, pleased with an excuse for stretching her magnificent limbs.

"Ay ; but mayhap he will not come back with *you* : will he, Dick ?"

"That he will, like a lamb." Dick wanted to look after the cattle.

"Yuke, my girl," said Phœbe, "listen. He has been a good friend of ours in trouble ; and now he is not quite right *here*. So be very kind to him ; but be sure and bring him back, or keep him till we come."

12*

"Me bring him back alive, certain sure," said Ucatella, smiling from ear to ear. She started with a sudden glide, like a boat taking the water, and appeared almost to saunter away, so easy was the motion; but, when you looked at the ground she was covering, the stride, or glide, or whatever it was, was amazing —

"She seemed in walking to devour the way."

Christopher walked fast, but nothing like this; and as he stopped at times to botanize, and gaze at the violet hills, and interrogate the past, she came up with him about five miles from the halting-place.

She laid her hand quietly on his shoulder, and said with a broad, genial smile and a musical chuckle, "Ucatella come for you. Missy want to speak you."

"Oh! very well;" and he turned back with her directly; but she took him by the hand to make sure; and they marched back peaceably, in silence, and hand in hand. But he looked and looked at her; and at last he stopped dead short, and said a little arrogantly, "Come! I know you. You are not locked up:" and he inspected her point-blank. She stood like an antique statue, and faced the examination. "You are 'the noble savage,'" said he, having concluded his inspection.

"Nay," said she. "I be the house-maid."

"The house-maid!"

"Iss, the house-maid, Ucatella. So come on." And she drew him along, sore perplexed.

They met the cavalcade a mile from the halting-place; and Phœbe apologized a little to Christopher. "I hope you'll excuse me, sir," said she; "but I am just for all the world like a hen with her chickens: if but one strays, I'm all in a flutter till I get him back."

"Madam," said Christopher, "I am very unhappy at the way things are locked up. Please tell me truly, is this 'the house-maid,' or the 'noble savage?'"

"Well, she is both, if you go to that, and the best creature ever breathed."

"Then she is the 'noble savage.'"

"Ay, so they call her, because she is black."

"Then, thank Heaven!" said Christopher, "the past is not all locked up."

That afternoon they stopped at an inn. But Dick slept in the cart. At three in the morning they took the road again, and creaked along supernaturally loud under a purple firmament studded with huge stars, all bright as moons, that lit the way quite clear, and showed black things innumerable flitting to and fro: these made Phœbe shudder, but were no doubt harmless; still Dick carried his double rifle, and a revolver in his belt.

They made a fine march in the cool, until some slight mists gathered, and then they halted, and breakfasted near a silvery kloof, and watered the cattle. While thus employed, suddenly a golden tinge seemed to fall like a lash on the vapors of night; they scudded away directly, as jackals before the lion. The stars paled; and with one incredible bound the mighty sun leaped into the horizon, and rose into the sky. In a moment all the lesser lamps of heaven were out, though late so glorious; and there was nothing but one vast vaulted turquoise, and a great flaming topaz mounting with eternal ardor to its centre.

This did not escape Christopher. "What is this?" said he. "No twilight. The tropics!" He managed to dig that word out of the past in a moment.

At ten o'clock the sun was so hot that they halted, and let the oxen loose till sundown. Then they began to climb the mountains.

The way was steep and rugged; indeed, so rough in places, that the cattle had to jump over the holes, and, as the wagon could not jump so cleverly, it jolted appallingly, and many a scream issued forth.

Near the summit, when the poor beasts were dead beat, they got into clouds and storms ; and the wind rushed howling at them through the narrow pass with such fury, it flattened the horses' ears, and bade fair to sweep the whole cavalcade to the plains below.

Christopher and Dick walked close behind under the lee of the wagon. Christopher said in Dick's ear, "D'ye hear that ? Time to reef topsails, captain."

"It is time to do *something*," said Dick. He took advantage of a jutting rock, drew the wagon half behind it and across the road, propped the wheels with stones ; and they all huddled to leeward, man and beast indiscriminately,

"Ah !" said Christopher approvingly : "we are lying to, — a very proper course."

They huddled and shivered three hours ; and then the sun leaped into the sky, and, lo ! a transformation scene. The cold clouds were first rosy fleeces, then golden ones, then gold-dust, then gone : the rain was big diamonds, then crystal sparks, then gone : the rocks and the bushes sparkled with gem-like drops, and shone and smiled.

The shivering party bustled, and toasted the potent luminary in hot coffee ; for Phœbe's wagon had a stove and chimney ; and then they yoked their miscellaneous cattle again, and breasted the hill. With many a jump and bump and jolt, and scream from inside, they reached the summit, and looked down on a vast slope flowering but arid, — a region of gaudy sterility.

The descent was more tremendous than the ascent ; and Phœbe got out, and told Christopher she would liever cross the ocean twice than this dreadful mountain once.

The Hottentot with the reins was now bent like a bow all the time, keeping the cattle from flowing diverse over precipices, and the Caffre with his kambok was here and there and everywhere, his whip flicking like a lancet, and cracking like a horse-pistol, and the pair vied like Apollo and Pan, not which could sing sweetest, but swear loudest. Having the lofty hill for some hours between them and the sun, they bumped and jolted, and stuck in mud-holes, and flogged and swore the cattle out of them again, till at last they got to the bottom, where ran a turbid kloof, or stream. It was fordable ; but the recent rains had licked away the slope : so the existing bank was two feet above the stream. Little recked the demon drivers or the parched cattle : in they plunged promiscuously, with a flop like thunder, followed by an awful splashing. The wagon stuck fast in the mud, the horses tied themselves in a knot, and, rolled about in the stream, and the oxen drank, imperturbable.

"Oh the salt ! the salt !" screamed Phœbe ; and the rocks re-echoed her lamentations.

The wagon was inextricable, the cattle done up, the savages lazy : so they staid for several hours. Christopher botanized, but not alone. Phœbe drew Ucatella apart, and explained to her, that, when a man is a little wrong in the head, it makes a child of him. "So," said she, "you must think he is your child, and never let him out of your sight."

"All right," said the sable Juno, who spoke English ridiculously well, and rapped out idioms, especially "Come on," and "All right."

About dusk what the drivers had foreseen, though they had not the sense to explain it, took place : the kloof dwindled to a mere gutter, and the wagon stuck high and dry. Phœbe waved her handkerchief to Ucatella. Ucatella, who had dogged Christopher about four hours without a word, now took his hand,

and said, "My child, missy wants us; come on;" and so led him unresistingly.

The drivers, flogging like devils, cursing like troopers, and yelling like hyenas gone mad, tried to get the wagon off; but it was fast as a rock. Then Dick and the Hottentot put their shoulders to one wheel, and tried to pry it up, while the Caffre *encouraged* the cattle with his thong. Observing this, Christopher went in, with his sable custodian at his heels, and heaved at the other embedded wheel. The wagon was lifted directly, so that the cattle tugged it out, and they got clear. On examination, the salt had just escaped.

Says Ucatella to Phœbe a little ostentatiously, "My child is strong and useful; make little missy a good slave."

"A slave! Heaven forbid!" said Phœbe. "He'll be a father to us all, once he gets his head back; and I do think it is coming — but very slow."

The next three days offered the ordinary incidents of African travel, but nothing that operated much on Christopher's mind, which is the true point of this narrative; and, as there are many admirable books of African travel, it is the more proper I should confine myself to what may be called the relevant incidents of the journey.

On the sixth day from Cape Town they came up with a large wagon stuck in a mudhole. There was quite a party of Boers, Hottentots, Caffres, round it, armed with whips, kamboks, and oaths, lashing and cursing without intermission, or any good effect; and there were the wretched beasts straining in vain at their choking yokes, moaning with anguish, trembling with terror, their poor mild eyes dilated with agony and fear; and often, when the blows of the cruel kamboks cut open their bleeding flesh, they bellowed to Heaven their miserable and vain protest against this devil's work.

Then the past opened its stores, and lent Christopher a word.

"BARBARIANS!" he roared, and seized a gigantic Caffre by the throat, just as his kambok descended for the hundredth time. There was a mighty struggle, as of two Titans; dust flew round the combatants in a cloud; a whirling of big bodies, and down they both went with an awful thud, the Saxon uppermost, by Nature's law.

The Caffre's companions, amazed at first, began to roll their eyes and draw a knife or two; but Dick ran forward, and said, "Don't hurt him: he is wrong *here*."

This representation pacified them more readily than one might have expected. Dick added hastily, "We'll get you out of the hole *our* way, and cry quits."

The proposal was favorably received; and the next minute Christopher and Ucatella at one wheel, and Dick and the Hottentot at the other, with no other help than two pointed iron bars bought for their shepherds, had effected what sixteen oxen could not. To do this Dick Dale had bared his arm to the shoulder. It was a stalwart limb, like his sister's; and he now held it out all swollen and corded, and slapped it with his other hand. "Look'ee here, you chaps," said he. "The worst use a man can put that there to is to go cutting out a poor beast's heart for not doing more than he can. You are good fellows, you Caffres; but I think you have sworn never to put your shoulder to a wheel. But, bless your poor silly hearts! a little strength put on at the right place is better than a deal at the wrong."

"You hear that, you Caffre chaps?" inquired Ucatella a little arrogantly — for a Caffre.

The Caffres, who had stood quite silent to imbibe these remarks, bowed their heads with all the dignity and politeness of Roman senators, Spanish grandees, &c.; and one of the said party replied gravely, "The words of the white man are always wise."

"And his arm blanked [1] strong," said Christopher's late opponent, from whose mind, however, all resentment had vanished.

Thus spake the Caffres, yet to this day never hath a man of all their tribe put his shoulder to a wheel, so strong is custom in South Africa, probably in all Africa; since I remember St. Augustin found it stronger than he liked at Carthage.

Ucatella went to Phœbe, and said, "Missy, my child is good and brave."

"Bother you and your child!" said poor Phœbe. "To think of his flying at a giant like that, and you letting of him. I'm all of a tremble from head to foot;" and Phœbe relieved herself with a cry.

"Oh, missy!" said Ucatella.

"There, never mind me. Do go and look after your child, and keep him out of more mischief. I wish we were safe at Dale's Kloof, I do."

Ucatella complied, and went botanizing with Dr. Staines; but that gentleman, in the course of his scientific researches into camomile flowers and blasted heath, which were all that lovely region afforded, suddenly succumbed, and stretched out his limbs, and said sleepily, "Good-night, U—cat"—and was off into the land of Nod.

The wagon, which, by the way, had passed the larger but slower vehicle, found him fast asleep, and Ucatella standing by him, as ordered, motionless and grand.

"Oh, dear! what now!" said Phœbe; but being a sensible woman, though in the hen and chickens line, she said, "'Tis the fighting and the excitement. 'Twill do him more good than harm, I think;" and she

had him bestowed in the wagon, and never disturbed him night nor day. He slept thirty-six hours at a stretch; and, when he awoke, she noticed a slight change in his eye. He looked at her with an interest he had not shown before, and said, "Madam, I know you."

"Thank God for that!" said Phœbe.

"You kept a little shop in the other world."

Phœbe opened her eyes with some little alarm.

"You understand—the world that is locked up—for the present."

"Well, sir, so I did, and sold you milk and butter. Don't you mind?"

"No—the milk and butter—they are locked up."

The country became wilder, the signs of life miserably sparse; about every twenty miles the farm-house or hut of a degenerate Boer, whose children and slaves pigged together, and all ran jostling, and the mistress screamed in her shrill Dutch, and the Hottentots all chirped together, and confusion reigned for want of method: often they went miles, and saw nothing but a hut or two, with a nude Hottentot eating flesh burned a little, but not cooked, at the door; and the kloofs became deeper and more turbid; and Phœbe was in agony about her salt; and Christopher advised her to break it in big lumps, and hang it all about the wagon in sacks; and she did, and Ucatella said profoundly, "My child is wise;" and they began to draw near home, and Phœbe to fidget; and she said to Christopher, "Oh, dear! I hope they are all alive and well: once you leave home, you don't know what may have happened by then you come back. One comfort, I've got Sophy: she is very dependable, and no beauty, thank my stars!"

That night, the last they had to travel, was cloudy for a wonder, and they groped with lanterns.

Ucatella and her child brought

---

[1] I take this very useful expression from a delightful volume by Mr. Boyle.

up the rear. Presently there was a light pattering behind them. The swift-eared Ucatella clutched Christopher's arm, and, turning round, pointed back, with eyeballs white and rolling. There were full a dozen animals following them, whose bodies seemed colorless as shadows, but their eyes little balls of flaming lime-light.

"GUN!" said Christie, and gave the Caffre's arm a pinch. She flew to the caravan: he walked backward, facing the foe. The wagon was halted; and Dick ran back with two loaded rifles. In his haste he gave one to Christopher, and repented at leisure; but Christopher took it, and handled it like an experienced person, and said with delight, "VOLUNTEER." But with this the cautious animals had vanished like bubbles. But Dick told Christopher they would be sure to come back. He ordered Ucatella into the wagon, and told her to warn Phœbe not to be frightened if guns should be fired. This soothing message brought Phœbe's white face out between the curtains; and she implored them to get into the wagon, and not tempt Providence.

"Not till I have got thee a kaross of jackal's fur."

"I'll never wear it!" said Phœbe violently, to divert him from his purpose.

"Time will show," said Dick dryly. "These varmint are on and off like shadows, and as cunning as old Nick. We two will walk on quite unconcerned like; and, as soon as ever the varmint are at our heels, you give us the office; and we'll pepper their fur, won't we, doctor?"

"We — will — pepper — their fur," said Christopher, repeating what to him was a lesson in the ancient and venerable English tongue.

So they walked on expectant; and by and by the four-footed shadows with large lime-light eyes came stealing on; and Phœbe shrieked, and they vanished before the men could draw a bead on them.

"Thou's no use at this work, Pheeb," said Dick. "Shut thy eyes, and let us have Yuke."

"Iss, master: here I be."

"You can bleat like a lamb; for I've heard ye."

"Iss, master. I bleats beautiful;" and she showed snowy teeth from ear to ear.

"Well, then, when the varmint are at our heels, draw in thy woolly head, and bleat like a young lamb. They won't turn from that, I know, the vagabonds."

Matters being thus prepared, they sauntered on; but the jackals were very wary. They came like shadows, so departed, — a great many times; but at last, being re-enforced, they lessened the distance, and got so close that Ucatella withdrew her head, and bleated faintly inside the wagon. The men turned, levelling their rifles, and found the troop within twenty yards of them. They wheeled directly; but the four barrels poured their flame, four loud reports startled the night, and one jackal lay dead as a stone, another limped behind the flying crowd, and one lay kicking. He was soon despatched, and both carcasses flung over the patient oxen; and good-by, jackals, for the rest of that journey.

Ucatella, with all a Caffre's love of fire-arms, clapped her hands with delight. "My child shoots loud and strong," said she.

"Ay, ay," replied Phœbe: "they are all alike. Wherever there's men, look for quarrelling and firing off. We had only to sit quiet in the wagon."

"Ay," said Dick, "the cattle especially, — for it is them the varmint were after, — and let 'em eat my Hottentots."

At this picture of the cattle inside the wagon, and the jackals supping on cold Hottentot alongside, Phœbe, who had no more humor than a cat, but a heart of gold, shut up, and turned red with confusion at her false estimate of the recent transaction in fur.

When the sun rose, they found themselves in a tract somewhat less arid and inhuman; and at last, at the rise of a gentle slope, they saw, half a mile before them, a large farmhouse partly clad with creepers, and a little plot of turf, the fruit of eternal watering; item, a flower bed; item, snow-white palings; item, an air of cleanliness and neatness scarcely known to those dirty descendants of clean ancestors, the Boers. At some distance a very large dam glittered in the sun, and a troop of snow-white sheep were watering at it.

"England!" cried Christopher.

"Ay, sir," said Phœbe; "as nigh as man can make it." But soon she began to fret. "Oh, dear! where are they all? If it was me, I'd be at the door looking out. Ah, there goes Yuke to rouse them up."

"Come, Pheeb, don't you fidget," said Dick kindly. "Why, the lazy lot are scarce out of their beds by this time."

"More shame for 'em! If they were away from me, and coming home, I should be at the door day and night, I know. Ah!"

She uttered a scream of delight; for just then out came Ucatella, with little Tommy on her shoulder, and danced along to meet her. As she came close, she raised the chubby child high in the air, and he crowed; and then she lowered him to his mother, who rushed at him, seized and devoured him with a hundred inarticulate cries of joy and love unspeakable.

"Nature!" said Christopher dogmatically, recognizing an old acquaintance, and booking it as one more conquest gained over the past. But there was too much excitement over the cherub to attend to him. So he watched the women gravely, and began to moralize with all his

might. "This," said he, "is what we used to call maternal love; and all animals had it, and that is why the noble savage went for him. It was very good of you, Miss Savage," said the poor soul sententiously.

"Good of her!" cried Phœbe. "She is all goodness. Savage! Find me a Dutchwoman like her. I'll give her a good cuddle for it." And she took the Caffre round the neck, and gave her a hearty kiss, and made the little boy kiss her too.

At this moment out came a collydog, hunting Ucatella by scent alone, which process landed him headlong in the group. He gave loud barks of recognition, fawned on Phœbe and Dick, smelled poor Christopher, gave a growl of suspicion, and lurked about, squinting, dissatisfied, and lowering his tail.

"Thou art wrong, lad, for once," said Dick; "for he's an old friend, and a good one."

"After the dog, perhaps some Christian will come to welcome us," said poor Phœbe.

Obedient to the wish, out walked Sophy, the English nurse, a scraggy woman, with a very cocked nose and thin pinched lips, and an air of respectability and pertness mingled. She dropped a short courtesy, shot the glance of a basilisk at Ucatella, and said stiffly, "You are welcome home, ma'am." Then she took the little boy as one having authority. Not that Phœbe would have surrendered him, but just then Mr. Falcon strolled out with a cigar in his mouth; and Phœbe, with her heart in *her* mouth, flew to meet him. There was a rapturous conjugal embrace, followed by mutual inquiries, and the wagon drew up at the door. Then, for the first time, Falcon observed Staines, saw at once he was a gentleman, and touched his hat to him, to which Christopher responded in kind, and remembered he had done so in the lockedup past.

Phœbe instantly drew her husband apart by the sleeve. "Who do you think that is? You'll never guess. 'Tis the great doctor that saved Dick's life in England with cutting of his throat. But oh, my dear, he is not the man he was. He is afflicted. Out of his mind partly. Well, we must cure him, and square the account for Dick. I'm a proud woman at finding him, and bringing him here to make him all right again, I can tell you. Oh! I am happy, I am happy. Little did I think to be so happy as I am. And, my dear, I have brought you a whole sackful of newspapers ·old and new."

"That is a good girl. But tell me a little more about him. What is his name?"

"Christie."

"Dr. Christie?"

"No doubt. He wasn't an apothecary or a chemist, you may be sure, but a high doctor, and the cleverest ever was or ever will be. And isn't it sad, love, to see him brought down so? My heart yearns for the poor man: and then his wife — the sweetest, loveliest creature you ever — oh!"

Phœbe stopped very short, for she remembered something all of a sudden; nor did she ever again give Falcon a chance of knowing that the woman whose presence had so disturbed him was this very Dr. Christie's wife. "Curious!" thought she to herself, "the world to be so large, and yet so small." Then aloud, "They are unpacking the wagon; come, dear. I don't think I have forgotten any thing of yours. There's cigars and tobacco, and powder and shot and bullets, and every thing to make you comfortable, as my duty 'tis; and — oh, but I'm a happy woman!"

Hottentots big and little clustered about the wagon. Treasure after treasure was delivered with cries of delight. The dogs found out it was a joyful time, and barked about the wheeled treasury; and the

place did not quiet down till sunset.

A plain but tidy little room was given to Christopher; and he slept there like a top. Next morning his nurse called him up to help her water the grass. She led the way with a tub on her head, and two buckets in it. She took him to the dam: when she got there, she took out the buckets, left one on the bank, and gave the other to Christie. She then went down the steps till the water was up to her neck, and bade Christie fill the tub. He poured eight bucketfuls in. Then she came slowly out, straight as an arrow, balancing this tub full on her head. Then she held out her hands for the two buckets. Christie filled them, wondering, and gave them to her. She took them like toy buckets, and glided slowly home with this enormous weight, and never spilled a drop. Indeed, the walk was more smooth and noble than ever, if possible.

When she reached the house, she hailed a Hottentot; and it cost the man and Christopher a great effort of strength to lower her tub between them.

"What a vertebral column you must have!" said Christopher.

"You must not speak bad words, my child," said she. "Now you water the grass and the flowers." She gave him a watering-pot, and watched him maternally, but did not put a hand to it. She evidently considered this part of the business as child's play, and not a fit exercise of her powers.

It was only by drowning that little oasis twice a day, that the grass was kept green and the flowers alive.

She found him other jobs in course of the day; and, indeed, he was always helping somebody or other, and became quite ruddy, bronzed, and plump of cheek, and wore a strange look of happiness, except at times when he got apart, and tried to recall the distant past. Then he would knit his brow, and look perplexed and sad.

They were getting quite used to him, and he to them, when one day he did not come in to dinner. Phœbe sent out for him; but they could not find him.

The sun set. Phœbe became greatly alarmed; and even Dick was anxious.

They all turned out with guns and dogs, and hunted for him beneath the stars.

Just before daybreak, Dick Dale saw a fire sparkle by the side of a distant thicket. He went to it; and there was Ucatella seated, calm and grand as antique statue, and Christopher lying by her side with a shawl thrown over him. As Dale came hurriedly up, she put her finger to her lips, and said, "My child sleeps. Do not wake him. When he sleeps, he hunts the past, as Colly hunts the springbok."

"Here's a go!" said Dick. Then, hearing a chuckle, he looked up, and was aware of a comical appendage to the scene. There hung, head downward, from a branch, a Caffre boy, who was in fact the brother of the stately Ucatella, only went farther into antiquity for his models of deportment; for, as she imitated the antique marbles, he reproduced the habits of that epoch when man roosted, and was arboreal. Wheel somersaults, and, above all, swinging head downward from a branch, were the sweetness of his existence.

"Oh! *you* are there, are you?" said Dick.

"Iss," said Ucatella. "Tim good boy. Tim found my child."

"Well," said Dick, "he has chosen a nice place. This is the clump the last lion came out of: at least they say so. For my part, I never saw an African lion. Falcon says they've all took ship, and gone to England. However, I shall stay here with my rifle till daybreak. 'Tis tempting Providence to lie down on the skirt of the wood for

Lord knows what to jump out on ye unawares."

Tim was sent home for Hottentots; and Christopher was carried home, still sleeping, and laid on his own bed.

He slept twenty-four hours more; and, when he was fairly awake, a sort of mist seemed to clear away in places, and he remembered things at random. He remembered being at sea on the raft with the dead body: that picture was quite vivid to him. He remembered, too, being in the hospital, and meeting Phœbe, and every succeeding incident; but, as respected the more distant past, he could not recall it by any effort of his will. His mind could only go into that remoter past by material stepping-stones; and what stepping-stones he had about him here led him back to general knowledge, but not to his private history.

In this condition he puzzled them all strangely at the farm: his mind was alternately so clear, and so obscure. He would chat with Phœbe, and sometimes give her a good practical hint, but the next moment helpless for want of memory,— that great faculty without which judgment cannot act, having no material.

After some days of this he had another great sleep. It brought him back the distant past in chapters, — his wedding-day, his wife's face and dress upon that day, his parting with her, his whole voyage out; but, strange to say, it swept away one-half of that which he had recovered at his last sleep, and he no longer remembered clearly how he came to be at Dale's Kloof.

Thus his mind might be compared to one climbing a slippery place, who gains a foot or two, then slips back, but, on the whole, gains more than he loses.

He took a great liking to Falcon. That gentleman had the art of pleasing, and the tact never to offend.

Falcon affected to treat the poor

soul's want of memory as a common infirmity; pretended he was himself very often troubled in the same way, and advised him to read the news-papers. "My good wife," said he, "has brought me a whole file of the *Cape Gazette.* I'd read them if I was you. The deuse is in it, if you don't rake up something or other."

Christopher thanked him warmly for this: he got the papers to his own little room, and had always one or two in his pocket for reading. At first he found a good many hard words that puzzled him; and he borrowed a pencil of Phœbe, and noted them down. Strange to say, the words that puzzled him were always common words, that his un-accountable memory had forgotten: a hard word—he was sure to re-member that.

One day he had to ask Falcon the meaning of "spendthrift." Fal-con told him briefly. He could have illustrated the word by a strik-ing example; but he did not. He added, in his polite way, "No fellow can understand all the words in a newspaper. Now, here's a word in mine, 'Anemometer:' who the deuse can understand such a word?"

"Oh, *that* is a common word enough," said poor Christopher. "It means a machine for measur-ing the force of the wind."

"Oh, indeed!" said Falcon; but did not believe a word of it.

One sultry day Christopher had a violent headache, and complained to Ucatella. She told Phœbe, and they bound his brows with a wet handkerchief, and advised him to keep in-doors. He sat down in the coolest part of the house, and held his head with his hands, for it seemed as if it would explode into two great fragments.

All in a moment the sky was overcast with angry clouds, whirl-ing this way and that. Huge drops of hail pattered down, and the next minute came a tremendous flash of lightning, accompanied, rather than followed, by a crash of thunder close over their heads.

This was the opening. Down came a deluge out of clouds that looked mountains of pitch, and made the day night but for the fast and furious strokes of lightning that fired the air. The scream of wind and awful peals of thunder completed the horrors of the scene.

In the midst of this, by what agency I know no more than science or a sheep does, something went off inside Christopher's head, like a pistol-shot. He gave a sort of scream, and dashed out into the weather.

Phœbe heard his scream and his flying footstep, and uttered an ejaculation of fear. The whole household was alarmed, and, under other circumstances, would have followed him; but you could not see ten yards.

A chill sense of impending mis-fortune settled on the house. Phœbe threw her apron over her head, and rocked in her chair.

Dick himself looked very grave.

Ucatella would have tried to fol-low him; but Dick forbade her. "'Tis no use," said he. "When it clears, we that be men will go for him."

"Pray Heaven you may find him alive."

"I don't think but what we shall. There's nowhere he can fall down to hurt himself, nor yet drown him-self, but our dam; and he has not gone that way. But"—

"But what?"

"If we do find him, we must take him back to Cape Town, before he does himself, or some one, a mis-chief. Why, Phœbe, don't you see the man has gone raving mad?"

———◆———

CHAPTER XVIII.

THE electrified man rushed out into the storm; but he scarcely felt it in his body : the effect on his mind overpowered hailstones. The lightning seemed to light up the past; the mighty explosions of thunder seemed cannon-strokes knocking down a wall, and letting in his whole life.

Six hours the storm raged; and before it ended he had recovered nearly his whole past. Except his voyage with Capt. Dodd — that, indeed, he never recovered — and the things that happened to him in the hospital before he met Phœbe Falcon and her brother; and, as soon as he had recovered his lost memory, his body began to shiver at the hail and rain. He tried to find his way home, but missed it; not so much, however, but that he recovered it as soon as it began to clear; and, just as they were coming out to look for him, he appeared before them, dripping, shivering, very pale and worn, with the handkerchief still about his head.

At sight of him, Dick slipped back to his sister, and said rather roughly, " There now, you may leave off crying : he is come home; and to-morrow I take him to Cape Town."

Christopher crept in, a dismal, sinister figure.

"O sir !" said Phœbe, "was this a day for a Christian to be out in ? How could you go and frighten us so ? "

"Forgive me, madam," said Christopher humbly. "I was not myself."

"The best thing you can do now is to go to bed, and let us send you up something warm."

"You are very good," said Christopher, and retired with the air of one too full of great amazing thoughts to gossip

He slept thirty hours at a stretch; and then, awaking in the dead of night, he saw the past even more clear and vivid. He lighted his candle, and began to grope in the *Cape Gazette*. As to dates, he now remembered when he had sailed from England, and also from Madeira. Following up this clew, he found in the *Gazette* a notice that H. M. ship *Amphitrite* had been spoken off the Cape, and had reported the melancholy loss of a promising physician and man of science, Dr. Staines.

The account said every exertion had been made to save him, but in vain.

Staines ground his teeth with rage at this. "Every exertion ! the false-hearted curs ! they left me to drown without one manly effort to save me. Curse them, and curse all the world ! "

Pursuing his researches rapidly, he found a much longer account of a raft picked up by Capt. Dodd, with a white man on it and a dead body, the white man having on him a considerable sum in money and jewels.

Then a new anxiety chilled him. There was not a word to identify him with Dr. Staines. The idea had never occurred to the editor of the *Cape Gazette*. Still less would it occur to any one in England. At this moment his wife must be mourning for him. "Poor, poor Rosa ! "

But perhaps the fatal news might not have reached her.

That hope was dashed away as soon as found. Why, these were all *old newspapers*. That gentlemanly man who had lent them to him had said so.

Old ! yet they completed the year 1867.

He now tore through them for the dates alone, and soon found they went to 1868. Yet they were old papers. He had sailed in May, 1867.

"My God !" he cried in agony, "I HAVE LOST A YEAR."

This thought crushed him. By and by he began to carry this awful thought into details. "My Rosa has worn mourning for me, and put it off again. I am dead to her and to all the world."

He wept long and bitterly.

Those tears cleared his brain still more. For all that, he was not yet himself, at least I doubt it : his insanity, driven from the intellect, fastened one lingering claw into his moral nature, and hung on by it. His soul filled with bitterness and a desire to be revenged on mankind for their injustice ; and this thought possessed him more than reason.

He joined the family at breakfast, and never a word all the time. But when he got up to go he said in a strange, dogged way, as if it went against the grain, "God bless the house that succors the afflicted!" Then he went out to brood alone.

"Dick," said Phœbe, "there's a change, I'll never part with him : and look, there's Colly following him, that never could abide him."

"Part with him ?" said Reginald. "Of course not. He is a gentleman, and they are not so common in Africa."

Dick, who hated Falcon, ignored this speech entirely, and said, "Well, Phœbe, you and Colly are wiser than I am. Take your own way, and don't blame me if any thing happens."

And soon Christopher paid the penalty of returning reason. He suffered all the poignant agony a great heart can endure.

So this was his reward for his great act of self-denial in leaving his beloved wife. He had lost his patient ; he had lost the income from that patient ; his wife was worse off than before, and had doubtless suffered the anguish of a loving heart bereaved. His mind, which now seemed more vigorous than ever after its long rest, placed her before his very eyes, pale and worn with grief, in her widow's cap.

At the picture he cried like the rain. He could give her joy by writing ; but he could not prevent her from suffering a whole year of misery.

Turning this over in connection with their poverty, his evil genius whispered, "By this time she has received the six thousand pounds for your death. *She* would never think of that : but her father has ; and there is her comfort assured, in spite of the caitiffs who left her husband to drown like a dog."

"I know my Rosa," he thought. "She has swooned — ah, my poor darling ! — she has raved, she has wept," — he wept himself at the thought, — " she has mourned every indiscreet act as if it was a crime. But she *has* done all this. Her good and loving but shallow nature is now at rest from the agonies of bereavement, and nought remains but sad and tender regrets. She can better endure that than poverty, cursed poverty, which has brought her and me to this, and is the only real evil in the world but bodily pain."

Then came a struggle that lasted a whole week, and knitted his brows and took the color from his cheek; but it ended in the triumph of love and hate over conscience and common sense. His Rosa should not be poor ; and he would cheat some of those contemptible creatures called men, who had done him nothing but injustice, and at last had sacrificed his life like a rat's.

When the struggle was over, and the fatal resolution taken, then he became calmer, less solitary, and more sociable.

Phœbe, who was secretly watching him with a woman's eye, observed this change in him, and with benevolent intentions invited him one day to ride round the farm with her. He consented readily. She showed him the fields devoted to maize and wheat, and then the sheepfolds. Tim's sheep were apparently deserted; but he was discovered swinging, head downward, from the branch of a camel-thorn, and, seeing him, it did strike one, that, if he had had a tail, he would have been swinging by that. Phœbe called to him. He never answered, but set off running to her, and landed himself un-der her nose in a wheel somersault.

"I hope you are watching them, Tim," said his mistress.

"Iss, missy, always washing 'em."

"Why, there's one straying to-ward the wood now."

": He not go far," said Tim coolly. The young monkey stole off a little way, then fell flat, and uttered the cry of a jackal with startling pre-cision. Back went the sheep to his comrades post-haste; and Tim af-fected a somersault and a chuckle.

"You are a clever boy," said Phœbe. "So that is how you man-age them."

"Dat one way, missy," said Tim, not caring to reveal all his resources at once.

Then Phœbe rode on, and showed Christopher the ostrich pan. It was a large basin, a form the soil often takes in these parts; and in it strut-ted several full grown ostriches and their young, bred on the premises. There was a little dam of water, and plenty of food about. They were herded by a Caffre infant of about six, black, glossy, fat, and clean, being in the water six times a day.

Sometimes one of the older birds would show an inclination to stray out of the pan. Then the infant rolled after her, and tapped her an-kles with a wand. She instantly came back, but without any loss of dignity; for she strutted with her nose in the air, affecting completely to ignore the inferior little animal, that was nevertheless controlling her movements. "There's a farce," said Phœbe. "But you would not believe the money they cost me, nor the money they bring me in. Grain will not sell here for a quarter its value; and we can't afford to send it to Cape Town, twenty days and back: but finery, that sells every-where. I gather sixty pounds the year off those poor fowls' backs — clear profit."

She showed him the granary, and told him there wasn't such another

in Africa. This farm had belonged to one of the old Dutch settlers, and that breed had been going down this many a year. "You see, sir, Dick and I being English, and not down-right in want of money, we can't bring ourselves to sell grain to the middle-men for nothing: so we store it, hoping for better times, that may be will never come. Now I'll show you how the dam is made."

They inspected the dam all round. "This is our best friend of all," said she. "Without this the sun would turn us all to tinder,— crops, flowers, beasts, and folk."

"Oh, indeed!" said Staines. "Then it is a pity you have not built it more scientifically. I must have a look at this."

"Ay, do, sir, and advise us if you see any thing wrong. But hark! it is milking-time. Come and see that." So she led the way to some sheds; and there they found several cows being milked, each by a little calf and a little Hottentot at the same time, and both fighting and jostling each other for the udder. Now and then a young cow, unused to incon-gruous twins, would kick impatient-ly at both animals, and scatter them.

"That is their way," said Phœbe. "They have got it into their silly Hottentot heads as kye won't yield their milk if the calf is taken away; and it is no use arguing with 'em: they will have their own way: But they are very trusty and honest, poor things. We soon found that out. When we came here first, it was in a hired wagon, and Hotten-tot drivers: so, when we came to settle, I made ready for a bit of a wrangle. But my maid Sophy, that is nurse now, and a great de-spiser of heathens, she says, 'Don't you trouble; them nasty ignorant blacks never charges more than their due.' 'I forgive 'em,' says I. 'I wish all white folk was as nice.' However, I did give them a trifle over for luck: and then they got together, and chattered something near the door, hand in hand. ‘La, Sophy,’ says I, ‘what is up now?’ Says she, ‘They are blessing of us. Things is come to a pretty pass for ignorant Muslimmen heathen to be blessing Christian folk.’—‘Well,’ says I, ‘it won’t hurt us any.’—‘I don’t know,’ says she. ‘I don’t want the devil prayed over me.’ So she cocked that long nose of hers, and followed it in-doors.”

By this time they were near the house; and Phœbe was obliged to come to her postscript, for the sake of which, believe me, she had uttered every syllable of this varied chat. “Well, sir,” said she, affecting to proceed without any considerable change of topic, “and how do you find yourself? Have you discovered the past?”

“I have, madam. I remember every leading incident of my life.”

“And has it made you happier?” said Phœbe softly.

“No,” said Christopher gravely. “Memory has brought me misery.”

“I feared as much; for you have lost your fine color, and your eyes are hollow, and lines on your poor brow that were not there before. Are you not sorry you have discovered the past?”

“No, Mrs. Falcon. Give me the sovereign gift of reason, with all the torture it can inflict. I thank God for returning memory, even with the misery it brings.”

Phœbe was silent a long time: then she said in a low, gentle voice, and with the indirectness of a truly feminine nature, “I have plenty of writing-paper in the house; and the post goes south to-morrow, such as ’tis.”

Christopher struggled with his misery, and trembled.

He was silent a long time. Then he said, “No. It is her interest that I should be dead,”

“Well, but sir — take a thought.”

“Not a word more, I implore you. I am the most miserable man that ever breathed.” As he spoke, two bitter tears forced their way.

Phœbe cast a look of pity on him, and said no more; but she shook her head. Her plain common-sense revolted.

However, it did not follow he would be in the same mind next week: so she was in excellent spirits at her *protégé’s* recovery, and very proud of her cure, and celebrated the event with a roaring supper, including an English ham and a bottle of port-wine; and, ten to one, that was English too.

Dick Dale looked a little incredulous; but he did not spare the ham any the more for that.

After supper, in a pause of the conversation, Staines turned to Dick, and said rather abruptly, “Suppose that dam of yours were to burst, and empty its contents, would it not be a great misfortune to you?”

“Misfortune, sir! Don’t talk of it. Why, it would ruin us, beast and body.”

“Well, it will burst if it is not looked to.”

“Dale’s Kloof dam burst!—the biggest and strongest for a hundred miles round.”

“You deceive yourself. It is not scientifically built, to begin; and there is a cause at work that will infallibly burst it if not looked to in time.”

“And what is that, sir?”

“The dam is full of crabs.”

“So ’tis; but what of them?”

“I detected two of them that had perforated the dike from the wet side to the dry; and water was trickling through the channel they had made. Now, for me to catch two that had come right through, there must be a great many at work honey-combing your dike. Those channels, once made, will be enlarged by the permeating water; and a mere cupful of water forced into a dike by the great pressure of a heavy column has an expansive power quite out of proportion to the quantity forced in. Colossal dikes have been burst in this way with disastrous effects. Indeed, it is only a question of time; and I would not guarantee your dike twelve hours. It is full, too, with the heavy rains."

"Here's a go," said Dick, turning pale. "Well, if it is to burst, it must."

"Why so? You can make it safe in a few hours. You have got a clumsy contrivance for letting off the excess of water: let us go and relieve the dam at once of two feet of water. That will make it safe for a day or two: and to-morrow we will puddle it afresh, and demolish those busy excavators."

He spoke with such authority and earnestness, that they all got up from table. A horn was blown that soon brought the Hottentots; and they all proceeded to the dam. With infinite difficulty they opened the waste sluice, lowered the water two feet, and so drenched the arid soil, that in forty-eight hours flowers unknown sprang up.

Next morning, under the doctor's orders, all the black men and boys were diving with lumps of stiff clay, and puddling the endangered wall with a thick coat of it. This took all the people the whole day.

Next day, the clay wall was carried two feet higher; and then the doctor made them work on the other side, and buttress the dike with supports so enormous as seemed extravagant to Dick and Phœbe; but, after all, it was as well to be on the safe side, they thought. And soon they were sure of it; for the whole work was hardly finished, when news came in that the dike of a neighboring Boer, ten miles off, had exploded like a cannon, and emptied itself in five minutes, drowning the farm-yard, and floating the furniture, but leaving them all to perish of drought. And, indeed, the Boer's cart came every day, with empty barrels, for some time, to beg water of the Dales. Ucatella pondered all this, and said her doctor child was wise.

This brief excitement over, Staines went back to his own gloomy thoughts; and they scarcely saw him, except at supper-time.

One evening he surprised them all by asking if they would add to all their kindness by lending him a horse and a spade and a few pounds, to go to the diamond fields.

Dick Dale looked at his sister. She said, "We had rather lend them you to go home with, sir, if you must leave us. But, dear heart, I was half in hopes — Dick and I were talking it over only yesterday — that you would go partners like with us; ever since you saved the dam."

"I have too little to offer for that, Mrs. Falcon, and, besides, I am driven into a corner. I must make money quickly, or not at all: the diamonds are only three hundred miles off. For Heaven's sake, let me try my luck."

They tried to dissuade him, and told him not one in fifty did any good at it.

"Ay; but *I* shall," said he. "Great bad luck is followed by great good luck, and I feel my turn is come. Not that I rely on luck. An accident directed my attention to the diamond a few years ago; and I read a number of prime works upon the subject, that told me things not known to the miners. It is clear, from the Cape journals, that they are looking for diamonds in the river only. Now, I am sure that is a mistake. Diamonds, like gold, have their matrix; and it is comparatively few gems that get washed into the river. I am confident that I shall find the volcanic matrix, and perhaps make my fortune in a week or two."

When the dialogue took this turn, Reginald Falcon's cheek began to flush, and his eyes to glitter.

Christopher continued, "You

who have befriended me so will not turn back, I am sure, when I have such a chance before me ; and, as for the small sum of money I shall require, I will repay you some day, even if"—

"La, sir, don't talk so. If you put it that way, why, the best horse we have, and fifty pounds in good English gold, they are at your service to-morrow."

"And pick and spade to boot," said Dick, "and a double rifle; for there are lions, and Lord knows what, between this and the Vaal River."

"God bless you both!" said Christopher. "I will start to-morrow."

"And I'll go with you," said Reginald Falcon.

———◆———

CHAPTER XIX.

"'Heaven forbid!" said Phœbe. "No, my dear, no more diamonds for us. We never had but one ; and it brought us trouble."

"Nonsense, Phœbe!" replied Falcon: "it was not the diamond's fault. You know I have often wanted to go there; but you objected. You said you were afraid some evil would befall me. But now Solomon himself is going to the mines, let us have no more of that nonsense. We will take our rifles and our pistols."

"There, there, rifles and pistols!" cried Phœbe: "that shows."

"And we will be there in a week, stay a month, and home with our pockets full of diamonds."

"And find me dead of a broken heart."

"Broken fiddlestick! We have been parted longer than that; and yet here we are all right."

"Ay; but the pitcher that goes too often to the well gets broke at last. No, Reginald, now I have tasted three years' happiness and peace of mind, I cannot go through what I used in England. O doctor! have you the heart to part man and wife that have never been a day from each other all these years ?"

"Mrs. Falcon, I would not do it for all the diamonds in Brazil. No, Mr. Falcon, I need hardly say how charmed I should be to have your company, but that is a pleasure I shall certainly deny myself, after what your good wife has said. I owe her too much to cause her a single pang."

"Doctor," said the charming Reginald, "you are a gentleman, and side with the lady. Quite right. It adds to my esteem, if possible. Make your mind easy: I will go alone. I am not a farmer. I am dead sick of this monotonous life; and, since I am compelled to speak my mind, a little ashamed, as a gentleman, of living on my wife and brother, and doing nothing for myself. So I shall go to the Vaal River, and see a little life : here there's nothing but vegetation, and not much of that. Not a word more, Phœbe, if you please. I am a good, easy, affectionate husband; but I am a man, and not a child to be tied to a woman's apron-strings, however much I may love and respect her."

Dick put in his word. "Since you are so independent, you can *walk* to the Vaal River. I can't spare a couple of horses."

This hit the Sybarite hard; and he cast a bitter glance of hatred at his brother-in-law, and fell into a moody silence.

But when he got Phœbe to himself he descanted on her selfishness, Dick's rudeness, and his own wounded dignity, till he made her quite anxious he should have his own way. She came to Staines with red eyes, and said, "Tell me, doctor, will there be any women up there — to take care of you ?"

"Not a petticoat in the place, I believe. It is a very rough life ; and how Falcon could think of leaving you and sweet little Tommy, and this life of health and peace and comfort"—

"Yet *you* do leave us, sir."

"I am the most unfortunate man upon the earth: Falcon is one of the happiest. Would I leave wife and child to go there? Ah, me! I am dead to those I love. This is my one chance of seeing my darling again for many a long year perhaps. Oh! I must not speak of *her* it unmans me. My good, kind friend, I'll tell you what to do. When we are all at supper, let a horse be saddled and left in the yard for me. I'll bid you all good-night, and I'll put fifty miles between us before morning. Even then *he* need not be told I am gone. he will not follow me."

"You are very good, sir," said Phœbe; "but no. Too much has been said. I can't have him humbled by my brother, nor any one. He says I am selfish. Perhaps I am; though I never was called so. I can't bear he should think me selfish He *will* go; and so let us have no ill blood about it. Since he is to go, of course I'd much liever he should go with you than by himself. You are sure there are no women up there — to take care of — you — both? You must be purse-bearer, sir, and look to every penny. He is too generous when he has got money to spend."

In short, Reginald had played so upon her heart, that she now urged the joint expedition, only she asked a delay of a day or two to equip them, and steel herself to the separation.

Staines did not share those vague fears that overpowered the wife, whose bitter experiences were unknown to him; but he felt uncomfortable at her condition, — for now she was often in tears, — and he said all he could to comfort her; and he also advised her how to profit by these terrible diamonds, in her way. He pointed out to her that her farm lay right in the road to the diamonds; yet the traffic all shunned her, passing twenty miles to the westward. Said he, "You should profit by all your resources. You have wood, a great rarity in Africa. Order a portable forge; run up a building where miners can sleep, another where they can feed; the grain you have so wisely refused to sell, — grind it into flour."

"Dear heart! why, there's neither wind nor water to turn a mill."

"But there are oxen. I'll show you how to make an ox-mill. Send your Cape cart into Cape Town for iron lathes, for coffee and tea and groceries by the hundred-weight. The moment you are ready, — for success depends on the order in which we act, — then prepare great boards, and plant them twenty miles south. Write or paint on them, very large. 'The nearest way to the Diamond Mines, through Dale's Kloof, where is excellent accommodation for man and beast. Tea, coffee, home-made bread, fresh butter, &c., &c.' Do this, and you will soon leave off decrying diamonds. This is the sure way to coin them. I myself take the doubtful way; but I can't help it. I am a dead man; and swift good fortune will give me life You can afford to go the slower road and the surer."

Then he drew her the model of an ox-mill, and of a miners' dormitory, the partitions six feet six apart, so that these very partitions formed the bedstead; the bed-sacking being hooked to the uprights. He drew his model for twenty bedrooms.

The portable forge and the ox-mill pleased Dick Dale most; but the partitioned bedsteads charmed Phœbe. She said, "O doctor! how can one man's head hold so many things? If there's a man on earth I can trust my husband with, 'tis you. But, if things go cross up there, promise me you will come back at once and cast in your lot with us.

We have got money and stock, and you have got head-piece : we might do very well together. Indeed, indeed, we might. Promise me. Oh, do, please promise me ! ”

“ I promise you.”

And on this understanding Staines and Falcon were equipped with rifles, pickaxe, shovels, water-proofs, and full saddle-bags, and started, with many shakings of the hand and many tears from Phœbe, for the diamond washings.

CHAPTER XX.

Phœbe's tears at parting made Staines feel uncomfortable ; and he said so.

“ Pooh, pooh ! ” said Falcon : “ crying for nothing does a woman good.”

Christopher stared at him.

Falcon's spirits rose as they proceeded. He was like a boy let loose from school. His fluency and charm of manner served, however, to cheer a singularly dreary journey.

The travellers soon entered on a vast and forbidding region that wearied the eye : at their feet a dull rusty carpet of dried grass and wild camomile, with pale red sand peeping through the burned and scanty herbage. On the low mounds, that looked like heaps of sifted ashes, struggled now and then into sickliness a ragged, twisted shrub. There were flowers too, but so sparse, that they sparkled vainly in the colorless waste which stretched to the horizon. The farm-houses were twenty miles apart ; and nine out of ten were new ones built by the Boers since they degenerated into white savages, — mere huts with domed kitchens behind them. In the dwelling-house the whole family pigged together, with raw flesh drying on the rafters, stinking skins in a corner, parasitical vermin of all sorts blackening the floor, and par-

ticularly a small, biting, and odoriferous tortoise, compared with which the insect a London washer-woman brings into your house in her basket is a stroke with a feather ; and all this without the excuse of penury ; for many of these were shepherd kings, sheared four thousand fleeces a year, and owned a hundred horses and horned cattle.

These Boers are compelled, by unwritten law, to receive travellers, and water their cattle. But our travellers, after one or two experiences, ceased to trouble them ; for, added to the dirt, the men were sullen ; the women moody, silent, brainless ; the whole reception churlish. Staines detected in them an uneasy consciousness that they had descended, in more ways than one, from a civilized race ; and the superior bearing of a European seemed to remind them what they had been, and might have been, and were not : so, after an attempt or two, our adventurers avoided the Boers, and tried the Caffres. They found the savages socially superior ; though their moral character does not rank high.

The Caffre cabins they entered were caves, lighted only by the door, but deliciously cool, and quite clean ; the floors of puddled clay or ants' nests, and very clean. On entering these cool retreats, the flies, that had tormented them, shirked the cool grot, and buzzed off to the nearest farm to batten on congenial foulness. On the fat, round, glossy babies not a speck of dirt : whereas the little Boers were cakes thereof. The Caffre would meet them at the door, his clean black face all smiles and welcome. The women and grown girls would fling a spotless handkerchief over their shoulders in a moment, and display their snowy teeth in unaffected joy at sight of an Englishman.

At one of these huts one evening, they met with something St. Paul ranks above cleanliness even ; viz., Christianity. A neighboring lion had just eaten a Hottentot *faute de mieux*; and these good Caffres wanted the Europeans not to go on at night, and be eaten for dessert. But they could not speak a word of English; and pantomimic expression exists in theory alone. In vain the women held our travellers by the coat-tails, and pointed to a distant wood. In vain Caffre *père* went on all-fours, and growled sore. But at last a savage youth ran to the kitchen, — for they never cook in the house, — and came back with a brand, and sketched on the wall of the hut a lion with a mane down to the ground, and a saucer-eye not loving. The creature's paw rested on a hat and coat, and another fragment or two of a European. The rest was fore-shortened, or else eaten.

The picture completed, the females looked, approved, and raised a dismal howl.

" A lion on the road," said Christopher gravely.

Then the undaunted Falcon seized the charcoal, and drew an Englishman in a theatrical attitude, — left foot well forward, firing a gun, and a lion rolling head over heels like a buck rabbit, and blood squirting out of a hole in his perforated carcass.

The savages saw, and exulted. They were so off their guard as to confound representation with fact. They danced round the white warrior, and launched him to victory.

" Aha ! " said Falcon. " I took the shine out of their lion, didn't I ?"

" You did. And once there was a sculptor who showed a lion his marble group,— a man trampling a lion, extracting his tongue, and so on ; but report says it *did not convince the lion.*"

" Why, no, a lion is not an ass. But, for your comfort, there *are* no lions in this part of the world. They are myths. There were lions in Africa. But now they are all at the Zoo. And I wish I was there too."

" In what character, — of a discontented animal, with every blessing ?

They would not take you in ; too common in England. Halloo ! this is something new. What lots of bushes ! We should not have much chance with a lion here."

" There *are* no lions : it is not the Zoo," said Falcon ; but he spurred on faster.

The country, however, did not change its feature : bushes and little acacias prevailed, and presently dark forms began to glide across at intervals.

The travellers held their breath, and pushed on ; but at last their horses flagged : so they thought it best to stop and light a fire, and stand upon their guard.

They did so ; and Falcon sat with his rifle cocked, while Staines boiled coffee, and they drank it, and, after two hours' halt pushed on. And at last the bushes got more scattered, and they were on the dreary plain again. Falcon drew the rein with a sigh of relief; and they walked their horses side by side.

" Well, what is become of the lions ? " said Falcon jauntily. He turned in his saddle, and saw a large animal stealing behind them with its belly to the very earth, and eyes hot coals. He uttered an eldrich screech, fired both barrels, with no more aim than a baby, and spurred away, yelling like a demon. The animal fled another way, in equal trepidation at those tongues of flame and loud reports; and Christopher's horse reared and plunged, and deposited him promptly on the sward : but he held the bridle, mounted again, and rode after his companion. A stern chase is a long chase, and, for that or some other reason, he could never catch him again till sunrise ; being caught, he ignored the lioness with cool hauteur. He said he had ridden on to find comfortable quarters, and craved thanks.

This was literally the only incident worth recording that the companions met with in three hundred miles.

On the sixth day out, toward afternoon, they found, by inquiring, they were near the diamond washings; and the short route was pointed out by an exceptionally civil Boer.

But Christopher's eye had lighted upon a sort of chain of knolls, or little round hills, devoid of vegetation; and he told Falcon he would like to inspect these before going farther.

"Oh," said the Boer, "they are not on my farm, thank goodness! they are on my cousin Bulteel's;" and he pointed to a large white house about four miles distant, and quite off the road. Nevertheless, Staines insisted on going to it. But first they made up to one of these knolls, and examined it. It was about thirty feet high, and not a vestige of herbage on it: the surface was composed of sand and of lumps of gray limestone, very hard, diversified with lots of quartz, mica, and other old formations.

Staines got to the top of it with some difficulty, and examined the surface all over. He came down again, and said, "All these little hills mark hot volcanic action, — why, they are like boiling earth-bubbles, — which is the very thing, under certain conditions, to turn carbonate of lime into diamonds. Now, here is plenty of limestone unnaturally hard; and, being in a diamond country, I can fancy no place more likely to be the matrix than these earth-bubbles. Let us tether the horses, and use our shovels."

They did so, and found one or two common crystals, and some jasper, and a piece of chalcedony, all in little bubbles, but no diamonds. Falcon said it was wasting time.

Just then the proprietor, a gigantic, pasty colonist, came up, with his pipe, and stood calmly looking on. Staines came down, and made a sort of apology. Bulteel smiled quietly, and asked what harm they could do him, raking that rubbish. "Rake

it all avay, mine vriends," said he: "ve shall thank you moch."

He then invited them languidly to his house. They went with him; and, as he volunteered no more remarks, they questioned him, and learned his father had been a Hollander, and so had his vrow's. This accounted for the size and comparative cleanliness of his place. It was stuccoed with the lime of the country outside, and was four times as large as the miserable farm-houses of the degenerate Boers. For all this, the street door opened on the principal room, and that room was kitchen and parlor, only very large and wholesome. "But Lord" — as poor dear Pepys used to blurt out — "to see how some folk understand cleanliness!" The floor was made of powered ants' nests, and smeared with fresh cow-duug every day. Yet these people were the cleanliest Boers in the colony.

The vrow met them, with a snow-white collar and cuffs of Hamburg linen; and the brats had pasted faces round as pumpkins, but shone with soap. The vrow was also pasty-faced, but gentle, and welcomed them with a smile, languid but unequivocal.

The Hottentots took their horses as a matter of course. Their guns were put in a corner. A clean cloth was spread; and they saw they were to sup and sleep there, though the words of invitation were never spoken.

At supper, sun-dried flesh, cabbage, and a savory dish the travellers returned to with gusto. Staines asked what it was. The vrow told him, — locusts. They had stripped her garden, and filled her very rooms, and fallen in heaps under her walls: so she had pressed them, by the million, into cakes, had salted them lightly, and stored them; and they were excellent baked.

After supper, the accomplished Reginald, observing a wire guitar, tuned it with some difficulty, and so twanged it and sang ditties to it, that the flabby giant's pasty face wore a look of dreamy content over his everlasting pipe. And in the morning, after a silent breakfast, he said, " Mine vriends, stay here a year or two, and rake in mine rubbish. Ven you are tired, here are spring-bok and antelopes, and you can shoot mit your rifles, and ve vill cook them, and you shall zing us zongs of Vaderland."

They thanked him heartily, and said they would stay a few days at all events.

The placid Boer went a-farming; and the pair shouldered their pick and shovel, and worked on their heap all day, and found a number of pretty stones, but no diamond.

" Come, "said Falcon : " we must go to the river; " and Staines acqui-esced. "I bow to experience," said he.

At the threshold they found two of the little Bulteels playing with pieces of quartz, crystal, &c., on the door-stone. One of these stones caught Staines's eye directly. It sparkled in a different way from the others. He examined it : it was the size of a white haricot bean, and one side of it polished by friction. He looked at it, and looked, and saw that it refracted the light. He felt convinced it was a diamond.

" Give the boy a penny for it," said the ingenious Falcon on re-ceiving the information.

" Oh! " said Staines. " Take advantage of a child ? "

He borrowed it of the boy, and laid it on the table after supper. " Sir," said he, " this is what we were raking in your kopjes for, and could not find it. It belongs to lit-tle Hans. Will you sell it us ? We are not experts; but we think it may be a diamond. We will risk ten pounds on it."

" Ten pounds ! " said the farmer. " Nay, we rob not travellers, mine vriend."

" But, if it is a diamond, it is worth a hundred. See how it gains fire in the dusk ! "

In short, they forced the ten pounds on him, and the next day went to work on another kopje.

But the simple farmer's conscience smote him. It was a slack time : so he sent four Hottentots, with shov-els, to help these friendly maniacs. These worked away gayly ; and the white men set up a sorting table, and sorted the stuff, and hammered the nodules, and at last found a lit-tle stone as big as a pea, that refract-ed the light. Staines showed this to the Hottentots; and their quick eyes discovered two more that day, only smaller.

Next day nothing but a splinter or two.

Then Staines determined to dig deeper, contrary to the general im-pression. He gave his reason : " Diamonds don't fall from the sky. They work up from the ground ; and clearly the heat must be great-er farther down."

Acting on this, they tried the next strata, but found it entirely barren. After that, however, they came to a fresh layer of carbonate ; and here, Falcon hammering a large lump of conglomerate, out leaped, all of a sudden, a diamond big as a nut, that ran along the earth, gleaming like a star. It had polished angles and natural facets ; and even a nov-ice with an eye in his head could see it was a diamond of the purest water. Staines and Falcon shouted with delight, and made the blacks a present on the spot.

They showed the prize at night, and begged the farmer to take to digging. There was ten times more money beneath his soil than on it.

Not he. He was a farmer : did not believe in diamonds.

Two days afterward another great find. Seven small diamonds.

Next day a stone as large as a cob-nut, and with strange and beau-tiful streaks. They carried it home to dinner, and set it on the table, and told the family it was worth a thousand pounds. Bulteel scarcely looked at it; but the vrow trembled, and all the young folk glowered at it.

In the middle of dinner it exploded like a cracker, and went literally into diamond-dust.

"Dere goes von tousand pounds," said Bulteel, without moving a muscle.

Falcon swore. But Staines showed fortitude. "It was laminated," said he; "and exposure to the air was fatal."

Owing to the invaluable assistance of the Hottentots, they had in less than a month collected four large stones of pure water, and a wine-glassful of small stones, when one fine day, going to work calmly after breakfast, they found some tents pitched, and at least a score of dirty diggers, bearded like the pard, at work on the ground. Staines sent Falcon back to tell Bulteel, and suggest that he should at once order them off, or, better still, make terms with them. The phlegmatic Boer did neither.

In twenty-four hours it was too late. The place was rushed. In other words, diggers swarmed to the spot, with no idea of law but diggers' law.

A thousand tents rose like mushrooms; and poor Bulteel stood, smoking and staring, amazed, at his own door, and saw a veritable procession of wagons, Cape carts, and powdered travellers, file past him to take possession of his hillocks. Him, the proprietor, they simply ignored: they had a committee, who were to deal with all obstructions, landlords and tenants included. They themselves measured out Bulteel's farm into thirty-foot claims, and went to work with shovel and pick. They held Staines's claim sacred: that was diggers' law; but they confined it strictly to thirty feet square.

Had the friends resisted, their brains would have been knocked out. However, they gained this, that dealers poured in, and, the market being not yet glutted, the price was good. Staines sold a few of the small stones for two hundred pounds. He showed one of the larger stones. The dealer's eye glittered, but he offered only three hundred pounds, and this was so wide of the ascending scale on which a stone of that importance is priced that Staines reserved it for sale at Cape Town.

Nevertheless he afterward doubted whether he had not better have taken it; for the multitude of diggers turned out such a prodigious number of diamonds at Bulteel's pan that a sort of panic fell on the market.

These dry diggings were a revelation to the world. Men began to think the diamond, perhaps, was a commoner stone than any one had dreamed it to be.

As to the discovery of stones, Staines and Falcon lost nothing by being confined to a thirty-foot claim. Compelled to dig deeper, they got into richer strata, where they found garnets by the pint, and some small diamonds, and at last, one lucky day, their largest diamond. It weighed thirty-seven carats, and was a rich yellow. Now, when a diamond is clouded or off color, it is terribly depreciated; but a diamond with a positive color is called a fancy stone, and ranks with the purest stones.

"I wish I had this in Cape Town," said Staines.

"Why, I'll take it to Cape Town, if you like," said the changeable Falcon.

"You will?" said Christopher, surprised.

"Why not? I'm not much of a digger. I can serve our interest better by selling. I could get a thousand pounds for this at Cape Town."

"We will talk of that quietly," said Christopher.

Now the fact is, Falcon as a digger, was not worth a pin. He could not sort. His eyes would not bear the blinding glare of a tropical sun upon lime and dazzling bits of mica, quartz, crystal, white topaz, &c., in the midst of which the true glint of the royal stone had to be caught in a moment. He could not sort, and he had not the heart to dig. The only way to make him earn his half was to turn him into the travelling and selling partner.

Christopher was too generous to tell him this; but he acted on it, and said he thought his was an excellent proposal: indeed, he had better take all the diamonds they had got to Dale's Kloof first, and show them to his wife for her consolation. "And perhaps," said he, "in a matter of this importance, she will go to Cape Town with you, and try the market there."

"All right," said Falcon.

He sat and brooded over the matter a long time, and said, "Why make two bites of a cherry? They will only give us half the value at Cape Town. Why not go by the steamer to England, before the London market is glutted, and all the world finds out that diamonds are as common as dirt?"

"Go to England! What, without your wife? I'll never be a party to that. Me part man and wife! If you knew my own story"—

"Why, who wants you?", said Reginald. "You don't understand. Phœbe is dying to visit England again; but she has got no excuse If you like to give her one, she will be much obliged to you, I can tell you." •

"Oh, that is a very different matter! If Mrs. Falcon can leave her farm"—

"Oh! that brute of a brother of hers is a very honest fellow, for that matter. She can trust the farm to him. Besides, it is only a month's voyage by the mail steamer."

This suggestion of Falcon's set Christopher's heart bounding, and his eyes glistening. But he restrained himself, and said, "This takes me by surprise: let me smoke a pipe over it."

He not only did that; but he lay awake all night.

The fact is, that, for some time past, Christopher had felt sharp twinges of conscience, and deep misgivings, as to the course he had pursued in leaving his wife a single day in the dark. Complete convalescence had cleared his moral sentiments; and perhaps, after all, the discovery of the diamonds had co-operated: since now the insurance money was no longer necessary to keep his wife from starving.

"Ah!" said he, "faith is a great quality; and how I have lacked it!"

To do him justice, he knew his wife's excitable nature, and was not without fears of some disaster, should the news be communicated to her unskilfully.

But this proposal of Falcon's made the way clearer. Mrs. Falcon, though not a lady, had all a lady's delicacy, and all a woman's tact and tenderness. He knew no one in the world more fit to be trusted with the delicate task of breaking to his Rosa that the grave, for once, was baffled, and her husband lived. He now became quite anxious for Falcon's departure, and ardently hoped that worthy had not deceived himself as to Mrs. Falcon's desire to visit England.

In short, it was settled that Falcon should start for Dale's Kloof, taking with him the diamonds, believed to be worth altogether three thousand pounds at Cape Town, and nearly as much again in England, and a long letter to Mrs. Falcon, in which Staines revealed his true story, told her where to find his wife, or hear of her, viz., at Kent:

Villa, Gravesend, and sketched an outline of instructions as to the way, and cunning degrees by which the joyful news should be broken to her. With this he sent a long letter to be given to Rosa herself, but not till she should know all; and in this letter he enclosed the ruby ring she had given him. That ring had never left his finger, by sea or land, in sickness or health.

The letter to Rosa was sealed. The two letters made quite a packet; for in the letter to his beloved Rosa he told her every thing that had befallen him. It was a romance, and a picture of love, — a letter to lift a loving woman to heaven, and almost reconcile her to all her bereaved heart had suffered.

This letter, written with many tears from the heart that had so suffered, and was now softened by good fortune, and bounding with joy, Staines intrusted to Falcon, together with the other diamonds, and, with many warm shakings of the hand, started him on his way.

"But mind, Falcon," said Christopher, "I shall expect an answer from Mrs. Falcon in twenty days at farthest. I do not feel so sure as you do that she wants to go to England, and, if not, I must write to Uncle Philip. Give me your solemn promise, old fellow, — an answer in twenty days, if you have to send a Caffre on horseback."

"I give you my honor," said Falcon superbly.

"Send it to me at Bulteel's Farm."

"All right. 'Dr. Christie, Bulteel's Farm.'"

"Well, — no. Why should I conceal my real name any longer from such friends as you and your wife? Christie is short for Christopher: that *is* my Christian name; but my surname is Staines. Write to 'Dr. Staines.'"

"Dr. Staines!"

"Yes. Did you ever hear of me?"

Falcon wore a strange look. "I almost think I have. Down at Gravesend, or somewhere."

"That is curious. Yes, I married my Rosa there — poor thing! God bless her; God comfort her. She thinks me dead."

His voice trembled; he grasped Falcon's cold hand till the latter winced again; and so they parted; and Falcon rode off muttering "Dr. Staines! so, then, *you* are Dr. Staines."

CHAPTER XXI.

ROSA STAINES had youth on her side; and it is an old saying that youth will not be denied. Youth struggled with death for her, and won the battle.

But she came out of that terrible fight weak as a child. The sweet, pale face, the widow's cap, the suit of deep black — it was long ere these came down from the sick-room. And, when they did, oh the dead blank! the weary, listless life! the days spent in sighs and tears and desolation. Solitude, solitude! Her husband was gone; and a strange woman played the mother to her child before her eyes.

Uncle Philip was devotedly kind to her, and so was her father; but they could do nothing for her.

Months rolled on, and skinned the wound over. Months could not heal. Her boy became dearer and dearer; and it was from him came the first real drops of comfort, however feeble.

She used to read her lost one's diary every day, and worship in deep sorrow the mind she had scarcely respected until it was too late. She searched in this diary to find his will; and often she mourned that he had written on it so few things she could obey. Her desire to obey the dead, whom living she had often disobeyed, was really simple and touching. She would mourn to her father that there were so few commands to her in his diary. "But," said she, "memory brings me back his will in many things ; and to obey is now the only sad comfort I have."

It was in this spirit she now forced herself to keep accounts. No fear of her wearing stays now, no powder, no trimmings, no waste.

After the usual delay, her father told her she should instruct a solicitor to apply to the insurance company for the six thousand pounds. She refused with a burst of agony. "The price of his life," she screamed. "Never! I'd live on bread and water sooner than touch that vile money."

Her father remonstrated gently. But she was immovable. "No. It would be like consenting to his death."

Then Uncle Philip was sent for.

He set her child on her knee, and gave her a pen. "Come," said he sternly, "be a woman, and do your duty to little Christie."

She kissed the boy, cried, and did her duty meekly. But, when the money was brought her, she flew to Uncle Philip, and said, "There, there!" and threw it all before him, and cried as if her heart would break. He waited patiently, and asked her what he was to do with all that : invest it ?

"Yes, yes, for my little Christie."

"And pay you the interest quarterly ?"

"Oh, no, no! Dribble us out a little as we want it. That is the way to be truly kind to a simpleton. I hate that word."

"And suppose I run off with it ? Such confiding geese as you corrupt a man."

"I shall never corrupt you. Crusty people are the soul of honor."

"Crusty people!" cried Philip, affecting amazement. "What are they?"

She bit her lip, and colored a little, but answered adroitly, "They are people that pretend not to have good hearts, but have the best in the world, — far better ones than your smooth ones : that's crusty people."

"Very well," said Philip; "and I'll tell you what simpletons are. They are little transparent-looking creatures, that look shallow, but are as deep as old Nick, and make you love them in spite of your judgment. They are the most artful of their sex ; for they always achieve its great object, — to be loved, — the very thing that clever women sometimes fail in."

"Well, and, if we are not to be loved, why live at all, — such useless things as I am ?" said Rosa simply.

So Philip took charge of her money, and agreed to help her save money for her little Christopher. Poverty should never destroy him, as it had his father.

As months rolled on, she crept out into public a little, but always on foot, and a very little way from home.

Youth and sober life gradually restored her strength, but not her color nor her buoyancy.

Yet she was, perhaps, more beautiful than ever; for a holy sorrow chastened and sublimed her features : it was now a sweet, angelic, pensive beauty, that interested every feeling person at a glance.

She would visit no one; but, a twelvemonth after her bereavement, she received a few chosen visitors.

One day a young gentleman called, and sent up his card, "Lord Tadcaster," with a note from Lady Cicely Treherne, full of kindly feeling. Uncle Philip had reconciled her to Lady Cicely ; but they had never met.

Mrs. Staines was much agitated at the very name of Lord Tadcaster ; but she would not have missed seeing him for the world.

She received him, with her beautiful eyes wide open, to drink in every lineament of one who had seen the last of her Christopher.

Tadcaster was wonderfully improved : he had grown six inches out at sea, and, though still short, was not diminutive. He was a small Apollo, a model of symmetry, and had an engaging, girlish beauty, redeemed from downright effeminacy by a golden mustache like silk, and a tanned cheek that became him wonderfully.

He seemed dazzled at first by Mrs. Staines, but murmured that Lady Cicely had told him to come, or he would not have ventured.

"Who can be so welcome to me as you?" said she; and the tears came thick in her eyes directly.

Soon, he hardly knew how, he found himself talking of Staines, and telling her what a favorite he was, and all the clever things he had done.

The tears streamed down her cheeks, but she begged him to go on telling her, and omit nothing.

He complied heartily, and was even so moved by the telling of his friend's virtues, and her tears and sobs, that he mingled his tears with hers. She rewarded him by giving him her hand as she turned away her tearful face to indulge the fresh burst of grief his sympathy evoked.

When he was leaving, she said in her simple way, "Bless you!" — "Come again," she said : "you have done a poor widow good."

Lord Tadcaster was so interested and charmed, he would gladly have come back next day to see her; but he restrained that extravagance, and waited a week.

Then he visited her again. He had observed the villa was not rich in flowers, and he took her down a magnificent bouquet. cut from his father's hothouses. At sight of him, or at sight of it, or both, the color rose for once in her pale cheek; and her pensive face wore a sweet expression of satisfaction. She took his flowers, and thanked him

for them and for coming to see her.

Soon they got on the only topic she cared for; and, in the course of this second conversation, he took her into his confidence, and told her he owed every thing to Dr. Staines. "I was on the wrong road altogether, and he put me right. To tell you the truth, I used to disobey him now and then while he was alive, and I was always the worse for it; now he is gone, I never disobey him. I have written down a lot of wise, kind things he said to me ; and I never go against any one of them. I call it my book of oracles. Dear me, I might have brought it with me."

"Oh, yes ! why didn't you ? " rather reproachfully.

"I will bring it next time."

"Pray do."

Then she looked at him with her lovely swimming eyes, and said tenderly, "And so here is another that disobeyed him living, but obeys him dead. What will you think when I tell you that I, his wife, who now worship him when it is too late, often thwarted and vexed him when he was alive ? "

"No, no ! He told me you were an angel, and I believe it."

"An angel ! A good-for-nothing, foolish woman, who sees every thing too late."

"Nobody else should say so before me," said the little gentleman grandly. " I shall take *his* word before yours on this one subject. If ever there was an angel, you are one ; and oh ! what would I give if I could but say or do any thing in the world to comfort you ! "

"You can do nothing for *me*, dear, but come and see me often, and talk to me as you do, on the one sad theme my broken heart has room for."

This invitation delighted Lord Tadcaster; and the sweet word " dear " from her lovely lips entered his heart, and ran through all his veins like some rapturous but dangerous elixir. He did not say to himself, "She is a widow with a child, feels old with grief, and looks on me as a boy who has been kind to her." Such prudence and wariness were hardly to be expected from his age. He had admired her at first sight, very nearly loved her at their first interview; and now this sweet word opened a heavenly vista. The generous heart that beat in his small frame burned to console her with a life-long devotion and all the sweet offices of love.

He ordered his yacht to Gravesend (for he had become a sailor); and then he called on Mrs. Staines, and told her, with a sort of sheepish cunning, that now, as his yacht *happened* to be at Gravesend, he could come and see her very often. He watched her timidly to see how she would take that proposition.

She said with the utmost simplicity, "I'm very glad of it."

Then he produced his oracles; and she devoured them. Such precepts to Tadcaster as she could apply to her own case she instantly noted in her memory; and they became her law from that moment.

Then in her simplicity she said, "And I will show you some things in his own hand-writing that may be good for you. But I can't show you the whole book: some of it is sacred from every eye but his wife's. His wife's? Ah, me! his widow's."

Then she pointed out passages in the diary that she thought might be for his good; and he nestled to her side, and followed her white finger with loving eyes, and was in an Elysium, which she would certainly have put a stop to at that time had she divined it. But all wisdom does not come at once to an unguarded woman. Rosa Staines was wiser about her husband than she had been; but she had plenty to learn.

Lord Tadcaster anchored off Gravesend, and visited Mrs. Staines nearly every day. She received him with a pleasure that was not at all lively, but quite undisguised He could not doubt his welcome; for once, when he came, she said to the servant, "Not at home,"—a plain proof she did not wish his visit to be cut short by any one else.

And so these visits and devoted attentions of every kind went on unobserved by Lord Tadcaster's friends, because Rosa would never go out, even with him; but at last Mr. Lusignan saw plainly how this would end, unless he interfered.

Well, he did not interfere: on the contrary, he was careful to avoid putting his daughter on her guard. He said to himself, "Lord Tadcaster does her good. I'm afraid she would not marry him if he was to ask her now; but in time she might. She likes him a great deal better than any one else."

As for Philip, he was abroad for his health, somewhat impaired by his own long and faithful attendance on Rosa.

So now Lord Tadcaster was in constant attendance on Rosa. She was languid, but gentle and kind; and as mourners, like invalids, are apt to be egotistical, she saw nothing but that he was a comfort to her in her affliction.

While matters were so, the Earl of Miltshire, who had long been sinking, died; and Tadcaster succeeded to his honors and estates.

Rosa heard of it, and, thinking it was a great bereavement, wrote him one of those exquisite letters of condolence a lady alone can write. He took it to Lady Cicely, and showed it to her. She highly approved it.

He said, "The only thing—it makes me ashamed I do not feel my poor father's death more; but you know it has been so long expected." Then he was silent a long time; and then he asked her if such a woman as that would not make him happy, if he could win her.

It was on her ladyship's tongue to say, "She did not make her first happy;" but she forbore, and said coldly, that was maw than she could say.

Tadcaster seemed disappointed by that, and by and by Cicely took herself to task. She asked herself what were Tadcaster's chances in the lottery of wives. The heavy army of scheming mothers, and the light cavalry of artful daughters, rose before her cousinly and disinterested eyes, and she asked herself what chance poor little Tadcaster would have of catching a true love, with a hundred female artists manœuvring, wheeling, ambuscading, and charging upon his wealth and titles. She returned to the subject of her own accord, and told him she saw but one objection to such a match, — the lady had a son by a man of rare merit and misfortune. Could he, at his age, undertake to be a father to that son? "Othahwise," said Lady Cicely, "maak my words, you will quall over that poor child; and you will have two to quall with, because I shall be on her side."

Tadcaster declared to her that the child should be quite the opposite of a bone of contention. "I have thought of that," said he; "and I mean to be so kind to that boy, I shall *make* her love me for that."

On these terms Lady Cicely gave her consent.

Then he asked her should he write, or ask her in person.

Lady Cicely reflected. "If you write, I think she will say No."

"But if I go?"

"Then it will depend on how you do it. Rosa Staines is a true mourner. Whatever you may think, I don't believe the idea of a second union has ever entered her head. But then she is very unselfish; and she likes you better than any one else, I dare say. I don't think your title or your money will weigh with her now. But, if you show her your happiness depends on it, she may perhaps cry and sob at the very idea of it, and then, after all, say, 'Well, why not, if I can make the poor soul happy?'"

So, on this advice, Tadcaster went down to Gravesend, and Lady Cicely felt a certain self-satisfaction; for her well-meant interference having lost Rosa one husband, she was pleased to think she had done something to give her another.

Lord Tadcaster came to Rosa Staines. He found her seated with her head upon her white hand, thinking sadly of the past.

At sight of him in deep mourning she started, and said, "Oh!"

Then she said tenderly, "We are of one color now," and gave him her hand.

He sat down beside her, not knowing how to begin.

"I am not Tadcaster now. I am Earl of Miltshire."

"Ah, yes! I forgot," said she indifferently.

"This is my first visit to any one in that character."

"Thank you."

"It is an awfully important visit to me. I could not feel myself independent, and able to secure your comfort and little Christie's, without coming to the lady, the only lady I ever saw, that — O Mrs. Staines, Rosa! who could see you as I have done, mingle his tears with yours as I have done, and not love you, and long to offer you his love!"

"Love! to me a broken-hearted woman, with nothing to live for but his memory and his child!"

She looked at him with a sort of scared amazement.

"His child shall be mine. His memory is almost as dear to me as to you."

"Nonsense, child, nonsense!" said she almost sternly.

"Was he not my best friend? Should I have the health I enjoy, or even be alive, but for him? O Mrs. Staines, Rosa! you will not live all your life unmarried ; and who will love you as I do ? You are my first and only love : my happiness depends on you."

"Your happiness depend on me ! Heaven forbid ! — a woman of my age, that feels so old, old, old."

"You are not old : you are young and sad and beautiful, and my happiness depends on you." She began to tremble a little. Then he kneeled at her knees, and implored her ; and his hot tears fell upon the hand she put out to stop him, while she turned her head away, and the tears began to run.

Oh! never can the cold dissecting pen tell what rushes over the heart that has loved and lost, when another true love first kneels and implores for love or pity, or any thing the bereaved can give.

◆

CHAPTER XXII.

When Falcon went, luck seemed to desert their claim. Day after day went by without a find ; and the discoveries on every side made this the more mortifying.

By this time, the diggers at Bul teel's pan were as miscellaneous as the audience at Drury Lane Theatre, only mixed more closely : the gallery folk and the stalls worked cheek by jowl. Here a gentleman with an affected lisp, and close by an honest fellow who could not deliver a sentence without an oath, or some still more horrible expletive that meant nothing at all in reality, but served to make respectable flesh creep ; interspersed with these, Hottentots, Caffres, and wild blue-blacks gayly clad in an ostrich-feather, a scarlet ribbon, and a Tower musket sold them by some good Christian for a modern rifle.

On one side of Staines were two swells, who lay on their backs, and talked opera half the day, but seldom condescended to work without finding a diamond of some sort.

After a week's deplorable luck, his Caffre boy struck work on account of a sore in his leg : the sore was due to a very common cause, — the burning sand had got into a scratch, and festered. Staines, out of humanity, examined the sore ; and, proceeding to clean it before bandaging, out popped a diamond worth forty pounds even in the depreciated market. Staines quietly pocketed it, and bandaged the leg. This made him suspect his blacks had been cheating him on a large scale; and he borrowed Hans Bulteel to watch them, giving him a third, with which Master Hans was mightily pleased. But they could only find small diamonds ; and by this time prodigious slices of luck were reported on every side. Caffres and Boers, that would not dig, but traversed large tracts of ground when the sun was shining, stumbled over diamonds. One Boer pointed to a wagon and eight oxen, and said that one lucky glance on the sand had given him that lot ; but day after day Staines returned home, covered with dust, and almost blinded, yet with little or nothing to show for it.

One evening, complaining of his change of luck, Bulteel quietly proposed to him migration. "I am going," said he resignedly ; "and you can come with me."

"You leave your farm, sir ? Why, they pay you ten shillings a claim, and that must make a large return : the pan is fifteen acres."

"Yes, mine vriend," said the poor Hollander, "dey pay ; but deir money it cost too dear. Vere is mine peace ? Dis farm is six tousand acres. If de cursed diamonds was farther off, den it vas vell. Bud dey are too near. Once I could smoke in peace, and zleep. Now diamonds is come, and zleep and peace is fled. Dere is four tousand tents, and to each tent a dawg : dat dawg bark at four tousand oder dawgs all night ; and dey bark at him and at each oder. Den de masters of de dawgs dey get angry, and fire four tousand pistole at de four tousand dawgs, and make my bed shake wid de trembling of mine vrow. My vamily is wid diamonds infected. Dey vill not vork. Dey takes long valks, and always looks on de ground. Mine childre shall be hump-backed, round-shouldered, looking down for diamonds. Dey shall forget Gott. He is on high: deir eyes are always on de earth. De diggers found a diamond in mine plaster of mine wall of mine house. Dat plaster vas limestone; it come from dose kopjes de good Gott made in his anger against man for his vickedness. I zay so. Dey not believe me. Dey tink dem abominable stones grow in mine house, and break out in mine plaster like de measle: dey vaunt to dig in mine wall, in mine garden, in mine floor. One day dey shall dig in mine body. I vill go. Better I love peace dan money. Here is English company make me offer for mine varm. Dey forgive de diamonds."

"You have not accepted it?" cried Staines in alarm.

"No, but I vill. I have said I shall tink of it. Dat is my vay. So I say yah."

"An English company? They will cheat you without mercy. No, they shall not, though; for I will have a hand in the bargain."

He set to work directly, added up the value of the claims, at ten shillings per month, and amazed the poor Hollander by his statement of the value of those fifteen acres, capitalized.

And, to close this part of the subject, the obnoxious diamonds obtained him three times as much money as his father had paid for the whole six thousand acres.

The company got a great bargain; but Bulteel received what for him was a large capital, and, settling far to the south, this lineal descendant of "le philosophe sans le savoir" carried his godliness, his cleanliness, and his love of peace, out of the turmoil, and was happier than ever; since now he could compare his placid existence with one year of noise and clamor.

But, long before this, events more pertinent to my story had occurred.

One day a Hottentot came into Bulteel's farm, and went about among the diggers till he found Staines. The Hottentot was one employed at Dale's Kloof, and knew him. He brought Staines a letter.

Staines opened the letter, and another letter fell out: it was directed to "Reginald Falcon, Esq."

"Why," thought Staines, "what a time this letter must have been on the road! So much for private messengers."

The letter ran thus:—

"DEAR SIR,—This leaves us all well at Dale's Kloof, as I hope it shall find you and my dear husband at the diggings. Sir, I am happy to say I have good news for you. When you got well, by God's mercy, I wrote to the doctor at the hospital, and told him so. I wrote unbeknown to you, because I had promised him. Well, sir, he has written back to say you have two hundred pounds in money, and a great many valuable things, such as gold and jewels. They are all at the old bank in Cape Town; and the cashier has seen you, and will deliver them on demand. So that is the first of my good news, because it is good news to you. But, dear sir, I think you will be pleased to hear that Dick and I are thriving wonderfully, thanks to your good advice. The wooden house it is built, and a great oven. But, sir, the traffic came almost before we were ready, and the miners that call here, coming and going, every day, you would not believe, likewise wagons and carts. It is all bustle, morn till night; and dear Reginald will never be dull here now. I hope you will be so kind as tell him so; for I do long to see you both home again.

"Sir we are making our fortunes. The grain we could not sell at a fair price we sell as bread, and higher than in England ever so much ! Tea and coffee the same ; and the poor things praise us, too, for being so moderate. So, sir, Dick bids me say that we owe this to you, and, if so be you are minded to share, why nothing would please us better. Head-piece is always worth money in these parts ; and, if it hurts your pride to be our partner without money, why you can throw in what you have at the Cape, though we don't ask that. And, besides, we are offered diamonds, a bargain every day, but are afraid to deal for want of experience ; but if you were in it with us, you must know them well by this time, and we might turn many a good pound that way. Dear sir, I hope you will not be offended ; but I think this is the only way we have, Dick and I, to show our respect and good-will.

"Dear sir, digging is hard work, and not fit for you and Reginald, that are gentlemen, among a lot of rough fellows, that their talk makes my hair stand on end ; though I dare say they mean no harm.

"Your bedroom is always ready, sir. I never will let it to any one of them, hoping now to see you every day. You that know every thing can guess how I long to see you both home. My very good-fortune seems not to taste like good-fortune, without those I love and esteem to share it. I shall count how many days this letter will take to reach you ; and then I shall pray for your safety harder than ever till the blessed hour comes when I see my husband and my good friend, never to part again, I hope in this world.

"I am, sir your dutiful servant and friend,   PHŒBE DALE.

"P.S. — There is regular travelling to and from Cape Town, and a post now to Pniel ; but I thought it surest to send by one that knows you."

Staines read this letter with great satisfaction. He remembered his two hundred pounds ; but his gold and jewels puzzled him. Still it was good news, and pleased him not a little. Phœbe's good-fortune gratified him too, and her offer of a partnership, especially in the purchase of diamonds from returning diggers. He saw a large fortune to be made ; and wearied and disgusted with recent ill luck, blear-eyed, and almost blinded with sorting in the blazing sun, he resolved to go at once to Dale's Kloof. Should Mrs. Falcon be gone to England with the diamonds, he would stay there, and Rosa should come out to him ; or he would go and fetch her.

He went home and washed himself, and told Bulteel he had had good news, and should leave the diggings at once. He gave him up the claim, and told him to sell it by auction. It was worth two hundred pounds still. The good people sympathized with him ; and he started within an hour. He left his pickaxe and shovel, and took only his double rifle, — an admirable one, — some ammunition, including conical bullets and projectile shells given him by Falcon, a bag full of carbuncles and garnets he had collected for Ucatella, a few small diamonds, and one hundred pounds, — all that remained to him, since he had been paying wages and other things for months, and had given Falcon twenty for his journey.

He rode away, and soon put twenty miles between him and the diggings.

He came to a little store that bought diamonds, and sold groceries and tobacco. He haltered his horse to a hook, and went in. He offered a small diamond for sale. The master was out ; and the assistant said there was a glut of these small stones : he did not care to give money for it.

"Well, give me three dozen cigars."

While they were chaffering, in walked a Hottentot, and said, " Will you buy this ? " and laid a clear, glittering stone on the counter as large as a walnut.

" Yes," said the young man. " How much ? "

" Two hundred pounds."

" Two hundred pounds ! Let us look at it." He examined it, and said he thought it was a diamond; but these large stones were so deceitful he dared not give two hundred pounds. " Come again in an hour," said he; " then the master will be in."

" No," said the Hottentot quietly, and walked out.

Staines, who had been literally perspiring at the sight of this stone, mounted his horse, and followed the man. When he came up to him, he asked leave to examine the gem. The Hottentot quietly assented.

Staines looked at it all over. It had a rough side and a polished side ; and the latter was of amazing softness and lustre. It made him tremble. He said, " Look here, I have only one hundred pounds in my pocket."

The Hottentot shook his head.

" But, if you will go back with me to Bulteel's farm, I'll borrow the other hundred."

The Hottentot declined, and told him he could get four hundred pounds for it by going back to Pniel. " But," said he, " my face is turned so ; and, when Squat turn his face so, he going home. Not can bear go the other way then ; " and he held out his hand for the diamond.

Staines gave it him, and was in despair at seeing such a prize so near, yet leaving him.

He made another effort. " Well, but," said he, " how far are you going this way ? "

" Ten days."

" Why, so am I. Come with me to Dale's Kloof, and I will give the other hundred. See, I am in ear-nest; for here is one hundred, at all events."

Staines made this proposal, trembling with excitement. To his surprise and joy, the Hottentot assented, though with an air of indifference ; and on these terms they became fellow-travellers, and Staines gave him a cigar. They went on side by side, and halted for the night forty miles from Bulteel's farm.

They slept in a Boer's outhouse ; and the vrow was civil, and lent Staines a jackal's skin. In the morning he bought it for a diamond, a carbuncle, and a score of garnets ; for a horrible thought had occurred to him, — if they stopped at any place where miners were, somebody might buy the great diamond over his head. This fear, and others, grew on him ; and, with all his philosophy, he went on thorns, and was the slave of the diamond.

He resolved to keep his Hottentot all to himself if possible. He shot a springbok that crossed the road ; and they roasted a portion of the animal, and the Hottentot carried some on with him.

Seeing he admired the rifle, Staines offered it him for the odd hundred pounds ; but, though Squat's eye glittered a moment, he declined.

Finding that they met too many diggers and carts, Staines asked his Hottentot was there no nearer way to reach that star, pointing to one he knew was just over Dale's Kloof.

Oh, yes ! he knew a nearer way, where there were trees and shade and grass, and many beasts to shoot.

" Let us take that way," said Staines.

The Hottentot, ductile as wax, except about the price of the diamond, assented-calmly ; and next day they diverged, and got into forest scenery ; and their eyes were soothed with green glades here and there, wherever the clumps of trees

Sheltered the grass from the panting sun. Animals abounded, and were tame. Staines, an excellent marksman, shot the Hottentot his supper without any trouble.

Sleeping in the woods, with not a creature near but Squat, a sombre thought struck Staines. Suppose this Hottentot should assassinate him for his money, who would ever know? The thought was horrible; and he awoke with a start ten times that night. The Hottentot slept like a stone, and never feared for his own life and precious booty. Staines was compelled to own to himself he had less faith in human goodness than the savage had. He said to himself, "He is my superior. He is the master of this dreadful diamond, and I am its slave."

Next day they went on till noon; and then they halted at a really delightful spot. A silver kloof ran along a bottom; and there was a little clump of three acacia-trees that lowered their long tresses pining for the stream, and sometimes getting a cool, grateful kiss from it when the water was high.

They haltered the horse, bathed in the stream, and lay luxurious under the acacias. All was delicious languor and enjoyment of life.

The Hottentot made a fire, and burned the remains of a little sort of kangaroo Staines had shot him the evening before; but it did not suffice his maw; and, looking about him, he saw three elands leisurely feeding about three hundred yards off. They were cropping the rich herbage close to the shelter of a wood.

The Hottentot suggested that this was an excellent opportunity. He would borrow Staines's rifle, steal into the wood, crawl on his belly close up to them, and send a bullet through one.

Staines did not relish the proposal. He had seen the savage's eye repeatedly gloat on the rifle, and was not without hopes he might

even yet relent, and give the great diamond for the hundred pounds and this rifle; and he was so demoralized by the diamond, and filled with suspicions, that he feared the savage, if he once had the rifle in his possession, might cut, and be seen no more, in which case he, Staines, still the slave of the diamond, might hang himself on the nearest tree, and so secure his Rosa the insurance money, at all events. In short, he he had really diamond on the brain.

He hemmed and hawed a little at Squat's proposal, and then got out of it by saying, "That is not necessary. I can shoot it from here."

"It is too far," objected Blacky.

"Too far! This is an Enfield rifle. I could kill the poor beast at three times that distance."

Blacky was amazed. "An Enfeel rifle," said he, in the soft, musical murmur of his tribe, which is the one charm of the poor Hottentot; "and shoot three times so far."

"Yes," said Christopher. Then, seeing his companion's hesitation, he conceived a hope. "If I kill that eland from here, will you give me the diamond for my horse and the wonderful rifle? No Hottentot has such a rifle."

Squat became cold directly. "The price of the diamond is two hundred pounds."

Staines groaned with disappointment, and thought to himself, with rage, "Anybody but me would club the rifle, give the obstinate black brute a stunner, and take the diamond — God forgive me!"

Says the Hottentot cunningly, "I can't think so far as white man. Let me see the eland dead, and then I shall know how far the rifle shoot."

"Very well," said Staines. But he felt sure the savage only wanted his meal, and would never part with the diamond except for the odd money.

However, he loaded his left barrel

with one of the explosive projectiles Falcon had given him : it was a little fulminating shell with a steel point. It was with this barrel he had shot the murcat overnight ; and he had found he shot better with this barrel than the other. He loaded his right barrel then, saw the powder well up, capped it, and cut away a strip of the acacia with his knife to see clear, and lying down in volunteer fashion, elbow on ground, drew his head steadily on an eland that presented him her broadside, her back being turned to the wood. The sun shone on her soft coat, and never was a fairer mark ; the sportsman's deadly eye being in the cool shade, the animal in the sun.

He aimed long and steadily. But, just as he was about to pull the trigger, Mind interposed ; and he lowered the deadly weapon. "Poor creature !" he said, "I am going to take her life — for what ? for a single meal. She is as big as a pony ; and I am to lay her carcass on the plain, that we may eat two pounds of it. This is how the weasel kills the rabbit ; sucks an ounce of blood for his food, and wastes the rest. So the demoralized sheep-dog tears out the poor creature's kidneys, and wastes the rest. Man, armed by science with such powers of slaying, should be less egotistical than weasels and perverted sheep-dogs. I will not kill her. I will not lay that beautiful body of hers low, and glaze those tender, loving eyes that never gleamed with hate or rage at man, and fix those innocent jaws that never bit the life out of any thing, not even of the grass she feeds on, and does it more good than harm. Feed on, poor innocent. And you be blanked,—you and your diamond, that I begin to wish I had never seen ; for it would corrupt an angel." •

Squat understood one word in ten ; but he managed to reply. "This is nonsense-talk," said he

gravely. "The life is no bigger in that than in the murcat you shot last shoot."

"No more it is," said Staines. "I am a fool. It is come to this, then, — Caffres teach us theology, and Hottentots morality. I bow to my intellectual superior. I'll shoot the eland." He raised his rifle again.

"No, no, no, no, no, no !" murmured the Hottentot, in a sweet voice scarcely audible, yet so keen in its entreaty, that Staines turned hastily round to look at him. His face was ashy, his teeth chattering, his limbs shaking. Before Staines could ask him what was the matter, he pointed through an aperture of the acacias into the wood hard by the elands. Staines looked, and saw what seemed to him a very long dog, or some such animal, crawling from tree to tree. He did not at all share the terror of his companion, nor understand it. But a terrible explanation followed. This creature, having got to the skirt of the wood, expanded, by some strange magic, to an incredible size, and sprang into the open with a growl, a mighty lion : he seemed to ricochet from the ground, so immense was his second bound, that carried him to the eland ; and he struck her one blow on the head with his terrible paw, and felled her as if with a thunder-bolt. Down went her body, with all the legs doubled, and her poor head turned over, and the nose kissed the ground. The lion stood motionless. Presently the eland, who was not dead, but stunned, began to recover, and struggle feebly up. Then the lion sprang on her with a roar, and rolled her over, and, with two tremendous bites and a shake, tore her entrails out, and laid her dying. He sat composedly down, and contemplated her last convulsions without touching her again.

At his roar, though not loud, the horse, though he had never heard or seen a lion, trembled, and pulled at his halter.

Blacky crept into the water, and Staines was struck with such an awe as he had never felt. Nevertheless, the king of beasts being at a distance, and occupied, and Staines a brave man, and out of sight, he kept his ground and watched, and by those means saw a sight never to be forgotten. The lion rose up, and stood in the sun, incredibly beautiful as well as terrible. His was not the mangy hue of the caged lion, but a skin tawny, golden, glossy as a race-horse, and of exquisite tint that shone like pure gold in the sun; his eye a lustrous jewel of richest hue, and his mane sublime. He looked toward the wood, and uttered a full roar. This was so tremendous, that the horse shook all over as if in an ague, and began to lather. Staines recoiled, and his flesh crept; and the Hottentot went under water, and did not emerge for ever so long.

After a pause, the lion roared again; and all the beasts and birds of prey seemed to know the meaning of that terrible roar. Till then the place had been a solitude; but now it began to fill in the strangest way, as if the lord of the forest could call all his subjects together with a trumpet roar. First came two lion cubs, to whom, in fact, the roar had been addressed. The lion rubbed himself several times against the eland, but did not eat a morsel; and the cubs went in, and feasted on the prey. The lion politely and paternally drew back, and watched the young people enjoying themselves.

Meantime approached, on tiptoe, jackals and hyenas, but dared not come too near. Slate-colored vultures settled at a little distance; but not a soul dared interfere with the cubs. They saw the lion was acting sentinel, and they knew better than come near.

After a time, papa feared for the digestion of those brats, or else his own mouth watered; for he came up, knocked them head over heels with his velvet paw, and they took the gentle hint, and ran into the wood double-quick.

Then the lion began tearing away at the eland, and bolting huge morsels greedily. This made the rabble's mouth water. The hyenas and jackals and vultures formed a circle ludicrous to behold; and that circle kept narrowing as the lion tore away at his prey. They increased in numbers; and at last hunger overcame prudence. The rear rank shoved on the front, as among men; and a general attack seemed imminent.

Then the lion looked up at these invaders, uttered a reproachful growl, and went at them, patting them right and left, and knocking them over. He never touched a vulture, nor, indeed, did he kill an animal. He was a lion, and only killed to eat: yet he soon cleared the place, because he knocked over a few hyenas and jackals; and the rest, being active, tumbled over the vultures before they could spread their heavy wings. After this warning, they made a respectful circle again, through which, in due course, the gorged lion stalked into the wood.

A savage's sentiments change quickly; and the Hottentot, fearing little from a full lion, was now giggling at Staines's side. Staines asked him which he thought was the lord of all creatures, — a man, or lion.

"A lion," said Blacky, amazed at such a shallow question.

Staines now got up, and proposed to continue their journey. But Blacky was for waiting till the lion was gone to sleep after his meal.

While they discussed the question, the lion burst out of the wood within hearing of their voices, as his pricked-up ears showed, and made straight for them at a distance of scarcely thirty yards.

Now, the chances are, the lion knew nothing about them, and only came to drink at the kloof after his meal, and perhaps lie under the acacias; but who can think calmly when his first lion bursts out on him a few paces off? Staines shouldered his rifle, took a hasty, flurried aim, and sent a bullet at him.

If he had missed him, perhaps the report might have turned the lion; but he wounded him, and not mortally. Instantly the enraged beast uttered a terrific roar, and came at him with his mane distended with rage, his eyes glaring, his mouth open, and his whole body dilated with fury.

At that terrible moment, Staines recovered his wits enough to see that what little chance he had was to fire into the destroyer, not at him. He kneeled, and levelled at the centre of the lion's chest, and not till he was within five yards did he fire. Through the smoke he saw the lion in the air above him, and rolled shrieking into the stream, and crawled like a worm under the bank, by one motion, and there lay trembling.

A few seconds of sick stupor passed: all was silent. Had the lion lost him? Was it possible he might yet escape?

All was silent.

He listened, in agony, for the sniffing of the lion, puzzling him out by scent.

No: all was silent.

Staines looked round, and saw a woolly head, and two saucer eyes, and open nostrils close by him. It was the Hottentot, more dead than alive.

Staines whispered him, "I think he is gone."

The Hottentot whispered, "Gone a little way to watch. He is wise as well as strong." With this he disappeared beneath the water.

Still no sound but the screaming of the vultures, and snarling of the hyenas and jackals over the eland.

"Take a look," said Staines.

"Yes," said Squat; "but not to-day. Wait here a day or two. Den he forget and forgive."

Now, Staines, having seen the lion lie down and watch the dying eland, was a great deal impressed by this; and, as he had now good hopes of saving his life, he would not throw away a chance. He kept his head just above water, and never moved.

In this freezing situation they remained.

Presently there was a rustling that made both crouch.

It was followed by a croaking noise.

Christopher made himself small.

The Hottentot, on the contrary, raised his head, and ventured a little way into the stream.

By these means he saw it. was something very foul. but not terrible. It was a large vulture that had settled on the very top of the nearest acacia.

At this the Hottentot got bolder still, and, to the great surprise of Staines, began to crawl cautiously into some rushes, and through them up the bank.

The next moment he burst into a mixture of yelling and chirping and singing, and other sounds so manifestly jubilant, that. the vulture flapped heavily away, and Staines emerged in turn, but very cautiously.

Could he believe his eyes? There lay the lion, dead as a stone, on his back, with his four legs in the air, like wooden legs, they were so very dead; and the valiant Squat dancing about him, and on him, and over him.

Staines, unable to change his sentiments so quickly, eyed even the dead body of the royal beast with awe and wonder. What, had he really laid that terrible monarch low, and with a tube made in a London shop by men who never saw a lion spring, nor heard his awful roar shake the air? He stood with his heart still beating, and said not a word. The shallow Hottentot whipped out a large knife, and began to skin the king of beasts. Staines wondered he could so profane that masterpiece of nature. He felt more inclined to thank God for so great a preservation, and then pass reverently on, and leave the dead king undesecrated.

He was roused from his solemn thoughts by the reflection that there might be a lioness about, since there were cubs. He took a piece of paper, emptied his remaining powder into it, and proceeded to dry it in the sun. This was soon done; and then he loaded both barrels.

By this time the adroit Hottentot had flayed the carcass sufficiently to reveal the mortal injury. The projectile had entered the chest, and, slanting upward, had burst among the vitals, reducing them to a gory pulp. The lion must have died in the air, when he bounded on receiving the fatal shot.

The Hottentot uttered a cry of admiration. "Not the lion king of all, nor even the white man," he said, "but Enfeel rifle!"

Staines's eyes glittered. "You shall have it and the horse for your diamond," said he eagerly. .

The black seemed a little shaken, but did not reply. He got out of it by going on with his lion; and Staines eyed him, and was bitterly disappointed at not getting the diamond even on these terms. He began to feel he should never get it. They were near the high-road; he could not keep the Hottentot to himself much longer. He felt sick at heart. He had wild and wicked thoughts; half hoped the lioness would come and kill the Hottentot, and liberate the jewel that possessed his soul.

At last the skin was off; and the Hottentot said, "Me take this to my kraal, and dey all say, 'Squat a great shooter; kill um lion.'"

Then Staines saw another chance for him, and summoned all his address for a last effort. "No, Squat," said he, "that skin belongs to me. I shot the lion with the only rifle that can kill a lion like a cat. Yet you would not give me a diamond,—a paltry stone for it. No, Squat, if you were to go into your village with that lion's skin, why, the old men would bend their heads to you, and say, 'Great is Squat! He killed the lion, and wears his skin.' The young women would all fight which should be the wife of Squat. Squat would be king of the village."

Squat's eyes began to roll.

"And shall I give the skin and the glory that is my due to an ill-natured fellow who refuses me his paltry diamond for a good horse—look at him; and for the rifle that kills lions like rabbits—behold it; and a hundred pounds in good gold and Dutch notes—see; and for the lion's skin and glory and honor and a rich wife, and to be king of Africa? Never."

The Hottentot's hands and toes began to work convulsively. "Good master, Squat ask pardon. Squat was blind. Squat will give the diamond; the great diamond of Africa, for the lion's skin, and the king rifle, and the little horse, and the gold, and Dutch notes every one of them. Dat make just two hundred pounds."

"More like four hundred," cried Staines very loud. "And how do I know it is a diamond? These large stones are the most deceitful. Show it me this instant," said he imperiously.

"Iss, master," said the crushed Hottentot, with the voice of a mouse, and put the stone into his hand with a child-like faith that almost melted Staines; but he saw he must be firm. "Where did you find it?" he bawled.

"Master," said poor Squat, in deprecating tones, "my little master at the farm wanted plaster. He send to Bulteel's pan: dere was large lumps. Squat say to miners, 'May we take de large lumps?'

Dey say, 'Yes: take de cursed lumps we no can break.' We took de cursed lumps. We ride 'em in de cart to farm, twenty milses. I beat 'em with my hammer. Dey is very hard. More dey break my heart dan I break deir cursed heads. One day I use strong words, like white man, and I hit one large lump too hard : he break, and out come de white clear stone. Iss, him diamond. Long time we know him in our kraal, because he hard. Long time before ever white man know him, tousand years ago, we find him, and he make us lilly hole in big stone for make wheat dust. Him a diamond, blank my eyes!"

This was intended as a solemn form of asseveration adapted to the white man's habits.

Yes, reader, he told the truth; and, strange to say, the miners knew the largest stones were in those great lumps of carbonate. But then the lumps were so cruelly hard, they lost all patience with them; and so, finding it was no use to break some of them, and not all, they rejected them all, with curses; and thus this great stone was carted away as rubbish from the mine, and found, like a toad in a hole, by Squat.

"Well," said Christopher, "after all, you are an honest fellow, and I think I will buy it. But first you must show me out of this wood : I am not going to be eaten alive in it for want of the king of rifles."

Squat assented eagerly; and they started at once. They passed the skeleton of the eland : its very bones were polished, and its head carried into the wood; and, looking back, they saw vultures busy on the lion. They soon cleared the wood.

Squat handed Staines the diamond, — when it touched his hand as his own, a bolt of ice seemed to run down his back, and hot water to follow it, — and the money, horse, rifle, and skin were made over to Squat.

"Shake hands over it, Squat," said Staines. "You are hard; but you are honest."

"Iss, master, I a good much hard, and honest," said Squat.

"Good-by, old fellow!"

"Good-by, master!"

And Squat strutted away, with the halter in his hand, horse following him, rifle under his arm, and the lion's skin over his shoulders, and the tail trailing, a figure sublime in his own eyes, ridiculous in creation's. So vanity triumphed even in the wilds of Africa.

Staines hurried forward on foot, loading his revolver as he went; for the very vicinity of the wood alarmed him now he had parted with his trusty rifle.

That night he lay down on the open veldt, in his jackal's skin, with no weapon but his revolver, and woke with a start a dozen times. Just before daybreak, he scanned the stars carefully, and, noting exactly where the sun rose, made a rough guess at his course, and followed it till the sun was too hot; then he crept under a ragged bush, hung up his jackal's skin, and sweated there, parched with thirst, and gnawed with hunger. When it was cooler, he crept on, and found water, but no food. He was in torture, and began to be frightened; for he was in a desert. He found an ostrich-egg, and ate it ravenously.

Next day hunger took a new form, —faintness. He could not walk for it : his jackal's skin oppressed him. He lay down, exhausted. A horror seized his dejected soul. The diamond! — it would be his death. No man must so long for any earthly thing as he had for this glittering traitor. "Oh, my good horse! my trusty rifle!" he cried. "For what have I thrown you away? For starvation. Misers have been found stretched over their gold; and some day my skeleton will be found, and nothing to tell the base death I died of, and deserved,—nothing but the cursed diamond Ay, fiend! glare in my eyes, do!" He felt delirium creeping over him; and at that a new terror froze him. His reason, that he had lost once—was he to lose it again? He prayed, he wept, he dozed, and forgot all. When he woke again, a cool air was fanning his cheeks, it revived him a little. It became almost a breeze.

And this breeze, as it happened, carried on its wings the curse of Africa. There loomed in the north-west a cloud of singular density, that seemed to expand in size as it drew nearer, yet to be still more solid, and darken the air. It seemed a dust-storm. Staines took out his handkerchief, prepared to wrap his face in it, not to be stifled.

But soon there was a whirring and a whizzing; and hundreds of locusts flew over his head: they were followed by thousands,—the swiftest of the mighty host. They thickened and thickened, till the air looked solid, and even that glaring sun was blackened by the rushing mass. Birds of all sorts whirled above, and swooped among them. They peppered Staines all over like shot. They stuck in his beard, and all over him: they clogged the bushes, carpeted the ground; while the darkened air sang as with the whirl of machinery. Every bird in the air, and beast of the field, granivorous or carnivorous, was gorged with them; and to these animals was added man, for Staines, being famished, and remembering the vrow Bulteel, lighted a fire, and roasted a handful or two on a flat stone: they were delicious. The fire once lighted, they cooked themselves; for they kept flying into it Three hours, without interruption, did they darken nature, and before the column ceased all the beasts of the field came after, gorging them so recklessly, that Staines could

have shot an antelope dead wit his pistol within a yard of him.

But, to tell the horrible truth, the cooked locusts were so nice, that he preferred to gorge on them along with the other animals.

He roasted another lot for future use, and marched on with a good heart.

But now he got on some rough, scrubby ground, and damaged his shoes, and tore his trousers.

This lasted a terrible distance; but at the end of it came the usual arid ground; and at last he came upon the track of wheels and hoofs. He struck it at an acute angle, and that showed him he had made a good line. He limped along it a little way slowly, being foot-sore.

By and by, looking back, he saw a lot of rough fellows swaggering along behind him. Then he was alarmed, terribly alarmed, for his diamond. He tore a strip off his handkerchief, and tied it cunningly under his arm-pit as he hobbled on.

The men came up with him.

"Halloo, mate! Come from the diggins?"

"Yes."

"What luck?"

"Very good."

"Haw, haw! What, found a fifty carat? Show it us."

"We found five big stones, my mate and me. He is gone to Cape Town to sell them. I had no luck when he left me, so I have cut it; going to turn farmer. Can you tell me how far it is to Dale's Kloof?"

No, they could not tell him that. They swung on; and to Staines their backs were a cordial, as we say in Scotland.

However, his travels were near an end. Next morning he saw Dale's Kloof in the distance; and, as soon as the heat moderated, he pushed on with one shoe and tattered trousers; and, half an hour before sunset, he hobbled up to the place.

It was all bustle. Travellers at

the door; their wagons and carts under a long shed.

Ueatella was the first to see him coming, and came and fawned on him with delight. Her eyes glistened, her teeth gleamed. She patted both his cheeks, and then his shoulders, and even his knees, and then flew indoors, crying, "My doctor child is come home!" This amused three travellers, and brought out Dick with a hearty welcome.

"But Lordsake, sir, why have you come afoot, and a rough road too? Look at your shoes! Halloo! What is come of the horse?"

"I exchanged him for a diamond."

"The deuse you did! And the rifle?"

"Exchanged that for the same diamond."

"It ought to be a big un."

"It is."

Dick made a wry face. "Well, sir, you know best. You are welcome, on horse or afoot. You are just in time: Phœbe and me are just sitting down to dinner."

He took him into a little room they had built for their own privacy, for they liked to be quiet now and then, being country bred; and Phœbe was putting their dinner on the table when Staines limped in.

She gave a joyful cry, and turned red all over. "O doctor!" Then his travel-torn appearance struck her. "But, dear heart! what a figure! Where's Reginald? Oh, he's not far off, *I* know!"

And she flung open the window, and almost flew through it in a moment to look for her husband.

"Reginald!" said Staines. Then, turning to Dick Dale, "Why, he is here; isn't he?"

"No, sir; not without he is just come with you."

"With me?—no. You know, we parted at the diggings. Come, Mr. Dale, he may not be here now; but he has been here: he must have been here."

Phœbe, who had not lost a word, turned round, with all her high color gone, and her cheeks getting paler and paler. "O Dick! what is this?"

"I don't understand it," said Dick. "What ever made you think he was here, sir?"

"Why, I tell you he left me to come here."

"Left you, sir!" faltered Phœbe. "Why, when, where?"

"At the diggings,—ever so long ago."

"Blank him! That is just like him, the uneasy fool!" roared Dick.

"No, Mr. Dale, you should not say that. He left me, with my consent, to come to Mrs. Falcon here, and consult her about disposing of our diamonds."

"Diamonds, diamonds!" cried Phœbe "Oh! they make me tremble. How *could* you let him go alone? You didn't let *him* go on foot, I hope?"

"Oh, no! Mrs. Falcon. He had his horse and his rifle, and money to spend on the road."

"How long ago did he leave you, sir?"

"I—I am sorry to say it was five weeks ago."

"Five weeks, and not come yet. Ah! the wild beasts! the diggers! the murderers! He is dead!"

"God forbid!" faltered Staines; but his own blood began to run cold.

"He is dead. He has died between this and the dreadful diamonds. I shall never see my darling again. He is dead; he is dead."

She rushed out of the room and out of the house, throwing her arms above her head in despair, and uttering those words of agony again and again in every variety of anguish.

At such horrible moments women always swoon—if we are to believe the dramatists. I doubt if there is one grain of truth in this. Women seldom swoon at all, unless their bodies are unhealthy, or weakened by the re-action that follows so terrible a shock as this. At all events, Phœbe, at first, was strong and wild as a lion, and went to and fro outside the house, unconscious of her body's motion, frenzied with agony, and but one word on her lips, "He is dead; he is dead!"

Dick followed her, crying like a child, but master of himself: he got his people about her, and half carried her in again; then shut the door in all their faces.

He got the poor creature to sit down; and she began to rock and moan, with her apron over her head, and her brown hair loose about her.

"Why should he be dead?" said Dick. "Don't give a man up like that, Phœbe.—Doctor, tell us more about it. O man! how could you let him out of your sight? You knew how fond the poor creature was of him."

"But that was it, Mr. Dale," said Staines. "I knew his wife must pine for him; and we had found six large diamonds, and a handful of small ones. But the market was glutted; and, to get a better price, he wanted to go straight to Cape Town. But I said, 'No: go and show them to your wife, and see whether she will go to Cape Town.'"

Phœbe began to listen, as was evident by her moaning more softly.

"Might he not have gone straight to Cape Town?" Staines hazarded this timidly.

"Why should he do that, sir? Dale's Kloof is on the road."

"Only on one road. Mr. Dale, he was well armed with rifle and revolver; and I cautioned him not to show a diamond on the road. Who would molest him? Diamonds don't show, like gold. Who was to know he had three thousand pounds hidden under his armpits and in two barrels of his revolver?"

"Three thousand pounds!" cried Dale. "You trusted *him* with three thousand pounds?"

"Certainly. They were worth about three thousand pounds in Cape Town, and half as much again in" —

Phœbe started up in a moment. "Thank God!" she cried. "There's hope for me. O Dick! he is not dead: HE HAS ONLY DESERTED ME."

And with these strange and pitiable words, she fell to sobbing, as if her great heart would burst at last.

CHAPTER XXIII.

THERE came a re-action; and Phœbe was prostrated with grief and alarm. Her brother never doubted now that Reginald had run to Cape Town for a lark. But Phœbe, though she thought so too, could not be sure; and so the double agony of bereavement and desertion tortured her by turns, and almost together. For the first time these many years, she was so crushed she could not go about her business, but lay on a little sofa in her own room, and had the blinds down; for her head ached so she could not bear the light.

She conceived a bitter resentment against Staines, and told Dick never to let him into her sight, if he did not want to be her death.

In vain Dick made excuses for him: she would hear none. For once she was as unreasonable as any other living woman. She could see nothing but that she had been happy, after years of misery, and should be happy now if this man had never entered her house. "Ah, Colly!" she cried, "you were wiser than I was. You as good as told me he would make me smart for lodging and curing him. And I was *so* happy!"

Dale communicated this as delicately as he could to Staines. Christopher was deeply grieved and wounded. He thought it unjust; but he knew it was natural. He said humbly, "I feel guilty myself, Mr. Dale; and yet, unless I had possessed omniscience, what could I do? I thought of her in all,—poor thing, poor thing!"

The tears were in his eyes; and Dick Dale went away scratching his head, and thinking it over. The more he thought, the less he was inclined to condemn him.

Staines himself was much troubled in mind, and lived on thorns. He wanted to be off to England; grudged every day, every hour, he spent in Africa. But Mrs. Falcon was his benefactress: he had been for months and months garnering up a heap of gratitude toward her. He had not the heart to leave her bad friends, and in misery. He kept hoping Falcon would return or write.

Two days after his return, he was seated, disconsolate, gluing garnets and carbuncles on to a broad tapering bit of lamb-skin, when Ucatella came to him and said, "My doctor child sick?"

"No, not sick, but miserable." And he explained to her, as well as he could, what had passed. "But," said he, "I would not mind the loss of the diamonds now, if I was only sure he was alive. I think most of poor, poor Mrs. Falcon."

While Ucatella pondered this, but with one eye of demure curiosity on the coronet he was making, he told her it was for her: he had not forgot her at the mines. "These stones," said he, "are not valued there; but see how glorious they are!"

In a few minutes he had finished the coronet, and gave it her. She uttered a chuckle of delight, and, with instinctive art, bound it, in a turn of her hand, about her brow; and then Staines himself was struck dumb with amazement. The carbuncles gathered from those mines look like rubies, so full of fire are they, and of enormous size. The chaplet had twelve great carbuncles in the centre, and went off by gradations into smaller garnets by the thousand. They flashed their blood-red flames in the African sun; and the head of Ucatella, grand before, became the head of the Sphinx, encircled with a coronet of fire. She bestowed a look of rapturous gratitude on Staines, and then glided away, like the stately Juno, to admire herself in the nearest glass, like any other coquette, black, brown, yellow, copper, or white.

That very day, toward sunset, she burst upon Staines quite suddenly, with her coronet gleaming on her magnificent head, and her eyes like coals of fire, and under her magnificent arm, hard as a rock, a boy kicking and struggling in vain. She was furiously excited, and, for the first time, showed signs of the savage in the whites of her eyes, which seemed to turn the glorious pupils into semi-circles. She clutched Staines by the shoulder with her left hand, and swept along with the pair, like dark Fate, or as potent justice sweeps away a pair of culprits, and carried them to the little window, and cried, "Open, open!"

Dick Dale was at dinner. Phœbe lying down. Dick got up rather crossly, and threw open the window. "What is up now?" said he crossly. He was like two or three more Englishmen,—hated to be bothered at dinner-time.

"Dar," screamed Ucatella, setting down Tim, but holding him tight by the shoulder: "now, you tell what you see that night, you lilly Caffir trash: if you not tell, I kill you DEAD. And she showed the whites of her eyes, like a wild beast.

Tim, thoroughly alarmed, quivered out that he had seen lilly master ride up to the gate one bright night, and look in, and Tim thought he was going in; but he changed his mind, and galloped away that way: and the monkey pointed south.

"And why couldn't you tell us this before ?" questioned Dick.

"Me mind de sheep," said Tim apologetically. "Me not mind de lilly master : jackals not eat him."

"You no more sense dan a sheep yourself," said Ucatella loftily.

"No, no ! God bless you both," cried poor Phœbe. "Now I know the worst ;" and a great burst of tears relieved her suffering heart.

Dick went out softly. When he got outside the door, he drew them all apart, and said, "Yuke, you *are* a good-hearted girl. I'll never forget this while I live. And, Tim, there's a shilling for thee ; but don't you go and spend it in Cape smoke : that is poison to whites, and destruction to blacks."

"No, master," said Tim. "I shall buy much bread, and make my tomach tiff ; " then, with a glance of reproach at the domestic caterer, Ucatella, " I almost never have my tomach tiff."

Dick left his sister alone an hour or two, to have her cry out.

When he went back to her there was a change. The brave woman no longer lay prostrate. She went about her business ; only she was always either crying, or drowning her tears.

He brought Dr. Staines in. Phœbe instantly turned her back on him with a shudder there was no mistaking.

"I had better go," said Staines. "Mrs. Falcon will never forgive me."

"She will have to quarrel with me else," said Dick steadily. "Sit you down, doctor. Honest folk like you and me and Phœbe wasn't made to quarrel for want of looking a thing all round. My sister, she hasn't looked it all round, and I have. — Come, Pheeb, 'tis no use your blinding yourself. How was the poor doctor to know your husband is a blackguard ?"

"He is not a blackguard. How dare you say that to my face ?"

"He is a blackguard, and always was ; and now he is a thief to boot. He has stolen those diamonds : you know that very well."

"Gently, Mr. Dale ; you forget : they are as much his as mine."

"Well, and if half a sheep is mine, and I take the whole and sell him, and keep the money, what is that but stealing ? Why, I wonder at you, Pheeb ! You was always honest yourself ; and yet you see the doctor robbed by your man, and that does not trouble you. What has he done to deserve it ? He has been a good friend to us. He has put us on the road. We did little more than keep the pot boiling before he came — well, yes, we stored grain : but whose advice has turned that grain to gold, I might say ? Well, what's his offence ? He trusted the diamonds to your man, and sent him to you. Is he the first honest man that has trusted a rogue ? How was he to know ? Likely he judged the husband by the wife. Answer me one thing, Pheeb. If he makes away with fifteen hundred pounds that is his, or partly yours, — for he has eaten your bread ever since I knew him, — and fifteen hundred more that is the doctor's, where shall we find fifteen hundred pounds all in a moment to pay the doctor back his own ?"

"My honest friend," said Staines, "you are tormenting yourself with shadows. I don't believe Mr. Falcon will wrong me of a shilling ; and, if he does, I shall quietly repay myself out of the big diamond. Yes, my dear friends, I did not throw away your horse, nor your rifle, nor your money : I gave them all, and the lion's skin — I gave them all — for this."

And he laid the big diamond on the table.

It was as big as a walnut, and of the purest water.

Dick Dale glanced at it stupidly. Phœbe turned her back on it with a cry of horror, and then came slowly round by degrees ; and her eyes were fascinated by the royal gem.

"Yes," said Staines sadly, "I had to strip myself of all to buy it; and, when I had got it, how proud I was! and how happy I thought we should all be over it! for it is half yours, half mine. Yes, Mr. Dale, there lies six thousand pounds that belong to Mrs. Falcon."

"Six thousand pounds!" cried Dick.

"I am sure of it. And so, if your suspicions are correct, and poor Falcon should yield to a sudden temptation, and spend all that money, I shall just coolly deduct it from your share of this wonderful stone: so make your mind easy. But no: if Falcon is really so wicked as to desert his happy home, and so mad as to spend thousands in a month or two, let us go and save him."

"That is my business," said Phœbe. "I am going in the mail-cart to-morrow."

"Well, you won't go alone," said Dick.

"Mrs. Falcon," said Staines imploringly, "let me go with you."

"Thank you, sir. My brother can take care of me."

"Me! You had better not take me. If I catch hold of him, by —— I'll break his neck, or his back, or his leg, or something: he'll never run away from you again if I lay hands on him," replied Dick.

"I'll go alone. You are both against me."

"No, Mrs. Falcon. I am not," said Staines. "My heart bleeds for you."

"Don't you demean yourself, praying her," said Dick. "It's a public conveyance: you have no need to ask *her* leave."

"That is true: I cannot hinder folk from going to Cape Town the same day," said Phœbe sullenly.

"If I might presume to advise, I would take little Tommy."

"What! all that road! Do you want me to lose my child as well as my man?"

"Oh! Mrs. Falcon!"

"Don't speak to her, doctor, to get your nose snapped off: give her time. She'll come to her senses before she dies."

Next day Mrs. Falcon and Staines started for Cape Town. Staines paid her every attention when opportunity offered. But she was sullen and gloomy, and held no converse with him.

He landed her at an inn, and then told her he would go at once to the jeweller's. He asked her piteously would she lend him a pound or two to prosecute his researches. She took out her purse without a word, and lent him two pounds. He began to scour the town. The jewellers he visited could tell him nothing. At last he came to a shop, and there he found Mrs. Falcon making her inquiries independently. She said coldly, "You had better come with me, and get your money and things."

She took him to the bank, — it happened to be the one she did business with, — and said, "This is Dr. Christie, come for his money and jewels."

There was some demur at this: but the cashier recognized him; and, Phœbe making herself responsible, the money and jewels were handed over.

Staines whispered Phœbe. "Are you sure the jewels are mine?"

"They were found on you, sir."

Staines took them, looking confused. He did not know what to think. When they got into the street again, he told her it was very kind of her to think of his interest at all.

No answer. She was not going to make friends with him over such a trifle as that.

By degrees, however, Christopher's zeal on her behalf broke the ice; and besides, as the search proved unavailing, she needed sympathy; and he gave it her, and did not abuse her husband, as Dick Dale did.

One day, in the street, after a long thought, she said to him, "Didn't you say, sir, you gave him a letter for me?"

"I gave him two letters: one of them was to you."

"Could you remember what you said in it?"

"Perfectly. I begged you, if you should go to England, to break the truth to my wife. She is very excitable; and sudden joy has killed ere now. I gave you particular instructions."

"And you were very wise. But whatever could make you think I would go to England?"

"He told me you only wanted an excuse."

"Oh!"

"When he told me that, I caught at it, of course. It was all the world to me to get my Rosa told by such a kind, good, sensible friend as you: and, Mrs. Falcon, I had no scruple about troubling you; because I knew the stones would sell for at least a thousand pounds more in England than here, and that would pay your expenses."

"I see, sir; I see. 'Twas very natural: you love your wife."

"Better than my life."

"And he told you I only wanted an excuse to go to England?"

"He did, indeed. It was not true?"

"It was any thing but true. I had suffered so in England! I had been so happy here! — too happy to last. Ah! well, it is all over. Let us think of the matter in hand. Sure that was not the only letter you gave my husband? Didn't you write to *her*?"

"Of course I did; but that was enclosed to you, and not to be given to her until you had broken the joyful news to her. Yes, Mrs. Falcon, I wrote, and told her every thing, — my loss at sea; how I was saved, after, by your kindness; our jour-

neys — from Cape Town, and then to the diggings; my sudden good-fortune, my hopes, my joy. O my poor Rosa! and now I suppose she will never get it. It is too cruel of him. I shall go home by the next steamer. I *can't* stay here any longer, for you or anybody. Oh! and I enclosed my ruby ring, that she gave me; for I* thought she might not believe you without that."

"Let me think," said Phœbe, turning ashy pale. "For mercy's sake, let me think."

"He has read both those letters, sir. She will never see hers, any more than I shall see mine."

She paused again, thinking harder and harder.

"We must take two places in the next mail-steamer. I must look after my husband, AND YOU AFTER YOUR WIFE."

CHAPTER XXIV.

MRS. FALCON'S bitter feeling against Dr. Staines did not subside: it merely went out of sight a little. They were thrown together by potent circumstances, and, in a manner, connected by mutual obligations; and an open rupture seemed too unnatural. Still Phœbe was a woman, and, blinded by her love for her husband, could not forgive the innocent cause of their present unhappy separation; though the fault lay entirely with Falcon.

Staines took her on board the steamer, and paid her every attention. She was also civil to him; but it was a cold and constrained civility.

About a hundred miles from land, the steamer stopped; and the passengers soon learned there was something wrong with her machinery.

In fact, after due consultation, the captain decided to put back.

This irritated and distressed Mrs. Falcon so, that the captain, desirous to oblige her, hailed a fast schooner that tacked across her bows, and gave Mrs. Falcon the option of going back with him, or going on in the schooner with whose skipper he was acquainted.

Staines advised her on no account to trust to sails, when she could have steam with only a delay of four or five days. But she said, "Any thing, sooner than go back. I can't, I can't, on such an errand."

Accordingly, she was put on board the schooner; and Staines, after some hesitation, felt bound to accompany her.

It proved a sad error. Contrary winds assailed them the very next day, and with such severity, that they had repeatedly to lie to.

On one of these occasions, with a ship reeling under them like a restive horse, and the waves running mountains high, poor Phœbe's terrors overmastered both her hostility and her reserve. "Doctor," said she, "I believe 'tis God's will we shall never see England. I must try and die more like a Christian than I have lived, forgiving all who have wronged me, and you, that have been my good friend and my worst enemy; but you did not mean it. Sir, what has turned me against you so — your wife was my husband's sweetheart before he married me."

"My wife your husband's — you are dreaming."

"Nay, sir: once she came in my shop, and I saw directly I was nothing to him, and he owned it all to me. He had courted her, and she jilted him. So he said. Why should he tell me a lie about that ? I'd lay my life 'tis true. And now you have sent him to her your own self; and, at sight of her, I shall be nothing again. Well, when this ship goes down, they can marry, and I hope he will be happy, happier than I can make him, that tried my best, God knows."

This conversation surprised Staines not a little. However, he said, with great warmth, it was false. His wife had danced and flirted with some young gentleman at one time, when there was a brief misunderstanding between him and her; but sweetheart she had never had, except him. He had courted her fresh from school. "Now, my good soul," said he, "make your mind easy. The ship is a good one, and well handled, and in no danger whatever; and my wife is in no danger from your husband. Since you and your brother tell me that he is a villain, I am bound to believe you. But my wife is an angel. In our miserable hour of parting she vowed not to marry again, should I be taken from her. Marry again ! what am I talking of ? Why, if he visits her at all, it will be to let her know I am alive, and give her my letter. Do you mean to tell me she will listen to vows of love from him, when her whole heart is in rapture for me ? Such nonsense ! "

This burst of his did not affront her, and did comfort her.

At last the wind abated ; and, after a wearisome calm, a light breeze came, and the schooner crept homeward.

Phœbe restrained herself for several days ; but at last she came back to the subject : this time it was in an apologetic tone at starting. "I know you think me a foolish woman," she said ; " but my poor Reginald could never resist a pretty face ; and she is so lovely ! And you should have seen how he turned when she came in to my place. Oh, sir ! there has been more between them than you know of ; and, when I think that he will have been in England so many months before we get there, O doctor ! sometimes I feel as I should go mad. My head

it is like a furnace, and see, my brow
is all wrinkled again."

Then Staines tried to comfort
her; assured her she was tormenting herself idly: her husband would,
perhaps, have spent some of the
diamond money on his amusement;
but what if he had, he should deduct
it out of the big diamond, which was
also their joint property; and the
loss would hardly be felt. "As to
my wife, madam, I have but one
anxiety,—lest he should go blurting
it out that I am alive, and almost
kill her with joy."

"He will not do that, sir. He is
no fool."

"I am glad of it; for there is
nothing else to fear."

"Man, I tell you there is every
thing to fear. You don't know
him as I do, nor his power over
'women."

"Mrs. Falcon, are you bent on
affronting me?"

"No, sir: Heaven forbid!"

"Then please to close this subject
forever. In three weeks we shall
be in England."

"Ay; but he has been there six
months."

He bowed stiffly to her, went to his
cabin, and avoided the poor foolish
woman as much as he could without seeming too unkind.

* * *

CHAPTER XXV.

MRS. STAINES made one or two
movements — to stop Lord Tadcaster — with her hand, that expressive
feature with which, at such times,
a sensitive woman can do all but
speak.

When, at last, he paused for her
reply, she said, "Me marry again!
Oh, for shame!"

"Mrs. Staines, Rosa, you will
marry again some day."

"Never. Me take another husband after such a man as I have

lost! I should be a monster. Besides"—

"Besides what?"

"No matter. O Lord Tadcaster! you have been so kind to me,
so sympathizing! You made me
believe you loved my Christopher
too; and now you have spoiled all.
It is too cruel."

"Oh, Mrs. Staines, do you think
me capable of feigning? don't you
see my love for you has taken me
by surprise? But how could I visit
you, look on you, hear you,
mingle my regrets with yours?
Yours were the deepest, of course;
but mine were honest."

"I believe it." And she gave him
her hand. He held it, and kissed it,
and cried over it, as the young will,
and implored her, on his knees, not
to condemn herself to life-long wi-
dowhood, and him to despair.

Then she cried too; but she was
firm, and by degrees she made him
see that her heart was inaccessible.

Then, at last, he submitted, with
tearful eyes, but a valiant heart.

She offered friendship timidly.

But he was too much of a man to
fall into that trap. "No," he said:
"I could not, I could not. Love,
or nothing."

"You are right," said she pity-
ingly. "Forgive me. In my selfishness and my usual folly, I did not see
this coming on, or I would have
spared you this mortification."

"Never mind that," gulped the
little earl. "I shall always be
proud I knew you, and proud I
loved you, and offered you my
hand."

Then the magnanimous little fellow blessed her, and left her, and
discontinued his visits.

Mr. Lusignan found her crying,
and got the truth out of her. He
was in despair. He remonstrated
kindly, but firmly. Truth compels
me to say that she politely ignored
him. He observed that phenomenon,
and said, "Very well, then, I shall
telegraph for Uncle Philip."

“Do,” said the rebel. “He is always welcome.”

Philip telegraphed; came down that evening; likewise his little black bag. He found them in the drawing-room; papa with the *Pall Mall Gazette*, Rosa seated, sewing, at a lamp. She made little Christie’s clothes herself; fancy that!

Having ascertained that the little boy was well, Philip, adroitly hiding that he had come down torn with anxiety on that head, inquired, with a show of contemptuous indifference, whose cat was dead.

“Nobody’s,” said Lusignan crossly. “Do you see that young lady, stitching there so demurely?”

Philip put on his spectacles.

“I see her,” said he. “She does look a little too innocent. None of them are really so innocent as all that. Has she been swearing at the nurse, and boxing her ears?”

“Worse than that. She has been and refused the Earl of Tadcaster.”

“Refused him? What! has that little monkey had the audacity?”

“The condescension, you mean?”

“Yes.”

“And she has refused him?”

“And twenty thousand a year.”

“What immorality!”

“Worse. What absurdity!”

“How is it to be accounted for? Is it the old story: ‘I could never love him’? No: that’s inadequate; for they all love a title and twenty thousand a year.”

Rosa sewed on in demure and absolute silence.

“She ignores us,” said Philip. “It is intolerable. She does not appreciate our politeness in talking at her. Let us arraign her before our sacred tribunal, and have her into court. Now, mistress, the Senate of Venice is assembled; and you must be pleased to tell us why you refused a title and twenty thousand a year, with a small but symmetrical earl tacked on.”

Rosa laid down her work, and said quietly, “Uncle, almost the last words that passed between me and my Christopher, we promised each other solemnly never to marry again till death should us part. You know how deep my sorrow has been that I can find so few wishes of my lost Christopher to obey. Well, to-day I have had an opportunity at last. I have obeyed my own lost one. It has cost me a tear or two; but, for all that, it has given me one little gleam of happiness. Ah, foolish woman, that obeys too late!”

And with this the tears began to run.

All this seemed a little too high-flown to Mr. Lusignan. “There,” said he, “see on what a straw her mind turns! So, but for that, you would have done the right thing, and married the earl?”

“I daresay I should — at the time — to stop his crying.”

And, with this listless remark, she quietly took up her sewing again.

The sagacious Philip looked at her sadly. He thought to himself how piteous it was to see so young and lovely a creature that had given up all hope of happiness for herself. These being his real thoughts, he expressed himself as follows: “We had better drop this subject, sir. This young lady will take us potent, grave, and reverend signors out of our depth, if we don’t mind.”

But the moment he got her alone he kissed her paternally, and said, “Rosa, it is not lost on me, your fidelity to the dead. As years roll on, and your deep wound first closes, then skins, then heals” —

“Ah, let me die first” —

“Time and nature will absolve you from that vow; but bless you for thinking this can never be. Rosa, your folly of this day has made you my heir: so never let money tempt you, for you have enough, and will have more than enough when I go.”

He was as good as his word;

a'tered his will next day, and made Rosa his residuary legatee.

When he had done this, foreseeing no fresh occasion for his services, he prepared for a long visit to Italy. He was packing up his things to go there, when he received a line from Lady Cicely Treherne, asking him to call on her professionally. As the lady's servant brought it, he sent back a line to say he no longer practised medicine, but would call on her as a friend in an hour's time.

He found her reclining, the picture of lassitude. "How good of you to come!" she drawled.

"What's the matter?" said he bruskly.

"I wish to cawnsnlt you about myself. I think, if anybody can brighten me up, it is you I feel such a languor! such a want of spirit! and I get palaa, and that is not desiwable."

He examined her tongue and the white of her eye, and told her, in his blunt way, she ate and drank too much.

"Excuse me, sir," said she stiffly.

"I mean too often. Now, let's see. Cup of tea in bed, of a morning?"

"Yaas."

"Dinner at two?"

"We call it luncheon."

"Are you a ventriloquist?"

"No."

"Then it is only your lips call it luncheon. Your poor stomach, could it speak, would call it dinner. Afternoon tea?"

"Yaas"

"At half-past seven another dinner. Tea after that. Your poor unhappy stomach gets no rest. You eat pastry?"

"I confess it."

"And sugar in a dozen forms?"
She nodded.

"Well, sugar is a poison to your temperament. Now, I'll set you up, if you can obey. Give up your morning dram, or" —

"What dwam?"

"Tea in bed, before eating. Can't you see that is a dram? Animal food twice a day. No wine but a little claret and water; no pastry, no sweets, and play battledoor with one of your male subjects."

"Battledaw! Won't a lady do for that?"

"No: you will get talking, and not play *ad sudorem.*"

"Ad sudawem! what is that?"

"In earnest."

"And will sudawem and the west put me in better spiwits, and give me a tinge?"

"It will incarnadine the lily, and make you the happiest young lady in England, as you are the best."

"Oh, dear! I should like to be much happier than I am good, if we could manage it among us."

"We will manage it *among* us; for, if the diet allowed should not make you boisterously gay, I have a remedy behind, suited to your temperament. I am old-fashioned, and believe in the temperaments."

"And what is that wemedy?"

"Try diet and hard exercise first."

"Oh, yes! but let me know that wemedy."

"I warn you it is what we call in medicine an heroic one."

"Never mind. I am despewate."

"Well, then, the heroic remedy — to be used only as a desperate resnrt, mind — you must marry an Irishman."
This took the lady's breath away.

"Mawwy an ice man?"

"A nice man; no! That means a fool. Marry scientifically, — a thing eternally neglected. Marry an Hibernian gentleman, a being as mercurial as you are lymphatic."

"Mercurial! lymphatic!" —

"Oh! hard words break no bones, ma'am."

"No, sir. And it is very curious. No, I won't tell you. Yes, I will. Hem! — I think I have noticed one."

“ One what ? ”

“ One Irishman dangling after me.”

“ Then your ladyship has only to tighten the cord, and *he's* done for.”

Having administered this prescription, our laughing philosopher went off to Italy ; and there fell in with some countrymen to his mind : so he accompanied them to Egypt and Palestine.

His absence, and Lord Tadcaster's, made Rosa Staines's life extremely monotonous. Day followed day, and week followed week, each so unvarying, that, on a retrospect, three months seemed like one day.

And I think, at last, youth and nature began to rebel, and secretly to crave some little change or incident to ruffle the stagnant pool. Yet she would not go into society, and would only receive two or three dull people at the villa : so she made the very monotony which was beginning to tire her, and nursed a sacred grief she had no need to nurse, it was so truly genuine.

She was in this forlorn condition, when, one morning, a carriage drove to the door, and a card was brought up to her — “ Mr. Reginald Falcon.”

Falcon's history, between this and our last advices, is soon disposed of.

When, after a little struggle with his better angel, he rode past his wife's gate, he intended, at first, only to go to Cape Town, sell the diamonds, have a lark, and bring home the balance ; but, as he rode south, his views expanded. He could have ten times the fun in London, and cheaper : since he could sell the diamonds for more money, and also conceal the true price. This was the Bohemian's whole mind in the business. He had no designs whatever on Mrs. Staines, nor did he intend to steal the diamonds, but to embezzle a portion of the purchase-money, and enjoy the pleasures and vices of the capital for a few months ; then back to his milch cow, Phœbe, and lead a quiet life till the next uncontrollable fit should come upon him along with the means of satisfying it.

On the way, he read Staines's letter to Mrs. Falcon very carefully. He never broke the seal of the letter to Mrs. Staines. That was to be given her when he had broken the good news to her ; and this he determined to do with such skill as should make Dr. Staines very unwilling to look suspiciously or ill-naturedly into money accounts.

He reached London, and, being a thorough egotist, attended first to his own interests. He never went near Mrs. Staines until he had visited every diamond merchant and dealer in the metropolis. He showed the small stones to them all ; but he showed no more than one large stone to each.

At last he got an offer of 1,200*l.* for the small stones, and the same for the large yellow stone, and 900*l.* for the second largest stone. He took this 900*l.*, and instantly wrote to Phœbe, telling her he had a sudden inspiration to bring the diamonds to England, which he could not regret, since he had never done a wiser thing. He had sold a single stone for 800*l.*, and had sent the doctor's 400*l.* to her account in Cape Town ; and, as each sale was effected, the half would be so remitted. She would see by that he was wiser than in former days. He should only stay so long as might be necessary to sell them all equally well. His own share he would apply to paying off mortgages on the family estate, of which he hoped some day to see her the mistress, or he would send it direct to her, whichever she might prefer.

Now, the main object of this artful letter was to keep Phœbe quiet, and not have her coming after him, of which he felt she was very capable.

The money got safe to Cape Town; but the letter to Phœbe miscarried. How this happened was never positively known; but the servant of the lodging-house was afterwards detected cutting stamps off a letter: so, perhaps, she had played that game on this occasion.

By this means, matters took a curious turn. Falcon, intending to lull his wife into a false security, lulled himself into that state instead.

When he had taken care of himself, and got 500*l*. to play the fool with, then he condescended to remember his errand of mercy; and he came down to Gravesend to see Mrs. Staines.

On the road, he gave his mind seriously to the delicate and dangerous task. It did not, however, disquiet him as it would you, sir, or you, madam. He had a great advantage over you. He was a liar,—a smooth, ready, accomplished liar, —and he knew it.

This was the outline he had traced in his mind He should appear very subdued and sad; should wear an air of condolence. But, after a while, should say, "And yet men have been lost like that, and escaped. A man was picked up on a raft in those very latitudes, and brought into Cape Town. A friend of mine saw him, months after, at the hospital. His memory was shaken; could not tell his name: but in other respects he was all right again."

If Mrs. Staines took fire at this, he would say his friend knew all the particulars, and he would ask him, and so leave that to rankle till next visit. And, having planted his germ of hope, he would grow it and water it, by visits and correspondence, till he could throw off the mask, and say he was convinced Staines was alive; and from

that, by other degrees, till he could say, on his wife's authority, that the man picked up at sea, and cured at her house, was the very physician who had saved her brother's life, and so on to the overwhelming proof he carried in the ruby ring and the letter.

I am afraid the cunning and dexterity, the subtlety and tact, required, interested him more in the commission than did the benevolence.

He called, sent up his card, and composed his countenance for his part, like an actor at the wing.

"Not at home."

He stared with amazement.

The history of a "Not at home," is not, in general, worth recording; but this is an exception.

On receiving Falcon's card, Mrs. Staines gave a little start, and colored faintly. She instantly resolved not to see him. What! the man she had flirted with, almost jilted, and refused to marry — he dared to be alive when her Christopher was dead, and had come there to show her *he* was alive!

She said "Not at home" with a tone of unusual sharpness and decision, which left the servant in no doubt he must be equally decided at the hall door.

Falcon received the sudden freezer with amazement. "Nonsense," said he. "Not at home at this time of the morning — to an old friend!"

"Not at home!" said the man doggedly.

"Oh, very well!" said Falcon with a bitter sneer, and returned to London.

He felt sure she was at home; and, being a tremendous egotist, he said, "Oh! all right. If she would rather not know her husband is alive, it is all one to me." And he actually took no more notice of her for full a week, and never thought of her except to chuckle over the penalty she was paying for daring to affront his vanity.

However, Sunday came. He saw a dull day before him; and so he relented, and thought he would give her another trial.

He went down to Gravesend by boat, and strolled towards the villa.

When he was about a hundred yards from the villa, a lady, all in black, came out with a nurse and child.

Falcon knew her figure all that way off, and it gave him a curious thrill that surprised him. He followed her, and was not very far behind her when she reached the church. She turned at the porch, kissed the child earnestly, and gave the nurse some directions; then entered the church.

"Come," said Falcon, "I'll have a look at her, any way."

He went into the church, and walked up a side aisle to a pillar, from which he thought he might be able to see the whole congregation. And, sure enough, there she sat a few yards from him. She was lovelier than ever. Mind had grown on her face with trouble. An angelic expression illuminated her beauty; he gazed on her, fascinated. He drank and drank her beauty two mortal hours; and when the church broke up, and she went home, he was half afraid to follow her, for he felt how hard it would be to say any thing to her but that the old love had returned on him with double force.

However, having watched her home, he walked slowly to and fro, composing himself for the interview.

He now determined to make the process of informing her a very long one. He would spin it out, and so secure many a sweet interview with her: and, who knows? he might fascinate her as she had him, and ripen gratitude into love, as he understood that word.

He called; he sent in his card. The man went in, and came back with a sonorous "Not at home."

"Not at home? Nonsense. Why she is just come in from church."

"Not at home," said the man, evidently strong in his instructions.

Falcon turned white with rage at this second affront. "All the worse for her," said he, and turned on his heel.

He went home raging with disappointment and wounded vanity; and — since such love as his is seldom very far from hate — he swore she should never know from him that her husband was alive. He even moralized. "This comes of being so unselfish," said he. "I'll give that game up forever."

By and by a mere negative revenge was not enough for him; and he set his wits to work to make her smart and see it.

He wrote to her from his lodgings : —

"DEAR MADAM, — What a pity you are never at home to me. I had something to say about your husband, that I thought might interest you.

　　　　"Yours truly,
　　　　　　"R. FALCON."

Imagine the effect of this abominable note. It was like a rock flung into a placid pool. It set Rosa trembling all over. What could he mean?

She ran with it to her father, and asked him what Mr. Falcon could mean.

"I have no idea," said he. "You had better ask him, not me."

"I am afraid it is only to get to see me. You know he admired me once. Ah, how suspicious I am getting !"

Rosa wrote to Falcon : —

"DEAR SIR, — Since my bereavement I see scarcely anybody. My servant did not know you : so I hope you will excuse me. If it is too much trouble to call again, would you kindly explain your note to me by letter.

"Yours respectfully,
"ROSA STAINES."

Falcon chuckled bitterly over this. "No, my lady," said he, "I'll serve you out. You shall run after me like a little dog. I have got the bone that will draw you."

He wrote back coldly to say that the matter he had wished to communicate was too delicate and important to put on paper; that he would try and get down to Gravesend again some day or other, but was much occupied, and had already put himself to inconvenience. He added, in a postscript, that he was always at home from four to five.

Next day he got hold of the servant, and gave her minute instructions and a guinea.

Then the wretch got some tools, and bored a hole in the partition-wall of his sitting-room. The paper had large flowers. He was artist enough to conceal the trick with water-colors. In his bedroom the hole came behind the curtains.

That very afternoon, as he had foreseen, Mrs. Staines called on him. The maid, duly instructed, said Mr. Falcon was out, but would soon return, and she could wait his return. The maid being so very civil, Mrs. Staines said she would wait a little while, and was immediately ushered into Falcon's sitting-room. There she sat down, but was evidently ill at ease, restless, flushed. She could not sit quiet, and at last began to walk up and down the room, almost wildly. Her beautiful eyes glittered, and the whole woman seemed on fire. The caitiff, who was watching her, saw and gloated on all this, and enjoyed to the full her beauty and agitation, and his revenge for her "Not at homes."

But, after a long time, there was a re-action. She sat down, and uttered some plaintive sounds inarti-culate, or nearly; and at last she began to cry.

Then it cost Faclon an effort not to come in and comfort her; but he controlled himself, and kept quiet.

She rang the bell. She asked for writing paper; and she wrote her unseen tormentor a humble note, begging him, for old acquaintance, to call on her, and tell her what his mysterious words meant that had filled her with agitation.

This done, she went away, with a deep sigh; and Falcon emerged, and pounced upon her letter.

He kissed it; he read it a dozen times. He sat down where she had sat; and his baseless passion overpowered him. Her beauty, her agitation, her fear, her tears, all combined to madden him, and do the devil's work in his false, selfish heart, so open to violent passions, so dead to conscience.

For once in his life he was violently agitated, and torn by conflicting feelings. He walked about the room more wildly than his victim had; and if it be true, that in certain great temptations, good and bad angels fight for a man, here you might have seen as fierce a battle of that kind as ever was.

At last he rushed out into the air, and did not return till ten o'clock at night. He came back pale and haggard, and with a look of crime in his face.

True Bohemian as he was, he sent for a pint of brandy.

So, then, the die was cast; and something was to be done that needed brandy.

He bolted himself in, and drank a wine-glass of it neat; then another; then another.

Now his pale cheek is flushed, and his eye glitters. Drink forever! great ruin of English souls, as well as bodies.

He put the poker in the fire, and heated it red hot.

He brought Staines's letter, and softened the sealing-wax with the hot poker; then, with his pen-knife, made a neat incision in the wax, and opened the letter. He took out the ring, and put it carefully away. Then he lighted a cigar, and read the letter, and studied it. Many a man, capable of murder in heat of passion, could not have resisted the pathos of this letter. Many a Newgate thief, after reading it, would have felt such pity for the loving husband who had suffered to the verge of death, and then to the brink of madness, and for the poor bereaved wife, that he would have taken the letter down to Gravesend that very night, though he picked two fresh pockets to defray the expenses of the road.

But this was an egotist. Good-nature had curbed his egotism a little while; but now vanity and passion had swept away all unselfish feelings, and the pure egotist alone remained.

Now, the pure egotist has been defined as a man who will burn down his *neighbor's* house to cook *himself* an egg. Murder is but egotism carried out to its natural climax. What is murder to a pure egotist, especially a brandied one?

I knew an egotist who met a female acquaintance in Newhaven village. She had a one-pound note, and offered to treat him. She changed this note to treat him. Fish she gave him, and much whiskey. Cost her four shillings. He ate and drank with her at her expense; and, his principal blood-vessel being warmed with her whiskey, he murdered her for the change, — the odd sixteen shillings.

I had the pleasure of seeing that egotist hung, with these eyes. It was a slice of luck, that, I grieve to say, has not occurred again to me.

So much for a whiskeyed egotist.

His less truculent, but equally remorseless, brother in villany, the brandied egotist, Falcon, could read that poor husband's letter without blenching. The love and the antici-pations of rapture — these made him writhe a little with jealousy; but they roused not a grain of pity. He was a true egotist, blind, remorse-less.

In this his true character he studied the letter profoundly, and mastered all the facts, and digested them well.

All manner of diabolical artifices presented themselves to his brain, barren of true intellect, yet fertile in fraud, but in that, and all low cunning and subtlety, far more than a match for Solomon or Bacon.

His sinister studies were persisted in far into the night. Then he went to bed; and his unbounded egotism gave him the sleep a grander criminal would have courted in vain on the verge of a monstrous and deliberate crime.

Next day he went to a fashionable tailor, and ordered a complete suit of black. This was made in forty-eight hours: the interval was spent mainly in concocting lies to be incorporated with the number of minute facts he had gathered from Staines's letter, and in making close imitations of his handwriting.

Thus armed, and crammed with more lies than the " Menteur " of Corneille, but not such innocent ones, he went down to Gravesend, all in deep mourning, with crape round his hat.

He presented himself at the villa.

The servant was all obsequiousness. Yes, Mrs. Staines received few visitors; but she was at home to *him*. He even began to falter excuses. " Nonsense," said Falcon, and slipped a sovereign into his hand. " You are a good servant," and obey orders."

The servant's respect doubled; and he ushered the visitor into the drawing-room, as one whose name was a passport. " Mr. Reginald Falcon, madam."

Mrs. Staines was alone. She rose to meet him. Her color came and went. Her full eye fell on him, and took in all at a glance, — that he was all in black, and that he had a beard, and looked pale, and ill at ease.

Little dreaming that this was the anxiety of a felon about to take the actual plunge into a novel crime, she was rather prepossessed by it. The beard gave him dignity, and hid his cruel mouth. His black suit seemed to say he, too, had lost some one dear to him; and that was a ground of sympathy.

She received him kindly, and thanked him for taking the trouble to come again. She begged him to be seated, and then, woman-like, she waited for him to explain.

But he was in no hurry, and waited for her. He knew she would speak if he was silent.

She could not keep him waiting long. "Mr. Falcon," said she, hesitating a little, "you have something to say to me about him I have lost."

"Yes," said he softly. "I have something I could say; and I think I ought to say it: but I am afraid; because I don't know what will be the result. I fear to make you more unhappy."

"Me! more unhappy? Me, whose dear husband lies at the bottom of the ocean. Other poor wounded creatures have the wretched comfort of knowing where he lies, of carrying flowers to his tomb; but I — O Mr. Falcon! I am bereaved of all: even his poor remains lost, lost." She could say no more.

Even that craven heart began to quake at what he was doing, — quaked, yet persevered; but his own voice quivered, and his cheek grew ashy pale. No wonder. If ever God condescended to pour his lightning on a skunk, surely now was the time.

Shaking and sweating with terror at his own act, he stammered out, "Would it be the least comfort to you to know that you are not denied that poor consolation? Suppose he died not so miserable as you think? Suppose he was picked up at sea, in a dying state?"

"Ah!"

"Suppose he lingered, nursed by kind and sympathizing hands, that almost saved him? Suppose he was laid in hallowed ground, and a great many tears shed over his grave?"

"Ah, that would indeed be a comfort! And it was to say this you came. I thank you! I bless you! But my good, kind friend, you are deceived. You don't know my husband. You never saw him. He perished at sea."

"Will it be kind, or unkind, to tell you why I think he died as I tell you, and not at sea?"

"Kind, but impossible. You deceive yourself. Ah! I see. You found some poor sufferer, and were good to him; but it was not my poor Christie. Oh, if it were, I should worship you! But I thank you, as it is. It was very kind to want to give me this little, little crumb of comfort; for I know I did not behave well to you, sir: but you are generous, and have forgiven a poor heart-broken creature that never was very wise."

He gave her time to cry, and then said to her, "I only wanted to be sure it *would* be any comfort to you. Mrs. Staines, it is true I did not even know his name, nor yours. When I met, in this very room, the great disappointment that has saddened my own life, I left England directly. I collected funds, went to Natal, and turned landowner and farmer. I have made a large fortune; but I need not tell you I am not happy. Well, I had a yacht, and, sailing from Cape Town to Algoa Bay, I picked up a raft with a dying man on it. He was perishing of exhaustion and exposure. I got a little brandy between his lips, and kept him alive. I landed with him at once: and we nursed him on shore. We had to be very cautious. He improved. We got him to take egg-flip. He smiled on us at first, and then he thanked us. I nursed him day and night for ten days. He got much stronger. He spoke to me, thanked me again and again, and told me his name was Christopher Staines. He told me he should never get well. I implored him to have courage. He said he did not want for courage; but nature had been tried too hard. We got so fond of each other. Oh!"— and the caitiff pretended to break down; and his feigned grief mingled with Rosa's despairing sobs.

He made an apparent effort, and said, "He spoke to me of his wife, his darling Rosa. The name made me start; but I could not know it was you. At last he was strong enough to write a few lines; and he made me promise to take them to his wife."

"Ah?" said Rosa. "Show them me."

"I will."

"This moment!" And her hands began to work convulsively.

"I cannot," said Falcon. "I have not brought them with me."

Rosa cast a keen eye of suspicion and terror on him. His not bringing the letter seemed monstrous; and so, indeed, it was. The fact is, the letter was not written.

Falcon affected not to notice her keen look. He flowed on, "The address he put on that letter astonished me. 'Kent Villa.' Of course I knew Kent Villa: and he called you 'Rosa.'"

"How could you come to me without that letter?" cried Rosa, wringing her hands. "How am I to know? It is all so strange, so incredible!"

"Don't you believe me?" said Falcon sadly. "Why should I deceive you? The first time I came down to tell you all this, I did not know who Mrs. Staines was. I suspected, but no more. The second time, I saw you in the church; and then I knew, and followed you, to try and tell you all this; and you were not at home to me."

"Forgive me," said Rosa carelessly: then, earnestly, "The letter —when can I see it?"

"I will send or bring it."

"Bring it! I am in agony till I see it. O my darling! my darling! It can't be true. It was not my Christie. He lies in the depths of ocean. Lord Tadcaster was in the ship, and he says so: everybody says so."

"And I say he sleeps in hallowed ground; and these hands laid him there."

Rosa lifted her hands to heaven, and cried piteously, "I don't know what to think. You would not willingly deceive me. But how can this be? O Uncle Philip! why are you away from me? Sir, you say he gave you a letter."

"Yes."

"Oh! why, why, did you not bring it?"

"Because he told me the contents; and I thought he prized my poor efforts too highly. It did not occur to me you would doubt my word."

"Oh, no! no more I do. But I fear it was not my Christie."

"I'll go for the letter at once, Mrs. Staines."

"Oh, thank you! Bless you! Yes, this minute!"

The artful rogue did not go; never intended.

He rose *to go*, but had a sudden inspiration; very sudden, of course. "Had he nothing about him you could recognize him by?"

"Yes, he had a ring I gave him."

Falcon took a black-edged envelope out of his pocket.

"A ruby ring," said she, beginning to tremble at his quiet action.

"Is that it?" and he handed her a ruby ring.

CHAPTER XXI.

Mrs. Staines uttered a sharp cry, and seized the ring. Her eyes dilated over it, and she began to tremble in every limb; and at last she sank slowly back, and her head fell on one side like a broken lily. The sudden sight of the ring overpowered her almost to fainting.

Falcon rose to call for assistance; but she made him a feeble motion not to do so.

She got the better of her faintness; and then she fell to kissing the ring in an agony of love, and wept over it, and still held it, and gazed at it through her blinding tears.

Falcon eyed her uneasily.

But he soon found he had nothing to fear. For a long time she seemed scarcely aware of his presence; and, when she noticed him, it was to thank him almost passionately.

"It was my Christie you were so good to. May Heaven bless you for it! And you will bring me his letter; will you not?"

"Of course I will."

"Oh! do not go yet. It is all so strange, so sad! I seem to have lost my poor Christie again, since he did not die at sea. But no: I am ungrateful to God, and ungrateful to the kind friend that nursed him to the last. Ah, I envy you that! Tell me all. Never mind my crying. I have seen the time I could not cry. It was worse then than now. I shall always cry when I speak of him; ay, to my dying day. Tell me, tell me all."

Her passion frightened the egotist, but did not turn him. He had gone too far. He told her, that, after raising all their hopes, Dr. Staines had suddenly changed for the worst, and sunk rapidly; that his last words had been about her; and he had said, "My poor Rosa: who will protect her?" That, to comfort him, he had said he would

protect her. Then the dying man had managed to write a line or two, and to address it. Almost his last words had been, "Be a father to my child."

"That is strange."

"You have no child? Then it must have been you he meant. He spoke of you as a child more than once."

"Mr. Falcon, I have a child, but born since I lost my poor child's father."

"Then I think he knew it. They say that dying men can see all over the world; and I remember, when he said it, his eyes seemed fixed very strangely, as if on something distant. Oh, how strange this all is! May I see his child, to whom I promised"—

The artist in lies left his sentence half completed.

Rosa rang, and sent for her little boy.

Mr. Falcon admired his beauty, and said quietly, "I shall keep my vow."

He then left her with a promise to come back early next morning with the letter.

She let him go only on those conditions.

As soon as her father came in, she ran to him with this strange story.

"I don't believe it," said he. "It is impossible."

She showed him the proof,—the ruby ring.

Then he became very uneasy, and begged her not to tell a soul. He did not tell her the reason; but he feared the insurance office would hear of it, and require proofs of Christopher's decease: whereas they had accepted it without a murmur, on the evidence of Capt. Hamilton and the *Amphitrite's* log-book.

As for Falcon, he went carefully through Staines's two letters; and, wherever he found a word that suited his purpose, he traced it by the usual process; and so, in the

course of a few hours, he concoct-
ed a short letter, all the words in
which, except three, were facsimiles,
only here and there a little shaky.
The three odd words he had to imitate by observation of the letters.
The signature he got to perfection
by tracing.

He inserted this letter in the original envelope, and sealed it very
carefully, so as to hide that the seal
had been tampered with.

Thus armed, he went down to
Gravesend. There he hired a horse,
and rode to Kent Villa.

Why he hired a horse, he knew
how hard it is to forge handwriting;
and he chose to have the means of
escape at hand.

He came into the drawing-room,
ghastly pale, and almost immediately gave her the letter; then
turned his back, feigning delicacy.
In reality, he was quaking with
fear, lest she should suspect the
handwriting. But the envelope was
addressed by Staines, and paved the
way for the letter. She was unsus-
picious and good; and her heart
cried out for her husband's last
written words. At such a moment
what chance had judgment and suspicion in an innocent and loving
soul?

Her eloquent sighs and sobs soon
told the craven he had nothing to
fear.

The letter ran thus: —

"MY OWN ROSA, —

"All that a brother could do for
a beloved brother Falcon has done.
He nursed me night and day. But
it is vain. I shall never see you
again in this world. I send you a
protector, and a father to your child.
Value him. He has promised to
be your stay on earth; and my spirit
shall watch over you.

"To my last breath,

"Your loving husband,

"CHRISTOPHER STAINES."

Falcon rose, and began to steal
on tiptoe out of the room.

Rosa stopped him. "You need
not go," said she. "You are our
friend. By and by I hope I shall
find words to thank you."

"Pray let me retire a moment,"
said the hypocrite. "A husband's
last words; too sacred — a stranger." And he went out into the
garden. There he found the nursemaid Emily, and the little boy.

He stopped the child, and made
love to the nursemaid; showed her
his diamonds (he carried them all
about him); told her he had thirty
thousand acres in Cape Colony, and
diamonds on them; and was going
to buy thirty thousand more of the
government. "Here, take one,"
said he. "Oh! you needn't be shy.
They are common enough on my
estates. I'll tell you what, though,
you could not buy that for less than
thirty pounds at any shop in London. Could she, my little duck?
Never mind, it is no brighter than
her eyes. Now, do you know what
she will do with that, Master Christie? She will give it to some duff-
er to put in a pin."

"She won't do nothing of the
kind," said Emily, flushing all over.
"She is not such a fool." She then
volunteered to tell him she had no
sweetheart, and did not trouble her
head about young men at all. He
interpreted this to mean she was
looking out for one. So do I.

"No sweetheart!" said he; "and
the prettiest girl I have seen since
I landed. Then I put in for the situation."

Here, seeing the footman coming,
he bestowed a most paternal kiss on
little Christie, and saying, "Not a
word to John, or no more diamonds
from me," he moved carefully away,
leaving the girl all in a flutter
with extravagant hopes.

The next moment this wolf in the
sheepfold entered the drawing-room.
Mrs. Staines was not there. He
waited and waited, and began to
get rather uneasy, as men will who
walk among pitfalls.

Presently the footman came to say that Mrs. Staines was with her father, in his study; but she would come to him in five minutes.

This increased his anxiety. What! She was taking advice of an older head. He began to be very seriously alarmed, and indeed had pretty well made up his mind to go down and gallop off, when the door opened, and Rosa came hastily in. Her eyes were very red with weeping. She came to him with both hands extended to him. He gave her his timidly. She pressed them with such earnestness and power as he could not have suspected; and thanked him and blessed him with such a torrent of eloquence, that he hung his head with shame. And being unable to face it out, villain as he was, yet still artful to the core, he pretended to burst out crying, and ran out of the room, and rode away.

He waited two days, and then called again. Rosa reproached him sweetly for going before she had half thanked him.

"All the better," said he. "I have been thanked a great deal too much already. Who would not do his best for a dying countryman, and fight night and day to save him for his wife and child at home? If I had succeeded, then I would be greedy of praise: but now it makes me blush; it makes me very sad."

"You did your best," said Rosa tearfully.

"Ah! that I did. Indeed I was ill for weeks after myself, through the strain upon my mind, and the disappointment, and going so many nights without sleep. But don't let us talk of that."

"Do you know what my darling says to me in my letter?"

"No."

"Would you like to see it?"

"Indeed I should; but I have no right."

"Every right. It is the only mark of esteem, worth any thing, I can show you."

She handed him the letter, and buried her own face in her hands.

He read it, and acted the deepest emotion.

He handed it back without a word.

CHAPTER XXII.

FROM this time Falcon was always welcome at Kent Villa. He fascinated everybody in the house. He renewed his acquaintance with Mr. Lusignan, and got asked to stay a week in the house. He showed Rosa and her father the diamonds; and, the truth must be owned, they made Rosa's eyes sparkle for the first time this eighteen months. He insinuated, rather than declared, his enormous wealth.

In reply to the old man's eager questions, as the large diamonds lay glittering on the table, and pointed every word, he said that a few of his Hottentots had found these for him. He had made them dig on a diamondiferous part of his estate, just by way of testing the matter; and this was the result, — this, and a much larger stone, for which he had received eight thousand pounds from Posno.

"If I was a young man," said Lusignan, "I would go out directly, and dig on your estate."

"I would not let you do any thing so paltry," said "le menteur." "Why, my dear sir, there are no fortunes to be made by grubbing for diamonds. The fortunes are made out of the diamonds, but not in that way. Now, I have thirty thousand acres, and am just concluding a bargain for thirty thousand more, on which I happen to know there are diamonds in a sly corner. Well, on my thirty thousand tried acres, a hundred only are diamondiferous. But I have four thousand thirty-foot claims, leased at ten shillings per month. Count that up."

"Why, it is twenty-four thousand pounds a year."

"Excuse me: you must deduct a thousand a year for the expenses of collection. But that is only one phase of the business. I have a large inn upon each of the three great routes from the diamonds to the coast; and these inns are supplied with the produce of my own farms. Mark the effect of the diamonds on property. My sixty thousand acres which are not diamondiferous will very soon be worth as much as sixty thousand English acres, say two pounds the acre, per annum. That is under the mark; because, in Africa, the land is not burdened with poor-rates, tithes, and all the other iniquities that crush the English landowner, as I know to my cost. But that is not all, sir. Would you believe it? Even after the diamonds were declared, the people out there had so little foresight, that they allowed me to buy land all round. Port Elizabeth, Natal, and Cape Town, the three ports through which the world gets at the diamonds, and the diamonds get at the world, — I have got a girdle of land round those three outlets, bought by the acre: in two years I shall sell it by the yard. Believe me, sir, English fortunes, even the largest, are mere child's play, compared with the colossal wealth a man can accumulate, if he looks beyond these great discoveries to their consequences, and lets others grub for him. But what is the use of it all to me?" said this Bohemian with a sigh. "I have no taste for luxuries, no love of display. I have not even charity to dispense on a large scale; for there are no deserving poor out there. And the poverty that springs from vice — that I never will encourage."

John heard nearly all this, and took it into the kitchen; and hence-

forth Adoration was the only word for this prince of men, this rare combination of the Adonis and the millionnaire.

He seldom held such discourses before Rosa, but talked her father into an impression of his boundless wealth, and half reconciled him to Rosa's refusal of Lord Tadcaster; since here was an old suitor, who, doubtless, with a little encouragement, would soon come on again.

Under this impression, Mr. Lusignan gave Falcon more than a little encouragement; and, as Rosa did not resist, he became a constant visitor at the villa, and was always there from Saturday to Monday.

He exerted all his art of pleasing; and he succeeded. He was welcome to Rosa, and she made no secret of it.

Emily threw herself in his way, and had many a sly talk with him while he was pretending to be engaged with young Christie. He flattered her, and made her sweet on him, but was too much in love with Rosa, after his fashion, to flirt seriously with her. He thought he might want her services: so he worked upon her after this fashion, — asked her if she would like to keep an inn.

"Wouldn't I just?" said she frankly.

Then he told her, that, if all went to his wish in England, she should be landlady of one of his inns in the Cape Colony. "And you will get a good husband out there directly," said he. "Beauty is a very uncommon thing in those parts. But I shall ask you to marry somebody who can help you in the business, or not to marry at all."

"I wish I had the inn!" said Emily. "Husbands are soon got when a girl hasn't her face only to look to."

"Well, I promise you the inn," said he, "and a good outfit of clothes, and money in both pockets, if you will do me a good turn here in England."

"That I· would, sir. But laws, what can a poor girl like me do for a rich gentleman like you ?"

"Can you keep a secret, Emily ?"

"Nobody better. You try me, sir."

He looked at her well; saw she was one of those who could keep a secret if she chose; and he resolved to risk it.

"Emily, my girl," said he sadly, "I am an unhappy man."

"You, sir ! Why you didn't ought to be."

"I am, then. I am in love, and cannot win her."

Then he told the girl a pretty tender tale, that he had loved Mrs. Staines when she was Miss Lusignan; had thought himself beloved in turn, but was rejected. And now, though she was a widow, he had not the courage to court her: her heart was in the grave. He spoke in such a broken voice that the girl's good nature fought against her little pique at finding how little he was smitten with *her*; and Falcon soon found means to array her cupidity on the side of her good nature. He gave her a five-pound note to buy gloves, and promised her a fortune; and she undertook to be secret as the grave, and say certain things adroitly to Mrs. Staines.

Accordingly, this young woman omitted no opportunity of dropping a word in favor of Falcon. For one thing, she said to Mrs. Staines, "Mr. Falcon must be very fond of children, ma'am. Why, he worships Master Christic."

"Indeed ! I have not observed that."

"Why, no, ma'am. He is rather shy over it; but, when he sees us alone, he is sure to come to us, and say, 'Let me look at my child, nurse:' and he do seem fit to eat him. Onst he says to me, 'This boy is my heir, nurse.' What did he mean by that, ma'am ?"

"I don't know."

"Is he any kin to you, ma'am ? "

"None whatever. You must have misunderstood him. You should not repeat all that people say."

"No, ma'am : only I did think it so odd. Poor gentleman ! I don't think he is happy, for all his money."

"He is too good to be unhappy all his life."

"So I think, ma'am."

These conversations were always short; for Rosa, though she was too kind and gentle to snub the girl, was also too delicate to give the least encouragement to her gossip.

But Rosa's was a mind that could be worked upon; and these short but repeated eulogies were not altogether without effect.

At last, the insidious Falcon, by not making his approaches in a way to alarm her, acquired her friendship as well as her gratitude; and, in short, she got used to him, and liked him. Not being bound by any limit of fact whatever, he entertained her, and took her out of herself a little by extemporaneous pictures. He told her all his thrilling adventures by flood and field, not one of which had ever occurred; yet he made them all sound like truth. He invented strange characters, and set them talking. He went after great whales, and harpooned one, which slapped his boat into fragments with one stroke of its tail, then died; and he hung on by the harpoon protruding from the carcass till a ship came and picked him up. He shot a lion that was carrying off his favorite Hottentot. He encountered another ; wounded him with both barrels; was seized, and dragged along the ground, and gave himself up for lost; but kept firing his revolver down the monster's throat, till at last he sickened that one, and so escaped out of death's maw. He did *not* say how he had fired in the air, and ridden fourteen miles on end at the bare sight of a lion's cub; but, to compensate that one reserve, plunged into a raging torrent, and saved a drowning woman by her long hair, which he caught in his teeth. He rode a race on an ostrich against a friend on a zebra, which went faster, but threw his rider, and screamed with rage at not being able to eat him; he, Falcon, having declined to run unless his friend's zebra was muzzled. He fed the hungry, clothed the naked, and shot a wild elephant in the eye; and all this he enlivened with pictorial descriptions of no mean beauty, and as like South Africa as if it had been feu George Robins advertising the Continent for sale.

In short, never was there a more voluble and interesting liar by word of mouth; and never was there a more agreeable creature interposed between a bereaved widow and her daily grief and regrets. He took her a little out of herself, and did her good.

At last, such was the charm of infinite lying, she missed him on the days he did not come, and was brighter when he did come and lie.

Things went smoothly, and so pleasantly, that he would gladly have prolonged this form of courtship for a month or two longer sooner than risk a premature declaration. But more than one cause drove him to a bolder course, — his passion, which increased in violence by contact with its beautiful object, and also a great uneasiness he felt at not hearing from Phœbe. This silence was ominous. He and she knew each other, and what the other was capable of. He knew she was the woman to cross the seas after him, if Staines left the diggings, and any explanation took place that might point to his whereabouts.

These double causes precipitated matters; and at last he began to throw more devotion into his manner. And, having so prepared her for a few days, he took his opportunity, and said one day, "We are both unhappy. Give me the right to console you."

She colored high, and said, "You have consoled me more than all the world. But there is a limit; always will be."

One less adroit would have brought her to the point; but this artist only sighed, and let the arrow rankle. By this means he outfenced her; for now she had listened to a declaration, and not stopped it short.

He played melancholy for a day or two; and then he tried her another way. He said, "I promised your dying husband to be your protector, and a father to his child. I see but one way to keep my word; and that gives me courage to speak : without that, I never could. Rosa, I loved you years ago : I am unmarried for your sake. Let me be your husband, and a father to your child."

Rosa shook her head. "I *could* not marry again. I esteem you; I am very grateful to you; and I know I behaved ill to you before. If I could marry again, it would be you. But I cannot. Oh, never, never ! "

"Then we are both to be unhappy all our days."

"I shall, as I ought to be. You will not, I hope. I shall miss you sadly; but, for all that, I advise you to leave me. You will carry my everlasting gratitude, go where you will : that and my esteem are all I have to give."

"I will go," said he; "and I hope he who is gone will forgive my want of courage."

"He who is gone took my promise never to marry again."

"Dying men see clearer. I am sure he wished — no matter. It is too delicate." He kissed her hand and went out, a picture of dejection.

Mrs. Staines shed a tear for him. Nothing was heard of him for several days; and Rosa pitied him more and more, and felt a certain discontent with herself, and doubt whether she had done right.

Matters were in this state, when, one morning, Emily came screaming in from the garden, "The child! Master Christie! Where is he? Where is he?"

The house was alarmed. The garden searched, the adjoining paddock. The child was gone.

Emily was examined, and owned, with many sobs and hysterical cries, that she had put him down in the summer-house for a minute, while she went to ask the gardener for some balm,—balm-tea being a favorite drink of hers. "But there was nobody near, that I saw," she sobbed.

Further inquiry proved, however, that a tall gypsy woman had been seen prowling about that morning; and suspicion instantly fastened on her. Servants were sent out right and left, but nothing discovered; and the agonized mother, terrified out of her wits, had Falcon telegraphed to immediately.

He came galloping down that very evening, and heard the story. He galloped into Gravesend, and, after seeing the police, sent word out he should advertise. He placarded Gravesend with rewards, and a reward of a thousand pounds; the child to be brought to him, and no questions asked.

Meantime, the police and many of the neighboring gentry came about the miserable mother with their vague ideas.

Down comes Falcon again next day; tells what he has done, and treats them all with contempt. "Don't you be afraid, Mrs. Staines," said he. "You will get him back. I have taken the sure way. This sort of rogues dare not go near the police; and the police can't find them. You have no enemies: it is only some woman that has fancied a beautiful child. Well, she can have them by the score for a thousand pounds."

He was the only one with a real idea: the woman saw it, and clung to him. He left late at night.

Next morning, out came the advertisements; and he sent her a handful by special messenger. His zeal and activity kept her bereaved heart from utter despair.

At eleven that night came a telegraph:—

"I have got him. Coming down by special train."

Then what a burst of joy and gratitude! The very walls of the house seemed to ring with it as a harp rings with music. A special train too! He would not let the mother yearn all night.

At one in the morning, he drove up with the child and a hired nurse.

Imagine the scene!—the mother's screams of joy, her furious kisses, her cooing, her tears, and all the miracles of nature at such a time. The servants all mingled with their employers in the general rapture; and Emily, who was pale as death, cried and sobbed, and said, "O ma'am! I'll never let him out of my sight again, no, not for one minute." Falcon made her a signal, and went out. She met him in the garden.

She was much agitated, and cried, "Oh, you did well to bring him to-day. I could not have kept it another hour. I'm a wretch!"

"You are a good kind girl; and here's the fifty pounds I promised you."

"Well, and I have earned it."

"Of course you have. Meet me in the garden to-morrow morning, and I'll show you you have done a kind thing to your mistress, as well as me. And, as for the fifty pounds, that is *nothing*; do you hear? It is nothing at all, compared with what I will do for you, if you will be true to me, and hold your tongue."

"Oh! as for that, my tongue sha'n't betray you, nor shame *me*. You are a gentleman, and I do think you love her, or I would not help you."

So she salved her nursemaid's conscience with the help of the fifty pounds.

The mother was left to her rapture that night. In the morning Falcon told his tale. At two, P.M., a man had called on him, and had produced one of his advertisements, and had asked him if that was all square, — no bobbies on the ·lurk. "'All square, my fine fellow,' said I. 'Well,' said he, 'I suppose you are a gentleman.' —'I am of that opinion too,' said I. 'Well, sir,' says he, 'I know a party as has *found* a young gent as comes werry nigh your advertisement.' — 'It will be a very lucky find to that party,' I said, 'if he is on the square.' — 'Oh! *we* are always on the square, when the blunt is put down.' — 'The blunt for the child, when you like, and where you like,' said I. 'You are the right sort,' said he. 'I am,' replied I. 'Will you come and see if it is all right ?' said he. 'In a minute,' said I. Stepped into my bedroom, and loaded my six-shooter."

"What is that ? " said Lusignan.

"A revolver with six barrels : by the by, the very same I killed the lion with. Ugh! I never think of that scene without feeling a little quiver ; and my nerves are pretty good too. Well, he took me into an awful part of the town, down a filthy close, into some boozing den, — I beg pardon, some thieves' public-house."

"Oh, my dear friend ! " said Rosa, "were you not frightened ? "

"Shall I tell you the truth, or play the hero ? I think I'll tell *you* the truth. I felt a little frightened, lest they should get my money and my life without my getting my godson : that is what I call him now. Well, two ugly dogs came in, and said, 'Let us see the flimsies before you see the kid.' "

"'That is rather sharp practice, I think,' said I ; 'however, here's the swag, and here's the watch-dog.' So I put down the notes, and my hand over them, with my revolver cocked, and ready to fire."

"Yes, yes," said Rosa pantingly. "Ah, you were a match for them ! "

"Well, Mrs. Staines, if I was writing you a novel, I suppose I should tell you the rogues recoiled ; but the truth is they only laughed, and were quite pleased. 'Swell's in earnest,' said one. 'Jem, show the kid.' Jem whistled ; and in came a great, tall, black gypsy woman, with the darling. My heart was in my mouth ; but I would not let them see it. I said, 'It is all right. Take half the notes here, and half at the door.' They agreed, and then I did it quick, — walked to the door ; took the child ; gave them the odd notes ; and made off as fast as I could ; hired a nurse at the hospital ; and the rest you know."

"Papa," said Rosa with enthusiasm, "there is but one man in England who would have got me back my child ; and this he."

When they were alone, Falcon told her she had said words that had gladdened his very heart. "You admit I can carry out one-half of his wishes ? " said he.

Mrs. Staines said " Yes ; " then colored high ; then, to turn it off, said, "But I cannot allow you to lose that large sum of money. You must let me repay you."

"Large sum of money ! " said he. "It is no more to me than sixpence to most people. I don't know what to do with my money ; and I never shall know, unless you will make a sacrifice of your own feelings to the wishes of the dead. O Mrs. Staines, Rosa ! do pray consider that a man of that wisdom sees the future, and gives wise advice. Sure am I, that, if you could overcome your natural repugnance to a second marriage, it would be the best thing for your little boy (I love him already as if he were my own), and in time would bring you peace and comfort, and some day, years hence, even happiness. You are my only love; yet I should never have come to you again if *he* had not sent me. Do consider how strange it all is, and what it points to, and don't let me have the misery of losing you again, when you can do no better now, alas! than reward my fidelity."

She was much moved at this artful appeal, and said, "If I was sure I was obeying his will. But how can I feel that, when we both promised never to wed again?"

"A man's dying words are more sacred than any other. You have his letter."

"Yes; but he does not say 'marry again.'"

"That is what he meant, though."

"How can you say that? How can you know?"

"Because I put the words he said to me together with that short line to you. Mind, I don't say that he did not exaggerate my poor merits: on the contrary, I think he did; but I declare to you that he did hope I should take charge of you and your child. Right or wrong, it was his wish: so pray do not deceive yourself on that point."

This made more impression on her than any thing else he could say; and she said, "I promise you one thing, — I will never marry any man but you."

Instead of pressing her further, as an inferior artist would, he broke into raptures, kissed her hand tenderly, and was in such high spirits, and so voluble all day, that she smiled sweetly on him, and thought to herself, "Poor soul! how happy I could make him with a word!"

As he was always watching her face, — a practice he carried further than any male person living, — he divined that sentiment, and wrought upon it so, that at last he tormented her into saying she would marry him *some day*.

When he had brought her to that, he raged inwardly to think he had not two years to work in; for it was evident she would marry him in time : but no, it had taken him more than four months, close siege, to bring her to that. No word from Phœbe. An ominous dread hung over his own soul. His wife would be upon him, or, worse still, her brother Dick, who, he knew, would beat him to a mummy on the spot, or, worst of all, the husband of Rosa Staines, who would kill him, or fling him into a prison. He *must* make a push.

In this emergency he used his ally, Mr. Lusignan. He told him Mrs. Staines had promised to marry him, but at some distant date. This would not do : he must look after his enormous interests in the colony, and he was so much in love, he could not leave her.

The old gentleman was desperately fond of Falcon, and bent on the match ; and he actually consented to give his daughter what Falcon called a little push.

The little push was a very great one, I think.

It consisted in directing the clergyman to call in church the banns of marriage between Reginald Falcon and Rosa Staines.

They were both in church together when this was done. Rosa all but screamed, and then turned red as fire, and white as a ghost, by turns. She never stood up again all the service ; and, in going home, refused Falcon's arm, and walked swiftly home by herself. Not that she had the slightest intention of passing this monstrous thing by in silence. On the contrary, her wrath was boiling over, and so hot, that she knew she should make a scene in the street if she said a word there.

Once inside the house, she turned

on Falcon, with a white cheek and a flashing eye, and said, "Follow me, sir, if you please." She led the way to her father's study. "Papa," said she, "I throw myself on your protection. Mr. Falcon has affronted me."

"O Rosa!" cried Falcon, affecting utter dismay.

"Publicly, publicly. He has had the banns of marriage cried in the church without my permission."

"Don't raise your voice so loud, child. All the house will hear you."

"I choose all the house to hear me. I will not endure it. I will never marry you now,—never!"

"Rosa, my child," said Lusignan, "you need not scold poor Falcon; for I am the culprit. It was I who ordered the banns to be cried."

"O papa! you had no right to do such a thing as that."

"I think I had. I exercised parental authority for once, and for your good and for the good of a true and faithful lover of yours, whom you jilted once, and now you trifle with his affection and his interests. He loves you too well to leave you; yet you know his vast estates and interests require his supervision."

"That for his vast estates!" said Rosa contemptuously. "I am not to be driven to the altar like this, when my heart is in the grave. Don't you do it again, papa, or I'll get up and forbid the banns; affront for affront."

"I should like to see that," said the old gentleman dryly.

Rosa vouchsafed no reply, but swept out of the room with burning cheeks and glittering eyes, and was not seen all day; would not dine with them, in spite of three humble, deprecating notes Falcon sent her.

"Let the spiteful cat alone," said old Lusignan. "You and I will dine together in peace and quiet."

It was a dull dinner; but Falcon took advantage of the opportunity, impregnated the father with his views, and got him to promise to have the banns cried next Sunday. He consented.

Rosa learned next Sunday morning that this was to be done; and her courage failed her. She did not go to church at all.

She cried a great deal, and submitted to violence, as your true women are too apt to do. They had compromised her, and so conquered her. The permanent feelings of gratitude and esteem caused a re-action after her passion; and she gave up open resistance as hopeless.

Falcon renewed his visits, and was received with the mere sullen languor of a woman who has given in.

The banns were cried the third time.

Then the patient Rosa bought laudanum enough to re-unite her to her Christopher in spite of them all, and, having provided herself with this resource, became more cheerful, and even kind and caressing.

She declined to name the day at present; and that was awkward. Nevertheless the conspirators felt sure they should tire her out into doing that before long; for they saw their way clear: and she was perplexed in the extreme.

In her perplexity she used to talk to a certain beautiful star she called her Christopher. She loved to fancy he was now an inhabitant of that bright star; and often, on a clear night, she would look up, and beg for guidance from this star. This I consider foolish: but then I am old and sceptical; she was still young and innocent, and sorely puzzled to know her husband's real will.

I don't suppose the star had any thing to do with it, except as a focus of her thoughts; but one fine night, after a long inspection of Christopher's star, she dreamed a dream. She thought that a lovely wedding-dress hung over a chair; that a crown of diamonds as large as an almond sparkled ready for her on the dressing-table, and she was undoing her black gown, and about to take it off, when suddenly the diamonds began to pale, and the white satin dress to melt away; and in its place there rose a pale face and a long beard, and Christopher Staines stood before her, and said quietly, "Is this how you keep your vow?" Then he sank slowly; and the white dress was black, and the diamonds were jet: and she awoke with his gentle words of remonstrance, and his very tones, ringing in her ear.

This dream, co-operating with her previous agitation and misgivings, shook her very much. She did not come down stairs till near dinner-time; and both her father and Falcon, who came as a matter of course to spend his Sunday, were struck with her appearance. She was pale, gloomy, morose, and had an air of desperation about her.

Falcon would not see it. He knew that it is safest to let her sex alone when they look like that, and the storm sometimes subsides of itself.

After dinner Rosa retired early; and, soon after, she was heard walking rapidly up and down the dressing-room.

This was quite unusual, and made a noise.

Papa Lusignan thought it inconsiderate; and after a while, remarking gently that he was not particularly fond of noise, he proposed they should smoke the pipe of peace on the lawn.

They did so; but after a while, finding that Falcon was not smoking, he said, "Don't let me detain you. Rosa is alone."

Falcon took the hint, and went to the drawing-room. Rosa met him on the stairs, with a scarf over her shoulders. "I must speak to papa," said she. "Where is he?"

"He is on the lawn, dear Rosa," said Falcon in his most dulcet tones. He was sure of his ally, and very glad to use him as a buffer to receive the first shock.

So he went into the drawing-room, where all the lights were burning, and quietly took up a book. But he did not read a line: he was too occupied in trying to read his own future.

The mean villain who is incapable of remorse is, of all men, most capable of fear. His villany had, to all appearance, reached the goal; for he felt sure that all Rosa's struggles would, sooner or later, succumb to her sense of gratitude and his strong will and patient temper. But, when the victory was won, what a life! He must fly with her to some foreign country, pursued from pillar to post by an enraged husband and by the offended law. And, if he escaped the vindictive foe a year or two, how could he escape that other enemy he knew and dreaded, — poverty? He foresaw he should come to hate the woman he was about to wrong, and she would instantly revenge herself by making him an exile, and, soon or late, a prisoner or a pauper.

While these misgivings battled with his base but ardent passion, strange things were going on out of doors, which, however, will be best related in another sequence of events, to which, indeed, they fairly belong.

CHAPTER XXIII.

STAINES and Mrs. Falcon landed at Plymouth, and went up to town by the same train. They parted in London, — Staines to go down to Gravesend, Mrs. Falcon to visit her husband's old haunts, and see if she could find him.

She did not find him; but she heard of him, and learned that he always went down to Gravesend from Saturday till Monday.

Notwithstanding all she had said to Staines, the actual information startled her, and gave her a turn. She was obliged to sit down; for her knees seemed to give way. It was but a momentary weakness. She was now a wife and a mother, and had her rights. She said to herself, "My rogue has turned that poor woman's head long before this, no doubt. But I shall go down, and just bring him away by the ear."

For once her bitter indignation overpowered every other sentiment, and she lost no time, but, late as it was, went down to Gravesend, ordered a private sitting-room and bedroom for the night, and took a fly to Kent Villa.

But Christopher Staines had the start of her. He had already gone down to Gravesend with his carpet bag, left it at the inn, and walked to Kent Villa that lovely summer night, the happiest husband in England.

His heart had never for one instant been disturbed by Mrs. Falcon's monstrous suspicion. He looked on her as a monomaniac, a sensible woman insane on one point, — her husband.

When he reached the villa, however, he thought it prudent to make sure that Falcon had come to England at all, and discharged his commission. He would not run the risk, small as he thought it, of pouncing unexpected on his Rosa, being taken for a ghost, and terrifying her, or exciting her to madness.

Now, the premises of Kent Villa were admirably adapted to what they call in war a reconnoissance. The lawn was studded with laurustinas and other shrubs that had grown magnificently in that Kentish air.

Staines had no sooner set his foot on the lawn than he heard voices. He crept towards them from bush to bush; and, standing in impenetrable shade, he saw in the clear moonlight two figures, — Mr. Lusignan and Reginald Falcon.

These two dropped out only a word or two at intervals; but what they did say struck Staines as odd. For one thing, Lusignan remarked, "I suppose you will want to go back to the Cape. Such enormous estates as yours will want looking after."

"Enormous estates!" said Staines to himself. "Then they must have grown very fast in a few months."

"Oh, yes!" said Falcon; "but I think of showing her a little of Europe first."

Staines thought this still more mysterious. He waited to hear more; but the succeeding remarks were of an ordinary kind.

He noticed, however, that Falcon spoke of his wife by her Christian name, and that neither party mentioned Christopher Staines. He seemed quite out of their little world.

Staines began to feel a strange chill creep down him.

Presently Falcon went off to join Rosa; and Staines thought it was quite time to ask the old gentleman whether Falcon had executed his commission, or not.

He was only hesitating how to do it, not liking to pounce in the dark on a man who abhorred every thing like excitement; when Rosa herself came flying out in great agitation.

Oh the thrill he felt at the sight of her! With all his self-possession, he would have sprung forward, and taken her in his arms with a mighty cry of love, if she had not immediately spoken words that rooted him to the spot with horror. But she came with the words in her very mouth, "Papa, I am come to tell you I cannot and will not marry Mr. Falcon."

"Oh, yes! you will, my dear."

"Never! I'll die sooner. Not that you will care for that. I tell you I saw my Christopher last night, — in a dream. He had a beard; but I saw him, oh, so plain! and he said, 'Is this the way you keep your promise?' That is enough for me. I have prayed again and again to his star for light. I am so perplexed and harassed by you all, and you make me believe what you like. Well, I have had a revelation. It is not my poor lost darling's wish I should wed again. I don't believe Mr. Falcon any more. I hear nothing but lies by day. The truth comes to my bedside at night. I will not marry this man."

"Consider, Rosa, your credit is pledged. You must not be always jilting him heartlessly. Dreams! nonsense. There — I love peace. It is no use your storming at me. Rave to the moon and the stars, if you like, and, when you have done, do pray come in and behave like a rational woman, who has pledged her faith to an honorable man, and a man of vast estates, — a man that nursed your husband in his last illness, found your child, at a great expense, when you had lost him, and merits eternal gratitude, not eternal jilting. I have no patience with you."

The old gentleman retired in high dudgeon.

Staines stood in the black shade of his cedar-tree, rooted to the ground by this revelation of male villany and female credulity.

He did not know what on earth to do. He wanted to kill Falcon, but not to terrify his own wife to death. It was now too clear she thought he was dead.

Rosa watched her father's retiring figure out of sight. "Very well," said she, clinching her teeth. Then suddenly she turned, and looked up to heaven. "Do you hear?" said she. "My Christie's star! I am a poor perplexed creature. I asked you for a sign; and that very night I saw him in a dream. Why should I marry out of gratitude? Why should I marry one man when I love another? What does it matter his being dead? I love him too well to

be wife to any living man. They persuade me, they coax me, they pull me, they push me. I see they will make me; but I will outwit them. See, see!" and she held up a little phial in the moonlight. "This shall cut the knot for me: this shall keep me true to my Christie, and save me from breaking promises I ought never to have made. This shall unite me once more with him I killed and loved."

She meant she would kill herself the night before the wedding; which perhaps she would not, and perhaps she would. Who can tell? The weak are violent. But Christopher, seeing the poison so near her lips, was perplexed, took two strides, wrenched it out of her hand with a snarl of rage, and instantly plunged into the shade again.

Rosa uttered a shriek, and flew into the house.

The farther she got, the more terrified she became; and soon Christopher heard her screaming in the drawing-room in an alarming way. They were like the screams of the insane.

He got terribly anxious, and followed her. All the doors were open.

As he went up stairs, he heard her cry, "His ghost, his ghost! I have seen his ghost! No, no! I feel his hand upon my arm now. A beard! and so he had in the dream. He is alive. My darling is alive. You have deceived me. You are an impostor, a villain. Out of the house this moment, or he shall kill you."

"Are you mad?" cried Falcon. "How can he be alive when I saw him dead?"

This was too much. Staines gave the door a blow with his arm, and strode into the apartment, looking white and tremendous.

Falcon saw death in his face; gave a shriek, drew his revolver, and fired at him with as little aim as he had at the lioness; then made for the open window. Staines seized a chair, followed him, and hurled it at him ; and the chair and the man went through the window together, and then there was a strange thud heard outside.

Rosa gave a loud scream, and swooned away.

Staines laid his wife flat on the floor, got the women about her ; and at last she began to give the usual signs of returning life.

Staines said to the oldest woman there, " If she sees me, she will go off again. Carry her to her room, and tell her, by degrees, that I am a'ive."

All this time Papa Lusignan had sat trembling and whimpering in a chair, moaning, " This is a painful scene, very painful." But at last an idea struck him,—" WHY, YOU HAVE ROBBED THE OFFICE ! "

Scarcely was Mrs. Staines out of the room, when a fly drove up ; and this was immediately followed by violent and continuous screaming close under the window.

" Oh, dear ! " sighed Papa Lusignan. " But never mind."

They ran down, and found Falcon impaled at full length on the spikes of the villa, and Phœbe screaming over him, and trying in vain to lift him off them. He had struggled a little, in silent terror, but had then fainted from fear and loss of blood ; and lying rather inside the rails, which were high, he could not be extricated from the outside.

As soon as his miserable condition was discovered, the servants ran down into the kitchen, and so up to the rails by the area steps. These rails had caught him : one had gone clean through his arm ; the other had penetrated the fleshy part of the thigh ; and a third through his ear.

They got him off ; but he was insensible, and the place drenched with his blood.

Phœbe clutched Staines by the arm. " Let me know the worst," said she. " Is he dead ? "

Staines examined him, and said, " No."

" Can you save him ? "

" I ? "

" Yes. Who can, if you cannot ? Oh, have mercy on me ! " And she went on her knees to him, and put her head on his knees.

He was touched by her simple faith ; and the noble traditions of his profession sided with his gratitude to this injured woman. " My poor friend," said he, " I will do my best, for *your* sake."

He took immediate steps for stanching the blood ; and the fly carried Phœbe and her villain to the inn at Gravesend.

Falcon came to on the road, but, finding himself alone with Phœbe, shammed unconsciousness of every thing but pain.

Staines, being thoroughly enraged with Rosa, yet remembering his solemn vow never to abuse her again, saw her father, and told him to tell her he should think over her conduct quietly, not wishing to be harder upon her than she deserved.

Rosa, who had been screaming and crying for joy ever since she came to her senses, was not so much afflicted at this message as one might have expected. He was alive ; and all things else were trifles.

Nevertheless, when day after day went by, and not even a line from Christopher, she began to fear he would cast her off entirely ; the more so as she heard he was now and then at Gravesend to visit Mrs. Falcon at the inn.

While matters were thus, Uncle Philip burst on her like a bomb. " He is alive ! he is alive ! he is alive ! " And they had a cuddle over it.

" O Uncle Philip ! Have you seen him ? "

" Seen him ? Yes. He caught me on the hop, just as I came in from Italy. I took him for a ghost."

"Oh! weren't you frightened?"

"Not a bit. I don't mind ghosts. I'd have half a dozen to dinner every day, if I might choose 'em. I couldn't stand stupid ones. But I say, his temper isn't improved by all this dying. He is in an awful rage with you; and what for?"

"O uncle! what for? Because I'm the vilest of women."

"Vilest of fiddlesticks! It's his fault, not yours. Shouldn't have died. It's always a dangerous experiment."

"*I* shall die if he will not forgive me. He keeps away from me and from his child."

"I'll tell you. He heard in Gravesend your banns had been cried: that has moved the peevish fellow's bile."

"It was done without my consent: papa will tell you so. And oh, uncle! if you knew the arts, the forged letter in my darling's hand, the way he wrought on me. O villain, villain! Uncle, forgive your poor silly niece, that the world is too wicked and too clever for her to live in it."

"Because you are too good and innocent," said Uncle Philip. "There, don't you be downhearted. I'll soon bring you two together again,—a couple of ninnies. I'll tell you what is the first thing. You must come and live with me. Come at once, bag and baggage. He won't show here, the sulky brute."

Philip Staines had a large house in Cavendish Square, a crusty old patient, like himself, had left him. It was his humor to live in a corner of this mansion; though the whole was capitally furnished by his judicious purchases at auctions.

He gave Rosa, and her boy, and his nurse, the entire first floor, and told her she was there for life. "Look here," said he, "this last affair has opened my eyes. Such women as you are the sweeteners of existence. You leave my roof no more. Your husband will make the same discovery. Let him run about and be miserable a bit. He will have to come to book."

She shook her head sadly.

"My Christopher will never say a harsh word to me. All the worse for me. He will quietly abandon a creature so inferior to him."

"Stuff!"

Now she was always running to the window in hope that Christopher would call on his uncle, and that she might see him; and one day she gave a scream so eloquent, Philip knew what it meant. "Get you behind that screen, you and your boy," said he, "and be as still as mice. Stop — give me that letter the scoundrel forged, and the ring."

This was hardly done, and Rosa out of sight, and trembling from head to foot, when Christopher was announced. Philip received him very affectionately, but wasted no time. "Been to Kent Villa yet?"

"No," was the grim reply.

"Why not?"

"Because I have sworn never to say an angry word to her again; and, if I was to go there, I should say a good many angry ones. Oh! when I think that her folly drove me to sea, to do my best for her, and that I was nearer death for that woman than ever man was, and lost my reason for her, and went through toil, privations, hunger, exile, mainly for her; and then to find the banns cried in open church with that scoundrel — say no more, uncle. I shall never reproach her, and never forgive her."

"She was deceived."

"I don't doubt that; but nobody has a right to be so great a fool as all that."

"It was not her folly, but her innocence, that was imposed on. You a philosopher, and not know that wisdom itself is sometimes imposed on and deceived by cunning folly! Have you forgotten your Milton?—

"At Wisdom's gate Suspicion sleeps,
And deems no ill where no ill seems."

Come, come: are you sure you are not a little to blame? Did you write home the moment you found you were not dead?"

Christopher colored high.

"Evidently not," said the keen old man. "Aha! my fine fellow, have I found the flaw in your own armor?"

"I did wrong; but it was for her. I sinned—for her. I could not bear her to be without money; and I knew the insurance. I sinned for her. She has sinned *against* me"

"And she had much better have sinned against God, hadn't she? He is more forgiving than we perfect creatures, that cheat insurance companies. And so, my fine fellow, you hid the truth from her for two or three months."

No answer.

"Strike off those two or three months: would the banns have ever been cried?"

"Well, uncle," said Christopher, hard pressed, "I am glad she has got a champion; and I hope you will always keep your eye on her."

"I mean to."

"Good-morning."

"No: don't be in a hurry. I have something else to say, not so provoking. Do you know the arts by which she was made to believe you wished her to marry again?"

"I wished her to marry again! Are you mad, uncle?"

"Whose handwriting is on this envelope?"

"Mine, to be sure."

"Now read the letter."

Christopher read the forged letter.

"Oh, monstrous!"

"This was given her with your ruby ring, and a tale so artful that nothing we read about the devil comes near it. This was what did it. The Earl of Tadcaster brought her title and wealth and love."

"What, he too! The little cub I saved, and lost myself for. Blank him! blank him!"

"Why, you stupid ninny! you forget you were dead. And he could not help loving her: how could he? Well, but you see she refused him; and why? Because he came without a forged letter from *you*. Do you doubt her love for you?"

"Of course I do. She never loved me as I loved her."

"Christopher, don't you say that before me, or you and I shall quarrel. Poor girl! she lay, in my sight, as near death for you as you were for her. I'll show you something."

He went to a cabinet, and took out a silver paper: he unpinned it, and laid Rosa's beautiful black hair upon her husband's knees. "Look at that, you hard-hearted brute!" he roared to Christopher, who sat, any thing but hard-hearted, his eyes filling fast at the sad proof of his wife's love and suffering.

Rosa could bear no more. She came out with her boy in her hand. "O uncle! do not speak harshly to him, or you will kill me quite."

She came across the room, a picture of timidity and penitence, with her whole eloquent body bent forward at an angle. She kneeled at his knees, with streaming eyes, and held her boy up to him. "Plead for your poor mother, my darling: she mourns her fault, and will never excuse it."

The cause was soon decided. All Philip's logic was nothing, compared with mighty nature. Christopher gave one great sob, and took his darling to his heart without one word; and he and Rosa clung together, and cried over each other. Philip slipped out of the room, and left the restored ones together.

I have something more to say about my hero and heroine, but must first deal with other characters, not wholly uninteresting to the reader, I hope.

Dr. Staines directed Phœbe Falcon how to treat her husband. No medicine, no stimulants; very wholesome food, in moderation, and the temperature of the body regulated by tepid water. Under these instructions, the injured but still devoted wife was the real healer. He pulled through, but was lame for life, and ridiculously lame; for he went with a spring halt, a sort of hop-and-go-one that made the girls laugh, and vexed Adonis.

Phœbe found the diamonds, and offered them all to Staines in expiation of his villany. "See," she said, "he has only spent one."

Staines said he was glad of it for her sake; for he must be just to his own family. He sold them for three thousand two hundred pounds. But for the big diamond he got twelve thousand pounds; and I believe it was worth double the money.

Counting the two sums, and deducting six hundred for the stone Mr. Falcon had embezzled, he gave her over seven thousand pounds.

She stared at him, and changed color at so large a sum. "But I have no claim on that, sir."

"That is a good joke," said he. "Why, you and I are partners in the whole thing, — you and I and Dick. Why, it was with his horse and rifle I bought the big diamond. Poor, dear, honest, manly Dick. No, the money is honestly yours, Mrs. Falcon; but don't trust a penny to your husband."

"He will never see it, sir. I shall take him back, and give him all his heart can ask for, with this; but he will be little more than a servant in the house now, as long as Dick is single: I know that." And she could still cry at the humiliation of her villain.

Staines made her promise to write to him; and she did write him a sweet womanly letter, to say that they were making an enormous fortune, and hoped to end their days

18*

in England. Dick sent his kind love and thanks.

I will add, what she only said by implication, that she was happy, after all. She still contrived to love the thing she could not respect. Once, when an officious friend pitied her for her husband's lameness, she said, "Find me a face, like his. The lamer the better: he can't run after the girls, like *some*."

Dr. Staines called on Lady Cicely Treherne. The footman stared. He left his card.

A week afterwards she called on him. She had a pink tinge in her cheeks, a general animation, and her face full of brightness and archness.

"Bless me!" said he bluntly, "is this you? How you are improved!"

"Yes," said she. "And I am come to thank you for your pwescwiption. I followed it to the lettaa."

"Woe is me! I have forgotten it."

"You diwected me to mawwy an ice man."

"Never: I hate a nice man."

"No, no, an Iwishman; and I have done it."

"Good gracious! you don't mean that! I must be more cautious in my prescriptions. After all, it seems to agree."

"Admiwably."

"He loves you?"

"To distwaction."

"He amuses you?"

"Pwodigiously. Come and see."

Dr. and Mrs. Staines live with Uncle Philip. The insurance money is returned; but the diamond money makes them very easy. Staines follows his profession now under great advantages, — a noble house, rent free; the curiosity that attaches to a man who has been canted out of a ship in mid-ocean, and lives to tell it. And then Lord Tadcaster, married into another noble house, swears by him, and talks of him: so does Lady Cicely

Munster, late Treherne; and, when such friends as these are warm, it makes a physician the centre of an important *clientelle*; but his best friend of all is his unflagging industry, and his truly wonderful diagnosis, which resembles divination. He has the ball at his feet, and, above all, that without which worldly success soon palls, — a happy home, a fireside warm with sympathy.

Mrs. Staines is an admiring, sympathizing wife, and an admirable housekeeper. She still utters inadvertencies now and then, commits new errors at odd times, but never repeats them when exposed. Observing which docility, Uncle Philip has been heard to express a fear, that, in twenty years, she will be the wisest woman in England. "But, thank Heaven!" he adds, "I shall be gone before that."

Her conduct and conversation affords this cynic constant food for observation; and he has delivered himself oracularly at various stages of the study: but I cannot say that his observations, taken as a whole, present that consistency which entitles them to be regarded as a body of philosophy. Examples: in the second month after Mrs. Staines came to live with him, he delivered himself thus: "My niece Rosa is an anomaly. She gives you the impression she is shallow. Mind your eye: in one moment she will take you out of your depth, or any man's depth. She is like those country streams I used to fish for pike when I was young. You go along, seeing the bottom everywhere; but presently you come to a corner, and it is fifteen feet deep all in a moment, and souse you go over head and ears: that's my niece Rosa."

In six months he had got to this, —and, mind you, each successive dogma was delivered in a loud, aggressive tone, and in sublime oblivion of the preceding oracle, "My niece Rosa is the most artful woman.

(You may haw, haw, haw! as much as you like. You have not found out her little game: I have.) What is the aim of all women? To be beloved by an unconscionable number of people. Well, she sets up for a simpleton, and so disarms all the brilliant people, and they love her. Everybody loves her. Just you put her down in a room with six clever women, and you will see who is the favorite. She looks as shallow as a pond, and she as deep as the ocean."

At the end of the year he threw off the mask altogether. "The *great* sweetener of a man's life," said he, "is a simpleton. I shall not go abroad any more: my house has become attractive: I've got a simpleton. When I have a headache, her eyes fill with tender concern, and she hovers about me, and pesters me with pillows. When I am cross with her, she is afraid I am ill. When I die, and leave her a lot of money, she will howl for months, and say, 'I don't want his money: I waw-waw-waw-waw-want my Uncle Philip, to love me and scold me.' One day she told me, with a sigh, I hadn't lectured her for a month. 'I am afraid I have offended you,' says she, 'or else worn you out, dear.' When I am well, give me a simpleton, to make me laugh. When I am ill, give me a simpleton, to soothe me with her innocent tenderness. A simpleton shall wipe the dews of death, and close my eyes; and, when I cross the river of death, let me be met by a band of the heavenly host, who were all simpletons here on earth, and too good for such a hole, so now they are in heaven, and their garments always white — because there are no laundresses there."

Arrived at this point, I advise the Anglo-Saxon race to retire, grinning, to fresh pastures, and leave this champion of "a simpleton" to thunder paradoxes in a desert.

THE WANDERING HEIR.

Vixere fortes ante Ortona.

CHAPTER I.

ONE raw, windy day in the spring of 1726, there was a strange buzzing by the side of a public road in the very heart of old Ireland. It came from a great many boys, seated by the roadside, plying their books and slates, with here and there a neighborly prod, followed by invectives, whispered, — for the pedagogue was marching up and down the line with a keen eye, and an immensely long black ruler, well known to the back and limbs of the scholars, except three or four whose fathers asked him to dine on poultry or butcher's meat, whenever those rarities were at the fire. The schoolroom stood opposite, and still belched through its one window the peat-smoke that had driven out the hive. There was a chimney, but so constructed, that, on a windy day, the smoke pooh-poohed it, and sought the sky by vents more congenial to the habits of the nation.

The boys were mostly farmers' sons, in long frieze coats, breeches loose at the knee, clouted shoes tied with strips of raw neat-skin, and slovenly caubeens; but there was a sprinkling of broadcloth, plain three-cornered hats, and shoe-buckles; there were also five or six bare-footed urchins, not the worst schol-ars there; for this strange anomalous people, with many traits of the pure savage, had been leaders in mediæval literature, had founded the University of Paris, and had still a noble reverence for learning. The humblest would struggle to pay a sharp boy's schooling, and so qualify him for business, perhaps for the priesthood itself, — pinnacle of an Irish peasant's ambition.

Aloof from this motley line stood a single, timid figure, — a boy with delicate skin and exquisite golden hair, his face pale and anxious. He wore a straight-cut coat, scarlet once, but now a rusty red, no hat, shoes with steel buckles — and holes. This decayed little gentleman peered anxiously round a corner of the building, and, as soon as ever the school broke up with horrid yells, ran and hid himself.

Too late. One quick young eye had seen him; and while the rest dispersed, — two or three galloping off on rough ponies, neck or nought, in a style to set their unfortunate mothers screaming to the saints, — a little party of five, eager for diversion on the spot where they had suffered study, chased that golden-haired boy, with an appalling whoop. Fear gave him wings; but numbers prevailed. They caught him, and plagued him sore; jibed him, poked him, pinched him, got him by the -

Missing Page

Missing Page

head and legs, and flogged a tree with him, and, in the exuberance of their gay hearts, pumped on his head till he gasped, and cried for mercy — in vain.

"That is foul play — five to one," said a cheerful voice, — *crick, crack, crick, crack, crack,* — and in a moment Master Matthews, one of the superior scholars, made all five heads ring with a light shillelah, but not a grain of malice: only he was a promising young cudgel-player, and must be diverted as well as the younger ones. The obstreperous mirth turned, with ludicrous swiftness, to yells of dismay; but the warlike spirit of the O'Tooles and the O'Shaughnessies soon revived; the pedagogue and his solitary servant Norah ran out staring, just in time to see battle arrayed with traditionary skill; here a crescent of five armed with stones, there Master Matthews, with a tree at his back, the lid of a slop-pail for shield, and a shillelah for sword, grinding his teeth, and looking dangerous, the fair-haired boy clasping his hands apart.

"Och, ye disperadoes! ye murtherin' villins: what is this at all?" cried Mr. Hoolaghan.

Then each side set to work to talk him over. "Masther avick," whined the army, "he hroke our heads, and kilt us with his murtherin' shillelah, the maraudin' villin, intirely."

"Masther, dear, they were five to one, torminting the life out of this little boccawn. Why didn't ye catch up a flint and crack their skulls like nuts at Hallowe'en?"

"Och! hear to the fungaleering ruffin!" And five hands were lifted high in a moment, each armed with a pebble.

Then the pedagogue grew warm, and gave them what he called his "tall English." "The first that rises a hand I'll poolverize um. Lay down your bellicose weapons, ye insurrectionary thaves, or Norah shall perforate ye — bring the spit out,

wench — and transfix ye to the primises, while I flagellate ye by dozens, till the blood pours down yer heels; lay down yer sprig of homicide, and stand on it this minit, ye vagabone, or I'll baste you with the kitchen poker till your back is coorant jelly and your head is a mashed turnup."

Mrs. Malaprop observed, in the next generation, that "there is nothing so conciliating to young people as a little severity;" and so it proved even in this. The weapons were laid down; and then Matthew Hoolaghan, changing at once to the most affectionate and dulcet tones, said, "Now, honeys, we'll discoorse the matter, not like the barbarian voolgar, that can only ratiocinate with a bludgeon, but like good Chrischins and rale Piripatetic philosophers that I have insensed in polite larning, multiplication, and all the humauities, glory be to God! Spake first, ye omadhaun, ye causa titirrima belly; and revale your crime."

"Masther, sir," said the victim, "I never done no crime. They do be always torminting me. I never offinded them. Spake the truth, now: did iver I offind you?"

"Sowl, ye did, thin! Masther, dear, look at um: he's got a Protestant face."

"Oh, fie! my father is a good Catholic; isn't he, then, sir?"

The pedagogue took fright at this turn. "Och, murther, murther!" he shrieked. "Ye conthrairy divils, would ye import the apple o' discord, an' set my two parishes cracking skulls and starving me? Would ye conflagrate the Timple of the Muses with ojum Theologicum? The first that divairges to controvarsial polimics in this Acadimy, I'll go to my brother, the priest, and have him exkimminicated alive. Face! it is a likely face enough, I'm thinkin'."

"It's the purtiest in the school, ony way," said Norah, the argument having now come within her scope, "and a dale the clanest." Whereupon one of these ready imps reminded her it was the oftenest pumped- on.

Said another, "He shouldn't pretind to be a lord's son, then, the little glorigotcen."

"But I am a lord's son," said the boy stoutly. Then there was a roar of derision. But the boy persisted that he was Lord Altham's son, and half the county of Wexford belonged to his father. Both sides appealed to the master; but he only said, "Hum!" So Norah put in her word, and said the boy had been brought there by a great lord, in a coach and six; and the lord had kissed him tenderly, and called him his darling Jemmy in her sight and hearing.

Mr. Hoolaghan admitted all that, but said, "If he was my lord's *real* son, would my lord leave his board, lodging, and schooling unpaid these fourteen months?"

"Divil a one of him!" replied an urchin with the modest promptitude of his tribe.

Jemmy was himself struck by this argument. "Alas, then!" said he, "I fear he must be dead. He was always good to me before. I was never away from him in all my life till now. Norah, when we were at Kinna, I had a little horse and boots, and rode with him a-hunting. I went to a day-school, then; and mine was the only laced hat in the school. I brought it here."

"Thrue for you, ma bouchal," said Norah; "and by the same token 'twas that thief o' the warld, Tim Doolan, that stripped it, and gave the lace to his cross-eyed wench, bad luck to the pair of 'em!"

"O master!" cried James, all of a sudden, clasping his hands, "you that knows every thing, tell me, is my father dead? The only friend I have. Ochoon! Ochoon!"

"Nay, nay," said Hoolaghan, touched by this cry of despair.

"Jemmy avick, if Lord Altham is your father, ye needn't cry, and wring your hands; for he. is alive, had eess to him: my cousin seen him in Dublin a sennight ago, spinding money like wather, and divil a tinpenny has he paid me this fourteen months."

"Masther, sir," said Jemmy firmly, "how far is it to Dublin, av ye plase?"

"A hundre miles and more."

"Then I'll go to him there, sir." There was an ironical shout.

"Give me one good male to start on, and I'll go; for I'm a lost boy here: and I'm ashamed to be in this place, an' him not paying for me, like the rest."

Now, this sudden resolution was quite agreeable to Hoolaghan. Norah took the boy into the kitchen to feed him for the journey. The cubs began to feel rather sorry; for they were thoughtless, not bad-hearted. They scraped together four-pence for his journey. Norah gave him an old hat, and kisses, and a word of feminine advice. "Ma-bouchal," said she, "wheniver you are in trouble, spake to the women; they will be *your* best friends; but keep clear of your own color — not intirely — only brown women and yellow women is more prifirabler, by raison you are fair, like an angel herself."

The boys set him on his road a mile; then stopped, and blessed him, and asked his forgiveness, being, to tell the truth, now quaking in the shoes of superstition, lest he should put "the hard word" on them at parting, — and him "a piece of an orphan," as the biggest remarked. But his nature was too gentle for that. He forgave them, and blessed them; and they all kissed him, and he kissed them; and they went their way. But Matthews would go another mile with him. At parting, he said, "Tell me God's truth. Are ye that lord's son?"

"Indeed, then, I am, sir."

"I wish I had known before. Let me look at thee well. I wonder whether I shall ever meet thee again, purty Jemmy."

"Indeed, and I hope so, sir; for you are all the friend I iver found in this place."

"Jemmy, it seems hard to make friends one afternoon, and then to part forever," said the elder boy, philosophizing.

Jemmy's heart was swelling already; and at this the lonely boy began to cry piteously. Then Matthews blubbered right out; and so they cried together, and kissed one another many times: and James Annesley began his wanderings.

He walked on till dusk, and saw a small farm. He went by Norah's advice, — made up straight to the farmer's wife, and asked her leave to sleep on the premises. She looked at him full before she answered; gave him some potatoes and buttermilk, and let him sleep in a little barn. He walked on the next day, and fared much the same; but by the third day he got footsore, and could only limp along; but he persevered. He sometimes got a lift in a cart; and sometimes, when a farmer's wife or daughter, on horseback, overtook him, he would appeal to her, especially if she was dark. And, true it was, the dark women, of whom there were plenty in Ireland, would generally take him up, and give him a ride before or behind, as might be most convenient.

Still creeping on, he got into a county where the people had faces unlike those he had left behind; and both men and women wore long frieze cloaks, and the women linen head-dresses, and sometimes a handkerchief over that. And he limped into a village where was a sort of fair; but he had no money left to spend, and he sat down on the shaft of a cart, disconsolate, and, seeing others so merry, began to weep with fatigue, hunger, and sorrow. By and by a man saw him, and asked him what ailed him; and he told his sad case. "Nay, then, sir," said the man, "you must come to the O'Brien." He took him to a little old man, exceedingly shabby, on a little white horse. He doffed his caubeen, and said, "An it plase your Honor's worship, this is a gintleman's son in throuble: he's hunting his own father. Glory be to God!"

"Who is your father, friend?" asked the O'Brien.

"An please your Worship, he is my Lord Altham."

The O'Brien made a wry face. "That is not Oirish," said he. "Some mushroom lord; maybe one of William's men."

"Nay, sir; he is a good Catholic. Glory be to the saints!"

By this time there was a bit of a crowd collected to hear; but the dialogue was interrupted by a simple fellow who had lost his wife. He burst in wildly, crying, "Arrab, people, people, did ye see Mary Sullivan, — a tall woman, a tall yellow woman, not very yellow intirely, — with a white pipe in her cheek?" They roared at him; but he just rushed on, repeating that strange formula. The fair rang with it. Well, the little old scarecrow, descended from Ireland's kings, took Jemmy home on his saddle-bow. Caubeens were lifted in the village, wherever this decayed noble passed. He told the boy the whole county belonged to him and his ancestors; and he should sup and sleep where he liked. Finally, he showed him a large mansion and a cabin, not far apart; let him know that these houses were his; only various families had lived in the mansion for the last few centuries. "Now, sir," said he, "will you slape in my large house, where other people live this five hundred years, by my lave, or in my small house, where I live — at prisent — for my convayuience?" Says Jemmy, "Sir, the small house, if it please you; by reason I desire your company, as well as your house." The mighty scarecrow was pleased with this answer, and took him to his mud cabin. He sent his one servant, a bare-legged girl, to demand a rasher from a neighboring farmer. No doubt she said the O'Brien had company; for eggs and perch were sent directly, as well as a large piece of bacon. The two personages supped together, and slept on one heap of straw.

In the morning, one peasant brought buttermilk, and another trout, and another oatmeal, and another a vehicle, the body of which was a square box, suspended on a strap; and the O'Brien's guest was taken five miles on his road, and his blessing sought by his conductor, a simple peasant, who discoursed on the grandeur of the O'Brien, and boasted that neither he nor his race had ever done a hand's turn of work — and would never be allowed to — in the country. James limped out of that county into another, and met with no adventure till he came to Dunnyshallan, and was turned into a dice-box. The young men of the village had cut a gigantic back-gammon-board on the green, very neat: it occupied the sixth part of an acre; and they had black and white flagstones to play with. Their dice-box was always a boy; and, catching sight of James, one sang out, "*Hurrooh! here's a strange gossoon. We'll have luck all round.*"

So James was seated on high, with his back to the players, and ordered, on pain of death, to sing out sixes, fours, quatre-ace, and all the combinations *ad libitum*. He complied, to avoid worse; and then it was he learned the literature of curses, in which this one small island was so fertile and ingenious, that all the blasphemy in all the rest of Europe was poor and mo-

notonous by comparison. The infinite maledictions would doubtless have instructed and amused him, had they been levelled at another; but, being fired at him whenever he called a number that did not suit the player, and uttered with every appearance of fury, they frightened him, and he began to tremble and snivel.

"Now, thin, ye vagabone, give me a good number, or may St. Anthony's sow trample out your intrails!"

"Oh, oh, oh! Sixes."

"Sixes! ye conthrary villin! Is it sixes I'm asking? The divil go a buck-hunting with ye!"

"Oh, oh, oh!"

"Never heed the bally-ragging ruffin. Cry for me now, honey."

"Oh! I'm afraid. Deuce-ace."

"Och! ye're a broth of a boy. May ye live till the skirts of your coat knock your brains out! Now cry for Barney."

"Oh! I am afraid to spake. The Virgin be good to me! Deuce-ace."

"Och! ye thafe o' the world. May you die with a caper in your heel, and give the crows a puddin'!"

And so on till dark, when a losing player threatened to murther the Dice. A winner objected. The two quarrelled: shillelahs crossed; a ring was made; and there was much subtle play, and the whistling cudgels parried, or met with a clash, and bent over each other, till at last Jemmy's friend parried an excessive blow, and, rising nimbly, delivered such a crasher on the other's skull, that it literally shot him to the ground like a bullet, and he rolled over by the impetus after he landed.

Then Jemmy screamed with dismay; but the more experienced laughed at his notion of what the true old Irish skull would bear; and the victor took him home to supper and bed, i.e., stirabout and straw.

He came to a fall in a river, eight feet high, and saw salmon glittering prismatic in the sun, like rainbows, as they leaped; but they struck the descending column a foot too low, struggled in it a moment, then came down as stupid as tin fish. And here he saw a sight he might have travelled creation, and never seen elsewhere, — a corpse-like man lying flat in a coffin, and towed gingerly up to the fall by his bare-armed wife straddling on a rock: the man caught the salmon on the ground, one after the other, by the belly, with a cart-rope and three barbed hooks that would have landed a whale. 'Twas his own coffin, ordered by his uneasy wife, with true Hibernian judgment, the moment he was expected to die. But the salmon came up from the sea, and began to leap like mad. Pat put off dying directly, and took to poaching We are creatures of habit; and salmon-slaughtering was his custom at that time of year, not dying.

The woman being dark, — partly with dirt, — James besought her for a fish supper. She boiled him half a salmon, and threw the rest to the pig; but she told James that in the big towns there were fools who would give 4s. a hundred-weight for the trash. Within fifteen miles of the capital he witnessed two abductions, — one real, one sham; both commonish customs. The imitation was the lineal descendant of the real; and the men hallooed and galloped so much alike in both pageants, and the two brides screamed so much alike, that he never knew for certain which was the Pseudo-Sabine, which the real, and never will. His feet were bleeding; his clothes only just hung together; his little heart was faint; when at last he mounted a hill, and looked down on a city, which, by its buildings, its size, and its blue-slated roofs, far transcended all that he had ever imagined of a mortal city. The town did not then overflow into pretty villas. Mud cabins prevailed up to

the city gates; and from them this weary, wondering child plunged into streets and mansions. At the very first street he stopped, and asked a decent man where Lord Altham lived. The decent man met this question by another: "How was he to know?" The same answer was returned in the next street, and the next; and this poor little mite of humanity wandered up and down in vain. Then a great and new fear fell on him: this Dublin was not a town, like Ross; it was another world, — a world of stone and slate, and hard hearts, not like the simple country folk. He might as well grope for his father in all Ireland as in this wilderness of labyrinths of stone. Snubbed, sneered at, rejected on all sides, he cried his sick heart and his hungry stomach to sleep in a church porch; and so he passed his first night in the capital.

Day after day the same, till at last he found a dark woman, a gentleman's cook, who listened to his tale, and gave him some broken victuals. She was an Englishwoman; her name was Martha. One day Jemmy came for his dinner, as usual, but was disappointed. Kathleen, the kitchen-maid, informed him, with a marked elevation of the nose, that Madam had gone out for the day, and locked up the safe, like a mane, miserly Sassenach as she was, bad cess to her and all her dhirty breed; but she'd be back again by five. Hungry Jemmy attended faithfully at five, in spite of the rain; and great was his surprise and awe when two chairmen brought up a chair, and there emerged from it — a duchess? No; but a fair imitation thereof; Mrs. Martha, with her income on her back, and two little black patches on her cheeks. She smiled at his adoration, paid the chairmen loftily, who retired with expressions of adulation, and sly satirical looks at each other; and she took James by the hand,

and led him to her sanctum. "Sir," said she, instead of "child," or "my dear," as heretofore, "I have been visiting my friends; and, from one to another, I have found ye my Lord Altham; as luck would have it, a countrywoman of mine, one Elizabeth Grainger, she lives in the house; but she tells me she shall give her notice."—"O madam! dear, good madam!" began Jemmy — "Nay, sir," said she, "but you must hear me out. I'm afeard you will not be so welcome as you ought to be. You are a sensible little gentleman as e'er I saw; so I'll e'en tell you the truth; Mrs Betty did let me know my lord is in ill hands; this Dame Gregory and her daughter have got him: the old woman goes about her own house like a servant; but miss, she is mistress, and games with the quality, and spends money like dirt; they are betrothed to each other, and his wife lying sick in the town, on her way back to England. Poor soul! she rues the day she ever saw this hole of a country, I'll go bail. They look for her to die — for their convenience. Well, if I was her, I'd spite 'em; I'd play the woman, and outlive the brute and the hussy both, saving your presence."

"O madam, an' if it please you, where does my father live?"

"'Tis in Frapper Lane, the corner house. What, will you be going, and no supper? Nay, then, God speed you. Give me a kiss, sweetheart. So. Your breath is honey. Sir," said she, courtesying to him all of a sudden, "I do wish you well. When you come into your estate, sir, prithee remember Martha Knatchbull, that took your part when Fortune frowned."

"Ay, that I will, good, kind lady," said James, still overpowered by her glorious costume; and so he shuffled off, limping fast, and, in the hunger of his longing heart, forgot his hungry belly for a time.

To give the reader some idea of the house he was going to, I will sketch the domestic performances from nine, P.M., on the previous evening. Lord Altham and friends had a drinking bout, at the end of which he was assisted to bed, and his friends sent home in chairs. But the ladies did not drink; they gamed their lives away. Mistress Anne Gregory received Lady Dace and Mistress Carmichael, and other ladies gloriously dressed, and, at first starting, most polite and ceremonious; they drank tea, and soon warmed into scandal, — each accusing some other lady of her own especial vice, — till at last they got upon politics. Inflamed by this topic, they soon boiled over: voices rose over voices; not a single tongue was mute a moment; and such was the babel, that at last the fat, lazy lapdog wriggled himself erect, and looked furiously at the disturbers of his peace. Then a Neptune arose to still the raging voices: in other words, Mrs. Betty set out the card-tables. Down they sat, and soon their eyes were gleaming, and their flesh trembling with excitement. Mistress Anne Gregory held bad cards; she had to pawn ring after ring, — for these ladies, being well acquainted with each other, never played on parole, — and she kept bemoaning her bad luck. "Betty, I knew how 'twould be. The parson called to-day — This odious chair, why will you stick me in it? — Stand further, girl. I always lose when you look on." Mrs. Betty tossed her head, and went behind another lady. Miss Gregory still lost, and had to pawn her snuff-box to Lady Dace. She consoled herself by an insinuation: "My lady, you touched your wedding-ring. That was a sign to your partner here."

"Nay, madam, 'twas but a sign my finger itched. But, if you go to that, you spoke a word which began with H. Then she knew you had the king of hearts."

"That is like miss, here," said another matron : "she rubs her chair when she hath Matadore in hand."

"Set a thief to catch a thief, madam," was miss's ingenious and polished reply.

"Hey-dey!" cries one. "Here's Spadillo got a mark on the back : a child might know it in the dark. Mistress Pigot, I wish you'd be pleased to pare your nails."

In short, they said things to each other all night, the slightest of which, among men, would have filled the Phœnix Park next morning with drawn swords : but it went for little here : they were all cheats, and knew it, and knew the others knew it, and didn't care. It was four o'clock before they broke up, huddled on their cloaks and hoods, and their chairs took them home with cold feet and aching heads.

At twelve next day, Miss Gregory was prematurely disturbed by her lapdog, barking like a demon for his breakfast. She stretched, gaped, unglued her eyes, and rang for Betty. No answer. She rang again, and beat the wall viciously with her slipper. Betty came in yawning.

"Here, child. Let in some light. Nay, not so much : wouldst blind me!—I'm dead of the vapors. Get me a dram of citron-water. So.— Now bring me a looking-glass. I will lie abed. Alack! I look frightfully to-day. If ever I touch a card again. Didst ever see such luck as mine? Four Matadores, and lose Codille!"

"Nay, madam," said Mrs. Betty, who was infected with the tastes of her betters, "with submission, you played bad cards."

"Hoity toity, wench!" cried the lady : "was ever such assurance? What is the world coming to?" And she packed her off contemptuously, to get her tea and cream.

Betty turned pale with wrath, but retired. Once outside the door, she said, "I'll be even with the jade. I'm as good as she."

Miss Gregory was at her glass when Betty returned with the tea. "Madam," said she, with a sly sneer, "the goldsmith waits below, to know if you'll redeem the silver cup."

"There, give him that for interest."

"And my Lady Dace has sent her maid."

"That is for her winnings. Never was such a dun. Here, take these ten pistoles my lord left for the wine merchant. They are all light, thank heaven!"

At two, being half-dressed, and the room tidied, but not a window opened, she received the visit of a fop. He paid her hyperbolical compliments, at which you should have seen Mrs. Betty's lip curl, and was consulted as to where she should put her patches ; but was driven out, like chaff before the wind, by a creature more attractive, to wit, a mercer with silks, patterns, and laces, from Paris : so the toilet was not complete at four, when a footman knocked at the door with, "Madam, dinner stays."

"Then the cook must keep it back. I never can have time to dress ; and I am sure no living woman takes less."

However, she soon came down, distended with an enormous hoop, glorious with brocaded skirt and quilted petticoat, and cocked up on red high-heeled shoes ; bedizened, belaced, powdered, pomatumed, pulvilloed, patched, perfumed, and everything else — except washed ; yet less savage than the men in one respect ; the commode and all the pyramidal, scaffolded heads had gone out : her hair was her own, and, though long, was compressed into a small compass, whereas the gentlemen had full-bottomed wigs that smothered their heads, contracted their cheeks, flowed over their shoulders, and beflowered their backs.

·My Lord Altham and two or three other gentlemen were there, and three ladies. Lord Altham, a little dark man with a loud voice, received her with great respect, and told her they waited only for his brother, Capt. Richard Annesley.

"Nay, he will not come, methinks," said she. "He and I had words t'other day."

"Nay, then, let the churl hang. Who waits?"

A flaring footman appeared, as if his string had been pulled.

"Bid them serve the dinner."

"I will, my lord."

For the conversation during dinner, see "Swift's Polite Conversation." You will be a gainer by the exchange; for the discourse at Lord Altham's board was half as coarse, and not half so witty.

Soon after dinner the host proposed "Church and State."

From that moment the ladies were evidently on their guard, and ready for flight.

"Parson," says my lord, "I'll tell you a merry story."

The ladies rose like one, and retired. My lord, having achieved his end, for at this time of night the bottle was his mistress until it became his master, substituted a toast for his song:—

"The finest sight beneath the moon
Is to see the ladies quit the room."

He then ordered the present bottles and glasses to be exchanged for others that would not stand upright, the stems of the glasses having been knocked off, and the decanters being made like a soda-water bottle. This insured so brisk a circulation, that, although they were gentlemen who had all "made their heads" in early life, the claret began to tell, as was proved by the swift alternations of superfluous ire and hyperbolical affection and peals of idiotic laughter; when, in the midst of the din, an altercation was heard in the hall. The disputants were three, and each

voice had its own key: first there was a sweet little quavering soprano, appealing to a flaming footman; then there was a flaming footman, objurgating the cherubic voice an octave lower; then came the commanding alto of Mrs. Betty.

"What is to do?" roared Lord Altham.

"Why," said Mrs. Betty, seizing this opportunity, "'tis a young gentleman that hath travelled an hundred miles to see my lord, and my lord's valet denied him, being stained with travel: but 'twas ill done, and him of kin to my lord."

"Of kin to my lord! Nay, then, Mistress Betty, he is welcome to all here."

Betty, who had her cue from the English cook, and who was already interested in the fair, sorrowful young face and golden hair, made no more ado, but led James into the room by the hand. The numerous lights in the candelabra dazzled him at first, and the fine clothes and perukes awed him; he hid against Betty's capacious apron, that descended from waist to ankle. Then he peered, and saw Lord Altham standing up, looking half-pleased, half-vexed; he gave a loud cry, as if his heart was flying out of his body, stretched out his arms, and flew to him. "O father, father!" The sorrow he had endured, the joy and infinite trust that swallowed all sorrow up at sight of his father, both spoke in that one wild cry; it thrilled; it startled; it sent Mrs. Betty's apron to her eyes in a moment, and pierced the heart even of this silly, brutal lord.

"My boy! my sweet Jemmy!" he cried, and sat down, and folded him in his arm, and kissed him tenderly, with a mawkish tear or two.

The guests then stood up respectfully, and drank welcome to the young gentleman. "Not forgetting Mrs. Betty, that brought him to us," said the chaplain, who had a sheep's eye to her and her savings: she was a Sassenach, and sure to have savings ; Irish savings were not.

"Father," said Jemmy, " they used me very crule at that school : bad luck to it. They were always bating me ; and the mastber would not rise a hand for me bekase you sent him no money for my schoolin.' Why didn't you send him his money ?"

This, which would have made a Sassenach father blush, did but divert my lord and his company. " I kept it for yourself, Jemmy," said he.

"My lord is a great saver, sir. Long life to him," said another.

"Father avick, does my mother live here ?" said Jemmy.

Now, this question made the company very uncomfortable. It quite staggered Lord Altham for a minute. But he burst out furiously, " Thou hast no mother."

"Nay, father ; then what hatb come of the gentlewoman that had red shoes, two pair, made for me in Ross ; and the likely woman that brought me woollen hose she had made for me herself, and called me her child ?" Then, seeing my lord silent, and much disturbed, he bethought himself, and said, " Well, if my mothers are both dead, I must love thee all the more."

Betty, who was watching Lord Altham's face very keenly all the time, now stepped forward, and took James away. She fed him, and then proceeded to ablutions. The cleanliness of his skin, dusty but not grimed, surprised her : but, above all, his head " Gramercy !" said she ; " not one to be seen, and they swarm in my lady's. To be sure, that same powder is a convenient habitation."

She put him to bed ; and, being a notable woman, sat up half the night, and made him a loose habit and a little hat. With this, and clean linen, and a cambric tie, she brought him to Lord Altham while Miss Gregory was abed. Lord Al-

tham was surprised and pleased, and took him out in a cbair, and had him shod on the spot, and measured for a fine suit from top to toe. He was petted by everybody, and especially by Miss Gregory. This was a very clever young lady : she was not going to risk Lord Altham's affections by snubbing his son, a pretty, amiable boy. Mrs. Betty's shot missed fire : Miss Gregory went with the stream, and had two riding-suits made, one for James and one for herself, and she got him a pony, and he was her cavalier. They were the glory of Dublin and the Phœnix, and had often a crowd at their tails. Their accoutrement was as follows : each had a beaver hat, gold laced, looped, and with a handsome feather ; a coat and waistcoat blazing with gold lace and gold buttons : only the lady ended in a petticoat of the same stuff, clinging close to her as a blister. She had also a little powdered peruke, like a man ; her object being to seem a smart cavalier by day and a finicking fine lady, hooped and furbelowed, at night. The only drawback was that this exquisite costume brought her mercer's bill to a climax ; and he demanded payment of the following trifles, and threatened law : Fine Holland smock, one guinea ; Marseilles quilted silk petticoat, three pound six ; hooped petticoat, two pound five ; Italian quilted ditto, ten pounds ; mantua and petticoat of French brocade, seventy-eight pounds ; English stays, three pounds ; Italian fan, five pounds ; a laced head, of Flanders point, sixty pounds ; silk stockings, one pound ; a black-laced hood, and a French silk à la mode hood, six pounds ; French garters, one pound five ; French bosom-knot, one pound twelve ; beaver hat and feather, three pounds ; ditto for James, two pounds ; embroidered riding-suit of Lyons velvet and gold lace, forty-seven pounds ; ditto for my young lord, nineteen pounds ; sable muff, five pounds; red shoes (English), two guineas; tippet, seven guineas; French kid gloves, two shillings and sixpence; with innumerable other articles, all for outside wear, the body linen being in the proportion of the bread to the sack in Falstaff's tavern-bill. Many of these articles could have been had for half the price, if the lady would have listened to Dr. Swift, and bought Irish goods; but she would almost rather have gone bare. No, she was Irish to the core; so every thing she wore must come from England or the Continent.

This bill, and the man's threats, brought on a fit of the vapors; another fashionable importation. She rode out with Jemmy one day, to shake them off, and they met a gentleman riding, in a scarlet coat, and a hat like a bishop's mitre. He drew up, and saluted Miss Gregory stiffly, and cast a sour look at Jemmy. "Odzooks," said he; "have you got that boy in the house?"

"What matters it to you, sir," said the lady, firing up, "since you do never come there?"

The officer explained that he and his brother, Lord Altham, had been out for some time. "To tell the truth, we are like cat and dog. Naught but want of money brings us together. You will see me now every day," said he, with a sneer: then, lowering his voice, "madam, I desire some private conference with you. Will it please you to be at home this afternoon?"

"Certainly, sir; in one hour."

When he was gone, she asked the boy if he knew the gentleman. James answered very gravely, that it was his uncle, Richard Annesley, and no friend to him, — "Never gave me a good word nor a look in his life."

"Perhaps you are in his way," said she, with a laugh.

She gave Capt. Annesley the *tête-à-tête* he had asked for, and he came to the point in a moment.

Lord Altham and himself were both in want of money, and, in order to get it, had patched up their quarrels: parading Jemmy about the streets of Dublin was unseasonable, and just the thing to stop the business, or at least retard it. The money-lenders might hesitate, and say there was another interest to be thought of.

"Nay," said Miss Gregory, "that would never do; for here I am threatened for £200 and more."

Capt. Annesley worked on her cupidity till she consented to part father and son; but she refused to do it with a high hand, or with brutal severity. She could never urge the father to turn his son out of the house. Richard Annesley, as artful as he was unscrupulous, offered her his house at Inchicore; and they settled that Lord Altham should be taken out there, and every means employed to separate him from James till the money was raised. This artful pair now put their heads together every day, and the first thing done was to discharge Mrs. Betty. She went back to England, leaving James in the house. Next all the servants were discharged, except two, who were sent on to Inchicore, and an old woman left in charge of the house and Jemmy.

Miss Gregory so worked on Lord Altham that he hid from James where he was going, stipulating only, like a sot as he was, that Richard should look to the boy, and see he wanted for nothing.

After all, the money-lenders hesitated, on account of the previous mortgages; and my lord remained in hiding with Mrs. Gregory and her daughter, and had to cut down his expenses, and live upon his rents. James Annesley staid in the house, hoping every day he should be sent for; till one day an execution was put in for rent, his riding-suit was seized, and he was turned out into the streets with nothing but what he carried on his back.

Then he began to wonder and fear.

He ran to Mrs. Martha, whom he had neglected in his prosperity. She had left the town. He was amazed, confused, heart-sick. He wandered to and fro, wondering what this might mean. He had to sell his fine suit for a plain one and a very little money ; and, when that was done, starvation stared him in the face. Deserted and penniless, he had hard work to live. At first á playmate, one Byrne, brought him morsels of food in secret, and lodged him in a hay-loft. Then he got into the college, and used to run errands and black shoes. Vacation came, and even that resource failed ; and then he held horses, for a halfpenny or a farthing, in Ormond Market, and was almost in rags : no other ragged boy so unhappy as he, since under those rags there beat the heart of a little gentleman, and rankled the deep sense of injustice and unnatural cruelty. Of late he had avoided speaking of his parentage ; but one day insults dragged it out of him. A bigger boy was abusing him, because a gentleman, liking his face, had selected him to hold his horse : the boy called him a blackguard, a beggar, and other opprobrious terms. "You lie," said James, losing all patience : "I am come of better folk than thou. My father is a lord, and I am heir to great estates, and have been served by thy betters, and so should now, if the world was not so wicked." These words did not fall unheeded : henceforth he was the scoff of all the dirty boys in the place ; and they cried "My lord" after him. One Farrell, that kept a shop on the quay, heard them at it, and said to his shopman, "Why, I see no hump on him ! the boy is straight enough, and fair, if he were cleaned." He called James to him, and asked him why they called him "My lord." The boy hung his head, and would not say at first, he was so used to be jeered ; but being pressed, and seeing a kindly face enough, began to tell his tale. But Farrell interrupted him. "Lord Altham," said he, "I know him, — to my cost. Well, I do remember one time I went to Dunmaine for my money, and got mulled claret instead on't, there was a child there with my lady and his nurse." James said eagerly, that was himself. "Nay, then," said Farrell, "why not seek thy mother, Lady Altham, if she be thy mother ?"

"Oh, sir !" said James, "I thought my mother was gone back to England. O dear, good sir ! have pity on me, and take me to her, if she is in this wicked place."

"Child," said the man, "I know that my Lady Altham sojourned with her friend, Alderman King ; but you are not fit to go there so. Come you home with me." So he took him home, and bade his wife clean him, and lend an old suit of his son that was away at school. The wife complied, with no great cordiality ; and Farrell sent a line about him to Alderman King, and then called at the alderman's house, and asked for my Lady Altham. "Nay," said the alderman, "my lady sailed for England a se'nnight ago. But, Master Farrell, what tale is this you bring me ? Why, my lady never had a son."

"Oh !" cried James, as if he had been struck.

Farrell looked blank ; but said, "Sure, your worship is mistook."

"I tell ye, Master Farrell, she was eight months in this house, and spoke of all her troubles, and she never breathed a word about a son of hers. Did she, Mistress Avice ?" turning to his housekeeper.

"She did — to me, sir," said the woman coolly. "My lady was my countrywoman, and opened her heart to me. She spoke once of her son, and said the greatest of her grief was she could never see him."

Here the alderman was called away, and Farrell took James home in tears. "Keep a stout heart, sir," said he : "your mother is gone ; but

I'll soon find your father, if he is above ground." Farrell wanted to keep him, but his wife would not hear of it. "We have lost above £50 by that Lord Altham already. I'll have none of his breed in this house, bad scran to the dirty clan of 'em."

Now, Farrell had a friend, a very honest fellow, one Purcell; so he told him the whole story one day, over a pipe. "Let me see him," said Purcell. "If I like his looks, —why, we can afford to keep something young about us. But I must see him first."

So these two went to one likely place and another; and presently Farrell saw Jemmy in Smithfield riding a horse, and pointed him out to Purcell. "Stand you aside," said Purcell, "and be not seen." He took a good look at the boy, and liked his face. "Child," said he, "what is your name?"

"James Annesley, sir."

"Whose son are you?"

"Alas, sir," said James, "prithee, do not ask me. It makes me cry so. I'm a lost boy."

Then the honest man's bowels were moved for the child; but he would not show it all at once. "Are you Lord Altham's son?" said he, a little roughly. "Indeed, then, I am, sir," said he, and looked him in the face. "Then," says Purcell, still a little roughly, "get you off that horse; for if you will be a good boy, I'll take you home with me; and," says he warmly, "you shall never want while I have it." Then Jemmy stared at him; and the next moment fell on his knees in the market-place, and gave him a thousand blessings: "for oh, sir!" said he, "I am almost lost;" and he trembled greatly.

"Have a good heart, sir," said Purcell, and took him by the hand, all shabby and dirty as he was, and brought him home to his wife that was busy cooking, being a right good housewife. "There," says he,

"Mary, here's a little gentleman for thee." So she looked at him and smiled, and asked who he was. "Thou'lt know anon," said he; "but take care of him as if he was thine own." Now, she was not like Farrell's wife, but one that had a good man, and knew it "Go thy ways," said she, and gave him a merry push, "and come thou here no more till supper-time." Then he went away; and she soon had a great pot on the fire, and made the boy wash in a two-eared tub, and put decent clothes on him, and drew all his history from him with her kind words and ways; and, when the honest man came home, he started at the door, for there sat his wife knitting, in her best apron; and there sat a lovely little gentleman with golden hair, leaning on her shoulder, and they were pratttling together; and one was " My child," and the other was "Mammy," already. It was the happiest fireside in Ireland that night; and it deserved to be.

Here was a respite to all James Annesley's troubles. He grew, he fattened, he brightened; he loved his Mammy and stout John Purcell, and they loved him.

Unfortunately, Farrell found out Lord Altham at Inchicore, and went to dun him, and told him about Jemmy. Lord Altham was shocked, and promised to remunerate both Farrell and Purcell as soon as he could raise money. Meantime he blustered to Miss Gregory, and she must have told Richard Annesley; for one September afternoon there walked into Purcell's shop a gentleman with a gun and a setter, and inquired, "Is there not one Purcell lives here?"

"Yes, sir," said Purcell, "I am the man."

Then the gentleman called for a pot of beer, and sat down by the fire, inviting Purcell to partake. When the gentleman had drunk a drop, he asked Purcell if he had not a boy called James Annesley. Purcell said yes; and the gentleman said he desired to see him. Now Jemmy had been ailing a little, and was in the parlor with Mrs. Purcell, in an armchair, by the fire; so Purcell went in to tell him, and found him in tears. "Why, what is the matter?" said Purcell. Says the boy, "It is that gentleman: the sight of him has put such a dread on me, I don't know what to do with myself."

"Nay," said Purcell, "the gentleman is civil enough. Come and speak to him." So he came very unwillingly. The gentleman said, "So, James, how do you do?" The boy answered, stiffly, "Sir, I thank you, I am pretty well." The gentleman said, "And I am glad you have fallen into such good hands." The boy said gravely, "Sir, I have reason to thank God for it. They are kinder to me than my own kin." The gentleman said he must not say so, and asked him if he knew him.

"I know you well," said he: "you are my uncle, Richard Annesley." And, at the first opportunity, slipped back to his "Mammy," as he called her. He was all trembling; and she asked him why he was so, and he said, "That's a wicked man; he hates me; he hates me. He never came near me but to hurt me. I'd liever meet the Devil. Some day he will kill me."

Whilst Dame Purcell was comforting him, and telling him nobody should harm him under her wing, Richard Annesley treated Purcell, and told him Lord Altham should recompense him; but Purcell declined that favor, and said rather contemptuously, "When he is man enough to take his own flesh and blood into the ·house, he knows where to find him; but I ask no pay: I can keep a lord's son, if his father can't, and I can love one, if his father can't; for there never was a better boy stood in the walls of a house."

Three months after this, Lord Altham had a short illness, and died. He was to be buried at Christ Church, and the sexton told Mrs. Purcell the afternoon before the funeral. They buried at night in those days. Mrs. Purcell had not the heart to keep it from the boy: he turned very pale, but he did not cry. Only he would go to the funeral. Purcell dissuaded him, and then he began to wring his hands. Mrs. Purcell had her way for once, and got him weepers, to attend.

It was a fine-funeral, by torchlight, — velvets, plumes, mutes, flambeaux. One thing only was wanting, — mourners. The tenants of his vast estates — his numerous boon companions, his wife, his betrothed, his brothers, Lord Anglesey and Richard Annesley — all drinking, or gaming, or minding their own business. There stood by this wretched noble's open grave only two that cared, — an old coachman, Weedon, and the poor boy he had so basely abandoned. The rest were strangers, brought there by hard curiosity.

When the coffin began to sink out of sight, the tender heart of the deserted one almost burst with grief and wasted love.

"O MY FATHER, MY FATHER!" cried the desolate child; and that wild cry of woe rang in ears that remembered it, and spoke of it years after.

When he came back, all in tears, Purcell said, "There, dame, I knew how 'twould be;" and he was almost angry.

"But 'tis best so, John," said she: "dear heart, when he comes to be old, would you have him remember he could not find a tear for his father, and him no more?"

"O mammy, mammy!" said James, "only one old man and me to weep for him: those he loved before me never cared for him;"

and then his tears burst out afresh.

A day or two after this, a message came to James Annesley that his uncle wanted to see him, at Mr. Jones's in the market. The boy refused to go. "It is not for any good, I know," said he. But he consented to accompany Mr. Purcell, if he would go armed. Stout-hearted Purcell laughed at his fears, but yielded to his entreaties, and took a thick stick. James held him fast by the skirt all the way. In the entry to Jones's three fellows slouched against the wall. "Oho!" thought John Purcell.

Mr. Annesley met him, and Purcell took off his hat, and Mr. Annesley gave him good-morning, and then, without more ceremony, called to one of the fellows to seize that thieving rogue, and take him to the proper place.

"Who do you call a thief?" said Purcell sternly.

"Confound you," says the gentleman, "I am not speaking to you." Then he ordered the fellows again to take Jemmy away. But Purcell put the boy between his legs, and raised his stick high. "The first of you," said he, "lays a hand on him, I'll knock his brains out." Hearing him raise his voice in anger, one or two people came about the entry, and the bullies sneaked off. "You a gentleman!" said John Purcell, "and would go to destroy this poor creature you were never man enough to maintain."

"Go you and talk to his nurse," said Richard Annesley spitefully: "she knows more of him than you do."

"This is idle chat," said John Purcell. "He has neither father, mother, nor nurse left in this kingdom, but my dame and me. Let us go home, Jemmy. We have fallen in ill company."

But from that day there were always fellows lurking about John Purcell's house; sometimes bailiffs or constables, or sharks disguised as such; and the boy one day lost his nerve and ran away: he entered the service of a Mr. Tighe, and sent word to Purcell that his life was not safe so long as his uncle knew where to find him; and he also feared to bring him and his mammy into trouble.

For this cowardice he paid dear. He had been watched, and an opportunity was taken to seize him one day in the open street, by men disguised as bailiffs, on a charge of theft; and, instead of being taken to a court, he was brought to Richard Annesley's house. Richard Annesley charged him with stealing a silver spoon. The boy was quiet till he saw that fatal face, and then he began to scream, and to cry, "He will kill me, or transport me." Annesley's eyes glittered fiendishly. "Ay, thou knave," said he, "I have been insulted enough for thee, and my very title denied me, because of thy noise. Away with him!"

Then the men put him into a coach, and took him along by the quay, screaming and crying for help. "They will kill me; they will transport me, because I am Lord Altham's son;" and people followed the coach, and murmured loud. But the men were quick and resolute; and, while one told some lie or other to the people, the others got him into a boat, and pulled lustily out to a ship that lay ready to cross the bar, for all this had been timed beforehand; and, once on board that wooden hell, he had no chance. He was thrust into the hold.

The law protected Englishmen from this, in theory, but not in practice. Some agent of Richard Annesley's indented James Annesley as his nearest friend: acting *at his request,* and the sole record of this act of villany read like an act of plain, unobjectionable business. He was kept in the hold, and his cries unregarded. The ship spread her pinions, and away. Then the boy was allowed to come on deck and take his last look of Ireland. He asked a sailor-boy where they were going. "Bonnd for Philadelphia," was the reply. At the bare word the poor little wretch uttered shriek upon shriek, and ran aft, to throw himself into the sea. The man at the wheel caught him by his skirt, and had much ado to hold him, till a sailor ran up, and they got him on board again, screaming and biting like a wild-cat: the gentle boy was quite changed by desperation; for Philadelphia, though it means "Brotherly Love" in Greek, meant "White Slavery" to poor betrayed creatures from the mother country.

Finally, after superhuman struggles, and shrieks of despair, so piteous that even the rugged sailors began to look blank, he went off into a dead swoon, and was white as ashes, and his lips blue. "He is dead," was the cry.

"Lord forbid!" said the captain. "Stand aloof, ye fools, and give him air."

"O humane captain!" says my reader; but "O good trader captain!" would be nearer the mark. This Richard Annesley, to save his purse, had given the captain an interest in the boy's life. The captain was to sell him over the water, and pocket the money. This fatal oversight elevated a human creature into merchandise. The worthy captain set himself in earnest to keep it alive. He fanned his merchandise, sprinkled his merchandise; and when his merchandise came to, and, with a stare and a loud scream, went off into heart-rending and distracting cries, he comforted his merchandise, and gave it a sup of rum and water, and hurried it down into a cabin, and set a guard on it night and day, with orders to be kind to it, but very watchful: this done, he gave his mind to sailing the good ship "James of Dublin."

But next day he was informed that the merchandise would not eat, nor drink, but was resolved to die. "Die! Not a bit of it; drench him," said the stout-hearted captain. "Drench him yourself," said the mate. "I'm sick on 't."

Then the captain bade the cook prepare a savory dish, and brought it down to James: "Eat this, sir," said he, as one used to be obeyed. The young gentleman made no reply, but his eyes gleamed. The captain drew his hanger with one hand, and stuck a two-pronged fork into a morsel with the other. "Eat that, ye contrary toad," said he, "or I'll make minced collops of thee." The boy took the morsel. "So!" said the captain, sneering over his shoulder at the mate. The boy spat it furiously in his face. "May God sink thy ship, thou knave, that wouldst steal away a nobleman's son, and sell him for a slave!"

The captain drew back a moment, like a dog a hen has flown at, and had hard work not to cut him in two: but he forebore, and said, "Starve then, and feed the fishes," and so left the cabin. The mate, at his back all the time, told the boatswain young master was a nobleman's son, and was being spirited away, and there was "foul play" in it. Some remarks were made which it was intended the captain should hear. He took them up directly. "A nobleman's son!" said he; "ay, but only a merrybegot, and so given to thieving he will do no good at home. Why, 'twas his own uncle shipped him, for his good." This quieted the men directly; and from that moment they made light of the matter.

When James was downright faint with hunger, the captain took quite another way with him,—went to him and said he feared there was some mistake, and he was sorry he had been led to take him on board, but the matter should be set right on landing. "No, no," said James, "I shall be bound as a slave. May God revenge me on my wicked uncle! I see now why he has done this,—to rob me of my estate and my title."

"Indeed, I begin to think he is to blame," said the captain. "But why take fright at a word, sir? None can make you a slave for life, as the negroes are, but only an apprentice for a time."

"I am beholden to you, sir," said James; "but, call it what you will, 'tis slavery, and I'd liever die. But promise to send me back by the first ship, and I will give you a hatful of money when I come to my rights, and pray for you all my days."

"Ay, but if I do so, will you eat and drink, and be of good heart?"

"That will I, sir."

"Then 'tis a bargain."

They shook hands upon it; and, from that hour, were good friends. James was treated like a guest: he ate and drank so heartily that the captain began to wince at his appetite; and, in a word, what with the sea-air, plentiful diet, and a mind relieved from fear of slavery, the young gentleman's cheeks plumped out, and became rosy; he grew an inch and a half in height, and landed at Philadelphia a picture of a little Briton.

The planters boarded the ship. The captain threw off the mask, and sold him directly for a high price to one Drummond.

James raged and cried, and demanded to be taken before a justice.

Then, for the first time, the captain produced papers, all prepared by Richard Annesley, under legal advice. The colony wanted labor, and was ill disposed to sift the evidence that furnished it: it all ended in Drummond carrying his white slave home to Newcastle County.

Next morning at five o'clock he found himself engaged, with other slaves, black and white, cutting pipe-staves, and an overseer standing by,

provided with a whip of very superior construction to any thing he ever saw in Ireland.

Being only a boy, and new at the work, he was first ridiculed, then threatened; and, before the day ended, the whip fell on his shoulders, stinging, branding, burning his back much, his heart more: for then this noble boy felt, with all his soul and all his body, what he was come to,—an ox, an ass, a beast, a slave.

———◆———

CHAPTER II.

IN this miserable condition of servitude James Annesley remained nearly seven years, having been indented for an extreme period; and many a sigh he heaved, and many a tear he shed in solitude, thinking of what he had been, and what he had a right to be, and what he was. But, being now a full-grown young man, tall, and very robust, he could do his work; and his misery was alleviated by caution, but, above all, by the blessed thought that his servitude was drawing to an end, since a white man could only be bound for a limited term.

But let all shallow statesmen and pedantic lawyers, who trifle with the equal rights of humanity, be warned that you cannot play fast and loose with things so sacred. The mother country, in its stupidity, allowed its citizens to be made slaves for a time: the pilgrim fathers and their grandchildren, though no men ever valued liberty more in their own persons, or talked more about it, had not that *disinterested* respect for it which marks their noble descendants; and so they, by a by-law or custom, enlarged the term of servitude; this they contrived by ordering that if one of these temporary slaves misbehaved grossly, and, above all, attempted escape, his term of servitude could be enlarged in proportion by judges who were in the interest of the planters.

So the game was, when the white slave's term of servitude drew near, to make his life intolerable : then, in his despair, he rebelled, or ran for it, and was recaptured, and re-enslaved, by this by-law passed in the colony.

"Where there's a multitude, there's a mixture," and not every planter played this heartless dodge; but too many did, and no man more barbarously than this Drummond. By the help of an unscrupulous overseer, who did and said whatever he was ordered, he starved, he insulted, he flogged, he made his slaves' life intolerable: and so, in a fit of desperation, James started one night for the Delaware River: he armed himself with a little billhook, for he was quite resolved not to be taken alive.

In the morning they found he was gone, and followed him horse and foot. But they did not catch him, for rather a curious reason : he had the ill-luck to miss his road, and got to the Susquehanna instead.

He found his mistake when too late ; but he did not give up all hope ; for he saw some ships, and a town, into which he resolved to penetrate at nightfall : it was then about ten o'clock. Meantime, he thought it best to hide ; and coming to two roads, one of which turned to his right and passed through a wood, he turned off that way, and lay down in shelter, and unseen, though close to the roadside. Here fatigue overpowered him, and he went to sleep, fast as a church, and slept till four in the afternoon. Then he awoke, with voices in his ears ; and, peeping through the leafy screen, he saw, with surprise, that there was company close to him : there was a man haltering a horse to a tree near him, and another already haltered ; a gentlewoman in a riding-habit stood looking on, while another man drew provisions and wine from some

saddlebags, and spread a cloth on the grass, and made every preparation for a repast.

Then they all three sat down and enjoyed themselves, so that poor hungry James sighed involuntarily, and peeped through the leaves. The lady heard him, turned, saw him, screamed, pointed at him, and in a moment the men were upon him with drawn swords, crying, "Traitor ! Spy !"

But James whipped behind a tree, and parleyed. "No traitor, sir, but a poor runaway slave, who never set eyes on you before." The men hesitated, and he soon convinced them of his innocence. One of them laughed, and said, "Why, then there's naught to fear from thee."

The lady, however, still anxious, cross-questioned him herself. His answers satisfied her, his appearance pleased her, and it ended to his advantage ; they made him sit down with them, and eat and drink heartily.

At last the lady let out they were fugitives too, and could feel for him ; and she said, "We are going on board a ship bound for Holland. She lies at anchor waiting for us ; and, if you can run with us, we will e'en take you on board ; but, in sooth, we must lose no time." They started. The gentleman had the lady behind him, and James ran with his hand on the other horse's mane ; but, losing breath, the man, who was well mounted, took him up behind him. Night fell, and then they went more slowly ; and James, to ease the good horse, walked by his side.

But presently there was a fierce galloping of horses behind them, and lights seemed flying at them from behind. The lady looked back, and screamed, "'Tis he, himself ; we are lost !"

The men had only time to dismount and draw their swords, when the party was upon them with a score of blades flashing in the torchlight. The men defended themselves; and James, forgetting it was no quarrel of his, laid about him with his bill-hook: but the combat was too unequal. In three minutes the lady, in a dead swoon, was laid before one horseman, her lover and his servant were bound upon their own horses, and James was worse treated still, for his hands were tied together, and fastened to a horse's tail.

In this wretched plight they were carried to the nearest village, and well guarded for the night in separate rooms.

At daybreak they were marched again; and James Annesley, in that horrible attitude of a captive felon, was drawn at a horse's tail through four hooting villages, and lodged in Chester jail.

Law did not halt here: they were all four put to the bar; and then first he learned, by the evidence, who his companions were, and what he had been doing when he drew bill-hook in their favor. The lady was daughter of a trader in this very town of Chester. Her father, finding her in love with some one beneath her, had compelled her to marry a rich planter. She hated him, and, in evil hour, listened to her lover, who persuaded her to fly with all she could lay her hands on. The money and jewels were found in the saddle-bags. The husband was vindictive, the crime two-fold. The guilty pair, the servant, and James, who was taken fighting on their side, were condemned.

James made an effort to separate his fate from the others. He told the judge who he was, and what master he had run away from; declared it was a mere accident his being there; he had been surprised by the sudden attack on persons, who, whatever their faults, had been good to him. The judge took a note while he was pleading in arrest of judgment, but said nothing; and they were all four condemned to stand on the gallows for one hour with a rope round their necks, to be whipped on their bare backs with so many lashes *well laid* on, and then imprisoned for several years.

<hr>

CHAPTER III.

Two little rivers meet, and run to the sea as naturally as if they had always meant to unite: yet, go to their sources in the hills, how wide apart! How unlikely to come together, or even approach each other! Why, one rises south, and the other north-east, and they do not even look the same way, at starting! It is hard to believe they are doomed to trickle hither and thither, meander and curve, and meet at last, to part no more.

And so it is with many human lives: the facts of this story compel me to trace, from their tiny sources, two human currents, that I think will bear out my simile. The James Annesley river is set flowing; so now for the Joanna Philippa Chester, and old England. .

She was the orphan daughter of two very superior people, who died too young. Her mother was a Spaniard, her father an Englishman, and a lawyer of great promise. They had but this child. She inherited her mother's jewels and thirteen thousand pounds: her father, impressed by some cruel experience in his own family, had an almost morbid fear lest she should be caught up by some fortune-hunter, and married for her money, she being a black-browed girl with no great promise of beauty at that time. During his last illness he thought much of this, and spoke of it very earnestly to the two gentleman he had appointed her trustees. These two, Mr. Hanway and Mr. Thomas Chester, hated each other decently, but sincerely. Mr. Chester knew that, and, with a lawyer's shrewdness, counted a little on it, as well as on their attachment to himself, to get his views carried out. He made them promise him, in writing, that Joanna's fortune should be concealed from her until she should be twenty-four, or some worthy person, unacquainted with her means, should offer her a marriage of affection : she was to be brought up soberly, taught to read and write very well, and cast accounts, and do plain stitching, but never to sit at a harpsichord nor a sampler. She was to live with Mr. Hanway, at Colebrook, till she was seventeen, and then with Mr. Thomas Chester, her uncle, till her marriage. Each trustee, in turn, to receive £100 a year, for her board and instruction. Her fortune was all out at good mortgage, paying larger interest than is to be had on that security nowadays.

The £100 a year was of some importance to Mr. Hanway; and he was not at all sorry that Joanna Philippa was to be taught only what he and his housekeeper could teach her : that saved expense. He did teach her, an hour every day; and she was so quick, that, at ten years old, she could read and write and sum better than a good many duchesses. But the rest of the day she was entirely neglected; so she was nearly always out of doors, acquiring more health and strength and freckles than a girl is entitled to, and playing pranks that ought to have been restrained. She was, at this time, a most daring girl; and she always played with the boys, and picked up their ways, and, by superior intelligence, became their leader. From them she learned to look down on her own sex; and the women, in return, called her a tomboy and a witch : indeed, there was something witch-like in her agility, her unbounded daring, and her great, keen, gray eyes, with thickish eyebrows, black as jet, that actually met, not on her brows, but

—with a slight dip—on the bridge of her nose.

One summer afternoon, being then about eleven, she had just ridden one of Farmer Newton's horses into the water to drink, according to her custom, and driven the others in before her, when she became aware of a gentleman in black, with a pale, but noble face, looking thoughtfully at her. It was the new vicar, a learned clerk from Oxford. He smiled on her, and said, "My young madam, may I speak with you?" He knew who she was.

"Ay, sir," says she; and in a moment, from riding astride like a boy, she whipped one leg over and was seated like a woman, and brought the horse out, and slid off his fat ribs, and lighted like a bird down at the parson's feet, and took her hat off to him, instead of courtesying. "Here be I," said the imp. "My dear," says the vicar, "that is not a pastime for a young gentlewoman." Joanna hung her head.

"Not," said the parson, "that I would deprive you of amusement, at your age; that were cruel : but—have you no little horse of your own to ride?"

"Nay, not so much as a Jenny ass. Daddy Hanway is—I know what he is, but I won't say till we are better acquainted."

"Come, come, we are to be better acquainted, then."

"Ay, an' you will. Now may I go, sir?"

"Why, we have not half made acquaintance. Madam, I desire to show you my house."

"Alack! And I am dying to see it. So come on!" and she caught him by the hand with a fiery little grasp.

"Have with you, then!" cried the parson, affecting excitement, and proposed a race to the vicarage : so they sped across the meadow. His reverence was careful to pound the earth, and make a great fuss, but not to beat the imp, who, indeed, skimmed along like a swallow.

"There," said she, panting, "there's none can beat me at running, in this parish, except that Dick Caulfield. Od rabbit him." The vicar allowed that refined expression to pass, for the present, and took her into his study. "O Jiminy!" she cried; "here's books. I ne'er thought there were as many in the world."

"What! you are fond of books?" said he, eagerly.

"I dote ou 'em, especially voyages. I have read every book in our house twice over; there's the Bible, and 'Culpepper's Herbal,' and 'Pilgrim's Progress,' and the 'Ready Reckoner,' and the 'Prayer Book,' and a volume of the *Spectator*, and the book of receipts, and the 'Book of Thieves.'"

"And which do you like the best of all those?"

"Why, the 'Pilgrim's Progress,' to be sure; 'tis all travels!"

"Strange," said the clergyman, half to himself, "that a girl born in a country village should be so fond of travels."

"Country village!" said she. "Drat the country village. I ran away from it once; but they caught me at Hounslow. I was only eight; better luck next time, parson."

"Nay, Mistress Joanna"—

"An't please you, call me Philippa. I like that name best."

"Well, then, Mistress Philippa, I am of your mind about travelling. My studies, and a narrow income somewhat drawn upon by poor relations, have kept me at home; but my mind has travelled on the wings of books, as yours shall, Mistress Philippa, if you please. See, here's Purchase for you, and Dampier, Cowley, Sharpe, Woodes Rogers, where you shall find the cream of 'Robinson Crusoe,' 'Stout John Dunton,' and 'Montaigne's Travels,' short, but priceless. Here be 'Coryat's Crudities,' and 'Mory-

son's Itinerary,' two travellers of the good old school, that footed Europe, and told no lies. Ay, Philippa, often as I sat in my study, or meditated beneath the stars, have I longed to escape the narrow terms of this small island, and see the strange and beautiful world: first of all, the Holy Land, where still the vine, the olive-tree, and the cornfield grow side by side; where the Dead Sea rolls o'er those wicked cities, and Lot's wife, in salten pillar, still looks on: to see Rome, that immortal city where ancient and modern history meet and mingle in monuments of surpassing grandeur and beauty. Then would I run east again, and behold the mighty caves of Elephanta, monument of a race that is no more; the Pyramids of Egypt, and her temples approached by avenues of colossal sphinxes a -mile long. Thence to the pole, and see its spectral glories, great temples and palaces of prismatic ice, of which this new poet, Mr. Pope, singeth well,—

'As Atlas fixed, each hoary pile appears
The gathered winter of a thousand years.'

Then away to sunny lands, where forever the sky is blue and flowers spring spontaneous, and the earth poureth forth pines and melons and luscious fruits, without the hand of man,—

'And universal Pan,
Knit with the graces and the hours in dance,
Leads on the eternal Spring.'

"Then I would see the famous mountains of the world,—Ararat, where the ark rested, as the waters of the flood abated; Teneriffe's peak, shaped like a sugar-loaf, and by mariners seen often in the clear glassy sky one hundred miles at sea; and above all the mighty Andes, so high that no aspiring cloud may reach his bosom, and his great eye looks out ever calm, from the empyrean, upon half the world."

The scholar would have gone on, dreaming aloud, an hour more; but his words, that to him were only words, were fire to the aspiring girl, and set her pale and panting. "O parson!" she cried, "for the love of God take hat and come along to all those places;" and she crammed his hat into his hand, and tugged at him amain.

"My young mistress," said he gravely, "you do use that sacred name too lightly."

"Well, then, for the love of the Devil: I care not, so we do go this minute."

Then he held up his finger, and, with kind and soothing words, cooled this fiery creature down a little, and put Dampier's voyages into her hand. Down she flung herself, — for it was erect as a dart, or flat as a pancake, with this young gentlewoman; no half measures — and sucked the book like an egg.

He gave her the right to come and read when she pleased; and from this beginning, by degrees, she became his pupil very willingly.

He played the viol da gamba himself; so he asked her did she like music?

"No," said she: "I hate it."

Would she like to draw, and color?

"Ay. But not to keep me from my travels."

It turned out that she had an excellent gift at drawing, and a fine eye for color; so, with instruction, she soon got to draw from nature, and to color very prettily; the only objection was, in less than six months from the first lesson, every roadside barn-door within five miles presented a gross caricature, in chalk, of the farmer who owned it, and often of his wife and family into the bargain. The number and distance of these "sculptures," as she was pleased to call them (why, I know not), revealed an active foot,

a skilful hand, and a heart not to be daunted by moonlight.

The parson tried to break her spirit — with arithmetic. But no: she was all docility and goodness by his side — she would learn arithmetic, or any thing else, with a rapidity that nothing but a precocious girl ever equalled, — but a daring demon when he was not at her back.

In vain he begged her to consider that she was now thirteen years old, and must begin to play the gentlewoman: "I cannot," said she; "gentlewomen are such mincing apes. The boys, they scorn them; and so do I; they make me sick. Parson," said she, "I love you;" and she made but one spring, and her arms were round his neck with the same movement. "Grant me a favor," said she, "because I love you. Have me made a boy; 'twill not cost much."

The parson looked at her, gazing imploringly right into him with her great eyes, and was sore puzzled what she would be at now. However, the explanation followed in due course.

"Why," said she, "'tis but the price of a coat and waistcoat and breeches, instead of these things," slapping her petticoats contemptuously; "and then I am a boy. Oh, 'twill be sweet to have my freedom, and not to be checked at every word, because I am a she!"

"Why, what stuff is this, child?" said his reverence: "putting thee in boy's clothes will not make thee a boy."

"Yes, it will. You know it will; nay, to be sure, there 's my hair; but I can soon cut that."

"Now, Philippa," said her preceptor, "I cannot have you cutting your beautiful hair, which is a woman's crown, and talking nonsense. Hum! — the truth is — ahem! when once one has been christened Joanna Philippa in the church, one is a girl forever."

"Alas!" whined Philippa, "and is it so? Methought it was the clothes the old folk put us in that did our business." Then, going into a fury, "Oh! why did not I scratch their eyes out, when they came to christen me a girl? Why cried I not aloud, 'No! No! No! —A Boy!—A Boy'?"

"Well, we must make the best of it, my dear. I will read you what Erasmus saith, in his 'Gun-æco-Synedrion,' of the female estate, and its advantages. Then you will see that each condition of life hath its comforts and its drawbacks."

The compass of my tale does not permit me to deal largely in conversations; otherwise, the intercourse of this gentle scholar's mind and this sharp girl's was curious and interesting enough. It left Philippa, at fourteen years of age, very superior to the ladies of the period, in reading, writing, arithmetic, drawing, walking, leaping, and running; but far more innocent, in spite of her wildness, than if she had consorted with the women of that day, whose tongues were too often foul.

At this time the good parson fell ill, and, having friends in office, obtained leave to go on the Continent.

He returned in two years, and found his pupil transformed into a tall, beautiful girl; even her black brows became her now, and dazzled the beholder. But such a change! She was now extremely shy; avoided the boys, blushed whenever they spoke to her, and played the prude even with her late preceptor. She had a great many new ideas in her head: need I say that love was one of them? But as there was nobody in the parish that approached the being she had fixed on,—young, beautiful, fair, brave, good, and that had made the grand tour, —her favorite companion, after all, was the good parson; only she now approached even him with a vast show of timidity. To tell the truth, she had just as much devil in her as ever; but, on the surface, was mighty guarded, demure, and bashful.

And now, all of a sudden, came a lover. Mr. Hanway, seeing the time draw near when he must surrender to the other trustee, could not resist the temptation of trying to get her for his son Silas. Silas was older than she, though he looked but a hobbadehoy. The old man, to carry out his scheme, indulged miss with a pony, and a moderately masculine riding-dress, with a little purple velvet cap and white feather, very neat, and set Silas to ride with her. She used to pace out of sight demurely, then dash out of the road into the fields and away, as the crow flies, over hedge and ditch, depositing Silas in the latter now and then. She treated his clumsy courtship with queenly contempt, and once, when he went to kiss her, she fetched him a slap that made his ears ring famously.

One day, when Mr. Hanway was out, this young lady, who was now mighty curious, and always prying about the house, gave the old gentleman's desk a shake with both hands. She had often admired this desk: it was of enormous size and weight, and sculptured at the sides, —an antique piece of furniture. When she shook it, something metallic seemed to ring at the bottom. She looked inside, and there was nothing but papers. "That is odd," thought Joanna Philippa. She shook it again. Same metallic sound. Then, with some difficulty, though she was a most sinewy girl, she turned it over, and saw a little button, scarcely perceptible. She pressed it, and lo! a drawer flew out at quite another part of the desk. That drawer dazzled her: it was literally full of sparkling jewels, some of them very beautiful and valuable. She screamed with surprise. She screamed again with delight. She knew, in a moment, they were her mother's jewels, which Mr. Hanway had told her were a few trifling things, not to be shown her till her twenty-first birthday, and then she was to have them for her own.

"Oh, thou old knave!" said she. She did not hesitate one moment. "I'll have them, and keep them too, if I hang for it; for they are mine." So she swept them all into her apron, and flew up stairs with them and hid them; then back again, and put the desk straight.

That night she had them all on, one after another, before she went to bed, and marched about the room, like a peacock, surveying herself.

Next day she took fright, and carried them out of the house, and hid them in the thatch of an old cart-house that was never used nowadays, so not likely to he repaired

On moonlight nights she would sometimes take a little hand-glass out, and wear the diamond cross and brooch, and parade with them, sparkling in the moonlight. Her bedroom commanded a view of this sacred cart-shed; aud she always took a look at it the last thing before she went to sleep.

Silas was to go to London, to be articled as a lawyer's clerk. His father thought now was the time to make a lasting impression; so he provided the youth with a ring to give her, and instructed him that he must kiss her at parting, say he loved her dearly, and get her to betroth herself to him, and so put the ring on her finger. When the time came, Miss was on the lawn hoeing weeds out of the gravel. Silas went to her with the ring. Mr. Hanway was dressing; but he managed to peep behind a curtain at the approaching ceremony.

It did not go smooth. The girl was ready to give Silas a civil goodby; but, at the very mention of love, she laughed him to scorn. That nettled him; and he told her

she would he very lucky to get as good a husband. "Come, sweetheart," said he, "here's the ring. E'en let me put it on thy hand, and give us a buss at parting."

"I'll take no ring of thine," said the girl, beginning to pant at the double proposal. "I'd rather die than wed thee."

"And I'd rather die than not wed thee." He threw his arms round her neck, and dragged her to him.

"Let me go," she screamed. "You are a churl and a ruffian. I'll not be used so."

She struggled violently, and screamed; and, when nothing else would do, she tore herself clear, with a fierce cry, all on fire with outraged modesty and repugnance, and gave him a savage blow on the bridge of the nose with her little hoe; it brought him to one knee: and with that she was gone like the wind, and flung herself, sobbing, into a garden seat out of sight.

Now this severe blow was not dangerous, but it made the lover's nose bleed profusely. It bled a great deal as he kneeled, half-stupefied; and, when he got up a little way, it bled freely again: he thought it would never leave off. His love was cooled forever. All he cared about now was not spoiling his new clothes; so, after a while, he walked away very slowly, with his nose projecting, like a gander's; and he was scarcely clear of the premises, when Joanna Philippa, who had peeped, and seen him off, came back to her occupation, looking as demure and innocent as any young lady you ever saw. She was rather dismayed, though, when she found the grass incarnadined, and the gardener's turfcutter literally drenched with blood, both blade and handle.

While she was contemplating this grim sight, and wishing she had not hit so hard, the old man came at her all of a sudden, white with rage. "Ay, look at your work, you monster!" he cried, "and the poor boy leaving us for good. You have killed him, or nearly, and I'll trounce you for it." He griped her by the arm, and raised his cane over her head.

She was terrified, and cried for mercy. "O° uncle! I did not mean. Oh, pray don't kill me! Don't kill me!"

He did not mean to kill her, nor even hurt her; but, in his paternal rage, he struck her a great many times about her petticoats, which made a great noise. She screamed all the time; only at first it was "Don't kill me!" and then "Don't degrade me!"

"There," said he, "let that teach thee not to be so ready with thy hands, thou barbarous, ungrateful jade!"

But now she confronted him in silence, with a face as white as death, and eyes that glared, and her black brows that looked terrible by the contrast with her ashy cheek, a child no more, but a beautiful woman outraged. She said nothing, but gave him that one tremendous look, then fled, with a cry of shame and anguish. She flew to the cart-house, took out her jewels, and, in three minutes, she was out of the premises. She darted down one lane, and up another, till she got on the high road to London. She entered the city at ten o'clock that evening, and slept at an inn.

Next morning she lay in bed a while, thinking what she should do to avoid being captured, as in her childish days. She thought the best thing was to make a change in her costume; so she sold one of her rings, and took a modest lodging, and bought some stuffs, and set to work to make a suit such as she saw worn by tradesman's daughters of the better sort. All her fear was to be captured, and her mother's jewels taken from her. They were

all her fortune, she thought; and, besides, she loved them.

One day, just before the new clothes were ready, and being weary of confinement, she strolled abroad, and, seeing a chocolate house, whipped on her mask, and entered it. While she was sipping her chocolate, a spark handed her the *Daily Post*, with a low bow, by way of preliminary to making her acquaintance. She thanked him so modestly, he hesitated, and let her read the paper in peace. It was a miserable sheet, with very little in it; but there was a curious advertisement:—

"April 26. Lost, or mislaid, one pair large brilliant ear-rings, with drops of the first water: one diamond cross; three large bars for the breast (diamonds of the first water): large pearl necklace; brooch of sapphire and brilliants; one large ruby ring; one emerald and brilliants; one locket, set with amethyst and rose diamonds. If offered to be sold, pawned, or valued, pray stop 'em (*sic*) and THE PARTY, especially if a young lady, and give notice to Mr. Drummond, goldsmith, at Charing Cross, and you shall receive 200 guineas reward."

The paper almost fell from her hands at first: yet, with the fine defensive cunning of her sex, she sipped her chocolate quite slowly, feeling very cold all the time; and then she went home.

The advertisement was very well worded for others; but falling, unluckily, into her hands, it disquieted as well as terrified her. "My jewels!" said she; "not me. He means to steal them. Well, he shall never see them, nor me again."

She carried her new dress to a shop that sold masquerade dresses, and she easily exchanged it for a seaman's holiday dress, a merchant captain's, or mate's. She brought it home in a bundle. She purchased ed a trunk, and paid her landlady, and then she had only a crown left and her jewels.

She took a coach, it being now dark, and had the hardihood to change her clothes in the coach. The seafaring man's dress fitted her so loosely she had no trouble. The moment she had got into it her native courage revived, and she was ready to dance for joy. "Now find your young gentlewoman and her jewels," said she. "Nay, but I'll put the sea between us rather." She had noticed some clean-looking lodgings; so she made the coachman stop there. When he let her out, he started at the metamorphosis; but she put her finger to her lips, and said, "Only a masquerading folly," and gave him her last shilling.

The landlady received the handsome young mate, all smiles; and they soon came to terms. In the morning she melted a jewel, and paid the landlady a week in advance. Then she took out her female costume, and pawned it. She purchased shirts and good stockings of wool and cotton, and marched about with a little hanger by her side, but was mighty civil, not feeling desirous to draw the said hanger. She always gave a fine gentleman the wall.

"She now asked the prices of jewels at many places; and, hearing of a good ship bound for America, she sold a ring, called herself a merchant's son, dressed accordingly, and sailed, a passenger to Boston, in the bay of Massachusetts.

Her first intention was to be a woman again, as soon as she got there. But there was what they called, in those days, a "Spirit" on board the ship, a gasconading agent, working for the planters; he told her such a tale about the American colonies, and how any man could dig a fortune there, that she agreed to indent as servant and book-keeper, and see whether it would suit her. She thought it was no use being idle in man's clothes : indeed, she had too much energy. She was easily led into signing an indenture, the full effect of which she did not comprehend : yet she was sharp enough to read the paper, and bargain that she was to do no work but keeping accounts and overlooking laborers; and this the agent wrote in, sooner than lose the prettiest young fellow he had ever seen; and, to make a long story short, a rich planter from Delaware acquired this prize, and carried her off to a first-rate farm near Willingtown.

There she remained a year, affording perfect satisfaction to her employer, reading every book she could lay hold of, taking in knowledge at every pore, flattering, and so winning the women, and watching the men like a very cat, to know their minds. This study amused her greatly.

She left the seeds of trouble behind her. At seven o'clock that very evening she ran away, Mr. Hanway's gardener, whose cottage was on the premises, took in his turf-cutter, and showed it to his wife, all bloody. He laughed, and said, "Why, one would think they had been a pig-killing, with this here!"

His wife, instead of laughing, gave a scream, and then fell a trembling. "Oh, dear!" said she, "we shall hear more of this." Then she told him she had heard some poor creature crying for mercy, and saying, "Oh! don't kill me; don't kill me!" and, after that, she had heard heavy blows. "O John!" said she, "put it away from me; for I do feel sick at sight on't." So he went and put the turf-cutter away in the tool-house, just as it was. When he came back, he asked her if she knew whose voice it was that had cried for mercy.

"How can I tell, all that way off?" said she. "'Twas a woman's voice, for certain : alack! ask me not, John; I'm afeard of my own thoughts."

"Well, keep them to thyself, then : we have got a good place. Least said is soonest mended."

Next morning the news was that Joanna had run away. The gardener told his wife at breakfast. She shook her head. "Run away, poor thing! She'll never run no more : she'll never be seen no more, without you do find her, digging about."

"Hush!" said the man. "Hold thy tongue : we have eaten his bread a many years."

"I shall never bear the sight of him again, I tell thee."

"Well, keep out of his sight, then : he won't come after thee, I trow; but if ye go hanging of him, with your tongue, and losing me a good place, I shall twist thy neck, sweetheart; and then there will be a pair hung instead of one."

These dark suspicions smouldered for many months. Mr. Hanway went to Mr. Chester, and told him the girl was a thief, and had run away with the jewels.

"A thief, Master Hanway!" said the other coldly. "The jewels were her mother's, and coming to her."

"Ay, but she knew not that," said the old man, who was bitterly incensed against her. Not a word did he say to Thomas Chester about either of the violent scenes in the garden. Mr. Chester advised him to advertise, and drew the advertisement for him.

Months rolled on; all hope of seeing Joanna oozed away : both trustees were unhappy about it and on ill terms; for Hanway thought his allowance ought to go on; but Chester ridiculed the idea; and so it stopped, since the money could only be drawn under both signatures.

Presently there arose in the village a vague, horrid whisper of "foul play." It reached Lawyer Chester. He tried to trace it: it was impalpable at first, like a sudden smell of carrion. But this keen lawyer tracked it and tracked it, and discovered that an old blind man, walking in his garden, which adjoined Mr. Hanway's, had heard a voice cry, "O uncle! don't kill me! don't kill me!" and then several heavy blows. He learned, too, that the gardener's wife had lately thrown out mysterious hints as to what would become of some people, if she were to tell all she knew. Then Mr. Chester began to fear a crime had been committed : only he could see no motive. But murders are not always motived : the passions slay as well as the interests. Being a just man, and feeling that his dislike to Hanway might prejudice him, he carried his notes to a neighboring justice, and left the matter in his hands.

This magistrate was young and zealous : he had seen Joanna riding across country, and admired her : he went into the matter a little too much like a crown solicitor.

Mr. Hanway was summoned to London to attend his son Silas, who had caught a violent fever. The magistrate in question heard of his absence, and took that opportunity to call on the gardener. He found the wife alone, and by coaxing and threatening soon got her story out of her. He took possession of the turf-cutter, which tool she and the gardener had avoided with horror ever since; and the sight of it, added to the other evidence, gave him a shock, and convinced him he saw before him the proofs of a bloody murder.

Everything was therefore prepared for the arrest of Mr. Hanway, on his return. But that return was delayed by a truly pitiable cause. Silas was insensible when his father came; and died a few hours after. The bereaved father had a shell made for the remains, and brought them down to Colebrook. The sad burden was but just taken into the hall, when the officers of justice, who had rigorous orders, arrested the bereaved father on a charge of murder.

He stared at them stupidly, and said, "Are ye mad?"

They told him no: the evidence was strong.

"Is it so?" said he languidly. "Well, let me bury my child; and I'll go to the gallows, or where you will: I have nought left to live for."

Then the officers of justice were puzzled what to do. However, as it happened, the magistrate himself came up; and, when he heard, he directed them to let the funeral proceed, but be careful the mourner did not escape.

The grave was already dug, and the clergyman waiting: so poor Silas was buried, attended by the whole parish, in strange silence; for their horror of the murderer was checked by their pity for the desolate father, to whom the charge of murder was, at that heavy hour, a feather-stroke compared with his bereavement.

He went home alone: the officers kept a little aloof from him, and so did the people. He was examined in his own house, and confronted with the witnesses. The turf-cutter was also produced.

He told the simple truth: not a soul believed it. He was committed for trial, and a reward of £50 offered to whoever should find the *corpus delictæ*, which was the one link in the evidence wanting.

Months passed on, and no *corpus delictæ*. At last some bones were found in a peat heath hard by, and brought to the justice, followed by a crowd.

"She is found! she is found!" was the cry. "The old rogue will be hanged now;" and all day folk dropped in to see the bones of poor Joanna. The parson and Mr. Chester, who were good friends, went together. Says the parson, "I know these bones well"—

"There! there!" was the cry: "Parson can swear to 'em: that is enow."

"—I know them," continued the parson, calmly, "for the bones of the moose-deer, which ran in these parts four thousand years ago. I do bid against the crown for these. I will give five shillings, and ten for the horns."

That very evening two young men came to the vicarage, and told the maid, with a sheepish look, they had brought parson the gentlewoman's horns. They had dug a little farther.

But this did not shake the general impression that a foul murder had been done and artfully concealed. Mr. Chester, however, who had started the inquiry, now felt uneasy in his mind at what he had done. He called on Mr. Hanway in prison, and found him piteously depressed. Mr. Hanway asked his forgiveness, if ever he had offended him.

"Nay, sir," said Chester, "I did never affect you much, nor you me; but, in truth, you never wronged me, that I know of: and, seeing you in this plight, I blame myself, and would serve you. Come, courage, man. If she is alive, there is a way to find her."

"Would to God I knew that way!"

"Advertise for her. Let her know your trouble, and that she is an heiress. That will be against the letter of her father's wish, but not the spirit. Write the advertisement yourself, and I will see it sent abroad."

Then Hanway plucked up a little heart, and wrote a humble, touching advertisement, describing his peril. Mr. Chester took it, and, having read it, was fain to wipe a tear from his eye, and straightway dropped the judicial character, and shut his eyes to the evidence, and, resuming old habits, retained himself solicitor for the defendant. In that self-assumed character, he spared not his own purse, but scattered the advertisements far and wide, not in England only, but Scotland, Ireland, and every country that spoke the English tongue.

———◆———

CHAPTER IV.

JAMES ANNESLEY remained in prison, awaiting his sentence. He was not without hope : but his fear was greater ; and this fear soon rose to agony. For the unhappy pair, whose kindness had brought him to this, were led out to receive the first part of their sentence within sight of the grated windows of his cell. They had to sit under the gallows one hour, with a rope round their necks, and then received, the lover forty lashes, the woman thirty, and the servant twenty-one, all on their bare backs, and well laid on. Their groans and shrieks rent the air, and froze James Annesley to the bone ; for he looked for his own turn to come next, and behind the cutting lash frowned the grim prison.

A week passed, and a spark of hope was reviving, when one morning the jailer and another officer came and told him he must go with them. His knees failed him. He groaned, and lay back almost insensible. They gave him a drop of brandy, and, seeing his mistake, told him to pluck up courage. " You are to be exposed every market-day, and not to be whipped, till somebody in Chester shall 'prove you were in the town before you came in a prisoner."

He was so exposed every market-day for a month. A large paper was pinned on his breast, inviting all good citizens to testify what they knew of him.

On the fourth market-day, casting his eyes wistfully round, who should he see but Drummond : he had come all that way to buy horses, and was so intent on business that he noticed nothing else. James made signs to him in vain. He called to him ; he did every thing to attract this cruel master's attention, whom he had run from. At last a man went for him to Drummond, and brought him up. Drummond started at first, then surveyed him with a cruel countenance. " What would you of me, young man ?"

" Do but take me home, and I will serve you faithfully."

Drummond, to torment him, turned on his heel without a word. However, he went to the justices, and claimed him ; showed, by an entry in his pocket-book, when he ran away, and from what place, and knocked the indictment to atoms. In twenty-four hours James Annesley was riding home, at Drummond's back. When he got him home, Drummond sued him for penalties and damages : the penalty, five days for every day's absence, came to a year ; but the damages, being paid in service, came to two years and a half.

Upon this decision, James Annesley began to fret, and pine away ; and Drummond, who had lost one or two that way, sold him to Jedediah Surefoot, a flourishing planter, near Willingtown, in Delaware. This was a beautiful place, and had an extraordinary story, which was then fresh in men's minds. William Shipley, a Leicestershire man, was settled at Ridley, with his second wife, Elizabeth Levis, of Springfield, in the county Chester. She was a distinguished minister in the society of " Friends," and a remarkable woman. Soon after her marriage, she dreamed a dream. She was riding through a wild country, on what errand she knew not, and mounted a lofty hill. From this hill burst on her eyes a landscape of surpassing beauty, — a wide valley, green with sloping lawns, studded with clumps of trees and settlers' cabins. The sun streamed golden through partial clearings made by the axe ; even now it tinkled unseen : and broad rivers ran, and little brooks sparkled silver, and meandered to the extreme limits of vision. She sat entranced upon her horse, and was speechless a while with delight. Then she asked her guide what country this was.

"Elizabeth," said he, "it is thy home."

"Nay," said she, "my earthly home is Ridley."

"Not so," said he. "This sweet place cries out for thee, and for the Word. Submit thyself, then, to the will of heaven, and come hither; so shalt thou do much good to the place and the people ; and the blessing of God shall be on thy house, and on their labors in the Lord."

Elizabeth told this dream to her husband, with all the warmth and freshness in the world ; and he made this sublime answer, "We are doing pretty well here ; " and the subject dropped.

Full three years afterwards, Elizabeth Shipley was invited to a meeting of Friends, between the Delaware and Chesapeake Bays.

She rode alone, and without fear, till she came to the Brandywine River ; and then, though the water was low, she took a guide : he led her some distance to " the old ford," and she got through, and went up the hill, by " the king's road." At the top of the hill she checked her horse, and uttered a cry of amazement and delight; for lo! there was the paradise of her dream before her, — ay, down to the minutest feature of the landscape, and the axe that tinkled unseen. She sat, like a statue, on her horse, just as she had done in her dream.

After this, she constantly entreated William Shipley to ride with her and see the lovely place. He thought it a waste of time : did not believe in dreams, though he durst not say so. So, at last, she said to him, " William, settle all thou hast in Ridley on thy children by thy first wife. I and mine will stand or fall by the place the Lord doth call me to."

The prophetess knew her lord and master : he came with her directly to see Willingtown, and it struck him all of a heat. He examined it nearer and found it was seated between the finger and thumb of two rivers, — one impetuous, and admirable for turning mills, the other tidal, and navigable to the sea. "Why, Elizabeth," said he, "a man might grind his corn here with one hand, and ship it with t'other ! "

So, what with her faith in power divine, and his in water-power, the Shipleys settled at Willingtown, now called Wilmington, and gave that rising place a wonderful impulse. William Shipley bought land between the streams, and set up mill and factory. Elizabeth became a shining light, and drew the cream of the Quakers thither ; and even poor James Annesley profited a little by her virtues ; for she preached and practised humanity to slaves : and Dame Surefoot, a simple motherly woman, was her pupil, though her senior ; so there was no starving of slaves, nor frolicsome flagellation, on Surefoot's farm. Servitude was robbed of its fangs — though nothing could remove its sting — in the circle of which that pious woman was the centre.

But the beauty of the place, and the milder servitude, came too late for poor James Annesley. The long persecution of fortune, the almost unintermittent sufferings of his soul and body, had broken his spirit and clouded his youth. He was worn out, dejected, hopeless. His mind might be compared to a ship, which has been so tossed, baffled, and battered by storm upon storm that at last it leaks, and sinks quietly in the golden ripple and placid sunlight of a calm.

He did his work well enough, but

in dogged silence; and nothing ever came from him but sighs: his face was handsome, but full of misery. Dame Surefoot noticed this, after a time, and asked him one day what was the matter. "Nothing, madam," said he, "thank you." — "Then why so sad? Most servants are glad to come to us from Drummond."

"And so ought I to be, madam. I will try to be more cheerful. But three years more!" And he groaned.

"What is three years!" said Mrs. Surefoot. "Alas! young man, 'twill pass like a shadow. You have got this new trouble, the vapors, with keeping too much alone. I shall find you a companion; for you are a civil-spoken young man."

So, that very evening she went to her favorite. When could any woman govern without one? "Philip," said she, "prithee, speak to this new servant, James, and be good to him. He is well to look at, and no idler, but so eaten up with sadness."

"Mayhap he is in love," said Philip, "I'll soon find what ails him, mother."

This Philip was a black-eyed youth, as sharp as a needle, who kept all the accounts, and sometimes rode on business. He flattered the mistress finely, and had got the length of her shoe, as the saying is. The master valued him on other grounds: he was saucy, but honest, and kept the books, though rather complicated, with marvellous precision and neatness. Thus, valued on both sides, Philip, who by the by was older than he looked, gave himself considerable airs; and it was in rather a condescending tone he danced up to James Annesley, and invited him to leave off sighing, and walk with him into the town of Willingtown.

"Thank you, sir," said James; "but I prefer to meditate."

"To mope, you mean. 'Tis the worst thing for you: and I hate to walk alone. So be not churlish now. Why, man, we are countrymen!"

"Sir, I shall be sorry company."

"But I shall be merry company. So come on."

"Well, if I must," said James, and went with him reluctantly.

Master Philip chattered away for both, and stole a glance at his companion now and then. Young Annesley's replies were civil, but reserved. "You are no mill-clack," said Philip ironically. "I am not," said James humbly.

Philip carried an enormous basket. He had to bring groceries home, and salt, and medicinal herbs from Mrs. Dean, the Dutch widow, and coarse sugar, and a jar of vinegar. When all these were on board, the basket was very heavy; and James said, "I will carry that."

"Nay," said Philip, pretending to resist. "I carried it hither, and I will carry it home."

"That you shall not," said James, and laid hold of it, and fairly wrenched it from him.

"You are a rude bear," said Philip. "You have hurt my thumb."

"Where?" asked James, catching at it to see.

"Somewhere," said Philip, and whipped it behind his back.

"Well, I am sorry for that," replied James. "I am much older than you, and stronger; and the least I could do was to carry your burden, since you put up with my dull company."

"Speak not to me. I'll never speak to you again, bear."

"And what else am I good for, now, but to carry burdens?"

"Oh! say not that, James. Alas! why are you so sad? You are young, you are well-looking, rather. What beautiful hair you have got! I declare I did never see such hair: 'tis like silk. I'd never despond, if I had such hair as that, instead of my black stuff. You should flatter the women; that is the way to get forward. Look at me. I get my own way in every thing, and that is my strategy. Tell me, James, — I won't tell a soul — are you in love ? "

" No."

" But you have been ? "

" Never. I was but a boy when I was kidnapped, and sent over here ; and my heart has always been too heavy for those idle fancies."

" What, you did not come here of your good-will ? "

" Consent to be a slave ? Who would be so base ? "

James said this with a certain majesty that quelled his merry companion for a moment. He drew instinctively a little farther off, and walked with thoughtful, downcast eyes. Nor did he say much more in fact, but brooded over what his companion had said. However, he chattered away fast enough to Mrs. Surefoot ; and they agreed that James was not a sullen churl, but a fine, melancholy, interesting young man. Then they fell into speculations as to why he had been kidnapped and sent out. This wise conversation was uttered within hearing of Maria Surefoot, a demure, romantic girl of seventeen. She drank in every word, but said nothing ; only, thenceforth, James became an object of vast curiosity and interest to her.

One day that some very heavy work in loading of timber was done near the house, James was very zealous and active, and so athletic that Philip drew Mrs. Surefoot's attention to his prowess.

" Yes, in truth," said the worthy dame. " Here, Maria, run you and get him a can of wine, and take it to him : he has earned it right well."

Maria soon appeared with the can, and went to James : he was now seated on a bank, in sight, and, the brief stimulus of labor over, had fallen into his usual pensive state.

The girl approached him timidly and softly, and stood looking at him a considerable time. " Is she afraid to speak to him ? " said Philip pet-

tishly. " What should she be afraid of ? " said Mrs. Surefoot.

The girl spoke to James, and he instantly rose, and removed his cap. She held him out the wine, blushing like a rose, and said, " Prithee, drink this : my mother sends it."

" I wish her every blessing," said James piously ; " and the same to you, Mistress Maria."

" You cannot wish me better than I wish you, James," murmured the girl, all in a flutter. " I have heard about you ; and, if there is any thing in the world I can do — for I pity you with all my heart." She turned, and went away in a tremor and confusion which did not escape the keen gray eyes of Master Philip. Dame Surefoot was older ; so perhaps her eye could not seize all the minutiæ by which a girl's very body indicates when love has seized her.

The coast was no sooner clear than Philip ran out, and invited James into his office : " It is cooler there," said he.

As soon as ever he got James into his office, he said sharply, " What did Mistress Maria say to you ? "

" I could not say : I paid no attention."

" I like not that young gentlewoman : she is a forward minx."

" Is she ? You know best. You have been here longest. How cool it is here ; and you have flowers in your window. What a luxurious boy ! And what a many books ! "

" Yes, I am the only one that reads much here. So our dame lets me have all the library. Are you fond of learning ? "

" I love it, of all things. But, alas ! I have been so ill brought up ; and, whenever I got to my books, some cruelty or other came and took me from them. It is my grief and my shame that I, a gentleman's son, have the education of a porter ? "

" What then," said Philip, " tell me, if I were to teach you, would that make you happier, and to leave off sighing so?"

"Indeed, I think it would. I burn with desire of instruction."

"Well, then, I will give you a lesson every evening. Then you will be out of the way of all these forward minxes."

"I trouble not my head about them. I would liever be at the books with you. Let us begin at once."

Then Philip gave James a book to read, and he read it, but badly: gave him a letter to write, and he wrote it vilely.

"Come," said Philip, with a curious air of satisfaction, "I have a year's work before me, with thee."

He taught James, every evening, after work, with a patience and an untiring amiability that he had not shown in conversation; and James ploughed at it with all his heart, and was pathetically docile and grateful. Out of this arose, by degrees, a tender friendship, and loyal partisanship, that belongs to youth; and so, one day, being now such friends, Philip urged him by their friendship to tell him his whole story. He hesitated. "Philip," said he, "I never told it yet but some ill luck did follow straight. No matter; sit by me, my one friend, and I'll tell it thee, — ay, ever since I was four years old."

Then he told his story, but broke down once or twice; then went manfully on, the more so that, while he was telling it, a brown but shapely hand stole into his, and was seldom idle, but ever speaking as variously as a voice, with its gentle pressure of sympathy and sudden grasps at danger; but when he came to his being kidnapped and swooning dead away in the ship, it trembled, and Philip turned his head away, and never looked towards him again, and by then he was flung into jail and cast for death the narrator discovered that Philip was crying.

"O Philip!" said he, "do not you cry. Ah! how many a time I have cried over it all; but now my eyes are dry. Sweet Philip! how kind you are to cry for me. Ah, miserable me!" and all of a sudden Philip's tears drew forth his own once more, the first he had shed for years. They did him a world of good. "O my dear Philip!" he cried, "you have saved me from despair: a cloud clears from my mind. Whilst I have one friend who will shed a tear for me, it were ungrateful to despair;" and he took Philip in his arms, and was going to kiss him heartily; but the boy panted, and put up both his hands, and said, "No, no! I am choking. Prithee, go get me a cup of wine."

James went accordingly; and the first person he saw was Mistress Maria: he asked her to oblige him with a cup of wine.

"Ay, that I will, James," said she tenderly, and brought it him in a moment, and told him she must have the pleasure of seeing him drink.

"I will taste it, madam," said he; "but, indeed, 'tis for Philip. He is not well."

"For Philip!" said she disdainfully. "I hope the next time 'twill be for yourself."

James ran with the cup to Philip. Philip was not to be found.

"Was ever such a boy?" said James. However, he left the cup of wine on a table: and the early negroes picked up that worm, as the saying is.

Next evening he went for his lesson, as usual. Philip was busy over a ledger, and only noticed him with a supercilious nod.

"Philip," said he, "I brought you the wine as fast I could."

Philip never looked off his ledger. "You brought it so fast that I was gone to bed. You were too busy with Mistress Maria to think of me, I trow."

"Nay, I did stay not two minutes with her."

"There — there, there, I thought as much: you *were* with her."

"Foolish boy, have I the key of the cellar? I asked the first I met."

"Well, I guessed she was the butler; so I did not drink a drop, — not a drop, sir."

"I am sorry for that."

"No, you are not."

"Yes, I am, Philip."

"Do not contradict *me*. I am very angry with you. You made me cry with your romance: that I do not believe a word of. Do not contradict *me*. And I am not so fond of crying as you are; it makes me ill: and so now I'll just give you a piece of advice; for I see every thing from this window. My nose may be in my ledger, but my eye is on you all; so tremble! I tell thee, young women are the artfullest creatures; they are not like men, who get gray and cunning. Girls are born artful: and two or three of these girls are setting their caps at you, after their manner. There's that Indian girl, Turquoise, she makes no disguise, being a savage; she lets all the world see she is ready to eat you up. Then there's the master's niece,—great fat thing, —she comes here six times for once she is wanted, and sits watching you with her great gray eyes, like a cat watches for a mouse: she will catch you too, some day, if you take not the better heed: and then there's Mistress Maria that is the worst of them all, because she is always here, and has so many opportunities. She is ever throwing herself in your way."

"Nay, nay," said James.

"Do you not meet her in lonely places, whenever you take your walks without me?"

"Sometimes, by pure chance."

"Chance! foolish man; that shows how little you are fit to cope with them."

"Very well, Philip," said James: "since you give me the benefit of your age and experience, I'll give *you* a piece of advice. Do not you trouble about me; for I am not in love with any young woman, and never was. What I love is the liberty I have lost, and the country I have been banished from. Love is not for a slave. If ever I get home again, I may fall in love; but I think it will be a dark woman: they have always been my best friends. So never you mind me. 'Tis you that are in danger from these girls, not I."

"Me? ha! ha!"

"Ay! why, your head is full of them. I never knew a boy of your age talk so much about women, nor think so much about them."

"Do I talk as if I loved them?"

"No; but you do study them, and abuse them beyond reason: and those are the men that are caught the first, I've heard."

"Well, this is idle chat. Come, sit down, and I'll give you your lesson, James. Now, then. How dark is your sweetheart to be? Copper, like Turquoise; or lampblack, like Chloe?"

"Thank you, Philip. I prefer a white skin. But her hair, and her eyebrows, and her eyes, I care not if they are dark as "—

"The Devil's," suggested Philip.

"Nay, yours will be dark enough for me. They are the blackest ever I saw; long life to 'em."

Philip colored high with pleasure; and then said, with arrogance, "Come, sir, this is idle chat. Let us to something more profitable, if you please."

The snubbed scholar submitted with a smile. He was getting used to Master Philip's caprices: they amused him.

James Annesley's spirits improved; his fine eyes began to beam at times, and color to come into his cheek.

Mistress Maria, on the contrary, began to sicken and pine; and the vigilant Philip determined to be her doctor, and prescribe her change of air. One morning he asked an interview with the master and mistress: they were breakfasting in the parlor. Philip was admitted.

Now, Jedediah Surefoot was not like his wife, who treated her servants as her children: he was humane but very short with them. Philip stood in awe of him, and had prepared a little speech beforehand. "Master," said he, "I think a good servant should tell his employer in time, if he sees any thing going on that might take an ill turn: so I am come to tell you something."

"Then why not tell it at once?" said Jedediah.

"Nay, sir, only for fear you should be hasty, and blame him who is guiltless in the matter. The truth is, master, and I hope you will forgive me, and set it down to my zeal and duty, if I do make so free, but it is about my young mistress."

"Ay," said Jedediah, frowning, "and what canst thou have to say about her?"

"She is sick, sir; and will be while she bides here."

"Why, the air is wholesome enough. I never was better in my life than I am here."

"'Tis not the air that is amiss, sir, saving your presence. 'Tis the mind."

"Speak plainer, thou jackanapes, if thou hast aught to say at all."

"Nay, then; Mistress Maria hath cast her eyes on James Annesley, and 'tis for him she is love-sick. Would you cure her, 't is but to send her elsewhere for a year. Change, and the sight of other men, will soon restore her."

Jedediah was taken all aback by this revelation. "Patience," said he, "can this be so?"

"Nay, Jedediah," said she, "I hope not; but Philip is not one that lies. Alas! what is to be done?"

"The first thing to be done is to know the truth."

He called a negro, and bade him clear the room, and bring an easy-chair into it. This done, he sent the negro to his daughter's room, and ordered her to come and sit in his arm-chair by the fire. When he heard her step on the stairs, he turned his wife and Philip out by another door (for the room had two), and left that door ajar. "Now bide you there," said he, "and still as mice."

He then went and ordered James Annesley to bring in billets of wood and fill the great basket in the parlor. This done, he stole back on tiptoe to his wife and Philip, and shook his fist at them, to keep their uneasy tongues quiet. They were on thorns, both of them, — the mother for her daughter, and Philip for his friend. "Master," he whispered, "think what you do. James is a good young man. He will never be so unfaithful as to seek her out and offer love to her; but seeing her all alone, and sick for love of him, 'tis too much for flesh and blood. Why, 'tis like the Devil, to tempt a weak mortal so."

"Hold thy tongue, jackanapes," was the stern reply.

"Nay, but I cannot. This goes against my conscience. Do as you will, sir; but I wash my hands on't." And he was walking off with dignity.

A rude hand was laid on his collar; and Jedediah, in a stern whisper, said, "Wouldst go and tell thy friend James, and put him on guard? Budge but one inch, and I'll have thee whipped, and soundly, the first this three years."

Then Philip turned very pale, and began to shake like a leaf. His quick spirit saw the terrible mistake he had made; and all the possible consequences flashed on him at once. What more likely than that James should commit a folly in an unguarded moment; and then the stern old man would punish him ; and O agony ! he would have been the traitor to betray his unfortunate friend ; ay, and that friend would know it. Such was the distress this cost him, that beads of perspiration rose on his brow, though his body was cold all over.

And the miserable suspense was so long ! It seemed an age before they heard James come into the room, and put down his heavy basket of wood ; and then the time he was placing the billets in the large basket ! and all passed in silence till the billets were placed.

At last a soft female voice said, "Thank you, James : you are very good."

"Nay, madam," James was heard to say, " 'tis little to do for you, and you in sickness ; but I hope you are better, Mistress Maria."

"No, James," sighed the young girl, " and never shall be till you are my doctor."

"I, madam !" said James, "why, I have no skill."

" 'Tis not the skill, but the will, that lacketh. You dull, insensible man, see you not 'tis your unkindness that is killing me ? Nay, dissemble no more. Oh that I could hate thee as I ought for slighting my affection ! Alas ! James, what is it in me that displeases you ? I am young ; they say I am fair : am I not better worth thy love than that Indian girl, that is forever hanging about thee, and so I hate her ? Speak to me, James, for mercy's sake ! do not make me woo thee in vain, and sue where I have a right to command. Oh, how I shall hate you now, if you are ungrateful ! Hate you, alas ! I cannot : thou hast bewitched me. I love thee to distraction. For pity's sake speak to me !"

James was much troubled and abashed. "Madam," said he, " for Heaven's sake bethink you. A slave is not a thing to love, nor to be loved. You are young, you are lovely ; and I wonder that I can be so much your friend as to affront you. But you spoke of gratitude. Do I owe none to your good mother, who has softened my slavery ? What would her feelings be, and your father's too, were I to be a traitor, and rob them of their only child ? No, madam, I have not the excuse of passion ; and I will not be a villain in cold blood."

"My parents ! Hypocrite ! You are a coward, and dare not love above you. Begone to your Indian maid ! Wretch, I hate the sight of you !"

"I obey you, Mistress Maria."

"James, James, James ! Come back. You might say you do not hate me. You might tell me you are sorry for me."

"I am, madam. I pity you from my soul."

"Pity me ? I scorn your pity. You must choose between love or hate."

"I will never love you, madam, if I can help it ; and I will never hate you, after what you have said to me — till you give me cause."

So ended this strange interview. James retired with a sigh ; and the young lady, as soon as he was gone, had a cruel fit of sobbing.

Philip's face was now radiant with unhoped-for triumph, and poor Mrs. Surefoot's red with maternal shame, and the tears streaming. As for Jedediah, he looked terribly disturbed and gloomy. "Not one word of this to any soul that breathes : that is my order," said he. "If you disobey me, look to it."

They obeyed him to the letter ; but they indemnified themselves by long discussions amongst themselves. Philip urged the temporary retirement of Mistress Maria. The good woman, who was like butter in Philip's hands, carried this advice to her husband ; but he received it ill. "Banish my daughter for a servant !" said he. "Think of some other way."

. "May I?" said she. "Then, sweetheart, if I might have my will, I'd part them as becomes us. 'Twas rare fidelity and modesty. O Jedediah! I know what Mistress Shipley would say: Give the young man his liberty, that pines for it, and hath earned it of us by his good deed."

"Now you talk sense," said Jedediah: "I will think on't."

Then Mrs. Surefoot went, all in a hurry, and told Mrs. Shipley her trouble; and Mrs. Shipley gave her religious comfort and advice, and highly approved Jedediah's giving James his liberty. "'Tis the least he can do," said she, "and a new suit to boot. If the young man is willing to try his fortune in these parts, I will give him an axe and a hoe, and a meal a day for three months, and William shall let him a few acres of wood for nothing the first year, and thereafter for a payment in kind. We have planted many a poor man so, that now doth well enow." Mrs. Surefoot told Philip all this, and, to her surprise, Philip looked blank. His little project had always been to banish Maria, not James. But one day Mrs. Surefoot came into the office with a face full of pain and concern, and said, "O Philip! I spoke too fast. The master will not give James his liberty."

"What a shame!" said Philip: "but no matter. He is happier now."

"Alas!" said Mrs. Surefoot, "you mistake me. James is to go for certain; but the master will not free him, but sell him to McCarthy, that is always willing to buy them."

Philip was struck dumb by this sudden blow. He was too much surprised and shocked to comment on Jedediah's conduct and character.

Mrs. Surefoot babbled on, unheeded almost. "What will Dame Shipley say? She will discourse on it till I shall wish I had ne'er been born. I am a miserable woman. The world is too hard for me. But, alas! I'm a wife, and sworn to obedience; and he is a good husband, and a good man; but what he hath bought for money that he never will give for nought. The Lord forgive him, and me for not knowing how to manage him as Elizabeth does her goodman, for all he is as hard as flint by nature."

Philip repaid her twaddle with a swift glance of scorn, then asked her, with affected composure, when McCarthy was to be expected. She told him the first of next month, without fail, and meantime Maria was to keep her chamber.

Soon after this Philip fell ill, and kept his bedroom. Mrs. Surefoot visited him often, and sent James to Katy Dean for simples. Philip got worse, and yet insisted on doing his work. At his request a couch was sent up to his little room, and he lay on his back and still kept the accounts, though groaning with pain. James became very anxious, and was always running up to see how he was, and sat gazing at his pale face piteously, and often implored him to say if there was any thing he could do for him. Generally Philip answered rather pettishly, and told James not to come there wasting his time. But one day, seeing James gazing at him with the tear in his eye, and a look of wonderful affection and sorrow on his noble though simple face, the boy gave a great gulp, and whined out in rather a tearful way, "James, do not you be a fool. What is the man snivelling for?" James hid his face in both hands, and groaned aloud.

"Come near me," said the boy, "and I will tell you a secret. Will you keep it faithfully?"

"Ay, that I will."

"Then you must know I am not ill a bit: I am only feigning."

"What! Alas! thy poor white face."

"Chalk, stupid. I tell thee, when you are all abed, I rise, and dance about the place, and shake my fist at you all, especially at that old knave Jedediah, and that dish of skim-milk, his wife, that has got a man, and lets him be her master, instead of making him her head slave, as I would."

Philip's laugh and sparkling eye amazed James Annesley; and he cried out, "Oh, thou dear, good, sweet wicked boy, for playing so with the hearts that love thee! let me kiss thee." And he rushed at him to embrace him; but Philip caught up the ink-stand in a moment, and threatened him. "Let me be," cried he: "I hate to be slobbered. Sit down, thou foolish, and talk sense."

"Nay," said James, "talk it thyself, and tell me why thou art such a dear, good, artful young fellow, to sport with the feelings of those that love thee; and, moreover, 'tis unlucky to feign sickness."

"Here's an ungrateful toad," said Philip: "why, 'tis for thee I do it."

"For me, Philip?"

"Ay, thou innocent, — for thee. O James! I could not abear to be parted from thee." Philip said this with a world of tenderness, and then hid his face in his hands, and blushed like a rose.

James's face showed he was sore puzzled. Philip, who could change his mood like lightning, darted off into his favorite tone of lofty assumption. "Why, thou coxcomb," said he, "dost thou really think thou art fit to go to a new master, without me at thy back? Come, James," added he patronizingly, "you are a good, worthy young man; but you know you are somewhat of a milksop. You are not fit to go alone. You cannot beat the men, nor flatter the women. I can do both, especially make fools of the women, and turn 'em to butter with my tongue. And I know not how it is," continued he, assuming now an air of philosophical meditation, "but custom governs us strangely: once get into the habit of taking care of a child, or a dog, or a James Annesley, or any foolish, helpless sort of a pet, and, in truth, you get so used to it, you can't let it go alone: you still come clucking after it, like a hen after her duckling. Is it not laughable?"

"No: for I am as fond of thee, Philip, as thou art of me."

"That you may easily be; for I am not fond of you at all; but I am warmly and sincerely and truly accustomed to you, sir; and so I can't part. I won't, neither. I'll kill everybody dead first, and die myself. But there's no need of that: I've got the key to that hunks: Avarice, James, avarice! Come, no more idle talk, but be a good lad: obey thy friend and protector, and let's to work. Give me that piece of chalk. So. Now, go you to Jedediah, and ask him to see me alone, before I die. Tell him I have somewhat to say I would not trust even to our dame."

James did as he was bid; and Jedediah, in the course of a few hours, when he had nothing more remunerative to do, went to Philip's room. He found him lying pale and exhausted, with a little table by him. He sat down by him, and said he hoped that he was better.

"Master," said the boy, "I shall never be better. I have got the complaint my father died of, and in a few days I shall leave you. What vexes me is you will lose a faithful servant."

"It can't be helped. God's will be done."

"And you will have to bury me; and that is like flinging money away. Nothing comes of it."

"It cannot be helped," said Jedediah, with a little groan.

"Not by you; but I think I could

help it. Why should you lose the money you paid for me, and the money for the coffin, and all?"

"It is a sore dispensation. But it cannot be helped."

"Yes, sir, it can. McCarthy comes here to-morrow to buy slaves." Jedediah nodded. "He got the better of you in that sale of wood." Jedediah groaned.

"It's your turn now. I'll seem well, or nearly, when he comes. You shall say, 'James Annesley will fret without his friend;' then McCarthy will buy us both; and I shall die on his premises, not yours."

Jedediah's little keen eye flashed. He subdued it, and said, "But I doubt me whether that would be fair trade. What thinkest thou? Is it lawful to spoil the Egyptians?"

"It is a Christian duty. And think of me, master. I shall die miserable if you have to bury me, and lose so much by me."

"Nay, I will not have thee die unhappy. That were cruel. Thou hast been indeed a faithful servant, and I'll humor thee in this thing."

"Good master, kind master! Then I pray you go at once to Mistress Maria's chamber, and fetch me her pot of red. Ask her not for it; or she'll deny you, and swear to't. 'Tis in the drawer of her table whereon stands her glass."

"My daughter paint her face?"

"Ay, and her lips and all, at odd times. Fetch it me, sir, privately; for without it McCarthy will see the trick, and never buy me."

Jedediah went straight for the cosmetic, looking black as thunder.

Philip chuckled with delight. "Aha!" said this sweet, harmless boy. "I have lent that minx a dig into the bargain."

Next day McCarthy came, and, at sight of James, offered a fair price. Jedediah appeared cool on it, and at last let out that there was such a close friendship between James and the book-keeper, he did not care to part them.

"Book-keeper?" said McCarthy.

"Ay," said Jedediah, and showed him the books.

At this juncture, the dialogue having purposely been carried on in sight of Philip's window, out ran the book-keeper, looking the picture of health. McCarthy was astonished at his youth and his book-keeping, and determined to purchase him: however, he concealed his enthusiasm, like a wary trader, and said he really only needed one servant, but would give the same price for Philip, if Jedediah would not part them.

The bargain was struck; and in less than an hour the two friends' bundles were in McCarthy's light wagon, and they were marching behind it.

With them, to their infinite surprise, walked Jedediah Surefoot, a short, thick riding-whip in his hand.

The fact is, his daughter had slipped out, taking advantage of her mother being at Willingtown; and he was afraid she had resolved to have a tender parting with James, or some worse folly; and who knows, exasperated at being sold, instead of rewarded, James's good faith might melt before a second temptation of the sort. So he said grimly to his late servants, "I'll set ye on your way." He stalked along with them in silence. They thought he would go a mile, and then give them his blessing; but, no: mile after mile, this kill-joy stuck to them, and was irksome; for they both wanted to talk, and congratulate each other on being still together.

At last Philip lost all patience, and resolved to make the intruder smart. He whispered James to fall back a little, and suddenly putting on his saucy swagger, that was quite new to Jedediah, he said, "Come, old man, hand forth my veil."

"Thy veil, boy?"

"Ay. Do you think I shall let

you bite my worthy master there, and not have my nibble? Two gold-pieces I demand. Give them, or I'll reveal the bubble to McCarthy, and have thee trounced, thou dealer in man's flesh, thou hypocritical knave, that wouldst rob a church, and go to prayers before the deed and after"

Jedediah was stupefied at first by this sudden hail-storm of insolence; but amazement soon gave way to rage. He gave a roar, and rushed at Philip. Philip screamed, and tried to escape, but could not. He clutched him fiercely by the collar, and raised his whip on high; but it never came down; for, at Philip's first scream, James rushed on Jedediah with equal fury, and seized his arm, and caught him by the throat so felly, that in a moment his face was purple. Then James seized his whip, and, mad with rage himself, whirled him round in a circle, and thrashed him furiously; you might have heard the blows a mile off; then put his foot to Jedediah's stomach, and, with one amazing thrust, spurned him head forward to the ground, that he rolled over, and the dust rose round his helpless body like a cloud. This done, he flung his whip at him where he lay.

Philip clung, sobbing and trembling, to his arm.

James stood like a Colossus, his feet wide apart, his eyes glaring.

"Nay, be not alarmed, sweet Philip," said he. "He is no master of ours, but only a knave I have taught a lesson. None shall lay whip on thee while I am by."

He coaxed and encouraged him, and they walked slowly on; but Philip, in walking, still clung to James's strong arm, and trembled.

When he was a little better, he looked up and gazed on James with quite a new sentiment of admiration, and said, "Oh, how grand and strong and brave and

beautiful you were! I did not think 'twas in you."

Having thus delivered himself, he lowered his head again suddenly, and clung to James's arm again.

"Nay," said James, "I am not a brave man : my want of courage was the first cause of all my misery. Child, 'twas only rage, not courage. No matter; I have but one friend : I'll not see him abused."

"Bless you, James!" He suddenly took James's hand, and kissed it with a gentle devotion he had never exhibited before. "Dear James," he said, "I cannot bear a blow. 'Twas for a blow I left my home and all my friends."

"Ay, indeed! Pluck up heart now, and tell me all about that."

"Tell thee my story? Not for all the world."

"Why, I told thee mine."

"Ay : you have nought to blush for. I'd rather die than tell thee mine. What have I done? I have put a barrier between me and the man I—Nay, heed not what I say. I am ill. I am sick. I have been frightened. I shall faint. I shall die."

"Nay, nay," said James. "Take not on so, for nought. Is this he who called me a milksop?"

"Ay," said Philip, weeping. Then, with a piteous effort at his little hectoring way, "and will again, if I pee-pee-please."

"Meantime," said James, "I'll bestow thy valor in yon cart." Caught up the weeping Hector in a moment, and carried him in his strong arms, striding away, till he overtook the cart. "Master, poor Philip hath been ill of late, and he is aweary. May I put him in the cart?"

"And welcome. There is room for thee an' all."

"Nay, sir. I will not weight the good horse."

In a very few minutes there was a good deal of talking and laughing in the covered cart. Master

Philip was amusing his new master, and taking the length of his foot.

"Dear heart!" thought Annesley, "what a strange boy 'tis! He changes like the wind. Sure, his mother's milk is scarce out of him."

Late at night they reached McCarthy's, a large farm, about sixty miles from Philadelphia.

CHAPTER V.

McCarthy was a widower; and the house was kept by his daughter, —a lady of very striking appearance. She was very tall and commanding and fair. Some thought her beautiful: others were repelled by the extreme haughtiness of her features, with which her deportment and manners corresponded.

The two friends, of course, talked everybody over with whom they were likely to come in contact; and they differed about Mistress Christina McCarthy. James thought her the most beautiful woman he had ever seen. Philip screamed, "What! a nose like a man's, foxy eyebrows, white eyelashes, and a cold cruel eye. She's not a woman," said this candid critic : "she is a cat."

"I never heard thee praise a woman yet," objected James.

"That is their fault, not mine," retorted Philip, who had long ago resumed the upper hand. "You will be pleased to avoid that cat, like poison," said Philip. "And if she runs after you, — and I hear she has had a dozen beaux already, — you will come to me for advice, or our friendship is at an end, sir. I shall have my eye on her."

The effect of Philip's espionage was this : he discovered that Christina McCarthy passed James and him as if they were dirt, her lofty affections being fixed on a big mulatto slave. Such an attachment was repugnant to the feelings of white men, and contrary to law. They kept it very close, in consequence; and nobody on the farm dreamed of such a thing, until this Argus-eyed Philip came, and found it out by their secret glances and signals, and a deal of subtle evidence.

He told James of it, and made merry over the lady's hauteur.

"That is so like the jades ! Whenever one of them knows herself baser than all the rest, she puts on a mask of transcendent pride to throw dust in folk's eyes ; but they cannot throw dust in mine."

James hoped it was not true : "for 'tis disgraceful," said he, "and contrary to nature. And, poor man, she is his only child."

"Don't contradict me," said Philip. "I tell you 'tis so; and I'll show you the law." He had picked out a copy of the State laws, on purpose to ascertain the probable fate of this haughty beauty, whose superb carriage had roused a most vindictive feeling in Master Philip.

James was not so curious in love affairs as Philip, and saw nothing to justify the libel. The lady passed often before his eyes, a model of cold dignity and feminine reserve. He scouted the notion, and almost scolded Philip for his uncharitableness towards women.

But one evening, having done his work, he took "Plutarch's Lives," which Philip had borrowed for him from the master, and lay down under a hedge of the prickly pear to read it. He was so absorbed in this book, and lay so still, that the little birds came about him, and did not mind him. The dusk came on, and still, with his young eyes, he went on reading, till suddenly he heard footsteps on the other side of the hedge, and, after the footsteps, voices.

Now, James was outside the hedge; but these speakers were inside, and well hidden by the shadow of some lofty trees. This, in fact, was the favorite rendezvous of Christina and the mulatto Regulus. James knew the young lady's voice directly; and, though they spoke low and hurriedly, he heard enough to show him they were lovers, and that she was going to elope with the fellow as soon as she could lay her hands on a large sum of money her father was about to receive for the sale of another plantation. James listened with horror, and asked himself what on earth he should do. At last these ill-assorted lovers parted; that is to say, Regulus went off, leaving his young mistress to follow at such an interval of time as might lead to no suspicion. Then James thought he would not tell the old man, but would, at all events, try first to show the young woman her folly. He ran hastily to a gate, penetrated the wood, and came swiftly through the trees to her; for he saw her white dress still standing there. Seeing him come straight to her so fast, she took him for Regulus come back with news; and she was so unguarded as to say, "Why, what now, my dear Regulus?" A strange voice answered her, at whose first tone she uttered a faint cry of alarm. "'Tis not Regulus, madam, but one who has more real good wishes towards you than he has." Christina trembled violently, but defended herself. She drew up haughtily, and said, "Why, 'tis James Annesley. How dare you speak to me? What are you doing here at this time? Have you been here long?"

"Long enough to learn something that astonishes and pains me; and I hope I may be in time to prevent it. Madam, I saw you and Regulus together."

"Wonderful! And now you see me and another of my slaves together. I was giving Regulus an order; and now I give you an order. Go home, and sleep the liquor off that hath made thee so bold as to speak to me. Begone, or dread the whip, thou malapert!" James stood his ground. "Before I go, tell me what I ought to do. I am your father's servant, madam, not yours. Both you and I, we eat his bread. Ought I to let him be robbed of his daughter and his money, and never breathe a word?" Then she began to pant, and said, "What mean you?" Then he told her that he had overheard every word that had passed between her and Regulus.

"Indeed!" said she with an attempt at defiance belied by her short breath. "Repeat it, then," said she ironically.

"I will," said he gravely. And he did repeat it, and at such length, and with such exact fidelity, that, as he went on, shame and infinite terror crawled over her. Her knees smote each other; and her haughty frame cringed and writhed; and she sank half down upon a wood-pile that was near, and her white hands fell helpless, one in front of her, and the other by her side. Never was a proud creature so stricken down in a moment.

Then this good young man pitied her, and hoped to save her. He said, "Madam, for Heaven's sake, look at the consequences. What good can come of it? If you fly with Regulus, and take your father's money, you will be caught one day, and set on the gallows, and be publicly whipped; for I have seen one as young and fair as you served so."

A moan from the crushed woman was the only comment.

"And if you steal nought, yet marry a mulatto, 'tis against the law, and your children will be illegitimate, and you will lose your father's estate, and break his heart."

Christina interrupted him. "Oh, say no more, James, for pity's sake! I have been mad. Oh! what a precipice! James, do not thrust me over! Do not tell my father, for mercy's sake!"

"Not if you will promise to forego this mad design. Sure, that mulatto must have bewitched you. That one so fair as you should cast an eye of love on any thing so foul."

She caught at this directly. "Ay," she cried, " 'twas witchcraft, and no other thing. But you have opened my eyes, good James, —too late, too late!" and she burst into a flood of tears.

"That depends on yourself. If you will swear to hold no more converse with that mulatto, I shall not feel bound to utter one word of what I know."

"James," said the lady, "you are my guardian angel: you have saved me from a crime, and from an act of frenzy I now look back upon with horror. Do but continue your good work. Advise me at every step, and all will be well."

James was surprised into consenting to that; and she then begged him to conduct her home. "Alas!" said she, "I can scarce stand." She leaned on James's shoulder, and went very slowly and feebly. This gave her time to say some of those vague things with which such women think to excuse their follies. "If you knew all, you would pity me even more than you condemn me." And again, with her white hand leaning on his arm, she said, "How sorcery blinds us!" And what with this, and her gentle pressure of his hand at parting, she disturbed even this Joseph's mind a little, and set him thinking it would not be very hard to cure her of her insane caprice.

Next day she sent for him openly, and told him her plan. "I shall keep out of his way; I shall not move from my own apartments; or, if I do, you shall be with me. And now here is a letter I will beg you to take him. Read it first, before I seal it."

The letter ran thus:—

"An accident has frustrated our design for the present. My father has not yet brought the money into the house. I hurt my foot last night, and shall not, I fear, be able to come to our rendezvous for some days. Burn this before the face of whatever person I may send it by, or I shall think you do not mean fair to
"THE WRITER."

James highly disapproved this letter, and told her so. "Why," said he, "it cannot fail to keep hope alive in him."

"Exactly," said she; "and so he will not blab of my folly."

"No more he will if you break off all connection with him. And why write at all? Such a letter is worse than silence."

However, she talked him over, and convinced him that she was resolved, in a cowardly and artful way, to detach herself gradually from the deplorable connection; so that he half consented to take the letter. Then she took a slice of cake out of her closet, and a pint of rich wine, and sat close to him while he drank it, and showed him such signs of favor, that he was the more inclined to believe she would readily detach herself from Regulus. So he consented to take the letter.

The mulatto eyed him keenly, took the letter, read it, burned it before his eyes, and said, "Tell her what you have seen me do : that is all."

Christina now showed James so many marks of favor, and so open, that Philip took him to task. "My poor mouse," said he scornfully, "are you going to let that cat catch you so easily?" When that produced no effect, he remonstrated, advised, scolded, and at last quarrelled with him downright, and would not speak to him.

Now, James was really rather smitten with Christina. Her tenderness and cajoleries, following upon her haughty demeanor, had wonderfully tickled his vanity, and even grazed his heart; but he was not so far gone as to part with Philip's friendship. So one day he came to him, and said, "Dear Philip, do not you quarrel with me in a mistake. I will tell thee the truth about Mistress Christina; but first you must swear to me, on the big Bible, never to reveal one word of that I tell thee."

Philip turned pale at this, but took the oath; and then James told him all.

He was more alarmed than surprised. "I knew she was nought, the minute I clapped eyes on her. Look at her white lashes and her cold, cruel eye. The unnatural beast! that would rob her own father, and wed with a brown! And what sort of a man are you? Why went you not straight to her father, like an honest man? What had you to do to go to her, and get cozened, you silly oaf! Are you a match for that artful jade, think you?"

"Nay, she seems very penitent, and keeps away from him; and — whisper, Philip. If I chose, I could take the brown's place, as you call him, any day; and, really 'tis a temptation."

"You love the wretch?"

"Nay; not quite love. But she is fair: and she was so haughty, and now is so tender. I own I think more about her than I ever did of any woman yet. To be sure, I am very proud of saving her, and that makes the heart soft towards the fair creature I have rescued from ' a precipice.' "

Philip's face turned green, and his lips pale. His face was distorted and discolored with the anguish these words cost him; and he sat mute as a statue.

James did not happen to look at him, and went maundering on: " The only thing I like not is that letter to Regulus. What think you of it, Philip?"

Philip, though sick at heart, made a great effort, and said faintly, "The letter was writ to show him he must temporize, but not despair. Prithee, James, leave me a while: I have work to do. Come in an hour; and we will see what all this really means."

He went; and then Philip began to sigh and moan at the confession James had made; and, for a long while, he could think only of his own misery at being supplanted in James's heart. But of course his hatred of this rival soon led him into a keen and hostile examination of her conduct; and the consequence was a new and more disinterested anxiety arose, which led him to put a very keen question to James the moment he entered the room. "Has the mulatto shown you any enmity?"

"None whatever."

"Yet he sees his mistress bestow favors on you. Then all is clear. She has told him. You are their dupe. How that woman must hate you!"

"Nay," said James, smiling conceitedly, "that I'll be sworn she does not."

"What, not when you have come between her and her fancy, and do keep them apart? Think you, when once a woman hath loved a woolly mulatto, she can so come back to wholesome affections? She hates you, and spends her days and nights scheming to destroy you. Oh, those cunning lashes, and that cruel eye! They make me tremble for you. Let me think what she is about at this very minute."

He resumed, after a pause, " She will draw you on to offer her some innocent freedom; then fly out, and accuse you of wooing her. Who will believe you, — a slave, — when the young mistress swears! "

"I'll not give her the occasion."

"How can you tell? And, if you do not, why, then she will get rid of you some other way. You shall be stabbed in the back some dark night, and never know who struck you. But I shall know; and I shall kill *her* — before I die."

So strong were Philip's fears, that he armed James with an enormous knife, and made him promise never to go to any lonely place without it. James assented, to quiet him, but, in his heart, made light of these extravagant fears. On the other hand, he felt piqued by Philip's insinuation that the mulatto and his penitent were duping him; and so he used often to get up in the dead of the night, and make his rounds with stealthy foot, to watch. The effect of this vigilance was, that one moonlight night, coming softly round a corner, he found Regulus under the young mistress's bedroom window; which window was open, the weather being warm. James collared him directly. "What do you do here at this time of night?"

"I do what you do," said the mulatto.

"Not so," said James; "for I guard my master's goods against a knave."

"Knave thyself, and meddler and fool!" cried the mulatto, whose rage had been simmering this many a day.

From words they came to blows, and struck each other hard and fast, without much parrying; in the midst of which Christina put her head out of her window on the first floor, and looked steadily down at them. After a few moments of self-possessed observation, she said in a keen whisper, "Kill him!"

In this combat, the white struck at the face, and the black at the body: by this means the black's face was soon covered with blood; but the white man was most hurt, and felt instinctively that he should soon be overpowered: so he closed with his dark antagonist. They wrestled fiercely; but it ended in James throwing him, and falling on him. The ground was hard; and the fall of the two heavy bodies on it tremendous: it drove the wind out of Regulus for a moment; and James got him by the ears, and pounded his bullet head on the ground.

Christina now screamed loudly. A window or two were opened; nightcapped heads popped out; and the combatants separated by mutual consent, and retired, glaring at each other.

James had not gone far when he was seized with a violent sickness; and, after that, he crawled to his bed, bruised and seriously hurt by the body blows he had received. Next morning he was too stiff and ill to go to his work.

Philip heard a vague report that James and the mulatto had been fighting in the dead of night, and sent a message directly to James, desiring to speak to him. The servant came back, and said he was too ill to leave his bed. Philip was much concerned at this, and, after a slight hesitation, went and knocked at the door of James's room. He slept over the stables. A faint voice said, "Come in." Philip lifted the latch. He found James lying on the bed, just as he had come from the battle, and his face two or three colors. Philip had intended to scold him; but this was no time. He came softly to him, and said, "Alas! my poor James, how is it with thee?"

"But badly, in truth," said James, still in a faint voice.

"How came it about?"

He told him the truth.

"Ah!" said Philip sadly. "Jealousy. How men do love ill women! That old cat — thirty if she is a day — to have two lovers and two nations, after a manner, fighting for her o' nights beneath her very window. Did she see you?"

"Indeed she did."

"And smiled, I'll be bound, at what would make a good woman scream to part the fools. Did she say nought?"

"She said, 'Kill him.'"

"Kill whom?"

" The black, I do suppose."

" I am not so sure of that." And Philip fell into a revery. It was broken by James going suddenly back on something Philip had said. " I do believe thou art right," said he, " and finding him under her window, I felt a sort of jealousy as well as wrath at his continuing to tempt her : if 'twas so, I am rightly served : but flout me not for 't, Philip, for I think I am sped."

" Now, heaven forbid ! Where is thy hurt ? "

" All over me. I made a great mistake. I kept beating him about his bullet head; but he still belabored my ribs. Oh ! I am all pains and aches : it hurts me e'en to speak."

" Alas, alas ! " said Philip, and laid a cool, consoling hand on the hot brow : then he suddenly ground his teeth, and said, " Curses on them all ! I will end this to-night; no later."

James asked him what he meant. He refused to say ; but the fact is he was resolved to go that very night to McCarthy, who was then on a visit to his brother, five miles off, and tell him the whole story. Knowing that James would remonstrate, he kept his resolution to himself, and went off for the present to prepare a composing draught for his patient, after the receipt of Patience Surefoot. He made the decoction, in which, I believe, the flowers of the lime-tree were a principal ingredient; and, while it was simmering, he took up the *Philadelphia Post*, that had just been brought into the office. He always read every line of that journal. It was a single quarto sheet, and came out twice a week.

That journal contained an advertisement that set the paper shaking in Philip's hand, and his eyes glowing : —

" I, Jonas Hanway, now lying in jail, charged with the murder of my ward, Joanna Philippa Chester, take this way to let her know my evil plight, and beg her, for pity's sake, to come back, or write of her welfare. Poor Silas, that made the mischief, is in his grave, and nought awaits her here but my true repentance, and the kind affection of my co-trustee, Mr. Thomas Chester, under whose care she now is, if only she could be found. And, for a further inducement to return, I do now, with my co-trustee's consent, inform her that she is heiress to a fortune of thirteen thousand pounds, or more, which knowledge was withheld from her by her father's express desire, lest any man should wed her for her dower, and not for true love of her : but now 'tis thought best to let her know the truth, lest she throw herself away. The said Joanna is now nineteen years of age, tall and active, and of singular beauty; hath eyebrows black as jet, and do meet so remarkably, as, in an Englishwoman, must needs draw notice. She hath been traced to London ; and it is thought she hath crossed the seas. Whoever will give information respecting her shall receive a reward of

FIVE HUNDRED GUINEAS.

" She had her mother's jewels with her. But they are now her own.

" From my prison at Staines, January, 1739–40."

Advertisement ! — it was a cry from a prison, and a cry from home, that knocked at her very heart. She uttered a responsive cry herself, as if the prisoner's cry had sounded in her ears ; and then she devoured the words once more, feeding on every syllable in great amazement. But presently the letters grew hazy ; her filling eyes saw them no more, and in their place came the pleasant meads of Colebrook, the English landscape, humble but sweet, the gray old church, the parson's scholarly face, the white-headed children, and poor old England stretching out her hands to her lost daughter, with words of sorrow and love. Then her heart gushed to her eyes in a stream; and the wanderer lay softly back in her chair, quite motionless, and let the sweet tears flow.

Then came the desire to act, — to fly home, and save that poor bereaved father, and live amongst her folk. How should she manage it? She had jewels secreted about her, any one of which was worth more than a slave's ransom. Why not go to McCarthy, tell him who she was, and offer him a diamond ring for her liberty? Why not? Because he might have her seized for wearing man's clothes, and throw her into prison for life, so severe was this colony in that matter. No: she could not endure the shame, nor run the risk. She would take one of his horses, and ride by night to Philadelphia, and make terms with him through some other party. One thing alone she did resolve, — not to lose an hour, but to be gone that very night. One day lost, and the prisoner's life might pay for it. Yes, she would go, and take James Annesley with her. She took up the sleeping draught, and went to his room. She made him drink it, and then covered him up warm, and took his hand in hers. "James, dear," said she, " I am a happy — creature. I have news from England, — sad news, after a manner, yet sweet; and I am going home."

"Going! — Ah, well! God's blessing and mine go with thee."

"Why, thou foolish man, I go not without thee. This very night we ride to Philadelphia, and thence to England."

James shook his head sorrowfully. "There is no escape for a slave. I have tried it."

"Ay, all alone, and on foot, without money or means. But 'tis different now. I shall command the expedition, — I, who, by your leave, possess the two capital gifts of a commander, which are forecast and courage, — forecast, by which I do foresee all possible accidents, and provide for them; and courage, whereby I overcome and trample under foot those petty dangers that scare a mere ordinary man like thee. What's this?"

"What is what?"

"I smell a smell I never could abide. 'Tis a cat. I know 'tis a cat. There! there she is, coiled in the mouth of that sack. I shall faint, I shall die."

"Why, here's a coil about poor puss. 'Tis the stable-cat, and loves to come here."

"Well, she goes forth, or I."

"Open the door then, and fling thy cap at the poor harmless thing."

"I call not foul things harmless, especially when they are all claws. I like not your cats, even when they are called Christinas."

While Philip was driving out the "harmless, necessary cat," James criticised him. "Why, 'tis like a girl, to be afeard of a cat! But indeed you are more like a girl than a boy, in many things. You hate women more than is natural, and you turn your toes out in walking, and you carry your hand so oddly when you walk."

"Mercy on us, how?"

"Why, you turn it out sideways, and show the fingers. I walk with my thumb straight down."

Philip turned very red, but said pertly, "All which proves that I was born of a woman. Now, you were born of a goose. I'm man enough to be your master; and this very evening you shall ride with me to Philadelphia."

"You are my master, and I own it," said James, — "my master by superior learning, wit, and daring; only the courage comes and goes most strangely. But good my master, for all that, I cannot ride with thee to-night."

"Oh! say not so, James. Why not?"

"I could not sit a horse, for my life."

"Alas! how unfortunate we are! James, think me not unkind; but I must go to-night—with thee or without thee."

"You must go without me, then; for indeed I am not able."

"But perhaps you may be by nightfall. Have a good sweat and a good sleep; and I'll come again at dusk; for, O James! I *must* go; and I am loath to leave thee."

Then Philippa retired, and went and made some slight preparation for the journey she had resolved to take; but, in the midst of it all, her hands fell helpless, and her heart revealed itself to her. She could not go. Love burst through all self-deception at last. She loved him; had loved him long; and now loved him to distraction. Leave him on his sick-bed, and among enemies? No, not for a day! She had honestly intended—if he could not come—to fly to Philadelphia, sell her jewels, and buy him of McCarthy; but, now it came to the point, she burst out crying, and found she could not leave him in trouble,—no, not for an hour. "Nay," said she to herself, "but I will come at night, and hector him, and taunt him, and coax him, and try all my wicked arts to get him to go with me; then, if he cannot, I will pretend to go without him; but I'll slip back softly, and lie on the mat at my darling's door. None shall come to hurt him but over my body."

Meantime, James received another unexpected visitor. There was a gentle tap at the door; and Mistress Christina glided in. He was surprised, and tried to rise and receive her; but she put up her white hand that he should not move. Then she sat down by him, and, with the most cajoling tenderness, expressed her regret at what had occurred. "Why," said she, "will you trouble about that man, whom you know I have discarded?"

"He was there to tempt you, madam."

"More likely through jealousy. Seeing me favor you, perhaps he suspected me of speaking to you at all hours. But once more, James, trouble not about him. Has he hurt you?"

"Nay, madam, not much," said James; "a few bruises, that I am to sleep away. He got as good as he gave, I know."

"That is true," said she gravely. "He is much cut about the face; and you have knocked out one of his front teeth."

"I will knock his head off next time."

"I will give you leave to kill him—*next time*," said the lady calmly. "Meantime, prithee get well—for my sake. I'll send you something to do you good." She then kissed her hand to him, and went softly out.

Before she had been long gone, Philip's potion began to work; and James fell into a fine sleep and a violent perspiration.

Presently there was another tap at the door; and, as the sleeper did not reply, Chloe entered with a large basin of strong soup prepared by the white hands of Christina herself. Chloe was followed by the late discarded cat, returning now with lofty tail, sniffing the savory mess. Chloe, finding the patient asleep and perspiring, had the sense not to awaken him; only, as she thought it a pity the soup should cool, she put it down by his bedside, calculating that the smell might waken him as it would her. To keep it warm, she put "Plutarch's Lives" over it, and then retired: it was about four o'clock.

Now, if James was asleep, puss was not. He turned about the leg of the table, sniffing; and at last sprang boldly on to the bed, and from the bed to the table. Here he found an obstacle in Plutarch. Plutarch covered the soup not entirely, but too much for puss to get a nose in. He sat quiet a few minutes, then he applied his forepaw and nose, and made a sufficient aperture. Then he found the soup too hot. Then he sat on the table a whole hour, waiting. Then he arose, and gradually licked up nearly half the soup; then he retired quietly, and coiled himself up.

James still slept on his balmy sleep, till just before sunset. Then he was awakened by a violent knocking.

He looked up, and there was the poor cat in violent convulsions, springing up to an incredible height, and hammering the floor with his head when he came down.

James got up, unconscious of his late pains, and threw some water over him. He thought it a fit; but after a few violent convulsions came piteous cries; and the poor creature stretched his limbs, and died foaming at the mouth.

James soon discovered the cause in the stolen soup.

His blood ran cold. He fell on his knees, and thanked God he was alive. But how long? What would not hate so diabolical as this attempt? He seized his knife, and prepared to sally forth.

At this moment he heard a whistle under his window.

"Ah!" thought he, "a signal of assassins." He instantly dragged his bed and other things to the door, to impede an attack from that quarter, and then went cautiously to the window. To his great relief it was Philip who had given that signal. He opened the window directly. "O Philip! They have tried to poison me!!"

"Ah! who, who?"

"Christina herself. Sent me soup. The cat stole some whilst I slept, thanks to your medicine!—You are my preserver. And see, the poor cat is dead." He took the cat's body, and flung it out. Philip recoiled with a cry of horror. "Come forth!" he cried. "Come forth! or they will murder thee yet. Oh, my love! come forth to me."

"I will, I will." And in a moment he tore away the bed and other things from the door, and ran down to Philip. Philip had lost not a moment, but was getting the two best horses out. James helped him. Without a word more, they saddled and bridled them; and Philip sprang into the saddle: his black eyes were gleaming with a strange fire.

"Take that dead beast before thee," said he, "and I'll give thee liberty and vengeance."

They galloped off, over the soft ground, Philip leading, and took the road to Philadelphia.

They did not venture to speak till they got clear of McCarthy's premises; but then James told Philip of Christina's visit and cajoleries, followed by murder.

Philip said, "'Twas in her eye. Ah! thou foul cat; but I'll be even with thee." And Philip ground his teeth audibly; and his eye shot fire in the moonlight. "My poor James!" said he, "that would not harm a mouse."

About five miles from McCarthy's they passed his brother's farm. They passed it a hundred yards or so; and then Philip drew the rein, and haltered his horse to a gate, and made James do the same. "Now take that dead Christina in thy hand," said he bitterly, "and follow me." He marched up to the farm, and asked for William McCarthy.

"What want you?"

"We are two servants of his, come with news of life and death."

"You shall find him at supper with the rest."

Philip walked boldly into the noisy supper-room, followed by

James. "Silence all!" said he, with a voice like a clarion; and the room was still in a moment.

"Master, have you money in your house?"

"Ay," cried McCarthy, half rising, and turning pale,—more than I can bear to lose. But 'tis in the safe, boy. None knows of it but my daughter."

"Am I your daughter? Yet I know it. Your daughter has a mulatto to her lover; and they have planned to rob you of your money, and fly."

"The proof!" roared McCarthy.

"The proof is this: James there overheard Christina and Regulus plan the robbery. He taxed Christina with it; and she tried to cajole him; but failing in that, and knowing he would tell you, like a faithful servant as he is, she this day essayed to poison him."

Here there were some exclamations. "Ay, sir," continued he: "the cat, by God's mercy, stole a little of the soup while he slept. Now look at that cat's body, and judge for yourselves."

The cat was instantly examined.

Philip did not stop for that. "Now, master, take your weapons, and to horse this moment, and save your goods, if there be yet time." Mr. McCarthy, and his brother, and two or three men, ran out. Philip turned to the others, and, folding his arms, said boldly, "Sirs, ye are Christian men, and white men like ourselves: is it your will that good servants of your own flesh and blood shall be poisoned like rats?" There was a roar of honest disclamation. "And all because Christina McCarthy is so lost to shame as to wed a black, and rob her own flesh and blood. Then, sirs, to your justice we, too, commend our cause. There is the poisoned beast to prove our words, and half the poisoned soup in this good young man's room over the stable. Punish them with every thing short of death.

James and I will keep away a little while; for, if we testify, the judge might hang her. Give you good e'en."

Having delivered this bold but artful speech, he retired with James, and, the moment he got outside the door, whispered him, "Now run for't, or they will keep us to testify in their courts." They ran off like the wind, untethered their horses, and, springing into their saddles, rode rapidly off, keeping the side of the road at first, to dull their horses' hoofs. They rode all night, and with the earliest streak of dawn entered the fair town of Philadelphia.

McCarthy and his party, twelve in all, caught the mulatto and Christina in the very act of levanting with McCarthy's money. They made short work of them; bound Regulus to a tree, and flogged him within an inch of his life, with Christina tied to a chair close by, and the dead cat in her lap. Then they drummed the mulatto out of the district, and sent Christina to a farm in Massachusetts, to clean pots and pans in the kitchen for a twelvemonth and a day.

----♦----

CHAPTER VI.

PHILIP, being commander, sent James to one inn, and went to another himself. He said that was most prudent to avoid discovery; but his real motive was different.

He had a very difficult game to play. His wit, however, proved equal to it. Remembering that his father was a lawyer, he inquired for an old lawyer, a gray-headed one: he stipulated severely for gray hairs. When he had found his gray-headed lawyer, and liked his countenance, he did not make two bites of a cherry, but told him all, and showed him the advertisement.

The lawyer easily got her eighty

gold-pieces on the security of her diamond cross, and gave her a room on his own premises, where she could dress herself in any costume she liked, without being reported.

Meantime, James Annesley was not idle. He saw a notice up that Admiral Vernon's ship was short of hands; and he went and engaged himself to serve on board her: he promised to bring a much smarter fellow next day, meaning his mate Philip.

When they met in the evening, he told Philip this; and Philip was much vexed at first. "Oh! why will you do things without asking me?"

However, on reflection, she acquiesced, and, with true feminine tact, altered all her plans to meet this unexpected move. She told James she would go on board the ship, but in another capacity. She had friends and money, and would work for both. Only, for a day or two, he must not expect to see much of her.

The lawyer sent the horses to McCarthy, and advised him not to trouble any more about the servants, as they were under his care; and he might have to go into the poisoning business, if they were molested.

Soon after this a young lady in her mask called on Admiral Vernon at his lodgings, and asked him if he would take her home in his ship.

"Zounds, madam, no!" said the admiral; "no petticoats aboard the king's ship."

"Alas, sir, say not so! do but cast your eye over this advertisement. Indeed 'tis no common case: 'tis a matter of life and death, my going in your ship." The admiral read the advertisement, and cried out, "What! Accused of murder? Gadzooks! what fools these landsmen be! And are you indeed the gentlewoman they seek?"

"Ay, noble admiral. Deign to regard my foul eyebrows, that are all published to the world so barbarously in this advertisement;" and the sly puss removed her mask, and burst on the sailor in all her sunlike beauty. At this blaze he began to falter a little. "'tis pity to deny you; but why not go in the first ship of burden?"

"Sir, none sail this week; and they are too slow for my need; and, in truth, I'm afeard to be drowned if I go in any other ship but the one you do command. O admiral! you are too brave to deny the weak and helpless in their trouble."

"Madam!" said the admiral, "you mistake the matter. 'Tis of you I think. I am a father; and a ship of war is not the place for young gentlewomen."

"But, sir, I am discreet, and know the world; and I can wear my mask, and keep close. O noble sir! have pity on me, and let me sail in your good ship." Then, with her lovely eyes, she turned on what I, laboring to be satirical, call the waters of the Nile. Then the admiral rapped out the usual oaths of the sea and century, and said she had done his business: "a sailor was never yet proof against salt water from a woman's eye."

He then told her where his ship lay in the bay of Delaware, and his day and hour of sailing. She must come out in a boat; and he would charge an officer beforehand to see her safe aboard.

Philippa returned to her lawyer in high spirits, and sent him to James, with a note in her own hand, directing him to go on board the English flag-ship next day at six in the evening, and she would follow the day after, before the ship sailed. James did as he was bid. At noon next day, a boat brought a lady in her mask alongside; and James, who was looking out anxiously for Philip, saw her taken on board, with her boxes, — for she had found time to shop furiously, — and handed respectfully to her cabin; but

James did not recognize her, nor dream this tall gentlewoman was little Philip.

At two, P.M., the admiral was seen coming out; the yards were manned directly, and he mounted the quarter-deck, with due honors; and the next minute the pipe was going, and the men's feet tramping to the capstan, whilst others hoisted a sail or two; and the anchor was secured; and the ship bowed and glided, and burst into canvas; and the busy seamen all bustled and shouldered poor James out of the way, with salt curses, as he ran about the ship asking wildly for Philip, and describing him to coarse fellows who only jeered him.

One faint hope remained, — Philip might be down below; but the next day dissipated this. Philip never showed his face; and this puzzled and grieved James Annesley so, that even the prospect of liberty and home could not reconcile him to the loss and seeming desertion of this tender and faithful friend.

The officer in charge of the new hands now called on James to do some very simple act of seamanship. He bungled it; and there was a good deal of hoarse derision, to which he replied at last, a little sadly, but with good temper, "Men are not born sailors; are they?"

An officer at the other side of the deck heard this reply, and was struck with the voice, or the face, or perhaps with all three, and called to him. He came respectfully, and removed his cap.

"Sure, I have seen that face before," said the officer.

James started, and said, "I have seen yours, sir, but where?"

Said the officer, "I'll tell you that. Is not your name James?"

"Indeed, sir, it is."

"Son of Lord Altham that was."

"Yes, sir; but how— Oh! 'tis my kind school-fellow."

"Ah, I am Mat Matthews, that set you on your way to Dublin. I took a good look at you that day; and I seldom forget a face I look at so. But what means this disguise, in Heaven's name? You have been reported dead in Ireland this many a year. Where have you been? Is this a frolic, good sir, or hath fortune used you crossly?"

"Sir," said James, "I'll tell you in a word, but a word full of misery. My Uncle Richard kidnapped me, and sent me to the plantations: there have I been a slave this many a long year, and even now escaped by a miracle."

"A slave! You, a lord's son, a slave! Kidnapped; and by Richard Annesley, say you? Why, 'tis he now holds your father's lands and titles. Perdition! Here is foul play! The knave! 'Twas to steal your lands and titles he spirited you away."

"Indeed, sir, I always did suspect it. Such villany was never yet done for love of God."

"Sir," said Capt. Matthews, "sit you down; and not another rope shall you handle in this ship." He ran, with his heart in his mouth, to the admiral; and his warm-hearted Irish eloquence, burning with his school-fellow's wrongs, soon fired the honest sailor. They agreed that this was the real earl, and his uncle a felon, whom the sight of the true heir would blast. "And, now I think on't," said Matthews, "Arthur Lord Anglesey is dead, and Richard Annesley has succeeded to *his* lands and titles too; so that there is one of the greatest noblemen in England and Ireland a sailor on board this ship, — and a very bad one."

"That may not be," said the admiral. "Overhaul the wardrobe straight, and rig him like a lord, as he is, and make us acquainted." He added, with a touch of delicacy one would hardly have expected, "I'll not see him in his sailor's jacket, nor seem to know he hath been brought so low."

CHAPTER VII.

It was a beautiful moonlight night; the great ocean was calm, and the light airs so gentle, that snow-white.studding-sails were set aloft to catch them.

The Honorable James Annesley, in a suit of blue velvet laced with silver, gold-laced hat, and jewel-hilted sword, paced the deck, and admired the solemn scene, the incredible sheen of the rippling ocean kissed by moonbeams, the ship's gigantic shadow, that ran trembling alongside, and the waves, like molten diamonds, that sparkled to the horizon.

His tide had turned : finery on his back; a hundred gold-pieces in his pocket, that Matthews, a man of large fortune, had insisted on lending him; a popular admiral conveying him home an honored guest !

Yet it seemed there was something wanting; for, after he had enjoyed the scene a while, he sat down upon a gun, and meditated; and his meditation was not gay, for soon he heaved a sigh.

Now, this sigh caught the quick ear of a young lady who had not long emerged upon deck. It was Joanna Philippa Chester, who never showed herself by day, but took the air at night, and even then had always her little mask in hand, ready to whip on. Joanna was farther still from complete happiness than James was. Her breast was torn with doubts and fears and shames, for which my reader, who has only seen her fitful audacity in boy's clothes, may not be quite prepared. She was now all tremors and misgivings, and paid the penalty of her disguise. Under that disguise she had fallen deep in love with James Annesley, yet inspired him with no tenderer feeling than friendship for a boy. That knowledge of the heart which an inexperienced but thoughtful woman sometimes attains by constantly thinking on its mysteries told her that between love and friendship there is a gulf, and that gulf sometimes impassable.

Philip might stand forever between James and Philippa.

And, besides this, for a girl to wear boy's clothes was indelicate : it was condemned by law; it was scouted by public opinion. James Annesley, even in his humble condition, had shown a great sense of propriety; and she felt, with a cold chill running down her back, that he was not the man to overlook indelicacy in her sex, much less make an Amazon his wife; and now, as she had learned with her sharp ears, the story he had told her was confirmed, and he was the real Earl of Anglesey, and all the less likely to honor a tomboy with his hand. For three whole days she had longed and pined to speak to him; yet fear and modesty had held her back. She could not bear to be Philip any more; yet she dreaded to be Philippa, lest she should lose even Philip's place in his regard.

Even now, the moment she saw him seated, with the moon glittering on his silver lace and his jewelled sword, and his dear, shapely head lowered in pensive thought, her first impulse was to recoil, slip down into her cabin again, and torture herself with misgivings, as she had been doing all the voyage.

But love would not let her go without a single look. She turned her eyes on him, that soon began to swim with tenderness as she looked at him. She stole a long drink of ineffable love, and the next moment she would have been gone; but he sighed deeply, and she heard it. Then the habit of consoling him, and her yearning heart, were too much for her. By a sudden impulse she whipped on her mask, and stole towards him. She trembled, she blushed; but all the woman was now in arms to defend that love which was her life.

He heard her coming, looked up, and saw a tall young lady close upon him, dressed in the fashion, with a little silk hood, and a mask that hid all but her mouth. He rose, removed his hat, and bowed ceremoniously. She courtesied in the same style.

"Forgive me, sir," said she, "I fear I interrupt your meditations."

"Most agreeably, madam."

"Methought I heard you sigh, sir."

"I dare say I did, madam."

"I was surprised, sir; for I hear you are a gentleman of quality, going home to high Fortune, after encountering her frowns. Sure, that should make her smiles the sweeter."

"Madam, it may be so; but my enemies are powerful. I may find it very hard to dispossess the wrongful owners."

"And 'twas for that you sighed?"

"Not at all, madam. I sighed for the loss of a dear friend."

"Alas! What — dead?"

"Now God forbid!"

"False, then, no doubt."

"I hope not. But I am sore perplexed; for he never failed me before."

"He? What, 'twas only a man, then, after all?"

"'Twas a boy, for that matter. But what a boy! You never saw his fellow, madam. His head was all wit, his heart all tenderness, his face all sunshine. He brightened my adversity; and now, when fortune seems to shine, he has deserted me. O Philip, Philip!"

"Philip! was that his name?"

"Yes, madam."

"Is he a very dark boy?"

"Yes, madam, yes."

"About my height?"

"Oh, no, madam! not by half a head."

Philippa smiled at that, and said, "Then, sir, you shall sigh no more on his account; for I happen to know that same Philip is here in this very ship."

"Is it possible? God bless you for that good news, madam. O madam! pray bring him to me; for my heart yearns for him. Why, why, has he hidden himself from me?"

"Nay, sir, you must have patience. The boy is not so much to blame. He is in trouble, and dare not show his face on deck. I wonder whether I may tell you the truth?"

"Yes, madam, for Heaven's sake!"

"Well, then, the truth is — ahem — he is here disguised as a woman."

"You amaze me, madam."

"And, if you were to accost him as Philip, 'twould be overheard, and might be his ruin. If you can be so much his friend as to fall into this disguise, and treat him with distant civility while he is on board the ship, I'll answer for him he will come to you — not to-night, but to-morrow night at this time."

James Annesley eagerly subscribed to these terms.

Next evening he paced the deck impatiently; and, in due course, a young gentlewoman came towards him, with Philip's very face, but blushing and beaming.

James ran to meet her; devoured her face; and then cried, "It is, it is! — oh, my sweet Philip!"

The young lady drew back instantly in alarm, and said, "Is this what you promised? Call me Philip again, or offer the slightest freedom, and you shall never see me again. My name is Philippa."

"So be it, thou capricious toad. I am too overjoyed at sight of thee to thwart thy humors. Thou wert never like any other he that breathes."

"I shall be more unlike them than ever now," said she. "Methinks my disposition is changed since I put off my boy's attire; and, the worst of it is, all my courage hath oozed away."

"It had always a trick of coming and going, Philip."

"Philippa, or I leave the ship."

"Well, Philippa, then."

"What sort of a gentlewoman do I make?"

"Nay, if I knew not the trick, I should take you for the most beautiful woman I ever saw."

Philippa blushed with pleasure. "And you look beautiful too," said she. "Fine feathers make fine birds."

He then scolded her gently, and asked her why she had deserted him.

"Well, I'll tell you the truth," said she, and delivered him a whole string of fibs.

She met him next evening, and the next, and so mystified him by her beauty and her bashfulness, that he questioned Matthews and the admiral about the young lady; but Matthews knew nothing, and the admiral pretended to know nothing, she having sworn him to secrecy.

Philippa was offended at his curiosity, and sent him word he had done very ill to ask other persons about her: she should not come on deck for ever so long.

She kept her word, though it cost her dear. Even when they touched at Jamaica, and everybody else landed, she kept her cabin. But, when they left Jamaica, she took another line. She came openly on deck now and then in the daytime, and removed her mask.

The effect may be divined. The officers of the ship treated her like a queen, and courted her with all possible attentions: these she received with singular modesty, politeness, and prudence; and, her heart being sincerely devoted to one, her head was not to be turned.

James Annesley looked on with wonder and a dash of satire to see men all but kneeling to a boy. But he soon got jealous, and the other men opened his eyes, and he began to ponder over many things. The truth flashed on him, and Philippa saw it in his face. Then she coquetted with her happiness; and, when he begged a private interview, she put him off.

But, when they passed Lizard Point, she came to her senses, and gave him his opportunity.

He was much agitated: she was more so, but hid it better. "Tell me the truth," he cried. "You were always Philippa, and I a blind fool." She hid her red face in her hands.

"Philippa," he cried, "you have killed the friend of my bosom. Will you give me nothing in exchange for him?"

"Alas, James!" she cried, "what can I give you that you will love as you did him? *I hate that boy.*"

"Nay, do not hate him; but for him I had never know the greatest, truest, tenderest heart that ever beat in woman. O Philippa! you saved me from despair, you saved me from servitude. I never could love another, now you are a woman. Be my bosom friend still, but by a dearer title; be my sweetheart, my darling, my wife."

"Ay, that or the grave," she cried; and the next moment he held her curling round his neck, and cooling her hot cheeks with tears of joy.

They landed at Portsmouth, took a kind leave of the admiral, to whom they owed so much, and, accompanied by Capt. Matthews, dashed up to Staines with post-horses, four at every relay. When they came near to the town, she bade the driver post to the prison. She demanded to see Jonas Hanway. He was called into the yard, and, at the sight of her, gave a scream of joy, and they had a cry together, and forgave each other. She feed the jailer to send to the proper authorities, and take the necessary steps for his liberation.

Then she went on to Thomas Chester, who lived outside the town by the river-side; but Matthews left them in the town, and went on to London, on his way to Ireland. He had inherited large estates, and was about to leave the king's service.

Thomas Chester, though a man not easily moved, gave a loud shout when his niece ran to him. He folded her in his arms, and thanked God aloud, in a broken voice, again· and again.

When they were a little calmer, he said to his man, "Send abroad, and let them ring all the church-bells for three miles about. I'll find the ale. And thou, Thomas, bring in our young lady's things. She is mistress of the house."

Then they went out, and found two boxes, and one James Annesley seated peaceable. "And who is this?" said the old man, staring not a little.

"'Tis only my — my James," said she, as if every young gentlewoman had a James; but the next moment her cheeks were dyed with blushes. "Dear uncle, he has been my friend and companion in servitude; and some do say he is the —

"Whoever he is, he hath brought me thee, my sweet long-lost niece, and must lie at my house this happy night." So he received James cordially, and put off all inquiries till the morrow. The next morning James told him, of his own accord, he loved Philippa, and was so happy as to have won her affections. He also spoke of his wrongs, and said he was Lord Altham's son, and dispossessed by the uncle who had kidnapped him; and he should go into Ireland at once, and hoped to punish his uncle, and make Philippa Lady Anglesey. He proved himself in earnest by starting for Ireland this very day. The parting with Philippa was very tender, and left her almost inconsolable, being their first real separation since they knew each other.

So the wise old lawyer let her have her cry out. Next day he told her what the young man had said.

"Alas!" said she, "he is gone on a wild-goose errand, I fear; and, as for me, I would not give one straw to be Lady Anglesey: to be Mrs. James is heaven enough for me. And, oh! if any ill befall him in that savage Ireland, I shall always think 'twas because I was not by him, as heretofore; and you will have but one more trouble with me, — to bury me."

"Niece," said the old man, "craving your pardon, you are pretty far gone."

"Never was woman farther," said she frankly. "I am fair sick with love. My James carries my heart and my life in his bosom, go where he will." And she leaned her head prettily on his shoulder.

"Hum!" said the lawyer, and dropped that subject, not possessing even its vocabulary.

He waited a reasonable time, and then cross-examined her. "My young mistress," said he, "have you told your sweetheart you have thirteen thousand pounds? and, now I think on't 'tis nearer fourteen thousand, by reason of your folly in going and getting your own living, instead of spending on't."

"Have I told James? No; not yet. I found out my father's will by that advertisement; and, since he wished it kept secret, I have held that wish sacred."

Mr. Chester told her she had done well. Lord Anglesey had been long in possession; and it was not likely he would be ousted. without a fearful litigation, in which her little fortune might easily be swamped. "No, Philippa," said he, "still go by your father's will and by my lights, and let us not risk one shilling of your fortune. Your husband can never be a pauper while that remains in *your* hands." She caught that idea in a moment, and gave her solemn promise.

The first letter from Ireland served to confirm her uncle's wisdom. James wrote to say that he had been to a dozen attorneys; and they all refused to take up his cause against a nobleman so powerful as Lord Anglesey, and who had been years in possession, without a voice raised against his title.

However, a day or two after writing this, James Annesley fell in with a long-headed attorney called McKercher, who listened to his story more thoughtfully than the others, and went so far as to ask him for a list of the people he thought could bear out his statements. Having got this, Mr. McKercher found Farrell and Purcell, and, by means of them, one or two more not known to James Annesley; and they established the kidnapping.

Then McKercher began to think more seriously of the case. He called on Mr. Annesley at his lodgings, and found him and Matthews taking a friendly glass, and talking the matter over. McKercher made three, and said, over the said glass, that the kidnapping was certainly a fine point; but it would be worthless without direct evidence to Mr. Annesley's parentage: and money would be required to ransack the county of Meath for evidence, and for other purposes; for money would certainly be used against them freely.

The warm-hearted Matthews offered a thousand pounds directly to begin: thereupon McKercher's eyes glittered, and he hesitated no longer. All three went out to Mr. Matthews's house that day in ringsend cars; and next day rode on his own horses to ransack Meath and Wexford for evidence.

They found some little evidence, and McKercher secured it; but there were two enemies in the field before them. Death was one, Lord Anglesey the other. This nobleman had got a fortnight's start in rather a curious way. Admiral Vernon anchored off Jamaica a few days. It got wind that he was bringing home the real Lord Anglesey. The *Daily Post* announced it, and the *Gentleman's Magazine* copied, as indeed may be seen in the *Gentleman's Magazine* for February, 1841.

Death, the other antagonist, had been unusually busy since James Annesley crossed over the bar of Dublin. Lady Altham, dead. Mrs. Avice, to whom she had spoken of a son, dead; the chaplain who he believed had christened him, dead: his sponsors, male and female, dead.

But McKercher was not to be baffled. He hunted up the old servants of Dunmaine House; and, from one to another, he began to create that pile of testimony which even now stands on record to prove this obscure man the Napoleon of all attorneys, living or dead. He and James and Matthews rode hundreds of miles after evidence; till one night Annesley was fired at from the edge of a wood; and two slugs whistled close by his head.

They all spurred away in great alarm.

When they got to the town they were going to, tactful McKercher set to work that moment, and printed bills, describing the attempt, offering a thousand pounds' reward, and, by subtle insinuation, accused Lord Anglesey of the crime. He got up what we now call a demonstration; showed his handsome client to the public, on a veranda stuck over with bills thus worded:—

"THIS IS THE HEIR. COME, LET US KILL HIM; THAT THE INHERITANCE MAY BE OURS."

For all that, he sent Annesley back to England directly. "It is too pretty a suit to be abated by a bullet," said keen McKercher.

James Annesley returned to Staines, and found the roses leaving Philippa's cheek. Ere he had been back a week, they bloomed again.

MeKercher circulated his bills in Dublin, with a guarded account of the attempted assassination, just keeping clear of an indictment for libel. One of the bills was sent over to Lord Anglesey by a friend.

That nobleman, at this period, began to lose heart. His estates were large, but encumbered. He had been for years amusing himself with trigamy; and trigamy had entailed its expenses. All the ladies had to be dressed as if there was but one Lady Anglesey; and you may see by Miss Gregory's bill that those noble brocades, though cheaper in the end than the trash we call silk, were dear at first. Then the three ladies had children; and one of the three was so ill bred as to indict my lord, and had to be bought off.

Then he had Charles Annesley and Frank Annesley on his back. Francis Annesley, an English barrister, claimed a large portion of the estates, and filed his bill in England. Charles Annesley had a large claim under Earl James's will, which claim Richard Lord Anglesey had lately compromised for a third, and then, with his usual perfidy, evaded the compromise, whereon Charles obtained a decree with costs, and a sequestration, under the terms of which Charles now received all the Irish rents, and paid himself his share. The earl, therefore, was in the power of Charles Annesley for his very subsistence.

On the top of all this came James Annesley, armed with McKercher, and hard cash, of which his lordship, like many other Irish proprietors, had mighty little, compared with the value of his estates.

Thus attacked on all sides, and influenced, probably, by some reasons not easy to penetrate so long after the event, he began to falter; and being at his house in Bolton Row, which house the writer of these lines (be it said in passing) occupied for some years, a century later, he sent for his London solicitor, Giffard, and directed him to try and effect a compromise with Jemmy, as he called him.

Giffard was too cautious to commit his client to writing in a matter so dangerous; but he intimated to McKercher that he had something important to say, if McKercher would come to London. McKercher wrote back very courteously to say he was very busy collecting evidence, but would wait on Mr. Giffard in a fortnight. In anticipation of this conference, Lord Anglesey told Giffard on what terms he would resign his estates, and live in France. He even went so far as to engage a French tutor.

Meantime, James Annesley was a guest of Mr. Thomas Chester, and a favored suitor for his niece's hand. The old lawyer liked James, and, at this time, hardly doubted he was the real heir to the late Lord Altham; and he intimated plainly, that if Mr. Annesley would allow Philippa's dower, whatever it might be, to be settled on herself, they might marry as soon as they chose, for him.

Young Annesley smiled at this stipulation. "I hope to settle half the counties of Wexford and Meath on her, besides," said he. So one Sunday morning that the lovers were seated in a pew, with their heads over one prayer-book, her dear old tutor delivered certain ephemeral words that seemed to this happy pair to have a strange vitality, compared with the immortal part of the liturgy. Said he in a sonorous yet kindly voice, "I publish — the banns — of marriage — between the Honorable James Annesley, bachelor, of the parish of Dunmaine in Ireland, and Mistress Joanna Philippa Chester, spinster, of this parish. This is the first time of asking. If any of you know cause or just impediment why these two persons should not be joined together in holy wedlock, ye are now to declare it."

While these words were delivered,

Philippa's face was a picture: her eyes lowered, her cheeks mantling with a gentle blush. The words rang strangely in those lovers' ears.

How tight custom holds civilized men and women, and flies them but with a string! Both had led adventurous lives, had been slaves in a distant colony; and this demure lass, with long black lashes lowered, had played a fine caper in boy's clothes. Yet there they must sit at last, over one prayer-book, in Staines Church, and hear their banns cried in one breath with two more couple that had never budged out of Middlesex.

Let the reader now contemplate this pretty picture, and James Annesley's prospects, — a rose-colored panorama. In Ireland, his interests pushed by that rarest of all friends, an able and zealous attorney; in London, his arch enemy losing heart, and preparing to accept an income, and retire from the disputed estates to Paris; in Staines, his hand in his sweet Philippa's; and holy wedlock, the sacred union of two pure and well-tried hearts, awaiting him in one little fortnight; even that fortnight to be spent in sight of paradise, and the gate ajar.

Even writers are human. And I feel myself linger here; for it grieves even hardened me to have to plunge again into the misfortunes of the good: but now are my wings of fancy clipped. Hard fact holds me with remorseless grasp; and I am constrained to show how all this bright picture was shivered in a day, and by the man's own hand.

CHAPTER VIII.

Mr. Thomas Chester had retired from the law with a comfortable fortune. He was now a bit of a sportsman: rented of Sir John Dolben the right of fishing the Thames for some distance, and of shooting over a part of the manor; and paid half Sir John's gamekeeper. He was a man that respected the rights of others, and stickled for his own. He did not mind a stray cockney fishing his perch, roach, and gudgeons with the hook, for that was fair sport; but he was bitter against all who poached on his water with nets: for he said, "They rob not me only of my fish, but my fish of their lives · 'tis not sport, 'tis larceny."

Annesley had often heard him say this. One day Annesley came out with his gun to Redding, the gamekeeper; and they were about to go out together shooting waterfowl. This was the only sport to be had; for it was the first of May.

As they were about to start, Redding cast his eyes round, and saw one Thomas Eaglestone and his son casting a net from Sylvester's meadow. "There is that old rogue again!" said he. "Let us have his net." He set off to run; and Annesley ran after him to help. Redding came up first, and collared Eaglestone; but he, to save his net, threw it half into the river: then young Eaglestone seized the cord, cut it, and jumped into the river. Annesley snatched at the net; and his gun went off. Old Eaglestone cried, "Villain, you have slain me!" and fell, scorched and bleeding, on the ground, and never spoke more. The boy swam away to the other bank; and the smoke of the gun drifting away revealed the man lying in the agonies of death, and Annesley and Redding so stupefied and appalled, that they did not move hand or foot, but gazed with terror at each other and at their bloody work.

They had but just realized that the man was shot, and in the agonies of death, when young Eaglestone was heard to cry across the water, "My father! They have murdered him."

Then Redding seized Annesley by the arm. "Heard you that?

They will hang us," and set off instantly to run ; which cowardly and imprudent course Annesley, who was quiet unnerved, unhappily imitated, scarcely knowing what he did. They got to Redding's house; and Redding laid his hand on all the money he could, and fled the country. But Annesley would go no farther. He said, "I have slain an innocent man ; and let me die for it." He sat a little while, with his head and his hands all of a heap, and then fell on the floor in a fainting-fit. There were three women in the house. They raised him ; and just then the constables were seen coming with young Eaglestone. What did these wise women do, but drag him up stairs, and hide him in a sort of partition between two floors ; and there the constables, who had sure information he was in the house, found him without any trouble. This hiding told heavily against him both then and afterwards. In such terrible cases courage is the better part of discretion.

They found him in a state so deplorable, that they set him in a chair in the yard, and sprinkled his face with water ; and he was some time before he could command his limbs, and walk with them to the justice.

A number of people followed the officers ; and, when they came upon the bridge, James stopped, and said, "Have I no friends here?" Then there was a cry of "Ay!" for indeed he was already respected in that part. "Then," said he, "I do implore you throw me over the bridge, and end me ; for I have slain an innocent man, and shall never more know peace."

The justice sent them to Sir Thomas Reynell ; and he heard the evidence, and committed him.

They had five miles to go, and all drank together on the road ; and things were said over the liquor that afterwards affected the case.

As for James Annesley, he fell now into a dull resignation ; and his regret was greater than his fear, except for Philippa. He gave one William Duffell a crown-piece to go to Philippa, and beg her not to believe one word she should hear, except from his own lips. "Speak comfortably to her, good William, or this will kill her too." And then, for the first time, he began to cry and bemoan himself.

Duffell sped on his errand ; but others had been before him. Remorseless Rumor came open mouthed to Mr. Chester's house, and told Philippa James Annesley had murdered a man.

She was white as a sheet in a moment, and trembled ; but her faith supported her. "'Tis false!" said she. But tongue followed tongue ; and, as the vulgar always exaggerate and add, a crop of lies was ingrafted into the little bit of truth ; and threats and oaths were said to have preceded the firing of the gun. Even Philippa's faith was giving way under repeated attacks, when Duffell came in with that comfortable message.

She cried out, as if he could hear her, "Believe thee a wilful murderer? That I never will! Unfortunate thou always wast, but guilty never." Then she said she would go to him on the instant. "Where is he?"

"In the Cage at Hounslow."

She was with him in less than an hour ; and, with the two pale faces close together, he told her how it had happened. She believed him ; she consoled him ; she treated it as a simple misfortune, for which he must grieve, but could never be punished ; and she left him greatly encouraged. But her words were bolder than her heart ; and, when she reached home, the great restraint she had put upon herself for love of him gave way. Her body overpowered her great spirit ; and she had faintings one after another that laid her low. Though prostrated herself, this noble girl dictated words of comfort to her unfortunate lover every day; and Thomas Chester carried them. Mr. Chester exerted himself to bail James Annesley, and appeared likely to succeed, when suddenly one Giffard, a London solicitor, appeared for young Eaglestone, and objected with such ability and weight, that Sir Thomas Reynell said he must consider the matter, and take advice. Then Mr. Chester saw that Annesley was to be prosecuted vindictively; and he conceived some grave suspicions, and began sadly to fear the final result of this unhappy business.

What I have now to relate will show the reader his suspicions were well founded.

CHAPTER IX.

It was eleven o'clock on the 2d of May. The Earl of Anglesey lay in state, receiving visits in bed. On the sheets beside him lay his peruke superbly powdered, and adorned with a Ramilies tie. A servant held a small glass before him; and, while he talked to his visitors, he tinged his cheeks with carmine, and put on his patches, as openly as if these things were essential parts of a toilet.

His conversation was mighty vapid, affected, and lisping, until his courier, Lawler, knocked loudly at the door, and said, "I must speak with my lord on the instant."

"Ask him where he comes from," said my lord, laying aside his affectation.

The man burst into the room, and answered, "From Staines, where you left me to watch James Annesley; and, my lord, I bring strange news."

"Fling a bottle of scent over him, and leave us in private," said Lord Anglesey

This was done; and Lawler told him James Annesley had killed a man at Staines, and was now in the cage at Hounslow.

"What fool's tale is this? I can't be so fortunate."

"Nay, my lord, 'tis the truth: but some say 'twas accident; others say 'twas done of malice."

Lord Anglesey's eyes glittered fiendishly. "So say I; and I will prove it, if money can do't."

He gave the man a gold-piece, and dismissed him; dressed himself in half an hour instead of two hours, as usual, and went at once to his attorney, Giffard; told him the good news, and that all thought of a compromise was at an end. "Go down to Staines on the instant," said he, "and tell me can we hang that knave."

Giffard went down, and saw young Eaglestone and others, and reported that John Eaglestone could hang or transport James Annesley. "Then," said Lord Anglesey, "you must be his lawyer; and I will find the money, if I pawn my diamond ring."

Giffard did not much like the business; but he undertook it, sooner than lose his noble client. He advised Lord Anglesey on no account to appear in the business, or he would prejudice the prosecution; and he himself saw young Eaglestone, and easily moulded him to Lord Anglesey's purpose by rousing his cupidity, and also his desire of vengeance for his father's slaughter.

Thus the crown was used as an instrument of private vengeance. Yet who could object? Only the son and his attorney were seen. The ruthless man who bribed the witnesses and spurred the law was in the dark.

But they were not to have it all their own way. James had written, post-haste, to McKercher. He handed over the other business to his clerk, Pat Higgins, and came at once to Hounslow; saw the prisoner; found Giffard was in it, whom he knew to be Lord Anglesey's attorney; saw Anglesey behind Giffard: and his very first move in the case was one that had never occurred to Thomas Chester, nor to any other friend of Annesley's; though many were coming about him now. He put Lord Anglesey under a system of espionage as complete and subtle as ever Fouché brought to bear on a man; and he told nobody but Philippa, and bound her to secrecy. This done, he proceeded to the legitimate defence, and left no stone unturned. But he could never get at the most dangerous witness, young Eaglestone. Giffard kept him too close.

He encountered Giffard once or twice, and always treated him with profound respect; separated him entirely from his client, and charmed him with his good-temper and urbanity. "Ah, sir," said he, "if you knew Mr. Annesley, his goodness and his misfortunes, you would regret the severity you are compelled to show him."·

"I regret it now," said Giffard.

Just before the trial, Philippa, who was all zeal and intelligence, secured a piece of evidence to prove that the boy Eaglestone had not been so confident the gun was fired purposely, until Giffard came on the scene. But, with all her efforts, that was all she could do for her lover now. How different from former times when she was a boy!

She spoke of her helplessness to McKercher, with tears in her eyes, and told him it had not been always so.

"Helpless, madam!" said McKercher: "by the hoky, beauty is never helpless. You have found him a witness that I'd never have heerd of maybe; and ye can do him a good turn at the trile, if you have the courage to come."

"The courage to come!" cried she. "I have the courage to die for him, or die with him. Of course, I will be there, with my hand in his all the time, to show them there's one who knows he is not a murderer."

"Ah! if they'd only let us," said McKercher, with a sigh. "But I'll have you on the bench, ony way; an' I'll find some way to let the jury know they'll have to strike at his head through your heart, alanna." And the warm-hearted sharper was very near crying.

The dreadful day of the trial came at last. Philippa was seated on the right hand of the judge's seat, but on a lower bench. She was dressed, by McKercher's advice, in black silk, with a small head-dress of white lace, and no ornament but a diamond cross on her bosom. There she sat in a frame of mind beyond the pen to paint. This was her first court of law, her first trial. The solemnity, the ancient usages, and all the panoply of justice, struck upon her young mind in one blow with the danger of him whose young life was bound up in hers; and·for this reason I shall briefly describe this trial from her point of view; and the reader who has imagination will do well to co-operate with me by putting himself in her place, as well as in the place of the accused.

First there was the usual hardened buzz of lawyers, to whom this terrible scene was but an every-day business. Philippa heard with wonder and horror. What! could men chatter when a life, and such a life,· was at stake?

Then came in the judge, in ermine and scarlet; and all stood up. Philippa eyed him as a divinity, on whom her darling's life depended.

Then the prisoners were brought to the bar; Redding having surrendered. Philippa uttered a faint cry, instantly suppressed; and her eye and her lover's met in a gaze that was beyond words.

But here the proceedings were disturbed for a moment by the entrance of a gorgeous gentleman, in scarlet and gold, powdered peruke, and Ramilies tie, who stalked in, and seated himself by the judge. This was Lord Anglesey, come to gloat over the criminal, and keep the witnesses for the prosecution up to the mark. He stared on the public as on so many dogs, and on James Annesley with a bitter sneer. James was all in black velvet, with weepers, as one who mourned the death he had caused.

Silence having been obtained, the prisoners were arraigned, and the indictment charged against James Annesley, laborer,— that he, not having God before his eyes, but moved by the instigation of the Devil, on the 1st of May, with force and arms, in and upon one Thomas Eaglestone, feloniously, wilfully, and of malice aforethought, did make an assault; and that he, the said James Annesley, with a certain gun of the value of 5s., being charged with powder and leaden shot, did discharge and shoot out of the said gun, by force of the gunpowder as aforesaid; and him the said Thomas ·Eaglestone, in and upon the left side of the breast of the said Thomas, did strike and penetrate, giving to him, the said Thomas, on the said side of his said breast, one mortal wound, of the breadth of one inch, and of the depth of four inches, whereof the aforesaid Thomas then and there instantly died.

The indictment then repeated the nature of the act, describing it, in the usual terms, as wilful murder, and against the peace of our lord the king, his crown and dignity.

The virulent terms of the indictment, being new to poor Philippa, made her blood run cold; for it seemed to her that the crown thirsted for his blood, and would not stick at any exaggeration to hang him.·

The clerk of arraigns now put the usual question, in a loud voice: "How say you, James Annesley,—

are you guilty·of this felony, or not guilty?"

James Annesley, thus called upon before judge, jury, enemy, and sweetheart, showed unexpected qualities. Though a man of unsteady nerves when hurried, he lacked neither dignity nor courage, give him time; and what little hile he had·in his nature was stirred by the sight of the man who had kidnapped him as a child, now hunting him down as a man. Instead of simply pleading not guilty, he objected to the terms·of·the indictment. "I observe, my lord," said he to the judge respectfully but firmly, "that I am indicted as a laborer. This is ·malicious, and comes from those who are my personal enemies for the very reason that I claim to be Earl of Anglesey, and a peer of this realm. However, with this protest, I plead not guilty to this indictment, and will be tried by God and my country. But in respect of my quality, and to wipe out that impertinence in the indictment, I ask your lordship of your courtesy to let me be tried within the bar."

"Certainly, Mr. Annesley," said my lord. But he thought to himself, "I shall have to hang you all the same."

Then both prisoners were allowed to sit within the bar.

Then the jury were sworn; and Sergeant Gupper opened the case in the close, dry way of a counsel who feels that the facts can be trusted to do the work. He stated that the Eaglestones were fishing in a meadow that belonged to one Sylvester; and that Annesley and Redding came on to the ground, and first threatened Thomas with foul language, and then shot him, and, even after that, threatened John; but he escaped across the river, and brought the constables after the prisoners, who, well knowing their guilt, had fled. But Annesley was found hidden in Redding's house, and dragged forth, and afterwards offered the boy money not to come against him; but he said, "I will not sell my father's blood."

When this neat outline was delivered with perfect sobriety, everybody looked at the prisoners, and Annesley in particular, as dead men. But he maintained a calm though sad demeanor, and did not blench.

The counsel for the crown called John Eaglestone first. He swore to the preliminary matter, which was, indeed, undisputed, and declared, that, while Redding was collaring his father, Annesley threatened the old man's life, with a ruffian-like oath, if he did not give up his net; and then, not waiting for the old man's answer, *shouldered* his gun, and shot him dead; and afterwards threatened *him* with the but-end of his piece: but he escaped by swimming, and ran instantly for the constables. He swore also to the hiding of Annesley, and his subsequent attempt at bribery.

Philippa at this stage felt all the bitterness of death, and could scarcely sit upright.

In cross-examination, John Eaglestone was asked whether he had not given a different account to three persons, — Duffin and Dalton and Thomas Chester. He looked staggered a moment, but boldly swore he had not.

McKercher then showed his teeth. Counsel, carefully instructed by him, drew from the witness that he was now living with one Williams, whom he had not known before this trial; was called his servant, but dined at his table.

Counsel. — "Of course you have seen my Lord Anglesey at Williams's?"

The Court here interrupted, and said the question was improper.

Counsel. — "I bow to your lordship. But no nobleman who is worthy of the name need fear the truth."

A juryman, however, asked this boy a very pertinent question, — whether there was no jostling or struggling for the net between Annesley and him. He said, "No."

Many other witnesses were called for the crown; but they were all at some distance, and only proved the killing. Fisher, indeed, one of these witnesses, said that he saw Annesley snatch at the net; and then the gun went off.

This rather contradicted Eaglestone, and gratified the juryman aforesaid.

This Fisher, though a witness for the crown, admitted under cross-examination, that, within two hours of the event, young Eaglestone had told him he believed the act was not done designedly.

Counsel for the crown then commented on the evidence, dwelt upon the sanguinary threats that had been proved, and not disproved on cross-examination, and demanded a verdict.

This closed the case for the crown.

The Court then called on James Annesley in these terms: "Mr. Annesley, you are indicted in a very unhappy case. What have you to say?"

James Annesley then surprised his friends again. He rose like a tower, and spoke as follows: "My lord, I am quite unable to make a proper defence, having been kidnapped when a child by him who now seeks my life under the disguise of a public prosecutor; and so I lost the education I was entitled to by my birth."

He paused long on these words, and turned his eyes so full on Lord Anglesey, that every soul in court turned too, and looked at him. A shiver ran through the Court. It was indeed a remarkable combination, a remarkable situation. In fact, considering that the defendant here was to be the plaintiff in a great civil suit, if he could save his neck, and that the nobleman who sat by the judge in England to see him hanged was to be defendant in that suit, should this indictment fail, the situation was, perhaps, without a parallel in all time.

James Annesley resumed, " My lord, you have heard a true and deplorable accident falsely and maliciously described in this court, with a view to stopping lawful proceedings in the Court of Exchequer in Ireland. The simple truth is, that neither I nor my most innocent fellow-prisoner were trespassers. He is gamekeeper to the lord of the manor. It was his duty to seize a poacher's net; and I ran with him to help him. The deceased threw the net half into the river. The boy jumped in to swim across with it. I stepped to seize one of the ropes that trailed on the ground; and the gun went off, to my great surprise and grief, and killed a poor man, whose name I did not then know; and he never wronged *me*; and I had no malice against him, nor ground of malice.

"My lord, and gentlemen, mine has been a life of strange misfortunes; but, believe me, whatever your verdict may be, it must always be my greatest grief that I have caused the death of an innocent man."

These words, delivered with great decency and touching resignation, drew tears from many eyes besides Philippa's; and even the judge bowed his head slightly in sober but profound approval of the prisoner's concluding sentence.

Redding, called on for his defence, said that he had seized the net in discharge of his duty; that, when the man fell, Mr. Annesley did not know he had shot him, and would not believe him till he turned up the flap of the man's coat, and found the wound; and then Mr. Annesley showed such grief and concern, that he felt sure it was as pure an accident as ever happened in this world.

The judge then retired for some refreshment, and there was a buzz of conversation; and, by the time the judge returned, everybody in court understood the relation of the parties, — the lovers both in black; and that shameless peer, who would hang the young man in England to stop his lawsuit in Ireland; and the judge sitting in his place between the defendant's true lover and his enemy.

THE EVIDENCE FOR THE DEFENCE.

They proved, by documents and evidence, that Sir J. Dolben was lord of the manor, and Redding his gamekeeper, with full' powers to seize nets, &c.; then by Dalton, who was Philippa's witness, that, on the day of the killing, young Eaglestone had said distinctly he believed it was done undesignedly; then, by two more respectable witnesses, that he had said the same thing next day.

Then they traced his change of mind to Giffard.

Then they went on, and connected Giffard with Anglesey.

Then they went further, and proved that Anglesey was constantly with Williams, and that Williams was keeping young Eaglestone *like a gentleman*.

Thereupon Anglesey turned pale as ashes, and fidgeted on his seat; and Philippa, looking like a woman at the jurymen's faces, turned red, and her eyes flashed, for she saw them cast looks of disgust and contempt at him.

Then they brought two medical men of high character, who had probed Eaglestone's wound, and declared the shot had gone not downwards but upwards, and, indeed, at a considerable angle, and that the blisters at the *back of the body*, caused by the shot, were several inches higher than the wound. This double proof was irresistible. It agreed with Annesley's account and Fisher's; and it destroyed Eaglestone's testimony that the gun had been shouldered.

This closed the defendant's case.

The judge summed up briefly. He said that the sting of the indictment lay in John Eaglestone's evidence. The other witnesses for the crown had proved nothing but the killing, which was superfluous, since the prisoners admitted it. That, as to Eaglestone's evidence, it was highly damnatory, but unsupported by any other witness, and contradicted in one vital part of it by the two surgeons: in another respect, viz., as to whether the act was intentional, the same witness was contradicted by himself, and in the worst possible way; for, while the act was fresh in his memory, he had said repeatedly that it was accidental; and it was only when his mind had been worked upon by some person or persons not present at the act, that he had come to say it was intentional. Against Redding there was not the shadow of a case. Against Annesley, the charge of murder had failed; but they must consider whether it was manslaughter, or chance-medley. If they thought the gun went off accidentally, it was chance-medley.

The jury, being invited to retire and consider their verdict, said, through their foreman, there was no need for that, as they had made up their minds long ago; and thereupon brought it in chance-medley, which was, in fact, a verdict of acquittal.

The Court then discharged the prisoners on the spot; and in five minutes Philippa and James were rattling down to Staines in a chaise and four, which McKercher, who knew he had made the verdict safe, had provided, and ribboned the horses. He followed in a chaise and pair, with Redding.

James and Philippa sat hand in hand all the way, with hearts almost too full for words; and the church-bells rang for his escape, as they had for hers.

Philippa flung her arms round McKercher that night, and kissed him and blessed him so, that the good-hearted sharper shed a tear. He told her all the blood in his heart was at her service; and what he had done for James that day in England was child's play compared with what he would do for him in Ireland.

He was off to Ireland next day; but he left a sting behind him. Ere he had been gone a month, out came a volume, called "Memoirs of an Unfortunate Young Nobleman," in which, under the thin disguise of "Anglia" for "Anglesey," "Altamont" for "Altham," and so on, a full and interesting account was given of James Annesley's wrongs and Lord Anglesey's vices, including his trigamy, and other matters not relevant to James Annesley's concerns.

Lord Anglesey, at this time, was in a stupid, sullen state. He had left the Court disappointed, rebuked, and exposed. He stormed at Giffard for his defeat, and quarrelled with him, and would only pay half his costs. Whereupon Giffard sued him. Anglesey employed a solicitor. He subjected Giffard to interrogatories. McKercher heard of them, and subpœnaed Giffard for the Irish trial. Anglesey, though he swore he would run his sword through McKercher at the first opportunity, dared not indict his publisher for the "Memoirs," though libellous. He lay quiet even when the "Gentleman's Magazine" came out with the whole substance of the book, and made him a by-word throughout the nation.

Nevertheless, this stirred him up an unexpected friend. Charles Annesley wrote to him and said, "This is a very serious matter. We had better lay aside all differences, and make common cause against this upstart, James Annesley." Lord Anglesey replied that he did not know which way to turn; he had drained himself already in trying to unmask that impostor in Ireland, and hang him in England.

Charles Annesley replied that he would find ten thousand pounds that year, sooner than see the estates and title transferred to this upstart by perjury and lying romances.

Thus encouraged, Lord Anglesey drew largely on Charles Annesley, and went into Ireland, and employed agents of all sorts, and poured out money like water.

His presence and influence were soon marked by a sinister event. Pat Higgins, McKercher's clerk, returning to Dublin with valuable notes of evidence, disappeared, together with his papers. McKercher, whose own corrupt practices were bloodless, vowed he had been bought by Lord Anglesey's men, and sent out of the country. But he was never heard of again; and it is the general opinion in Ireland now, that he was made away with by persons in the employ of Anglesey.

McKercher now got leases signed by James Annesley, and put his lessees into possession of several farms in Meath. Anglesey ousted them by force; and Campbell Craig, one of the tenants so ousted, who was a tool of McKercher's, served a writ of ejectment on Lord Anglesey in the Irish Court of Exchequer. This brought the matter to an issue; and the cause was set down for trial. Though the actual property in litigation was small, all the Irish estates of Lord Anglesey depended on the verdict in Craig *vs.* Anglesey: of that the parties were agreed.

But meantime James Annesley had fallen into deep dejection of spirits. The malicious prosecution had done him good: it had stirred up his resistance; but, now a jury had acquitted him, he could not forgive himself for having killed a man.

McKercher comforted him, rallied him, but all in vain. He actually wanted to drop the proceedings against Lord Anglesey. "He will beat me," said he. "I shall never thrive. I have shed innocent blood."

McKercher was first sorry, then angry, then alarmed. He wrote seriously to Philippa about him, and she wrote back directly, "Send him to me."

In anticipation of his arrival, Philippa made Mr. Chester buy James a horse; and she had a riding-dress made so masculine, that she could speak her mind more freely in it. She had also a country dress for walking, made; and, when he came, she encountered his melancholy point blank with hilarity. "Your spirits want a *Philip*, sir," said she, "and I must give them one." She rode with him, she walked huge walks with him, she would not let him mope or pine. She was Philip one moment, all vivacity and cheerfulness; Philippa the next, all tenderness; and neither out of place. Her resolution, with her wit and her tenderness, attacked his despondency with so many weapons, and such minute pertinacity, that at last she drove the dark cloud away; and the man plucked up heart again to fight his enemies, and love his sweetheart as she deserved. And here I cannot help observing, that if this man's misfortunes were almost unparalleled, so his good fortune in finding so rare a woman as this to love him was almost as singular. I believe that, at this juncture, she saved him from the madhouse. Well, she had her reward; she saw the color creep back to the beloved cheek, the brilliancy to the dull eye; she saw the shapely head held up again, and at last she heard the beloved tongue bless her for what she had done.

And now I really think they would have been married, but for Thomas Chester. He had been for some time growing rather cold to young Annesley, but, seeing him so down-hearted, had not spoken his mind; but he now took an opportunity, and had it out with him. He said, "Mr. Annesley, if you had come to me as a poor gentleman, of no pretensions, I think I should have said to you, 'Show yourself willing to make a livelihood, and you shall have my niece, since matters have gone so far between you.' But you call yourself the son of Lord and Lady Altham, and others say you are not so, for my lady never had a son."

"I assure you, sir, on my honor "—

"And I assure you, on my honor, that you do not remember the circumstances of your birth any more than I do mine. Therefore, sir, by the kindness that is between us, I beg of you not to abuse your influence with my niece by urging her to marry you, unless you can make good your pretensions. I could show you it would be unwise to take any other course on account of the singular powers Mr. Hanway and myself possess under her father's will; but I prefer to appeal first to your honor and delicacy."

James Annesley replied with perfect dignity, "Mr. Chester, after the stain that has fallen on me, I have never asked my dear Philippa to marry me; but, since you offer her to me on condition that I can prove my birth before a jury of my countrymen, I take you at your word; and so be it. And, sir, I bear you no ill-will for this. You are an honest man, and Philippa's true friend; and to be her friend is to be mine."

"That is very handsomely said, young man," said Mr. Chester.

Annesley thought over this for an hour or two; and after dinner he burst out before Philippa, "Sir, you have roused me from my lethargy. I value Philippa's hand more than I do the lands and title I have been robbed of. I shall start for Ireland to-morrow."

"So soon ?" said Philippa.

"Ay, sweet one," said he; "and, if I am not the true Earl of Anglesey, I will never trouble you again, nor your good uncle."

Philippa turned pale, and knit her black brows at Mr. Chester. "Uncle," said she, "you have been saying something to him."

"No more than my own conscience says to me," replied Annesley before the old lawyer could speak a word.

James Annesley stood firm, and parted from Philippa tenderly, but hopefully, next day. Philippa was inconsolable, and kept her room. When she did re-appear, her uncle saw, with regret, that he had lost her affection.

She scarcely spoke to him, never volunteered a remark, and treated him with a bitter coldness that distressed him. However, he felt sure he had done his duty, and his niece would see that, too, some day. So he remained firm. But he was uncomfortable, to say the least. She went about the house pale and gloomy, knitting her magnificent brows, and never speaking nor smiling, except when she got a letter from James; and then it was as if the dead had come to life; ardent kisses on the paper, eager devouring of the contents, eyes streaming; and then away to some secret place to read it again all alone.

At last he made an appeal to her one day. He said gently, "Philippa, let me ask thee a question. Dost thou really think Thomas Chester is thine enemy ?"

The girl hesitated, and then said, "Why, n-n-no."

"Thou knowest he is not, but loved thy father dearly, and loveth thee. Then would it not become thine years to say, 'This is an old, experienced man, who loves me. Let me not condemn him hastily, lest I fight against my own good.' "

The sullen eyes began to fill at that, but never a word.

However, he said no more; for he saw the shaft had gone home.

But two days after this came a letter; to say that the trial, after several postponements, was to be that day month, by special appointment; and that McKercher was hopeful, though not confident. The assassination, or spiriting-away, of Higgins, with his notes, the fruit of two months' research, was very unfortunate.

The letter had been a week coming.

Philippa brought it to Mr. Chester, and coolly putting her arm round his neck, as if their attachment had never been interrupted, she said, "Uncle dear, please you read that."

So he smiled, well pleased at being "Uncle deared" again all of a sudden; and he read the letter. "Well," said he, "at all events it will end his suspense and yours."

"Uncle dear," said the young lady, "you asked me, Did I doubt your affection? Well, of course you cannot love as *he* doth; but I do think you love me a little in your way. But that I shall soon know; for I shall put it to the proof. Uncle dear, if you love me, go with me straightway to Dublin."

He started, and then said, "That is as if you should say, ' Sweet uncle, —I know you love me, — take me into the pit of destruction.' "

"Oh, fie, fie!"

"What else is litigation? If I take you to Dublin, you will be every day in court, as you were at the Old Bailey, sore against my wish: and here 't will be ten times worse; for you will hear him taunted by counsel, and exposed by a score of witnesses, and defeated in the end."

The young lady smiled superbly. "Uncle," said she, "you are learned in the law, no doubt, but most un-

learned in women's hearts. Each word you have spoken, it is a chain of steel, and draws me to Dublin by the heart. Had you but said, ' He will surely win, and can be happy without thee for a time,' I had yielded; but when you tell me he shall be defeated and shamed over there, then am I here on hot coals, and cannot bide. Know that I love him, as men, methinks, cannot love. I grudge him no triumph all to himself, no solitary joy. But trouble —and I not have my part! shame —and I not blush with him! Nay, but I tell you, not one sup of grief, sorrow, shame, or any mortal ill, shall *ever* reach his lips but I *will* have my share on't, by the God that made me, —ay, made me for no other use that I know of, but to console my darling, that is the very pearl of goodness, and the butt of misfortune from his birth."

She clasped her hands with angelic fervor, and was gone, with the words.

The old lawyer looked after her admiringly, but sadly. "She is too good to last," thought he. "I fear she is like her father, and will ne'er make old bones." Then he fell into one of the long reveries a thoughtful old man is subject to, since the past offers a larger landscape to him than to the young.

He had been thus an hour or more, when in came a swift foot. He looked up, and there stood — Philip, in the very clothes he had last worn at Wilmington. He had put on with them his old audacity, with which, however, a hot blush was doing battle.

"Now, uncle," said he sharply, "how is it to be? Will you go to Dublin with Philippa, that is a poor timid creature, afraid of men and mice, and every thing? or shall Philip go alone? — Philip, that fears nought, and feels like Alexander the Great at this moment. The Lord be praised for doublet and hose!"

Mr. Chester interrupted her

"Thou brazen toad, come hither, and let me look at thee. What, is this indeed the disguise thou didst prank thyself in out there?"

"Ay, uncle, and will again if you are unkind. Come now, old man. Time flies. How is't to be?"

Mr. Chester uttered a groan of resignation. "Needs must, when such as you drive," said he. "Go you up stairs this minute, and d'off that masquerade. To-morrow we will set forth, and be in Dublin this day week, God willing.

CHAPTER X.

Philippa was welcomed with surprise and rapture by James Annesley.

McKercher wore a blank look, that did not escape Philippa; but he recovered himself, and was rather violent in his expressions of satisfaction. Nevertheless, his original face of utter dismay imprinted itself on her memory, and puzzled her for some time. She told him she should be present at the trial. He assented, with a great show of warmth, and, having assented, began to raise one objection after another.

"It will be the longest trial ever known."

"No longer for me than for him."

"The court will be crowded to suffocation."

"What strangers can bear I can."

"'Twill be a bitter fight this time." She did not deign a reply. "'Tis pity you should hear him taunted by their counsel and their witnesses."

"I have borne to hear him charged with murder."

"There will be hard swearing: they have forty witnesses."

"When I know all that malice can say against him, then I shall be the better able to comfort him."

Her face, with its native power and indomitable resolution, lent double effect to her words. McKercher gave in, and said with a sort of admiring sigh, "Och, sure thin, go which way it will, he's a lucky man!"

She was too lofty to affect to misunderstand him. She said, simply, "It is the one piece of good fortune in his hard, his cruel lot;" and then a gentle tear stole down the lovely cheek, and McKercher was subdued entirely, and, keeping his misgivings to himself, made it his business to get her and Thomas Chester excellent seats at the trial. It was one of great expectation. When Philippa entered the court, a very large and commodious one, the floor was already crowded with the public; and, before she had been there ten minutes — for she went early — all the seats about the bench, and below the bench, were filled with Irish peers and peeresses, gorgeously dressed, and the gallery crowded with citizens and their wives.

Presently the claimant entered with his friends; not dressed in black, as at the last trial, but in a rich suit of purple velvet, and a gold sword-hilt. He wore an air of composure; but Philippa could see that he was flushed with excitement.

A sort of doubtful murmur ran round the court when he took his seat; but several of the ladies whispered in favor of his personal appearance, which, indeed, was captivating.

Lord Anglesey and his friends came in soon after; and he took his seat; but first he looked round the court, and exchanged bows with all the most distinguished persons present.

His eyes and James Annesley's met; and James turned a little pale at the sight of this implacable foe. He remembered the day he was kidnapped. The earl, more self-possessed, stared at him with a sort of overlooking air, and after that ignored him utterly, — the general feeling was in favor of Lord Anglesey. They were great worshippers of rank in Ireland, and his lordship's rank was established : the chances were, this claimant was an upstart.

Every thing betokened an extraordinary battle, — the prodigious number and various dresses of the witnesses on both sides, and the number of counsel engaged, thirteen for the claimant, led by Mr. Marshall, second sergeant, and fifteen for the defendant, led by prime Sergeant Malone, the ablest counsellor of that day, either in Ireland or England.

And now the judges were announced. Hooped dresses rustled as that brilliant assembly rose ; and no less than three judges entered, in their scarlet and ermine, to sit on this important trial.

The jury was called. They were all gentlemen of good position. There was a baronet and a right honorable amongst them ; and the only objection to any of them was that a couple had unexpired leases under Lord Anglesey. McKercher, however, declined to object to them on that score. Their swords were girded on them in court, and the trial began.

Mr. Sergeant Marshall opened the case of the plaintiff's lessor, which I shall ask leave to call the claimant's case.

It was one that lent itself to a rhetorical opening ; but the learned sergeant took the other great line. In a speech which is worth study as a model of condensation and strong sobriety, he articulated his topics, and marshalled an army of facts to prove, first, that James Annesley was the son of Lord and Lady Altham ; second, that the defendant had kidnapped him, and sent him out of the country, and, failing in that attempt to get rid of him, compassed his death in London by a

prosecution, the character of which he should not describe, but leave it to the witnesses.

But able speeches of counsel are no rarity ; and this trial offered something not only rare, but marvellous, — two piles of evidence, each as high as a tower, and each contradicting the other in nearly all the particulars directly affecting the issue.

They proved by *Mrs. Cole* and by two servants, that, in 1714, Lady Altham had expectation of offspring, and *Mrs. Heath*, her gentlewoman, knew it.

They then advanced a step, and proved by *John Turner*, seneschal to successive Earls of Anglesey, that, in the spring of 1715, Lady Altham was manifestly expecting her confinement ; and a year or so after he saw her teaching a child to walk. By *Bartholomew Furlong*, a peasant farmer, that in 1715 her condition was notorious ; that, as ladies of rank never nursed their own children, he applied personally to Lord and Lady Altham for his wife to be the nurse, and came to terms with them, subject to Dr. Brown's approval. But Dr. Brown did not approve of Mrs. Furlong. This was confirmed by *Dennis Redmond*, a groom at Dunmaine 1714-16, who said the doctor selected for wet-nurse *Foan Landy*, a cleanly, bright girl that lived on Lord Altham's land.

By *Dennis Redmond*. — That early in the summer of 1715, *Mrs. Heath* sent him to Ross, — three miles from Dunmaine, — to fetch Mrs. Shiel, a pofessional person, since dead ; and he brought Mrs. Shiel to Dunmaine on a pillion, and that same day a son was born.

By *Joan Laffan*, chambermaid. — That she was in the *house* when this son was born.

By *Mary Doyle* and *Elinor Murphy*. — That they were in the *room* when this son was born.

By *Capt. Fitzgerald*. — That he,

being quartered at Ross, Lord Altham asked him to dinner, and to *tap the groaning drink.* (What we call caudle.) That he came to Dunmaine House, saw the baby in the nurse's arms, and gave her half a guinea. Had seen the same nurse in court that day. "I took notice of her, sir, because she was very handsome, if you will have the truth of it."

By *Alderman Barnes* of Ross. — That Lord Altham dined with him in Ross on the alderman's return from a visit, and said over the bottle, "Tom, I'll tell you good news. I've a son by Moll Sheffield." Whereupon he shook his head in disapproval. "Zoons, man!" says my lord. "Why, she's my wife!" "Then I begged his lordship's pardon ; for I remembered my Lady Altham was daughter to Sheffield, Duke of Buckingham."

Redmond, Doyle, Murphy, and *Laffan,* servants in the house at the time, and *Christopher Brown,* servant to Anthony Cliff, at Ross, swore to the subsequent christening, accompanied with a bonfire , and such carousing that some of them were "*drunk in the ditches to the next morning.*" They all named as the sponsors three persons, who were since dead, — Anthony Colclough, Counsellor Cliff, Madame Pigot, and the clergyman, dead too.

To cure this excess of death in part, they proved by *Southweil Pigot, Esq.,* it was always received in the Pigot family that Lady Altham had a child.

They proved by *Joan Laffan* that this child was nursed by *Joan Landy* at her own house, a cabin ; and that the said cabin was embellished on this occasion, and a coach road made to it by which Lady Altham went daily to see the child. That in due time Master James was weaned, and then came into Dunmaine House; and there she, Laffan, was his dry-nurse and sole attendant. That in February, 1716,

Lord and Lady Altham parted in an angry manner about Tom Palliser, "whose ear," said she coolly, "I saw cut off," and Master James pointed to the blood on the floor. Laffan and Redmond both swore that they saw the actual parting ; and Lady Altham cried, and begged to have James. But Lord Altham would not let her.

This witness went on and swore that Lady Altham retired to Ross, and the Dunmaine servants took James to her clandestinely, which was confirmed by *Lutwyche,* a shoemaker at Ross, who swore Lady Altham ordered child's shoes of him, and bemoaned herself. "I had better be the wife of the poorest tradesman in Ross, for then I could see my child every day ; but now I can only see him by stealth."

To conclude their evidence about the deceased Lady Altham they followed her to Dublin ; and *John Walsh, Esq.,* swore she had cried to him over her husband's cruelty, but had thanked God "for an indulgent father and a promising young son, who would be a prop to her old age ;" and *Mrs. Hodgers,* who let lodgings in Dublin, deposed to a solitary conversation, in which Lady Altham, finding her to be English, gossiped with her, and told her she had a son.

They followed James from Dunmaine to Kinna, Carrickduffe, and other places where Lord Altham had resided, and proved by several witnesses he had been always dressed, powdered, booted, and horsed like a nobleman's son till he was more than ten years of age. Then they proved Lord Altham's entanglement with Miss Gregory, and also his poverty, to account in some degree for the boy being deserted at that time. In proof of his poverty, one witness swore that *when he kept hounds one hound would eat another.*

They then opened a vein of indirect evidence founded on the words and deeds of Lord Anglesey, the defendant. They grafted this into the case very neatly, thus:—

They proved by several witnesses that Lord Angelsey was constantly in communication with Lord Altham, and often at Dunmaine and other places; and they made it clear that Lord Anglesey knew for certain whether James Annesley was or was not his brother Altham's lawful son. This done, they proved by *Laffan* that she knew defendant well, and that he came home to Dunmaine a few months after the parting, and asked after Jemmy; and she told him my lady had begged hard for him, but my lord would not let her have him. Then the defendant swore an oath, which she repeated verbatim when questioned, and attested that blessed name to which all Christians bow, that *he* would have let Lady Altham have the boy, and take him to the devil; "for," said he, "I would keep none of the breed of her."

Having grafted this branch, they grew it high.

They called *Dominick Farrell* and *John Purcell*, the latter lamish, and with a staff, but sturdy still. Foreseeing the terrible difficulty under which I now labor, I stuck close to Purcell's sworn evidence in those earlier scenes he figures in. So please turn back to those scenes, and imagine every word you find there sworn to in open court before the principal actors in the scene; the child, now grown to man's estate, and the barbarous uncle, both glaring at each other, also before Philippa and her eyes that poured black lightning at her lover's treacherous enemy, and before the excitable Irish crowd, that roared and raged like wild beasts at Purcell's every other sentence. He told how he had taken the claimant off a horse in Smithfield, and carried him to his wife, &c.; the first visit of Capt. Annesley to his house, when the boy was all terror, but Richard Annesley all politeness; Lord Altham's death; Richard Annesley's changed behavior, and attempt to kidnap him. He told his tale simply, yet well. Anybody could see by his emotion and earnestness, he was not inventing, but living a real romance over again. Once or twice, in relating his sturdy answers to Lord Anglesey, he involuntarily struck his stick down upon the table, and so pointed his speech; but, when he came to the first attempt at kidnapping, and told how he put the boy between his legs, and dared that craven lord and his three bullies with his single cudgel, he suddenly waved his staff round his head with a gesture so impulsive, that a roar of admiration and sympathy burst from the crowd, followed by a buzz that interrupted the proceedings for some minutes.

Tenderer feelings were aroused among the tenderer; for, upon this, all the scene came back to James Annesley, and he made an eloquent motion of his hand toward the champion of his childhood, and then buried his face in his handkerchief. Many tears were shed all round.

Asked to identify poor little Jemmy, if he could, John Purcell pointed at once to James Annesley, and said with manly emotion, "That is the gentleman. *I know him as well as I know the hand now upon my heart.*"

This witness's cross-examination only led to fresh triumphs. He was asked with a sneer whether all those persons could not have taken the child from him had they really meditated violence. He replied, "No, sir," and struck the table with his staff. "*I'd have lost my life before I'd have lost the child.*"

At this there was a loud huzza; and the very peeresses about the bench waved their handkerchiefs to the honest fellow; and Philippa could have hugged them for that.

Having admitted he had afterwards seen him in a livery, he was asked if he still thought he was

Lord Altham: he replied frankly that it had staggered him, "but still I thought so in my conscience; *for might may overcome right.*"

This line rang in Dublin that day, and a century after rang round the world; for the Wizard of the North wove stout John Purcell's very line, and one more out of this marvellous trial, into his immortal romance.

Andrew Connor, proprietor of the ship *James* of Dublin, proved by the ship's books that James Annesley sailed in her for Pennsylvania at a certain date.

James Reilly and *Mark Byrne*, two rakehelly fellows, swore they were bribed by Anglesey to kidnap him at that date. They added to my account some particulars of the boy's cries and tears, and the impotent curses of the crowd as they hurried him on board the ship *James* of Dublin.

Being now the sixth day of the trial, they closed this vein of evidence and the claimant's case, by calling the defendant's own English attorney, Giffard. He deposed that he had been, for a long time, Lord Anglesey's man of business in England, and knew his affairs. Having suits with Lord Haversham and the Annesleys, and being now menaced by the claimant, defendant said to Giffard he would be glad to compound for two or three thousand a year, and surrender titles and estates to James Annesley, for it was his right; and, for his part, he would rather his brother's son should have all than ·Frank and Charles Annesley; and, in that case, he would live in France. Accordingly, he sent for Mr. Stephen Hayes, to teach him the French tongue.

Q. —" And pray what altered his resolution ?"

Giffard, in reply, told the truth, as you see it in my narrative, about the homicide at Staines, with this addition: " He said he did not care if it cost him ten thousand pounds, if he could get James Annesley hanged." He also described the clandestine way in which it was managed, the money wanted in the prosecution coming to him through Jans, Lord Anglesey's factotum.

The plaintiff's case closed, leaving Lord Anglesey an object of immense horror and disgust, and James Annesley the darling of the public.

Said Philippa, " After this, why do they not give him his rights, and have done with it ? That miserable old man might have spared himself this exposure by merely giving his title and estates to the rightful owner."

Says Chester, " It *is* odd, how people cling to these trifles when they have held them undisturbed for a few years." Then, more gravely, " Niece, do not deceive yourself. We know nothing of the other party's case, as yet; and our own is prejudiced by this conduct of McKercher. He has done a monstrous thing: he has published a libel of the defendant."

" A libel of the defendant! Who can libel that old villain? Who can paint him half as black as Nature has made him ? "

" The blacker he is, the less need to write a novel about him. Why, in England, the defendant would have attached him for contempt of court. A pretty attorney ! "

" He is a lawyer with a heart: that is all his fault. My James had been kidnapped by the old villain, and all but hanged; and he tried to assassinate him here in Ireland: and you cry out because poor, good kind McKercher replies to bullets, halters, and ten years slavery with a book, a few words that break no bones, a few home-truths that the villain himself hath made to be so. This is your justice ! This is how you cold-blooded lawyers hold the balance. Oh ! if my eyes could kill the caitiffs, body and soul, I'd give you something more to cry for! Prithee speak to me no more. Men with hearts are a sealed book to you. There—I would not forget the respect I owe you. I have done it once. For pity's sake, uncle—That prince of villains hath fifteen counsel to gloze his crimes for him; why need you make the sixteenth, and drive me mad?" She trembled, and her hands worked, and her eyes flashed fire.

The old man looked at her, thought of her father, and said softly, "That is true; and I am silenced, completely silenced."

"Better so than for us to quarrel. Forgive me, uncle; but I do not love my James by halves; and indeed I am but a woman, and so strung up by this terrible trial, as I should quarrel with my own father, if he said one word against my James."

"Nay," said the old man: "I never said a word against thy James, and never will. He is an honest man, and hath been cruelly used; and he is not to blame that his attorney writes novels *pendente lite.*"

The defendant now opened his case, and called a cloud of witnesses.

Aaron Lambert, Esq.—Lived near Dunmaine; never heard of nor saw a child of Lord and Lady Altham's. He impeached *Joan Laffan's* credit. Unshaken by her cross-examination. He said, "Nobody would believe, her in my opinion, if she swore all the oaths in the universe."

Thomas Palliser, Esq., a squireen. —Lived but three miles from Dunmaine, and visited there. Never heard of a son and heir; but had understood there was a boy about, whose mother was one *Joan Landy.*

William Napper swore that Lord Altham was not succeeded in his estates by the present defendant, but by Arthur, the then Lord Au-

glesey; that he, the witness, acted for Earl Arthur, and took possession of the Ross estate, on which were near a hundred tenants, and not one made any scruple, nor mentioned a child of Lord Altham's.

Thomas Pallisser, jun, delivered a romance illustrative of the time. He was young, and intimate with Lord and Lady Altham. Lord Altham told him one day he was determined to part with her, because he had no child by her; subsequently, by a "principle of selection" that looks rather odd to us English, my lord made his confidant the handle. He asked him to breakfast on mulled claret in a little room of Dunmaine House, called "Sot's hole" (a name that would have been more correctly applied to the mansion in general), and after breakfast made what the French dramatists call a *fausse sortie;* pretended to go to church, of all places. Palliser, having no other company, went to my lady's room, and sat on a stool. Presently there was a whistle. My lord and his servants burst in, cudgelled him, and, while he was insensible, *" Cut off this ear; and they might as well have killed me as done that."* He then swore there was no child in the house at that time, contradicting *Laffan.*

William Elms confirmed *Palliser, jun.,* that the child came into the house after Lady Altham's departure. He swore *Joan Landy* had a child that lived with her, and was miserably dressed till Lady Altham left. Then it was taken into the house, and clothed. After that he came to Dunmaine one day, and saw the child playing at Lord Altham's feet, and Joan Landy came to the gate, and peeped in; and my lord swore, and told the man to let the hounds out, and set them at her. He then said he would not for £500. The child should know that jade was his mother.

Thomas Rolph swore he was butler at Dunmaine until Michaelmas, 1715; between Michaelmas and Christmas, 1715, was discharged, by letter from Dublin, for *beating the gardener very heartily.* Now, this covered the period of the birth; and all the plaintiff's witnesses but one had sworn Charles Mugher was the butler at this period. Rolph could name more servants than any of the claimant's witnesses could. There was no *Joan Laffy* there in all his time. *Juggy Lundy*, as he called her, was discharged, and her child was born soon after; and he went to her hut to see her. "She lay upon straw covered with a caddow, and a hurdle at her head to keep the air of the door from her. There was a place at the feet of the bed, where her brother lay, and on the other side her father and mother; and there were stakes drove into the ground, and wattled to keep the straw together." When he first visited her, her child was but a few days old; and he asked her whom she called the father, and she told him. He deposed that he had often seen the child after that, and given the mother broken victuals at the stables; and before he left in Michaelmas, 1715, the child could go alone, and ran about with a sort of blanket on its shoulders, and nothing else. This child was christened at Nash by *Father Michael Downes.* Lady Altham never visited Joan's cabin, that he knew of. She was as proud a woman as any in Ireland. She had heard a scandal, and forbade the woman the house.

This closed that day's proceedings; and poor Philippa's throat was very dry, and her heart sick, and her mind amazed, to hear people swear such contrary things. "Ah, my child," said Thomas Chester, "why would you come here?"

Mrs. Anne Giffard lived near Dunmaine. Was familiar with Lady Altham. Never knew her to have a child. Undertook to prove an "ALIBI" for her at the time assigned for the birth. She went in a coach with Lady Altham to the spring assizes at Wexford, 1715. Lord Altham and *Mrs. Heath* rode with them on horseback. Jack Walsh of Moniseed, Masterton, his nephew, and one Doyle, an English clergyman, all Pretender's men, were tried. She and Lady Altham were in court; and *Cæsar Colclough, Esq.*, sat by them all day.

This "ALIBI" was sworn to by *Rolph* also, and *Mrs. Heath.*

Now came a pictorial figure of another class; for, if all the costumes in this single trial could be faithfully produced, the miserable meagreness of our authorities on that head would be very striking. It was a priest, with his cassock, his huge shoes with iron buckles, and his cockle hat, — *Father Michael Downes.* Had now lived forty-two years one mile from Dunmaine House. Dunmaine is in his parish. "No one could have a child in that parish, and I not know it." Lady Altham never had one; and Joan Landy had: it was in the year 1714. He was asked to christen it, but *was rather shy of doing that.* Finally, he bethought himself *there could be no harm done to him for making a Christian: so he christened him.*

He deposed, further, that Lord Altham afterwards asked him, had he christened Joan Landy's child. "I said, 'I have; *but I have got no retribution*,' meaning christening money. 'Well, well,' says he, 'I'll requite you hereafter.'"

He deposed, further, that, some years after, he saw the boy at Dunmaine House, and Lord Altham swore at the child, and said, "Why don't you get up and make a bow to him that made you a Christian?"

He kept a registry, and, by his own account, kept it vilely. *Thought* he would have registered a legitimate child by Lord Altham, *if my lord had desired him.* Was not used to register illegitimate children, and gave his "exquisite reasons," as Shakspeare hath it.

There now stepped upon the table one of the main pillars of the defence,—a tall, elderly Englishwoman, a glance at whom showed her condition. There was an air of decency about her. Her clothes were well made, though they were not rich, her full apron from waist to ankle, her snowy cap, puckered, and some lawn about her bosom, were very fine, and beautifully clean, and showed she had lived with gentlefolks. This was *Mrs. Mary Heath*, referred to by so many of the plaintiff's and defendant's witnesses. She swore that she was Lady Altham's woman, and came over from England with her in October, 1713, and lived with her till the day of her death. Remembered going down to Dunmaine. Remembered some of the servants,—Setwright, the housekeeper; Rolph, the butler, Anthony Dyer; Michael, the cook; and his scullery girl, Juggy Landy, who left soon after, and had a child. Hearing some scandal, she was curious to see who this child was like: so asked the coachman's wife to have it brought to the gate for her to see. She did see it: it was about six weeks old then, and had nothing but a clean blanket. She gave it several things, amongst the rest a fine cambric neckcloth she had brought from England amongst her own things.

Her mistress never had a child, nor any expectation of one. She often confided to the witness her regret; and once, in particular, she came up stairs, after dinner, crying, and said that brute below (meaning the defendant) had said he wished she might never have a child. And my lady said she wished she might but have a child, to inherit; and she did not care if she was to die the next hour. Was at Ross, with her lady, after the separation, and had no knowledge of *Lutwyche*, a

shoemaker. Her lady wore braided shoes, but white damask never, all the time she knew her. No child ever visited her at Ross.

Q — "Was there any child brought to my lady as her child?"

A. — "*No, never was. She had no child; I can say no more, if they rack me to death.*"

She swore that McKercher had called at her home in Holborn, and she had said to him, *inter alia*, "Think you, if a child had been born to such an estate, they would not have had his birth registered?"

This witness was violent, and argued the case too much; yet, under cross-examination, she gave, unconsciously, a picture of her fidelity and affection that made it hard to believe she could be the woman to lie her unhappy lady's son out of his estate, if she believed he was her son. Counsel was cross-examining her to prove that Lady Altham's memory was impaired long before she died in 1729,—in fact, when she came from Ross to Dublin.

"Was not she troubled with a dead palsy?"

"I cannot call it a dead palsy, sir."

"Did not that disorder deprive her of the use of her limbs?"

"She lost her limbs by that disorder; but it came by degrees. *When she came from Ross, she could go about with holding by one hand. When we first went to London, with one hand I could lead her about the room; and then with both hands; and then not at all. I was forced to put her in a chair, and wheel her about. But her mind was clear. She kept her own accounts.*"

That touching though incidental picture of fidelity did not appear to strike the court; but it did Philippa Chester, and she felt sorely staggered and sick at heart. She was silent this evening, while James and Chester and McKercher discussed the evidence.

Mr. Chester said her evidence was crushing, if true; but her manner was rather against her. "I think you may perhaps get over *her*," said he. "Are there many more?"

"Plenty," said McKercher; "but Heath is the only one I fear. She is an Englishwoman and a Protestant. Bad luck to her!"

Martin Neif had seen Joan Landy with a child of her own at Dunmaine. Saw the same child afterwards at Dunmaine House; saw him afterwards with my lord, at Kinna. Has heard my lord say he would not, for any money, the boy should know Juggy Landy was his mother.

Arthur Herd was a barber's apprentice, and went out to shave Lord Altham at Carrickduffe. When he had shaved him, Lord Altham said, "Come and live with me: you shall never want a piece of money in your pocket, a gun to shoot with, a horse to ride on, nor a lass to walk with." On this picture of domestic service, he ran away from his master without scruple. He found a boy in my lord's house called Jemmy Annesley. He had a scarlet coat and a laced hat. Knew my lord to correct him once, and say, "He has the thieving blood of the Landys in him. His grandfather used to steal the cauls out of his sheep, and half thresh his corn, and make the sheaves up."

Witness used to go sometimes and see his friends at Ross. On these occasions Master Annesley would send his duty to his mother: she was then in the service of a baker at Ross. Since Mr. Annesley's return, had seen him and Mr. McKercher. Mr. McKercher asked him who was James Annesley's mother; and he told him it was Joan, or Juggy, Landy. He then reminded Mr. Annesley he had taken several duties from him to his mother, and brought several blessings from his mother to him, and reminded him of a pair of stockings he brought him of his mother's knitting; and Mr. Annes-

ley trembled and turned pale at this discourse.

The claimant's case was now considered desperate. He himself seemed like a man awaking from a dream.

Philippa was sick at heart. "Oh!" she moaned, "will these dreadful witnesses never leave off?"

As for McKercher, he disappeared that night.

Philippa went to the court next morning, pale and disturbed, all her alacrity gone. She went like one to execution. Yet no entreaties could keep her away: no, she would know the worst.

This day came a new costume, *Alderman King* in his robes, out of respect for the court. He deposed that Lady Altham lived in his house nine months as his guest a little before she left Ireland. She used to converse freely of her affairs, but never mentioned to him that she had a son.

This closed the defendant's evidence.

What now remained but the speeches of counsel and a verdict for the defendant? Not much, only to conquer the Napoleon of all attorneys, living or dead. McKercher re-appeared, and claimed, through his counsel, to prove PERJURY on the part of certain witnesses for the defence. The Court allowed this, with the usual limitation, — he must state his points first, and keep strictly within them.

Claimant's counsel stated four points, and then called to defeat the "*alibi*" aforesaid.

Cæsar Colclough, Esq. — He swore that he was at Wexford spring assizes, 1715. Was in court all day at Masterton's trial; did not sit by Lady Altham and Mrs. Giffard; did not believe they were in court; and Parson Doyle was not tried that day, but just one twelvemonth after, and he, Colclough, was a juryman.

On the same line *Thomas Higginson*, collector of rents, swore Lord

Altham went to those very assizes alone; and he called at Dunmaine with money due, and Lady Altham gave to him two glasses of white wine and at the second he wished her a happy delivery.

Against Mrs. Heath they called an acquaintance of hers, one *John Hussey*, who swore, that when the news of Mr. Annesley coming to claim his rights first reached London from Jamaica, and before the defendant's agents could get to her, she spoke of him to deponent as Lady Altham's son, and a much wronged man. *William Stephens* and *William Houghton*, persons intimate with *Arthur Herd*, swore that this formidable witness for the defendant had told quite a different tale to them before the trial. Houghton gave some particulars of gossip. One Mrs. Symons had come into his place, and told him *Herd had turned tail to Mr. Annesley*, and the trial was going against him. "Why, madam," said I, "I heard Arthur Herd express himself that Mr. Annesley was the heir." Pressed for the exact words of Herd, he said, "Upon my oath, and upon my salvation, and upon every thing, he said he did believe him to be the true heir of the estate the Earl of Anglesey now possesses." Both opponents swore that a remarkable saying which was now ringing through every street in Dublin came first out of Herd's mouth, viz., Annesley is the right heir, if right might take place.

Father John Ryan swore that Father Michael Downes had told him he was to get £200 for his evidence, and if he made a mistake he must get absolution.

This closed the plaintiff's evidence in reply.

Then came an incident without a parallel. The judges had now before them the greatest mass of perjury ever delivered in Great Britain; and, not being clear on which side the perjury predominated, they took

unusual means to test the witnesses. They confronted them on the same table, and took the examination into their own hands. Thus, whereas in an ordinary case there are two battles of evidence, in this immortal trial there were four; and the last deserves a distinct heading.

THE DUELS ON A TABLE.

William Elms, who had said Joan Laffan was a person not to be believed on her oath, was put on the table, and then *Joan Laffan* was ordered up. When she came on the table she courtesied, and said, "Your servant, Mr. Elms."

The Court. — "Woman, do you know that gentleman?"

Joan. — "Yes: since I knew anybody."

Court. — "Did you tell him at Dunmaine you were nursing Lady Altham's child?" *A.* — "I don't know, my lord: I never saw him to speak to at Dunmaine but once."

Elms. — "I was high constable, and I spoke to her several times at Dunmaine, when I went to collect the public money. Don't you remember that? Can you deny it?"

Joan. — "I protest I know nothing of it."

The Court. — "What was the nature of your service?"

Joan. — "I was chambermaid."

Elms. — "She was laundry-maid."

Joan (ironically). — Very well, Mr. Elms."

The Court, having brought them to this issue, looked into the matter, and found, by the evidence of Heath and others, she was chambermaid, and not laundry-maid.

About Joan Landy's cabin, Joan said she only knew it while the child was there. It was then a handsome house, with handsome things in it.

The Court (to Elms) — "Pray

was there any such fine room as she describes ? "

Elms. — " I never saw it, *without it was underground.* I saw no furniture at all : there was a wall made up of sods and stones."

Joan Laffan. — " Oh, fie, Mr. Elms ! I wonder you'll say so. Then she clasped her hands. " *By the Holy Evangelists there was never a sod in the house* "

They continued again about the coach-road ; and this much abused witness, Laffan, distinctly proved that the respectable Mr. Elms and Rolph had lied and prevaricated about the coach-road ; and that it did not go where they said it did, but only to Joan Landy's cabin.

The Court (to Joan Laffan). — " Was it known by the neighbors that my lady had a son, and that the child you nursed was that son ? "

Joan (composedly). — *My lord, it is known by two thousand people ; and everybody knows it if they will please to speak truth.*"

Elms. — " *I never heard of it for one.*"

The two priests were now put on the table cheek by jowl.

Father Downes denied that he ever rode and conversed with Father Ryan on any Sunday morning ; but, on Ryan reminding him of a circumstance, he conceded the riding, but denied that he had ever conversed about this trial on a Sunday morning.

Then the Court made Ryan repeat to his face about the £200, &c.

Downes. — " Does this man swear this ? "

Court. — " He does."

Downes. — " Well, then, I'll tell you, by virtue of my oath — I never was promised a farthing ; and, *if you believe this gentleman, you may hang me ; for he is a vile, drunken, licentious dog in the country.*"

The next duel was between *John Hussy* and *Mary Heath.* They were put on the table together ; and the Court asked Mrs. Heath if Hussy had drank tea with her since the account came from abroad about Mr. Annesley.

Mrs. Heath. — " Several times."

Court. — " Had you any conversation with him thereupon ? "

Mrs. Heath. — " I have often said to him what a vile thing it was to take away the earl's right. My lady never had a child. And I can't say no more if you rack me to death."

Court. — " What is Mr. Hussy's character ? "

Mrs. Heath. — " I can say no more than that some said he was a gentleman's servant, and some said he lived by gaming."

The Court. — " Repeat the words you say she said before you."

Hussy. — " She told me the Duchess of Buckingham sent for her ; and then she said, ' Poor gentleman, I'm sorry for him from my heart, for no one has reason to know his affairs better than I do ; for I lived long with Lady Altham, his mother.'"

Mrs. Heath. — " *By all that's good and great I never said any such word.*" Then, turning on Hussy, " I never thought you were such a man I've heard people say you were a gamester, and lived in an odd way ; but I would never believe it till now. I took your part, and always said you behaved like a gentleman."

Hussy. — " I am a gentleman, and a man of family. Indeed, I heard you say it, and with all the regret and concern imaginable."

Thus ended the greatest conflict of direct and heterogeneous evidence ever known in this country before or since : and, if it does not interest my readers more than the rest of this story, let us have no more of the miserable cant about truth being superior to fiction ; for truth has very few pearls to offer comparable to this great trial.

The Court adjourned; and Philippa and James Annesley both thanked God it was over, and agreed they would never have gone through it, had they known what they were to endure.

"Sweetheart," said she to him, "I have much need to see you gain your estates; for I have lost my youth. I was so young before this dreadful trial, and now they have made me old. They have shown me mankind too near. What! is it really so, that Christian men and women can stand up side by side, and take the Gospels of their Redeemer in hand, and one swear black and t'other white, of things they both do know? and all we, looking on amazed, can see nought in either face but truth and honesty. Land and titles, quotha! What are they that men and women should fling away their souls? Why, if each of these false witnesses were to be Ireland's richest land-owner, and England's highest earl, still 'tis the Devil that hath the best of the bargain. Oh! I am sick, sick. Shall England ever come to this? Then, methinks, 'twere time for honest men and women to run into the sea, and so to another world for truth."

Having relieved her swelling soul, the noble girl laid her hand on James's shoulder, and said pathetically, "I have but one comfort in this wicked world,—that he I love is an honest man."

"Yes, I am an honest man; too honest to trouble you any more if the jury shall say I am that woman's son."

"O James! what words are these? Think you I care whose son men say you are?"

She made light of it, not knowing at the time the gloomy resolution James had come to.

Yet after all, now I think of it, she may have had some vague mis-

giving; for she said to Thomas Chester, almost crying, "Uncle dear, if it goes against him, you will be very kind to him for my sake?"

"I will. Why should I not? But if you mean give him my niece and her fortune all the same, why, no,—not till he resigns litigation, that is a curse, and takes to some honest trade."

Next day Philippa had a terrible headache; but nothing would keep her out of court.

Four counsel for the defendant spoke in turn: of these Malone was one; and he spoke four hours, with all the zeal and cogency of a great forensic reasoner. Often during his speech, poor Philippa said, "Oh! will he never leave off?" and, when he did leave off, the claimant's case seemed prostrate.

Nevertheless, next day Counsellor Marshall for the plaintiff spoke one hour only, but with such lucid order, such neatness, cogency, and power of condensation, that he set the claimant's case on its legs again. He was followed by three more.

I shall give one point of the many on which they countered; but I give it only because the judges, by some strange delusion unaccountable in men so able, actually omitted to say one word upon the point, though, to my mind, the case lay there.

Prime Sergeant Malone cited, "It is a rule well known, that every case ought to be proved by the best testimony the nature of the thing will admit; and surely this Joan Landy was the very best witness that could have been produced on the side of the plaintiff. It is sworn for her, by others, that she took this child from its mother, and nursed it for fifteen months. Why, then, is not she produced? She is named on their list of witnesses; and the gentlemen on the other side did, very early in the case, promise we should see her. But by and by they told us she was a weak woman, and might be put off the thread of her story. But this was plainly not the real reason. The weakest man or woman can speak truth, and will probably, on their oath, say no other. It is a hardship for a weak mind, that knows a fact not to be true, to color it, or make it appear true. Their consciousness that Joan Landy was unwilling or unable to do this must have been their only reason for not producing her. Good-will to the plaintiff she could not lack: she is, by their account, his wet-nurse; and an Irish nurse, as Mr. McKercher told those who suspected this woman of being something more to the claimant, has a maternal affection, and is willing, *by all honest means*, to promote her nursling's welfare. Joan Landy knows better than any one whether she had a son by Lord Altham, or not. Yet she is not called; and so, because Joan Landy knew too much about the sham to stand an examination, Joan Laffan, the pretended dry-nurse, is put forward to give Joan Landy's evidence.

Sergeant Marshall cited, in reply to the above:—

"What we said to the gentlemen was "that Joan Landy had been *tampered with;* ' and we repeat it. On that account we did not examine her; but we offered her to the gentlemen on the other side, if they pleased to examine her; and they declined. Yet she is their witness. She plays in their case the part Lady Altham plays in ours. Their refusing to examine her is as if we should refuse to examine Lady Altham, were she alive; yet we had Joan Landy in court for them, and they declined her."

The last conflict was over: the three judges summed up. Baron Dawson flimsily: the chief Baron and Baron Mountney with great pains, closeness, method, and impartiality on every point but the conduct of the counsel in not calling Joan Landy. This, by some strange crook of the Celtic intellect, they all ignored.

The jury retired.

James Annesley waited a few minutes, and then, unable to bear it any longer, cast a look of agony at Philippa, and left the court. McKercher followed him.

Philippa sat in all the tortures of suspense.

While she sat twisting her hands, a line from McKercher was brought her. "My dear young lady, keep your eye on him. He has bespoke a passage to Pennsylvania."

She handed it to her uncle, and clasped her hands.

"No," said Thomas Chester, "there is no need for that. We must think of something. What! the jury come back so soon? Well, they are agreed then. I was afraid they never would. Better so, my child, than to go through this all again."

"SILENCE!"

Then the usual question was put to the jury; and their foreman delivered

A VERDICT FOR THE PLAINTIFF.

There was loud "Huzza" from the crowded court. Ladies waved their handkerchiefs; and Philippa gave a cry, and was carried almost fainting from the court.

She had not been at home many minutes when in rushed her lover, exalted in proportion to his recent despondence, and demanded her hand in marriage that very minute.

What woman, however much in love, could put up with such conduct? She coquetted with her happiness directly, like any other daughter of Eve. "Marriage! time enough for that." At present she preferred to revel in her lover's triumph, and "not talk nonsense," —so she said, however. Her lover then informed her that the Irish estates and the title in perspective would not compensate him for what he had endured. McKercher had been fighting for land and honors; but he for her.

' Mr. Chester put in his word. "Come, niece, a bargain is a bargain. Prithee make me not a liar I ne'er broke faith when I was young; and shall I begin in my old age?"

"I would do much to oblige *you*, uncle," says the young lady, smiling, and coloring high at what she saw coming.

In ran McKercher, boiling over, to say he had arranged bonfires, bells, and a torchlight procession.

"The marriage first," said Annesley, "or none of your public shows for me."

Finding him as obstinate as a mule, the pliable McKercher shifted his helm; got a parson and distinguished witnesses all in an hour; and the deed of settlement was produced by Chester, and signed, sealed and witnessed, and the marriage solemnized in private, as usual among the great; and Matthews rode home to prepare his house to receive the bride and bridegroom.

At night McKercher, all in his glory, arranged the torchlight procession, with all the bells a-ringing, and bonfires blazing on the neighboring heights. It was a splendid cavalcade, both of men and women: for the young lord, as they called him now, was the darling of the hour; and all the quality clustered round him. Then James must show his darling Philippa all the places where he had suffered privation and misery. They made a progress. They went in triumph to Frapper Lane, and other of the places; to Smithfield, where he had held horses and to Ormond Quay.

One incident occurred worth mentioning. They passed John Purcell's door; and the old man stood in his doorway to see the show, as all the neighbors did. Annesley caught sight of him, instantly dismounted, and fairly flung his arms round the old man's neck, and kissed him on both cheeks. The old man kissed him in turn, and sobbed a word or two; but, when James looked for his mammy, he shook his head. She was gone from the joys and troubles of the world: and this is the sorest wound to gentle hearts, that those who have been kindest to us in adversity cannot stay below to share our prosperity.

The crowd huzzaed louder than ever when the young lord kissed the humble, sturdy benefactor of his youth; and then the bright cavalcade resumed its march. They took that sore-tried but now triumphant pair a mile out of Dublin; then they broke into two companies: the larger rode back to drink their healths in Dublin; the smaller rode with them to Capt. Matthews's, waving torches, and hurrahing lustily at times. He kept them all, and their horses, that night, with Irish hospitality.

How sweet is pleasure after pain! Such a day as this comes to few, and to the happiest but once in a life; and all the past trouble, mortification, doubt, and suspense made it sweeter still, indeed, scarcely credible, it was such rapture.

I could tell more about the "Wandering Heir;" but fiction is not history, and I claim my rights. Even the "Iliad" is but a slice out of Troy's siege: so, surely, I may take these marvellous passages of an eventful life, then drop the curtain on the doubtful future.

Whether or not he holds his estates, and gets his title from the peers, he has been poor, and now is well-to-do; a slave, and now is free; alone in the world, and now blessed with Philippa: there lies his best chance of enduring happiness when all is done; for few things in this world keep their high flavor, custom blunts them so. Wealth palls by habit; titles cease to ring in sated ears; French dishes pall the appetite in time; power and reputation have no spells against satiety. Only pure conjugal love seems never old nor stale, but ever sweet : if it declines in passion, it gains in affection ; it multiplieth joy ; it divideth sorrow, and here in this sorry world is the thing likest heaven.

NOTE.

As this story is historical, many real names figure in it. Should the same names still exist, please do not connect their present owners with my characters, who died a century ago. Example: The Earl of Anglesey, who plays so ill a part in these pages, was an Annesley, and no relation whatever to the chivalrous Pagets. The old earldom expired in 1771. In 1815 Parliament bestowed the title on one of the heroes of Waterloo, by whose direct descendant it is held. C. R.